In Love
and War

In Love
and War

EILEEN TOWNSEND

GRAFTON BOOKS

A Division of the Collins Publishing Group

LONDON GLASGOW
TORONTO SYDNEY AUCKLAND

Grafton Books
A Division of the Collins Publishing Group
8 Grafton Street, London W1X 3LA

Published by Grafton Books 1989

A CIP catalogue record for this book is available
from the British Library

ISBN 0–246–13482–8
ISBN 0–246–13548–4 (Pbk)

Phototypeset by Computape (Pickering) Ltd, North Yorkshire
Printed in Great Britain by
William Collins Sons & Co. Ltd, Glasgow

'Lie in the Dark and Listen' from *Collected Verse*
by Noël Coward is reproduced by permission of
Methuen, London

Prologue

On Thursday 31 August 1939, as the first shadows of evening fell across Europe and the sweet scents of late summer drifted on the light breeze through open windows into the homes of Britain, two women, a mother and daughter, sat sipping an after-dinner drink in the drawing-room of their Georgian terraced home in one of London's most elegant squares. The port tasted mellow on the tongue and imparted a feeling of contentment and well-being at the end of a busy day.

But this was not an evening to be spent in England's capital city. It was the type that made the elder of the two long for the peace and tranquillity of a garden she had known once in another life, a garden that had once been hers, but was a thousand miles away from her now: the garden at Wolfsberg, the country estate of one of Germany's most noble families, the von Stellings.

Sitting here now, with her daughter Lara humming softly to herself in the chair opposite, as the melodic strains of a Strauss waltz filled the room, it seemed impossible that she, Beth Mallory, had once been a von Stelling. She – as proud an Englishwoman as they come – was once Mistress of Wolfsberg and a member of one of Germany's most noble families.

But all that was a long time ago now; Lara, her beloved daughter, was now a young woman – almost exactly the age she had been then. Yes, a whole generation had passed since she had taken the vow to love, honour and obey the man who was Master of Wolfsberg, till death did them part.

'Till death do us part … *für immer und ewig* … ' Beth's lips soundlessly formed the words, and her eyes clouded at the memory as she took another sip of the ruby liquid and leaned her head back against the soft hide of the chair. There had been more than death to torture her soul in that last summer she had spent as a young wife and mother beneath those cloudless foreign skies.

A shudder ran through her as the emotions she had struggled to bury deep within her for a whole generation fought to break free.

How many times had she endured just such a struggle? How often had her spirit refused to remain a prisoner, casting aside the mental chains that bound it to the here and now and returning to that land in the east that still today held her heart as captive as it had all those years ago?

Her eyes closed as she rested her head against the soft brown hide of the armchair and allowed her thoughts to wing their way across half a continent, to Wolfsberg, and Silesia, that beautiful land, haunted by its past and fearful for its future. A land that had changed hands between Germany and Poland more times over the generations than its inhabitants cared to remember. A land that today was on the minds of so many who walked the corridors of power in this country and across the sea. A land whose fate could seal the destinies of so many other nations, including her own.

And, that same evening of 31 August, as Beth's thoughts returned to the place that had once been home, to the present inhabitants of that troubled land that straddled the German–Polish border, the sky seemed an even deeper blue than usual, the air warm and balmy, without the oppressive heat of high summer. The leaves that quivered in the faint breeze had not yet turned to gold and, as far as the eye could see, fields of tall maize lay, ripe for harvest, in shimmering complement to the shining orb of the setting sun.

Beyond the golden fields ablaze with scarlet poppies, and the acres of gently stirring flax now ready for the waiting looms of Vilna, the pine-covered hills stretched to the far horizon.

In the shelter of the valleys, small farmsteads clustered, their orchards heavy with rosy-cheeked apples and dusky purple plums, and old men gathered in big-hearted, wine-red cabbages from well-tended gardens. Never had there been such an autumn or such a harvest, they told their younger neighbours.

In the countryside around Wolfsberg, both German and Polish voices could be heard extolling the bounties of nature and thanking God for his goodness to them and their families. Yes, here, in this most blessed of lands, Germans and Poles had lived side by side since time immemorial. But time was rapidly running out for the Polish population. Only nine days previously, on 22 August, Adolf Hitler had declared, 'I keep my Death's Head Battalions ready, without mercy or pity, to kill men, women and children of Polish origin. That is the only way we shall get the living space we need.'

Unknown to all but a few, the moment to create that living space – the coveted *Lebensraum* – was here at last …

One and a half million German troops were already amassed on the Polish border. And at 4.45 A.M., the first German air attack on Poland began. One hour later, in the wake of the *Luftwaffe*'s bombers, the German troops and tanks crossed the border and moved rapidly towards the growing light in the sky. The *blitzkrieg* had begun while Beth Mallory, along with her daughter Lara, and the rest of Europe continued to slumber, unaware that they were sleeping through the last moments of peace they would know for six years.

And, as the blood-red glow filled the heavens, less than two hours' drive from the advancing tanks, a man in his early fifties paced the polished wood floor of his study and stared out through the tall windows of the ancient Polish castle that had been his family home for seven generations. He could not understand why he was so on edge this evening. Something was stirring in his psyche – an uneasy feeling that life here would never be the same again.

His brown eyes gazed out over the forested hills that separated his own estate of Jarosbork from the neighbouring Wolfsberg of the von Stellings. The von Stellings … The muscles of his jaw tightened automatically at the very name, and the look in his eyes hardened as he stared into the distance. The German castle was hidden from view by the tallest hill of the range that divided the two estates; pine-clad and jagged, it pierced the evening sky – a jewel of darkest jade framed in a setting of pure gold, as the sun sank slowly behind it.

Motionless, he watched as the golden glory faded and the rich crimson spread across the heavens, transforming the dark green of the mountains to a deep purple. There was something strange about the sky this night. Something beautiful, yet fearful. A terrible beauty that tugged at the heart and brought tears to the eyes. At moments like this he knew that he loved this land with a passion he had known only once before in his fifty-one years.

As he stood there his mind returned to the words of Slowacki, the Polish poet and patriot:

'He who has chosen to nest on the heights of the eagle rather than the hearthstone will know how to sleep when the horizon is red with the storm, and the mutterings of demons are heard in the wind among the pines.'

The unease grew within him, as the crimson canopy of the heavens parted to reveal shimmering silver bands which grew broader and broader. Soon the red and gold of the evening would give way to the darker hues of the approaching night.

3

The moon was high in the sky; it drew his gaze as it had on so many nights like this over the years. How many times had he stood here and wondered if, a thousand miles away, she was looking at it too?

BOOK ONE

'Blood, Smoke and Flame'

———

I did not lose my heart in summer's even,
When roses to the moonrise burst apart;
When plumes were under heel and lead was flying,
In blood and smoke and flame I lost my heart.

A. E. Housman

Chapter One

'Tell me, Beth ... Tell me, *mein Schatz* ... Is the baby mine? Is Lara my child?'

Beth von Lessing stared down at the face on the pillow, the face of her husband of less than two years, Count Hans Heinrich von Lessing. Beads of sweat stood out on his pale brow like diamonds on the finest parchment. She knew what it had cost him to utter that question; the question that had haunted his mind since the day he had first held his newly-born daughter in his arms almost six months ago, only weeks before a growth in his groin had transformed him from the healthy giant she had married into a pale shadow of the man recognized throughout Upper Silesia as the Master of Wolfsberg, one of the greatest estates east of the Oder–Neisse line. The red-rimmed eyes looked up into hers, pleading for the truth.

How could she deny him what he craved more than all the world to hear? 'Yes, Hans. Yes, *Liebling*. Lara is your child.'

A deep sigh emitted from the cracked lips of the shrunken figure on the bed. It was the answer he had hoped for, had prayed for, for all these months.

Beth von Lessing closed her eyes. She could no longer meet his gaze. Tears were swimming beneath the tightly shut lids. *May God forgive me for this lie ... May the dear Lord forgive me, for I never will ...*

Forgive me, Hans, forgive me. The words cavorted crazily in her head, then spilled from her lips in a strangled shout, 'Forgive me ...', as a high-pitched wailing sound drowned her cry and penetrated her subconscious.

Clasping her hands to her ears, she sat up in the dishevelled bed, as the sound of the air-raid siren brought her tumbling back to reality. She was no longer in the faraway land of Silesia in the summer of 1920, she was right here in the bleak mid-winter of war-torn London, 1940.

'Are you all right, Mum?'

Beth's green eyes opened abruptly, spilling hot tears down her cheeks as she turned and blinked in confusion in the direction of the voice from the bedroom door.

'I asked if you're all right, Mum. The siren's gone. Didn't you hear it?'

Beth looked at her daughter and shook her head as she fought to control her breathing. That damned nightmare. How long must she relive her guilt? How long, dear Lord, how long?

The film of sweat that covered her skin made her face shine in the dull glow of the bedside light, and the palms of her hands were damp as she ran them through the wayward strands of brown hair plastered to her brow. Her voice came faintly, as if from afar, as she struggled back to full consciousness. 'Yes, Lara dear, I heard it. I was dreaming, that's all ... You go on down to the shelter. Don't bother waiting for me. I'll be right behind you.'

Lara Cameron, *née* von Lessing, smiled indulgently. 'You're tired. You do too much these days. I keep telling you that.'

The bedroom door closed softly behind her and Beth stared at it dully as she flopped back on the pillows. Between the air-raids and these nightmares, sometimes she thought she wouldn't give a damn if the *Luftwaffe* found its target on 29 Atholl Square, London W1 one night and put an end to everything, once and for all.

With a sigh, she got up from the bed and reached for her dressing-gown. These were defeatist thoughts, she ought to be ashamed of herself. Lara was right. She was tired, that was all. Everyone was. This damned war was seeing to that.

She tightened the belt of her robe around her waist as the drone of the first wave of bombers penetrated the heavy velvet of the curtains and the black-out material beyond. A shudder ran through her. How much more could they take? It was now fifteen months since that day when the whole country had held its breath as the Prime Minister, Neville Chamberlain, informed them they were now at war with Germany.

She had been alone in the house that morning, Sunday 3 September 1939. She remembered the sun had been shining after a night of thunderstorms across the country. She had poured herself a dry sherry as the Prime Minister's tinny tones filled the room, resonating from the walnut depths of the KB wireless on the side-table:

'... I have to tell you now that no such undertaking has been received, and that consequently this country is at war with Germany ... The situation in which no word given by Germany's ruler could be trusted and no people or country could feel itself safe, has become intolerable. Now we have resolved to finish it ... May God bless you all. May He defend the right, for it is evil things that we shall be fighting against – brute force, bad faith, injustice, oppression and persecution; and against them I am certain that the right will prevail ... '

'Evil things ... ' Beth repeated the words, reliving once more the cold chill that had filled her soul as she had switched off the small Bakelite knob of the wireless set and stared with unseeing eyes out of the window at the sunlit street beyond. It had all seemed so unreal. Did people really declare war on a bright, sunny morning like this? Perhaps she was dreaming it. Perhaps it was another of those awful nightmares that had plagued her life for so many years.

But it had been no nightmare. And some of those evil things that Chamberlain had warned them against were heading their way right now, causing havoc and destruction unimaginable fifteen short months ago. They said that Victoria Station got it last night. But it was difficult to verify things right away. The newspapers were very careful about what they published. Morale must be kept high at all costs. The droning outside the window was louder now. They could be no more than a few streets away. The muffled sound of the retaliatory ack-ack sent a shiver through her, but brought comfort, nevertheless.

It would be Christmas in less than two weeks. Would that mean the raids would get better or worse? She shrugged in silent response to her own question as she reached for her book. Margaret Irwin's *The Stranger Prince* was far too large a tome to fit into her pocket, and she slipped it down the front of her dressing-gown as she slid her feet into her warmest slippers.

Her fur coat hung waiting on the back of the bedroom door and she pulled it on top of her dressing-gown. She gave a wry smile as she always did when she caught sight of herself dressed like this in the dressing-table mirror. If they were hit, what an incongruous sight she would make, standing outside the Pearly Gates in a fur coat, night-gown and bedroom slippers. A bomb exploded with a dull crunch in the distance, adding credence to her fears.

The others were already settled comfortably into their usual positions in the wine cellars when she got there. Half the house had been requisitioned for members of the Polish Embassy, and she could see the huddled figures of Mr Kulinski, a second secretary, Mr Kador, a translator, and Mr and Mrs Malinowski in the dim lamplight of the room beyond. The Poles usually played cards before dropping off to

9

sleep and, by the faint tinkle of glass, it seemed they were well enough supplied with Poland's national drink to keep out the worst of the cold tonight.

In their own part of the cellar, Lara was curled up on an old *chaise-longue*, with a tartan car-rug over her knees. Mrs Bates, their housekeeper of ten years' standing, was already snoring fitfully on a camp-bed close by. She never waited for the siren these days, but had taken to coming down here at twelve o'clock every night, after locking up. 'The bleeders just wait till you've got all comfy in your bed before they decide to come,' she had complained. 'I've had enough of it.' And no one could argue with her. One of the worst things about the bombing was the fact that the sirens seemed to go off just as you were sitting down to a meal or had begun to doze off in bed. No wonder many folk had resorted to a permanent subterranean life-style.

Heaving Humphrey the ginger tom from her lap, Lara pulled something from beneath the car-rug as Beth approached and held it out towards her. 'Here. I knew you wouldn't bother filling one for yourself.'

Her mother gave a shamefaced smile as she took the proffered hot water bottle. 'Thank you, dear. That was a sweet thought.' Removing the book, she tucked the bottle between her fur coat and dressing-gown and settled into the old leather library chair she had claimed for her own for the duration of their cellar existence. A paisley-patterned eiderdown that had seen better days was then tucked around her lap and the book laid on top. When comfortably settled, she smiled across at her daughter and said softly, so as not to waken Mrs Bates, 'I never asked at tea, but did you hear from Ken today?'

Lara shook her head in the lamplight and snuggled down further on the *chaise*, as Humphrey sprang back up to claim his place beside her. 'No, but I didn't really expect to. His last letter was from Tangmere, but they haven't got much time to write just now. In his last letter he was still hopeful of getting home on a twenty-four-hour pass over Christmas, though.'

A wry smile flickered momentarily at the corners of her lips. It would be their first wedding anniversary on Boxing Day. She prayed every night he would make it back for that. It was now over six months since his squadron had abandoned its base in France, in the wake of the Germans goose-stepping into Paris on 14 June. She knew he had been actively engaged in all the fighting over the Channel and south coast that had taken place between then and the end of September, referred to by the newspapers as the Battle of Britain, but as to his movements since – well, they were really anybody's guess.

'Is he still making forays over France?' The question was asked tentatively. Operations in the RAF, like everything else in this war, were classified, if not top secret, and they both knew it.

'I think so. From the snippets of information I've been able to put together, it seems Number One Squadron still spend most of their time over or around the Channel.'

'As long as they're just over or around it and not *in* it, you should thank God for small mercies!'

Lara gave a wistful smile. 'I just wish Judy or some of the other wives lived nearer, then we could swap notes ... ' Her voice tailed off as she sank into thought. It was a mixed blessing to be married to a pilot in the RAF's premier fighter squadron, and, while she was inordinately proud of the sandy-haired, moustached Scotsman she had married twelve months ago, she often wished he had chosen a diplomatic career instead. In her own job at the Foreign Office she could appreciate more than most what a relatively secure life His Majesty's public servants led.

'Did I hear you say something earlier about going into work tomorrow?' her mother asked.

'You did.'

'But tomorrow's Saturday!' Beth protested. 'You've already worked two out of the past three. Surely you must have some time off, even if there *is* a war on!'

Lara shivered as a low rumble from somewhere in the direction of the next terrace sent a faint tremor through their own walls. 'It's my own choice,' she said softly. 'I'm being seconded to the American Embassy for a few days from Monday. They've been having problems with so many of their secretarial staff going down with this 'flu bug that's going the rounds, and there's been some trouble about getting hold of enough replacements with High Security clearance at short notice. It should only be for a few days though, thank God.'

'The Yanks are not that bad, surely?'

'Oh, they're all right, I suppose – in small doses. Anyway, I've not much choice in the matter. They seem very keen that we should feel at home. I've been told I'm very welcome to take a walk over there tomorrow to get the feel of the place, so I'll be raring to go first thing Monday morning. I'll actually be working from the Embassy Residence at 14 Princes Gate – you know, the place where the Kennedys used to live.'

Beth's interest grew. There could be hardly a soul in London who hadn't been intrigued by Ambassador Joe Kennedy, his glamorous wife Rose, and their enormous brood of children. His recent resignation and departure for Washington in October, however, had left the American diplomatic scene in London in a state of flux, and public interest was keen to learn who would replace the larger-than-life Irish-American as Ambassador to Britain.

'That should be quite an experience, the way things are at the moment. It's a pity you couldn't have been assigned to Princes Gate before the war broke out and Rose took the family back to America – I'm told that the two eldest boys, Joe Junior and his younger brother Jack, are quite something!'

'Shame on you, Mother! I'm sure neither of them can hold a candle to Ken, anyway!'

'There speaks a true and faithful wife.' Beth smiled. 'And I'm sure you're right. So you intend to take them up on their suggestion to go over there tomorrow?'

Lara nodded. 'It's not a bad idea really. It'll help break the ice. I'd feel like the new girl on her first day at school on Monday, otherwise. But what about you? You're not on duty tomorrow, are you?'

Beth shook her head. Her part-time job as an ambulance driver had given her her first weekend off for a month, air-raids permitting. 'Count Raczynski, the Polish Ambassador, has very kindly invited me to a reception at their Embassy in Portland Place tomorrow evening. Mrs Malinowska passed on the invitation. I think she's been feeling sorry for me of late and thought a night out might just cheer me up.'

'Mmm,' Lara looked suitably impressed. 'I hope she's right. There's no doubt about it, you *have* been overdoing things recently. You'll wear your gold brocade, won't you? That always makes you feel on top of the world.'

'But of course.' Just the thought of her Molyneux gown brought a warm glow. It was identical to the one that Princess Marina, the beautiful Greek wife of the Duke of Kent, had worn to the Coronation two and a half years ago. Jack Mallory, the man she had married after Hans Heinrich's death, had been alive then, and they had been lucky enough to be invited to the ceremony in Westminster Abbey itself, then to the reception afterwards, where lunch was served in a huge marquee next to the Abbey. She had been unable to take her eyes off the beautiful gown worn by the Duchess of Kent and, seeing how much she had admired it, Jack had ordered an exact replica in her size to be sent specially from Paris. The gesture had been so typical of him and the gown had remained one of her firm favourites, although she had never worn it since his death just over two years ago.

A silence settled in the chill of the cellar, punctuated by the familiar sounds of the air-raid outside and the faint murmur of voices and occasional muffled laugh from the adjoining room.

Mrs Bates was snoring now through her nose, a high-pitched whistling sound that had become a familiar nightly accompaniment to the sounds of the planes and ack-ack outside. Her teeth were sitting in a glass on top of a cabin trunk next to her bed, her toothless lower jaw resting slackly on the loose rolls of skin that made up her triple chin. Beth found it hard to believe the housekeeper was the same age as herself – forty-two years old. Peggy Bates's ample figure, once voluptuous in her twenties and thirties, had now gone to seed; a fact even the most armour-plated corsetry could do little to disguise. Not that Beth herself felt much of a *femme fatale* right now. She glanced down at the winceyette nightdress beneath her fur coat. It would be a blessed relief to get dressed up for the reception at the Polish Embassy tomorrow night. She could scarcely remember the last time she had donned an evening gown.

Things had been so very different before the war when Jack was still alive. Then she had danced the night away several times a week at this time of year. She closed her eyes and sighed deeply as the ghosts of Christmas Past came back to haunt her once more. She had still not got used to finding herself a widow for the second time in twenty years. Perhaps she never would.

Jack Mallory, one of the Foreign Office's most respected mandarins, diplomatic adviser to three Prime Ministers, and Beth's second husband, had died unexpectedly on 1 October 1938, just as Neville Chamberlain flew back from Munich, after his meeting with Hitler, waving his 'Peace for our Time' scrap of paper.

It was funny really, things had seemed to go downhill both for the country and for herself from that moment on. She could never claim to have been madly in love with Jack, even he would have been the first to acknowledge that fact, but since meeting him in 1925, five years after Hans Heinrich's death and her return to England, he had become her whole life. It had never seemed to matter that he was almost twenty-five years her senior. He had been one of her father's dearest friends and that had been a good enough reason to accept that first invitation to have dinner with him. He had picked her up in his brand-new Rolls-Royce Phantom, but, to her surprise, he had not booked a table at a fashionable restaurant; instead, they had dined here in his town house at 29 Atholl Square, and she had had her first taste of gracious living in half a decade.

No one had really believed that as the widow of Count Hans Heinrich von Lessing she could be anything but extremely wealthy when she returned to London in 1920. But Carl Christian, Hans's twin brother, had made it very clear there would be little surplus cash available to send abroad if she chose to renege on her responsibilities to the Wolfsberg estate and return to England. The Great War had cut deep into the coffers of the German landed classes and nerves were fraught all over the Fatherland at the thought of what more punitive measures the victorious powers would come up with at Versailles and afterwards. Lloyd George was on record as threatening to squeeze Germany like a lemon till the pips squeaked, and no one doubted for a minute he would succeed. The fiery Welshman, as well as the French across the Channel, had many backers in their mutual desire to inflict punitive financial retribution on the Fatherland.

Her own parents, although supportive in every other way, could do little to help financially. The salary of an Oxford don did not stretch to supporting widowed daughters and, anyway, she would have been much too proud to allow that. No, she had kept her poverty well enough hidden to fool just about everyone. Just about everyone, that was, until she met Jack Mallory again, this time as a grown woman, on the occasion of her father's funeral. He had come up from London to pay his last respects to his old friend and, after the service, she had invited him back to her own tiny flat for a meal. This small kindness had been done out of consideration for her mother, who was taking the bereavement especially hard and was in no fit state to entertain. But within minutes of finding herself alone with the tall, grey-haired man with the slight limp from the trenches of 1914, Beth knew it was to herself that she had done the greatest favour.

After the emotional turmoil of Lara's birth, the shock of Hans Heinrich's death, then the struggle to bring up her child alone, to meet a pillar of security as companionable as Jack seemed like a dream come true, a safe haven after the storms of the past few years. Their wedding, six months later, had come as the natural conclusion to a relationship that had flowered into a deep love that, although it had very little to do with passion on her part, was to prove as deep and lasting as she knew she had any right to expect in this world.

What she had done to Hans Heinrich – the betrayal of her marriage vows – had left a deep and still livid wound that time could not heal. And, even today, twenty years later, the hurt was still there, a deep, abiding pain within her heart. She found herself shivering, despite the warmth of the quilt wrapped around her, as she looked across at her daughter, now a beautiful young woman of twenty.

Lara gave an encouraging smile. Her mother had been looking pale of late and the prospect of an evening out couldn't have come at a

14

better time, she was certain of that. It should be just what she needed to boost her flagging spirits. 'Did you pick up much Polish when you were out in Silesia?'

Beth's shoulders shrugged slightly beneath the quilt. 'A little. Enough to get by. Let's just say it wasn't exactly encouraged in the circles we moved in, although most of our servants were Polish.'

Lara nodded pensively, her eyes fixed on her mother's face. 'You've never talked much about that part of your life, have you, Mum? It's always struck me as rather odd, with my real father being German and all that ...'

And all that ... For Beth, volumes lay behind those three words. But, as far as Lara was concerned, her mother's reticence to talk about the Silesian years stemmed from another source – her unhappiness at having to leave behind her small stepson, Otto von Lessing, all those years ago.

Neither of them had spoken of the von Lessing side of the family since Britain had gone to war with Germany. Wolfsberg and their earlier life in Silesia had simply dropped from the conversation. How *could* they talk of it when Otto, dear, dear Otto, was now fighting for Hitler in this terrible war?

Just thinking about her stepson could still bring tears to Beth's eyes. He had been only four years old when she had brought her baby daughter back to live in England after Hans Heinrich's death. She had wanted to bring back Otto too, but the remaining von Lessing family would not hear of it. Hans Heinrich's twin brother, Carl Christian, had been running the adjoining estate of Adlerberg, and acting as Regent for Wolfsberg until Otto, the heir, came of age. He had been adamant that his dead brother's only son must remain in Silesia. Only by doing that could the child be prepared to be worthy one day of the title that was now his – Count Otto von Lessing und Wolfsberg.

Perhaps if she had lived in Silesia for longer than those two years as Hans's wife, things might have been different. But two years was not long enough for her ever to consider herself a German. She was English through and through, and all she wanted after her husband's death was to bring her baby daughter back to London. Her brother-in-law, Carl Christian, was much better fitted to run Wolfsberg than she could ever be. Anyway, the castle and estate would be Otto's when he grew up and what would happen to her then? If she had chosen to stay and had grown to love the place, what would have become of her when the time came to hand it over? She could not imagine her future as the ageing Dowager Countess von Lessing in a land that was not and could never be her own. No, all she had wanted was to bring Lara back to the people and places she knew and loved best. Her daughter must be brought up as an Englishwoman. Suddenly that had become very important to her. And now, all these years later, she knew the decision had been the right one.

'You still have friends over there presumably. But you've never kept in touch with them. Was there a reason for that?'

Beth tensed, her fingers gripping the smooth stoneware of the hot water bottle beneath the quilt. But this was neither the time nor the place to go into it. Perhaps some other day, some other time when the world was not so fraught a place, some time in the distant future when she was very old and felt the need to unburden herself of the secret that had weighed so heavily on her heart for all these years. Yes, perhaps then ... or perhaps never, who was to know? Who was to know anything these days? Who was to know if they would even be alive in the morning?

She feigned a yawn and snuggled down further in the chair as the foundations of the old house shook to the dull thud of another bomb detonating in the darkness outside. 'I'm tired, darling. Very tired. Perhaps some other time ...'

Lara looked across at her mother, a slight frown creasing the skin between her brows. The shutters were coming down again, as they always did when she probed too deeply into that part of her mother's life. It had happened so often in the past. But it was late, too late, to pursue the matter. Tomorrow was another day, and a glance at her watch told her it was here already.

Chapter Two

The American Ambassador's residence at 14 Princes Gate was an enormous, six-storey house of thirty-six rooms that overlooked Kensington Gardens at the front and at the back looked out over a large, enclosed expanse of lawn and gardens, which it shared with the other houses in the terrace. Most of the rooms on the lower floors were given over to the secretarial staff, and it was with a distinct feeling of apprehension that Lara walked up the steps and in through the front door to become part of their number.

The reception area was bright and welcoming as she walked in and announced herself, in a hesitant voice, to the young woman behind the desk.

'Mrs Cameron? Oh, yes, Mr Somerville informed me you'd be taking Margot's place on Monday. Welcome on board.' The neatly coiffured young woman with the Bette Davis eyes looked up from the appointments book in front of her and offered a slender hand to be shaken. 'I'll show you to your office. I'm Sheila, Sheila Cassidy.'

Lara followed as the receptionist led the way through to the lift that would take her to her own office. Why did all American women she met look as if they had just stepped out of a bandbox? Sheila Cassidy's high-heels clicked briskly on the highly polished floor and Lara could not help noticing that she was wearing real nylons. She felt a sense of inferiority growing by the minute as she glanced down at her own best pair of silk stockings, now so well washed that they wrinkled embarrassingly around the knees and ankles.

They stopped outside the heavy metal doors of the biggest, most ornamental cage of a lift that Lara had ever come across, and the Bette Davis eyes turned on her once more. 'You can use the stairs, but why tire yourself out needlessly? Your office is on the second floor, room 12a. It's through room 12. You'll excuse me if I don't come all the way up. I'm not really supposed to leave the desk for more than a couple of minutes at a time.'

Lara gave a mechanical smile and murmured her thanks. She hated lifts. It was a throwback to her childhood. She had got stuck in one once at a friend's house when celebrating a tenth birthday party. She had chosen to conceal herself in the service lift during a game of hide and seek and, to her alarm, could not get the door open again. She grimaced at the memory as the metal cage clanked its way up on a system of wires and pulleys to the second floor and shuddered to a stop.

Room 12 proved to be a smallish office at the back of the building, overlooking the lawn and gardens. The door was half open. After receiving no response to her knock, she entered tentatively, closing it quietly behind her. With its pale cream wallpaper, varnished wood-work and two-tone striped brown curtains, it had a distinctly masculine look to it. The desk and filing cabinets that lined the wall opposite the Adam-style fireplace were made of oak and were thirties in style. Lara grimaced; the last decade was not her favourite period. The room smelt vaguely of cigarette smoke, as if it had been recently vacated, and a man's grey, soft felt hat hung at a rakish angle on the coatstand, along with a darker grey Harris tweed coat and a black and white checked woollen scarf. Papers lay scattered on top of the desk and a half-drunk cup of black coffee sat next to an ashtray containing a crumpled pack of Camels.

A small door to the left of the window had the number 12a in brass letters on it. Her room. A tingle of anticipation ran through her as she crossed the floor, clasped the brass knob and pushed it open.

The room she found herself in was less than half the size of the outer office and contained little more than a desk and chair. A row of oak filing cabinets ran along the back wall and, on the same side as the window, two pictures hung rather incongruously next to each other – an official black and white photograph of the President, Franklin Delano Roosevelt, and a garishly coloured one of Clark Gable dressed as Rhett Butler, from *Gone With the Wind*. The office's last occupant had obviously been quite a fan.

That was the only outward evidence, however, of the secretary she was to replace. Unlike the outer office, there was no other visible sign of human habitation. The desk-top was devoid of everything but a clean blotter, an inkwell and pencil tray, and a clean ashtray with an advertisement for Lucky Strikes around the rim.

Curiosity got the better of her and she went over to the tallest of the filing cabinets and pulled open the top drawer. At least it would give her some idea of what type of work she would be doing in here for the next few days.

'Who the hell are you?'

The male voice from the open door made her whirl round immediately, dropping the file she had extracted from the drawer with a clatter. Her eyes met those of a tall, dark-haired man, in his middle to late thirties, with looks not unlike the film star on the wall, although the face was leaner, the brows thicker, and the hair slightly curlier.

Embarrassment and guilt suffused Lara's cheeks with a deep shade of pink. Redheads blushed all too easily and she could feel her face positively burning as she stooped to pick up the folder. Its pages were scattered over the brown linoleum and she was aware of her stockings bagging even more at the ankles as she squatted down to retrieve the papers. The fact that most of them seemed to be stamped 'Highly Confidential' only added to her consternation.

'Leave that and identify yourself, please.' The question was rapped out. The stranger was obviously annoyed.

'Cameron – Mrs Lara Cameron,' she stammered. 'I – I work here. At least I will do as from Monday.'

'You don't say!' For the first time the features beneath the thatch of dark hair relaxed a little. 'Well, a piece of advice, Mrs Lara Cameron. Don't ever walk into anyone's office unannounced around here. Especially mine.'

'Yours,' Lara said faintly. But this could not be her new boss. She had been told she would be working for a Harvey J. Ledbetter, an official of some thirty-five years' standing. 'You're Mr Ledbetter?' Either he was an incredibly well preserved fifty-five-year-old, or she had been drastically misinformed.

The dark brows quirked and the blue eyes took on an amused look. 'Do I look like him?'

Lara shrugged helplessly. 'I really don't know. I've never met the gentleman.'

'And you're never liable to now, I'm afraid. Harve was recalled a few days ago. His wife's had a heart attack and he's been transferred back to Washington. I'm his replacement.'

Her heart sank. 'How do you do, Mr ... ?'

'Adams. Mike Adams.' His handshake was almost too firm, causing the gold signet ring on the middle finger of her right hand to dig into the flesh. The blue eyes continued to regard her sceptically. 'Been a secretary long, Mrs Cameron?'

'Almost two years.'

'Mmm. Long enough to know better than to go in for breaking and entering like this.'

The colour flooded back into Lara's cheeks. 'The door was open ... I – I presumed the receptionist at the desk downstairs would have rung you to say I was on my way up.'

He grinned, a lopsided affair that creased the skin around his eyes on the left side of his face. 'So she did, most probably. But I was in the john.'

He was nothing if not direct. Lara averted her eyes and made an attempt to make for the outer office, but his huge bulk was taking up most of the space between her and the door. For no accountable reason, Mr Mike Adams made her nervous. And, worst of all, she knew he could sense it.

'I understand you're not a permanent member of our staff.'

'No, I usually work at the Foreign Office, but I often get drafted in as a temp wherever one with High Security vetting is required at short notice.'

'Mmm. So you're obviously used to coping with the foibles of different bosses.'

Lara gave a quiet smile. 'I've had my share of characters.'

'Anyone I know?' He still stood wedged between her and the door to the outer office, making it impossible for her to do anything but stand there and answer his questions.

'A few. Churchill, Bevin ... '

The names, so casually dropped, could not fail to impress, but surprisingly, except for a slight upward quirk of the left eyebrow, he gave no indication of it. 'Fancy a coffee?'

She relaxed slightly. Even if working for two of Britain's greatest statesmen cut no ice with this particular American, perhaps he was human after all. 'I'd love one.'

'Great. I could do with another myself. What's left of mine's gone cold by now. You'll get all you need in the little ante-room at the end of the corridor.'

'What?'

'The coffee. You'll get all you require to make two coffees in that small scullery at the foot of the corridor.'

Lara stared at him. He was perfectly serious.

'You *have* been assigned as my secretary, haven't you?'

She nodded dumbly. But, thank God, not for long. 'How many sugars?'

'No sugar and no milk. I take it as it comes – just as I do life, Mrs Cameron. You might remember that.'

He was sitting behind his desk in the outer office when she got back, his suede shoes crossed and balancing on the edge of a small filing cabinet. He smiled his thanks as she sat the cup and saucer in front of him, then, never lifting his gaze from her, he extracted a new pack of Camels from the inside pocket of his jacket. 'Smoke?'

'I don't, thanks.' The words came out more primly than she had intended.

'You don't mind if I do?'

She shook her head.

He lit the cigarette with a quick flick of his lighter, then drew the smoke deep into his lungs before letting it out slowly through his nostrils. Much to her discomfort, he continued to survey her critically from behind the desk. 'I get the feeling you don't care too much for this transfer, Mrs Cameron. Or maybe you just don't care too much for Americans in general.' The quirky smile returned. 'Or is it just me in particular you take exception to?'

Lara bristled. What he said was too close to the truth for comfort. He had her on the defensive, but she was determined not to let it show. 'I don't know what makes you say that.'

'Oh, just a feeling, I guess. You get a nose for these things. From what I've heard since I've been here, we Americans have had a pretty bad press so far amongst you British. At least those poor guys have who've joined up and come over here of their own accord to help you out of this mess you've gotten yourselves into in Europe.'

Lara's eyebrows rose along with her hackles. So he was coming the 'nobody over here appreciates us and what we're doing for you' line, was he? 'Really? Well, I can assure you your self-pity is totally unwarranted. If Yanks are unpopular in certain quarters, that most definitely doesn't apply to a particular contingent of the female population. On the contrary, you Americans are quite amazingly popular with, shall we say, the less discriminating section of the female populace over here.'

'Only the less discriminating, huh?' His left eyebrow quirked upwards, as he mimicked her accent almost too perfectly. 'Well now, I don't know so much about that. From what I've heard the vast majority of you British gals are wearing utility knickers these days.'

'I beg your pardon?'

His grin was broader now as her discomfort increased. 'Utility knickers, Mrs Cameron, ma'am. Now don't tell me you've never heard of them. What is it they say about them again? One Yank and they're off!'

Lara could feel the blood rush to her cheeks once more. 'Mr Adams, that was hardly the remark of a gentleman!'

The grin grew broader as he straightened up in the chair and flicked his ash in the vague direction of the ashtray. 'Crap, Mrs Cameron, there's no such critter as "a gentleman", as you so quaintly put it. There are only men.'

'Then you are not a very nice man.' She was aware of sounding hopelessly prudish as she uttered the words.

He shook his head. 'The bottom of this trashcan we call a world is full of "nice guys", Mrs Cameron. Only the cream and the bastards rise to the top.'

'And which one are you?'

'I'll leave that for you to find out.'

Travelling back to Atholl Square on the bus, Lara shifted uncomfortably in her seat as she relived the encounter with her new boss. He seemed the typical caricature of what she had chosen to believe about Americans over here. But she had more than a sneaking suspicion that that was exactly the impression he had intended to convey. He had deliberately set out to shock her, imagining her to be one of those strait-laced English Misses that they in their turn imagined all British females to be.

She gave a rueful sigh as she stared at her reflection in the window of the bus. If only he knew. No one could work for the Foreign Office for any length of time and remain a prude. She had spent a few weeks last summer as a temporary secretary to Ernest Bevin, the Minister of Labour and National Service. For the initial few days, she had worked in a constantly puce-faced state, but after that she had become totally inured to whatever bad language or risqué jokes she heard around her from the male of the species.

No, she certainly wasn't shocked by her meeting with her new boss this morning. What really disturbed her was the suspicion that perhaps there was some truth in Mike Adams's accusation. Maybe she was just the tiniest bit anti-American. But it was hard not to be these days, wasn't it? There they were, the richest country in the world, just standing by while Hitler rode roughshod over Europe and blitzed Britain to pieces. It was no secret that Joe Kennedy's resignation as Ambassador and his departure for America several weeks ago was the inevitable outcome of his very vocal condemnation of any moves by his President to get more involved in this war. He had announced loud and clear to all who would listen that he could no longer continue representing an Administration that was seen to be actively supporting one side over the other. He saw Roosevelt's tentative moves in that direction as the first steps in active involvement and, as one of the staunchest advocates of appeasement, that was something he could never countenance. Lara frowned into the dirty glass of the window. With friends like him in the American Embassy, who needed enemies?

The journey home seemed to take longer every evening, as the nightly bombing raids took their toll of the roads. If it wasn't a detour they had to put up with, because whole streets had been closed off due to bomb craters, then it was the driver weaving his way around the series of gaping holes in the road that no amount of repair squads could ever keep up with.

She stared out at the grey pavements. They were coming to a bus stop, but there was hardly a child in sight. In fact, the whole city was almost bereft of children, so many thousands had been evacuated to safer areas in the country over the past few months. Who would have thought that was what war was all about – a world without children? It was a depressing thought.

She looked at her watch impatiently as the bus juddered to a full stop in the slush-filled street and a handful of bedraggled people got on.

She moved over in her seat to make room for a young woman in the uniform of the Women's Royal Army Corps to sit down. They exchanged polite smiles, then the girl took a pack of Lucky Strike cigarettes from her breast pocket and offered Lara one.

'They're Yank. Better than ours.'

'No thanks. I don't smoke.'

'Please yourself.'

As one of the cigarettes was puffed into life and the WRAC settled back in her seat, the sight of the cigarettes sent Lara's mind returning to Americans in general, and her new boss in particular. Perhaps half the problem was that every American male over twenty seemed to think he was God's gift to women. And the infuriating thing was that most of the female population seemed to agree with him. Even Joe Kennedy himself had been regarded as quite a one with the ladies, so was it surprising that the Embassy should have the likes of Mike Adams amongst the other senior members of its staff?

Despite her attempts to turn her mind to other things, her encounter with the acerbic Mr Adams was still on her mind when she entered the front hall of 29 Atholl Square and found the envelope with the familiar spikey handwriting waiting for her on the side table. 'Ken!' Her heart raced as she snatched up the envelope and tore it open.

My darling,

I'm writing this while trying to snatch an hour's kip before reporting for duty. I'm grounded at the moment, but it's nothing to worry about. I had to eject a couple of days ago when an ME 109 shell at 12,000 feet did for my machine. Luckily, my injuries were fairly minor and the parachute drop almost enjoyable! The jar dislocated my left shoulder and I've got a few splinter punctures here and there, but nothing that won't be mended fairly soon. I'm hoping the CO takes enough pity on me to let me off for a couple of days so I can make it back to the Big Smoke for Christmas. I thought I'd better let you know about the scratches in case you heard from Judy or one of the other wives and began to worry. Honestly, sweetheart, it's nothing – and the skirmish might just have done us a favour when it comes to deciding who gets leave at the end of the month and who doesn't.

I hope the old place is still standing up to the pounding from Jerry. The blighters had better not drop anything in the vicinity of Atholl Square! How is your Ma and Mrs B. and that old rat-bag Humphrey? Give them my love.

My old boss 'Bing' Crosby bought it last weekend – somewhere over the Channel, I think. You may remember, we met two years ago at Tangmere. He taught me almost all I know about Hurricane aerobatics. Some pretty hairy stuff, but he had absolutely no fear. He assured me he would die in bed at the end of it all and leave his body to medical science. I told him medical science would probably contest the will! He liked that and agreed with me. He was a good bloke. What more can I say?

Duty calls, my darling. Keep safe for me. I think of you constantly.

All love, as always,
Ken

Lara stared at the letter in her hands for a long time. Just feasting her eyes on his handwriting seemed to bring him closer somehow. He had been injured. God only knew how badly. He always was one for underplaying everything. Not for the first time, the south coast of England seemed a million miles away. She wanted to drop everything and go to him, but that wouldn't do any good. There was hardly a wife in the whole squadron who didn't feel the same. It seemed an age since they had spent any time together. What a first year of marriage this had turned out to be!

They had met at a party given by Judy Martin, one of her old school friends. Ken had arrived with Judy's brother Bob and a few more of their fighter pilot pals. They were all stationed with Number One Squadron at Tangmere, the Sussex RAF base of Number One and Forty-three Squadrons that nestled between the South Downs and Selsey Bill on the Channel coast.

She had been attracted to him at once. A sandy-haired Scot from Dundee, of medium height, he had none of the cockiness she had come to associate with the usual 'Brylcreem Boys' that frequented the Martin household when Judy's brother was around. Although, if she were entirely honest with herself, his first words to her made her think she had come face to face with the cockiest of the lot. She had been standing by the window of the Martins' drawing room, looking out at the sun setting behind the high beech hedge that bordered the garden, and wishing she had never accepted Judy's invitation to this particular party, when one of the laughing crowd of young men clustered around the piano left the group and came over to her. 'I've been watching you standing here for some time,' he said, extending a hand. 'I don't believe we've met. I'm Mr Right.' The memory still made her smile. And his words were to prove so true. She was to be head over heels in love with him before the night was out.

He had wanted to fly ever since hearing stories as a small child of his father's exploits before and during the Great War with the Royal Flying Corps at Farnborough in Hampshire. He even carried a sepia-coloured photograph around with him of Sandy Cameron in the cockpit of his Havilland Scout. But the flying that Ken was doing was a far cry from those early days of flight. The week before they had met he had been admitted to Number One Squadron's crack aerobatic team. The Air Ministry had forbidden formation aerobatics being carried out in Hurricanes, or aerobatic manoeuvres at below 5,000 feet, but Ken had demonstrated that the Hurricane could be safely employed both in formation manoeuvres and below the stipulated 5,000 feet.

His pioneering bravery in the cockpit had been the talk not only of their own 'drome, but of every squadron in the country. He had not told her this himself, of course. That would have been too much like boasting. Bob Martin had revealed it during a night out, in August of last year, when a gang of them had gone to see Emlyn Williams and Sybil Thorndike in the former's play, *The Corn is Green*, at the Duchess Theatre. It was only two weeks before war broke out; three months before their wedding. Ken's best friend, Dai Jenkins from Bridgend, Glamorgan, had been the best man, and Judy had made a picture of a bridesmaid. The pair of them had followed them up the aisle as man and wife only two months later. It all seemed a million years ago now.

Carefully folding the letter and slotting it back in its envelope, she placed it in her handbag and snapped the catch shut. A glance at her watch told her it was past lunchtime but, with a bit of luck, Mrs Bates might have something worth eating left in the kitchen. Before she could begin the descent to the lower floor, the buxom figure of Mrs Malinowska appeared at the top of the stairs.

'Larisa, my dear!' Sophie Malinowska did not believe in the diminutive form of names. 'You are looking forward to tonight?'

'Tonight?'

Mrs Malinowska looked abashed. 'The reception! How could you forget!'

Realization dawned on Lara's face. 'Oh, but it's my mother who's going, not me, I'm afraid.'

'Dear me ... Your mother is going with another partner, perhaps?'

'Well, no. Not that I know of ...'

Mrs Malinowska looked puzzled. 'But the invitation was for Mrs Mallory and Partner – and you are not coming? But you *must* join us tonight. I insist upon it. I cannot imagine why your dear mother hasn't mentioned it.' She gave Lara a reassuring squeeze on the arm. 'I shall look forward to seeing you tonight. You tell your Mama so. The change will be good for you both.' She pulled the chinchilla collar of her coat up around her neck and made for the front door and her luncheon date at the Dorchester, leaving a pensive Lara in her wake.

It was strange indeed that her mother hadn't mentioned that the invitation was for two. And she was pretty certain that she wasn't going with anyone else. Lunch forgotten, she made for the stairs. With a bit of luck her mother should be at home, unless she had popped out to do some shopping.

Beth was in the drawing-room on the first floor, toying with a letter to her mother in Oxford. She looked up from the writing desk by the window as her daughter entered. 'Lara, dear! You're back earlier than I'd anticipated. Have you eaten?'

Ignoring the question, Lara wagged an admonishing finger. 'You're a dark horse and no mistake! What's all this about you getting a double invitation to that "do" at the Polish Embassy and not telling me?'

The colour drained momentarily from Beth's cheeks. The omission had been deliberate. To take her daughter along with her tonight would somehow seem wrong. But why she felt it to be so wrong, and exactly how wrong, only she must ever know. She forced a smile to her lips. 'Oh my dear, I never imagined you would want to go to anything so boring!'

'Boring! From what I've heard at the FO, the Poles know better than most how to let their hair down. Before this beastly war broke out, invitations to their parties were more sought after than to any bashes at the German Embassy. Certainly old "Brick-en-drop", the illustrious Ambassador Joachim von Ribbentrop, may well have once been a champagne salesman, but there was very little of that in evidence at any reception I was ever invited to there!'

'You mean you really would like to come?'

'Of course I would! And I'm mortally offended you could think otherwise.' The two women looked at one another, then Lara laughed and hurried across the Indian carpet to hug her mother. 'Oh, come on, don't look so tragic! I'm only joking. I'm not really angry. But I *would* like to come – if that's all right with you. I just fancy a night out – a real night out for once.'

'Then you shall have one, Lara dear. And I apologize for being so remiss as not to ask you before now.' Beth's heart sank as she spoke the words. But there seemed very little choice.

Both women dressed with special care that evening. Beth because she had decided to wear the gold brocade Molyneux, and that meant doing her nut-brown hair into a special figure of eight chignon instead of the normal bun at the nape of her neck, and fishing out her favourite pieces of gold jewellery to complement the gown. And Lara because she knew that to compete with her mother on a night out was difficult enough, even without the Molyneux.

She often wished she had inherited her mother's colouring, instead of this infuriating red hair and the obligatory freckles, which even the most liberal helping of Coty's Air-spun face powder did little to disguise. Heaven only knew where she got her colouring from, for pictures of her father showed him as a typical example of Teutonic manhood, with the blondest of hair and bluest of eyes. She squinted closer to the mirror as she applied the faintest touch of pale-blue powder to her upper lids. Hazel would be the kindest description of her eye-colour, she supposed, if that stretched to the greenish brown colour she detested. Oh, to have her mother's pure sea-green eyes!

She stepped back from the mirror and stared critically at her reflection. Mmm, not too bad. She twirled on one heel and examined herself from the back. The expanse of fair, naked skin, from the shining pageboy that skimmed her shoulders, to the narrow, hand-span waist, was flawless. She had put on this particular gown only once before, for a party she was going to with Ken shortly before their marriage and, quite frankly, he had been horrified.

'The front's all right,' he had admitted grudgingly, eyeing the modest sweetheart neckline, well-fitting bodice and straight skirt, 'but where the hell's the back of it?'

She had stared at him in a mixture of disappointment and indignation. 'It doesn't have a back because that's the latest fashion,' she had protested.

But he would not be moved. It was his Calvinistic Scottish background, of course, and she had told him so in no uncertain terms, although it had made no difference to the outcome. His grandfather had been a Free Church Minister in Arbroath. Ken had told her he had spent his life haunted by the thought that someone, somewhere might be enjoying themselves.

But no matter how his grandson could make fun at the old man's expense, Lara knew there was still a strongly Presbyterian, amazingly prudish heart beating beneath the airforce-blue serge of his uniform jacket. Nevertheless, she had taken off the dress that night – and would do so again tonight, if only she could have him back with her.

She sighed and picked up her fur wrap from the bed. There was little point in dreaming. The taxi would be waiting and, with a bit of luck and the *Luftwaffe* permitting, they just might make it round to Portland Place in one piece.

Chapter Three

Beth gripped Lara's arm as they entered the two large basement rooms at 47 Portland Place that had been given over for the Embassy reception. She recognized several of the faces in the crowd of immaculately turned out guests, many in uniform, nodding her head in greeting and smiling politely as they moved through the throng to where Count Edward Raczynski, the Ambassador, was standing next to the elegant figure of his wife Cesia. They were in a small group consisting of Sir John and Lady Anderson; Lady Granville, the President of the Anglo-Polish Society; Lord Queensberry, and a stocky, serious-faced man in the uniform of a Colonel in the Polish Army. All, except the Army officer, were old friends who required no introduction. The Count raised his glass in acknowledgement of Beth's presence, and gestured for her and Lara to join them.

'Countess – how nice to see you again!' He could never bring himself to refer to Beth by any title other than her Silesian one. His smile of welcome was genuine and the group moved apart slightly to allow them to join it. 'And – don't tell me – this is Lara.' His eyes moved appreciatively from the top of the shining red hair to Lara's black satin slippers. 'How time flies ... You were a fresh-faced eighteen-year-old, just finishing secretarial college, I believe, when we last met.'

'Lara is a married woman now. Aren't you, my dear?' Lady Granville smiled. 'Married to one of our brave fighter pilots, no less. Tell me, my dear, your husband is holding his own against that beastly Goering's *Luftwaffe*, I trust?'

Lara gave a rueful smile and experienced a momentary twinge of guilt at the mention of Ken. What wouldn't she give to have him here with her right now? It seemed quite wrong to be enjoying herself without him. 'Yes – thank you. Although I did get a letter today telling me he's been shot down and slightly injured.'

'Lara!' Beth looked truly shocked. 'For heaven's sake, you never said a word about that to me.'

Count Raczynski gave a knowing laugh. 'Since when did our children tell us everything? Lara has simply not wished to worry you, my dear Countess. Heaven knows, we all have worries enough as it is these days, wouldn't you agree?'

Beth nodded wryly. He was right, of course. Lara had simply not wanted to add to her load. 'That's what makes an evening like this all the more welcome,' she smiled. 'It helps lighten these dark days for us all. But not only that, it allows us to show in a tangible way that we are right behind your fellow countrymen in their fight against that monstrous man Hitler. Whatever we may be going through here, we know that the Polish people are suffering so much more. The hearts of all of us are with your poor people at this awful time. We can only thank God that so many of your country's leaders have made it over here to keep freedom's hopes alive for Poland – and all of us.'

There was a momentary silence after Beth had spoken and she felt a flush of embarrassment at her impromptu little speech, but she had spoken the truth and knew that her words were echoed in the hearts of all those present.

The Count nodded, appreciation of the sentiment expressed obvious in his eyes. 'And more of those leaders join us by the week, my dear lady. That is the reason for the reception this evening – partly to raise funds for our cause, and partly to welcome some more of Poland's sons and daughters to our midst. I will be introducing our new arrivals to the assembled company in a few moments …' Extracting a gold fob watch from the pocket of his waistcoat, he glanced at it and sighed. 'In fact, duty calls right now. If you will excuse me, please, ladies and gentlemen.'

As the Ambassador took his leave, Lord Queensberry replaced his half-empty glass on a side table and announced, 'Time for the formalities, dear friends! The vodka can wait.' He led the way to the edge of the floor and the others took their cue from him, forming themselves into an informal line along the walls.

As they awaited the return of the Count, and the expectant buzz of conversation grew louder in her ears, Beth found herself gripping Lara's arm once more. Just hearing Polish spoken all around her and listening to the attractive but unmistakable accent of the Count had had a curiously unsettling effect on her.

'Are you all right, Mum?' Lara's brow furrowed beneath the fringe of wispy curls. 'You're not feeling faint or anything, are you? It is rather hot in here.'

'I'm fine, honestly,' Beth said much too quickly, removing her hand from her daughter's arm. It was ridiculous that she should be feeling so edgy tonight. Mrs Malinowska was probably right – she was overtired, that was all. She had been doing too much recently, what with her ambulance driving, running the household, and doing a stint at fire-watching into the bargain. She took a deep breath and let it out slowly. Poise, she must retain her poise …

The Count had now re-entered the room, leading a small group of Polish exiles in his wake.

'I wish I could speak the language,' Lara whispered, as the introductions began. 'It would make them feel so much more at home.' Being able to speak only basic French and German, as well as her native English, her lack of complete fluency in a foreign tongue was a never-ending source of regret to her, although from what she could see almost all the Poles were chatting quite freely in English to the British guests as they were introduced. They, in their turn, were nodding politely and making the appropriate welcoming noises to the new arrivals.

The faces moved before them until there were only two left – a plumpish, but still pretty, middle-aged woman with blonde hair and her much taller, grey-haired husband. 'Now, my dear Countess – Mrs Mallory – we have a couple from a part of the world that you knew well, I believe – Upper Silesia. Allow me to introduce Count Jan Jarosinski and his wife Leni.'

The Countess's beringed fingers gripped Beth's hand. Beth was aware of responding mechanically as they exchanged pleasantries, but what she actually said she had no idea. Her eyes were riveted on the man next to her, whose gold-flecked brown eyes were staring down incredulously into her own.

'Countess.' Count Jan Jarosinski took Beth's hand into his own. His skin was cold to the touch, as if he had just come in from the outside, but his grip was firm. Her breath caught in her throat, causing her to gasp out loud. She opened her mouth to speak but her throat had closed up, making sound impossible. It was the first time in twenty years that they had touched. She could feel the room dissolve around her as her gaze remained locked in his. She was aware of the Ambassador's voice talking less than a yard away, but could hear and see nothing of the other guests. All her senses were centred on the man in front of her.

'Count, Countess Jarosinski, allow me to introduce Lara Mal … forgive me, I should say Mrs Cameron now, or so I'm reliably informed. Mrs Lara Cameron is Mrs Mallory's – the former Countess von Lessing's – daughter.'

Beth's eyes remained locked with those of the man in front of her, in a visual embrace that was totally physical in its intensity. Her heart pounded mercilessly beneath the gold brocade of her gown as a delicate sweat broke on her skin. Then the Ambassador, impatient to get the introductions over with, repeated Lara's name.

Count Raczynski's voice, more insistent now in tone, floated somewhere in the distance. But he no longer existed. No one did. There was no one else in the place. Only them. Only herself and Jan Jarosinski. Only the two of them. Time stood still as the years rolled away. And still he looked at her. Then, slowly, very slowly, his hand withdrew from hers and his eyes tore away from her own as his fingers reached for those of her daughter. Her daughter ... Dear God, dear God ...

A muscle tightened in his cheek and the blood pulsated beneath a livid scar that ran from the corner of his left eye to the side of his mouth as his eyes met those of the redheaded young woman in front of him. He had never believed – no, not in his wildest dreams – that he would ever live to see this day. 'Mrs Cameron ...' His voice sounded huskier than Beth remembered it, as emotion clutched at his vocal chords.

She stared at them both, transfixed. The two profiles – that of her daughter and that of the man she had once loved with all her heart and soul – both so similar. The high foreheads and wide, high cheekbones, the straight noses, with the well-formed lips and almost stubborn chin beneath. The resemblance was startling. More obvious than she could ever have imagined. And if she could see it, so surely could everyone in the room?

He was less than two feet away and she longed to reach out, to touch him once more. Just once more, before he melted into the crowd. Why had she been such a coward? Why had she ever left Silesia – left him – to return here, knowing they might never meet again? One of the reasons was now moving on down the line beside him. His wife Leni.

'What an attractive man.' Lara's voice in her ear brought her tumbling back to reality. 'They're from Silesia, too, so the Ambassador said. I think he expected you to know each other. It's funny that you never met before. I would have thought that all the aristocracy stuck together over there. It's not that big a place, is it?'

Beth shook her head as her eyes followed the tall, dark-suited figure down the line of guests. Her heart was still beating erratically in her breast and she was aware of her voice sounding ragged as she spoke.

'He's Polish, Lara. Hans Heinrich – your father – was German. There was a world of difference, although they inhabited the same land.'

'The land our Herr Hitler now claims he needs for his *Lebensraum*.' Lara grimaced as she turned back to her mother. 'Well, whose land is it, for heaven's sake?'

Beth sighed. Her daughter was asking the question that had plagued politicians and people alike for centuries. 'Heaven only knows the answer to that one. Both sides have regarded it as home for generations. The von Lessings and the Jarosinskis would both claim to have God *and* history on their side.'

Lara shrugged and adjusted her gloves at the elbow. 'Why they couldn't just settle it amongst themselves, I'll never know. Why things had to get out of hand and involve people like Ken seems so unfair. Why should he be expected to die for a country he scarcely knows – and cares even less about?' It was impossible to keep the bitterness from her voice.

Her mother had no answer. Her daughter was still young and this was neither the time nor the place for philosophical justifications of the war. Her eyes were still on the tall figure of Jan as the group of new arrivals, their introductions over, formed a line at the end of the room. Then Count Raczynski held up his hand for silence. As those nearest him fell silent, he rapped on a nearby table for the attention of the others, using a wooden serving spoon as a makeshift gavel:

'Ladies and Gentlemen, a few words, please, before we begin. It has been our pleasure and privilege to welcome to our midst tonight several more dear friends from the motherland. You will soon learn that what they have to tell us – what they have witnessed before joining us here – does not make for pleasant listening. But it is a story that must be told, nevertheless. To tell it in total would take much more time than we have available, but, let me welcome now a man who in very few words can paint a picture for us that must, if we are to help Poland, remain imprinted on our minds as we leave here tonight. Count Jan Jarosinski.'

A buzz of expectation went round the company. It subsided immediately the tall, grey-haired figure in the dark evening suit took the floor. Jan Jarosinski stood silently for a moment or so, as if composing his thoughts. What he had to say was of the greatest importance to him. His country was in agony – tortured and bleeding to death, its wounds inflicted by an ancient enemy using the most modern weapons. The speech he had rehearsed so carefully in his head all day had gone. It had vanished the moment he had set eyes on the two women now standing only a few yards away.

33

His mouth was dry as he opened it to speak. But, when he began, he found the words flooding back as the present receded and his mind returned to the land he had just left:

'My lords, ladies and gentlemen, *panstwo, panstwa*, dear friends of Poland, thank you from the bottom of all our hearts for your warm welcome here tonight. It is not so very long ago that none of us believed we would ever live to see this moment. And we would not have been alone ... The extermination of the leaders in our country affects all political parties and all classes of society. Quite apart from the old established families like my own, men and women from every walk in life have been affected and our political parties have been particularly cruelly hit. In my own homeland of Silesia, thousands have been executed and imprisoned without trial, including many representatives of the Polish Labour Party, with which I have been closely associated. In the western provinces, virtually all the leaders of the National Party have been murdered, along with most village and community leaders, and active members of the Peasants' Party. Trade Union leaders, leaders of business, industry, the arts, scientists and intellectuals ...'

His voice tailed off as he shook his head, 'The terrible fate of the professors of the Jagellonian University in Cracow, of which perhaps you have read, will go down as one of the most heinous crimes in the annals of civilized man. And their fate has been shared by colleagues from all our other universities and seats of learning.

'I myself was in Warsaw in May of this year when I heard that a dear friend of mine, Maciej Rataj, one of our most respected politicians, a former Speaker of our Parliament and leader of the Peasant Party, had been tortured to death in that very city. He had been imprisoned by the Germans last winter and forced to endure indescribable tortures before being finally murdered. I personally can vouch for the suffering that he endured, for I was myself imprisoned in the next cell for many weeks. The walls of that cell transmitted sounds that even today echo through my every waking hour and return to haunt my every night.'

A buzz ran through the assembled guests and a cold shiver ran through Beth as all eyes remained fixed on the man in front of them. Even in the subdued lighting of the cellar, the deep furrows that ran across the high brow and down each side of the well-formed mouth were all too obvious. The scar that disfigured the fine features now required no explanation. It was the face of a man who had seen and experienced suffering, who knew more than most the real truth of what this war was all about.

His voice faltered slightly as he continued, 'In June of this year, yet more mass executions were carried out by the Germans in Palmiry. Among those to perish was a man known to many of you here tonight – Mieczyslaw Niedzialkowski, an old friend of mine and one of our most prominent Socialists, who for many years was deputy to the Sejm, and the editor of *Robotnik*.

'It is true to say that almost every leader of note in our country who has not already fled, has been imprisoned, or already killed. The list is endless and includes Wincenty Witos, a man who served our country several times as Prime Minister, and our heroic Mayor of Warsaw, Stefan Starzynski ... '

He paused, as if unable to comprehend the enormity of what he was now relating. 'I could go on and on, but, as our friend the Ambassador has already pointed out, unlike the suffering, our time is not endless. Let it suffice to say, that up to the time I left my homeland two weeks ago, the number of our countrymen and women killed by the Gestapo alone in what the Germans like to refer to as the "incorporated territories" is estimated at more than 70,000. And this figure takes no account of the tens of thousands tortured to death in the prisons and concentration camps. No one is exempt. My own brother, Father Stefan Jarosinski, was shot out of hand by the Gestapo, in the vicarage in Mszczonow, near Warsaw, along with the vicar, Father Paciorkowski, and two curates.'

Beth gasped aloud. Not Stefan. No, not Stefan. She shook her head as tears sprang to her eyes. His brother was the gentlest of men – a truly good human being who, even as a young man, had gladly forfeited the privileges of his class to devote his life to helping those less fortunate than himself.

Her eyes, now blurred with tears, remained fixed on Jan's face as he continued, 'My brother and his colleagues were not alone. Today, the Church estimates that over 3,000 of its priests are in concentration camps, with countless others already dead.'

His voice broke and he paused once more to clear his throat. 'Only two days before my brother was killed, on my release from prison, I went to see him in Mszczonow. He begged me to leave the country, to get to Britain before it was too late. I told him I couldn't go – I could never leave Poland. He shook his head. "You will never leave Poland, even though you go to Britain, my brother," he told me softly. "You will never leave Poland because, wherever you go in this world, Poland is here – right here." And he placed his hand on my heart ... '

His eyes dropped and, when he raised them once more to look

round at the assembled faces, there were tears shining in their golden brown depths as he placed his own right hand on his heart and said quietly, 'He was right. Poland is right here. We carry her with us, each one of us, every day of our lives. When one is born a Pole, one must of necessity be born a patriot. That is a lesson we learn very early, a bitter lesson that history has taught each and every one of us.

'Ladies and gentlemen, give generously of your time and money when you leave here tonight. It will never be in a better cause.'

With that he turned and abruptly left the room. Beth watched him go as tears flooded her own eyes, to stream silently down her cheeks. 'Jan … !'

Lara watched in astonishment as her mother left her side to push her way through the crowd and disappear in the direction of the open door out of which the speaker had just vanished.

Beth shivered as the cold air from outside the Embassy cellar brought the naked skin of her arms out in gooseflesh. There was no sign of Jan, but a sudden blast of even colder air told her he had headed for the door that led to the back courtyard.

Her high heels clattered on the stone flags as she picked up her skirts and ran on into the darkness, until a shaft of moonlight from the open door illuminated the dark-suited figure that stood quite motionless, gazing up into the starlit sky.

He did not turn as she approached, although he could not fail to have heard her. She halted less than an arm's length behind him, a sudden shyness engulfing her. What did you say, what could you say, to the man whom you had loved more than life itself, whose child you had borne, only to run out on his life forever? Tentatively, very tentatively, she reached across the twenty years and touched his arm.

Chapter Four

'You never told me,' he said softly. 'You never told me your daughter had red hair. A child of Hans Heinrich von Lessing could never have such a colour.'

Beth stared up at him in the moonlight and shook her head. No, she had never told him. In fact, she had made sure that he had never seen the child at all before she left Silesia for good. He had asked her, of course. He had never stopped asking her if the child she was expecting was his, but she had always denied it, denied it with every breath in her body. How could she do any other in the position she was in, and with his own wife, Leni, expecting a child of their own?

'All I ask is – is she happy? Is she happy, Beth? Are you both happy now?'

She avoided his gaze, her eyes darting sideways to the half-open door to the basement as she shrugged her shoulders helplessly. Was she happy? Had she ever been really happy since she left him that day by the banks of the small stream that sparkled its way through the flower-scented grass in front of the old castle of Jarosbork? 'As happy as you are, Jan,' she said quietly. It was the nearest she could get to the truth.

He nodded. There was too much to say, so he said nothing. Perhaps the time to speak would come later. Or perhaps it would never come. Perhaps the volumes that had filled his mind for the past two decades would never be spoken.

'And Anna, your daughter? How is Anna?' she asked. They were like two casual acquaintances going through the motions.

He took a step back and reached inside the pocket of his evening jacket for a cigarette which he snapped into life with an impatient flick of his lighter. 'Anna is still in Warsaw,' he said tersely. 'She would not leave.'

'She has a reason to stay behind?'

He was silent for a moment, drawing the smoke of the cigarette deeply into his lungs and letting it out in a hissing stream through clenched teeth. 'A reason certain women might not understand ... She refuses to leave the man she loves.' The innuendo was not lost on her, as he continued quickly, 'He is a Jew by the name of Leon Grossmann. May God help them, for no one else will.'

Beth caught her breath. Even she knew what that meant. 'Has she known him long?'

'They met last year. They were both medical students at the University together.'

A silence descended as Beth searched desperately for the right words to say. How would she have felt if she had had to leave Lara to a certain death?

The smoke of his cigarette wound a silver trail heavenwards in the moonlight. He watched it for a moment, then said quietly, 'By the way, I met one of your Silesian relatives during my stay in prison recently, as a guest of the SS. He was one of Mine Hosts.'

'Really – who?' Could it be that Carl Christian had been in Warsaw? She dismissed the idea instantly. Her former brother-in-law was far too old for the SS.

'It was Otto. He is now an SS officer. Obersturmbannführer Otto von Lessing, to be precise.'

A cold hand clutched at Beth's heart as she stared at him. He was joking. Please let him be joking. But people, especially Jan, did not joke about something like that. 'I can't believe it,' she whispered.

'I too found it hard to believe, but belief came quickly with my release from prison.'

Beth felt sick to her stomach, but her spirits rose slightly as she looked across at him. 'You mean he had something to do with that?'

Jan gave a bitter laugh and glanced down at the burning tip of the cigarette between his fingers. 'Something to do with it? My dear Beth, he had everything to do with it. It was in his name that I was arrested, then under his orders that I was released.'

It was all too much to take in. 'You mean you actually saw him? You spoke to Otto?' She could not reconcile the memory of the small, fair-haired, gentle-natured child in the brown lederhosen, with the picture of a jackbooted, black-uniformed SS officer.

Before he could answer, a voice from the doorway made them both turn abruptly. 'Mum ... Are you all right?'

Beth's heart sank at the sight of her daughter. 'Lara ... Of – of course I'm all right. I – I felt rather faint, that's all. I came out for a breath of fresh air. I – I was just congratulating the Count here on a most moving speech.' She spoke quickly, too quickly, her eyes darting from one to the other as the words tumbled out.

Jan stared at her as she spoke, then turned to look at the younger woman in the doorway. His daughter. Despite Beth's denials, he no longer had the slightest doubt. But it was almost impossible to reconcile this self-assured, sophisticated young woman with the vision of Anna, his beloved Anna, that he had left behind in his homeland. Anna was a pretty, diminutive blonde, just like her mother, but while Leni's once enviable figure had turned to fat in recent years, Anna's still retained the soft curves of youth. Yes, there was nothing visible of the Jarosinskis in Anna, she was a Kowalska through and through, just like her mother. But Lara – Lara was something else entirely. Tall and lean limbed, with that give-away titian-red hair. Lara was a Jarosinska.

'May I join my mother in offering my congratulations on your speech, sir. You must be very brave to have escaped like this.'

Jan Jarosinski shrugged impatiently. 'Running away is not an act of bravery, Mrs Cameron. The really brave are the ones who have remained behind, who ...'

'That's not true!' Beth cut in. 'You know perfectly well you risked your life making your way here to help carry on some sort of free government for your people! It's tor those who remain behind – people like Anna – that you've done this. She must be proud of you. Very proud of you.'

'Anna?' Lara looked puzzled.

'My daughter,' Jan said quietly. 'And, no, you are wrong. Anna is not proud of me. Anna is not proud of any of her fellow Poles who have meekly allowed their Jewish neighbours to be herded into the ghetto in our capital city and other Polish towns.' He paused, the pain in his eyes obvious, even in the semi-darkness. Then he said lightly, 'But enough of this. It is far too cold for you ladies to be out here any longer in such attire.' He bowed towards both, drawing the conversation to an end, 'Countess, Mrs Cameron ...'

Beth could understand why. Almost any topic could be a potential minefield between the three of them. 'The Count's right, Lara, dear. We'd better get back. They'll be wondering what's become of us inside.'

She gave a valiant attempt at a smile, but avoided Jan's eyes as she took her daughter by the arm and led her back into the basement. To her consternation, her legs were quivering beneath her. She tried to convince herself it was the cold, but knew better.

'What an intriguing man,' Lara murmured, as they made their

way back to the reception rooms. 'Just how well exactly do you two know one another? You can't tell me you've never met before in your lives!'

Beth could not see the face that turned to her in the darkness as they approached the door that would bring them back to the assembled guests, but she persuaded herself that the question was asked in all innocence. 'Well, funnily enough, it transpires we *have* met once or twice before in the past. But it was so long ago, it's hardly any wonder we didn't realize it at first!'

Lara's brows rose. In the light of the open door her mother had gone quite flushed. Two bright pink spots had appeared high up on her cheekbones that only surfaced when something had really unsettled her. She opened her mouth to pursue the matter further, then thought better of it. She was staring into the blue eyes of a tall, well-built man in the uniform of an American Army Colonel. Good God, it can't be! What in heaven's name was Mike Adams doing here – and in uniform?

He strode towards them, pushing his way through the company as deftly as politeness would allow. 'Mrs Cameron – well, this is a surprise!'

'I could say the same to you,' Lara said. At five feet nine inches in her stockinged feet there were very few men she had to look up to, but her new boss was one of them. 'You – you are in the Army, Mr Adams?'

'Military Intelligence, Mrs Cameron, ma'am. Some claim it to be a contradiction in terms, but I do my best.'

Lara's astonishment grew by the minute. 'And you have some connection with Poland?'

He grinned down at her. 'Only my blood. My father was from Cracow. His name was Michal Adamski, but by the time he had applied for American citizenship he had decided he was tired of being referred to as a "goddam Polak" and dropped the "ki". I'm thinking of reverting to it myself.'

'Good for you!' Beth could not resist cutting in.

'Oh, Mr Adams, I'd like you to meet my mother, Mrs Beth Mallory. Mum, this is Mr Mike Adams, my new boss – for a very short time – at the American Embassy.'

'It's a real pleasure, ma'am.' Mike Adams bowed politely as he shook Beth by the hand, then turned to Lara once more. 'You said that like you're going to make sure it really is just for a few days, Mrs Cameron. Good secretaries are hard to come by these days, and it may just be I can't afford to let you go all that easily.'

'Beth, dear,' Cesia Raczynska's voice interrupted the conversation. 'There are some people over here I'd like you to meet. You don't mind if I borrow your mother for a few moments, do you, Lara? I'm sure Colonel Adams here will be only too delighted to keep you entertained.'

'Now there goes a real classy lady – and your Mom's a real stunner to look at, too. Funny how you don't resemble her at all.'

Lara's teeth bit the inside of her cheek, a trick she had done since childhood, in an effort to curb her temper and stop herself from saying something she might later regret.

Sensing the ire rising within her, Mike Adams's face broke into the now familiar lop-sided grin. 'Hey, come on. I didn't exactly say you weren't as good-looking a dame as your Mom, did I now? On the contrary, Mrs Cameron, I've always had a soft spot for redheads myself. In fact, I'd go as far as to say that when it comes to women, you can keep your blondes and brunettes – red is my favourite colour!'

Lara looked up at him. For downright condescension the man was hard to beat! 'Really, Mr Adams?' She deliberately avoided his rank. 'Not the wisest of choices, I would have thought. Aren't you aware that in any circumstances red means stop?'

The grin grew broader as he took a swig of vodka, emptying the glass in his hand. 'Let's just say that where you're concerned I happily admit to being colour-blind!'

Their eyes met and held and, despite her determination not to be intimidated by his obviously cultivated chauvinism, Lara was disconcerted to find herself marvelling at how blue his eyes were, even in the subdued, black-out lighting of the cellar. This conversation had to get back to an even keel – and fast. 'You are here on a purely social visit this evening?'

Mike Adams shook his head. 'I don't think it's any secret that General Sikorski, Count Raczynski and the other Polish leaders over here have been doing their darndest to get some sort of North American Polish detachment of troops off the ground, and it so happens that I've got some friends back home that could do something towards bringing that about.'

'You're a man of influence, Mr Adams?'

'Let's just say, there are some four million Americans of Polish descent, Mrs Cameron – that's one heck of a lot of manpower if it can be harnessed effectively.'

Lara nodded. She had the distinct feeling that if any man could do it this one could. There was something about the Polish-American

Colonel that oozed confidence and a capability that she had known in very few men. No, not since her stints as personal secretary to Winston Churchill himself, or his doughty Labour colleague, Ernest Bevin, had she felt herself to be in the presence of a man who could be capable of accomplishing almost anything he set his mind to. 'But surely all that would take a great deal of money? Where might that come from?'

Mike Adams replaced his empty glass on the tray of a passing waiter and helped himself to another vodka. 'In Canada that wouldn't be a problem. The initial cost of setting up a Polish Corps could be met by the Polish Government's small holding of Canadian currency, although the equipping and arming of greater numbers of men would pose a bigger problem. As far as the States is concerned, I'm hoping that the Lend Lease bill will see the release of US dollars for just such a venture.'

'You really think the President will agree to it?'

'I've discussed the matter with Harry Hopkins and *he's* certainly in favour.'

The casual way in which the name of the President's closest adviser was dropped into the conversation did not fail to impress. 'You're very sure of yourself.'

'Young men shall see visions, Mrs Cameron, and old men shall dream dreams ... I may have turned thirty, but my visions are still as clear today as they were ten years ago. I want a free world for my kids to grow up in; and to have a free world we must first have a free Poland. We have no other choice in the matter. Poland must be freed from the Nazi menace, no matter what the cost.'

He took another swig of the neat vodka, downing the contents of the glass in one gulp, as Lara continued to look up at him through narrowed eyes. 'I see you like your convictions as undiluted as your vodka. I hope your kids appreciate the sacrifices that are being made right now by so many people on their behalf. How old are they?'

He gave an embarrassed half-grin. 'I don't have any – not that I own up to, anyway.'

'You're not married?'

'I didn't say that.'

'You *are* married, then?'

He nodded.

'Happily married – or shouldn't I ask?'

He shrugged, but his grin had a faintly strained look to it. 'Yeah, you could say that. I'm very happily married, Mrs Cameron. But my wife isn't.'

Lara's brows shot up. 'She's left you?' It was none of her business, but she could not resist the question.

'Let's just say, Joanne has decided that monogamy leaves a lot to be desired – innuendo intended!'

Lara flushed deeply. This conversation was going down a road she had no wish to follow. 'You – you've got yourself fixed up with decent lodgings in the city since you've been here?'

He laughed. 'You could say that. Like I told Jo when I last wrote – you get a better class of cockroaches here in London! But you won't see too many of them yourself, I guess.'

'If you mean I live in a decent house, then yes, yes I do, Mr Adams.' She wished she did not sound so defensive about it.

'Look, let's cut the Mr Adams – Mrs Cameron bit, can we? My name's Mike – and yours is Lara, right?'

'Right.' She accepted his proffered right hand with a slightly embarrassed smile. He was waving the flag of truce, she might at least accept it. 'You've made plans for tomorrow?' Suddenly the thought of him alone in the city on a Sunday didn't seem right somehow.

'I thought I'd give the National Gallery the once-over.'

'You – you collect pictures yourself, perhaps? You're interested in the Old Masters?'

He laughed. 'I might just take up collecting Old Masters at that. They fetch a better price than old mistresses, so they tell me!'

She found herself blushing once more, but could not stop the grin that spread across her flushed features. It was a joke, but she could not believe that Joanne Adams, his wife, was the only one in that relationship who found that monogamy left a lot to be desired. Perhaps inviting the good Colonel home to tea tomorrow wasn't such a good idea after all. She avoided his gaze. There was a certain look in his eye that gave her the most curious feeling. 'If you'll excuse me, Mr Adams – Mike – I see my mother beckoning me … '

He raised one dark eyebrow and the cynicism in his voice was obvious as they both glanced round at the gold brocade back of Beth's gown. 'Of course. I can see that your Mom's really desperate for your company. Don't let me keep you a moment longer. Till Monday, Lara … ' He raised his empty glass in silent salute.

Lara was aware of his eyes on her as she made her way across the floor to where her mother was in deep conversation, in the middle of a small knot of guests. It was odd how difficult it was to keep to a straight line when someone's eyes were following your every move.

Then, unaccountably, her own eyes moved to the other side of the room. Count Jan Jarosinski was standing alone by the fireplace, pensively smoking a cigarette. His eyes were on the back of her mother's head, and he had the most curious expression on his face. Wistful was the only word she could think of to describe it, but that had far too soppy a connotation. It was a look of almost infinite sadness. And she noted that same look on his face once more as the evening came to an end, when Barbara Syska, the wife of one of the new exiles, took the floor to recite from memory a moving Polish translation of Byron's *Childe Harold*:

> 'Bywaj zdrowy, kraju kochany
> Juz w mglistej nikniesz pomroce
> Świsnęły wiatry, szumią bałwany
> I morskie ptactwo świergoce!
> Dalej za słońcem, gdzie jasno głowe
> W zachodzie pogrążą piany,
> Tymczasem słońce bywaj mi zdrowe,
> Bywaj zdrów, kraju kochany!'

When she had done, Jan Jarosinski himself stepped forward and said quietly. 'For those of our friends who do not speak our native language, Mrs Syska has just expressed what we all felt as we crossed the cold waters of the Baltic two short days ago:

> 'Adieu, adieu! My native shore
> Fades o'er the waters blue;
> The night-winds sigh, the breakers roar,
> And shrieks the wild sea-mew.
> Yon sun that sets upon the sea
> We follow in his flight;
> Farewell awhile to him and thee,
> My native land – Good Night!'

It was a fitting note on which to end the evening, but few who made their way back out into the darkened pavements of Portland Place could say for certain which if any of them gathered there that evening would ever return to that native land. Despite what the newspapers assured them daily, there was no clear view of victory in sight. That 'Good Night' could very well prove to be 'Goodbye'. And as Beth and Lara took their leave of their own Polish house-guests inside the front hall of 29 Atholl Square some three-quarters of an hour later, they felt a new empathy enter into the relationship. They were all in this together: no longer did Lara resent the fact that Ken was out there somewhere, in the skies above them, risking his life day after day.

Beth held her daughter tighter than usual after their goodnight peck on the cheek. And as Lara's hazel eyes smiled back into hers, a shiver ran down her spine. They were *his* eyes smiling back at her.

'Goodnight, Mum, sleep tight. Let's hope we have one night without another of those awful air-raids for a change. I think we could all do with a proper night's sleep!'

A proper night's sleep! Beth could only smile wryly at the thought as she ascended the staircase to her room. That was the last thing she would get tonight, air-raid or no air-raid!

Chapter Five

Jan Jarosinski gazed out into the night sky, his lean fingers parting the black-out material at one of the windows of the Embassy's first-floor drawing-room. It was against regulations, of course, but who was around at three o'clock in the morning to report him? No one – not even the *Luftwaffe*, thank God, although the searchlights of the anti-aircraft batteries still seared the darkness beyond.

Behind him, stacked around the room, stood dozens of packing cases containing many of Poland's most treasured possessions. It gave him a special satisfaction to stand here now with the motley collection of wooden cases, tin boxes and cloth bundles around him. He prided himself in being partially responsible for their salvation. He had stood on the banks of the Vistula at Cracow, alongside the Curator of the Wawel Castle and his assistant, to see them aboard a barge which was to take them to safety from beneath the noses of the Germans.

Alas, the best laid schemes did not always go as planned, for they were to hear several hours later that the vessel had been bombed by the *Luftwaffe* at Kazimierz, near Lublin. Only the most frantic phone-calls and pulling of official strings had succeeded in obtaining enough trucks on which to transfer the precious cargo and take it on the hazardous journey by road all the way to Romania, then on via Italy to France, from where, with the help of their Polish refugee network, the boxes had been loaded on to a tramp steamer for the last leg of their journey to England.

The most valuable of the treasured articles, such as the famous Jagiellonian tapestries, the Coronation sword, and other items from the Wawel Castle, had been despatched to Canada in July of that year aboard the Polish ship *Batory*, but enough remained behind to make the work-space of the officials and secretaries at the Embassy even more cramped than usual.

Jan's fingers touched the still livid scar on his left cheek. This, along with other more painful wounds to his body, had been the reward for his part in the exercise. News of the exploit had been leaked to the Gestapo and he had been arrested for his part in it within days of arriving back at Jarosbork. There followed almost three months of hell as an unwilling guest of the Gestapo. His insides still quailed at the memory.

He had been taken first to Gestapo Headquarters on Szuch Avenue, in Warsaw, where he was kept for three weeks in the former Polish Ministry of Religion and Education, and interrogated until he felt there was nothing left in this life but pain. Cold sweats of fear would drench his pain-racked body night and day, as hour after never-ending hour he would beg, plead, would entreat them to believe, with every breath left in his body, that he knew nothing of any possible value to them.

Whether they finally believed him, or simply gave up because they had bigger fish to fry – whatever the reason – the weeks of torture finally came to an end and he was transferred to the Pawiak prison, where he was left to rot in a tiny cell before his proposed transport to that repository of all enemies of the Reich – a concentration camp.

There was no doubt in his mind that he would not be standing here now, but would have been tortured to death, or shot, like so many of his compatriots, had it not been for the intervention of the tall, blond SS Obersturmbannführer who had noticed his name on the list of prisoners to be transferred that day to the pride and joy of the Nazi regime in Poland – Auschwitz. He could still see Otto von Lessing's face as they confronted each other in that stinking cell. As a child it had been angelic: now there was a sickening irony in the beautiful Aryan face and body of a grown man who now devoted his life to serving the devil incarnate in Adolf Hitler.

As a playmate of his daughter Anna, the young Otto von Lessing had once called him 'Onkel Jan', but that morning in late October there was no such familiarity. There had not even been a shaking of hands as the German entered the small cell and stared silently down at the huddled figure of his old neighbour on the wooden bench-bed. At length he spoke. 'So it *is* you. I had to see for myself. I could not believe at first – that one so clever could be so careless as to get himself arrested for complicity in so stupid a crime.'

Jan had struggled to his feet, taking care to look the blond giant straight in the eye as he racked his befuddled brain to recognize the figure before him. 'Otto … ? Can it really be little Otto?' He had barely set eyes on Hans Heinrich's son since the child had been sent to military academy in Potsdam at the age of fourteen.

'Not so little now, my dear Count. And Obersturmbannführer von Lessing to you and all others of your traitorous race, if you please.'

'Traitorous?' Jan had replied in a quiet voice. 'Traitorous to whom?'

'To the Reich, *natürlich*. You Poles never could be trusted. But I must admit I thought that someone like you would have had the good sense not to get involved in crimes against the state – if not for your own sake, then for that of your family.' He had paused, his well-drawn features stiffening slightly. Several seconds silence followed before he asked quietly, 'How is the Countess ... and Anna?'

The incongruousness of the situation was not lost on either man as Jan replied politely that his wife was quite well and, as Otto already knew, his daughter was now studying medicine at the University here in Warsaw. Under any other circumstances he would have suggested that he look her up. Heaven knows, they had been almost inseparable for all those long hot summers before Otto had been packed off to Potsdam by his uncle, Carl Christian.

'A medical student, here in Warsaw? *Ah ja*, I remember.'

A thoughtful look crossed the young German's face and Jan's stomach had risen to his throat. What in heaven's name had possessed him to remind Otto of that? And Anna with a Jewish boyfriend of all things. 'Well, naturally, I can't vouch for the fact she's still in the city now that the University is all but closed down ...'

'Then if she is not in the city she will be at Jarosbork, *nicht wahr?*'

Jan shrugged. 'Perhaps. Who knows with young people these days? I am no longer my daughter's keeper, Herr Obersturmbann-führer.'

'More is the pity, Count. More is the pity.'

The two men had looked at one another, then without another word, Otto von Lessing had turned and walked out of the cell, leaving the door ajar behind him. It had been a portent of things to come; release had been granted less than two hours later that day.

Jan Jarosinski shivered in the darkness at the memory. Even all these weeks later he felt sick to his stomach when he recalled the events of that day and what had gone before. He bitterly regretted his slip in reminding him that Anna was in Warsaw, although in his wildest dreams he could not really imagine that any harm could come of it – not from him, not from Otto.

A frown creased the high brow and a nerve twitched spasmodically beneath the scar tissue at the corner of his left eye as he pondered on the creed that could transform a once personable youth into a monster. For that's what they all were, wasn't it? They could scarcely be anything else – those blue-eyed, blond-haired specimens of *Übermenschen* who had chosen to follow the Führer to hell and back on the road to building the Thousand Year Reich.

There had been something spine-chilling about sitting in the darkness of that cell, night after night, and listening to those jack-booted feet march past the window, their youthful voices echoing on the chill of the night air as the words of their 'Sturmabteilung Hitler' filled the dank, dark cell, then continued in his head to haunt the long hours of the night:

> '*Hakenkreuz am Stahlhelm*
> *Schwarzweissrotes Band,*
> *Sturmabteilung Hitler*
> *Werden wir genannt...*'

The black-out blind of the Embassy drawing-room twanged back into place as memories gave way to the reality of the present. Was there no escape? Would there never be an escape from the past? He leaned back against the wall and closed his eyes. There had been another part of the past that had caught up with him tonight. But another part of the past that he had no wish ever to be free of – and it had caught up with him in this very building.

'Beth ...' His lips formed the name and whispered it into the silence of the room. 'Elizabeth von Lessing.' But that was no longer her name, was it? Hadn't the Ambassador informed him that she had married again? An Englishman called Mallory, if he remembered rightly.

It was only to be expected, of course. Someone like her could never be alone for long. All the same, something inside him had winced with pain at the knowledge. She had chosen to go through a ceremony of marriage with another man after all that had happened, all they had been to each other ...

He stared into the darkness of the room with its grotesque shapes, and felt his way over to the mantelpiece. A three-pronged silver candelabra stood on either side of its marble top and, with three flicks of his cigarette lighter, he lit each of the candles of the one nearest and lifted it down to a small side-table next to a leather easy-chair that sat beside the long-dead fire.

As he settled himself down into it, his fingers reached into his dressing-gown pocket, touching a small leather-bound volume of Wordsworth poems that she had given him the day they had taken their last walk together along the banks of the Praszkawarthe, the meandering stream that bordered their two estates. *Der Himmelfluss* – the Heavenly River – she called it, where, beneath a sapphire sky, the evening sun had scattered spangles of gold across the rushing water, and swallows had soared and swooped above them, leaving long streamers of dazzling light in their wake.

He had held her close to him as the sun, like a globe of crimson fire, sank lower and lower behind the pine-covered hills, sending a last flash of colour across the tall, stone battlements of Jarosbork in the distance. She had not told him that day she was leaving for England the next, that tomorrow she would come and bid him goodbye forever. Perhaps she had come to do so, but the enchantment of the hour had prevented it. 'All this might have been yours, too, my love,' he had whispered, and cursed his God in heaven for not allowing him to meet her first.

They had walked back together along the path towards the small bridge that joined the two estates. And he had sat with her as she did her last drawing of the spot. He had asked her for it afterwards, but she had given a sad shake of the head. How was he to know what that last sketch would come to mean to her in the years that followed?

When she had finished and secreted it away in the canvas knapsack on her shoulder, they had resumed their walk, hand in hand. It was the nearest he had ever come to heaven on this earth. Leaves in every shade of green had formed a sea that whispered and undulated gently in the light breeze that swept down from the hills beyond, and from the hidden depths of the pine forests the music of a million songbirds had accompanied their every step.

They had looked up at the shimmering, pink-hued battlements of Jarosbork, then across at its rival, the tall grey walls of Wolfsberg, the von Lessing stronghold, in the distance. Viewed from across the waving green sea of foliage, the two castles were no longer the grim prisons they had seemed to her during her first days here in Silesia; they were enchanted places such as she would never know again.

Perhaps he had guessed something of what was in her mind that evening, for he had held her even more tightly when the time came to say goodbye. 'You will come tomorrow, my love?' he had whispered, and she had nodded, not trusting herself to speak. She had come tomorrow all right. She had come to say goodbye …

He lit a cigarette and watched the smoke spiral upwards in the lamplight to the ornate ceiling of the Embassy drawing-room, then his eyes dropped to the small book on his lap. There had been one page with the corner turned down when he had first opened it in the sanctuary of his own study that night so long ago, and his eyes had fallen on some lines the poet had composed a few miles above Tintern Abbey. She had meant them for his eyes only, when she had slipped the small volume into his hand. She had meant him to read them when she had gone and to keep on reading them; for they said it all, didn't they? They encapsulated so completely what had been theirs that glorious summer when their love was new, and what was yet to come was still hidden in the annals of fate.

Never again would she walk with him along the banks of their enchanted *Himmelfluss*. The next time he would walk alone, as he would continue to walk alone through all the long years that lay ahead. Very softly in the darkness he began to read the words that had sustained him down the years:

> 'Therefore let the moon
> Shine on thee in thy solitary walk;
> And let the misty mountain-winds be free
> To blow against thee: and, in after years,
> When these wild ecstasies shall be matured
> Into a sober pleasure ...
> Thy memory be as a dwelling-place
> For all sweet sounds and harmonies; oh! then,
> If solitude, or fear, or pain, or grief,
> Should be thy portion, with what healing thoughts
> Of tender joy wilt thou remember me ...
> If I should be where I no more can hear
> Thy voice, nor catch from thy wild eyes these gleams
> Of past existence – wilt thou then forget
> That on the banks of this delightful stream
> We stood together ...
> Nor wilt thou then forget,
> That after many wanderings, many years
> Of absence, these steep woods and lofty cliffs,
> And this green pastoral landscape, were to me
> More dear, both for themselves and for thy sake!'

His eyes were wet as the sound of the last word died on his lips; just as they had been every time he had repeated those lines to himself in the quiet, private moments of his life down the years. He had repeated them in the darkness and hellish cold of that cell in Pawiak prison, and tears had fallen down his beaten and bloodied cheeks there too. It was funny how he could not cry out of pain. All the beatings in the world could not bring a tear to his eye. Only memory could do that. The memory of a woman he had once loved more than life itself, but who he knew could never be his. What perverted quirk of fate had decided that both of them would meet and marry other people only a few short months before they met each other?

'Jan, what in God's name are you sitting here for at this time of night?' Leni Jarosinska's incredulous voice shattered the silence, bringing him tumbling back to the grim reality of the present.

He sat quite still, staring at her through the dim candlelight, this woman he had sworn his life to all those years ago. The woman who had borne his younger daughter only a few short months after the birth of his firstborn, Lara.

'Well, did you hear me, or have you gone deaf as well as stupid – sitting here in the dark and cold like this?'

He looked at her quite dispassionately; this small, overweight woman of almost fifty, with the bulging thyroid eyes and once blonde, but now peroxided hair done in a single plait that hung over her ample bosom, who was staring at him as she would at a madman.

He had never been in love with her. No, not even on their wedding day. Their marriage had been the thing to do, that was all. Their families had been friends for generations and, with the Great War over, and his thirtieth birthday looming on the horizon, there had been every reason to seek a Mistress for Jarosbork. The old castle had been missing a woman's touch ever since his mother had died a few years previously in the great 'flu epidemic of 1915 that had carried off thousands throughout Europe. And, with his younger brother Stefan serving the Good Lord and the Vatican in Holy Orders, it seemed he had run out of excuses when his friends and remaining family exhorted him to marry Leni Kowalska before she was snapped up by any one of the dozens of other young noblemen who had just been released from uniform. Such marriages had happened all the time then amongst people of their class. His lips twisted into the suspicion of a mirthless smile. Young people weren't so stupid these days, thank God. They made their own decisions. They married for love.

'Are you all right? You're not ill, are you?' Concern had replaced the annoyance in his wife's voice. There was no doubt about it, he had not been the same since his release from prison. And this evening he had been even worse. He had been distracted – distinctly edgy – ever since the beginning of that reception tonight.

He looked up at her and forced his lips into a reassuring smile. 'I'm all right, Leni. As all right as I'll ever be …'

His fingers concealed the small leather volume of poems as he slipped it into his dressing-gown pocket and eased himself out of the chair, wincing slightly at the spasm of rheumatism that gripped his left thigh and knee. Automatically his right arm went around his wife's shoulder and his lips found the brittle blonde fringe that adorned her brow. 'Time for bed, Leni my dear. Time for bed …'

Chapter Six

'Shining towers in the sky
The Torch of Liberty lifted high
Blazing lights of the Great White-way
Spelling glamour bright as day!
Flitting traffic everywhere
Bridges hanging in the air
Tooting tugboats, never still –
Sights and sounds which bring a thrill!
There's New York, where dreams come true.
Her magic skyline welcomes you!'

Lara perched on the edge of Mike Adams's oak desk in the Princes Gate office, and read the lines printed on the postcard, over the coloured cityscape of New York. Fascinated, she turned it over and stared down at the scrawling handwriting on the back:

Heading for LA. Don't call me – I'll call you! They tell me Hollywood is a sewer with service from the Waldorf! You don't have to worry about finding happiness there – you simply send out for it! Can't wait to find out for myself! Enjoy your war. You're welcome to it! All love –
Joanne xxx

'You in the habit of reading other people's mail?'
As if caught in the act of some heinous crime, Lara gasped aloud and dropped the postcard back on the desk-top as the tall figure of Mike Adams loomed in the open doorway.
'No – carry on. Why don't you? Read the whole lot! Start as you mean to go on.'
Lara's cheeks burned as she backed round behind the desk. 'Look, I'm terribly sorry. I – I really didn't mean to pry.'
'So we're "terribly" sorry, are we? Well, I'm most "frightfully" sorry to tell you that that makes two of us.' He could take off her accent to a T. 'I'm most "frightfully" sorry to tell you that whatever

passes between my wife and myself, whether on a postcard or not, is none of your goddam business ... Now where's my morning coffee? It's gone nine already – don't you English dames know you've got to get your priorities right when you come to work for Uncle Sam? And number one is coffee – first thing – pronto! Comprenez?'

'You – you've been at work long?' From the number of dog-ends in the ashtray it was a needless question. She glanced at the clock on the wall above the fireplace. It was exactly one minute past nine.

'Since just after eight, and I'm gasping for that Nescafé. Now are you going to make it, or do I have to do it myself?'

'You wouldn't!'

He grinned for the first time that day. 'Darned right I wouldn't. So scram, honeybunch, before I get mad in earnest. A guy gets all sorts of peculiar withdrawal symptoms without his shot of caffeine first thing, or haven't you learnt that yet?' He looked at her quizzically across the desk-top. 'How long did you say you'd been married?'

'I didn't, but it's one year.'

'He English?'

'Scottish, actually.'

'Same thing in a kilt. He in the Forces by any chance?'

'He's in the RAF. He's a fighter pilot.' It was impossible to keep the pride from her voice.

'Ho-hum! A Brylcreem Boy, huh? Stationed far from here?'

'Well, I'm not really supposed to say ... '

'Oh, for Chrissake, Mrs Cameron girl, who do you think you're working for – Hermann Goering and Co.? This is the American Embassy. We're on your side, remember?'

'I'm sorry. You get used to being careful, that's all. Careless talk costs lives and all that.'

'Yeah, I know, I know ... It's not your fault. The whole goddam country's paranoid, if you ask me. A few years back it was Reds under the bed back home, but here it's Jerries jumping out of every closet.'

He threw a folder of papers on to the desk. 'I'd like these dealt with some time today. Old Hersch's hollerin' for them.' This was an exaggeration. Herschel Johnson, the Chargé d'Affaires who was standing in for the absent Ambassador, was seldom known to raise his voice, but there was no advantage in letting your secretary know the day's work was anything less than urgent. 'FDR's announced he's bringing iron and steel within the export-licence system, to come into effect at the end of the year. Let's hope it does the harm it's intended to to those Nip bastards.'

He walked to the window, staring out over the barren gardens, his hands dug deep into the pockets of his trousers. In the distance, wraiths of black smoke rose from the fires still smouldering from the previous night's bombing. 'Some poor bastards got it in the next street to me last night, and my landlady's sister's family ended up on our doorstep at four o'clock this morning. The Rowland Galleries in Church Street got a direct hit and their place was just next door.'

He grimaced at the memory of the four red-eyed, bedraggled children who had stood with their mother on the doorstep of his lodgings, with all they had left in this world wrapped up in a salvaged patchwork bedspread. 'I reckon I've never hated those German sons of bitches as much as I did at that moment. It's a miracle we got through the night before that without one single raid.'

'You enjoyed the reception?'

He nodded, reaching into the inside pocket of his jacket and extracting a cigarette from a crumpled pack of Camels. '*Sehr interessant.*' His German accent was flawless. 'Yes, I learned quite a lot.'

'About the Polish situation?'

'About you.'

The colour flared in her cheeks again. He seemed to delight in tormenting her like this. 'And just what exactly did you learn, may I ask?'

He took a drag on the cigarette and aimed a lop-sided grin in her direction. 'You never told me you were born with a silver spoon in that pretty little mouth, for example. Not that I envy you it, of course. I'd have gagged on the darned thing, personally ... ' He exhaled the smoke in a thin stream and looked at her intently, as if gauging her reaction to his words. 'There's a lot to be said for being born on the wrong side of the tracks, Mrs Cameron, ma'am. It teaches you to survive in this world.'

'You mean you don't intend to feel inferior to me just because my natural father was an aristocrat?' She might as well play him at his own game.

'Your old man was a German, honey, let's get it right ... Or so I'm reliably informed. You can count yourself darned lucky you're not locked up on the Isle of Man, in one of those internment camps your government's setting up all over the place; collaring innocent little Eye-Tye ice-cream sellers and Jewish emigrés and the like to send to them. No, I don't feel one little bit inferior to the likes of you, Mrs Cameron. My mother may not have married some titled Hun – in fact, she spent most of her life working her butt off in the "five and dime" round the corner so she wouldn't have to clothe me from the local rummage sales like so many of the kids on our block. But she was more of a lady than just about any I've met with a legal claim to the title over here in Europe.'

He turned back to face her, looking her straight in the eyes as he continued. 'My old man once said to me that sitting on the loftiest thrones in the world we're still sitting on our own asses. Some folks would do well to remember that.'

She stared back at him, keen to take offence, but that crazy, quirky grin came back as he took another drag of his cigarette and glanced at his watch. The conversation was at an end. Being secretary to Colonel Mike Adams was going to be no easy ride, she could see that. 'One sugar or two?'

He shook his head in admonishment. 'Tut tut. Now what did I tell you the other day? I take it straight ... Like with vodka and sex, honey, it's the only way.'

'One straight black coffee coming up!'

Once made, she placed it in front of his desk and made to head for her own room.

'Si'down!'

'I beg your pardon?'

'Goddam it, girl, stop sounding like some prim little school-marm! We've got to work together. I didn't ask for you any more than you asked to work for me, but we're stuck with each other, right? So we might as well get to know each other.'

He glared at her from behind the desk as she stood looking down at him. He sat sprawled in his chair, looking every inch the typical Warner Brothers' hero. God, how she hated Americans! 'And what exactly would you like to know, pray?'

'What you do with yourself at night, for a start.'

Her breath caught in her throat at the sheer gall of the man. 'I stay true to my husband, Colonel Adams, that's what I do. You have no objections to that, I trust?'

His left eyebrow quirked upwards. 'Married in holy-deadlock, huh? *Fides servanda est* – a most noble sentiment!'

Ignoring his jibe, she mentally translated the Latin comment with difficulty; it had never been her strong point at school. 'We must keep our plighted word' – if her memory served her rightly. 'Quite so, Colonel, but I doubt if you'd appreciate it. Fidelity to you is probably not having more than one woman in bed at the same time!'

'Mrs Cameron, ma'am, how well you know me!'

They stared at one another across the desk-top, then both burst out laughing at the same time, his loud guffaw filling the office and echoing in the corridor outside.

'Doing anything special for lunch?'

She shook her head.

'Fancy a bite at the Piccadilly? They tell me Billy Gerhardi's band is quite something.'

'That would be very nice.' A wave of guilt washed over her the moment she accepted, but what the heck, she had to work with the man, didn't she?

And work was certainly the operative word. Most days there was hardly time to draw breath, let alone enjoy a leisurely lunch at one of London's best hotels. Top of the agenda today was a memo Mike Adams was drawing up on British–Russian co-operation. In October, the British Government had come up with a series of proposals for the mutual benefit of both countries that they had put to the Kremlin but, unfortunately, after Molotov's visit to Berlin, they seemed to have fallen on stony ground. Deputy Soviet Minister of Foreign Affairs, Andrei Vyshinsky, was doing his best to assure Sir Stafford Cripps that this German visit was not to be interpreted as an unfriendly act towards His Majesty's Government but, having spoken to Cripps, Mike knew the British Minister was of the opinion that the Russians had decided to throw in their lot with the Axis powers, as their own best means of defence.

The British were also stepping up their objections to the level of American exports to the Soviet Union and this was something that had to be clarified. Cripps himself was hopping mad, being constantly thwarted in his attempts to arrange a meeting with the Soviet Foreign Minister: one of Anthony Eden's first actions as Secretary of State for Foreign Affairs was to lodge a protest on Cripps's behalf.

Mike had been keeping his ear to the ground with both British and Soviet circles over the past week in an attempt to clarify the situation, and today was the time for his weekly report to be drawn up and submitted to the White House. Lara sighed as she sat down with the huge bundle of papers covered in her boss's slanting scrawl. Maybe she was going to need that lunchtime treat after all …

She had only been in the Louis XIV restaurant of the Piccadilly Hotel once before – as a very reluctant debutante – when her stepfather had treated her and her mother to a pre-Coming-Out dinner, just before her eighteenth birthday. The memory was a bitter-sweet one in her mind, for Jack Mallory had died only a few weeks afterwards. But, as she walked through the profusion of gilt and tapestry towards their table for two by the window, all thoughts of that occasion fled from her head. All she could think of was the tall American by her side and the sandy-haired Scotsman to whom she was married, probably at this minute flying somewhere in the overcast skies above them.

'You're thinking about him – your Kiltie, right?' her companion said quietly, as they sat nursing their pre-lunch drinks, whilst waiting for the first course to arrive. 'It doesn't pay, honey, honestly. Life's too short to live in the past, especially at a time like this. We could all be dead tomorrow, if old Jerry gets his way tonight. And there's certainly no need for you to feel guilty. Hell, I haven't asked you to share my bed tonight – only a pretty ordinary Wiener schnitzel!'

She looked across at him and smiled as a sigh shuddered through her. 'You're right, I know. It's just that I've never even shared as much as a cup of tea with another man since Ken and I were married.'

'Wrong. You've shared a coffee with me!'

She grinned and admitted defeat. 'You're right – made by myself.'

'It still counts.'

The waiter arrived with the seafood bisque they had ordered and, as they sipped the soup, she found herself wondering about this man sitting across the table from her. 'Tell me, Col …'

'Mike.'

She gave an embarrassed smile, 'Mike … Do you belong to New York?'

'You're thinking of that postcard, right?'

'Oh, no …'

'Well, you're right, I do. Born and bred. Ever heard of the Bronx?'

She nodded. 'Vaguely.'

'That's probably the best way to know it,' he said, with a wry grin, between spoonfuls of soup. 'Our street was mainly Jewish – as Catholic Polaks we stuck out like sore thumbs. To tell the truth, that's probably why I ended up a pagan: between Father O'Malley, our local priest, and all the rabbis in the block, I'd had it up to here with religion by the time I was out of Sixth Grade!'

'Are your parents still alive?'

He shook his head and his eyes clouded for a second, then the familiar grin reappeared. 'I'm a thirty-odd-year-old orphan. Doesn't that make you feel sorry for me?'

Lara finished the last drop of soup in the plate and dabbed her mouth with the corner of the damask napkin. 'Nothing, Colonel, could ever make me do that. You strike me as just about the most self-possessed person I've ever come across.'

He pushed his empty plate from him and leaned back in his seat, regarding her quietly for a moment. 'An arrogant Yank, huh?'

'No – I didn't say that!' she said quickly, realizing that that description was far from the whole truth. 'You Americans are different from us, that's all. Not worse, just different. To tell the truth, I haven't met all that many before, and you're the first ...'

'To ask you out?'

'Don't say that!'

He raised his hands in front of him in a gesture of mock acquiescence. 'OK. OK. We met by accident!' He was tempted to make a joke of it but, sensing her embarrassment, he resisted.

'Is your wife from the Bronx, too?'

'Joanne?' He laughed out loud at the suggestion. 'Hell, no. Her old man owns "Biltcliffe's", one of the fanciest stores on Fifth Avenue. She lived above the store, you could say – considering he owned the whole darned block!'

He fell silent for a moment, as a slight frown creased the lightly-tanned skin between his brows. 'It's not all her fault, you know, the fact that she's disillusioned with this marriage game. It was no fun being married to a lush.'

'A lush ... ?'

'A drunk, Lara honey. A common or garden drunk.'

'You ... ?' She looked across at him in incredulity.

'Oh, don't worry, those days are long over – for me, at least.'

'And for her?'

His lips twisted in a bitter half-smile. 'Let's just say, they have a disconcerting habit of living on in her memory.'

Lara toyed with the silver handle of her knife. 'I used to envy people who drank too much,' she said quietly. 'At least they had something to blame all their mistakes on.'

'Oh, I was good at that all right – the very best! Nothing was ever my fault. It was always the goddam drink. If I insulted her best friend – or worse, her beloved Poppa – it was always the Jack Daniels ...' He raised the remaining vodka in the glass in front of him. 'I wasn't on to the old motherland's brew at that time.'

'Did – did it affect your work, the drinking?'

He shook his head emphatically. 'Never.' A look almost of embarrassment crept into his face. 'I guess even then I had my priorities the right way round, in my eyes. Work first, women second.'

'And it's still like that?'

'That's for you to decide.' Their eyes met and, as the waiter discreetly removed the empty soup plates from the table, Mike waited till he had disappeared from view, then said softly, 'Let's just say, I'm no longer a lush, but I've never claimed to be on the wagon. I drink when I choose now. I have no need to pile the trash-can with bottles every week.'

She regarded him thoughtfully from across the table. He was honest, disconcertingly so. He had no need to tell her any of this. But there was more to it than the fact that he was once 'a lush', as he so colourfully put it. Something had been wrong, sadly wrong, in his previous life – in his life now, for all she knew. Looking at him sitting there so self-assured – in control of the whole world by the look of it – one could hardly believe it. But surely he wouldn't just spin her a line, would he?

'You're wondering what the hell type of guy you've got involved with, right?'

'Colonel … Mike, you have the most unfortunate choice of phrasing where we're concerned. I – I'm not "involved" with you, as you put it.'

'Would you like to be … ? If you weren't already married to Rob Roy, of course!'

'That's an impossible question!'

Their eyes met once more. His were incredibly blue, and he looked at her quizzically from beneath a thick fringe of dark lashes. 'An impertinent one, maybe. But not impossible.'

She shifted uncomfortably in her seat. Why was he deliberately trying to embarrass her like this? Was it some sort of test that he put all his secretaries through?

'You're wondering if I ask the same question to every dame I ask out to lunch, right?'

He was certainly perceptive. She nodded, without speaking, as the waiter laid the second course in front of them.

He dug his knife into the small portion of breaded veal and, pausing with the morsel half-way to his lips, he said quietly, 'Well, I can assure you I don't. I only ask the pretty ones!'

Despite herself she laughed out loud. 'You know, Mike Adams, I just don't know what to make of you!'

He grinned back at her. 'How about just plain happy?'

The small five-piece orchestra in the corner of the dining-room was playing softly in the background and she was suddenly aware of the music filling her head. The fingers of his left hand were tapping out the rhythm on the white damask of the table-cloth as he attacked the Wiener schnitzel with the fork in his right. 'I've always been a fan of Cole Porter,' he said, between mouthfuls. 'If anyone could make a eunuch horny, he could.'

A couple two tables down from them got up to dance, and she

could feel his eyes on her as she bent her head and attempted to concentrate on the food. He was humming now and she could feel his foot tapping next to hers beneath the table. As she toyed with a roast potato, he laid his fork down on his plate, then, half-rising from his seat, leaned across the table and took her hand. 'To hell with the schnitzel. Let's dance ...'

He led the way to the dance floor then, suddenly, she was in his arms. The skin of his cheek smelt of pine-scented soap intermingled with the faintest smell of tobacco, and it was slightly rough against her brow as he swept her into his arms and sang softly along with the music:

> 'The Dutch in old Amsterdam do it,
> Not to mention the Finns.
> Folks in Siam do it –
> Think of Siamese twins;
> Some Argentines without means do it,
> People say in Boston even beans do it;
> Let's do it, let's fall in love ...'

Dear Ken, forgive me, she prayed inwardly, as his arms moulded her body to his. Forgive me ... But exactly for what she was not quite sure.

Chapter Seven

The ambulance screeched to a halt in front of the pile of rubble that had once been the entrance to Victoria Station, and Beth slipped from the driving seat to aid her team who were already pulling survivors of the bomb from the debris. First a child was brought out, then an elderly man, and finally the fur-coated body of a woman became visible through the smoke and dust. She was lying face down, her toque hat perched on the back of her head. She was whimpering softly as her rescuers worked to clear the fragments of loose masonry from the lower half of her body, then she began to call out in a foreign tongue.

'Gawd only knows what we've got here, sounds like a bleedin' Russian spy to me!' Alf Barnes called over to Beth, as she made the small boy comfortable in the back of the ambulance. 'You speak German, don't you, Mrs M.? What d'ya make of this?'

Heaven only knew how speaking German qualified her to translate Russian, Beth thought, as she hurried over to the prostrate figure on what had once been the pavement, but she would help any way she could. She had already been on duty since two o'clock that afternoon and had been preparing to put on her coat for home when the call came at seven o'clock to say there had been a direct hit on Victoria Station.

Of her own volition, the woman was struggling over on to her back as Beth reached her. They stared at one another, then Beth caught her breath. Despite the dust and grime, the face that stared back at her was unmistakable. 'Leni ... !'

The Countess Jarosinska stared up into the face of her rescuer in disbelief. Surely it couldn't be ... ? But it was. It was that woman – Hans Heinrich von Lessing's widow – the one they had met again at the reception in the Embassy just after their arrival in England. Beth, wasn't it, her name was now ... ? Beth Mallory?

'Here, let me help you!' Beth knelt down beside her and gently wiped the dirt from the other's face. 'Are you hurt? Are you in pain anywhere?'

Leni Jarosinska shook her head. 'No, *Bogu dzieki*. I don't think so ... A little shocked, that's all.'

'We must get you to hospital, though. You never know, they may find something.'

'No! No! Please, no hospital!'

The vehemence with which the words were uttered made Beth start back in surprise. 'But ...'

'No. No ... *Nein, bitte*. Please, Mrs Mallory. I do not go to hospital!'

As the two male attendants helped Leni to her feet, Alf Barnes turned to Beth. 'Sounds like the lady has made up her mind, Mrs M. We can't force her, you know. Ain't got the power.'

'Then she can come home with me and rest for a while, after we've delivered the other two to Casualty.' It was said on impulse, but the offer was immediately taken up.

'*Tak* – that would be very kind.' Leni Jarosinska looked at her gratefully. 'Jan, my husband, he will worry to see me like this. Perhaps I could rest a little and then telephone the Embassy for a car to go home.'

'Fine, we'll do that.'

I must be mad. I must be stark raving mad, Beth told herself as, after having deposited the child and the elderly man at the nearest hospital, she drove the ambulance back to the depot to transfer to her own car and head for home. She had thought of almost nothing else this past week but Jan Jarosinski and his wife Leni. And now here she was volunteering to take the woman she had once regarded as her greatest rival back to her own home. Last Saturday apart, she had met Leni Jarosinska on only two or three occasions in her entire life – at the occasional house-party in Silesia – and had never had the slightest desire to become better acquainted. How could you make small-talk with the wife of the man you loved?

'Your house – it is beautiful, Mrs Mallory,' Leni said, as she stood in the entrance hall of 29 Atholl Square and looked around her at the discreet, ivory flock wallpaper and tasteful, pastoral oil paintings that adorned the walls.

'Beth, please – if you will allow me to call you Leni.'

Beth led the way into the first floor drawing-room and pulled one of the leather wing-backed chairs nearer to the glowing fire. 'Here, do sit down, and I'll ring for some tea. Or maybe you'd prefer

63

something a bit stronger – brandy, perhaps?'

Leni shook her head. 'No, tea – that is very nice, thank you.' Her plump pink hands tugged nervously at the edges of her tweed skirt, pulling it down over her torn stockings. She had never felt such a mess. Despite the rigorous brushing that her fur-coat had received in the ambulance depot, it was still smeared with dried mud, and particles of dirt stubbornly adhered to her carefully curled, blonde hair beneath the toque hat. 'Not in the bombing of Warsaw do I ever look like this,' she said, shaking her head. 'We escape the bombing in Poland to get such a thing here ...' she gestured in despair at her dishevelled clothing, 'here in England. Life is strange, no?'

Beth tugged the corded silk of the bell-pull by the mantelpiece to summon the housekeeper and nodded. 'It certainly is. Who would have thought, for instance, that we would meet again the other night after so long?'

Leni nodded. '*Tak.* Your face – I feel at the reception that I know it. I say to Jan – who is this lady? Twenty years – it is a long time. You regret sometime that you leave Wolfsberg?'

Beth turned away on the pretext of plumping up a cushion on her own chair, as the muscles of her face tightened. Regret? There was not a word strong enough in the English language for the mental anguish she had endured in making that decision.

'I tell my husband, never can I leave Poland,' Leni continued, not bothering to wait for an answer to her question. 'Jan – pfff ... !' She made an explosive gesture with her hands. 'We have so big an argument. I say I very happy to leave Jarosbork to the Germans. My God, they say it is a part of Fatherland for so long, no? I say they are welcome to it! But I tell Jan, for sure, I never can leave Poland, not with my Anna in Warsaw. I go to her and beg, you know.' She looked across at Beth, as tears sprang to the pale-blue eyes. 'I go on my knees and beg her to come with us ... I do that, you know. I go down like so ...' she pointed to the floor, 'I go to the floor for my daughter to come.'

'But she wouldn't.'

Leni shook her head. 'She is so – so ...' she searched for the right word in English, then remembering that Beth spoke German, her face lightened, 'she is so *stur.*'

'Stubborn,' Beth said, with an understanding smile.

'*Ja*, she is so stubborn, stubborn as her father; and like him she is so – can you say – deep?'

Beth nodded.

'Then she is deep – deep and stubborn, like Jan. Can you believe,

64

we know nothing about her love for that Jew? We know only that they are friends, then – poof – she is going to marry him, be his wife!'

She shook her head, unable to comprehend what had happened to make her only child behave in such a way. 'But she was always so. When she was a little girl ... ' she made a knee-high gesture with her hand. 'She was like her father – so *stur*! Not even the Holy Mother – not the good God Himself knows what is in my husband's mind. But I do not complain, he is a good husband to me.'

Leni fell silent and watched as Mrs Bates came into the room in response to the bell, and Beth ordered tea and cakes for two. Then, as the housekeeper took her leave, she sank back in the chair and shook her head. 'I have been lucky, Mrs Mallory ... Beth. I remember your husband, Hans Heinrich. He die so soon after your wedding.' Her mind went back to the tall, quiet German whom she would have once considered as a possible husband had he been of Polish blood. The whole of Silesia had been shocked when it was to England he turned for a bride to replace his dead wife, the pretty blonde Berliner. 'Tell me, how you meet Hans Heinrich? All our neighbours, they talk of nothing else when you marry him. How can such a thing be, they say? You, an English woman, and Hans, a German, and the war ... it was only a few months ended.'

Beth gave a strained smile as she bent down to place another log on the fire from the wicker basket by the side of the hearth. 'It seemed most peculiar to many people over here as well, I must admit. Some of my best friends made me feel as though I was consorting with the enemy, although the war had been over for almost three months when we announced our engagement.'

'But how you meet? Tell me that.'

'It was quite simple really,' Beth said, settling back in the armchair opposite. 'Hans Heinrich's father and mine were students together, both in Berlin and later in Oxford, and despite what happened between their two countries later – the Great War, I mean – our families remained very close. And we spent lots of holidays together before 1914. In fact, I was one of the youngest of the bridesmaids at Hans's first wedding.'

'*Ach, ja!* Hans was married before, *nicht wahr*? To that tall, blonde girl. What was her name? Lenchen ... Lotte ... ?'

'Liesel,' Beth replied quietly. 'Liesel von Hartmann.'

'And she die when little Otto is born.'

Beth nodded. It had been a tragic episode in a tragically short marriage. Hans Heinrich had married his third cousin, Liesel, a talented young musician from Berlin, in June 1914, a few months

65

before receiving his call-up papers for the Army. Everyone had believed the war would be over by Christmas, but it was to drag on for four long years and slaughter a whole generation of young men.

'It was terrible,' Beth said softly. 'She must have become pregnant on his only leave from the Front, in the summer of 1916, and was dead nine months later, without ever seeing her husband again. After the war, my father invited Hans, and little Otto, across to our home in Oxford to recuperate. Hans had some quite bad shrapnel wounds to his left arm that needed special treatment and Daddy knew a surgeon who could make a good job of it. Heaven only knows when he would have had it done otherwise – Germany was in such chaos then.'

She sighed as her memory returned to her first sight of the tall, gaunt-faced young man who had stood on the platform at Oxford station, clutching the small, flaxen-haired child by the hand. 'Daddy did right in asking him over. To have remained in Silesia would have had a terrible effect on him mentally. Wolfsberg had too many sad memories for him at that time.'

'So he came to England and meet you once again. His little bridesmaid is now a beautiful lady, no?'

Beth smiled. 'Well, I don't know about that, but he certainly came to England all right.' She gave a wistful laugh. 'He used to claim it was really Otto I fell in love with and only married him to get at his son.' The smile died on her lips as she spoke. There was more than a grain of truth in the claim.

'*Gewiss*, Otto was a beautiful child,' Leni nodded in agreement, as Mrs Bates entered with a tray containing tea and a plate of freshly made fairy-cakes. As the housekeeper put it down on a small side-table between them, and then served each one in turn, Leni's brow furrowed as she looked across at Beth. 'Do you – how do you say it – keep in touch with Otto?'

Beth gave an embarrassed shake of the head. 'Sadly, no. Our letters seemed to peter out after he joined the Army several years ago.'

'The SS,' Leni corrected. 'You do not know he is now a high-ranking officer in the SS?' She looked straight at Beth, and there was the faintest hint of accusation in her voice as she spoke.

Beth avoided her eyes and took a sip of tea before leaning over to take a cake from the stand on the tray. 'I believe I did hear something to that effect.'

'He was in Warsaw, but we hear he leave to go back to Berlin at Christmas. We believe he was the one – the reason for Jan to get out of prison. He come to see him in the cell, then – poof – just like that he is free!' The plump fingers of her left hand fluttered in the air to demonstrate the suddenness of his release, as she looked gravely at Beth. 'But we can not feel grateful, you understand, he should never be in there! It's a crime against all humanity what the Germans do to our country.'

Leni's blue eyes brimmed and she fell silent for a moment. 'Can you believe, those German pigs they even stop us for nothing in our own streets and arrest us if we can not produce a piece of paper to say we are a true German?'

She took a mouthful of cake and nodded vehemently. *Ja*, it is true. If a Pole he is stopped in what the pigs call the "incorporated territories" and can not produce a paper to say he is a *Volksdeutscher*, then he can be put in prison – just like that – poof!' Once more she made a violent gesture with her left hand, almost upsetting the cup in her right. 'Can you believe such a thing? It happened to my own brother Mikolaj, in Poznan. I think what we hear – it is just stories, then it happen to my own family. We cannot eat in our own restaurants and cafés any more – *strenglich verboten* for Poles!' She gave a bitter laugh. 'Not that there is anything left to eat in Poland any more. They have stripped it of all food and now they are stripping it of the Polish people themselves.'

'And Jarosbork?' Beth asked. 'What has become of Jarosbork?'

Leni shrugged as she sipped her tea. 'You must ask Otto and his friends the answer to that question. Only God and the *verdammt* Germans can answer that one. Not that it will be any great sorrow to me, I tell you! Who wants to live in such an old, cold barn of a place? Apart from Jan, that is!'

'He was very attached to it.' Beth spoke hesitantly. She still found it difficult to believe she was actually sitting here entertaining his wife.

'Attached to it? *Ja*, he was attached to it! All his life, I tell him, it is like a great stone around his neck. A great stone that he loves more than his own wife!' She took another bite of fairy-cake and shook her head at the stupidity of the man. 'How could he live there when he could live in a nice house in Warsaw?' She shook her head in wonder, then added in a confidential tone. 'You know, our marriage – it was almost kaput because of that place, because of Jarosbork!'

'Really?' Beth's interest was genuine.

'*Ach, ja*,' Leni continued between mouthfuls of cake. 'At first, our marriage – it was hell.' She pondered for a moment as if calculating back over the years. '*Ja*, the worst time was around 1920 – when you left Wolfsberg to return to England. For sure, I don't know why, but we could not talk at that time. There I was, *ja*, pregnant with Anna and hating the terrible old place I had to live in, with a husband who

67

did not even see me. Every day he was too busy – his beloved estate, *ja*? Well, I can tell you the truth, Beth. No woman like to play second fiddle, as you say here in England. To another woman – that is bad enough, *ja*? But to a piece of land and a heap of old stones like Jarosbork!'

There was a tightening in her stomach as Beth looked across at the woman she had envied more than any other for so many years. 'But, you must admit, it *is* a very beautiful place. Think of that lovely walk along the banks of the Praszkawarthe, for instance.' She almost choked on the words.

'Pah! That stupid little stream – what is so special about that? There are hundreds all over Silesia. Why should I feel happy walking beside such a thing when I can be walking along any of the beautiful shopping streets in Warsaw or Cracow? Tell me that, my dear Beth … Is it not crazy? *Mein Gott*, it would be better, *ja*, to live in some terrible industrial town like Gleiwitz or Katowice to living out there, with nothing but trees for company! *Und, gewiss*, it was even worse when you left to return to England. Then there was no one of my own age for miles around.'

She paused and frowned slightly, puckering the pink skin of her small, rosebud mouth. 'It was a pity we did not have time to get to know each other better before you go. I say to Jan one or two times, you know, that he invite you to visit; but he never did it. I think, maybe he have argument with Hans Heinrich over something … land, who knows. Then, of course, Hans Heinrich, he get that terrible cancer … He did not have much of a life, *nicht wahr*? His first wife, the Berliner, she die, then the war, and then that terrible, terrible illness?'

Tears sprang to Beth's eyes. It was true, he hadn't had much of a life. Listening to Leni brought it home to her once more that she had never really known the man who had been her husband for such a very short time. She had known from the beginning that she could only ever be a very poor replacement for Liesel in his eyes and, somehow, knowing that, she had not even bothered to try to inject any real romance into their life together. But then he had never exactly encouraged intimacy. Never, not once in the two years they had been together, had he ever told her he loved her.

At first she had convinced herself that it was simply his German reserve – they were not known to be the most emotional of races – but very soon she knew that was not the whole story. He had said, '*Ich liebe dich*' before, she was convinced of that. And he had written it too: many, many times. For she had found the cache of love letters in

68

a leather-bound notecase that Liesel had saved throughout her pregnancy, whilst he was far away fighting the British and French on the Western Front. Ever since that bright, sunlit morning, in the late spring of 1919, when, as a new bride, she had chanced upon them in an old army trunk in the attics of the castle, she had felt like an interloper in Wolfsberg.

She should not have been there. That was never her place. Only a perverse God could have determined that she should travel the thousand miles to that land, to live with a man she did not truly love, then to find love – real love – in the arms of another who was someone else's husband. She stared with glistening eyes into the fire. That someone else was sitting less than eight feet from her at this very moment.

Sensing the conversation had moved on to sensitive ground, Leni attempted to change it. She glanced at the ormolu clock on the mantelpiece and then down at her watch. 'It is late – almost twenty past eight. Jan he will think, what has happened to me? I can trouble you to telephone my husband at the Embassy for me, please? Tell him for sure I am all right, but I need a car to collect me. Tell him he may come now.'

The very thought of talking to him again, let alone meeting him, made Beth's mouth go dry as she said, much too quickly, 'Oh, there's no need for that. I'll drive you over there myself.'

Leni Jarosinska shook her blonde head emphatically. 'You will not. You do too much already. Just telephone, please. I know he will be so happy to hear from you again.'

Chapter Eight

'Who did you say is calling, please?' the man's voice queried. There was a faint trace of irritability in it, as if the last thing he needed this Saturday evening was the intrusive ring of the telephone.

Beth's mouth was dry, the palms of her hands damp, as she clutched the black mouthpiece even more tightly and repeated her name, 'Mallory – Beth Mallory.'

'Beth! Why didn't you say so more clearly?' Jan Jarosinski's voice was incredulous over the crackling line. This was the last thing he expected. 'Where are you?'

'At home. I'm calling from home,' she said, much too quickly, aware of the dishevelled figure of Leni seated less than fifteen feet away. 'I have Leni, your wife, here.'

'What? What did you say?'

'I have your wife here. She – she was involved in a slight accident this evening, so I brought her back here to recover. There's nothing at all to worry about, believe me. She was a bit shaken, that's all, but she's perfectly all right now.'

There was a long pause on the other end of the line, then his voice said: 'Look, I don't understand any of this, but tell her to stay where she is. I'll be right over.'

'But you don't know where I live.'

'Oh, yes I do. It was one of the first things I made it my business to find out.'

The phone at the other end of the line went dead, and she found herself staring into the black holes of the mouthpiece. Her hand was trembling and a glance in the gilt mirror on the wall beside her told her that her face was flushed, the two high spots of colour glowing like twin beacons high up on her cheekbones. She replaced the receiver in its cradle and took a deep breath. There was nothing she could do about it. The moment she had dreamt about – yes, and had nightmares about – night and day for the past week was here. He was coming over.

'You got through all right?' Leni asked, needlessly. 'Was it Jan himself you spoke to?' Seated comfortably in the armchair, nursing her second gin and tonic, she was not particularly interested in the reply. This place was a palace compared to their cramped accommodation in the Embassy. The first floor drawing room they were having to share with all those dusty crates was also partitioned off at one end to accommodate Stanislaw Stronski, the Minister of Information, and his staff – a situation which did not exactly lend itself to spacious living.

Yes, she was not a little envious of the other Poles she had since discovered were lucky enough to be living here along with Beth and her daughter. That fat cow Sophie Malinowska was one of them, if she remembered rightly. As classmates at school in Warsaw before the Great War, she had known Sophie and her elder sister well, and had no particularly fond memories of either of the Zalinska girls, as they were then. Trust Sophie to end up in a place like this. You could always rely on their great fat carcasses to bob to the surface when all about them were drowning. Leni's brow puckered as she sipped her drink. Perhaps something could be done about it. It was certainly food for thought.

'He's coming straight over,' Beth replied, interrupting the other's musing. Her voice had gone up an octave at the very idea. 'If you'll excuse me a moment, Leni ...'

She rushed from the room far more quickly than decorum decreed and made for her own room several doors along the landing. Closing the door behind her, she stared at her reflection in the swing mirror on the rosewood stand by the window. Ever since that night at the Embassy, she had imagined how it would be if they ever met again: how she would look, how he would look. And now look at her! Her eyes travelled in dismay over the creased and smudged uniform and at the long tendrils of hair that had crept out of her carefully arranged bun at the nape of her neck. The afternoon's duty on the ambulances had taken its toll.

Taking a clean white handkerchief from her dressing-table drawer and wetting it, she rubbed most of the offending smudges and pieces of grit from her face, then carefully re-applied a light coating of powder to her nose and cheeks before brightening her lips with a smear of Coty's Red Devil lipstick. There was no time to do anything about her hair so, ignoring it completely, she made do with splashing a liberal helping of 'Muguet des Bois' perfume on to her wrists and behind her ears.

I must keep calm. I must keep calm at all costs, she told herself, as she walked slowly back towards the drawing-room and Leni.

Although the all-clear had gone, the localized chaos caused by the seven o'clock raid meant that it took him the best part of half an hour to travel the short distance between Portland Place and Atholl Square. Because of the black-out, it was impossible to watch the car arrive, but she thanked God it was Mrs Bates's evening off and she could answer the door herself when, at almost twenty past nine, the bell rang twice.

He was standing on the top step looking down at her as she opened the door, and for one crazy moment she had to resist the urge to throw herself into his arms. Despite everything – despite the war, despite the intervening years, yes, and despite the woman waiting upstairs for him at this moment – he still had that effect on her. 'Jan. Won't you come in?' Her voice was almost primly polite as she stepped aside to allow him to enter.

'Is it true? Is Leni really here?' It was sleeting now outside and he shook the frozen droplets from his hat before closing the door behind him.

She looked up at him in amazement. 'Why on earth would I lie about a thing like that?'

Their eyes met and locked. They both knew why.

'I'm sorry, Beth. I should have known better.'

He got no further, there was a clattering of feet on the outside steps, the door was pushed open behind him and a breathless Lara entered. 'God, I'm sorry!' Gasping for breath, she gaped in surprise at the tall, overcoated figure in front of her. 'Don't I know you?'

'It's the Count Jarosinski, Lara dear. You met at the Polish Embassy last week,' Beth said quickly, stepping back into the entrance hall behind her to allow them both to enter in out of the coldness of the porch.

'It's a pleasure to make your acquaintance again, young lady.' Jan took Lara's gloved hand and raised it to his lips.

Lara beamed first at him, then at her mother. 'Oh, Mum, I'm so happy. I've been with Judy all afternoon. I ran into her in Oxford Street. She's in town for some last-minute Christmas shopping and guess what she said?'

'I really can't imagine.'

'Ken's got leave! She heard from Dai, her own husband, the other day, and he said a few forty-eight-hour passes had been allocated over the Christmas period and Ken's got one!'

'It's odd he hasn't told you.'

Lara shook her head vehemently. 'Oh no, it's not. He'll be keeping it as a surprise. Anyway, he wouldn't want to build up my hopes only to dash them again if anything cropped up that stopped him from getting home.'

'But that's wonderful!' Beth hugged her daughter, then turned back to the man by their side in embarrassment. 'Forgive us, please. They've only been married a year and have hardly seen each other during that time.'

He looked from one to the other, his brown eyes taking in the difference in appearance between the two. Both were very beautiful women, it was true, but there was almost no physical resemblance between the much smaller, darker Beth and the tall, titian-haired Lara. It was not Beth twenty years ago he saw when he looked at their daughter, it was his own mother's eyes that sparkled back at him from Lara's open, high-cheekboned face. No one who had ever seen the portrait in oils that hung above the mantelpiece in the main drawing-room at Jarosbork could doubt that fact. 'I'm very happy for you, Lara,' he said quietly. 'Being young and in love is a very special time in all our lives. Make the most of every moment, for they may never come again.' He looked straight at Beth as he finished the sentence.

She averted her gaze immediately. 'I really don't know what we're doing standing here freezing to death in the hallway. Do come in, both of you. Your wife is upstairs in the drawing-room, Jan. We'd better go straight up otherwise she'll be wondering what on earth's happened to us.'

Jan Jarosinski's eyes took in everything as he followed Beth up the wide staircase to the first floor. It was a beautiful house, and he was glad she had done well for herself back in England. Twenty years without a single word had been a long time, and there was no one left at Wolfsberg he could have asked about her after she had gone. Carl Christian, her brother-in-law, was not the type of man one could approach with such a question. Beth's return to England had caused a lot of bad feeling within the remaining von Lessing family. Yes, that had been the worst part – the not knowing.

At the top of the staircase hung a life-size painting of an elderly man in evening dress, whose good-humoured, slightly quizzical gaze, from beneath shaggy, silver brows, met his own as he reached the top step.

'That's Jack, my late husband,' Beth said quietly, seeing him pause to look at it. 'I had it done for his sixty-fifth birthday. It was one of the best decisions I ever made. He died a few months later.'

'His sixty-fifth birthday,' Jan repeated, still gazing at the face of the man before him. 'He was a great deal older than you.'

'Yes. He was my father's best friend. He was a wonderful man. Age never came into it.'

Jan looked from her to the portrait, then back again. 'So, firstly you marry the son of your father's best German friend then, when he dies, you marry your father's best English friend.'

Beth flushed. 'I – I never thought of it like that before,' she said defensively. 'They were both very worthy men in their own right ... Anyway, I really don't think I have to justify myself to anyone in my choice of husband!'

His eyes held hers. 'Not even to me?'

The colour flared even brighter in her cheeks, then she turned and walked quickly in the direction of the drawing-room. 'Your wife's waiting.'

When both Jan Jarosinski and his wife had gone, the best part of an hour later, she sat staring into the fire, in the chair he had just vacated. The smell of his cigarettes still hung in the air. It was funny how certain everyday scents could often evoke far more poignant memories than the most expensive of perfumes. Her fingers reached into the ashtray on the side-table beside her and picked out one of the longer dog-ends he had discarded. Carefully she smoothed it out and inserted it between her own lips, then, lifting the table-lighter, she lit it, inhaling the pungent smoke deep into her lungs. She was not used to smoking and the resultant bout of coughing was interrupted by Lara, now changed and ready for bed.

'Mum, what on earth are you doing?'

Beth threw the cigarette butt into the open fire and turned to her daughter in embarrassment. 'Lara dear, I didn't hear you come in.'

'Obviously.' Lara walked to the drinks' cabinet and pulled down the lid. 'This war must really be having an effect on you! Fancy a drink?'

'A sherry would be lovely.'

Lara poured two and handed one over, before sitting down in the chair opposite. 'Anything on the radio?'

Beth shrugged and leaned across to switch it on. The strains of Glenn Miller's orchestra filled the room. It was a saxophone solo of 'Let's Do It'.

Lara downed her sherry in one gulp as the vision of Mike Adams filled the room. She closed her eyes to banish it and leaned back in the chair. What would her mother say – what would anyone say – if they knew where she was last night; if they knew that she had been to the cinema to see Laurence Olivier in *The Divorce of Lady X* with her boss?

She had been on her way home when Mike Adams had caught up with her and announced it was his birthday. How could she allow him to go back to an overcrowded lodgings and celebrate it alone, amid the noise of his landlady and her bombed-out relatives? She had looked at him sceptically. 'How do I know you're telling the truth?'

'Prove I'm not.'

Finally, after a half-hearted argument on the steps outside 14 Princes Gate, she had given in. After all, it wasn't too heinous a crime, was it, simply enjoying watching your favourite actor on film with a colleague? And enjoy it she had. Mike Adams had been the perfect gentleman, which was no mean feat for him. In fact, he had been the perfect boss, give or take the odd eruption of male temperament, ever since they had lunched together at the Piccadilly on her first day at work.

In a curious way she was even growing fond of him, getting to know his quirky ways of working, and gaining an increasing respect for his ability to get on with the job in hand and do it with more flair and ability than just about anyone she had worked for before.

'Have you any plans for when Ken gets back?' Her mother's voice broke into her reverie.

Lara shrugged. 'Can anyone have plans with that blasted air-raid siren going off left, right and centre every night? Sometimes I wish we could just sail off somewhere into the sunset and forget all about this awful war. They don't know how lucky they are over in the States, being able to go to bed every night and know when their head hits the pillow, it's there until morning.'

'It says all the more for the likes of that young man you're now working for. With his brains he could quite easily have found himself a nice little niche in the Pentagon, but he didn't. He chose to come over here and take his chance with the rest of us.'

'It's funny, I've never thought of Mike Adams as a hero before.' The thought amused her, but there was more than a grain of truth in it, nevertheless. 'I suppose you're right, you know. There are more heroes in this world than the ones out there actively fighting the Germans. Look at that Count fellow – the one who was here with his wife tonight. I expect he could have stayed behind in Poland and taken up a gun against the Nazis, but he didn't, did he? He came over here to fight the enemy in an entirely different way that could prove even more effective in the long run. Incidentally, when are they moving in?'

'I beg your pardon?'

'When are they moving in here – that Count and his wife?'

Beth drained the last drop of sherry from the glass and shook her head. 'I don't know what you're talking about. They have rooms in the Polish Embassy.'

'Part of a room,' Lara corrected, 'which they share with heaven only knows how many other people. They're only there until they can find better accommodation.'

Beth's brows furrowed. 'And just how do you know all this, pray?'

'Mrs Malinowska,' Lara replied. 'She met the Jarosinskis in the street outside as they were getting into their car to head back to the Embassy. Seemingly the Countess had said something about envying her her luck in having such comfortable accommodation as they have here and Sophie, having the soft spot for nobility that she has, couldn't resist telling her she was sure they could squeeze in two more.'

Beth's jaw dropped open. 'I don't believe it! She couldn't have said that without consulting me.'

Lara shrugged as she got up to help herself to another sherry. 'Oh, she intends to "consult" you all right, but I don't think she expects any resistance. As she said to me on the stairs ten minutes ago, they'll be the ones to be inconvenienced, not us. She's going to ask Mr Kulinski and Mr Kador to double up together so that the Jarosinskis can have the big front bedroom that Mr Kulinski's in at the moment.'

Beth sat and stared at her, open-mouthed. 'She has it all worked out, hasn't she?'

'Seems like it. But it does seem quite a feasible idea to me, don't you agree? And, after all, you did say that the Count was once a sort of friend back in Silesia, didn't you?'

Her mother nodded dumbly, not trusting herself to speak. A sort of friend ... Her frozen features contorted into a mirthless smile. 'You could say that, Lara dear. You could say he was a sort of friend ... '

The telephone went at the other end of the room and Lara rose to get it. 'It'll probably be Judy. We were to arrange another meeting some time over the New Year.'

Flicking back the pageboy bob of hair behind her ear, she lifted the receiver, 'Hello?'

'Red?'

Only one voice ever called her by that name. 'Ken!' She turned to her mother watching from the fireside and positively screamed her delight, 'Mum, it's him – it's Ken!'

The soft Scots voice on the other end of the line reflected his amusement. 'Hey, hang on there – what's it going to be like when I'm really there in person, if you carry on like this over the phone?'

But Lara was in no mood for teasing. 'Oh, tell me, tell me! You're coming home! When, Ken, when?' She held her breath for the reply.

'Wait a minute – nobody's stolen my thunder, have they? Has somebody already tipped you off about this?' The thought obviously annoyed him.

'Of course not,' she lied. 'I simply presumed that was what you were phoning to tell me … '

'Well, you're right. I'm grounded at the moment and I'll be arriving some time over the next couple of days. With a bit of luck, and Jerry permitting, I'll be with you for Christmas.'

Lara sank back against the wall and let out an enormous, heartfelt sigh. 'Thank God!' Dreams could come true, after all!

Chapter Nine

'You look like you've lost a nickel and found a dime. Is it just the Christmas spirit that's got into you – from a bottle or otherwise – or what's happened?' Mike Adams stood in the open doorway of the office and took another look at the broad smile on his secretary's face, then nodded as it dawned on him. 'I get it ... Don't tell me, Rob Roy's coming home!'

Lara nodded excitedly. 'Any day now!'

'Well now, that's real nice for you, I'm sure.' His enthusiasm was not exactly reflected in his voice as he turned and walked out into the corridor again. He re-emerged a few seconds later, lugging two hefty cases behind him.

'What on earth are those for?' Lara stared at them in amazement. 'You're not leaving, are you?'

'My landlady's place, yes – Great Britain, no.'

'You mean you've been turned out of your lodgings?'

'Well, maybe that's putting it a bit strong. Let's just say we came to an amicable parting of the ways. I got a bit fed up sharing a pint pot of a house with a quart's worth of squalling kids, and two females who seemed to make it a point of honour to argue over every darned thing from who swiped the last cookie in the jar to whether to listen to the Light Programme or the Home Service on the radio.'

'You've left, then?'

'Darned right I have.'

'Have you somewhere else lined up?'

'Nope.'

Lara whistled softly. 'Accommodation isn't exactly thick on the ground, what with all the bombing ... I wish I could help.'

'I could've suggested you might have had a spare half to a double bed going a'begging, but it sounds like Kiltie's booked it over the next few days.'

'His name's Ken,' she reminded him with a barely suppressed smile. His quips no longer made her blush. 'And I doubt very much if there would have been an invitation forthcoming in that regard ... But that doesn't alter the question of where you go from here.'

The broad shoulders in the slate-grey suit shrugged. 'I'll bunk down here for the time being. There are plenty of spare rooms now that Joe and Rose's bunch have moved out. It won't be for long, though. Something will turn up. It always does.'

'You sound just like Mr Micawber.'

'Come again?'

'Forget it. I'll make you a coffee.'

He moved aside to let her pass and caught her arm before she reached the door. 'Look, honey, I really am glad about your old man gettin' home. If you need any extra time off over the next week ...'

Lara shook her head. 'I doubt if that'll be necessary, thanks all the same. He's not likely to get much more than a forty-eight-hour pass, and with a bit of luck that'll be for Christmas Day and Boxing Day.'

'A couple of days is better than nothing, huh?'

There was a wistfulness in his eyes that made her stop in her tracks. Here she was exulting over Ken getting home for Christmas when she already had all her friends and family around her anyway. His were thousands of miles away across the Atlantic. 'Have – have you made any special plans for Christmas? You're very welcome to come over to our place, you know.' He still had hold of her arm and she extracted it with difficulty from his grasp.

Their eyes held for a moment, then he shook his head. 'That's real sweet of you, and thanks, but no thanks. I wouldn't want to muscle in on your celebrations – not as things are.'

'You mean not with Ken being at home? It won't make much difference, really it won't. I'm living with my mother anyway at the moment and we'll have quite a houseful as it is.'

But still he shook his head. 'Tell you what, though – since it is so near Christmas, how about joining me in an after-work festive-season drink tonight?'

'Well, I ...'

'Oh, come on! What's the harm in a simple quick one at the Rose and Crown? You can bet your boots it'll be full of seasonal revellers, so you'll be in no moral danger from me – more's the pity. And, heaven knows, we'll probably need some "spiritual" fortification before the day is out.'

That was certainly true. Lord Lothian, the British Ambassador to Washington, had died two weeks previously, and Churchill had just appointed Lord Halifax in his place, the latter being replaced by Anthony Eden as Foreign Secretary, with David Margesson, the Conservative Chief Whip, becoming Secretary of State for War. The reshuffle had caused quite a stir, and the new appointments were going to mean an even bigger work load than usual that day, with extra files and assessments having to be drawn up for perusal by Herschel Johnson, the Chargé d'Affaires, before being passed on to FDR himself, and his aides.

Mike's main preoccupation at the moment was with what effects the reshuffle might have on Roosevelt's chances of getting the Lend-Lease bill through Congress. Would Lord Halifax, as the new British Ambassador, fight as hard as his predecessor for it, and would he have the full backing of his new Foreign Secretary and Secretary for War? Mike Adams's fervent hope was that they *would* lend their whole-hearted support to their Prime Minister's own efforts. The pro-Lend-Lease faction would need every voice it could raise, at home or abroad, to get the bill through. Back in the States there was still plenty of venom directed at any mention of sending concrete aid to Britain. Senator Burton K. Wheeler had coined a slogan stating that Lend-Lease was 'ploughing under every fourth American boy' and too many Americans were only too willing to believe that. Isolation-ism was still a factor to be reckoned with, for both American politicians and the public at large.

As far as Mike was concerned, the drafting of the Lend-Lease bill had simply meant the end of an ignominious period of sham, during which the US Administration had sought to protect itself by a series of bootlegging methods. He didn't need his background in Military Intelligence to tell him that US national security interests were inextricably linked with those of the British Empire. Britain was holding positions vital to American defence interests, so it was the duty of the American government either to strengthen the British, by all means possible, or to join in the fray themselves and send in American troops to occupy and defend those positions. In his book, you couldn't have it both ways.

Although he was quite convinced in his own mind of the rightness of America backing Britain to the hilt, somehow he couldn't quite come right out and say so to his secretary. He felt that Lara, in common with so many over here, seemed to enjoy feeling a sort of righteous indignation at how little America appeared to be doing for the British war effort and, while his own country was under such suspicion, he preferred simply to keep his counsel and beaver away behind the scenes, hoping that, in Lara's case at least, she would see by the tone of the memos he drafted where exactly his own sympathies lay.

Lara, for her part, had spent little time pondering on her boss's views of the Lend-Lease situation that day. There was simply far too much work to be done and, in such a situation, she could not tell at the end of the day if she had been typing out the latest Agatha Christie, or page after page of state secrets. She simply got on with the job, and was scarcely even aware of what words rattled through the keys of her typewriter. Luckily, she was quite used to having to work late, for it was twenty past six before her desk was sufficiently clear to call it a day. The same couldn't be said for Mike's, though, and she looked at it in sympathy as she reached for her coat.

He saw the look in her eyes and laughed. 'Don't you worry about that. I'm sleeping here tonight, remember. It'll keep me out of mischief.'

The pub was crowded to the door when they arrived, and it took a great deal of pushing and shoving to manoeuvre their way to the bar where Mike ordered himself a double vodka and Lara a glass of pink champagne. She looked at the rose-coloured liquid sparkling in the glass and smiled up at him in delight. 'What have I done to deserve this?'

His lips quirked into a secret smile, as if he knew the answer to that question but declined to answer it. Instead he looked down into his own drink, then raised his eyes to meet hers. 'I got the chance of having Margot back today.'

'Margot?' She looked at him blankly.

'The previous secretary. She's got over her 'flu.'

'Oh.' It was Lara's turn to look away. There had been no question when she arrived at the Embassy that she was to be anything but a very temporary secretary, but somehow she had put that knowledge to the back of her mind over the past week. 'What – what did you say to them?'

'I told them I was more than satisfied with the replacement.'

'Was that wise?'

'What do you think?'

Their eyes met once again. 'I ... They may not allow it ...' She shook her head in confusion, her voice trailing off. 'I'm only a temporary, remember. I don't even belong there.'

'Are you happy there – working for me?'

There was a strange intensity underlying the conversation, although both were doing their best to keep it light.

'You know I am.'

'Do I?'

His eyes held hers, making it impossible for her to look away. The area around the bar had become even more crowded, with a new influx of off-duty firemen from the station nearby. Her back was hard up against the wall at the corner of the bar nearest the door and the last surge of incomers had pressed Mike right up against her. Only their glasses, clasped protectively in front of them, prevented their bodies from being sandwiched together completely.

Even in the stuffy atmosphere of the bar, she was aware of that same, slightly pine-scented smell emanating from him. His breath was warm on her face and smelt faintly of the cigarette he had recently stubbed out in the ashtray at his elbow. She could feel a curious fluttering inside her; a sort of suppressed excitement, tinged with guilt. He was quite different from any man she had ever known. Especially Ken. There could not be many years between them, but he seemed so much older than her husband. Her mind flew back to the laughing crowd of flyers at the Martins' house-party last year. Looking at the man beside her, now they all seemed to be little more than boys and, in truth, that's exactly what many of them were. Hadn't Ken once told her himself that the RAF had no time for anyone over the age of twenty-six in the fighter squadrons, or on Bomber Command? With great difficulty, taking care not to spill any, she raised her glass to her lips and drained the champagne from it in one go.

Mike raised his hand to the barmaid. 'Same again, please. One pink champagne, one double vodka!'

'I'll get squiffy.'

'Does it matter?'

They watched as the two fresh drinks were poured, then he raised his in front of him. 'What'll it be, honey? What do we drink to?'

'I'll leave that up to you.'

He looked pensive for a moment, then said softly, 'Your old man was German, wasn't he? How about drinking to Life? It seems kinda appropriate at a time like this.' He touched his glass to hers. '*Und das Leben ist die Liebe!*'

She recognized the quote from Goethe immediately. 'And Life is Love,' she said softly.

'Right.'

They took their first sips of the new drinks in unison. A shiver ran up Lara's back. He knew she could speak German. He had deliberately chosen that quote. She downed the rest of the champagne almost immediately as a sudden anxiety welled within her. 'I – I'd better be going.'

She replaced her empty glass on the bar as another surge of humanity from the door brought them even closer together. She was aware of him putting down his own glass, then, before she could make another move, his arms had closed around her. Her ensuing gasp was smothered on her lips as his mouth came down to meet hers.

She was a married woman. What on earth was he doing? Completely pinned into the corner, she could not move a single inch as her mind went into a blind panic. She had a husband. Married women did not kiss other men in public. Well, maybe they did where he came from – but this was Britain!

Then, suddenly, his arms tightened around her and she could feel her frozen spine melt beneath his touch as his hands moulded her body to his. Her mind whirled as the jostling crowd dissolved and her eyes closed of their own volition. His mouth was warm on hers, but it was not a lover's kiss, although she could feel her lips parting of their own accord in invitation.

It lasted only a few short seconds and then he pulled himself away. Instead of feeling outraged, to her consternation Lara found herself feeling curiously cheated. She had never been kissed so chastely by a grown man before. What was wrong with her? Didn't she appeal to him enough, or was he simply trying to torment her? Her heart was pounding beneath the white silk of her blouse.

'Merry Christmas, Mrs C.,' he said softly.

She could not answer him, nor look at him, as she picked up her handbag from the bar counter and blindly pushed her way through the festive throng.

Once outside on the pavement, she looked back into the open door of the pub, immediately regretting her hasty exit. She half-expected, and found herself half-hoping that he would follow her, but he did not. Only an elderly man in a grease-stained trenchcoat came staggering out into the faint evening drizzle.

She leaned against the wall and closed her eyes as she fought to control her breathing. Her heart was beating erratically in her breast and her teeth were chattering, but she could not believe it was with the cold. Her whole body felt flushed and was bathed in a film of nervous perspiration. This was ridiculous, she was reacting like a silly young girl. Whatever could he think of her? She glanced back at the swing doors of the pub, as the veneer of sophistication she so carefully cultivated dissolved about her, but they remained firmly shut.

When she got home to Atholl Square, her dismay at the stupidity of her reaction to what was probably no more than a festive aberration was even more intense. She was met by the beaming figure of Mrs Bates in the hall. 'Your mother's in the drawing-room, Miss Lara. She'd like to see you.'

That was odd indeed. Her mother should have been on ambulance duty this evening. She found herself almost dragging her feet up the wide sweep of the staircase and along the few yards to the drawing-room door. She opened it feeling mildly irritated. The last thing she wanted was a prolonged conversation with her mother about the inconvenience of having the Jarosinskis move in with them. No, all she really wanted to do was to go to her own room and close her eyes. And, if she was really honest with herself, to ponder on what had just occurred during the past hour.

'No!'

'Yes!'

'I don't believe it!' With a shriek of delight she raced across the carpet to throw herself into the arms of her husband.

'Hey, easy on there! I'm a wounded man, remember.' Ken Cameron grinned down at her as he held her at arm's length.

'When ... ? How ... ?'

'Oh, just a couple of hours ago. I wanted to surprise you, that's why I got Mrs B. to say it was your Ma up here.' His right hand toyed with a stray lock of her hair and his brow furrowed slightly as he said softly: 'I called the Embassy. I thought you'd be home by now.'

Her breath caught in her throat. 'You called Princes Gate?'

He nodded. 'They said you'd already left.'

Thankfully there was no accusation in his voice and she breathed easier. 'We – we had to work late because of the new government appointments that've just been announced; then we went for a Christmas drink.'

'We?'

She could feel her face colour and hoped it didn't show. 'Oh, some of the other secretaries and me.' It was the first time she had ever lied to him.

'So, you're at least one up on me, are you? We'll see about that!' Taking her by the hand, he made his way to the drinks cabinet. 'What'll it be? It's daft to mix them, so you might as well have the same as before. What was it – G and T?'

The glasses of sparkling pink liquid flashed before her eyes as she nodded. 'Yes, yes, that's right – gin and tonic.'

They sat down side by side on the settee and he took her hand in his as he devoured her with his eyes. 'You look wonderful, Red.'

She looked back at him – at the fresh, freckled face, with its almost regulation RAF handlebar moustache, and the shock of sandy hair.

'What are you thinking?'

She smiled. 'If it wasn't for that face fungus, you'd pass for seventeen.' It was a back-handed compliment, but it was exactly what was passing through her mind.

'I'm older than you, young lady!'

'And wiser, most probably,' she smiled, raising her glass. 'What shall we drink to?'

'How about youth and beauty? May we grow old gracefully together and remain as happy as we are now.'

They touched glasses and, as the tart liquid found Lara's tongue, she felt a cold, sick feeling well within her that had nothing to do with the drink. She watched him down his whisky, then asked softly: 'That prang you had – the one you mentioned in the letter – how are the injuries? Are they as bad as the ones you received last summer?' Her eyes searched the boyish figure in the blue-grey uniform for any outward sign of disability. But, thankfully, none was visible.

'Scratches, that's all. I told you in the letter. And all above the belt, so you needn't worry too much.' He winked at her over the top of his whisky glass. 'What do you fancy doing tonight – apart from the obvious?'

'Oh, I don't know. Just being together, really.'

'I have tickets for a show. Look!' As if to dispel possible disbelief, he extracted two pink tickets from the top left-hand pocket of his tunic and flourished them in front of her. 'The Adelphi – "The Dancing Years". Don't ask me how I got them.'

'Another military secret, I suppose,' she smiled, as she sipped her drink. She didn't feel in the least like a night on the town, but couldn't disappoint him. 'That would be lovely, Ken.' She glanced at her watch, before downing the rest of her drink. 'I'd better get changed right away. With a bit of luck we might just make it by the end of the first interval.'

To their disappointment, they did not quite make it in time for the interval and had to enter the darkened auditorium without the fortification of a drink. They were not the only latecomers, however. The bomb-scarred streets and chaotic traffic conditions meant that many others found themselves squeezing along the rows of seated customers with whispered apologies.

By the time they had been seated for ten minutes, they had already suffered four interruptions. Anxious not to miss a moment of the show, they kept their eyes fixed firmly on the stage as the fifth couple began their disruptive journey along the row. Lara completely ignored the Jean-Harlow-type blonde in the chinchilla coat who squeezed past without a word, and was equally oblivious to the tall, broad-shouldered man in the grey, dog-tooth overcoat who followed in her wake, his hand protectively around the back of his companion's waist. It was his voice as he murmured his apologies that made Lara catch her breath.

'Excuse me, ma'am.'

Her head jerked round to stare at the back of the dark, half-bowed head. It couldn't be ... But it was. It was *him*. She remained half-standing, gaping after him – after her. How could he? How could he?

She sat back down on the seat with a clatter, bringing looks of irritation from those around her. It was less than an hour and a half since she had left him in the Rose and Crown. The whole episode had suddenly soured and left a bitter taste in her mouth. The guilt she had felt earlier suddenly vanished. The sense of betrayal was acute. Irrational, but acute.

When the lights went up three-quarters of an hour later, she deliberately dropped a glove on the floor so she could bend down and take a good look along the row. He was sitting with his arm around the back of the blonde's seat – and she was laughing. No doubt at one of his smart-alecky quips. He leaned forwards in his own seat and their eyes met. For a split second the smile died on his lips, only to reappear almost immediately when, with the most elaborate of gestures, he lifted his hat from his lap, placed it on his head and removed it, executing the deepest bow his confined circumstances would allow.

Lara could not match that now familiar, lop-sided grin as it spread across his face, for her lips froze in a grimace that barely passed for a smile before she turned back abruptly in her seat. The rat, she fumed inwardly. The absolute rat. She sank back in her seat and closed her eyes to those around her as they made to get out of theirs.

'Are you feeling all right, sweetheart?'

Ken's voice sounded from somewhere above her head and she opened her eyes and looked up into his concerned face.

Hot tears flooded her vision, and she blinked them back in a mixture of irritation and dismay. 'Dratted cigarette smoke,' she said, digging into her coat pocket for her handkerchief. 'They shouldn't allow it in confined places like this.'

Chapter Ten

Jan Jarosinski paced the reception area of the Polish Embassy with its gilt French furniture, now worn and shabby from the multitudes that crowded the area daily, refugees like himself from their homeland. There was nothing for it, he'd have to ring her. He would have to ring Beth.

He inhaled deeply on the cigarette gripped between his thumb and forefinger, drawing the smoke into his lungs and exhaling it in two thin streams through his nostrils. Drat Leni. Drat the woman ... But no, that was unfair. How was she to know?

He perched with one hip on the edge of the desk and pondered on the events of the day. Since her unexpected visit to Atholl Square, his wife was determined that Beth's elegant home was to be their new abode. All day she had pestered both Kulinski and Kador about it, asking them how they could possibly justify occupying two rooms in such a house when she and her husband were cooped up here with only a few feet of floor space to call their own. Eventually, they had been forced to agree with her. Of course they were being selfish. She was quite right: it was unthinkable that the situation should continue. They would talk to Mrs Mallory personally, reinforcing every word Sophie had already said to her on the subject.

He stared down at the telephone on the desk in front of him. He would have to do it before it was too late, before things went too far. He would have to talk to her. There was no way on earth he could ever move in there – into her home – with his wife.

Although he had never had to use it before, he had memorized her number off by heart. It took only seconds to get through – a miracle these days. And the sound of her voice brought the familiar quickening of blood in his veins that he had come to know so well.

'Beth Mallory speaking.'

'Beth – it's Jan.'

There was a momentary silence at the other end of the line. 'Jan ... ?'

'Beth, I must talk to you. It's very important. May I come over?'

'Now?' Her voice was barely audible.

'Now.'

'I'll be waiting.' She replaced the receiver with shaking fingers. That was the last thing she expected. She was sure it would have been Lara and Ken to say they were going on somewhere after the show and not to worry if they were late. She glanced at the clock on the mantelpiece. It was barely nine-thirty; they would still be in the theatre.

She looked down at her dressing-gown. Should she change back into something more respectable? In preparation for the air-raid she was certain would come that night, she had bathed early and donned her favourite white satin nightdress and quilted black velvet robe. With the possibility of having a last goodnight drink with her daughter and son-in-law, she was determined that Ken shouldn't see her in her usual ancient woollen affair and winceyette nightie.

Her hair, released from its daytime bun, hung long and loose over her shoulders, still as glossy and brown as the day she had first met the Master of Jarosbork, when she had stumbled by mistake from the path that divided his estate from that of Hans. He had thought at first she was one of the young parlour maids from Wolfsberg and had stared at her in amazement when she introduced herself as the new Countess von Lessing. She could still see the look in those golden-brown eyes to this day ...

No, she would not change, she decided. Whatever he had to say he could say to her like this. It would be ridiculous to change back. She was more decent, more covered-up in this than in anything she ever wore during the day.

Casting a last glance in the mirror, she left the room and made her way downstairs to the kitchen, where Mrs Bates was seated by the Aga, listening to the wireless and nursing Humphrey, the fat ginger tom.

'You can turn in whenever you wish now, Mrs B., dear. I'll see to supper if Lara and Ken want anything when they get back. But I shouldn't imagine they will. Wailing Winnie permitting, they'll probably go for a bite to eat after the show.'

'That bleedin' siren,' the housekeeper said, creaking her way out of the chair and shooing Humphrey off her lap. 'Had it up to the eyes, I have!' Her latest Ngaio Marsh library book lay on the table beside her newly prepared flask of tea, her flashlight, hot water bottle, and other essentials for the nightly trek to the cellar. She began to gather them up. The ritual had become second nature by now. 'Well, I'll be headin' down there, if it's all the same to you, ma'am. You sure there's nothing I can get you first?'

'No, really. Thanks all the same. I'll just wait up a bit to see Lara and Ken safely in and then head off for bed myself before too long.' Why hadn't she mentioned she was expecting a visitor? Why had she deliberately avoided mentioning Jan? She could make no excuses as she made her way back upstairs.

He arrived half an hour later; a tall figure in a grey trenchcoat and soft felt hat. They shook hands like strangers in the foyer and she took his coat and hat, hanging it on the ornamental hallstand just outside the inner door.

'There's a good fire in the drawing-room. We can talk there.'

He followed her upstairs, his eyes riveted to the heavy fall of nut-brown hair on the velvet shoulders of the robe. He had seen her hair free of its hairpinned prison only once before. The blood pulsed within him at the memory. It was he who had released it himself ...

'I thought you might prefer a whisky to a cup of tea – in the circumstances,' she said, making her way to the drinks' cabinet, and gesturing for him to take a seat by the fire.

'The circumstances?'

She shrugged uncomfortably as she extracted her finest malt whisky and held up the bottle for his approval. 'Glenlivet suit?' He nodded and she poured a large measure into a glass, following it with a sherry for herself. 'Well, it must be something fairly important to bring you over here at this time.'

She handed him the drink and he remained standing by the fire looking down at her. 'I couldn't come over here without a good reason, is that it?'

She took a sip of the sherry and stared into the flames of the fire, deliberately avoiding his eyes. 'You – you know you're very welcome to come here any time you wish.' Her face glowed in the firelight, the two pink spots had reappeared on her cheekbones, heightened now by the warmth of the flames and the two previous sherries she had downed whilst awaiting his arrival. 'But it's not purely a social call, is it, Jan?'

'You're right. And I think you already know what it's about.'

She nodded. 'Mrs Malinowska has spoken to me.'

'It won't work, you know. We can't come here ... I can't come here to live.'

Their eyes met. 'Would it be so very difficult?' she asked softly.

'You know it would. Do you think Leni is a complete fool? Don't you think she would notice eventually?'

'Notice? Notice what?' She whispered the words.

'The way we look at each other. The resemblance between Lara and myself.'

The colour flared even higher in Beth's face as she took a defensive step backwards. She stared at him in a mixture of horror and elation.

'Don't tell me you thought I never knew. Don't lie to me any more, Beth. Not now. Not now that I've seen her.'

'It was a long time ago …'

'The years have no significance.' His voice was almost harsh. 'She is as much my flesh and blood as she is yours. How do you think it will be for me living in the same house, seeing her every day and pretending to be no more than a casual acquaintance? Lara is *our* child, Beth. Born of our love. If that much is not obvious to the world at large, and my wife in particular, then what we mean to each other certainly will be.'

'It was a long time ago, Jan …' She repeated the words for want of anything better to say. Her mind was whirling as she looked up at him.

'Are you telling me that time kills love? Are you really saying that what we shared, what we knew then, has not survived; that there is nothing between us now; that you feel nothing when you look at me?'

How could she say that? How could she lie to him again? Her mouth parted but no words would come, and she shook her head slowly. She loved this man. She had always loved him, with a passion she had prayed had died all those years ago, but was now rekindling in her breast as she looked up at him. The years had not been kind to him. The flame-red hair had turned to silver and there were deep furrows lining the high forehead, and the scar – that terrible scar … But the eyes, the eyes would never change. They still burned with that same golden glow in their deep brown depths that had melted her heart, and her resolve, all those years ago. 'Love … what is love?' she whispered helplessly.

Discarding his drink, and taking hers from her hand, his fingers gripped her shoulders. Then, with the right index finger, he tilted her chin upwards. Their eyes met once more. 'Love, my beloved Beth, is a meeting of souls. And bodies, yes, that is true, but irrelevant. Once in our life, if fortune smiles on us, we may meet someone – someone that touches something deep within us that tells us that this is the person who will mean more very often than life itself.'

Tears welled in her eyes and spilled down over the flushed skin of her cheeks. He wiped them away gently with his fingers. 'The tragedy is if we meet that person, that very special person, when we are no longer free. I have never regretted loving you, no, not for a single second. But don't ask me to live in the same house as you. I am human, remember. I am a normal man ... How long could our secret hold?'

He was speaking the truth. If he did not crack, then she would. She had never been more sure of anything. Her whole body and soul was crying out for him. But why, why, after so long, should they deny themselves now? She wanted him. Wanted him more than she had ever wanted any man ... Just as she had wanted him that day in the warmth of the soft grass on the banks of the Praszkawarthe. Her arms slid up round his neck and gently pulled his face down to hers. He kissed the salt tears from her cheeks; his lips murmuring words of love in the language of his people that she knew but little of.

His hands undid the tie belt of her robe and slipped it over her shoulders. It slid silently to the floor as his lips moved down her neck to the soft swell of her breast beneath the satin nightgown ...

'Mother!'

The name froze every drop of blood in Beth's veins as Jan's arms released her and they turned to stare in unison at the two aghast faces in the open doorway.

'Lara ... Ken ... I didn't expect you back just yet ... ' It seemed an eternity to Beth before she could utter a word, and her embarrassment was all too obvious as Jan bent to retrieve the robe from the floor and slipped it over her shoulders.

'Obviously!' Lara glared, not at her mother, but at the man beside her. 'Your *wife's* not with you tonight I see, Count.'

The nerve at the side of Jan's jaw twitched as he shook his head and met the ice-cold glance of his daughter. 'No, she is not with me.' He looked across at Beth. Her consternation was obvious. Her hair was dishevelled and her cheeks flushed. She looked much younger than her years. Much younger. It was as if the young woman with the cold eyes staring at them from the doorway was the elder of the two. Lara was making judgements, he could see that. But judgements built on false premises. His arm slipped protectively around Beth's shoulders. He must shield her from that. There had already been far too many lies in all their lives. Perhaps the time for charades was over. They were all adults here. What was revealed in the cause of truth need go no further than these four walls. 'I think it's time, don't you, Beth ... ?'

She knew exactly what he meant and stared at him in horror. There could be no question of revealing the truth to Lara – not now, at any rate. All her life she had thought that Hans was her father and, though she never knew him, she had grown up to love and respect the memory of the man who had once been Master of Wolfsberg. For her to learn now that her mother had not only deceived her as to the truth of her paternity throughout the whole of her life, but had deceived Hans, the man she had married, within so short a time of their wedding ... Well, that would surely make a complete mockery of all she had believed in about the sanctity of marriage, and shatter whatever trust had been built up between them over the years.

She glanced in apprehension from one to the other. The look of distaste on Lara's face was obvious ... What must she be thinking of her? But if this shocked her, what on earth would her reaction be if the whole truth were to come out?

Yes, she could attempt to justify her past till kingdom come, she could make all the excuses in the world, but the fact remained she had committed the mortal sin of conceiving and bearing another man's child with her own husband already a dying man. How could she now explain to the child of that adulterous union that she had lied to her throughout the whole of her life? Out of shame for herself, or out of concern for her daughter – whatever the reason – she had lied, and this was no time to confess. Not with Lara's real father standing here beside her. No, it was quite unthinkable. 'No ... please!' The desperation in Beth's voice was obvious as her eyes moved from Jan to her daughter.

'We seem to have got our timing a bit out, I'm afraid ... arrived back rather too early by the looks of it.' It was Ken who spoke, coming out from behind his wife to throw his peaked cap on to the sideboard and look curiously at Jan, then across at his mother-in-law. A pink tinge of embarrassment was quite visible beneath the lightly freckled skin on his face, despite his deliberate, man-of-the-world air.

He drew a hand through the short, sand-coloured thatch and averted his eyes as Beth finished straightening her robe. He was annoyed to find himself quite nonplussed and was not quite sure how to handle it. These things went on, of course. You couldn't be in the Forces five minutes and not realize that – but his own mother-in-law? Beth, who was every inch the English lady in word and deed, a potential adulteress? Lord, what was the world coming to?

His wife's voice broke into the confusion of these thoughts. 'On the contrary, I think we timed it exactly right. Wouldn't you agree, Mum?'

There was a cutting edge to Lara's voice that Beth had only rarely heard before. She deliberately avoided her daughter's eyes as she fought to compose herself. There was nothing to do but brazen it out. And, after all, it wasn't as if they'd been actually caught in bed. No matter how unfortunate her apparel, there had been no major crime committed.

Her fingers automatically tightened the ties of her belt and she drew a smoothing hand over her hair. No, this was not the time to break down and confront anyone with the truth, let alone Lara in her present mood. She must simply make the best of a difficult situation. She glanced across at Ken. He caught her eye and gave an embarrassed half-smile. She could rely on him to help her out. 'Jan, this is my son-in-law, Ken Cameron – he's a fighter pilot in the RAF and is only here for a couple of days leave ...'

As the two men stepped towards each other, hands outstretched, she continued, 'Ken, this is Count Jan Jarosinski ... a – an old friend from my days in Silesia.'

'A *very* old friend, by the looks of it,' Lara put in, but her husband ignored the remark.

'I'm very pleased to make your acquaintance, sir. I have the greatest respect for what your airmen are doing over here.'

The flush that had come to Jan's cheeks subsided slightly and he found himself breathing easier as he grasped the younger man's hand. Thank God for the presence of others in the room. Had he been alone with Beth and Lara ... He dismissed the thought and cleared his throat as Ken's fingers clasped his. 'Well, thank you, young man. Coming from one in the front line, that's quite a compliment. Have you had much to do with them yourself?'

Ken nodded. 'My squadron was based in France for most of the past year, until the Germans took over, and there was a Polish Fighter Squadron formed across there last February – the *Groupe de chasse polonais*. Its main job was to give aid to the Finns.'

Jan's embarrassment receded as his interest in what Ken had to say quickened. Receiving first-hand information was always more interesting than reading reports, and usually far more accurate. He raised a quizzical eyebrow. 'Really? How were they equipped?' That was always the crucial question where the Free Polish Forces were concerned.

Ken looked faintly embarrassed. The lack of decent equipment for the Polish airmen disturbed them all. 'They weren't too badly off for planes in the beginning. Got thirty brand new Gordon-Cyclone fighters, if I remember rightly. Fairly fast jobs, although they were pretty useless at climbing – and, my God, were they badly armed! Only four machine guns, can you believe?' He shook his head in disbelief at the thought. 'The men from the old Polish Fighter Squadron were stationed at Villacoublay, just outside Paris, but there was another squadron of Poles at Etampes who were even worse off, if that's possible. It was a queer lot of mongrels they were using, all right – Dutch planes, with French engines, and Belgian armaments. They made the best of a bad job, though, I'll say that for them.'

Jan gave a weary smile, 'That seems to be the story of our lives, I'm afraid – making the best of a bad job. We Poles have learned to be patient in the quest for freedom and happiness ... both for ourselves and our country.' He looked straight at Beth as he finished the sentence.

She studiously avoided his eyes, running a hand over her hair and tucking a stray strand behind her ear as she said brightly, 'Well, at least our Air Force was well enough equipped to see off most of the *Luftwaffe* last summer. You and your friends did a marvellous job, Ken. It must have given Goering and the rest quite a shock to see what we were capable of.'

Jan nodded emphatically and looked appreciatively at Ken. 'Indeed. When the story of these years comes to be written, what you young men did then will live forever in the annals of heroism, not only in these islands, but in the world. What was it your Prime Minister said last August? "Never in the field of human conflict was so much owed by so many to so few." We can all echo that.' He looked across at Beth for confirmation, then back at Ken. 'Tell me, young man, what thoughts went through your head when you heard those words?'

Ken glanced at his wife and was silent for a moment, before giving a sheepish grin. 'If you honestly want to know, I thought he must be talking about our mess bill!'

The laughter that followed lightened the mood completely. Even Lara, Beth noticed, raised a smile. The tension was gone from the atmosphere. Much more composed now, she glanced at the clock. It was long past supper time. 'Well, on that note, I think it's time we should be thinking about some food and drink around here.' She looked in concern at Ken and Lara. 'You young people must be starving. Let me get you something to eat.' She turned to Jan. 'You *will* stay and join us, won't you?'

He gave an almost imperceptible bow. 'Thank you, no. I'd better be getting back. I have work to do at the Embassy still.' He gave a wry smile. 'We have to work out how these new appointments the British

Government has just made will affect our country. I have also a letter to draft to the Lord Provost of Aberdeen. Our Ambassador is just back from inaugurating an Appeal Committee for the Polish Relief Fund up there and they have already done some marvellous work.' He glanced across at Ken. 'You're a Scot yourself, aren't you?'

'I have that distinction,' Ken grinned. 'In fact, I know Aberdeen pretty well, coming from just down the coast in Dundee. Ever got that far north yourself?'

'No, but I may have to. Count Raczynski, our Ambassador, is very heavily committed at the moment, and I may have to stand in for him up in Scotland in the next week or so. These Relief Funds are our life blood at the moment.'

'Well, I hope you enjoy your trip. At least it should mean some respite from these darned air-raids.'

'Speaking of air-raids, I'd better be going before – what is it you call her? – your Moaning Minnie starts up again!'

'Wailing Winnie she's known as around here,' Beth smiled, 'but either way she's a confounded nuisance.' She watched, a curious mixture of emotions in her breast, as Jan shook hands with her son-in-law. Then her heart sank as Lara deliberately moved out of the way to avoid offering her own hand. Jan could not have failed to notice the slight. She forced a smile to her dry lips. 'I – I'll see you to the door.'

Jan glanced at Lara's face, then back to her mother. 'Thank you, but it won't be necessary. I can see myself out ... It's been a pleasure to meet you,' he said, bowing slightly in Ken's direction. Then he turned to Lara, 'Mrs Cameron ...'

Lara stared past him, then aware of the air of disapproval emanating from her husband beside her, she managed a fixed smile and gave a perfunctory nod of acknowledgement. She was still in a state of disbelief at what had occurred. And while part of her was annoyed at her own prudish reaction, by far the greater part was still in shock at what she had seen. The knowledge, brought home so dramatically, that her mother was still an active sexual being was something of a revelation, to say the least. And as for the Count – the gall of the man! How could he come here like that and attempt to make love to her mother – him with a wife waiting back at the Embassy!

Beth's heart sank at the look on her daughter's face as she walked to the drawing-room door. She had hoped that the lighter mood of the previous few minutes would have prevailed as they took their leave. An unbidden sigh shuddered through her. Lara could be a stubborn creature when she wanted to be.

Once outside on the landing, Jan held up his hand to prevent her from coming further, gesturing to her to rejoin Lara and Ken. '*Dobranoc, kochanie,*' he said softly in Polish. 'Goodnight, my love.'

She opened her mouth, but no words would come. Suddenly, she had tears in her eyes. He touched her lips with his fingertips. The gesture said more than any kiss. Then he was gone. She closed the door behind him and leaned back against it, the sight and sound of him still filling her senses.

'A fine one you are!'

Her daughter's accusation came hurtling across the room towards her.

'Lara, no!' Ken grabbed his wife's arm as Lara made towards her mother.

'Let me go, will you!' She twisted herself free and stood glaring at Beth. 'Just what kind of an exhibition do you call that? Don't you know he's a married man?'

'Come on, Red, lay off there!' Ken cut in. 'Since when has it been a crime to kiss a man just because he's married, for God's sake? Why, if that was so, they'd have to lock up half the female population during this damned war!'

'It's still wrong!' Lara would not be pacified. She didn't give a damn if the whole world *was* at it – this was her mother!

'Come off it! You mean to tell me you're such a Goody Two Shoes that you would never, under any circumstances whatsoever, kiss a married man?'

There was a degree of amusement in his voice as he spoke, but Lara had never felt less like smiling. The memory of a pair of blue eyes smiling down into hers in the Rose and Crown earlier that evening came flooding into her mind. Dear God, dear God, what a little hypocrite she was ...

She looked across at her mother, who had gone quite pale as she steadied herself against the varnished panels of the door. She had gone too far. She made a helpless gesture with her shoulders. 'I'm sorry, Mum. It was a bit of a shock, that's all ... ' Her voice fell to little more than a whisper. 'I suppose you don't like to think of your own parent as having a sex life. Stupid really, isn't it?'

Beth shook her head. No, it wasn't stupid. It wasn't stupid at all. 'It was a silly mistake, Lara dear. A silly mistake that will never be repeated.' But the assurance in her voice was far more emphatic than that in her own mind.

Chapter Eleven

Lara lay awake, staring at the crack in the black-out material that covered the tall window of the bedroom. It was over two hours now since the all-clear had sounded. Not that they had bothered getting out of bed to make their way down to the cellar to join the others. After so many months apart, every second together was far too precious. So they had remained where they were and braved the bombs. 'If we go, we go together, girl,' Ken had said to her, his face buried in the tangle of red hair on her pillow, as the sound of the ack-ack guns filled the silence of the night, and the heavy, ominous drone of the *Luftwaffe*'s bombers continued overhead.

Every now and again there would be the dull, crunching thud of a bomb hitting its target somewhere in the vicinity and they would cling together even more tightly. 'Some poor blighters are getting it over by the docks tonight. They'll not bother with us,' he had whispered by way of reassurance, but it hadn't worked. They were as liable to hit Atholl Square as anywhere.

She could feel the regularity of his breathing in the bed beside her. He was making a light whistling sound through his nose – she couldn't really call it a snore – and his left hand was sprawled across her breasts. Her husband was never one for pyjamas, and his body was warm, and felt slightly damp next to hers, despite the chill of the night air. He had been almost childlike in his attempts to please her tonight. Sensing the episode with her mother had upset her, he had gone out of his way to 'put on a good show' as he would say himself. Her lips twisted into a mirthless smile in the darkness. They had made love three times in as many hours. She should be grateful ... But was she?

Carefully lifting his arm from her and placing it across the mat of frizzy golden hair that covered his chest, she slipped out of the bed and made her way to the window, pulling back the blind to stare out into the darkness beyond. Part of the sky was still lit up by the occasional searchlight, the shaft of white light searing the night sky in search of the stray bomber that might not yet be on its way back across the Channel.

There was a scattering of fires in the distance over Lambeth way. But none in the direction of Princes Gate. She found herself breathing a sigh of relief as the dull, inky blackness of the sky in the direction of the American Embassy Residence told her that Mike Adams had had a relatively peaceful night. Unless he was with that blonde, that was.

Her fingers gripped tighter on the cord of the blind as the picture of the blonde in the fur-coat filled her mind. For all she knew she was some tart from the docklands and the two of them had already been blown to Kingdom Come ... But no, that was a terrible thing to think. He was safe. Of course he was safe. She let the blind twang back into place and let out an almighty sigh. Why, in heaven's name, did it matter so much? Why had she been able to think of almost nothing else in bed tonight but those few seconds in the Rose and Crown when her world had turned upside down?

Goody Two Shoes, Ken had called her tonight – and that's exactly what she had been until that American had walked into her life. She had had nothing but contempt for wives who cheated on their husbands, especially when their men were out there in the front line, fighting for them and their freedom. God, what a little hypocrite she had been! And all that righteous indignation tonight about her mother. Mind you, the sight of her in that Pole's arms had come as something of a shock, to say the least. It was funny really, she had never thought of her mother as a sexual being. She was her mother, that was all. And, as far as she knew, Beth had never looked at another man either throughout her stepfather's life or after it. Just who exactly was this Jarosinski person? One thing was for sure, if anything had been going on between them back in Silesia, her mother would never tell her. If she ever wanted to find out, then she would have to do so for herself. But enough of her mother's problems ... She had quite enough of her own to be going on with right now.

In the darkness, her eyes could just make out the sprawled figure of Ken on the bed. Until tonight she had never had the slightest doubt about their relationship. It was as solid as the rock of Gibraltar itself. But, if that was so, why had she found herself feeling curiously detached during the most passionate moments of their lovemaking? There was a dull, empty feeling within her that told her that something wasn't right. That wasn't how it should be. When, breathless and glowing, he had said to her afterwards, 'It was just as good, Red, wasn't it? It was just as good as before, girl?' she had nodded her reassurance almost too vigorously. 'Of course, Ken darling. Of course it was.' But all the time her mind had been elsewhere – had been in the company of a tall, wisecracking New Yorker, who was as far removed from her stocky, Calvinistic Dundonian as night was from day.

'What's wrong, sweetheart? Can't you sleep?'

Ken's voice from the bed brought a guilty flush to her face. 'I'm fine – I'm fine. Don't worry. I think maybe there's been a bit too much excitement tonight, that's all.'

He sat up in the bed, pulling the covers up over his naked shoulders for warmth. 'I'd like to think you were referring to what's gone on in here over the past couple of hours, but I suspect you're referring to your Ma and that Polish bloke ... Look, love, don't worry about it. So what if she's having a fling with him? Good luck to her. Good luck to them both, that's what I say.'

She gave a hoot of hollow laughter. 'That's rich, coming from a descendant of old John Knox himself! Since when did adultery become an acceptable thing in the Presbyterian Free Church, may I ask?'

'OK, OK. So my grandfather was a bit of a kill-joy. But we can't choose our ancestors, Red, any more than they can choose us. I expect you don't exactly feel hunky-dory about your old man being a Kraut, do you now?'

Lara grimaced. 'Leave him out of it, will you? I never even knew him.'

'No, but you can't deny his existence, all the same – any more than you can deny the existence of your half-brother, that SS bastard.'

'We have no contact with Otto now.'

'Maybe so, but you did have, didn't you? And he's still your brother.'

'Half-brother, remember. It makes a difference.'

'Bullshit. You shared the same father. If he hadn't died then you'd still be over there – a good little *Mädchen*, fighting for the Fatherland with the best of them.'

'Take that back!'

'I haven't said anything that isn't true.'

'You bastard!' Reaching out an arm, she grabbed a hairbrush from the top of the dressing-table and aimed it in the general direction of the bed. It hit him in the middle of the forehead and the ensuing yell brought her scrambling on to the quilt to comfort him. 'I'm sorry, Ken, really I am. I – I didn't mean it to hit you.'

He rubbed the developing bruise and put out a consoling arm. The gesture made him wince slightly: the dislocation of his shoulder a week or so back had left its mark. 'I've had worse than this aimed at me over the past year or so.'

She snuggled back down in the bed beside him. 'I know, and that's partly the trouble. We've all been living such a weird existence since this dratted war began that we say terrible things to each other we can't possibly mean.' Her fingers tenderly touched the splinter scars that marked the pale skin of his body, from the last skirmish and earlier ones that summer.

'They're nothing,' he said, but moved away slightly all the same. Some were still tender, even to the lightest touch. 'There are lots far worse off than me.'

He leaned back on the pillow and closed his eyes as his mind went back to his old boss, 'Bing' Crosby, to 'Snowy' White, 'Cuppa' Coffey, and all the others over the past year who had scrambled their aircraft never to return to base. He had joked with Bing when they had first heard that Churchill speech about 'The Few'. 'By Christ, he's right there, old boy,' Bing had commented, downing a pint. 'There are damned few of us left!' And now he was gone too.

'It must have been awful when you got these,' Lara said softly, her fingers still tenderly stroking the skin around the wounds. 'Although you probably can't remember too much about it now.'

Can't remember too much about it? How little she knew. How little she would ever know. The sanitized versions he had written home bore little relation to the reality that he relived in his memory almost every time he closed his eyes. They were closed now and he was back in that bloody cockpit again, one hot summer's morning last July, the voice of the Operations Controller coming over his head-phones. 'Operations calling Delta. Come in, please. What is your height?'

'Fifteen thousand. Repeat fifteen thousand feet.'

'Operations to Delta. Enemy bombers to your north and turning south. Height approximately eighteen thousand.'

His guts had knotted. Did he turn away or attempt to gain height? There could be little doubt where the bastards were heading. They would be over the 'drome in less than ten minutes. He radioed Operations for instructions.

'Up to you, old boy. They're heading this way.'

Jesus ... the poor sod in that Ops Room was sitting there ready to be blown to smithereens any second. And the only way to prevent it happening was for him and the others to get the hell after the Jerry bastards. And the only way you could shoot a Hun down was to get so close you were half-way up his backside, then really let him have it, with everything you'd got.

At fifteen thousand feet he was above the clouds, and the dazzling glare of the sun made it difficult to see even the next plane when turning. A Spitfire shot past in a half-roll. He had pulled the stick right back into his gut to make the turn. The force pinned him down in his seat, his eyeballs half-way out of their sockets. He was pulling one helluva lot of 'G': a few seconds became forever in this condition. He squinted into the sun as two black brutes with slightly longer fuselage and blunter wing-tips than theirs – two ME 109s – homed in. One sped past almost skimming his port wing, a flash of tracer just missing the cockpit. The other did a sort of half-roll and dived towards the ground, leaving a trail of black smoke behind him. One or two black puffs of anti-aircraft fire from the Channel defences dispersed in the atmosphere.

He knew just what to do at a moment like this. He chose his target – the other 109 – and let him have it, hoping like hell that he didn't overshoot and flash past him without having time to get him squarely in his sights.

His eyes zeroed in on the Messerschmitt's tail unit so that the two cross bars of the gunsight cut the fuselage behind the pilot's head. Then he let loose. Now! He could feel the shudder as the guns fired and saw the flash as they found their target. If he kept his finger on the trigger he'd be out of ammo in under fifteen seconds, so he aimed it in short bursts. There was a billow of black smoke and part of the 109's tail dropped off, causing the plane to reel crazily and lose speed. Then he was past him, and all the time he was weaving and turning, turning and shooting, in a desperate attempt to gain height, as the skies filled with the enemy.

Suddenly all the heavens were peppered with aircraft; the whole bloody shooting match were manoeuvring for position. A sudden flash of tracer skimmed the port wing. Another 109 was after him. As the tracer sprayed past the windscreen, he gave him a two-second burst of fire, ripping fabric from the German's wing. There was a burst of black smoke, followed by red flames, before the Messerschmitt spiralled out of sight. Machines were exploding in a mass of flame and black smoke and disintegrating in the air around him, the flaming wreckage spinning downwards towards the earth below. A Junkers 87 was on his tail, there was nothing for it but to use all the

·aerobatics they had ever taught at Tangmere.

The plane went into the most perfectly executed dive it had ever made. The extra speed made the controls stiff and difficult to manoeuvre and the noise increased. He could hear the whine of the slipstream of the Junkers as it rushed over the cockpit cover. The familiar red mist obscured his vision as the blood rushed from his eyes, almost causing him to black out, then suddenly the bloody seat collapsed. There had been too much 'G' and he had ended up on the floor as the bullets splattered the fuselage, pieces of which ended up in his body. A large star appeared in the thick bullet-proof wind-screen and, most worrying of all, thick black smoke was escaping from the floor of the cockpit. He could smell hot oil.

He was over the sea now, and an Air-Sea Rescue boat was skim-ming the breakers, leaving a long white wake as it sped towards a plummeting Hurricane. But he was heading for land. The ack-ack from the coast was becoming fiercer. Please God, let him get back, let him get back ...

How he ever came down in one piece he would never know. But survive he did – and that was more than could be said for four of his best mates on that particular little sortie. They had scrambled before him and he had lost sight of them before his first sighting of the Germans. Poor blighters, they could already have bought it by then and he never knew. He was too busy trying to save his own skin and those of the others on the 'drome down below.

A lump came to his throat as he remembered the scene in the dining-room back there. They had been joking and laughing as usual as they tucked into kippers that morning, when the ominous crackle came over the loudspeaker from the Ops Room and the Controller's voice warned them to prepare to scramble. They hadn't expected it – none of them. Not that morning. Jock and Paddy's lot had gone first, grabbing their Mae Wests, helmets, goggles and gloves, and harness-ing themselves into their 'chutes as they ran to their waiting aircraft.

Poor sods. Poor bloody sods. Not for them the dignity of a funeral with loved ones gathered round to pay their last respects. Their remains lay somewhere in that bloodied foreign field across the Channel known only to God. He could picture it now – the fuselage gleaming in the sunlight, the scattered remnants of what had once been a young man, barely in his prime. Bing, Snowy, Cuppa, Jock, Paddy, it could be any one of them:

> 'Ossements qu'animait un fier souffle naguère,
> Membres épars, débris sans nom, humain chaos ...
> Dieu vous reconnaîtra.'

'I don't speak French, Ken. You know I don't – not half as well as German, anyway.'

He was silent for a long time, then said softly, 'It's part of a poem I came across while over in France. I can only remember the first couple of lines:

'Heaps of bones once animated by the proud breath of life,
Scattered limbs, debris without a name, human chaos ...,
Known unto God.'

There were tears in his eyes when he finished, and he said brusquely: 'Of course my French translation's not really up to much ...'

She held him closer. There was nothing she could say.

She rang the Embassy next morning to say she wouldn't be in for work. It was Christmas Eve and she had decided to take her boss at his word about giving her some extra time off. Ken's pass was only for forty-eight hours, and twenty-four of them were up already. To her consternation she could not be put through to Mike Adams; he wasn't in the office and the disembodied female voice on the other end of the line had no idea when he would be back. He had left no message to that effect.

Her mother was in the kitchen giving Mrs Bates some last minute instructions for the Christmas meal when she finally emerged ready to face the day at a little after ten. It was a relief there was so much to be said and done in the way of preparation, for it helped overcome the residue of embarrassment from the previous night.

The Poles had all been invited out for Christmas Day, and would be gone from Midnight Mass on Christmas Eve to the following evening, so rather than the houseful that Beth had been expecting, it turned out that there would just be the three of them, and Mrs Bates, to celebrate the birth of their Saviour. 'I did warn you, ma'am – you can't say as I didn't,' the housekeeper reminded her, as she prodded the last remnant of chestnut stuffing into the turkey. 'There was no need to go getting a bird of this size. Gawd knows, it'll keep us going right through the New Year.'

'I doubt that, Mrs B.,' Lara cut in. 'Ken'll be only too happy to take his fair share of it back to the 'drome with him when he leaves.' She shooed Humphrey from his favourite seat on the rocker by the Aga and sat down herself. 'By the way, how's Vi these days?' Mrs Bates's only daughter had recently become a reluctant recruit for the

Women's Land Army, and was presently billeted down in deepest Dorset.

'Oh Lord, don't ask!' the housekeeper replied, wiping her hands on her apron. 'Got a Christmas present and a card from her this morning, I did. She sent me this, so I suppose I should be grateful.' She glanced down at a marcasite brooch in the shape of a crucifix that she had pinned to her ample bosom. 'Her taste in presents ain't so bad – but here, cop a look of this. Have a dekko at the card that came with it. Did you ever come across anything so daft in your life?' She reached over to the sideboard and lifted off a card bearing the insignia of the Women's Land Army and handed it to Lara.

There was a poem on the front page bearing the distinctly un-Christmassy title of 'Bread', as Lara announced in astonishment, and began to read aloud:

> 'Be gentle when you touch bread,
> Let it not lie uncared for, unwanted,
> Too often bread is taken for granted.
> There is such beauty in bread,
> Beauty of sun and soil,
> Beauty of patient toil,
> Wind and rain have caressed it,
> Christ often blessed it.
>
> Be gentle when you touch bread ...'

She could barely finish the final sentence for laughter.

'I told you, didn't I?' Mrs Bates exclaimed. 'They're all barmy, if you ask me. What's a bleedin' loaf of bread got to do with anything at Christmas?'

She retrieved the card from Lara with an incredulous shake of the head and stuck it at the back of the others on the sideboard. 'What our Vi needs is a decent fella to look after her. Gawd only knows what she's gettin' up to down there in Devon!'

'Dorset, isn't it?' Beth corrected.

'Same bleedin' thing! Still miles from anywhere.' Mrs Bates had never been out of London in her entire life, save for a day trip to Southend once as a child. 'What does that fella of yours want for 'is breakfast, Miss Lara? Porridge, no doubt.' She had a distinct suspicion of all foreigners, especially Scotsmen.

'Bacon and eggs would go down better, if we've got any.'

'Hmmm!' The answer did not please. But eventually a rasher was produced, plus one of the eggs she had been carefully collecting for the Christmas pudding, but hadn't needed. 'It's more than the rest of us gets, you know. Some of us have to make do with tea and toast!'

But the request was complied with all the same, and Lara carried the tray back upstairs to the bedroom. Ken was still in bed as she entered, his head turned from her on the pillow.

'Just put it down there, sweetheart.'

His voice sounded odd – thicker than usual. She put the tray down on the bedside table and walked round to the other side of the bed. 'You've been crying!' It was a tactless thing to say, but the sight had shocked her deeply. She had never seen a man cry before. 'What's wrong, Ken? For God's sake, tell me. What's wrong?'

He looked her straight in the eyes and shrugged his naked shoulders beneath the sheets. 'Only this bloody war, Red, girl,' he said wearily. 'Only this bloody war.'

Chapter Twelve

''Twas the night before Christmas and all through the house, not a creature was stirring, not even a mouse ...' Mike Adams threw his pen down on to the desk-top and repeated the words of the child's verse, with not a little irony, into the silence of the office. Some Christmas this was turning out to be! He extracted his last cigarette from the pack on the desk beside him and lit it, inhaling deeply before leaning back in his chair to watch the exhaled smoke spiral lazily upwards in the light of the desk lamp.

It wasn't as if he hadn't had an invitation to spend Christmas with anyone in England: he had had several, but the thought of forced conviviality within a strange family circle did not appeal.

This was the second Christmas he had spent alone: he should be getting used to it by now. Joanne had taken off for her parents' home on the Cape last year without even bothering to try to persuade him to follow. Not that Cape Cod was a favourite of his at the best of times, and Christmas with the Biltcliffes was enough to drive him back into the arms of Jack Daniels. But he had been off the bourbon almost a whole year by then, a whole year when their marriage should have been getting better instead of worse. In the early stages he had tried to analyse what had gone wrong, but in the end he had decided it was a fruitless exercise. A love affair, he decided, was like a war – easy to begin, but very hard to put an end to. By the time he realized he really wanted to put the brakes on, the Biltcliffes had taken over and the invitations to the wedding had gone out to anybody who was anybody in New York.

That was really when it began: the urge to blur the edges of reality just enough with the booze to convince himself that marriage to Joanne was what he really wanted. Heaven knows, she was one of the best looking dames he had ever come across. Even now he would have a hard job thinking of one to match up to the effect she had on him. Oh, he had had a couple of one night stands during the four years since they had tied the knot in St Patrick's Cathedral, but then she had never pretended to be Snow White herself. Thou shalt not commit adultery, unless in the mood, had always been Joanne's creed. And who was to say she was wrong? Certainly not him. Not after tonight, anyhow.

Despite his thirty-odd years he had actually felt like a kid at his first Junior Prom back there in the Rose and Crown with the Cameron dame. Odd really, she couldn't hold a candle to Joanne as far as looks went, but then they had always figured pretty far down his list of priorities with the opposite sex. No, it was something else – there was a chemistry between them that he knew she was every bit as aware of as he was.

His brows furrowed as he tapped his teeth thoughtfully with the end of his pencil and leaned forward in his chair, pulling a new folder off the pile. One thing was for sure – he certainly wasn't in the market for getting involved with some other guy's wife. Especially when the guy involved was out there somewhere doing his bit against these goddam Nazis ... This infernal war – just how would it all end? And how many of them would actually be around long enough to see the end of it?

The shrill ring of the telephone by his elbow broke the silence around him but not the mood, as he lifted the receiver and barked, 'Yes?' into the mouthpiece.

'Colonel Adams, I have a call for you from Washington. Will you accept it?' the operator's cool tone announced.

'Sure. Go right ahead.'

After a couple of minutes' delay and several crossed lines, he heard his name being called. 'Mike – is that you?' The male American voice on the other end was certainly familiar, but the crackling on the line made instant identification impossible.

'Yup. Mike Adams speaking.'

A sigh of relief was audible from the other end, between the crackles. 'Thank God for that. I thought I'd never get hold of you – tonight of all nights. It's Harry here – Harry Hopkins.'

'Harry, you old sonofabitch!' The President's aide was one of a very small band of his acquaintances he always had time for, no matter what his mood. 'How are things in Washington?'

'Hectic. That's why I'm calling. Have you any idea just how hard it is to get a call placed to England these days, even from the White House itself?'

'It figures: communications are in one helluva mess here with all the bombing. What's the big deal that you've got to call tonight, though? It's not to wish me a Merry Christmas, I presume.'

'Darned right it's not. I need your help.' There was a pause on the other end of the line, then the voice continued, 'You know the President's been fighting tooth and nail to get this Lend-Lease bill through.'

'It has reached my attention.' The comment was ironic. Roosevelt's determination to persuade the American Congress and people that concrete aid for Britain was also in the interests of the United States had been the main topic of conversation in the Embassy for weeks.

'Yeah, well, Ed Foley and Oscar Cox over at the Treasury have been working hell for leather in plugging all possible loopholes in the draft that the isolationists can grab hold of and exploit. They've even managed to dig an old statute out of the files – 1892, would you believe – whereby Congress can authorize the Secretary of War to lease Army property, to quote: "when in his discretion it will be for the public good". I guess it's our job to come up with enough to help the President convince the American people, not to mention Congress, that lending arms to Britain is for, quote, "the good" of the American people.'

'I appreciate the problem. And if I've learned one thing since I've been here, it's that the British public aren't too amused at the time we're taking to put this "good neighbour" policy into operation.'

'It's not just the British public that's belly-aching, believe me. Churchill's been bending the President's ear over it for weeks now. He's determined Britain will get the money and armaments she needs without too many strings attached. In fact, as far as I'm concerned, there'll be very little in the way of jollities this Christmas: I seem to be spending most of it right here in the Oval Office. I'm working on the speech FDR's to deliver on the 29th extolling the virtues of supporting Churchill and building up our own strength in the face of the Fascists. He's gonna say that we in America must be the great arsenal of democracy – a neat phrase, huh?'

'Neat but not original. I reckon Jean Monnet, for one, has come out with it before. But I support the sentiment. What are the odds on selling it to Congress?'

'Fifty-fifty at the most, I guess, but the tide's running our way. That's why I'm coming over there, to see how things are for myself. In fact, that's why I'm calling. I want you to get some low down on opinion over there in England about the main issues, so we can include them in the speech, and so I know what to concentrate on when I get over there myself next month.'

'You're coming over here?'

'Well, there's nothing official yet, but I reckon it's on the cards. The President wants as much firsthand evidence on how things are going over there as possible.'

'I thought Winston was keeping you up to date.'

There was a wry laugh. 'Winston keeps us up to date on his own pet topics – mainly the need for more arms and money. What we need is a fresh angle on such things as the danger to Ireland and the Azores. Regarding Ireland, in particular, Winston is getting pretty het up over continued Irish neutrality and has been hinting he'd like us to play some part in negotiations with De Valera. He's suggested that Joe Kennedy and Bill Donovan might act as some sort of emissaries between London and Dublin.'

'Sounds plausible.'

'Yeah, that's what we think. It'll be interesting seeing how things materialize there over the next few months. We'd also like the British Admiralty's views on the presence of our fleet in the Pacific and, of course, British opinion on the B-29s. Can you take some soundings and let us have them over the next few days?'

'Hell, Harry, it's Christmas Day tomorrow. Where am I meant to go for these opinions, for Chrissake? Do I go round knocking on doors just as they're setting to to carve the turkey?'

'Yes, if you have to. That's just what you do.'

'You're a hard man, buddy.'

'And you're a very capable one, soldier … You'll get back to me by, say, this time on the 27th? That should give us enough time to include anything in the speech you may come up with.'

Mike sighed and flicked a long, flaky column of ash in the general direction of the ashtray. 'Right, suh!'

'Good man, Colonel! I'll stand you one when I get over there.'

'Make it a double and you got a deal!'

A good-natured laugh sounded over the line before it went dead at the other end and a long, high-pitched buzzing assaulted his ears. Mike replaced the receiver in its cradle and took a last drag of his cigarette before stubbing it out in the ashtray. Good old Harry. His sense of timing was bang on as usual. Just how the hell did anybody, let alone an American like him, get hold of enough British over Christmas to satisfy them back at the White House?

A glance at his watch told him it was already after ten. It wouldn't be fair to ring anyone this time on Christmas Eve. No, it could wait till tomorrow. He would work on here for another hour or so and try to get through in the morning. With a bit of luck, and the British telephone system permitting, he could place a few calls to the right quarters just after breakfast. But just who exactly were 'the right quarters'? His brows furrowed. He had not been over here long enough to assess just whose opinion was worth listening to and whose wasn't. What he needed was some inside information on the best guys to call ... Now who did he know who was completely *au fait* with goings-on at the British Foreign Office? Lara. He would have to call Lara. She probably wouldn't be too amused at his intrusion into her private life now that her Kiltie was back with her, but what the hell ...

The phone rang in the drawing-room of 29 Atholl Square at precisely nine o'clock the next day, to be answered by Beth, still in her dressing gown. Irrationally, her hand automatically flew to her hair, to smooth the wayward locks, at the sound of the American's voice. 'Colonel Adams, why, this is a lovely surprise! ... Yes, Lara's around. She's just taken Ken's breakfast up to him. I'll get her for you ... But don't tell me you're actually working on Christmas Day!'

'Afraid so, ma'am.'

'But that's simply terrible! Don't they give you *any* time off over there? I trust you won't be in at the office all day?'

'Well, I wasn't planning on it.'

'I presume you'll be spending at least part of the day with the Winants or the Johnsons?'

'Well, no ...'

'You *are* going somewhere for Christmas dinner, aren't you?'

'Well ...'

'You're not!' Beth did not bother waiting for another word. The embarrassed tone to his voice said it all. 'But that's terrible!'

'Oh, I don't know ...'

'Look, we were expecting to entertain a whole lot more people here to Christmas dinner today than we've ended up having. Mrs Bates has been economizing with the ration cards for weeks now so we can have a real feast – and now all to no avail, as it turns out. Our Polish guests are going elsewhere. So you're not going to let all that turkey and chestnut stuffing go to waste now, are you?'

There was an embarrassed silence on the other end of the line.

'You're *not* now, are you?'

He could think of no real excuse without sounding ungrateful in the extreme. 'Well, that's real kind of you, ma'am.'

'Nonsense, it'll be our pleasure. I'm sure Lara will be delighted ... In fact, I think this's her now?' Beth turned as the drawing-room door opened and her daughter entered. 'Lara, dear, it's Colonel

Adams on the phone. He wants a word with you …'

'Colonel Adams?' Lara hurried across the room and snatched up the phone. 'Mike?'

'Lara … Sorry to bother you on Christmas Day, but something's come up. I've had a call from Washington. They want me to sound out British informed opinion on several political points regarding US involvement in the war. Can you suggest anyone? I'd like a cross-section – you know, a couple of Socialists, and the odd Liberal, as well as a few Tories. Nobody too high up. It's really grass-roots' opinion I'd like to canvas first.'

Lara's brow furrowed. This was a tall order off the top of her head. 'Well, as far as Labour is concerned you couldn't do much better than have a word with Ellen Wilkinson.'

'She sounds like a woman.'

'She is.' There was a long pause on the Princes Gate end of the line. She knew exactly what was going through his mind. 'Any objections?'

'No, no, go right ahead …'

'Well, there's Edith Summerskill, too.'

'Another dame?'

'I haven't known many men christened Edith.' She could almost see him fume at the other end of the phone.

'Continue, please.'

'Well, there's always Nye Bevan. He's worth listening to on any subject. As regards the Liberals, I'd go for Megan Lloyd George and, for the Tories, Bob Boothby always has his ear to the ground. I'd have him for starters, followed by Duff Cooper or Rab Butler, and ending up with Harold Macmillan. He's a Conservative with a social conscience – a rare bird, considering his aristocratic connections.'

'Right – I've got a note of them. I'm surprised you haven't come up with a female Tory.'

She smiled into the phone. 'I would've included Nancy Astor, but since she's an American herself, I doubt if her opinions would have been entirely objective … You're not actually going to phone all these people today, are you?'

'I'm gonna try.'

Lara shook her head in disbelief. 'Well, I wish you luck. And a very Merry Christmas to you!'

'Well, thank you kindly, ma'am!' he said in an affected Southern drawl. 'But you'll be able to say that in person this afternoon. I'm dining with you good people.'

'You're what?' She almost shouted the words.

Now it was his turn to smile into the phone. 'Your Mom has very kindly invited me to Christmas dinner and I have accepted. By the way, what time do you usually eat?'

'Four o'clock,' Lara replied faintly. 'We usually eat at four.'

Chapter Thirteen

'Another helping of stuffing, Colonel Adams?' Beth leaned across the table, proffering the silver serving dish with its crusty brown contents. 'At least chestnuts are not on ration!'

'Thank you, ma'am, I don't mind if I do.' Despite his initial misgivings, Mike Adams was really enjoying this meal. In fact, it was the best Christmas dinner he had had since marrying Joanne. The Mallory household was a darned sight more relaxed than the Biltcliffes, despite the false air-raid alarm that had sent them all scurrying to the cellars during their pre-dinner drink, only to re-emerge half an hour later to a slightly overdone bird and brown leather roast potatoes.

'Best meal I've had all year, Ma!' Ken said, as he nodded his acceptance of the dish of stuffing that Mike passed along the table.

'It must be a pretty tough life you're living at the moment,' Mike said, 'never knowing if you'll even get through a meal without being ... "scrambled" is it they call it?'

'You get used to it.'

Mike paused, a portion of turkey half-way to his mouth. 'I've really got to hand it to you guys. You know they reckon that the Jerries outnumber you in the air by two and a half to one, but you still succeeded in holding your own – and more – last summer.'

'It wasn't without its price.'

There was a momentary silence around the table, then Beth said quietly, 'I know mere buildings can't be compared with the loss of human life, but I called at what must be one of your old haunts the other day, Colonel – the United Service Club – and, oh dear, what a mess. Incendiaries had fallen through the roof, smashing the wonderful chandelier and setting fire to the grand stairway. By the time we got there to attend to the casualties, all the lovely oil paintings commemorating the Battles of Jutland and Passchendaele, as well as portraits of Wellington and Nelson done just after the Napoleonic wars, were ablaze. Oddly enough, the coffee room and restaurant were barely touched and the staff seemed more pleased about that than anything!'

'Quite right too!' Ken put in. 'Shows they've got their priorities right. You learn to appreciate your grub as much as anything in this war. Even if there's not usually very much of it!'

They all murmured their agreement on the importance of good food, and were lavish in their praise to Mrs Bates for her efforts on their behalf when, half an hour later, she removed the empty Christmas pudding plates and distributed the coffee and brandy-snaps. The housekeeper, however, was obviously flustered, and it was not due to the effusive compliments from around the table. 'You'll excuse me being a few minutes late with the coffee, ma'am,' she said, handing Beth the first cup. 'It's Vi, my girl – she's downstairs in the kitchen.'

'Vi's here in London – in the house!' Beth's surprise was obvious. 'But that's wonderful! Were you expecting her?'

'That I was not!' Peggy Bates said emphatically. 'Turned up like a bad penny, she has. Run off from that farm of hers in the country!'

'No!'

'As sure as God's my witness.'

'Was she very unhappy there?' Lara asked, reaching for her own coffee, then handing on Mike's to him.

'Quiet as the grave, she says it was. Spent all the hours God gives mucking out the pigs.'

'Can't blame her for feeling she's had enough,' Ken said, suppressing a smile. 'What will she do now?'

'End up in the bloody Tower, if you ask me – beggin' your pardon, ma'am,' Mrs Bates sighed, as she looked at Beth balefully.

Beth looked from one to the other at the table, then back to her housekeeper. 'Now, there's no question of that – no question of that at all. In fact, the poor girl must be very upset and thoroughly depressed. Why don't you ask her up to join us for an after-dinner drink in half an hour? And come up yourself. Goodness knows, after producing a magnificent dinner like this, you certainly deserve one!'

Mrs Bates's pink cheeks broke into a wide smile. 'Well, that's real kind of you, ma'am.' She looked round the table at the others to make sure there was no dissent, then nodded her acceptance. 'A nice glass of Wincarnis would go down a treat as far as I'm concerned, and I'm sure Vi would be all the better for a touch of something cheering inside of her. Not that she deserves it, mind! Her dear father would turn in his grave if he knew she'd deserted her post like this in such desperate times!'

'Yes, well I doubt if the whole of the British Empire's going to come crashing down about our ears just because Violet is no longer there to muck out somebody's pigs,' Beth said, with a smile. 'But I take your point. You go down and tell her you're both expected in the drawing-room in half an hour.'

They all watched, with barely suppressed mirth, as the housekeeper waddled her way to the dining-room door. 'You don't mind, do you?' Beth said to the others, once she was well out of earshot. 'Vi is – shall we say – a bit of a girl, but there's no real harm in her. And I'm sure if we left them down there alone together, the fur would be flying within a few minutes.'

'It'll probably be flying up here as well from what I can remember of Violet,' Lara commented, half under her breath. With her baby-blue eyes blinking out from behind the platinum blonde of her Veronica Lake hairdo, every man was fair game as far as the house-keeper's daughter was concerned. She had not set eyes on Violet since her marriage to Ken, but well remembered the play she had made for him when he was staying here for a few days after their engagement was announced last autumn. A few well-chosen words in Vi's shell-like ear had worked wonders then, but surely they wouldn't be necessary tonight?

They adjourned to the drawing-room about two minutes before Mrs Bates knocked tentatively on the door, and entered with Violet in her wake. Lara was aware of not only Ken's, but also Mike Adams's eyes grow wider at the sight of the curvaceous blonde in the tight-fitting, white angora sweater and pencil-slim black skirt.

When the introductions were made and the drinks distributed, Ken made for the gramophone. 'I think some music wouldn't go amiss. What'll it be – Glenn Miller, Tommy Dorsey? Requests taken, provided that the requestee winds the gramophone!'

'I'll wind the gramophone,' Beth volunteered, 'then you young people are free to dance. Mrs B. can sit by me and enjoy the heat of the fire.' She patted the leather cushion for the housekeeper to join her in the other wing-chair and motioned to Ken to bring the gramophone and sit it on the side-table beside them. 'Now, what about asking one of our guests to choose the music … Colonel Adams, is there anything in particular you'd like to hear? We have a pretty good selection, I can assure you.'

Mike glanced at Lara, then back at her mother. 'I'm rather partial to Glenn Miller's version of "Let's Do It", ma'am, if you have it.'

'I think that can be arranged.' After some ferreting in the record cabinet, the record was produced with a flourish, and placed on the turntable.

As the music filled the room, Mike turned to Ken and said quietly, 'Would you permit me the pleasure of having this dance with your wife?'

Ken looked slightly surprised at the request, but smiled nonetheless. 'Sure – go right ahead. Violet here and I will keep you company on the floor.'

'You did that on purpose!' Lara hissed in his ear, as Mike took her in his arms. 'How could you?'

'Quite easily, honey.' His breath was warm on her brow. 'And you needn't feel in the least bit guilty about us doing anything behind your better-half's back ... By the looks of it our Vi's got there before you!'

Lara's eyes swivelled to the right as Ken and the housekeeper's daughter swept past. Violet's crimson-tipped fingers were moving slowly up and down the fine grey worsted back of Ken's jacket and, from the look on his face, he was lodging no obvious objections.

'I have to see you again.' Mike's words were whispered so quietly into the hair at the side of her brow that at first she thought she was imagining things.

'What?'

'I must see you again, Lara.' He had not meant to come out with such a thing, but the several vodkas he had downed that day, along with the heat of the fire, the music, and the feel of her once again in his arms, had sent convention to the winds.

She stiffened in his arms. 'We see each other at work.'

'Don't play games. You know what I mean.'

'I can't, you know that.'

His right hand clutched her fingers even tighter in his, as his left pressed her closer to him. His chest was much broader than Ken's; broader and firmer. 'What's stopping you? What harm can it do?'

She remained silent, staring straight ahead over his shoulder as they swung rhythmically around the room. He was drunk; he must be to talk to her like this almost in front of Ken himself.

'You're hesitating, I can feel it.'

'No, I'm not!' It was difficult to keep her voice low enough so as not to attract the attention of the others. 'You're a bastard, Mike Adams, do you know that?'

He grinned and moved his body even closer to hers as they glided rhythmically into the window alcove, then danced on the spot for a moment. 'So you've made up your mind, have you? About whether I'm the cream that rises to the top or a bastard, I mean.'

She remembered their previous conversation only too well, but chose to ignore the remark. The cheek of the man was incredible. 'Doesn't the fact that I'm a married woman mean anything to you?' she hissed. 'Doesn't your own marriage mean anything at all? Or can it be that marriage as an institution doesn't rate at all in your book? What *does* it mean to you exactly? Tell me that.'

He looked down at her with an almost wistful look in his eyes. 'Marriage, my dear Mrs C., is the price men pay for sex; and, if I was really cynical, I could say the opposite is just as true – sex is the price women pay for marriage. Only somehow I feel that wouldn't be the whole story as far as you're concerned.'

The fingers of Lara's right hand twitched in his. She had an almost uncontrollable urge to slap his face. Sensing it, he gripped her hand even tighter. 'That's not an insult, honey. It means in my book you're not like most other dames. There's more to relationships where you're concerned. Much more.'

She had come almost to a full stop. 'You're right there, Colonel. Certain things *are* important to me. Like love, for instance.'

The faint hint of a smile flickered across his mouth as he said quietly, 'We'd better dance on. We wouldn't want the others to think there was something wrong between us now, would we?'

His arms tightened around her and, despite her anger, a frisson of excitement ran up her spine. This man infuriated her more than any other she had ever met. Infuriated her and excited her, if she was really honest with herself. The knowledge appalled her as she deliberately attempted to turn her body to wood in his arms.

They danced on in silence until the music stopped. There was no more to say short of having an all-out row with him on the subject of faithfulness in marriage. And the awful thing was he would probably win as usual. He had a disconcerting habit of making her feel like a silly little prude at times – as if the guilt she felt whenever they were alone together outside working hours was simply a product of her own mind attributing dirty connotations to their relationship that did not exist.

Although the record had ended, Ken and Vi still stood in the middle of the floor with their arms wrapped around each other. Taking care to avoid Mike's eyes, Lara extricated herself from his embrace, then called across to her mother, who was in the process of putting another record on the turntable. 'I hope you'll excuse us if

Ken and I slip away now, Mum. He's leaving in an hour or so, remember.'

Beth got up from the gramophone and glanced at her watch. 'Good heavens, is that the time! Of course, dear. We quite understand. It's so true what they say about time flying when you're having fun, isn't it?' The cliché was aimed at no one in particular, but the others all murmured their agreement as they stood up to shake hands with Ken.

Lara flinched inwardly as the two men faced each other across the Indian carpet, but there was nothing but the most casual of smiles on Mike Adams's face as he held out his hand to her husband. 'Well, here's wishing you happy landings, Ken, and many of them. I hope to see you again before my stint in England comes to an end.'

'Thanks, Mike. It was a real pleasure to meet you. Give my regards to New York when you get back there. It's a place I've always fancied visiting, and I might just do that when this crazy war is over. I did part of my training in Florida, but never quite made it that far north. Take care of Lara for me, won't you? Don't work her too hard.'

'Don't worry, I won't. Good secretaries are hard to come by these days.'

Lara could not even summon up the pretence of a smile as she came forward and took Ken's arm to shepherd him from the room. When they had gone, the others stood around in silence for a moment or two, then Beth said lightly, 'Well, I'm sure we all wish Ken the very best of luck now he's returning to his aerodrome, so how about another drink and something appropriate to send him off?'

Once the glasses had been replenished, she went back to the record cabinet and, after a certain amount of shuffling, extracted an appropriate song. Soon the strains of 'We'll keep the Home Fires Burning' filled the room, and she raised her glass, and said, with scarcely disguised emotion, 'It may well have applied to the last war, but it's equally valid for this. Let's keep the home fires burning till they all come home again to us. Let's drink to Ken and all those other brave boys who risk their lives in the skies above us every day!'

'To Ken!'

Mike downed his in one, to find himself the object of a lingering glance from the young woman by the fireplace. He returned Vi's smile and raised his empty glass in silent salute.

'You're a Yank, then?'

'Yes, I'm from New York.'

'It must get lonely for you being over here at this time of year. Although I've heard you've got some very good clubs – that one in

Piccadilly, for example, I've heard that's very good.' She looked directly at him as she spoke, and there was no mistaking the unspoken message in her words.

'You mean the Rainbow Club. Yeah, it's OK, I guess. A bit crowded usually.'

'I adore crowds.'

'It figures. Your Mom told us you'd been working on a farm as some sort of female swineherd, if I remember rightly. I can imagine that life down on the farm wasn't exactly a load of laughs.'

'You're right there.'

He regarded her quizzically for a moment, a look of mild amusement on his face. 'You really fancy going on somewhere, huh?'

Vi tapped the tips of her bottom teeth with her glass and looked up at him through curling eyelashes, as she gave a quiet smile and a slow nod of her head.

'Well now, I reckon we can come up with somewhere tonight that's lively enough for you – if you don't mind a walk, that is. I've got no transport tonight and the streets are pretty dirty with all that slush.'

Vi downed the rest of her drink and smiled up at him through Cupid Pink lips. 'I'm used to getting dirty, don't forget. Remember the pigs?'

Chapter Fourteen

Lara watched her husband throw the last pair of black socks into his kitbag then sit down on the bed beside her with a sigh. She stretched out a hand and touched his, her fingers tenderly stroking the soft down of golden hair that covered its back. 'We're nearly at the end of the year, my love,' she said softly. 'Surely there won't be too many more goodbyes? Surely this war can't go on forever?'

'Nothing is forever, Red,' he said quietly. 'I've learned that much over the past year or so – not life, not love, not anything.'

'Not love?'

He gave a bitter smile. 'Ever sat in a barracks and watched the bloke in the next bed cry like a baby over a Dear John letter? No? Well I have. Many times. And the last time it happened, it was to Taffy Hughes just before we were scrambled for the raid on Tangmere. He never came back. Went down in the sea off the Needles. One of our best pilots, he was. You'll never convince me that bloody letter didn't have something to do with it … No, not even love is forever now – especially not now. This damned war has changed everything.'

She had never seen him so down. 'Well, *we* are forever, Ken – you're sure of that, aren't you? You must be sure of that. I won't let you go until you tell me you are!' Her hand gripped his even tighter and she could feel the hot sting of tears in her eyes as they searched for his, but he avoided her gaze.

'It's time I was going.' He stood up, his hand still clasped in hers, and he raised it to his lips before letting go. 'Don't come to the door with me, it'll only upset you.'

'You want me to go now?' She looked at him bleakly. Didn't he know that every second was precious? All possible doubts she had had about their relationship since he had been home had vanished. She didn't want him to go. All she wanted on this earth was for them to be together – forever. To hell with this damned war. It wasn't even anything to do with them. It was a quarrel about a few areas of foreign land that had been blown up out of all proportion. Why should *her* husband have to die for a country that he might never set eyes on as long as he lived? 'Can't I stay in here with you for a few minutes more?'

He shook his head. 'I need a second or two on my own, that's all. A few seconds before I go.'

He wanted to pray. She was sure of it. Despite all his protestations about not needing the Kirk any more, the 'Wee Free' of his Grandfather Cameron was still in his blood; at a time like this he wanted a private moment or two to be alone with his God. They hugged one another in silence, her tears leaving a damp, darker blue patch on the collar of his shirt, then she left the room without looking back.

He sat back down on the edge of the bed and buried his face in his hands. It would be so easy to cry, but if the English had been taught from childhood to hide their emotions, then the Scots had had it ingrained even more so.

'Now don't be a Jessie, Kenneth!' He could hear his father's voice to this day. That had been the familiar entreaty in years gone by, whenever life had become too much for the small, sandy-haired boy in short trousers, in that sprawling, jute-spinning seaport of Dundee, on the windswept east coast of Scotland. 'Take it like a man!' he would say. 'Be a man, laddie! Be a man!' Well, now he was a man, but it felt no different.

The old man had sent him a diary for Christmas, and had written a message in it. A diary! Ken managed a mirthless smile. At least it showed his father had faith that his son would see the coming year out. The Scots never spent money needlessly.

He felt into the right-hand breast pocket of his tunic and extracted the small, cloth-bound book, with the pencil stuck down the spine. On the blue cover, in gold writing, was the word 'Diary' and the year '1941' beneath it. He opened it carefully and, leafing his way to the blank pages at the back marked 'Miscellaneous', he looked down at the inscription written in black ink. His father had chosen the words used by the King, George VI, in his address to the nation last Christmas:

'I said to the man who stood at the Gate of the Year, "Give me a light that I may tread safely into the unknown". And he replied, "Go out into the darkness, and put your hand into the Hand of God. That shall be to you better than the light, and safer than a known way".'

Ken's eyes misted at the memory of them all. Had they ever really existed? Had all those carefree summer afternoons spent as a child fishing off the end of Broughty pier, beneath the shadow of the castle, ever really happened? His old friends from the Eastern Primary – where were they now? It all seemed a world away from life down here, but the war was affecting them just the same. His cousin Alan was out there somewhere in North Africa, with the Seventh Royal Tank Regiment, helping in the offensive in the western desert against the Italian General Garibaldi's Tenth Army. Aunt Cissie, Alan's mother, had sworn never to buy a flat currant biscuit again as long as she lived.

A shuddering sigh ran through him as he pushed the diary back in his breast pocket and securely fastened the metal button. A glance at his watch told him it was gone seven and he was due at the station at eight. It was time he was going.

As Ken stood on the freezing platform three-quarters of an hour later, Mike Adams and Violet Bates stood in the flurrying snow outside the entrance to the Underground at Piccadilly Circus. Violet, who was wearing wildly impractical, ankle-strap, open-toed shoes, stamped her feet on the impacted snow of the pavement, as she attempted to keep her umbrella upright above her head. 'God, it's freezing!'

Mike put a comforting arm around her shoulders. 'What do you fancy doing? Personally, I'm easy.'

Despite the cold, she aimed a knowing smile up at him. 'So am I, ducks.'

'Figuratively speaking, I trust.'

'If I knew what you meant I could agree with you – or disagree, as the case may be.' She clung tightly to his arm as she spoke, and the turn of her head had a distinctly coquettish air to it, as did her tone of voice.

He pulled the brim of his hat down further over his brow in a vain attempt to prevent the swirling snow from blowing into his eyes. 'To put it crudely, honey, I was assuming you were not – how shall I put it – a lady of pleasure.'

'A lady of pleasure!' Vi hooted. 'Now there's a good old-fashioned phrase for you. And what might be wrong with grabbing a little pleasure where you can now and then, may I ask?'

Mike's eyebrows rose a fraction of an inch. 'Nothing. Absolutely nothing!'

'You think us English girls are incapable of enjoying a bit of slap and tickle, is that it?'

He grinned. 'Well, some say most young women over here prefer a good hot-water bottle to a good lay.'

'You Yanks – you make making love sound like it takes place in a hen-house!' She gave him a playful punch, then the coyest of smiles. 'I can think of much more comfortable places than that!'

'Really? Tell me more.'

Vi's coy smile increased, as they moved aside on the pavement to let two soldiers and their girlfriends pass. 'Well now, I've never been one for beating around the bush, and you strike me as a man of the world yourself, if you don't mind my saying so. Seems to me neither of us have got anything better to do tonight, so why not spend an hour or so havin' a bit of fun? I've got a friend whose old lady's got a boarding house down the Tottenham Court Road. She's always got a room available for a consideration.'

Mike looked down at her through another flurry of snowflakes. He would have to be deaf, dumb and blind not to get the implication. But what the hell … If she was that keen, what did he have to lose? You could bet your boots Joanne hadn't exactly been playing Snow White since he'd been away. 'I've got about ten pounds on me, I guess. Would that rate as "a consideration"?'

Vi looked dubious for a moment. 'Trust me to meet up with the only hard-up Yank in London! But it's far too bleedin' cold to argue!' The grip on his arm tightened as she steered him back towards the Underground entrance. 'Let's go before I'm so chilled to death that that hot-water bottle you were on about proves too big a temptation!'

They reached the 'Royal Duchess' guest house about half an hour later, to have the door opened by a buxom female of indeterminable age, with tightly-curled, hennaed hair. 'Well, bless my soul, if it isn't Violet!' The beady, blue-lidded eyes of the landlady turned from Vi to peer at the man by her side. 'And who 'ave we here, may I ask?'

'Merry Christmas Ede! We have here an American,' Vi declared proudly. 'From New York – where else! We need a room, Edie. Say you've got one – and quick about it – it's flippin' brass monkey weather out here!'

'On Christmas night? You're after a room on Christmas night? Lord preserve us!'

'You can do it, Edie,' Vi coaxed, blowing on her hands to bring some life back to them, as she stamped her frozen feet on the step. The snow had stopped now, but it was still freezing cold. 'Come on, you know you can do it.'

'For a consideration, of course,' Mike cut in, with not a little irony.

Both women looked up at him, then Edie took Vi by the arm and pulled her in over the red-polished step. 'You'd better come in before you catch your deaths out there. The back one's free on the second floor. If the fire won't light, the meter's under the stairs, with the number of your room on it. It's ten bob for half a night, a quid if you stay past midnight.'

'Thanks, Edie, you're a good 'un!'

Mike followed Vi up the dimly-lit staircase. A heavy oak wardrobe loomed out of the semi-darkness on the half-landing, and a whiff of mothballs caught his nostrils as they passed the partially open door. Their footsteps echoed on the frayed, brown linoleum treads as they ascended in single file. The whole place smelt vaguely of either stale boiled cabbage or urine: which of the two it was impossible to discern. After the heavy meal less than an hour before, he began to feel distinctly queasy.

At the top step, Vi halted and turned round, causing him to pause a few steps below her. Their eyes were level as she slid her arms around his neck and planted an open-mouthed kiss on his lips. 'In the mood already, eh?' Her breath smelt of the cigarette still burning between the fingers of her right hand, as her left played with the short hairs at the nape of his neck.

'You'll never know ... ' He tried hard to disguise the irony in his voice.

There were four other rooms on the floor, with light showing faintly beneath two of the doors. The one at the back stood ajar. 'This must be ours,' Vi said in a husky whisper, pushing it open even further to allow them to enter.

Mike switched on the light. A dim glow permeated the room from a single, shadeless bulb that swayed slightly in the draught from the open door. A one-bar gas fire was set in the middle of a cream ceramic fireplace, most of the tiles of which were discoloured and cracked; an Edwardian wardrobe loomed against the far wall, its door half-open, and a four-drawer chest stood in solitary splendour against the wall opposite, with a washbowl and ewer on top. In the middle of the room was a double bed, with a khaki Army issue blanket thrown over the faded pink bedspread, and two striped towels that had seen better days hung over the bed-end. A hand-printed notice was stuck into a framed Coronation print that hung above the bed. 'To whom it may concern. Would customers please use the towels in bed to save the sheets. Failure to do so may result in them having to pay laundry charges.' Mike read the message aloud, then turned to Vi. 'Romantic, huh?'

She had stubbed out her cigarette and was already shedding her coat and hanging it in the wardrobe. 'Take no notice. In this light, she'd never notice if a bottle of her bleedin' mother's ruin mixed with blackcurrant juice was spilt on them there sheets, never mind anythin' else! Light that fire, will you? It's bleedin' perishin' in 'ere!'

He fumbled in the pocket of his coat and extracted his cigarette lighter and, to his surprise, the bar with its broken filaments eventually spluttered into life. He held his frozen hands to it for a moment, but the heat was minimal.

Despite the cold, Vi continued to undress. He sat down on the edge of the bed and watched as, item by item, her clothes were removed, until she was down to her brassière, knickers, suspender-belt, stockings and shoes. Then, very deliberately, she raised one foot on to the edge of the bed beside him and undid one suspender. She was less than a foot away and emitted a distinct body odour that caused him to move back slightly on the blanket. 'Care to undo the rest?' Her voice was huskily low.

He shook his head. 'No, you go right ahead, honey. I'm enjoying the show!'

She looked at him suspiciously for a moment, then deciding his answer was genuine, she carefully slid one stocking down the first leg, to lie neatly rolled around her ankle as she undid the strap of her shoe. His eyes lit on a knot of blue veins just beneath the pale skin behind her knee, and he stared at them as if fixated. The second stocking was removed with rather less ceremony than the first, then she stood in front of him and slowly turned her back. 'Undo my bra, Yank,' she whispered.

His fingers, still frozen, fumbled with the intricate set of hooks and eyes, then slid the pink cotton straps over her shoulders. Still with her back to him, she slipped her arms out of them, then tossed the bra on to the floor.

'Well, what d'you think?' She turned to face him, now half-naked, with arms outstretched, a look of almost triumph on her face.

He stared at the small pendulous breasts, startlingly white in the dim light from the bulb. The body smell was stronger now, permeating through his nostrils down into his stomach, where the Christmas dinner and drinks were lying far too uneasily for comfort. Then, as he sat there staring, the contents of his gut began to churn unmistakably. He swallowed hard, but to no avail, as they continued to make their way back up into his gullet. For a moment longer he tried to fight it, then could hold back no longer.

'What the bleedin' hell's going on?'

With Vi's offended protest echoing in his ears, he rose from the bed and made a dash for the enamel washbowl sitting on top of the chest, as his Christmas dinner made its second appearance of the day.

Vi watched in a mixture of indignation and disgust. 'Well, don't that just beat everything!' She bent down and, snatching her brassière from the rag rug beneath her feet, she struggled back into it. 'They needn't talk to me about Yanks in future! Give me a bleedin' Englishman any day – they know how to treat a lady!'

Rising from the washbowl, Mike wiped his mouth with a handker-chief, then reached back into his pocket and extracted a five pound note. He tossed it into the middle of the khaki blanket on the bed with a wry smile. 'At least we won't have to pay the laundry charges!'

'And what about me, may I ask?' Vi glared at him from across the room, an incongruous figure in her brassière and creased French knickers. 'Don't I get anything for wasting my time?'

He reached back into his pocket and pulled out his remaining notes. There were four of them. 'You're welcome to them, honey. Anything to oblige a lady.'

He sat back down on the bed and watched blankly as she hurried back into her clothes, then disappeared out of the door; no doubt to cadge a drink off her friend Edie and complain loudly of her bad luck in ending up with a 'right rum 'un', as Ada, his office cleaner, would say.

As her feet clattered their way back down the stairs, he fumbled into the pocket of his overcoat for a cigarette, which he lit with shaking fingers. He drew the smoke deeply into his lungs, then blew it out in one long stream. He watched as it drifted slowly to the ceiling in the light of the single bulb. Christmas night and he had come down to this! What, in God's name, was happening to him? Was he really so desperately lonely that he would allow himself to be picked up by any cheap tart who happened to think she was on to a good thing? He continued to stare into the dim glow of the gas fire, as an emptiness such as he had never known welled within him. Maybe he was. God help him, maybe he was.

Chapter Fifteen

'You're sure you'll be all right, dear? You really don't mind staying here alone for a few days?' Beth looked at her daughter with genuine concern in her eyes, before closing her wardrobe door and turning the key.

'Alone,' Lara laughed. 'I'll hardly be that! It's only three days from Christmas, after all. We've still got quite a houseful – what with Mrs B. and all the Polish contingent still not back at work yet … No, don't you worry, Mum. It's much more important that you go up and spend a few peaceful days with Gran. Heaven knows it's long enough since you last saw her.'

Beth nodded. That was certainly true. It was almost four months since she had been up to Oxford to see her mother. Up until last year, the old lady had always spent Christmas with them in London, but with the almost continuous air-raids and increasing pain from her arthritis, she preferred to spend most of her time in her own home on the outskirts of the university city. With her father now dead, Beth would normally have been perturbed at the thought of her mother living there alone, but luckily that was no longer a problem. Jack's death had left Beth a relatively wealthy woman – wealthy enough, at least, to pay for the services of a full-time, live-in nurse for the old lady.

'Will you go by train or take the car?'

'I doubt if I'd get as far as Watford on the measly amount of petrol my coupons would supply,' Beth smiled. 'No, I think, all things considered, it'd better be the train.' She squeezed a pair of sensible, brown leather walking-shoes into the corner of her suitcase and, with a satisfied sigh, closed the lid. 'I shall think of you slaving away at your typewriter on Monday.'

Lara tensed, slipping down from the end of the bed and walking to the bedroom window to look out over the small flower-bed, edged by the short black stumps of what had once been ornamental, wrought-iron railings. 'It's such a pity they had to take down all the railings, isn't it? Ours were especially pretty, with all those pretty fleur-de-lis …' Her voice tailed off. It was no use, she'd have to tell her mother before she left for Oxford. 'I – I've handed in my notice. I won't be going back to Princes Gate on Monday.'

'You've what?'

'I've handed in my notice … It was meant to be a very temporary appointment, anyway.' It was hard to keep the defensiveness from her voice.

Beth looked genuinely astonished. 'But what's brought this on? I thought you really liked it there, and that Colonel Adams seems like such a nice fellow.'

Lara stared silently out over the black iron stumps to the pavement beyond. A small child was attempting to pull a wooden sledge over what was left of the snow. The metal runners bumped instead of sliding along past their window. 'He was all right, I suppose, as Americans go.'

'Was. So he's already in the past tense? Have you told him of your decision?'

'Not personally. I telephoned reception; Sheila Cassidy will pass on the message.'

'That was a bit mean.'

Lara's head jerked round. 'What do you mean by that?'

'Well, don't you think it was – just to leave like that, without even a reason, without a proper farewell? You could at least go round personally and say goodbye.'

Lara turned back to the window, avoiding her mother's eyes. Her teeth chewed nervously at the inside of her left cheek, a nervous habit from childhood that her mother was quick to note.

'There's nothing wrong, is there, Lara? You haven't done anything wrong?'

'If you mean, have I betrayed a state secret, or stolen from the petty cash, then no – no, there's nothing wrong.'

Beth looked at her daughter. She was hiding something, there was no doubt about that. But what? In all the time Lara had worked at the Foreign Office she could never remember her being anything but enthusiastic about her work. So, it wasn't the job … 'He – he hasn't done anything "improper", has he?' The word was spoken with difficulty. It seemed a ludicrous question.

Lara shook her head. 'No, Mum, *he* hasn't done anything improper.'

It was Beth's turn to tense. The implication was impossible to ignore. 'You – you mean, you're frightened *you* might? You don't trust yourself?' It was difficult to keep her voice calm.

Still staring out of the window, Lara gave an almost imperceptible nod of her head. 'Dreadful, isn't it?' She turned and faced her mother. 'Some people have names for women like me, you know – women who have only been married a short time and find other men attractive.'

'One other man, Lara … It *is* only him, isn't it?'

'Good God, isn't that enough? Of course it's only him. And yes, yes, I do find him attractive.'

'I see.'

The two women looked at one another from across the room, then Lara asked quietly, 'Do you? Can you really begin to understand?'

There was a helplessness bordering on despair in her voice that made Beth want to run and put her arms around her, comfort her as she had done so many times throughout her childhood. But her daughter was no longer a small child. She was a grown woman and was confiding in her something she had hoped she would never have to hear. 'But you and Ken – you seem so happy together.'

Lara made a despairing gesture with her hands. 'That's just it – we are! When he's here and we're together I can't imagine how I could ever have these thoughts about Mike Adams. But that's just the trouble, Mum, can't you see? Ken is not here and we're hardly ever together. I probably won't see him again for months.'

'But you would see Colonel Adams every day?'

'Quite.' Lara sat down on the edge of the bed and shook her head bleakly. 'And that's why I've determined to do something positive about it. If I'd let things just drift on, who knows where it would have led?' She gave a hollow laugh. 'Now there was a rhetorical question if I ever heard one! I'm afraid we both know very well where it would have led.'

'You haven't actually … ' Beth floundered for the right words.

'I haven't actually let him make love to me? If I had, would it shock you?'

Beth looked straight back into the questioning hazel eyes – his eyes, Jan's eyes. She paused before answering, then said slowly, 'It would sadden me, for Ken's sake. But it wouldn't shock me. In many ways I would understand. Colonel Adams is a fine man, Lara. You would not be the first woman in this world to meet the right man at the wrong time.' She paused once more. If ever there was a time for the truth it was now. Now was the moment she had been waiting for since perhaps the first moment she held her daughter in her arms as a tiny infant. The moment to confide in her the truth of her parentage. Now was the moment when, woman to woman, she could tell her that she too had had the misfortune to fall in love with a fine man at the wrong time. She could feel the palms of her hands grow damp as she searched for the words.

'Mum, are you all right?' Her mother had gone quite pale. 'It has upset you, hasn't it? I was stupid even to mention it – to burden you with my problems.'

Beth shook her head. 'No, please – don't say that. It means a lot to me that you feel you can confide in me … There was a time I would have been grateful for someone to have been there – just to listen, to understand … Having a gold ring on your finger doesn't mean you stop having feelings, Lara. That's something you've found out the hard way.'

Lara looked at her curiously. Two pink spots were appearing high up on Beth's cheeks. This conversation was making her mother distinctly uncomfortable, yet she seemed to wish to prolong it. She was trying to tell her something. To tell her that she understood – that she had been in that situation too.

Then, suddenly, before Lara's eyes flashed the sight of her mother kissing that Pole – what was his name? – Jarosinski. In all the turmoil of her own life, she had almost forgotten how shocked she had been at the sight of Beth in the Count's arms. A silence fell between them and, as Lara continued to stare at her mother, the conviction grew that she too had known what it was like to love a man other than her husband.

Countless questions whirled in her head. Questions that she knew she had no right to the answers to, yet longed to ask. Had she been in love with Jan Jarosinski? Was she still in love with him? Shame at her reaction that night burned within her. How could she have been so insensitive? Perhaps that was the moment her mother had been dreaming about for twenty years – the moment she found herself back in the arms of the man she loved. And she – her own daughter – had spoiled it for her.

Beth took her daughter's silence to mean she did not want to continue the conversation. In a way it was a relief. She attempted a bright smile that did not quite come off. 'Well, I'm sure all this soul-searching is doing no one any good. I'll slip down and see about a cup of tea. Would you fancy one?'

Lara nodded mutely, then found her voice. 'Yes, yes thanks. That would be lovely.' It was the English answer to everything.

Beth left the room quickly – almost too quickly, as if she couldn't wait to get away, and when she had gone the room seemed empty. Their words hung in the air. 'Oh, Lord …' Lara sighed deeply and ran her fingers through her hair as she stared at the closed door. Was she right to speak so freely, to reveal so many of her innermost thoughts? She felt suddenly very vulnerable, exposed, as if caught naked in public. But what was even harder to bear was that she felt she had made her mother feel the same. No longer were they parent and child, but two women who had shared an experience – an experience which, for her own part, she would rather not have had.

She got up from the edge of the bed, where she was perched, and walked to the fireplace. It was freezing in here. She shivered and rubbed the goose-fleshed skin of her arms beneath the beige wool of her cardigan, as she crouched down in front of the one glowing bar of the electric fire. If it wasn't for this infuriating rationing, they could have a decent fire in here instead of this pathetic thing. Nothing was right at the moment, nothing. And it had started going wrong the minute Mike Adams had walked into her life. What awful quirk of fate had decreed that Harvey Ledbetter should have been recalled to the States and Colonel Mike Adams be assigned to take his place?

She got wearily to her feet and stood with her back to the fire, her teeth chewing thoughtfully at the inside of her cheek as she stared out of the window at the grey, snow-filled sky beyond. It was funny how once you had confessed something it no longer assumed the proportions it once did in your mind. Maybe she had been making a mountain out of a molehill. The incongruousness of the analogy made her smile despite her sombre mood. Mike Adams would always rank as a mountain in her mind. There was no way on earth he could ever be classed as a molehill!

But it was true all the same. Maybe most of it was her imagination. When she got out of bed this morning, Mike Adams wasn't even on her mind, but then as the day wore on he began to fill more and more of her thoughts. She had even found herself sweating at the thought of that certain way he had of looking at her – definitely not the usual way a boss looked at his secretary, she was certain of that. She had found herself thinking of what had occurred between them in the past, and imagined what might happen in the future. Past conversations were gone over in detail in her head, imagined conversations of the future were concocted, her reactions to them analysed, until finally, that afternoon, she thought she would go mad. It was all so ridiculous when you thought about it rationally. She was in love with her husband, and yet this conceited, chauvinistic American seemed to haunt her every waking moment.

No, I've done the right thing, she decided. There was nothing for it other than to nip it in the bud – if 'it' actually existed outside her imagination. She had had no real alternative than to hand in her notice. There was nothing to be gained in tempting fate. In a few weeks, Colonel Mike Adams would be merely one more name to add to the growing list of bosses she had worked for since joining the Foreign Office two years ago.

Her eyes moved to a picture of herself on the bedside cabinet. It was taken on the day she graduated from secretarial college. It seemed only yesterday, yet so much had happened in the two years that had passed since then. This past year alone she had seen and done things the young graduate in the picture would never have dreamt possible. Who would have imagined that on the very eve of the Battle of Britain she would be sitting in the Cabinet Room itself as the Prime Minister, Winston Churchill, dictated the words that would harden the nation's resolve and prepare it for the invasion by air that summer: 'The whole fury and might of the enemy must be turned upon us. Hitler knows that he will have to break us in this island, or lose the war.' Six months later those words could still send a shiver down her spine.

She would remember that first day's note-taking as long as she lived. Entering the cavernous, yellow chamber that was the Cabinet Room was like entering the bowels of the earth itself. Some thirty-five feet below ground, it was about forty feet square, with ugly red girders slung across the ceiling. Their function was obvious – to prevent the building on top landing on them in the event of a direct hit during an air-raid. Even looking at them had brought on the most awful feeling of claustrophobia.

Above the door were two bare bulbs, one red, one green, to show whether an air-raid was in progress in the streets overhead. That night she had sat there, at the back of the room, and worn down pencil after pencil as the conversation went on and on, and the bulb above the door still glowed red.

When the blitz was at its height that night, the Prime Minister had left the table and made his way to the nearest rooftop to watch as the *Luftwaffe* pummelled his city to pieces.

Not all the Cabinet had accompanied him: most remained below, and she had sat with them, a silent observer in what had seemed at the time to be the very hub of the universe. She could see them all yet, seated on tubular metal chairs around the large, black baize table: the

Labour Party leader, Clement Attlee, as Lord Privy Seal; Herbert Morrison, the Home Secretary; Sir Kingsley Wood, Chancellor of the Exchequer; Lord Halifax, the Foreign Secretary, and the others ...

One chair, however, was different from the green, leather-seated, metal ones that the others occupied; it was made of dark wood and had rounded arms. On the table in front of it lay a clean blotter, four inkwells and a small pile of red labels, marked 'Action This Day'. She gave a wry smile. Oh, how she had come to fear those labels.

A small card stood on one side of the blotter, upon which were written Queen Victoria's immortal words: 'Please understand there is no pessimism in the House and we are not interested in the possibilities of defeat; they do not exist.' They had all come to believe that. They had to believe it if they were to survive this awful war.

It was usually late evening before she was called to the Cabinet Room itself, but all the aches and pains of the day would miraculously disappear as she became absorbed once more in the nation's decision-making. It would often be the early hours of the morning before her working day came to an end, but she would not have missed a minute of it.

It was funny really – by rights she should shudder at the very thought of that yellow-painted cell but, despite the constant tiredness, those had been the most exciting days of her life. Certain moments would live with her forever, such as the night the Prime Minister pointed to his chair and declared to all present, 'If the invasion takes place, that is where I shall sit. And I shall sit there until the Germans are driven back – or they shall carry me out dead.' And she had not the slightest doubt that he was speaking the truth.

Yes, she had worked for greater men than Mike Adams, and she would again. She hoped they would understand at the Foreign Office when she called to say that she was requesting a transfer back there, although there was bound to be some tut-tutting in certain quarters. It was not quite the done thing to offend the Americans at the moment, with their help so desperately needed against Germany. But, after all, they couldn't be too annoyed – she had been assured that the job at the American Embassy was only for a few days.

'Here we are, dear, two nice cups of Earl Grey, and two of Mrs B.'s freshly baked shortcake biscuits.' Her mother's voice broke into her musings, causing her to turn abruptly.

Beth made to close the door with her foot as she balanced the tray in front of her, but paused with it still ajar as she inclined her head to one side. 'Is somebody calling?'

'How should I know? You're nearer the stairs than me ... Here, let me take that.' Lara crossed the room and relieved her mother of the tray as a woman's voice called again from down below.

'It's Mrs B. ... What on earth does she want? I've just left the kitchen.' Puzzled, Beth glanced at Lara, who shrugged her shoulders as she placed the tray safely on a side table.

Beth held the door ajar, shivering slightly in the draught from the landing, as the housekeeper puffed her way up from the floor below.

'Gawd, these stairs'll be the death of me! It's the front door, ma'am. There's a gentleman at the front door and he's asking for you.'

Chapter Sixteen

'Jan!' Beth stared in astonishment at the overcoated figure on the front doorstep. 'This is a surprise!'

'Obviously.' There was no mistaking the disappointment in his voice as his eyes took in her thick tweed suit and high-heeled brown brogues. 'I seem to have caught you in the act of going out.'

What was he doing here? And why was he looking at her like that? Didn't he know the effect it had on her? 'I – I'm leaving for the station; but not for an hour or so.' She smoothed the neat chignon of hair at the nape of her neck as she backed into the hall. 'Come in – please.'

'You're leaving for the station?' The disappointment in his eyes and voice was even more obvious. 'To catch a train?'

She smiled awkwardly and attempted to keep a light-hearted tone to her voice. 'That's usually what one does at a station, isn't it? ... Actually, I'm only going as far as Oxford. I'm going up to spend a few days with my mother. She usually comes here for Christmas, but what with the bombing and one thing and another ...' She was aware she was prattling on much too quickly as nerves knotted in her stomach. What on earth had he come for? And what would Lara say? She was waiting for her upstairs in the bedroom. Oh, please, don't let her come to the landing and look down ...

They stood facing one another in the hall. Jan held his hat in his hand, nervously fingering the brim, as if ready to put it back on and depart at any moment. By the obvious embarrassment on his face, her impending departure had taken him by complete surprise. His eyes shifted nervously from her to the door, then back again.

Beth was aware of Mrs Bates watching them from half-way down the stairs, and she called out to her. 'Two fresh cups of tea, please, Mrs B. – in the drawing-room. And take the Count's hat and coat, otherwise he won't feel the good of them when he goes out. Oh, and tell Lara just to wait in my bedroom and I'll be up shortly.'

Jan paused once more, still unsure whether to stay or not. He had obviously arrived at an awkward time, but then no time was the right one for what he had to say. He looked across at Beth. Her cheeks were flushed and her eyes shining, whether in embarrassment at his sudden appearance, or in pleasure at seeing him again, it was impossible to tell. He hoped with all his heart it was the latter. Mrs Bates came down to take his things and he acquiesced, handing his hat to the housekeeper, then slipping off his coat and draping it over her waiting arms.

Beth smiled, trying hard to keep her expression and voice casual as she murmured, 'Follow me', and made for the staircase.

She glanced round as she reached the landing, and was aware of his eyes fixed once more on the oil painting of her husband at the top of the stairs, but this time neither made any comment on it. She darted a look up the next sweep of steps as they made their way along the landing, but luckily there was no sign of Lara. She gave an inward sigh of relief when the drawing-room door closed behind them.

They made uncomfortable small-talk until Mrs Bates reappeared with the tea-tray five minutes later, then, once the housekeeper had left, Jan got up from his seat and stood in front of the fire, his hands clasped behind his back, as he looked gravely at Beth. His eyes had a strangely intense expression, and the scar that ran down the side of his face seemed to stand out even more lividly than usual against his pale skin. His voice was husky when, at last, he spoke. 'I'm going back to Poland.'

'No!'

He nodded slowly, looking her straight in the eyes.

'When?' Her fingers clasped tightly in her lap as she looked up at him.

'Soon.'

'But why? It's suicide to return there, you know that!'

'I can't talk of the reasons – not yet. But believe me when I say there is no alternative.'

'I may never see you again.' The words stuck in her throat.

'I know. That's why I'm here ... Do you think I could bear that any more than you?'

She looked away, unable to bear the look in his eyes. What was she supposed to say? He was still another woman's husband. Her fingers nervously twisted her wedding ring round and round. 'When – when do you leave?' Her voice was scarcely above a whisper.

'Soon, but I have to go to Scotland first.'

'Scotland?' Her surprise was obvious. 'Why Scotland?'

'It's a favour for the Ambassador. They're doing a lot of fund raising on our behalf up there and he's been invited to Dundee to try to repeat the success they had in Aberdeen a few weeks ago. The trouble is he's already committed to too many other things at the moment, so he has asked me to stand in for him. I leave on the second of January.'

'The second ... This is Saturday, the twenty-eighth – that must be this Thursday!' Beth gripped the arms of the chair. 'But I probably won't be back from Oxford by then!'

Their eyes remained locked, and there was an intense glow in his as he said softly, 'I want you to come to Scotland with me, Beth. It's our last chance to be together. Our only chance. It – it's not a decision I've come to lightly. I've thought about it a lot over the past twenty-four hours since Edward asked me to take over the Scottish trip for him.'

'But I'm on my way to see my mother,' Beth said faintly. 'She's expecting me.'

'Then go. Go for a few days, then come to Dundee.'

She stared up at him, her heart pounding. Was it possible? He was asking her to share a few stolen days with him; a few stolen days that may have to last a lifetime.

Although he had given no hint, she was well aware how dangerous it was for him to return to Poland. He had been fortunate indeed in Otto securing his release, if that was in fact the reason behind it, but he would not be so lucky a second time. He was now a marked man in German-occupied Poland. If he were to fall into the hands of the Gestapo again it would mean certain death. And there was one thing more ... 'But, but Leni ... ?' It required a physical effort to speak the name of the woman who had stood between them all those years ago – who stood between them still.

The brown eyes clouded slightly. 'Leni is remaining here in London.'

'Oh.' She looked down at her hands. What did she say next? He was standing there waiting for her reply.

'I realize I am asking a lot. I am being selfish in my desire to be with you ... completely selfish. But what is a few days stolen from a lifetime, *kochanie*? These are terrible times we are living through, Beth. Not one of us knows if we will live through the coming day, never mind the coming year. Who among us can make plans for the future any more? The whole world is living for today. For some of us there may be no tomorrow.'

For some of us … The words rang in her head. He meant himself. Whatever he was going back to Poland to do, he knew he was signing his own death warrant. 'A few days …' she repeated softly. How could she deny him that? How could she deny herself? She got up from her seat and stood before him, her eyes searching his for the reassurance she so badly needed that she would be doing the right thing. 'When … ? Where … ?'

He reached inside his jacket pocket and removed a sealed envelope. 'The details of my hotel in Dundee and how and when to get there are inside. Come as soon as you can: I will be waiting.'

She took the envelope between shaking fingers then, without looking at it, slipped it into her jacket pocket. He looked down at her, wanting to reach out, to touch her, to reassure her that everything would be all right, that they were doing nothing wrong. He had searched his own heart before coming here tonight and he knew, without a doubt, he was doing nothing that he would be ashamed to stand up and account for before his God. A love such as they had known, and denied for half a lifetime, he could never believe to be a sin. Never. Never.

'I'll go now,' he said quietly. 'Don't come with me. I'll see myself out. There have been too many goodbyes already in our lives, *kochanie*; let us spare ourselves one more.'

She nodded, acutely aware of her hands hanging helplessly by her sides. She wanted to rush into his arms, to tell him of course she would come. How could he fear otherwise? But she made no move.

He looked so tired, so very tired. What he had been through in the past she could not begin to even guess at, and the thought of what was ahead of him in the future turned her blood to ice-water. His eyes, so golden-brown at the centre, seemed to burn into hers. Then, without another word, he turned and walked to the door, and was gone.

Her knees seemed to give way beneath her, and she sat back down heavily on the seat she had just vacated. She looked down at her hands, they were trembling. She was quivering like a leaf inside and out. She thought of Lara still waiting for her upstairs and felt a kinship she had never known before with her daughter. Whatever torment Lara was going through today, she herself had known with a vengeance in the past – and still knew. For absence did not kill love; it merely fed the flame, so that one fine day it might blaze into life again and engulf you, as it had done so suddenly that Silesian summer so long ago.

'Mum, do you know what the time is?'

Her daughter's voice from the doorway a few minutes later caused her to jump. She turned in the seat and did her best to keep her voice steady. 'I – I know, dear, I was just coming.' She got up awkwardly from the chair, relieved that the untouched cups of tea and biscuits were not visible behind the chair.

'Who was that at the door?'

Beth breathed an inward sigh of relief. Mrs B. obviously hadn't told her. 'Oh, just someone from the Ambulance Depot wanting me to work tomorrow, but I've had to disappoint them, I'm afraid. I feel bad about it, but I really can't let Mother down at this late stage.'

Lara was silent for a moment or two as they walked back upstairs, then said emphatically, 'Ring them up. Tell them I'll stand in for you.'

'You?' Beth looked round in surprise. 'But you've never done that sort of work before!'

'No, but neither had you until you began. And I can drive, can't I? Don't tell me they're so spoilt for volunteers that they can afford to turn people down!'

'Good heavens, no!'

'Well, that's settled then.' She glanced at her watch. 'It's just on quarter past three. What time did you say your train's due?'

'Four-twenty,' Beth said. 'The taxi's due in ten minutes. I'd better get a move on!'

'In that case don't bother calling to tell them at the Depot. You'll never get through anyway with so many lines down. I'll just go along there tomorrow morning and present myself as a willing helper – and we'll pray to God there's no air-raid so my services won't be called upon too much.'

'You know, Lara, that's a very noble offer.'

'Noble! Mother dear, that's the very last thing I feel today!'

The air-raid siren went next morning just as Lara was sitting down to breakfast. 'Bleedin' 'ell! Wouldn't you just believe it!' Peggy Bates exclaimed in dismay. 'The first Sunday after Christmas and the bleeders are at it again!'

Lara got up from the kitchen table immediately and, ramming a piece of toast in her mouth, she reached for her coat on the back of the door.

'Where in heaven's name are you going, Miss Lara? You can't go out there into them streets now.'

'I can, Mrs B. and I must. I promised Mum I'd take her place today. And with Wailing Winnie at it again, it seems they'll need me even more now!'

'And just when do you reckon on coming off duty, pray?'

'That'll depend entirely on the Germans. But don't bother about preparing any food. If I'm hungry when I get back I'll just grab a sandwich, or anything that's going.'

Mrs Bates threw up her hands in disgust. 'Well, far be it from me to argue with you, I'm sure. Are the others back from Mass yet, or will it just be me and Humphrey down in the cellar?'

'I honestly don't know.' Lara tied a headscarf around her hair and tucked the knotted end into her coat collar. 'You don't mind going down there on your own, do you? I'll stay for a bit, if you're really nervous about it.'

Mrs Bates scooped the cat up in her arms from the top of the kitchen table and deposited him on the floor, before lifting the steaming kettle from the Aga to fill her Thermos flask. 'Get away with you, Miss! After living with my old man for ten years before he finally met his Maker, it'll take more than the likes of old Hermann's lot to scare me! No, just be off with you, but for Gawd's sake take care.'

'I will, Mrs B.' Lara slung her handbag over her shoulder and bent to give Humphrey a final stroke before making for the door. 'Let's all keep our fingers crossed it's just a false alarm and then everyone can get back to reading the Sunday papers in peace.'

Her words had a hollow ring, however, as the day wore on and the bombs began to drop with increasing frequency on the city. To her disappointment, she was not, in fact, assigned to her mother's post as an ambulance driver, but was asked to assist in one of the Fire Brigade control centres, where calls for assistance were catalogued and assessed for gravity, as the incendiaries rained down around them.

The sound of the bombers was something she knew she could never get used to, for every one meant potential death. It seemed that her stomach was rising to meet her mouth every few minutes as another went over their roof-top with its deadly cargo. Her breath would catch in her throat until she was certain it had passed over-head, then occasionally a bomb went off in the vicinity and she would experience a strange mixture of sympathy for those who were catching it and relief that it was not them.

By six o'clock that evening she was emotionally and physically drained: they had listened to the planes go over in their hundreds and had charted over 1,400 fires in the centre of the City, most concentrated on the square mile around St Paul's Cathedral.

To add to the panic, they had been informed that the Thames was at a particularly low ebb that night, so water supplies to the Fire Brigade were almost non-existent. Every minute she sat at her post collating the information, the catalogue of disasters seemed to mount up: below Tower Bridge an unexploded land-mine had immobilized most of the fire-boats; and the only one that could have been brought into use was reported to have collided with a submerged wreck and sunk. Each succeeding mishap was read out to the others by the telephonist who received the information, and as the minutes ticked past and the casualties grew, they were all convinced they would be lucky to get out of the centre alive tonight.

It was one disaster after another, as firemen struggled hopelessly in the fifty feet of sticky black mud on the river bed in a vain attempt to get the fire-boat hose ashore. Most of the hoses that snaked along the smoke-filled streets like black spaghetti lay dry and useless, cast aside by frustrated firemen. A few directed pathetically small jets at the leaping flames.

As the evening wore on, in the wake of the hundreds of incendiaries rained down on the city came a hail of high-explosive bombs which succeeded in fracturing no less than twelve of the City's biggest water mains, including the one assigned to cope with all fire-fighting emergencies between the Thames and Regent's Park. With the emergency mains all burst by the bombs, the number of pumps operating caused the pressure on the remaining mains to dwindle to nothing, and one by one the static water tanks ran dry.

Word came in that, south of the river, Guy's Hospital was now ablaze and the patients were being evacuated. They could all well imagine the distress caused by that operation. It seemed that one historic landmark after another was falling prey to the exploding bombs. What would be left of the London they knew and loved when they left here tonight? *If* they left here tonight.

By nine o'clock, the fires were raging so intensely all around them that the 2,600 pumps that London Region had succeeded in mobilizing, and the 300 drafted in from elsewhere, could do little or nothing to stop the flaming carnage.

One of the firemen, a gritty little Irishman with red-rimmed eyes and a soot-blackened face, informed them that a gas-main was flaring outside the National Gallery in Trafalgar Square; then some of the girls on the switchboard began to read out the names of the most well-loved buildings as they fell one by one to the *Luftwaffe*. Lara wanted to cover her ears, but instead listened with a morbid fascination as the toll of destruction mounted. Among them were eight of Sir Christopher Wren's finest churches, including St Lawrence Jewry,

St Bride's, St Andrew's. Even his greatest masterpiece, St Paul's itself, was encircled in flames, and word had it that an incendiary had struck the magnificent 148-foot dome. She found herself praying inwardly that it wasn't true. Somehow, if St Paul's was to go, then the heart would be torn from the City, and from the citizens of London itself, if not from the whole country.

As the catalogue of horror and destruction mounted, and the casualty lists grew, the anger and frustration within the centre increased, and a creeping fear gnawed at their insides as word came through that first one, then another, of the fire control centres themselves had received direct hits. How long until it was their turn? An air of quiet desperation pervaded their beings, but no one dared to ask the question that tormented them all as, red-eyed and white with fatigue, they remained glued to their posts.

By ten o'clock that evening, Lara was still at her desk, despite several suggestions by her superiors that she return home. A few of the girls had already gone, to be replaced by fresh staff, but somehow she could not bring herself to return to Atholl Square. At least here she could feel she was doing something concrete. There was nothing worse than spending hours huddled impotently in an air-raid shelter at home.

At last, just after ten o'clock, someone came in with an urn of tea. She accepted a cup gratefully, getting up wearily from her chair to stretch her legs. Her bloodshot eyes stared dully at the chart on the wall listing the calls for assistance that had come in over the past few hours. It made for depressing reading, as she scanned the list at random. Call No. 1: 6.20 P.M. Knightrider Street to Victoria Street bombed; Call No. 59: 6.45 P.M. Eastcheap by Mark Lane, explosive incendiary bombs bursting all over the place; Call No. 62: 6.59 P.M. Queen Street by Mark Lane, well alight; Call No. 74b: 8.10 P.M. YMCA Building, 186 Aldersgate Street. Fire spreading rapidly; Call No. 137: 9.10 P.M. 26–27 Bush Lane. Help needed urgently; Call No. 171: 9.30 P.M. 12–16 Red Lion Court. Fire Brigade in attendance, but no water; Call No. 171a: 10.05 P.M. 27–35 Atholl Square, three incendiaries ...

Twenty-seven to thirty-five Atholl Square ... Her eyes reread the words on the sheet of paper, not once but twice. No – it couldn't be. She was tired, that was all. She was seeing things ...

'Are you all right, love?' One of the older women looked up from the desk to where Lara was standing, now ashen-faced, leaning against the wall. 'Can I get you anything?'

Mutely Lara shook her head, not trusting herself to speak.

'You've been here since morning. Don't you think it's time you were getting off home with you?'

Home … Lara stared at the words on the wall once more as her mouth went dry. 'I don't think I've got a home to go to any more, by the looks of this,' she said, quite unemotionally, before walking in a daze from the operations' room.

She declined all offers of a lift and made her own way out of the building into the smoke-filled street. It seemed the whole world was aflame. The night sky was a canopy of crimson and the pungent smell and crackle of burning wood filled the air. The whole night seemed to be a cacophony of brilliant colours and ear-splitting sounds, as blazing timbers cracked and crashed around her in the burning buildings and exhausted firemen yelled instructions to one another. And all the time the ack-ack of the anti-aircraft batteries pounded like a weird staccato symphony in her head.

Coming out into the open seemed like walking into the bowels of hell itself. The familiar streets had become unrecognizable alleyways of smoke and flame, down which strange, dark figures with red eyes ran and shouted directions that no one heard or heeded.

She stood transfixed in the middle of it all but, instead of repelling her, the fire seemed to draw her towards it. She began to walk towards the flames, in the general direction of the City's fifteenth-century Guildhall, the ancient meeting place that was now home to the City Corporation. And, as she turned down Aldermanbury, she could see to her horror that the beautiful old hall itself was already well alight.

As she gazed to her right, sheets of flame several hundreds of feet high had turned the sky above the Guildhall to a flaming orange-red. Gusting winds were fanning the flames and pushing them to the North and East, where it appeared that most of the square mile of the City around St Paul's Cathedral was already well ablaze.

As she stood on the crowded pavement, she could see the flames burning so fiercely within the Guildhall itself that all the coloured figures on its west windows were completely blotted out; only the tracery stood out in dark relief against the fierce glow within. Hundreds of years of history was disappearing before her eyes. Her city – the heart of the nation – was being consumed by the fires of hell itself.

She was not alone as she stood there transfixed. Onlookers stood in their hundreds along the pavements, beneath the crimson sky, as enormous mushroom clouds of black smoke streaked with orange flame climbed upwards to fill the heavens. Through the burnt-out windows they could see the flames sweeping from room to room, and hear the dry crackle of the burning beams and roof timbers that sent a shiver down the spines of all the onlookers; of the firemen especially, who stood impotent and frustrated beside them, holding their dry hoses. 'The bastards deliberately chose this night to do their damage,' one of them said bitterly to no one in particular. 'We might as well be pissin' on the flames of hell, for all the good we're doing! Don't tell me Hitler didn't know the tide was at its lowest ebb tonight.'

It wasn't only the Thames that was at its lowest ebb, Lara thought wearily, as she began the long trudge through the smoke-filled streets in the vague direction of Atholl Square, or what was left of it.

Chapter Seventeen

Lara was stopped at the edge of Atholl Square by the tall, burly, blue-uniformed figure of a policeman. 'Sorry, love, I wouldn't advise you to go any further. Those houses in the middle of the row that took the brunt of the damage just ain't safe.'

Lara stared past him. 'Those houses' he was referring to included her home. She pushed past him for a better view. Black smoke was still pouring from the blown-out windows of at least four in the tall, Georgian terrace. She stared at them bleakly through smarting, red-rimmed eyes. The middle one had been her home for as long as she could remember.

Furniture had either been blown out or pulled out into the small front gardens. These were now piled high with rubble and burning wood, which smouldered and sparked as firemen directed their pathetically inadequate water supplies at the flames still raging within. Their next-door-neighbour's pride and joy, a one-year-old Alfa Romeo 8C2900, lay crumpled beyond recognition at the kerb-side, a chimney pot sticking incongruously out of its smashed windscreen.

Small knots of people stood huddled in night-clothes around the edge of the Square, some of whom she recognized as neighbours. All looked as dazed as she felt. But what of the others who had been inside the buildings when the bomb fell? Her eyes scanned their faces; all were from houses further down the Square than theirs. What of Mrs Bates, Mr and Mrs Malinowski and the others? Where were they? Why weren't they out here? A cold fear gripped her. There was only one way to find out.

Ignoring the warning cries of the policeman and one of the firemen, she pushed past them and ran out into the road, intent on reaching what was left of her home.

'Hey, Miss, hold on there!' The policeman set off after her, cursing beneath his breath as he clambered over the hoses and ARP rescue artefacts that lay strewn across the road.

The fact that she was being pursued simply made Lara run even faster; so fast, in fact, that within fifty yards of what was left of Number 29, she tripped on a length of hose and went flying her whole length down on to the road.

'As if we haven't got enough to do without looking after members of the public who won't take a telling!' Even in the rosy glow of the fires, the policeman's face shone red with exertion as he puffed his way over to where Lara was lying, and bent down to help her to her feet. 'Just where did you think you were making for, Miss? Can't you .see it's highly dangerous around here still? For all we know there may still be an unexploded bomb in the debris.'

Both Lara's knees were bleeding and her pale-blue tweed coat was now a dirty grey with dust and dirt from the road, as she attempted to shrug herself free from the arms of the law. 'I have to get down there,' she protested, raising her voice against the crackle of the flames. 'I live down there!'

'One of them's *your* house?' The policeman's expression changed immediately. 'Lord, Miss, you've got your lucky stars to thank tonight!'

'My lucky stars?' Lara queried faintly. Giving thanks was the last thing she felt like doing.

'Too true! You could have been one of them poor sods they've been carrying out of the wreckage.' Then, realizing he could be sounding incredibly tactless, he asked gently, 'You didn't have family in there tonight, by any chance, did you?'

'Not family,' Lara shook her head. 'But friends, yes … Our house-keeper and the others. There are survivors, aren't there?' She looked around her, a feeling of panic welling within her at the sight of the dead the firemen had succeeded in bringing out, who were now lying covered in blankets on the pavement.

'I don't have the figures myself,' he replied tactfully. 'But you can ask at the hospital when you get there. You'll need to get into one of them ambulances and get down to Casualty yourself, anyway, to get those legs seen to.'

For the first time, she glanced down at the blood that streaked her shins. The sight of it came as a shock and, all of a sudden, the heat of the flames, the smell of the burning timbers, and the shouting of the firemen and the rescue services became too much. The policeman's ruddy face began to swim as her blood-stained legs gave way beneath her.

Then a strong arm gripped her from behind. It couldn't be the policeman; she was still conscious enough to realize that much: he was still standing there in front of her. Her head turned automatically over her right shoulder, so she was looking straight into a pair of familiar blue eyes.

'It's all right, officer, I'll take care of the young lady.' Mike Adams's arm around Lara's back gripped her even tighter as her head flopped in relief on his shoulder.

'You a friend of hers?'

'Yes, I'm a friend, and I'll be taking care of her from now on.'

The words were said quite emphatically and Lara knew she was in no state to argue. How he had got here she hadn't a clue, but an overwhelming feeling of relief swept through her as he hoisted her limp figure into his arms and carried her back towards the edge of the square, away from the flames and the wreckage of what had once been her home. A black Packard belonging to the American Embassy was parked at the edge of the kerb and he threw open the front passenger door and set her gently into the padded-hide seat.

She was aware of him arranging her coat so that the blood from her knees could do no further damage, then he closed the door and sprinted round the front of the car and got into the driver's seat beside her.

'How – how did you know?' She could hear herself ask the question, as if from a great distance.

'I didn't. But once the blitz began, I simply had to look out of my window this evening to see where most of the damage was being done. It was pretty obvious it was in the direction of your mother's place, and I'd have to have been one helluva jerk just to stand there and not bother to find out if you were OK or not.' He gave a mirthless smile. 'I may not be your regular Sir Galahad, but did you honestly think I could just sit there twiddling my thumbs in Princes Gate and not find out how my best-ever secretary was faring?'

She shook her head, as it rested against the brown hide of the seat. 'But I'm no longer ...'

He interrupted before she could finish the sentence. 'Yes, well, if you were going to refer to that stupid message you gave Sheila to pass on to me – we won't bother going into that right now. You were depressed after Ken leaving, I guess. Anyway, I took no notice of it; and now there are far more important things to deal with.' He switched on the ignition, and slid the car into gear, before carefully manoeuvring it past the other vehicles parked at the edge of the kerb.

She remained leaning back against the seat and closed her eyes. She was tired, much too tired to argue. The whole of this past hour seemed like a terrible nightmare from which she would soon awaken. What she had just seen had shocked her to the core. She shouldn't be here being driven away from the scene in comfort. She should be back there looking for them – for Mrs Bates and the others. Hot tears welled in her eyes at the very thought and she blinked them back, determined not to break down in front of him. 'Where are we going?'

'Back to Princes Gate, unless you've got a better idea.' She shook her head as he continued, 'I told you before, with all the Kennedy clan gone, they've got a few spare rooms round there. You can have one for as long as you need it.'

'I'm running away. I should be back there helping.' There was real anguish in her voice as she twisted round in her seat to cast a despairing eye at the scene of devastation around Atholl Square.

'Don't talk nonsense. You're in no fit state to help any one right now, not even yourself. What you need is a good rest, then maybe you can start thinking of helping other people.'

His words washed over her; though sharply said, they were a soothing balm on her tattered nerves. It was a relief simply to have someone to take care of everything, even if that person was the one she had been desperately trying to avoid for the past few days. Maybe he was right. Maybe she wasn't fit for much tonight. Her whole body was aching from fatigue and her eyes were smarting, whether from tears or the stinging smoke it was impossible to say.

It took the best part of an hour to drive the few miles to Princes Gate. The fires had raged through Fleet Street and across Ludgate Circus to St Paul's, and then along the length of Cheapside. The whole area around the Guildhall, along Moorgate, and into City Road was also still well ablaze, making a complete detour of the City area the only way out.

'It's like driving through hell itself,' Mike commented through gritted teeth, as the Packard crawled its way through the smoke-filled streets. The sky above them, for as far as the eye could see, was still a glowing red and, despite the car windows being tightly shut, Lara could smell the bitter odour of charred wood in her nostrils.

In the distance, looming dark and magnificent against the red of the sky, they caught the occasional glimpse of the giant dome of St Paul's still standing proudly above the fire-storms raging below. The sight of it offered a curious comfort, and she found herself praying inwardly that it would still be there in the morning, as the search-lights of the anti-aircraft batteries streaked the sky and the last of the

Luftwaffe bombers droned their way southwards towards the Channel to France and the Fatherland beyond.

Here, enclosed in the car as it crept its way through the smoke and flames, it felt as if they were somehow encapsulated in their own little world, unwilling witnesses on a journey through the fiery underworld itself. How many personal tragedies had taken place in this city tonight? How many thousands of Londoners had lost loved ones, homes, possessions?

Her thoughts returned time and time again to all those left behind in Atholl Square, and she prayed silently and fervently that they had escaped, that they had not perished in that inferno that had once been their home. That she herself had escaped was surely a miracle, a fact that it could take a long time to come to terms with. A curious guilt overwhelmed her: a guilt only the living could know, when all about them was death and destruction.

She glanced across at the man beside her. His face gave away little of his thoughts as he manoeuvred the Packard through the rubble-filled streets, and she wondered what exactly was going on in his mind. What did he feel about finding himself involved in a war that his own country still had no part in? 'Don't you wish you were back in New York?'

'No.' His answer was quite emphatic. 'I wouldn't have been able to play Sir Galahad and come to your rescue tonight if I were back in New York, would I?'

She made no reply. She was grateful, yes, but also confused; confused because her life was now even more entangled with his, and because she could see no immediate way out of it. She had no near relatives in London. Her mother had been an only child, of only children; she had almost no contact with the von Lessing side of the family, and Jack Mallory, her late stepfather, had no living relatives. It was ironic really: as far as family was concerned, she was almost as alone in London as Mike Adams himself.

Despite her overwhelming fatigue, her thoughts raced ahead. Decisions had to be made. Ken would have to be told, of course, but more immediately – should she telegraph her mother? Her brow creased at the thought. Her grandmother in Oxford was not on the telephone, but maybe that was just as well. There was no point in alarming her mother and bringing her rushing back to London until she herself knew exactly what the damage to their home amounted to, and she wouldn't know that until morning at the earliest. A yawn overtook her. Her body was rebelling. She huddled back down in her seat and closed her eyes.

Mike glanced across and gave the ghost of a smile. Sleep, if it would come, was what she needed more than anything right now.

Most of the inhabitants of the Embassy Residence were still in the cellar when they arrived at Princes Gate. 'Please don't broadcast what's happened to me,' Lara pleaded, as they entered the front door. 'I really couldn't bear a whole lot of people gathering around to sympathize with me tonight.'

'Sure. I understand. I'll fix you up with somewhere to sleep and clear it with the housekeeper in the morning.'

They travelled up together in the lift to the third floor, where Mike had taken up lodgings in one of the bedrooms overlooking the back gardens. 'It's not much,' he said, throwing open the door and ushering her into the white-walled room that was now his home, 'but it's a darned sight better than quite a lot of Londoners will have to resort to tonight, I bet.'

Lara nodded in agreement. If it hadn't been for him, she would now be sitting in a municipal shelter with hundreds of other bombed-out victims of the *Luftwaffe*. The very thought made her shudder, for she had witnessed such scenes herself before now when on fire-watching duty: dozens of dazed, helpless people, huddled together in whatever makeshift accommodation was available, usually a church hall or somewhere similar, and forced to change into a ghastly white hospital smock before being examined for head lice and the like. Surely that was the last thing they required at a time like that. The only thing the victims had in common was the fact that the *Luftwaffe* had chosen their home that night to wreak their havoc on ... No, this might not be the Ritz, but it was infinitely preferable to the alternative.

The room was simply furnished, with a double bed covered in a pale-blue bedspread, a bedroom suite in polished oak, and a three-seater couch covered in striped blue linen beneath the window. Alongside the couch was a drop-leaf writing desk, the lid of which was down. Writing-paper and envelopes were spread over it, as if he had been in the middle of writing a letter when he made his decision to come to her rescue.

Mike indicated the couch. 'Make yourself comfortable. I'll fix us a cup of coffee. Fancy anything to eat? I'm sure I could rustle up something acceptable.'

She shook her head. Food was the last thing on her mind. The very thought made her feel sick. But he meant well. 'No thanks, I couldn't eat a thing.'

Without even waiting to take off his coat and hat, he disappeared from the room, leaving her standing alone. Despite her tiredness, she found herself glancing idly at the writing-desk beside her. The top page of the writing-pad was covered in his familiar script. Without even realizing it, her eyes read the words on the top sheet of the pad, and the address on the envelope. The envelope was addressed to a firm of attorneys on Fifth Avenue, New York: Larsen, Ritchie and Kaldor. She moved an inch or two nearer, her eyes moving from the envelope to the top page of the pad.

Dear Lars,
    Your letter came as a surprise to say the least. I guess I can't claim to be so dumb as to believe that Joanne has been as pure as the driven snow over the past few years of our marriage – but she must've done one hell of a lot of drifting to end up wanting to marry that SOB Crawford. Tell her I won't stand in her way, although I would have appreciated hearing it from her first. If she's dead set on citing me to keep her own virtue intact as far as the Press goes, at least, then that's OK by me. No doubt it won't be too difficult to come up with some broad who will be only too willing to provide the 'evidence' you need. I'll work on it. You'll hear from me later …

Lara could read no further. She had no need to. He was giving his wife a divorce and was only too willing to provide her with the evidence … It wasn't going to be too difficult to provide himself with a 'broad' to do just that. A broad: even the very word brought a sick feeling to the pit of her stomach. So that's what this had been all about! All the attention, the wining and dining, the rescue tonight … What a set up!

Tears stung her eyes, blinding her vision as she rushed from the room and back down the corridor. Despite her tiredness, she ignored the lift. He would be using it himself any minute now to bring up her coffee. Her feet clattered down the curving sweep of staircase and on through the reception area to the front door.

Once outside she looked around her in dismay. Where on earth did she go from here? The tears that had welled in her eyes spilled in hot rivulets down her cold cheeks. Never in her life had she felt so helpless and utterly alone in the world.

Of their own accord, her feet started to walk back towards the flaming carnage, her eyes staring blindly into the crimson heavens. Where she was going she did not know, and she cared even less.

Chapter Eighteen

Lara tossed and turned in the narrow bed, listening to the sounds of the night from beyond the blacked-out window. Every so often there would be a burst of ack-ack fire and the distant drone of an aeroplane. She wondered how on earth they could be sure it was always the enemy they were firing at. Despite the searchlights it must often be very difficult in the darkness. What if it was one of theirs up there? What if it was Ken? A shiver ran through her as gloom mounted upon gloom. Here in the pitch-blackness of the strange bedroom, thinking back on the happenings of the past few hours, it seemed as if the whole world had turned against her.

Up till now the suffering had been a communal thing, and such things as bombings only happened to other people. A bombed-out house was something you read about in the papers in the morning, or passed in the bus on your way to work. But no longer. She had become one of the victims of the *Luftwaffe*'s deadly forays across the Channel and, unlike the refugees who were pouring into London from the Continent, she had had no time to salvage even as much as a suitcase of belongings from the wreckage.

It was strange the things you thought of at a time like this. Apart from the sickening knowledge that many of your friends and neighbours might be dead, you thought about the small, personal things you might never see again: Heather, the doll with real hair that said 'Mama' when you turned her upside down – Lara had received Heather for her seventh birthday and she had sat in pride of place on her dressing-table ever since; the moroccan-bound set of Charles Dickens she had been given by her grandmother on Matriculation; the album of Silesian family photographs – her only link with her father's homeland; the list went on and on in her mind as the lump in her throat grew bigger. She tried to close her mind to it all but, far from being sleepy any longer, all her senses seemed heightened. If only she could sleep. She had been like this ever since her head hit the pillow just after midnight.

The sheets had a curious feel and smell to them and she was convinced that she was not their first inhabitant, and would probably not be their last. But they would do. Anywhere to lay her head would have done on a night like this. The Abermarle Hotel might not be London's finest, but at least it was still standing and had offered shelter when she needed it most. She leaned over and switched on the bedside light. Ten past four. Just over three hours till they began to serve breakfast.

The forty watt bulb threw strange shadows on the far wall. Above the dressing chest at the foot of the bed was a print of Holman Hunt's *The Light of the World*. She found herself staring at the depiction of Christ carrying a lantern. She wished she believed more. She wished she had the faith to believe that they would all come out of this alive. Her mind went back to Atholl Square and the blazing pile of rubble that had once been Number 29. 'Dear God, let Mrs Bates and the others be all right,' she prayed. 'Let them have been brought out safely. Please, dear God, please ...'

The hours seemed to drag past until eight o'clock, and she was the first guest to be seated at the long table in the dining-room when the elderly waitress arrived with the huge urn of tea. By the look of her, she had probably spent the night in a shelter, like most Londoners, and Lara was grateful she made no attempt at conversation as she laid out the crockery on the stained damask cloth.

Breakfast was frugal: porridge, followed by toast and marmalade and tea. She had just started on the toast when she was joined by an elderly man in an old-fashioned wing-collar and a clerical-grey suit. They exchanged smiles.

'You from these parts, Miss?'

Lara nodded. 'Atholl Square, actually. I was bombed-out last night.'

The man stared across the table at her. 'Dear me, dear me, now that's a terrible thing, so it is ... And just what do you intend to do, young lady – lodge here permanently?' He had a southern Irish accent that Lara found herself warming to immediately.

'Good heavens, no! I'll probably have to see about renting a flat, but first I intend going back to Atholl Square to see the extent of the damage, then ... Well, then I'll just take it from there.'

Her companion adjusted his napkin on his lap before sprinkling a helping of sugar on his porridge that paid little heed to the weekly ration. 'And have you ways and means of getting there this morning?'

She shook her head. 'I'll have to walk, I suppose. I don't expect there'll be many buses heading into that part of London today.'

'You're quite right there, so you are. But you're very welcome to a lift in the general direction. It'll save shoe-leather, at least.'

'You – you have a car?'

'A 1932 Alvis. Not the latest model exactly, but it gets me where I want to go.'

'You do much travelling, Mr … ?'

'O'Leary – Phineas O'Leary. I travel in ladies' toiletries. No funny comments about that, if you please. I've heard the lot.'

'I wouldn't dream of it,' Lara smiled. 'And that would be very nice, thank you. Anywhere in the area will be a great help. To tell the truth I wasn't looking forward at all to that walk. The streets, or what's left of them, are unbelievable. There's rubble and pot-holes everywhere.'

'There is that. And it can only get worse before it gets better, so they say. They tell me yon madman Hitler's got all sorts of weird and not-so-wonderful weapons he's preparing to unleash on us poor folks in the next few weeks.'

Lara glanced up at him bleakly from her porridge. Phineas O'Leary was just the sort of tonic she needed this morning! 'You'd be better off back in Ireland by the sound of it.'

'True, m'dear. Quite true. But there's precious little call for my services around County Mayo at the moment. I'd have the divil's own job to keep myself in the necessities of life, never mind me family.'

'You have children?'

'Seven, counting the one that's up and gone. But we'll not dwell on them over breakfast if it's all the same to you. To tell the truth, with a houseful like that, it does me good to get away for a few days to deliver me orders.'

She could believe that. They exchanged smiles once more, then got on with their breakfast, as the dining-room slowly filled up with servicemen on leave and their wives or, in many cases, girlfriends. But no one was demanding marriage certificates or proof of anything right now. These days it was enough to be alive when morning came.

As Lara sat in Phineas O'Leary's Alvis half an hour later, their conversation was dominated by the previous night's bombing, as daylight revealed it in all its horrific reality. 'It'll be on Pathé News today, mark my words,' he said, as the car edged its way along Sloane Street. 'They won't be able to keep this lot hushed up.'

Pathé News! The words struck horror into Lara. If it was on the main cinema newsreels, then there was no way she could disguise it

154

from her mother. She would simply have to let her know before she learned it from elsewhere.

How to break the news to her mother was still on her mind when the Alvis drew up in the next street to Atholl Square. 'Is this near enough, m'dear?'

'Yes, yes, thank you. This is just fine.' She got out of the car and thanked Phineas O'Leary for his trouble.

'Pleasure's mine, m'dear. All mine. Hope to see you again at the Abermarle. I lodge there pretty regularly m'self, whenever I'm down this way with orders. I'll look out for you.' And with that he was gone, in a puff of exhaust fumes and with a friendly honk of the horn.

She stood on the pavement and watched him drive off into the distance. To take up any kind of permanent lodgings at the Abermarle was the last thing she wanted to do, but what was the alternative? With so many bombed-out people in the capital, accommodation was at a premium. She would be lucky if she ended up with a seedy room somewhere in the East End. With a sinking heart she began to walk round the corner to Atholl Square.

There were still lots of ARP people around, and a few firemen coping with the smouldering ruins in the middle of the terrace. From what she could see, it was the house on the left-hand side of theirs, number 27, that had taken the brunt of the bomb. There was almost nothing left of it at all. In her mind's eye she could see the old couple, the Hardys, who had lived there with their twenty-two-year-old son Harold. Where were they now? She felt sick at the thought.

Hardly daring to look ahead, she walked past what was left of their home towards her own house, and her heart turned over at the sight that met her eyes. Most of the front wall was still standing, but the roof had caved in completely. The top floors were hanging as if suspended in mid-air within the shell of the building, with the charred remains of what looked like a wardrobe hanging over the edge of the third floor. Other pieces of furniture lay in a blackened heap in the middle of the rubble, with only the springs of several beds easily identifiable.

Some sort of path had been cleared by the rescue services into the middle of it all in the search for survivors, and the steps to the cellars themselves, which went down at right-angles to the front gate, were now almost cleared. Turning up the collar of her coat to protect her nostrils from the terrible smell of burnt wood, she gazed down the stone staircase into what had once been their shelter, their place of safety from the bombs.

Pieces of charred belongings littered the steps: like everything else they were almost unidentifiable now in their blackened state. But about half-way down something glinted in the hazy morning sunshine. Her eyes fixed on it. What on earth was it? Curiosity got the better of her and, holding on to the wall for support, she edged her way down and stooped to pick it up. It was Mrs Bates's brooch: the one that Vi had given her for Christmas. She had been wearing it yesterday morning. It lay in the palm of Lara's hand, a twisted lump of metal, bereft of most of its stones, but the shape of the crucifix still discernible.

'You know anyone from round here, Miss?' A fireman's voice from the top of the steps made her turn round.

She looked up at him as tears sprang to her eyes, and nodded, not trusting herself to speak.

'Bloody shame. We could've done more if we'd had the water. As it was, most of them had perished before we even got here.'

'Perished ... ?' Her voice was barely audible. 'How – how many ... ?'

He scratched his head beneath the helmet. 'Can't say as I remember rightly. But I reckon they brought at least four or five out of here last night. Most were dug out before I came on duty myself. But they were just bringing a woman out – what was left of 'er, that is – when I arrived at the back of eight. Real stout, she was. They had one helluva job getting her body up the stairs ... Are you all right, Miss?'

Lara leaned back against the wall and closed her eyes, screwing them up tight to prevent the tears that threatened to cascade down her cold cheeks.

'Were they friends of yours, by any chance?'

She nodded mutely, her eyes still tightly closed against the devastation around her. Yes, yes, they were friends – all of them. The tears that had squeezed beneath her lashes tasted salty on her lips and she wiped them away with the back of a gloved hand.

'Well, I'm real sorry about that, ducks. We've seen things these past twenty-four hours that make us wonder what the human race has come to – awful things. I'd go home now if I were you. It'll do you no good hanging around here. Go home and have yourself a nice cup of tea. I wish to God I could do the same!'

'Go home ...' Lara repeated softly. 'Go home ...' This was her home – what was left of it. She looked around her in despair, managing a wan smile for the fireman before he went back to his job of sifting through the ruins of next door's garden. How was he to know? He was only trying to be of comfort.

She turned to make her way back up the steps, when from somewhere down in the blackened cellar she heard a sound like a baby crying. She paused and listened. Yes, there it was again. A chill ran through her. They had had no baby in the house. How could a baby get down there? How could anything have survived what occurred here last night?

With a thumping heart, she edged her way further down the cellar steps to where the sound was coming from. There it was again! It was coming from an overturned dustbin that lay at the front door to the main basement. Hesitantly she approached, and squatted down to look inside. 'Humphrey!'

The ginger tom let out an even louder miaow of recognition, but remained huddled in the far end of the bin. Lara put in her hand. He was quivering violently. 'You poor thing, you've been through it all, haven't you?' Heedless of her clothing, she lay down on the concrete and, pushing both arms as far into the bin as they would go, she grabbed hold of the animal.

Humphrey hissed and attempted to scratch her hands as she pulled him from his shelter. But, luckily, her gloves prevented any real damage. 'There, there, now ...'

She struggled back to her feet, the animal clutched tightly in her arms. His beautiful marmalade coat was the colour of slate from the smoke and dirt, and his green eyes a bright, painful shade of pink. 'You poor little devil. It was your home too, wasn't it?'

She buried her face in the smoke-scorched fur and gazed back into the black hole that had once been their shelter against the bombs. Hot tears scalded her cold cheeks and ran down to mingle with the cat's fur as she gripped the animal even tighter. 'Where do we go from here, old boy? What's left for us now?' There was no answer to her question.

She began to walk and did not stop until she had put the sight, sounds and smell of Atholl Square well behind her. She seemed to have been walking forever, but had just turned into Piccadilly and paused at the edge of the kerb to rest, for Humphrey was becoming a dead weight in her arms, when a black limousine pulled up just in front of her. A man wound down the back passenger window and leaned out, staring at her curiously for a moment or two before calling out, 'Lara!'

He had a grey Homburg hat pulled well down over his eyes and she squinted through the hazy winter sunshine to make out who it was. It was the scar that ran down the left-hand cheek that she recognized first. It was that Count – the Pole her mother seemed to be so enamoured with. What on earth did he want?

Jan Jarosinski got out of the car and walked quickly back along the pavement to where she was standing. 'Lara – I thought it was you, although I almost didn't recognize you at first.' His eyes travelled over the dirt-smeared coat, but he was too polite to make any further comment on her appearance. 'I am on my way back to the Embassy. May I offer you a lift?' He looked down at the battered-looking Humphrey in her arms. 'You look as if you need one. Are you taking him home?'

She gave a mirthless smile. 'I'm afraid "home" as such no longer exists for either of us, Count. Both Humphrey here and I were bombed out of house and home last night.'

'No!' Deep shock registered on his face. 'Your house got hit in the bombing? It can't be true!'

'It can and it is, I'm afraid,' Lara said quietly. 'There's nothing – and no one – left.'

He stared at her, as if waiting for her to admit it was some kind of joke, but her face remained totally expressionless as she mechanically stroked the animal in her arms and gazed into the middle-distance.

'But your mother ... ?'

'My mother is in Oxford, thank God,' Lara said.

'She knows nothing of this?'

'Not yet.'

'You have somewhere else to live?'

'Well, no ... not at the moment.' The Count looked thoughtful, then took her by the arm. 'You must come with me. You must accompany me back to the Embassy. We need time. We must think how to handle this – this terrible thing.'

At first she attempted to hang back. Just who was he to try to take over like this? But the fact she had no alternative weakened her resistance, and she allowed herself to be shepherded into the back of the Daimler.

'What did you do last night?' he asked, as the car pulled back out into the traffic and headed back in the direction of Portland Place. 'Where did you sleep?'

'I – I stayed in an hotel. I'll try to get somewhere else to live fixed up today.'

'You haven't been in touch with your mother yet, you said?'

'No.'

'She must be told,' Jan said quietly. 'But not yet. It would do her no good to rush back here with things as they are – with the ruins of last night's raid still smoking all over the city. She must be protected from that ... Yes, she is better off where she is at the moment.' He spoke quietly, almost under his breath, as if talking to himself, before turning in his seat to look straight at Lara. 'Today is one of my most busy, I'm afraid. I have an appointment in the Embassy in half an hour, and directly afterwards I am seeing the Ambassador to discuss his first official call on your new Foreign Secretary tomorrow. Then, as soon as that is over, I leave for the North, for Scotland. But I can easily break the journey to spend a few hours in Oxford. Would you like me to break the news to your mother?'

Lara looked at him curiously. Why should he be willing to put himself out like this? Just what was there between them? 'You – you seem on very personal terms with my mother.'

There was a slight pause. 'Yes – yes, you could say that.'

'And have been for a very long time.'

'A very long time.'

The words were spoken so softly she had to strain to catch them. She moved uncomfortably in her seat. She had no right to probe any deeper into their personal relationship, no right at all. There was a moment's silence. 'You – you knew my father too, presumably?'

She was aware of him catching his breath and his hands gripping the steering-wheel that bit tighter. 'Yes, yes Lara, I knew your father.'

She looked down at the animal in her lap, her fingers nervously stroking the matted fur of the cat's ears. 'My – my mother's very fond of you …' He made no response to the statement and it hung in the air between them. 'I think she may even be in love with you. Would that surprise you?'

A small pulse throbbed at the side of his temple and he stared even harder at the road ahead. 'No – no, it would not.'

'Are *you* in love with *her*?' She surprised even herself with the directness of the question.

He looked her straight in the eyes. Her forthrightness surprised him, but did not upset him. There was no point in lying, not to her. There had been enough lies throughout her lifetime. He owed it to her not to add to them. 'Yes, yes I am. I have been for over twenty years.'

'And she loves you?'

'You will have to ask her that question – although you seem to have already made up your mind on that score.'

Lara shook her head and gazed with unseeing eyes out through the windscreen of the car. 'To think you can live with someone all your life and never really know them – never really know what's going on in their private thoughts.' She paused. 'It must have been a very special kind of love to have lasted all those years.'

'Your mother is a very special kind of woman, my dear.'

Lara's head flopped back on the cushioned head-rest. He was certainly honest. She had not expected, nor deserved, so frank a reaction to such a personal conversation. It was really none of her business what had gone on in the past, or was still going on between him and her mother; yet there were a million and one more questions she wanted to ask and, by the honest, straightforward way he had answered the last ones, she would probably get truthful answers. But now was neither the time nor the place. 'I – I'd be very obliged if you would break the news of what's happened to Mum,' she said quietly. 'And don't let her come back here. Not yet, anyway. Not till I've managed to get things sorted out. It would only upset her.'

'I understand.'

They continued the rest of the journey to Portland Place in silence. Lara was too exhausted to even think of the future. The pain of learning that Mrs Bates and some of the others had almost certainly perished was almost unbearable. On top of that there were practical things to be done: a report to be made out to the authorities, identifications to be made, and heaven only knew what other pieces of red-tape to be untangled before things could begin to get back to normal. But all that would have to wait. Right now all she wanted was a cup of tea, and a saucer of milk for Humphrey. The cat snuggled deeper into her lap as the car made its way along Regent Street, across Langham Place, and on into the parking bays reserved for the Polish Embassy in Portland Place.

Jan Jarosinski took her arm and helped her out of the car and she smiled her thanks in return. He had a strangely familiar face that gave her the feeling she had known him for a very long time, which was not the case. But maybe she was simply feeling especially well-disposed towards any familiar face, no matter how recent the acquaintance. They entered the front door and squeezed their way past the perpetual queues of displaced persons that seemed to be a permanent feature of the Embassy these days.

'Make yourself comfortable in here, my dear,' Jan said, pushing open the door of an ante-room just off the main reception area.

He waited to see her settled into an arm-chair and then left in search of refreshments for herself and the cat.

She was too much on edge to rest, however, and, leaving the exhausted animal snoozing on the cushion of the chair, she got up and walked to the window. The ante-room overlooked the front door of the Embassy and a queue of refugees stretched all the way down the steps and on along the pavement. For the first time she felt a close affinity with these homeless people, the flotsam of the tides of war that were sweeping across Europe. But as well as their homes, they had lost their country – she, at least, still had that left. And Britain would fight on, with or without America's help, she was certain of that. If this experience had done anything, it had hardened her resolve to do all in her power to aid the war effort.

As she watched, a car drew up outside – a black Packard – and the driver's door opened. A man jumped out. A tall, broad-shouldered man in the uniform of a Colonel of the US Army. She had rarely seen him in uniform before. 'Mike …' She gasped his name aloud as he ascended the stone steps two at a time and entered the front door.

Chapter Nineteen

Jan Jarosinski placed the tea tray on the table by the window of the Embassy ante-room, and smiled across at Lara. 'Tea and biscuits and a saucer of milk for the cat. I would stay and join you, but someone important to our cause has just arrived to see me. It's necessary for me to see him before I leave for Scotland tomorrow.'

She knew he was talking about Mike Adams. 'This is very kind of you. Please feel free to have your meeting. I'll be quite all right here.'

He gave a slight bow. 'Thank you. I shall return just as soon as Colonel Adams has left.'

When he had gone, Lara put Humphrey's saucer of milk on the floor by the chair and lifted him off the cushion to enjoy it, before sitting down to drink her own tea. A pile of magazines stood alongside the tray on the table: most were in Polish, but a tattered copy of *Lilliput* lay amongst them. She picked it up and leafed through the pages. Instead of the usual batch of heartwarming stories that there had been before the war, there were now numerous articles full of anti-German propaganda. She skimmed through the pages. Despite her bitterness at what had happened, she could feel no real hate towards the German people themselves. Heaven knows, she was half-German herself, after all, even if she had never set eyes on that part of her family.

Her eyes fell on a drawing of an evil-looking Nazi officer in one of the stories. They were always depicted as square-headed, oafish brutes, but surely they weren't all like that? Her own half-brother Otto was one of them. It was a curious thought. When she was younger she had even cherished thoughts of visiting Wolfsberg and making his acquaintance, but the war had put paid to all that. Upper Silesia was now a battlefield; soon all Europe might be, and God only knew when things would get back to normal, or indeed if they would ever be normal again, even when all this bloodshed was at an end.

She thought of Ken down in Tangmere, or wherever he was based at the moment. A pang of guilt ran through her. She had hardly given him more than a passing thought since the air-raid. She would have to get in touch as soon as possible, but his squadron seemed to be moving about so much these days it was almost impossible to keep up with him. Wherever he was, she would have to inform him there was no point in addressing his letters to Atholl Square any more. But where else could he write to? Come what may, she would have to find new accommodation today. There was so much to do, so much to think about …

Humphrey, his thirst satiated, jumped back up on her lap and made himself comfortable. She leaned back in the chair and closed her eyes, as a great tiredness overcame her.

She was awakened twenty minutes later by a gentle shake of the shoulder. 'Lara …'

Her eyes blinked open to look straight into those of Mike Adams.

'The Count told me you were here.'

She struggled up in her chair. 'He had no right to!'

He ignored her protest. 'Why the hell did you run off like that last night? That was a damn-fool thing to do. I was worried sick about you.'

'I'm sorry … I mean I'm sorry you were worried; I'm not sorry I left.'

He stood looking down at her, a tall, unfamiliar figure in the Colonel's uniform. 'I reckon you owe me an explanation, don't you?'

Conscious of being in an inferior position so far below him, she got out of the chair, depositing Humphrey back on the cushion, and walked to the window. 'I owe you nothing.'

'Then what's brought on the big freeze treatment, for Chrissake? What's got into you, Lara? Just what do you think you're playing at these days?'

She turned back to face him. '*I'm* playing at nothing, Colonel,' she said through gritted teeth. 'What you should ask yourself is, what are *you* playing at, using me like that?'

'Using you?' He looked genuinely puzzled. 'What the devil's that supposed to mean?'

'Don't tell me you don't know what I'm talking about. You're giving your wife a divorce, aren't you?'

His brows knitted. 'What's that got to do with you?'

'You tell me!'

He shook his head. 'I don't know what the hell you're talking about, Lara, I swear I don't.'

163

He looked down at her. Despite her anger, she looked so vulnerable, standing there in that filthy coat, her eyes still bloodshot from the fatigue and smoke of the past twenty-four hours. 'Let me help you, Lara,' he said softly. 'Forget about the divorce. What the hell does that matter at a time like this? Joanne's marriage plans are immaterial to what's going on over here – to what you've just gone through last night. Let's talk about what really matters. Let me help you, for God's sake. I won't plead with you to come back to work for me, not if you don't want to. Just let me help you out of this mess.'

She looked up at him, then, unable to bear the intensity of his gaze, she dropped hers to the magazines on the table. Ignoring his attempt to change the subject, she asked quietly. 'You – you weren't intending to set me up as a co-respondent in your divorce from Joanne, then?'

'No, for Chrissake – a hundred times no! I wouldn't do that to you, Lara, not ever. What kind of a jerk do you take me for?'

'There must be someone else, though? There must be someone – some female – lined up who's willing to jump into bed with you to provide the evidence she needs?'

'Yeah, if you must know, there is someone.'

Quite ridiculously she felt a sudden stab of jealousy. 'Do I know her?'

He shrugged impatiently once more. 'Look, what the hell is this – the third degree?' Then, seeing the expression in her eyes, his voice softened. 'There is someone – I think you saw me with her once at the theatre that night ... '

'That blonde?' The words caught in her throat. 'You're sleeping with *her* to give your wife the evidence?' The vision of the peroxided Veronica Lake locks and the voluptuous figure in the fur-coat filled her mind. 'She's agreed to have sex with you for money, so that your wife can get her divorce? That's sordid, Mike, really sordid.'

He looked at her for a long time; there was a look almost of pity in his eyes. 'You're very good at jumping to assumptions, Lara. And even if it were as you like to imagine it to be, it doesn't make it automatically sordid, you know. On the contrary, I know a lot of guys who would argue with you on that one – who would say that the only difference between sex for money and sex for free is that sex for money usually costs less in the long run.'

'That's a very cynical viewpoint.'

'Yeah, well, maybe I've got a bit cynical of late. There are certain females of the species make you like that.'

'Maybe you just had the misfortune to meet the wrong women at the right time in your life.'

'And the right woman at the wrong time?'

Their eyes met and held, and both knew exactly what was meant. Lara broke the gaze first, as she felt herself colouring once more. 'I still think it's awful what you're doing with that blonde.'

'You really are a little innocent, aren't you? It's a business deal, that's all. We book in together to some dive of an hotel and Joanne's private eye comes along to take the photos. That's all there is to it. The blonde – Brenda's her name, by the way – gets enough to keep herself in gin and tonics for the next few months or so, and Joanne gets her divorce, without a stain on her lily-white name.'

'All neatly cut and dried. But you, Mike, what do you get out of it?' she asked softly.

'I get my freedom.'

She bit her lip, still avoiding his eyes. It sounded plausible enough.

'Look, if it's my virtue you're frightened for, I promise to keep on my shorts when I get into the double-bed with her. Will that suit you?' One eyebrow quirked upwards and that familiar, lop-sided grin reappeared.

The smile was infectious. 'I really don't know why we're even talking like this,' she said. 'Who you choose to sleep with, for whatever reason, has got nothing to do with me, has it?'

They looked at one another for a long time. And the question remained unanswered.

The rattle of the door-handle broke the silence and made them look round. Then the door opened and Jan Jarosinski entered. 'If you'll excuse me interrupting, I have an appointment with the Ambassador in five minutes, and I just wanted to say you are most welcome to remain here for as long as you wish, Lara.'

'Don't worry about Lara, Count,' Mike cut in. 'I know you've got problems yourself with accommodation. Seeing that lot waiting outside, and knowing what conditions you're living in yourself, you've got enough on your plate. I'll see that Lara's well taken care of today.'

Lara drew in her breath sharply, but had no chance to protest, as the Count's face lit up. 'Really? That's good news indeed, Colonel. You come here with hope for Poland, and now offer hope to Lara, too. Lara, my dear, I will leave you in the Colonel's capable hands for the time being. Please don't worry any more about informing your mother. I'll make it my business to stop off in Oxford myself to-morrow and break it to her.'

'Gently, please.'

'You have my promise.' He took her hand and raised it to his lips.

'Now, if you will excuse me ... ' He released her fingers and held out his hand to Mike. 'Colonel Adams, I can't thank you enough for the work you are doing personally for our country. Your news today about Mr Hopkins' visit gives us hope that your government is serious in its commitment to Europe. We shall all await what happens with the keenest interest. You keep the flag of hope flying for us, sir.'

Mike gave an embarrassed smile. 'I do what I can. Don't forget it's Polish blood that runs in these veins too, Count. I'll be only too glad to put your case to Harry when he arrives next week. It seems as if our reports have been doing some good of late. I guess all of us Americans over here have been heartened by the President's latest fireside chat to the nation last night.' He turned to Lara. 'I know you've had more pressing things on your mind, honey, but did you read the report of it in today's papers?'

She shook her head. 'I haven't had a chance to get hold of one today.'

'Then you must have this!' Jan Jarosinski delved into the briefcase in his hand, pulled out a copy of *The Times*, and handed it to her.

She looked down at it curiously, then, aware they were watching for her reaction, her eyes flicked over the columns devoted to Roosevelt's speech, and she began to read aloud the parts that particularly took her eye: 'This is not a fireside chat on war, it is a talk on national security ... The Nazi masters of Germany have made it clear that they intend not only to dominate all life and thought in their own country, but also to enslave the whole of Europe, and then to use the resources of Europe to dominate the rest of the world. There are two worlds that stand opposed to each other.'

'Hitler himself said the same sort of thing only three weeks ago,' Jan murmured. 'And who can doubt the truth of it after what has happened to my country?'

Mike nodded quietly in agreement, as she read on: 'The experience of the past two years has proved beyond doubt that no nation can appease the Nazis. No man can tame a tiger into a kitten by stroking it ... If Britain goes down, the Axis powers will control the Continents of Europe, Asia, Africa, Australasia and the high seas, and they will be in a position to bring enormous military and naval resources against this hemisphere. It is no exaggeration to say that all of us in all the Americas would be living at the point of a gun – a gun loaded with explosive bullets, economic as well as military ... I make the direct statement to the American people that there is far less chance of the United States getting into war if we do all we can now to support the nations defending themselves against attack by the

Axis than if we acquiesce in their defeat, submit tamely to an Axis victory, and wait our turn to be the object of attack in another war later on …'

Her eyes moved further down the column and she read on. 'You can, therefore, nail any talk about sending armies to Europe as a deliberate untruth. Our national policy is not directed toward war. Its sole purpose is to keep war away from our country and our people. We must be the great arsenal of democracy …'

'Harry's phrase,' Mike muttered. 'Sorry, Lara, please continue.'

She cleared her throat. 'I believe that the Axis powers are not going to win this war. I base that belief on the latest and best information …' Lara read the last two sentences in a much louder voice as she looked up at Mike Adams. She knew he was responsible for much of the information that winged its way across the Atlantic to Washington. 'You have great faith in us, Colonel Adams,' she smiled a trifle cynically, as she passed the newspaper back to the Count. 'I only wish more of your countrymen felt that way.'

'We must all have faith in America, Lara,' Jan said gravely. 'We have no choice. Although, God knows, I for one get very tired of walking on my knees to so-called friends.' He looked directly at Mike as he finished the sentence.

'Oh, come on now, Count. Since when did a Pole have to grovel to anyone?'

'Since the first of September last year, when Hitler invaded my country, my dear Colonel. My people are dying because our "friends", such as America, who certainly have the money, obviously do not have the will to supply us with either the weapons or the money to buy them.'

'It's true,' Lara interrupted. 'And, heaven knows, Roosevelt has made it pretty clear from that speech that he isn't willing to commit American troops to help out here in Europe either. You will understand why certain of us over here sometimes get a little tired of hearing platitudes in support of freedom being spouted forth from the other side of the Atlantic. Fine words don't stop the bombs.'

'Nor the Nazis from claiming my country for their own and sending thousands of my fellow Poles to their deaths, or to the concentration camps. You do not have to be a Jew or a Socialist to be hounded into the cattle-trucks any longer, Colonel Adams – being a Pole is quite enough.'

'Public opinion back in the States just won't buy going as far as sending troops at the moment,' Mike said, with a shrug. 'But if they're willing to swallow the idea of financing much of the British war effort, then that'll mean one helluva lot. In fact, as you well know, Lara – if you read my reports as well as type them – that means coming up with several billion dollars.'

'It's all figures on paper,' Lara said impatiently, 'and in the meantime, as the Count says, people are dying. Some of my friends – and his – were killed last night, while your government hummed and hawed.'

Mike held up his hands at the onslaught. 'OK. OK. I get the message. And don't think I haven't relayed it loud and clear to the chiefs back home.'

'I think we have attacked the good Colonel quite enough for one day, Lara, don't you?' Jan said, with an apologetic smile in Mike's direction. 'You must forgive us, Colonel Adams. We Europeans can get a little – how do you say it – "overheated" at times. All I would really like to say is that, when it comes to voting for all those billions of dollars, I hope your President will not forget the Polish people. After all, this whole terrible business was begun in the name of Polish freedom.'

Mike gave a conciliatory grin. 'You have my word for it, Count. Poland will be at the top of my agenda when I see Harry Hopkins next week.'

Jan Jarosinski extended his right hand. 'I do not doubt your word for one moment. Now, if you will excuse me, time is rather pressing today ... '

'The Count is leaving for Scotland this afternoon,' Lara informed Mike.

'Really? Then I hope we'll meet again on your return. I'll come round after Harry's visit to report – would that suit?'

Jan shook his head. 'Alas no, Colonel. I will be leaving the country for some time.'

'Leaving the country? You mean you're leaving Britain when you get back from Scotland?' Lara asked.

Jan looked uncomfortable. 'It – it is not really something I wish to talk about at the moment. My plans are still in the oven, so to speak.'

Mike frowned. Surely he wasn't thinking of returning to Poland? That would be a foolhardy thing to do – suicide even. Not that it was any of his business, and the Count was no fool; he must have weighed up the odds before making such a decision. 'Well, if you're heading back to the Continent, all I can say is that I wish you luck. You'll certainly need it.' Mike extended his arm, and the two men shook hands, then Jan turned to Lara.

'Don't worry about your mother, my dear. I'll see that she is well taken care of, have no fear.'

'Thank you,' Lara replied softly. 'I appreciate that.' She managed a strained smile, a feeling of guilt welling within her at the memory of her previous antagonism towards him. There was a lot more to this man than met the eye, and she was just beginning to realize what it was that her mother found so attractive about him. There was an innate dignity about him – something about the way he carried himself that personified the *Szlachta*, the Polish land-owning upper class, and commanded respect, unlike their German counterparts, the *Junkers*, whose overbearing qualities were well-known to all. Yes, there was something about this tall, lean-framed Pole, with the soft voice, that made you believe you had met someone of integrity, someone in whom you could put your entire trust.

After shaking hands with both in turn, and with a small bow towards each of them, Jan Jarosinski turned and walked from the room.

'That's quite a guy,' Mike said, as the door closed and they were alone once more. 'He holds the *Virtute Militari*, you know. Sikorski himself told me – the Count never would.'

'The *Virtute Militari*?'

'Poland's highest military honour for gallantry. He got it in 1919, while serving with Sikorski's own Fifth Army on the Wikra. He's done his bit for his country all right, and I can understand why he gets so frustrated about the lack of help forthcoming from their so-called "allies", but there's little I can do about it. I'm just a pretty minor cog in a very big wheel when it comes to the American war effort.'

'But you'll do your best.'

'Sure, I'll do my best. I really admire the guy. And he's an old friend of your mother's, I believe?'

'You could say that.'

He looked at her curiously. 'Do I detect a note of disapproval there?'

'My mother's in love with him.'

Mike's eyebrows rose a fraction, then he nodded thoughtfully, as if the news did not totally surprise him. 'The Count is a very attractive man. And not only that, he's a very brave one.'

'He's also a very married one.'

He raised his eyes to the ceiling, as he lit a cigarette. 'Do I detect a certain feeling of *déjà vu* about this conversation? Don't tell me – you reckon because a man or woman's got a ring on their finger it makes them immune from falling in love with someone else?' He looked right through her as he spoke.

'I'd really rather not get into a discussion on personal relationships at the moment. I've much more important things on my mind, if it's all the same to you.'

'You're right and I'm sorry. You look all in.'

'Well, thanks, that's really chivalrous!'

He ignored her protest. 'Had anything decent to eat today?'

'Yes … I had porridge and toast earlier on.'

'Anything *decent*, I said! Fancy a bite to eat somewhere nice?'

'If I can leave Humphrey here in peace for a while.'

'Humphrey?' He looked puzzled.

'My cat.' She bent down to pick him up, cuddling him to her defensively. 'He's all I've got left from home.'

'He survived the bomb?'

She nodded.

'In that case, he must have special treatment. I'll take him downstairs to the kitchens myself. He'll have a life of Reilly down there until you can provide him with a proper home again. And, as for you, you're going to have the finest lunch this battered old city can provide!'

He was as good as his word. They lunched at the Ritz, and even more than the food, Lara revelled in the twenty minutes she spent in the ladies' powder room, while Mike had a quiet pre-dinner drink at the bar. The mud was all brushed from her clothes, her face and hands washed, and her powder and lipstick carefully reapplied, before she indulged in an extravagant spray from the eau-de-Cologne bottle laid out for the customers' use. He was waiting at the table when she re-emerged.

'I took the liberty of ordering: Brown Windsor, followed by *Carré d'Agneau*. Suit you?'

'Lovely. I'm quite partial to lamb.'

He had also ordered a bottle of finest Bordeaux and, as they raised their glasses for the first sip, he gave a rueful smile, and sighed, 'Why do we do it, Lara – this continual getting at one another?'

She shook her head and looked down into the wine. 'I was just asking myself that same question on the way over here in the car.'

'And did you find the answer?'

She continued to stare down into the glass, then raised her eyes to meet his. 'Can I be honest with you, Mike?'

'Sure.' He tensed slightly in his seat and took a quick gulp of the wine.

'I – I don't know quite how to put this, but I think I owe you the truth. I handed in my notice because I feel if I work for you any longer I may run the risk of becoming too fond of you. I – I can't allow that to happen. Can you understand that?'

'Yes, I can understand that.'

'Well, then, you'll ... '

'I understand it,' he interrupted, 'because I feel exactly the same.'

She sat up in her seat as if stung. What on earth did she say now? This wasn't what she expected at all. She had decided in the car to be entirely honest with him. He would think all the more of her for it; then they could part with no ill feelings. She could return to the Foreign Office, get on with her work and her marriage to Ken, and forget in time that she had ever met a tall American with a lop-sided grin called Mike Adams.

'That surprises you, huh?'

'A little ... ' she flustered. 'Well, a lot, actually.'

'You know what I'm thinking as I sit here and look at you?'

She shook her head. This was getting too much for her to handle.

'I'm thinking I've fallen in love for the first time in my life.'

Chapter Twenty

'Please don't say any more,' Lara pleaded. 'It'll only make things worse.'

'It could hardly be any worse, could it?' Mike Adams could not disguise the bitterness in his voice. 'If it wasn't for this goddam war I could ask you to choose between him and me. But I can't, can I? Not with Ken up there in the skies risking his life like that.' He finished the remaining wine in the glass in one gulp, then refilled it from the bottle. 'It would take an even bigger bastard than I can claim to be to do that.'

Following his lead, Lara finished her own wine and held out her glass for a refill. 'You can always accept my resignation. That would be a gentlemanly thing to do.'

He grimaced. 'Don't use that word: it makes my skin crawl. I told you before, Lara, I'm no gentleman.'

'You will accept it, though – my resignation.'

He was silent for a moment, then looked straight at her. 'What if I said, No? What if I forgot all about playing it straight and putting your husband first? What if I forgot the fact he's one of your "boys in blue" and all that? What if I said to hell with accepting your resignation, I'm going to fight this one out? "All's fair in love and war", Mrs Cameron – and this is both!'

It was Lara's turn to fall silent. She looked across at him; his eyes were challenging hers across the table, his mouth set, with just the faintest quirk at one corner. 'It's an old maxim, Lara, but a true one,' he said quietly. 'Things are different now. They have to be when no one knows for certain if they'll even be alive this time tomorrow, never mind next week, or next year.'

'I know that. Don't you think I know that? But that's all the more reason to hang on to the things – the standards if you like – that were important before this awful war began.' She shrugged helplessly, searching for the right words. 'Everything falls apart otherwise ... Those standards – our moral code or whatever you want to call it – those things that were important then *must* remain important now, or that damned Hitler will have won a moral as well as a physical victory.'

'And there endeth the first lesson ...'

'I'm sorry, Mike. I didn't mean to preach. I suppose I'm trying to convince myself as much as you.'

He lifted his glass slowly to his lips and took a sip of the wine, watching her intently as he did so. 'I guess I'm not making it very easy for you, am I?'

She shook her head and gave a rueful half-smile. 'No, not really.'

'Tell me what you want me to say, Lara.' His voice was soft, but there was a disconcerting note of challenge in it again.

She returned his gaze unflinchingly. 'I want you to say you accept my resignation.'

His lips twisted into a mirthless smile. 'Sure ... if that's what you really want.'

She toyed with the stem of her glass. Of course it wasn't what she really wanted, and he knew it as well as she did. What she really wanted more than anything was to indulge this insatiable craving she had to know him body and soul; to find out what really went on behind that cynical, man-of-the-world smile; to touch the smooth, lightly-tanned skin beneath that high-ranking uniform ... Her cheeks flamed at the thoughts that tumbled through her mind, as the waiter arrived with the first course.

She could only toy with the soup and try to put out of her mind what he had admitted to her a few minutes ago. He was obviously as upset at the confession and her reaction to it as she was, for his face seemed set in an inscrutable mask as he got on with his meal. As the minutes ticked past and the conversation did not resume, she was glad of the small orchestra playing softly in the background, otherwise the silence between them would have been unbearable.

She saw him look at the almost full plate of soup that she handed back to the waiter, but he made no comment. Then, when the second course arrived, she toyed with it for several minutes then looked across at him in despair. 'I – I'm afraid our conversation has completely robbed me of my appetite; but I suppose I'd better try to finish it. If I don't I'll only regret it later. If I go back to that hotel again tonight it'll probably be pot-luck – and knowing the way the rationing's going at the moment that's no joke. It'll be toad-in-the-hole minus the sausage and bread-and-butter pudding minus the butter, or some such delicacy.'

'You won't have to go back there,' Mike said, dabbing his mouth and pushing his plate from him. 'There'll be no more draughty hotel corridors and bed bugs for you tonight: I've got you a nice little apartment lined up. It's just round the corner from the Embassy in Lower Belgrave Street.'

'You're joking!'

'Scout's honour!' He made the appropriate salute, dug into the pocket of his jacket for the keys and jingled them in front of her. 'Look, if you don't believe me!'

'But how … ?'

'One of the Embassy staff had it, but he's been transferred back to the States. It's been empty for two days.'

'I bet they offered it to you! You can't do this, Mike. I can't possibly accept a flat that you're supposed to have.'

'That's bullshit. I'm perfectly happy where I am for the time being – there's nothing like living over the shop. It couldn't be handier. Anyway, you'll have to have somewhere for your Mom to come back to, won't you? You can hardly book her into some crummy hotel. And if you think you can just walk into a decent apartment in this city just now, then forget it. There's just nowhere even half decent to be had. I know 'cause I've tried! God, Lara, there have been thousands – literally thousands – made homeless with this German Blitz. People are so desperate they're squatting down anywhere. You can bet your boots that half of those who spend their nights sleeping in the Tubes don't have any choice in the matter!'

'That's true, I suppose.' The thought of her mother's reaction to the loss of their home and having to end up in some communal shelter or, God help them, the Underground, sent a shudder through her.

'It's a real nice place, Lara. Four rooms, kitchen and bathroom; and all fully furnished. It's mainly Embassy personnel in the block, so you'll have decent neighbours – if you don't mind Americans, that is.' One dark eyebrow and the corner of his mouth quirked slightly at the last remark then, sensing she was in no mood for teasing, he said quietly, 'We can go on and take a look at it after lunch, if that's OK by you.'

She shook her head and sighed. 'I – I don't know what to say.'

'Then don't say anything. Just grab your coat and follow me. Unless you fancy a sweet and a coffee, that is?'

She declined with a smile. 'I couldn't touch another thing. I've had four glasses of wine, remember.'

'Who's counting? At least it's brought some colour back to those cheeks of yours.' He signalled for the bill.

The head waiter came across and bowed politely. 'The management wish to tell you, sir, that there's to be no charge for today's luncheon. The pleasure has been ours in playing host to a serving member of the US Army.'

When he had gone, Mike looked at Lara in amazement. 'Well, how about that?'

She smiled. 'I've heard of similar happenings before, but you really must have impressed them.'

'Old FDR did, most like, with his speech last night.' His grin grew broader. 'I guess we've got to cash in on the goodwill while it lasts. If the Congress vote against the Lend-Lease bill, they'll all be refusing to serve us, never mind entertaining us on the house!'

As she sat next to him in the front passenger seat of the Packard on their way to Lower Belgrave Street, she found herself struggling to make small-talk. The silences between them had become far too potent. Her own mind was still on the conversation in the restaurant, and she knew his was not a million miles from the same subject. 'I don't know how you manage it, I really don't – getting sufficient petrol coupons for this thing, I mean. My mother has the most awful job getting enough for her little Morris. In fact, if she didn't have that extra allowance for her voluntary work, heaven knows what she'd do.'

Mike shrugged. 'We're not too badly off for things like that. In fact, to be honest, we're hardly affected by the rationing at all. Lots of our essentials get sent over from the States, but that's getting increasingly dodgy these days with so much shipping being sunk. I can see us ending up being like your lot with your "make do and mend" and "dig for victory" carryings-on before too long!'

Lara fell silent for a moment, remembering all the drawers full of old clothes in her bedroom in Atholl Square that she had meant to get round to altering one of these fine days, and the old cardigan her mother was in the act of unpicking to knit up again before the worst of the winter was past. 'It's a weird thought, but Mum and I won't be able to do any "make do and mending" from now on. There's nothing left to give a new lease of life to.'

His grip tightened on the wheel. 'Look, Lara honey, I was going to say to you – if money's a problem, I've got a bank account here. You're welcome to whatever you need. And, of course, it goes without saying that the apartment you're about to see has been taken care of in that regard.'

'Oh no – thank you all the same. Whatever happens we'll pay our own way. And, thankfully, money really isn't a problem. I can't imagine what sort of compensation we'll get for what's happened, but it's really immaterial: my stepfather left us pretty well provided for.'

'He was a big shot in the Foreign Office, wasn't he?'

'He was big in every way – a marvellous man. I really admired him.'

'Went to the same school and belonged to the same clubs as Churchill, so I hear.'

Lara glanced across at him and nodded. 'You're remarkably well-informed. But yes, it's true, they went back a long way. Jack remained one of Winston's true friends when he was out of favour for so long with the political Establishment. The Prime Minister never forgot it.'

'And you worked for him – old Winnie – yourself, so I believe.'

'Yes, last summer.' It was hard to keep the pride from her voice. 'And I hope to again.'

'Now you're no longer working for me, that is.' His words had a bitter edge.

She shifted slightly in her seat. 'It wouldn't work, Mike. You know it wouldn't. Don't blame me too much.'

'We could give it a try.'

'What good would it do? We would only be torturing ourselves. And what if this war goes on for a few more years, heaven help us, what then? I would know you even better than I know the man I'm married to and, whether or not we had an affair, I would feel more married to you than to him – to Ken.' The words burst out of her, then she fell silent for a moment, pondering on such an event, before continuing in a quiet voice, 'Do you know I was tallying it up the other night just how long I spent in Ken's company before I married him. It's far less than I've spent in yours!'

'Time is immaterial, Lara. You can fall in love – or out of it – in five minutes.'

'Do you really believe that?' She looked across at him in curiosity. 'Yes I do.'

'You *do* believe in "love", then?' Despite what he said earlier, she found it hard to think of him as having a sentimental side, to reconcile a professed belief in such a romantic concept with his usual cynical outlook on life.

'That surprises you?'

'Well, yes, it does. You sometimes give the impression that to you love is just another four letter word.'

He glanced round at her, a look akin to hurt in his eyes, despite the smile on his lips. And there was a faint wistfulness in his voice as he said: 'To be honest, until fairly recently I was of the opinion that love was simply a dirty trick played on us by Mother Nature to perpetuate the human race ... I've modified that opinion recently.'

She tensed in her seat, waiting for him to continue. He did, darting another look at her as the Packard turned into Grosvenor Gardens. 'Sure, there's such a thing as love. If we're lucky, we can all expect to experience it at least once in our lives. But it has one arch-enemy – and that is life itself.'

He drew the car up in front of a large block of flats a few hundred yards into Lower Belgrave Street, and pointed up to a second floor window. 'See that one with the half-drawn blue curtains – that's yours.'

'You're very sure I'll take it.'

He made no response, but got out of his side of the car and came round to hold open the passenger door for her. He took her arm as they entered the building and made their way up the stairs. The front doors they passed were all freshly-painted and the place had a well-cared-for feel to it, even before they stepped inside the flat in question.

'Well, what do you think?' he asked when, a few minutes later, he had opened the door and they walked through the spacious hall and on into the neatly furnished living-room.

She looked around her. The wallpaper had a pale blue stripe, with sprigs of tiny forget-me-nots, and the blue was picked up again in the curtains and the linen covers of the three-piece suite. A fairly modern sideboard, coffee table, and bookcase made up the remainder of the furniture. 'It looks very nice,' she said truthfully, as she wandered over to the bookcase and plucked out a book at random. '*The East Wind of Love* by Compton MacKenzie ... Mmm, quite an up-to-date selection, by the looks of it.'

They wandered on through the dining-room, then into the kitchen, the half-tiled bathroom with an enormous copper shower contraption over the bath, and on into the smallest of the bedrooms, before ending up in the main bedroom that overlooked the street.

Lara pulled back the curtain and looked down at the Packard parked by the kerb, then out over the roof-tops beyond. He came across and joined her, standing just behind as they looked out at the wisps of grey smoke still spiralling skywards from the dozens of small fires not yet fully extinguished throughout the City.

'It's been one hell of a Christmas, one way and another, hasn't it?' Mike said softly. 'One hell of a Christmas.'

She nodded, her heart suddenly too full to speak. He was standing very close. It was all she could think of. He rested his left hand on her shoulder and she jumped, as if the touch had sent an electric shock through her.

'What will you do, Lara?' he asked softly. 'What will you do when you're no longer working for me?'

She shook her head. 'Go back to the Foreign Office, I expect. Carry on as before ... '

'As before we met?'

'Yes.' She whispered the word.

His fingers tightened round her shoulder. 'But we *did* meet, Lara. All the wishing in the world can't alter that fact. No matter how far you run, no matter how hard you try, nothing can ever change that. Sometime, somewhere, something will happen to bring the memories tumbling back. A face in the crowd, a certain tune,' he paused, and gave a wry smile, 'even a plate of Brown Windsor soup ... something will be there to remind you that we did exist, that there was a time when, in the midst of all this destruction and misery, we knew each other, and felt the spark that could have flamed into the love of a lifetime.'

His words flowed over her. The whole of her insides were quivering. What she was feeling now she had never felt before – no, not even with Ken. Her longing for him was a physical pain within her, as his fingers caressed her shoulder, then moved up to touch the pale skin at the nape of her neck. She trembled visibly beneath his touch. 'Don't, Mike, please don't ... ' But there was no conviction in her voice.

He had hold of both her shoulders now, and he turned her to him. 'I want you, Lara ... God help me, I want you ... ' His eyes seemed to burn deep into her very soul as his fingers moved to undo the buttons of her coat. It slipped from her shoulders and landed soundlessly at her feet. Then his arms went around her and his lips were raining kisses over her wet cheeks. 'You're crying, my love ... Don't cry, Lara, don't cry ... '

She felt herself tremble violently in his arms, as his mouth moved down the pale curve of her neck. 'It's wrong, Mike ... It's wrong ... ' The words came out in gasps. 'We must be sensible ... '

He pulled back and looked down at her, his blue eyes a dark navy in the pale afternoon light from the window. 'To love and be sensible at the same time is asking the impossible. And I love you, Lara. God help me, I love you.' He had never said those words voluntarily to another woman before, not even to Joanne. But he was saying them now and feeling no shame, no humiliation in exposing his deepest

178

feelings to another human being – to another man's wife. As he looked at her, he hated Ken Cameron. He hated him for meeting her first, for claiming what should rightly be his. He wanted her as he had never wanted another woman. As he would never want another woman.

His hands dug deeply into the soft flesh of her upper arms. 'You want me too, Lara. I can see it in your eyes. I can feel it in your touch. You want me as much as I want you.' His voice was husky with emotion. The chemistry between them was a tangible thing. It wrapped itself around them, making them oblivious to everything but their need for each other.

Tears were spilling down her cheeks, but she was not aware of crying. She was aware only of the blood pulsating through her body, as the longing for his became almost impossible to bear. There was a white heat between them that blotted out everything. Nothing and no one else mattered. She tried desperately to think of Ken, but her senses were filled with the man whose eyes were gazing down into hers, with a look that mirrored her own feelings completely.

His hands moved up and cupped her cheeks as his mouth found hers. This time there was no holding back. They kissed as lovers, his tongue sending pulsations of desire through her body as his kiss grew deeper and turned every fibre of her being to water. 'Say you want me, too, my love. Let me love you, Lara ... Now, my love, now ... '

She was not aware of wrenching herself from his grasp, but the sharp crack of the slap that followed echoed in her head. Her fingers stung from it as Mike took a staggering step backwards. His hand moved automatically to his cheek as it reddened beneath his fingers. She would remember the look on his face till her dying day.

He did not ask why. He simply turned from her and walked to the window. He gripped the sill until his knuckles turned white beneath the tanned skin, as he stared out at the buildings opposite.

'I – I'm sorry – so sorry ... Forgive me, Mike, forgive me ... ' She rushed to him, but stopped short before touching him, her fingers reaching out to halt a couple of inches from the back of his jacket. There was something about the hunch of his shoulders that told ner not to come any closer.

She sat down on the edge of the bed and stared at the back of his head through tear-soaked lashes. The magic of a moment ago was shattered. She had seen to that. It had exploded about their ears when she had lifted her hand and struck him. It was the only way to stop it: the thing that she wanted most in this world was about to happen, and she could not allow it to. She could not allow him to make love to her. She had to put a stop to it, but the passion remained – a deep throbbing ache within her. It had been an unforgiveable thing to do – to strike him like that. She had humiliated him and demeaned herself.

A deep anger welled within her as she sat staring bleakly at the back of his hunched shoulders: an anger directed at herself and at the perversity of life that had brought them to this. She wanted to lash out at everything and everyone. 'All right, I'll say it. I'll admit it. I love you. Heaven help me, I love you! Does that make you feel any better? It doesn't help me!' She found herself shouting as the tears began to flow again.

She got up off the bed and rushed to the window, grabbing him by the arm. 'I love you, Mike. I love you. But I can't be unfaithful to Ken. I just can't. Say you understand. Please say you understand!'

'I understand, Lara.' His voice was as expressionless as his face as he turned and faced her.

She let go his arm and her hands flailed helplessly at her sides. 'You don't understand. You don't understand at all. I can see it. You're angry and you're blaming me. This is what I was afraid would happen. Can't you see? This is exactly the situation I've been terrified of.'

'What are you afraid of, Lara? Of your own feelings?'

'Yes, dammit, yes! Because those feelings can hurt someone else.'

'You're hurting me now.'

'But I'm not married to you. I'm married to Ken. I can't hurt him.'

'Does not having a piece of paper with our names on it mean I hurt any the less?' There was a huskiness in his voice as he looked at her; his eyes seemed to see into her very soul.

She stared back at him. She had no answer to that. 'Don't make it any harder for me, please.'

'But it's true, Lara, isn't it? We don't hurt any the less just because we're not married to each other. The pain is just the same with or without the ring. I could turn your argument on its head. I could say that by sticking to your marriage vows you're hurting two people, not just one. You're inflicting twice as much hurt by denying our love, because you feel you should stand by your relationship with Ken. Who says that because someone went through a marriage ceremony they have the monopoly on being hurt, or on really deep feelings for the other person? How do you know that I don't love you ten times more than your Scotsman? I believe I do – do you?'

'Don't ask me that. Don't ask me to try to compare.'

'Why – because you daren't? Because you're too frightened of the answer you may come to?' He loosened the top button of his shirt and pulled at the knot of his tie. A bead of sweat had appeared on his upper lip. He was perspiring beneath the uniform and it showed. 'He's only a man like I am, Lara. We're both flesh and blood, God help us. We both have feelings.'

'I know ... Don't you think I know that better than any one? Do you imagine I wanted this to happen? How many times do I have to tell you, this is exactly the situation I wanted to avoid?' She gestured helplessly with her hands and ran her fingers through her hair. She was tired, very tired. Her brain seemed to have gone numb. She wished she had eaten something at lunch-time. Why were they shouting at each other like this? Her head was beginning to throb and her legs were turning to lead.

'Are you all right, honey?' He saw the blood drain from her face and took a step forward. The bitterness had gone from his voice as he put out a supportive hand. 'Here, let's sit down.' He led her to the edge of the bed and sat down alongside her on the blue coverlet. There was nothing but concern in his eyes as he put a comforting arm around her shoulders and murmured, 'You're all in ... '

He got up and very gently laid her down on the bed, adjusting her legs into the most comfortable position before lying down beside her. The passion of a few minutes earlier had given way to tenderness as he stretched out his arm and gathered her to him. The anger and frustration had disappeared. He felt nothing but an overwhelming concern as he smoothed the dishevelled strands of titian hair back from her brow. She had been through so much recently – much more than any one should ever have to go through in a lifetime in the past twenty-four hours alone. 'Just rest, honey,' he whispered softly. 'Just rest ... '

Chapter Twenty-one

Lara fell asleep in Mike's arms as he lay on the bed beside her and stared up at the ornate cornice of the ceiling. A spider had spun a web in the corner above the half-open door, and he watched it swaying slightly in the draught as it dangled from its fragile thread. If he wanted to be cynical he could feel that was exactly how she had him – dangling from a thread. But he knew that wasn't true. She hadn't wanted this to happen any more than he had. But, hell, you didn't choose the people you fell in love with any more than you chose your parents. It happened, that was all, often at the most inconvenient times, in the most unexpected of places. What it was exactly that ignited the vital spark between two people far better minds than his had tried to figure out over the years and had failed. It was either there or it wasn't, and the almost physical ache in his being for this woman beside him told him that in his case that spark was already well ablaze and there was nothing he could do about it. Or was there?

He closed his eyes as a frown etched itself between the dark brows. Just where *did* their relationship go from here? All was fair in love and war, so they said, but just how true was that old maxim? He wasn't exactly proud of the fact he had tried to make love to another man's wife, but everything he had said to Lara had been true. Who was to say that Ken Cameron loved her more than he did? Who was to say that she wouldn't have a far better life married to him, Mike Adams, than to that Scotsman?

She stirred slightly in her sleep and he moved over, gently extricating his arm from behind her head to allow her to rest more comfortably on the pillow. He glanced at his watch as he did so and grimaced. He should be back at the Embassy by now. He had an appointment with General Raymond Lee, his superior officer. Word had come in that very morning of the sinking of the *Merchant Prince* and the *Ville d'Arlan*, the former of which was carrying twenty-eight sacks of

Embassy mail, and the latter nine sacks. Their loss was incalculable, especially with Harry Hopkins on his way over here in the next few days.

Lee himself was in the midst of preparations for a return trip to the United States, and had passed a remark the other day about the possibility of Mike returning to Washington with him. Admiral Sir Dudley Pound, the British First Sea Lord, had informed them that the British had a series of plans to put to the American Administration that could not be trusted either to the cable or to a courier, but the information could be imparted to General Lee and his aides on the voyage across the Atlantic. 'They've got nervous as hell about committing anything to paper, Mike,' the General had said to him. 'After the French government falling so easily and everything being handed to the Jerries on a plate over in Paris, the British won't even commit a shopping list to paper, if they can avoid it.' The American Rear Admiral Robert Ghormley was to accompany him, but Lee was keen on the idea of the presence of another sharp mind on board. 'I'd appreciate it if you'd consider accompanying us,' he had said to Mike. 'It'll give you a chance to see something of your wife into the bargain.'

A mirthless grin twisted Mike's lips at the memory as he continued to gaze, with unseeing eyes, at the bedroom ceiling. How little Ray Lee knew. How little any of them knew …

He turned his head slightly on the pillow and feasted his eyes once more on the sleeping face of the young woman beside him. Why wasn't it her? Why wasn't it Lara he had married? But all the wishing in the world could not alter the fact that she was married to another man and, despite everything, he knew as he looked down at her that he could not take her from him. A Dear John letter was the last thing that poor guy Cameron needed before he set off on another foray against Goering's bunch.

Slowly and painfully the resolve hardened within him. Today she had been the stronger of the two, but now it was his turn. There must be no more self-doubt. He must take the lead, no matter how painful the decision. He would make it easy for her. He would disappear from her life. He would take Raymond Lee up on his suggestion and go back to the States with him. He leaned across and kissed her gently on the brow. A deep emptiness filled his soul as he made the decision, an emptiness he knew would be with him every mile of the way across that cold, grey Atlantic.

She slept for over an hour. When she awoke he was sitting in a chair by the window reading an old copy of the *Reader's Digest* from the bookcase next door. He put it down as soon as she stirred. 'Fancy a cup of tea?'

She blinked her eyes as she pulled herself up on the pillow. 'You mean there's room service here?'

He got up and gave a bow every bit as immaculate as the one delivered by the Head Waiter at the Ritz today. 'At your service, ma'am. What'll it be – tea or coffee?'

'A cup of tea would be lovely.' She swung her legs down from the bed. 'But don't you bother. You've done far too much already. I'll get it!'

That old grin returned. 'Lara honey, make the most of it. This is a quite unique event in the history of mankind … Well, in the history of this man, at any rate!'

She watched him as he headed for the kitchen, the smile fading on her lips as a great sadness overwhelmed her. She had awoken to another world. The moment had gone, never to return; that magic moment when they had admitted their love for each other. In doing so they had stood at a crossroads in both their lives. She could have gone on into a new life – with him. Even now a shiver ran through her at the prospect. Divorce was a scandal, it was true, but it had been done before, and would be again; it was becoming more common every day. She could have disappeared to America as Mrs Mike Adams and, after a little while, some other love affair would arise to take the place of theirs on the tongues of all their acquaintances. Why, even the King and Mrs Simpson had all but disappeared from the headlines now they were simply the Duke and Duchess of Windsor … But she had chosen the other path – the familiar one that she had already trodden for the past year with Ken. Was she right? Her head told her, of course she was. But what her heart said was quite another matter.

They sipped their tea sitting together on the edge of the bed. She knew he was doing his best to lighten the atmosphere between them, but his quips were as strained as the smiles she gave in return. It was all a charade and they both knew it, but both were equally resolved not to make it harder for the other by letting their true feelings show. They had reached the Rubicon and crossed it: there could be no turning back now. Whatever future awaited them, they could not share it together – the ring on her finger had seen to that.

'Do you feel up to a visit to the police station, or would you rather stay here and rest? I'm sure I can do all that's required in that regard.' Mike looked at her reflection in the mirror as he ran a comb through his hair half an hour later.

Lara paused, her lipstick halfway to her lips, and shook her head. 'That's kind of you, but I'd better go myself. And there's really no need for you to come. I'm sure you've got plenty to do at the Embassy without wasting your time with my affairs.'

He made no reply as he replaced the comb in his pocket, squared the cap on his head, and resolved to go with her.

They spoke little on the way there. The silence that hung heavily between them in the front seats of the car seemed to echo the hollowness they both felt inside.

But, as they neared the police station, the pain of their personal situation began to recede in Lara's mind as her apprehension grew about the task ahead. Reliving the horror of the bombing of 29 Atholl Square and enquiring about possible survivors was the last thing she felt up to at that moment.

The desk sergeant, a bald-headed, portly individual with half-moon spectacles, was not too happy at her delayed arrival. 'Don't you know, Miss, that if survivors don't come forward immediately and declare themselves, the rescue services are put to a whole lot of extra work? For all we know the poor blighters down there in Atholl Square could have been digging away for hours looking for you.'

'I'm terribly sorry,' Lara said, her face colouring. 'I really didn't mean to cause anyone any extra trouble. I honestly didn't think it would ... '

'Aye, well, that's just the trouble, isn't it? Folks don't bloody well think enough these days and it makes no end of bother for others, who've got quite enough on their plates as it is ... '

'Look here, fella,' Mike cut in. 'The lady was in a state of shock last night. Wouldn't you be, if you'd worked flat out all day and arrived home late at night to find your home bombed to the ground? Mrs Cameron came as quickly as she could. You should be grateful she's bothered, given the state of shock she's in.'

'Well, yes, Major, I appreciate that.' The sergeant unwittingly demoted Mike in his confusion. 'I didn't mean to cause any offence, believe me ... It's been a nightmare trying to catch up on all the casualties from last night. Bloody murder it was around here. Bloody murder.' He sighed deeply, as if to emphasize the point, then glanced up at Lara once more. 'Now, young lady, if you'll be kind enough to give me a list of all possible occupants of your house when the bomb fell last night, it'll help us greatly in completing our records.'

Lara haltingly began to reel off the names of the housekeeper and their Polish house-guests. Just repeating their names out loud was a painful process, and she stumbled on Mrs Bates's name, feeling sure in herself that the housekeeper who had been part of her family for so long was dead. She felt Mike's grip tighten on her arm in support as they watched the police officer scratch the names into his log book.

'And who exactly did the house belong to? Was it rented or privately owned?'

'The house was actually in my mother's name but, luckily, she had just left for my grandmother's in Oxford.'

'Lucky indeed.' The sergeant licked the end of his pencil. 'That's one less we have to worry about then, I take it. You don't know about the exact whereabouts of the others, though ... If they were in the house or not?' He flicked a nicotine-stained index finger through a sheaf of papers. 'I have a list here somewhere giving the number of bodies still unidentified from Atholl Square and thereabouts ... Ah, here we are ...'

Lara gripped Mike's arm. She could feel the blood drain from her face as the sergeant ran his forefinger down the typed list of streets and adjacent column of figures.

'Yes, here we are – Atholl Square. What number did we say again, Miss?'

'Twenty-nine. Number twenty-nine.' Her voice was barely audible.

'Twenty-nine, Atholl Square ... This is it. We have the right one here. Four bodies recovered there, by the looks of it – two female, two male. Is that what we reckoned it up to be?' He looked up at Lara, who was now trembling visibly.

Her mind reeled and, despite her resolve to remain in control of her emotions, tears rushed unbidden to her eyes. Four bodies ... Mrs B., the Malinowskis, Mr Kulinski, Mr Kador ... Four bodies ... Which ones? She shook her head, as she tried in vain to get her numbed brain to count.

'That means there's one still unaccounted for,' she heard Mike say. 'You won't know who it is, presumably?'

Protruding blue eyes looked up at him from behind the half-moon spectacles across the desk. 'Sorry, sir, we have no note of identification having taken place. That'll be up to the young lady, if she's the sole survivor.'

'Like hell it will. If anyone's going down to the morgue, or wherever they've taken them, then I'll do it. I've met them all at one time or another. There's no law says that the identification of bomb victims has to be done by a member of the household, is there?'

'Well, no. Not that I know of.' He searched his memory for a forgotten regulation, but came up with none. 'You have to be acquainted with all the deceased, of course.'

'Of course. Like I've said, I've met them all at one time or another.'

Lara squeezed his arm and shook her head. He was willing to do that most gruesome of tasks for her. She wanted to thank him, but her throat had closed and the words came only with difficulty. 'I – I can't ask you to do such a horrible duty for me.'

He looked down at her. Her face was ashen and tears hovered on her lower lashes. He knew just what she was going through. They had been good people, all of them – friends and neighbours alike. It would be bad enough for him going to identify the remains; there was no way he could allow her to go through that. He patted her hand. 'Who's asking me? I'm volunteering! Now say no more. I'll take you back to the apartment and see you settled in, then I'll go and do the needful, after I've reported back to the Embassy. All you'll have to worry about is what time you fancy getting out of bed tomorrow morning. And don't tell me you can't do with the sleep!'

'You do as the Major says, Miss. No use arguing with an officer, you know. Even if he ain't one of us!'

They arrived back at Lower Belgrave Street at just after four o'clock. Barely a single word passed between them on the return journey. Lara felt at her lowest ebb. The visit to the police station had brought the horror of the bombing back to the forefront of her mind, and her anguish at the possible fate of her friends was intensified by the thought of now losing the man sitting beside her; for if he were to disappear from her life he might as well be dead, mightn't he? He would no longer be part of her world. And if you never saw a person again then that in itself was akin to death, wasn't it?

Mike pulled the car into the kerbside and, without switching off the ignition, he reached into his pocket and fished out the keys to the flat. He placed them into the palm of her hand and closed her fingers over them. His eyes found hers and, when he spoke, the lightness of his voice belied the heaviness of his heart. 'They're yours now, Lara honey. For as long as you want. If you've any problems, the Embassy staff will be only too ready to help. And, of course, all your neighbours in the block are part of our diplomatic community, too. Any one of them will be only too glad to help out with anything that you feel you can't cope with yourself. They're a good bunch.'

She looked down at the keys, then back at him. His eyes were dark and unfathomable in the confines of the car. There was so much she wanted to say, but the lover of earlier in the day had become another person – a helpful friend in her hour of need. Had it all been a dream? What if she were to reach out right now and touch his cheek? What if … ? 'And what about you, Mike? Will you come back soon – just to see I'm settling in and all that?' Her voice was husky. She couldn't just let him go. Not like that, with no prospect of ever seeing him again, except by accident.

He looked at her quietly for a moment. Her eyes had an unnatural sparkle and he knew tears were not far from the surface. There was the trace of a tremor on her lower lip. He put out his hand and traced its outline with his fingertips, lifting the edges slightly into the semblance of a smile. 'I'll always be around, Lara. If you need me – really need me – just call and I'll be there.'

She smiled a genuine smile of relief. Maybe it wasn't quite the final curtain. Not quite yet, anyway. 'It'll be good to know that you're only half a mile or so away.'

Half a mile or so away … How little she guessed. His heart felt like stone in his chest. Half a world away would be nearer the mark.

He watched her get out of the car and walk up and into the front door. She turned and gave a small wave of her hand as she reached the step. He waved back, thankful she was not near enough to see that his own eyes were glistening. He had not shed a tear since his father died. But as he drove the short distance back to the Embassy, and attempted to focus his gaze on the way ahead, the world before him seemed suddenly a much colder, greyer place.

Chapter Twenty-two

'Beth, dear, there's a gentleman at the front door asking for you.'
Emily Sanders rested on her walking-stick at the foot of the stairs of
her neat, ivy-covered Edwardian house in north Oxford and called up
to her daughter.

'Ask him what he wants. I'm busy at the moment.' Beth paused, her
pen poised in mid-sentence above the letter she was writing, her voice
registering her annoyance. Just when she thought she had an evening
free to get on with her correspondence, someone had to call. It would
probably be one of the younger tutors from her father's old College
who had heard she was in town for a few days: unsolicited male
attentions, however platonic, were the last thing she wanted at the
moment.

'I really can't do that, dear, it seems terribly rude.'

With a sigh, Beth rose from the rosewood writing-desk in front of
the bedroom window, and drew aside the net curtain to peer over the
sill. He must already have come inside, for there was no sign of him
through the diamond-paned windows of the porch. She gave another
exasperated sigh and put down the pen. 'All right, I'll come down if I
must.'

Emily stood by the foot of the stairs in the narrow hallway and
watched curiously as her daughter went to greet the stranger. It was
rare that such attractive men graced the front step of The Hawthorns
these days. The most she could expect was old Professor Holmes,
who occasionally called in to change her library books for her when
the weather was bad enough to prevent her getting out. But Arthur
Holmes was pushing eighty, making this caller a positive youngster
in comparison. And, unlike Arthur, there was nothing shambling
about the visitor. There was something about his bearing that told
her this was no desk-bound, elderly academic. No, he wasn't from the
University, she was pretty sure of that. And although he spoke perfect

English, in a soft, well-modulated voice, there was just the slightest trace of an accent. There was something in his looks, too, that told her he was a foreigner – a certain height to the cheekbones, and width of brow that one didn't see every day on this side of the Channel. He wasn't German, though. She could recognize that accent all right. Heaven knows she had heard it often enough before the Great War, during all their holidays with the von Lessings.

She made her way into the sitting-room, leaving the door slightly ajar, so that she could hear what was said as Beth greeted him.

'Jan!' Beth gasped in astonishment at the sight of the man filling the door-frame. Her heart began to race wildly beneath the fair-isle pattern of her jumper. This was the last person she was expecting to find. 'What on earth brings you here? Shouldn't you be on your way to Scotland?'

He kissed her on both cheeks, but his smile was strained, and his brown eyes were serious as they looked down into hers. 'So I am, *kochanie*. But it was important that I speak to you first.'

'If – if it's about my travelling up North to join you, then I honestly don't know. I haven't made up my mind yet.' She spoke quickly, her voice deliberately low, knowing her mother would most certainly be listening. But she was only half speaking the truth. She had already found out the timetables for the north-bound trains.

He ignored her remark. This was not the time to discuss that particular matter. His gaze travelled past her, on into the hallway beyond. 'May I come in? What I have to say really is better said indoors.'

'Of course ... forgive me.'

Emily, now listening with growing curiosity from behind the sitting-room door, jumped back, causing a stab of pain from her arthritic knee to jar up through her hip. She let out an involuntary cry of pain as Beth stood aside to allow Jan into the narrow hallway.

Beth darted a look towards the sound, and knew exactly what had caused it. The conversation was going to be quite tricky over the next few minutes. Whatever brought Jan here, it must be of some importance for him to break his journey. She prayed inwardly it had nothing to do with their relationship, past or present. That was something her mother knew nothing of, and now was not the time to enlighten her.

Emily was at a diplomatic distance when they entered the comfortable, chintzy sitting-room, with its profusion of potted plants and polished brasses. She smiled graciously as her daughter ushered her visitor in through the door. 'Mum, this is Count Jan Jarosinski. He's an old friend from Silesia who's over here as part of the Polish Government in Exile ... Jan, this is my mother, Emily Sanders.'

Emily beamed as Jan took her hand in his and raised it to his lips. 'It is an honour to meet you, Mrs Sanders.'

'And you, Count ...' She never was much good with foreign names. It had taken her ages to remember Hans Heinrich's father's full title, even after Beth married into the family. 'The Polish Government in Exile, you say ... How interesting. I try to follow what's happening over there, you know. And I so much admire your General Sikorski. We met Marshal Pilsudski, your former leader, you know – my late husband and I. A born leader if ever there was one. And a fine country, Poland. A fine country.' She was gushing, and was well aware of it, but nerves always got the better of her at a time like this. 'It must be difficult for you being at such a distance from home. Do you manage to keep in touch with what's happening over there just now?'

'Of course. It is our duty to be informed.'

'You have *spies* over there?' Emily's interest grew. She had adored anything to do with counter-espionage since reading Erskine Childers's *Riddle of the Sands* as a young girl.

Jan smiled indulgently. There was a certain naïvety and charm about the old lady that caused the girl to be still visible in Emily Sanders, despite her advanced age. 'We have our ways of keeping in touch ... such as this, for example.' He pulled a copy of *Biuletyn Informacyjny* from the pocket of his coat and handed it to her. 'It may be of interest to you. It's produced in Warsaw – without the knowledge of the Germans, of course.'

Emily accepted it with a gracious smile. 'An underground newspaper? How exciting!'

Sensing her mother was about to monopolize the visitor for the next half-hour, Beth intervened. 'Mum, I'm sure the Count has come here on a very pressing errand ...'

'Oh, I'm so sorry. You're right, of course.' She directed a half-apologetic smile at Jan. 'At my age one gets so few exciting visitors these days.' She turned back to her daughter. 'Make sure our guest makes himself comfortable, Beth dear. Give him the seat nearest the fire and I'll pop into the kitchen and put the kettle on.' She paused on the way out to lay her hand on Jan's arm and whisper confidentially, 'My warder – that's what I call the nurse Beth here has thoughtfully provided for me – has taken a few days off now that I've got company, and it's bliss just to have the kitchen to myself again!'

They both watched, smiling indulgently, as the old lady hobbled painfully from the room; then the smile died on Beth's lips as she asked anxiously, 'Just why *are* you here, Jan? If it's nothing to do with us, it must be Lara.' Her voice rose an octave. 'It's not her, is it? Nothing's happened to her?'

'No, it's nothing to do with Lara. Not directly. But it was Lara who asked me to come to break the news.'

Fear clutched at Beth's throat as she remembered the radio reports and newspaper headlines of the past twenty-four hours. No amount of censorship could disguise what London had just gone through. 'It was the bombing, wasn't it? It was Sunday night's bombing raids. What's happened, Jan? Is it our house? Did we catch it?' She wanted to shout the questions, and it took all her effort to keep her voice low enough so her mother wouldn't hear.

He put an arm around her shoulders. 'Let's sit down.' He led her to the sofa in front of the fire and sat down beside her, holding her hands in his. She looked so helpless, so vulnerable. He wanted to gather her into his arms and smooth the furrows from her brow. Apart from her mother and Lara, she was all alone in the world now. She needed a man to lean on. He should be here – always. But all he could do was come on a fleeting visit like this – offer himself in snatches when she needed him most. His heart ached at the knowledge. 'You must be strong, Beth.'

'It *is* our house, isn't it?' Already she was seeing visions of 29 Atholl Square as a pile of smoking rubble. By the look on his face, she was right in her supposition. She had no doubt about it now. 'Is – is it completely gone?' The words stuck in her throat as tears welled in her eyes and she fought to hold them back.

He could only nod silently and hold her hands even tighter. He knew exactly what was going through her mind. He had been through it himself, when the Germans took over Jarosbork. To lose your home and all your possessions was to lose part of yourself. There was little he could say by way of comfort. Instead, he raised her fingers to his lips and kissed them gently.

She stared vacantly in front of her, giving no indication she was even aware of the gesture. When she finally spoke, her voice was urgent. 'But Lara's not hurt. You did say Lara's not hurt?'

'Lara's not hurt,' he assured her. 'She's well and is being taken good care of. Colonel Adams, from the American Embassy, has found her somewhere to live until you can get somewhere permanent arranged. I have her address. You can write to her today.'

'And the others? What about the others?' Her nails dug into the back of his hands as she asked the question, hardly daring to listen to the reply.

He could only shake his head. 'We do not know yet. Not for certain. But there seems very little hope for any one who was at home that night.'

The tears ran down her cheeks, blurring her vision, as she thought of Mrs B. and the others. There might be some hope for the Poles – the Malinowskis, Mr Kulinski and Mr Kador – they were often out quite late at night; but not Mrs B. She was always at home.

'I – I don't know what to say, *kochanie*,' Jan said softly, as he took a clean handkerchief from his pocket and tried to stem the flow of tears. 'If the words had been invented I would use them ...'

She took the handkerchief from him and shook her head as she wiped her wet face and dabbed her eyes. She was making it harder for him going to pieces like this. She had to control herself. After all, he had been through so much more. 'It's happening all the time to others. Why shouldn't it happen to us?' she asked abruptly. She felt guilty. Guilty that she should be living when they – Mrs B. and the others – they could all be dead. Unable to bear the look in his eyes, she stared into space somewhere beyond his head, as the tears continued to stream down her cheeks. Why should she have escaped? Why should she be the lucky one?

'I know what you are thinking,' Jan said quietly. 'Why you? Why should you be allowed to live, when all the others perished? We all feel like that, Beth. All of us who have lost friends and loved ones. I carry the guilt with me every day – for Stefan and all the others I have known and loved who are now dead. And for all the others I will never know. It is something that is always with you. You learn to live with it, that's all.'

'You're certain Lara is all right?' It was the one question that was uppermost in her mind. She scrutinized his face for any trace that he may be trying to spare her feelings. 'Should I go to her? Does she need me there? What about the house? Is anything salvageable?' A thousand questions whirled in her head and she looked to him for the answers.

'Lara is fine, Beth. She is well and has a roof over her head. I spoke to Mike Adams on the telephone this morning – the flat is hers for as long as she needs it, and he is seeing to such things as the identification of the bodies.'

She shuddered. 'Nothing was saved from the house, then? Nothing and nobody.'

He shook his head. 'You are better off here for the time being. I'm sure Lara would rather know you were in a safe place than that you were thinking of returning to London at a time like this.'

That made sense. And, although her first inclination was to take the first train back there, she knew there was nothing she could do in London, other than go round to Atholl Square to gaze at the ruins and upset herself even more. It was a peculiar feeling to sit there knowing that all her past life had just been wiped out overnight.

She looked across at him and knew now exactly how he must have felt at having to leave Poland – at having to leave Silesia and Jarosbork. But it wasn't places and possessions that mattered, it was people. And very soon she would lose him. He would return to Poland and she would never see him again. She looked down at their clasped hands, then met his eyes once more. Whatever remaining doubts she had had about allowing themselves a few snatched days from a lifetime lay buried in the ruins of Atholl Square. Life was too short for scruples. 'I've made up my mind,' she said softly. 'I'll come to Scotland, Jan. I'll join you up there.'

When he had gone, her mother, who had been shocked at the news of the bombing of Atholl Square, looked pityingly at her daughter. 'You know you are welcome to stay here for as long as you like, Beth dear. This can be your home too – yours and Lara's.'

'I know, Mum, and I appreciate the offer.' Beth stood at the sitting-room window, toying with the cream chintz curtain as, in her mind's eye, she watched his tall, spare figure walking back down the garden path once more. She had wanted to bury her head in his shoulder before he left, to sob all her hurt out into his arms. But it was impossible. Her mother had been seated there, in the armchair by the fire, watching every move, listening to every word.

'You can't go back to London – not just now, with these awful raids still going on almost every night.' Emily Sanders looked imploringly at her daughter. 'It's only asking for even more trouble, my dear.'

'I know that. I was thinking of going up North for a few days. I feel I could do with a change of scene.'

'Up North? You mean Yorkshire?' She had several cousins in and around Bridlington, a few of whom she still saw from time to time.

Beth shook her head. 'No, to Scotland, actually.'

'Scotland! Goodness – who on earth do we know in Scotland?'

Beth tensed. She hated deception of any sort. She had had enough of that in her life already. 'Well, there's all Ken's family for a start. I met his parents and other relatives at the wedding last year and I have a standing invitation to visit any time I feel like it. It seems to me that now's as good a time as any for a change of scene for a few days.'

Emily nodded. That made sense. 'And where is it Ken's from again?'

'Dundee,' Beth said quietly. Was it fate that had arranged for her son-in-law to come from that city?

Emily reached into a pocket in the loose cover of the armchair and pulled out her knitting, which she deposited in her lap with a sigh. 'Well, it won't be any picnic travelling away up there at this time of year, what with the cold weather and the trains full of troops, but I can't say that I blame you for wanting a change. Heaven only knows what this coming year will bring. Mind you, if some of us knew what the next day had in store sometimes, I doubt if we'd bother getting out of bed in the morning!'

Beth returned to her letter writing with peculiarly mixed feelings. Part of her was still numb – devastated at the loss of her home and her friends, but part of her was already looking ahead to her journey up North. Strangely, for the first time in her life, she felt no pangs of guilt towards Leni, Jan's wife. It was as though she had moved beyond that. Losing her own home, and some of her friends, had brought the reality of war that bit closer. You never really believed it would happen to you – that you too would become a casualty. When it did happen, it brought home to you the fragile hold you had on life. It could be snuffed out at any moment. No longer was old age a certainty. You could not live for tomorrow, never mind next year. You learned to live for today. That was all that mattered – that you were alive, and those you loved were still alive, for the time being at least. When the whole world was disintegrating around you, you had to cling on – cling on to hope, but most of all cling on to love, even when life itself seemed bent on its destruction.

What harm could she possibly do to Leni by going to Scotland to spend a few days with Jan? She would never even have to know. What she would be doing was snatching a few brief moments of happiness; a happiness they had denied each other for over twenty years.

She picked up the piece of paper Jan had given her before he left, with Lara's new address on it. She would write to her today and tell her she would join her in London in about a week's time. She would not mention Scotland. For the meantime, that was her secret. She would share it with no one but with the man she loved.

Chapter Twenty-three

On the evening of Thursday 9 January 1941, Colonel Mike Adams stood shivering beneath his military greatcoat on the platform at Waterloo Station, alongside the equally cold figure of the Chargé d'Affaires at the American Embassy, Herschel Johnson. The two men were awaiting the arrival in London of President Roosevelt's special envoy, Harry Hopkins. Mike glanced at his watch, then peered down the track. 'Just on seven. The train should be here any minute.'

No sooner had the words left his lips than the air-raid siren sounded. 'Holy Jeezuz! What a time for them to choose!' Mike turned to Herschel, as people started to run for the nearest air-raid shelters. 'What the hell do we do now?'

The question went unanswered as the rattle and smoke of the approaching train brought them walking smartly to the edge of the platform.

Harry Hopkins, a tall, gangling, gaunt-faced man with an easy smile, emerged first from the specially commissioned Pullman carriage, followed by the astrakhan-collared figure of Churchill's Parliamentary Private Secretary, Brendan Bracken. The American held out a hand to greet firstly Herschel Johnson, then his old friend. 'Mike, good to see you at last!'

'Harry – it's great to have you here!' The two men gripped each other by the shoulders, their delight at meeting again obvious to the others present.

Brendan Bracken, his features almost obscured by his black fedora and turned-up coat collar, hovered in the background. He had been sent by Churchill, on behalf of the British Government, to meet Hopkins's plane at Poole, on the south coast of England, on its arrival from Lisbon, and to accompany him on the last leg of the journey to London. He hung back diplomatically as the three Americans greeted one another, only to be immediately taken aside by the white-gloved Station Master, as the sound of exploding incendiaries became audible over the wail of the siren. 'Thank God, you've made it, sir. We've just been informed the Jerries have blown up the lines between here and Clapham Junction. You must have missed the bombs by seconds.'

'A baptism of fire!' Harry Hopkins overheard the remark and attempted a rueful grin in Mike's direction. 'I must admit I never expected such a show of fireworks quite so soon, although you must be pretty used to this kind of thing by now.'

'If you ever get used to it,' Mike replied. 'Wailing Winnie, as they call it round here, can still send a shiver up the best of spines.' He wanted to say something reassuring to his old friend, but the incessant wailing of the siren, and the muffled bangs in the distance, made a mockery of any platitudes he could have thought up. His friend looked older, much older, since he had last seen him, and tired. 'You look all in, Harry. It's been one helluva journey, I bet.'

'You could say that,' Harry replied truthfully, as the party moved towards the cars waiting at the station entrance. 'Fully five days it takes these days to get here from Washington, you know. There's no way round it but to go via Lisbon. I tell you, boy, I'm pooped!'

'How did you get to Lisbon?' Herschel Johnson asked, as he slid into the front seat of the limousine, next to the driver.

'Pan Am Clipper, and, if that wasn't bad enough, then a BOAC Clipper to Poole – and don't ask me how I enjoyed the journey!' Harry snapped.

Herschel looked a trifle hurt, but Mike smiled quietly to himself as he got into the back of the car with his old friend. This was the Harry of old, all right. He hated air travel so much he had once refused a Presidential invitation to make an inspection flight over the Boulder Dam, back home in the States, having no compunction about admitting to all and sundry, 'Goddam it, I'm scared!' A one-time social worker from Iowa, Harry was never one for beating about the bush. They played it straight in the Mid-West, and Mike liked that.

As the official car made its way through the bomb-scarred streets towards Claridge's Hotel in Brook Street, where a room had been booked for the visitor, incendiaries were raining down in their hundreds. Thankfully, however, mainly in the area they had just left, around Waterloo Station. 'Do you reckon they knew I was on my way and have laid on this little show in my honour?' Harry grinned nervously at Mike, only half-joking.

'If they didn't it's one hell of a coincidence!'

Although Harry was invited to dinner at 10 Downing Street by the Prime Minister that evening, he felt too tired and travel-sick to contemplate it. Instead he sent his apologies and settled for a quiet drink and a bite to eat in his hotel room with Herschel Johnson and Mike. As they spoke, they could hear the anti-aircraft batteries blazing away in nearby Hyde Park. It was as if the raid had been specially commissioned to demonstrate to the new arrival just what they had to put up with on an almost daily basis. Both Mike and Herschel Johnson were of the opinion that Americans back home still did not appreciate the seriousness of Britain's plight and the urgency of her need for immediate aid. Maybe this little demonstration tonight might just go some way to impressing at least one influential member of the Roosevelt Administration.

'We're relying on you, Harry. You've got to lay it on the line to the President,' Mike said, as he accepted a refill of his vodka glass. 'Just how exactly do you see your role over here?'

Hopkins thought for a moment, then grinned wryly, 'I suppose you could say that I've come here to try to find a way to be a catalytic agent between two prima donnas. With two egos such as those of FDR and Churchill, there's bound to be a clash. I see it as part of my job to smooth things over.' He paused to light a cigarette, then continued, 'I had an interesting chat with Jean Monnet before I left and his advice was not to waste time with the Minister of This or That in the British Cabinet, but to concentrate on the old man himself. He reckons Churchill *is* the British Cabinet. Would you guys go along with that?'

They did, and Harry nodded thoughtfully, grateful to have his own suspicions reinforced by those on the ground. 'I guess, most of all, I want to try to get some sort of understanding of Churchill and of the men he sees after midnight.'

Mike knew just what he meant. His mind went back to what Lara had told him of those legendary Cabinet meetings that went on into the wee small hours of the morning. They could do with her here right now. 'Just how do you see the war situation yourself at the moment?' he asked, as he took a sip of his drink. 'You do accept that Hitler intends to have a go at Britain, I take it?'

Hopkins nodded as he drew on his cigarette. 'Sure I do. But I don't believe he'll succeed with any invasion plans, if that's what you mean. As we see the situation to date, we reckon that Turkey will fight if the Germans move into Bulgaria, so Hitler is more likely to make his next move through Italy to attack the Greeks.'

Harry's assessment wasn't too far removed from Mike's own

reading of the situation. 'And Russia – what do you reckon's going to happen there?'

'Russia's terrified of a German invasion. Any fool can see that. She'll keep well out of it if she can.'

There was a difference of opinion on that point, and they went on to discuss the subject in greater detail, until Harry's white, drained face told them he was in no fit state to sit up half the night chewing the fat. The real talk could wait till morning.

As they shook hands at the door of his room, Harry held out a restraining arm as Mike turned to go. 'I'm seeing the Prime Minister tomorrow morning, Mike. I'd like you there, if that's possible.'

Mike could not disguise his surprise. 'At 10 Downing Street? You sure?'

'Sure I'm sure. Bracken is almost certain to be there, and probably some others. I don't take too kindly to feeling outnumbered.'

'I know what you mean. I've been feeling like that ever since I got here ... ' He gave his friend a reassuring slap on the shoulder. 'Don't worry, I'll be over first thing after breakfast.'

He slept little that night, thinking of the day to come, and the days that had just gone. Harry's arrival was the best thing that could have happened to him. It helped take his mind off what was happening to his personal life, which seemed to be in a real shambles at the moment. It wasn't Joanne's surprise divorce moves that bothered him. To be honest, it was a relief to have the sham of their marriage acknowledged at last. No, it was the fact that, for the first time in his life, he had admitted that he cared deeply about another human being – cared deeply enough to put her happiness before his own.

The feelings he had for Lara would never be satisfied by the occasional, furtive one-night stand behind her husband's back: that would be demeaning, for both of them. If their relationship were to continue, he knew he could be satisfied with nothing less than being the number one man in her life. And to be that he would have to be willing to stab Ken Cameron in the back. And what if he did succeed in swallowing his scruples and persuading her to ditch Ken – what then? What if the Scotsman were to be shot down and killed just after she had left him? Some start to a relationship that would be ... No, in going back to the States, he was doing the only honourable thing. An honourable man, that's what he was. He grinned mirthlessly in the dark of his bedroom at the thought. Who would have believed it?

Next morning, Harry Hopkins was already pacing the hotel lobby when Mike arrived. They talked very little on the way from Claridge's, down through Berkeley Square and Trafalgar Square to

Downing Street. It was the first time Mike had actually seen the Prime Minister's residence at such close quarters, and he was surprised at how shabby it looked. The Treasury next door had received some bomb damage, and he thought to himself that the whole place looked as war-weary as most of its inhabitants undoubtedly felt.

They were met at the door by Brendan Bracken, who greeted them politely, then led them into a small dining-room in the basement of the building and poured them both a sherry while they waited for the Prime Minister himself to appear.

Churchill arrived within a few minutes – a small, rotund figure, with a red, cherubic face. He was dressed not in the familiar siren suit, but in a short black coat and striped trousers. His hearty welcome to them both appeared genuine, and he insisted on showing them, with obvious pride, the latest photograph of his daughter-in-law and grandchild, before getting down to business. It was a human touch that appealed to Harry, in particular, as a family man himself.

Lunch was plain but wholesome: soup, cold meat served with a green salad, washed down with a light wine, cheese and coffee, with port to follow. Churchill took snuff from a small silver box and offered his guests a pinch, but both politely declined. By the time the cigar and cigarette stage was reached, Mike found himself warming to the old man, and felt sure his friend shared his opinion, despite earlier misgivings. Tentative plans were made for a supposedly accidental meeting between the Prime Minister and President Roosevelt in April, probably aboard a cruiser off the West Indies. Then Harry, believing honesty to be the best policy, admitted that a face-to-face meeting could do nothing but good. 'You see, Prime Minister, there's a definite feeling in some quarters that you simply don't like America, Americans, or our President.'

Mike shifted uncomfortably in his easy-chair as Churchill's naturally pink face turned a bright puce and he launched into a personal attack on Joe Kennedy, the former Ambassador, who he claimed was personally responsible for that misconception, which he denied vigorously. While Mike and Harry sat mute beneath the explosion, the Prime Minister insisted on sending for a Secretary to produce a copy of the telegram he had sent to the President expressing delight at his re-election. 'I couldn't have been more enthusiastic than that now, could I?' he asked rhetorically, waving the piece of paper in their faces. They were forced to agree.

Only when the conversation turned once again to the war effort did he calm down. 'I don't believe the Nazis will invade, you know,' he declared, puffing thoughtfully on his cigar. 'But if they do and succeed in gaining a toe-hold on the British mainland, we shall drive them out – have no fear of that. Besides our excellent coastal defences, we have twenty-five divisions trained in offensive warfare. They will drive Hitler's hoards into the sea, from whence they came – or blow them out of the air once again, as we did last summer.'

'The *Luftwaffe* still have it over you to a ratio of two and a half to one, though, you can't deny that,' Harry put in.

'Not for much longer,' Churchill growled. 'That will soon be reduced to one and a half to one. We can hold our own in the air, don't you worry about that.'

When the conversation turned to shipping, they were taken upstairs to the Cabinet Room where, on seeing their pale, pinched faces, the Prime Minister assured them there was a better fire. To their scarcely disguised relief there was, and there were also large maps pinned to the walls showing the convoys that were coming through Glasgow and Liverpool, and indicating the routes the German bombers were taking from France to Norway to intercept the British ships.

The talk then turned to the countries, such as France, that Hitler was now in command of, and Churchill was adamant that they should impress upon the President the foolhardiness of supplying those countries with food. 'I know I'll be accused of being an ogre for denying French children vitamins,' he said gruffly, stabbing his cigar in Harry's direction, 'but, as I see it, one of Hitler's greatest weaknesses must be that he controls territory inhabited by a dejected and despairing people.' The others fell silent at that remark, and he quickly followed it with a plea that they would not reveal his thoughts on that matter to the Press at the arranged Press conference that afternoon.

Two Press conferences were given, one for the British journalists, one for the American, and, while Harry was busy fending off their more awkward questions, Mike took the opportunity to slip back to Grosvenor Square and have a quiet word with his superior, General Lee.

Raymond Lee was in conference with Professor Hall, of the Ministry of Economic Affairs, when he arrived. The latter had just brought him a ten-page report the Americans had commissioned on how the United States could help in putting a stranglehold on Germany.

While Mike waited for his chief, he passed the time talking to Clegg, an FBI man who was over in London discussing security with Colonel Stewart Menzies, the head of the British Secret Intelligence

Services. As they chatted, Mike couldn't help feeling a twinge of regret that very soon he would be out of it all – out of the front line and back behind a desk in Washington. In fact, he was relieved when Ray Lee called him in; otherwise he was in imminent danger of having second thoughts on the matter.

General Lee was delighted with his junior officer's decision to accompany him on the trip back to Washington. In fact, everything seemed to be going his way today. He had just got back from a personal visit to the fashion house of Molyneux, where he had found just the thing to take back to his wife in the States. He had settled for a suit-length of brownish tweed, along with the patterns for having it made up, as there was no time for it to be done before they left England. 'They had some real nice stuff down there, Mike,' he said helpfully. 'I'd recommend a visit, if you haven't already got something to take back to Joanne.'

Mike gave a wry smile. 'Don't worry, sir, I've already got my wife all she wants from me.'

'Oh really?' His Chief's interest quickened. He was always on the lookout for something original to take back to Jeanette. 'Anything exciting that I should know about?'

Mike shook his head and picked up that day's edition of the *Manchester Guardian*, as if to close the subject, but the General would not be distracted. 'Come on then, out with it? What *are* you giving your good lady?'

'A divorce, General. I'm giving Joanne a divorce.'

Chapter Twenty-four

To Mike's surprise, the following day, Saturday, found him on his way to the small village of Ditchley, just north of Oxford. Harry Hopkins had asked Mike to accompany him as a weekend guest of the Prime Minister, Winston Churchill. Their destination was Ditchley Park, the beautiful seventeenth-century stately home of Ronald Tree, Parliamentary Secretary to Brendan Bracken. Normally at weekends Churchill went to Chequers, the official country residence of the British Prime Minister, but Security would not allow its use that weekend because the full moon made it too tempting a target for the *Luftwaffe*'s bombers.

As the car swept up the wide, tree-shaded drive, it was difficult to remember that Britain was a country at war. It seemed to the two Americans that by the look of the house and gardens nothing had changed in the 300 years of its existence. 'Gives you a sense of your own mortality, doesn't it?' Harry murmured, gazing out of the Packard window at the elegant, ivy-covered walls. 'And it'll still be standing in another three centuries, if those goddam Krauts don't take a fancy to it.'

Neither of them could remember ever having been in such impressive surroundings, aside from public buildings or museums. The gilt furniture, exquisite drapes and furnishings and magnificent oil paintings reminded both men of a Hollywood film set; the only difference being that this was for real. They were even more impressed to learn that the present house had, in fact, been built on the site of an earlier building, the family home of the Lee family, ancestors of the illustrious Confederate General of the American Civil War, Robert E. Lee.

Their interest continued as they were shown round on a preliminary guided tour of the building. They paused longest in the three well-appointed rooms on the ground floor that had been given over for the use of the Prime Minister and his staff.

Each room was fully equipped with every possible device to allow Churchill to keep abreast of war operations, and it appeared to be staffed around the clock. When they arrived, word was just coming in of the appearance of German Stuka dive bombers in the Mediterranean. British ships had been attacked off Pantelleria, first by two Italian torpedo boats, then by forty German Stukas and Ju 88 bombers. The air was electric as detail by detail the picture was built up. And Mike heard Harry give a low whistle as news came in that the British carrier *Illustrious* was reported to have received six direct hits. Other ships had also been damaged. Severe losses were reported. 'Looks like it's the first time the German X Fliegerkorps has been seen in action,' one of the Army personnel charting the action commented, quite unemotionally, to the two American visitors.

'That makes it a whole new ball-game, I presume?' Harry asked.

'You could say that. It certainly means that those of our convoys that have been covering Malta and Greece are in for a hell of a time in the future, if today is anything to go by.'

Harry grimaced. It was his first experience of the reality of warfare, and he was immediately struck by the matter-of-fact way in which the news was being received by the people around them. There was little outward sign of depression or dismay. Each man and woman simply got on with his job to the best of his or her ability. Typically British, he presumed.

'They can't afford to let it affect them,' Mike commented, as if reading his mind. 'If they did they'd be in a permanent state of trauma.'

Harry grinned. 'A bit like me since I arrived here.'

It became immediately apparent that most of the real business would be done in the evening. They had been well advised that the Prime Minister was at his most eloquent after dinner; the afternoon, they were informed, was their own to do with as they wished.

Harry decided to stay indoors: it was cold and he had letters to write. Mike, however, could not settle. Too much had happened over the past few days. He was on edge. 'I think I'll take a run over to Oxford,' he said, as they left the dining-room after lunch. The Embassy Packard looked just too tempting sitting out there in the driveway. And, if he was leaving England for good in a few days, he might as well see as much of it as he could. 'I'll take a run over to Oxford. I've always wanted to see the old place.'

'Who knows, those dreaming spires might just rub off on you. You might come back a wiser man!' Harry gave him a playful punch on the arm, as he left Mike and made his own way upstairs to his room.

A pale sun shone out of a grey, snow-filled sky as Mike drove the narrow country lanes between the small village of Ditchley and the ancient university town. It gave the countryside a fairy-tale appearance that seemed totally at odds with the realities of war.

Small children pulled sledges along the narrow edges of the tall, white-coated hedgerows, and mothers gathered armfuls of frozen washing from the lines that criss-crossed the snow-covered, postage-stamp lawns of the tiny, thatched cottages that bordered the roadside. Shirts and other items of clothing stuck out like frozen carcases in the women's arms as they carried them back indoors to be thawed out and dried.

His mind went back to the freezing winters in New York, when his own mother would bring in just such frozen items of laundry. Nothing changed, not really. Despite having their world turned upside down by politicians, young mothers still had to carry on as best they could. Life still had to be lived, although the world as you knew it was disintegrating around you.

A small child in a dark-blue coat and leggings waved at him from a garden gate and he returned the greeting with a tuneful honk of the horn. He would be leaving all this behind in a few days; leaving them all to their fate. He hoped passionately that Roosevelt and the Lend-Leasers would win the battle for the hearts and minds of Congress back home, and that America would send the aid that was so badly needed if the Nazi menace was to be defeated – if that small kid was to grow up in peace.

Compared to London, there seemed to be very little traffic in Oxford itself, and he marvelled at the courage, or foolhardiness, of the long-scarved students who precariously pedalled bicycles along the frozen roads. He parked the car near Magdalen Bridge and got out to stretch his legs. The air felt crisp and the cold stung his lungs as he stood on the edge of the pavement and took a deep breath. He glanced at his watch. It was just after two-thirty. He would take a leisurely walk around the Colleges, to see if those dreaming spires he had read so much about back home really did live up to their reputation.

He passed the University Botanic Garden, turning left into Rose Lane, and followed the path through Christ Church Meadow. The few male students he passed all looked very young, then he remembered that most of their older colleagues would already be out there fighting – doing a man's job before they had had time to be boys. It was at times like this that the guilt became almost too much. There they were, kids, fighting the Nazi menace, fighting for a world free from racial persecution and bigotry, while he was doing damn all. Oh, all right, he was over here doing his bit as far as his own country was concerned, but he was leaving in a few days; no doubt to take a cushy number of a desk job back at the Pentagon. He lit another cigarette and tried to blot the knowledge out of his head as he walked on through Christ Church College and out of Tom Gate.

A bitter wind, promising further snow, hit him as he turned right along St Aldate's. God, he could do with something to warm him up! There must be somewhere around here where he could get a cup of coffee, or even a cup of tea, if rationing wouldn't stretch as far as the little brown bean.

A few minutes walk brought him to a tiny tea-shop in Beaumont Street, with pink gingham drapes at the windows and a sign saying, The Tea-caddy.

He pushed open the door and an old-fashioned brass bell clanged above his head. The place was even tinier inside than it looked from the outside and appeared to be jam-packed with customers. Most of the heads turned, and the buzz of conversation halted momentarily as he stood in the half-open doorway. The place was obviously full, and he was on the point of turning to try his luck elsewhere when a female voice from somewhere in the crowd called out, 'Colonel! Colonel Adams!'

Mike stopped in his tracks and scanned the faces, the majority of whom seemed to be either very young students, or very old ladies.

'Colonel ... Colonel Adams! Over here!'

A hand was waving at him from the far side of the tea-room, next to the fireplace. Its owner was standing up and smiling at him – a pretty, dark-haired woman in a grey, turban-style hat and a beaver-lamb coat. At first he didn't recognize her, although there was no doubt she knew exactly who he was. Then realization dawned. 'Mrs Mallory ... Well, I'll be darned!'

Beth continued to smile, and pulled out the empty chair next to her as Mike squeezed his way between the tables. Lara's old boss was the last person she expected to see in her favourite Oxford tea-shop. 'Colonel Adams – what a lovely surprise!'

'Mike – please,' he insisted as they shook hands.

'What on earth are you doing here in Oxford? Or is it something terribly secret that I'm not allowed to ask about?'

He smiled as he removed his gloves and laid them on the table beside him. 'I'm a guest of the Prime Minister at Ditchley ... How's that for name-dropping?'

'I'm impressed.' Her green eyes sparkled for the first time in days as she smiled across at him. A waitress came to take the order and Mike looked a trifle perplexed. 'I'd recommend the toasted crumpet,' Beth advised. 'And I'd forgo the coffee, if I were you – it's ersatz. But the tea is very good, and quite genuine. I'm having the Assam.'

'Right, that settles it. We'll have another pot of Assam tea for two and two more hot toasted crumpets, please.'

The order arrived within a few minutes, which they spent talking about the weather. Then, as Mike took his first sip of the steaming liquid, his brows furrowed as he looked across at Beth. 'I feel I should say straight off how sorry I was to hear about Atholl Square.'

Beth looked down at her plate, her fingers toying with the bone handle of the tea-knife. 'Thank you, Mike.' She could feel that awful choking sensation in her throat and prayed she wouldn't break down in front of him. This should be a cheerful meeting of acquaintances, not a morbid reliving of the horrors of that terrible night. 'I – I should thank you for being so kind to Lara,' she said. 'I'm very grateful for the way you've looked after her. Jan – Count Jarosinski – told me how helpful you've been.'

'It was nothing.' He spoke more brusquely than he intended. He had no wish to bring the conversation round to her daughter.

Beth studied him closely as he reached inside his jacket and extracted his cigarette packet. He was obviously nervous about something, for his crumpet was still only half-eaten. She had touched on a raw nerve mentioning Lara, she could see that. She shook her head at the offer of one. 'But you go right ahead.'

She watched as he lit up and inhaled deeply. He was deliberately avoiding her eyes. A tenseness had come over him. Her mind went back to the conversation she had had with Lara over her resignation as his secretary. It was not a one-sided thing, she was certain of it. The feelings Lara had been fighting against had been entirely mutual. She would stake her life on it. 'You – you're very fond of my daughter, aren't you, Mike?'

His facial muscles froze. 'What makes you say that?'

'Oh, call it a woman's intuition if you like.'

He avoided her eyes, his gaze dwelling on the flaking plaster in the corner of the ceiling next to the window. He took another long drag on the cigarette and let the smoke out slowly through his nostrils. It seemed pointless to lie. Hell, he was leaving in a few days, wasn't he? 'I'll square with you, Mrs Mallory. I owe you the truth. I'm in love with Lara ...'

He paused, as if unsure exactly how much to say, and her heart stood still. It was one thing imagining that to be the truth, quite another to have it confirmed so bluntly. She swallowed loudly as she looked across at him. 'And … ?'

'And that's why I'm going back to the States.'

'You mean you're leaving England?'

'Next week.'

An enormous sense of relief flooded over her, mixed with an almost heartbreaking understanding of what he must now be going through. 'That couldn't have been an easy decision to make.'

'It was the only one possible in the circumstances.' He gave a short laugh. 'That makes me sound unbearably noble. It's not really the case. I resent it like hell, having to leave – both from a personal and a professional point of view.'

'I can understand that.'

'I'm glad you're not telling me I'll get over it!' He grinned across at her, making a valiant attempt to lighten the conversation.

'I'd never do that, Mike, never. You're not the only one to have been in this situation, you know. Some of us understand exactly how you feel.'

He looked at her closely. She had gone quite flushed about the face as she spoke. 'You sound like you speak from experience.'

Beth's heart was beating faster. She hadn't meant the conversation to take this sort of turning but, now it had, a curious excitement began to build up in her. Apart from Lara, she had never in all these years mentioned her love for Jan to a living soul, but here was a man who was feeling exactly as she had felt then; a man who loved her daughter as she had loved Lara's father; a man who was leaving this land for good very soon. 'Yes, I'm speaking from experience,' she said softly. 'You never get over it – never. Not if it's real.'

His mind went back to one of his last conversations with Lara. He knew exactly whom she was referring to, and a peculiar gut-feeling within him told him confession could sometimes be good for the soul. He decided to take the risk. 'Jan Jarosinski is a fine man,' he said quietly. 'They don't come any finer.'

The blood drained from Beth's face and her mouth dropped open as she stared across the table at him. Panic flooded through her. Was it so obvious? Did the whole world know?

His hand reached across and took hers. 'Don't worry … please don't worry. Keeping confidences is my job, remember.'

It was useless lying. He knew. He actually knew. 'It was all a long time ago,' she whispered. 'Twenty-one years, to be exact.'

A slight furrow of Mike's left eyebrow told her he was nobody's fool. He must have seen Lara's age from her Security Clearance file.

He was putting two and two together and coming up with the right answer.

'I know what you're thinking, and you're right,' she said, so softly that her words were barely audible above the tea-shop babble. 'You're right ... Jan is Lara's father.'

Mike let out a long, low whistle, before taking another drag of his cigarette. 'Does she know?'

Beth shook her head.

'Do you ever intend to tell her?'

'I don't know, Mike. I really don't know ... The more time passes, the harder it becomes.'

'It's none of my business, and you can tell me to keep my nose out of it if you like, but I'd have thought she would want to know – that it was her right to know. What if something were to happen to him? What if he were to be killed and she found out later, after the war is over, that he was her father – what then?'

Beth drew in her breath and stared down into her tea cup, feeling she had just been dealt a physical blow. He was right, of course. She had no right to keep the truth from Lara. But how did she go about it at this late stage? She tried to make light of what he said. 'Oh, I really don't think there's too much danger of anything untoward happening to Jan, do you? After all, he's well over forty-one, so he's not exactly in the front line any more.'

Mike's jaw tensed as he flicked a column of ash from his cigarette into the ashtray. She had no idea. She really had no idea about the danger that lay ahead of him if he went back to Poland. But then she had not seen the report that had landed on his desk yesterday. She had no idea he was to be part of the new SOE operation in Poland. The Special Operations Executive was still so highly secret an organization that its very name was classified. He had to be careful what he said. 'Has Jan told you anything of his plans for the immediate future?' he asked tentatively.

'He's told me he's going up to Scotland for a few days, then he's returning to Poland immediately he gets back.'

'Do you have any plans for seeing him again?'

'I rather think that's my affair, don't you?'

'I'm sorry, Mrs Mallory, I don't mean to pry. I was just going to suggest that, if you don't, then I'd make some if I were you. I'd arrange to see him double-quick before he heads back for Warsaw.'

Beth froze in her seat as she looked across at him. His eyes were grave as they looked back into hers. 'You're trying to tell me he's going out there to die, aren't you?' she whispered.

'They're your words, not mine.'

'But that's what you believe?'

He attempted a reassuring smile as he took a sip of the tea. 'I can't foretell the future, ma'am. I can only say what I'd do if I were in your place ... If you do manage to meet again, give him my best. I doubt if I'll ever have the pleasure of meeting him again – or any of you, come to that.'

She nodded, her heart too full to speak. He was leaving because he was in love with Lara, just as she had run away from her love for Jan. Nothing much changed. People – good, decent people – still fell in love with the right person at the wrong time and would go on doing so.

She glanced down at her half-eaten crumpet. She couldn't touch another crumb. If she remained here any longer it would be impossible to retain her composure. His advice about Jan still rang in her head. He was speaking from the heart, she had no doubt about that. But what he didn't know was that she had just spent a whole two months' clothing coupons on a new mock-silk nightgown and robe that were now lying, wrapped in brown paper, in one of the shopping bags at her feet. They would not see the light of day again until she unpacked them in Dundee.

Carefully she dabbed her mouth with her napkin, then pushed back her chair and offered her hand. 'It's not only the Count who is a fine man, Colonel – you're not so bad yourself. I really must go now, but I want you to know that. It's been a privilege to know you. May God go with you wherever you go.'

They stood up and shook hands across the table. 'Can I give you a lift anywhere?' he asked, sorry that she had to leave so soon, and concerned that he had spoken out of turn. But there was no sign in her face of offence having been taken, only a deep sadness in her eyes as she shook her head.

'No, thank you all the same. I can manage.'

He watched as she gathered up her shopping bags and, with a final small smile and wave in his direction, squeezed her way through the crowded tea-shop to the door. He would probably not set eyes on her again, nor on her daughter ...

Her daughter ... 'Lara ...' He spoke the name aloud, and was aware of a hot, stinging sensation in his eyes as he took another drag on the cigarette and drained the last of the tea in his cup.

He returned to Ditchley in time to bathe and dress for dinner which, thanks to the brilliantly chauvinistic and controversial rhetoric from the Prime Minister, proved to be a welcome distraction from his own sombre thoughts.

It was the first time Mike had listened to him at his best as, once the ladies had retired from the table and left the men to their cigars and port, Churchill expanded on Britain's war aims. Seeing Harry dispense with his own cigarettes and accept one of the best Havanas on offer, Mike did likewise, finding the smooth rounded taste a welcome relief from the pack of Camels he usually got through on such an occasion with their own Head of State back in Washington.

Harry, for his part, seemed to be at his most relaxed of the visit as he assured the Prime Minister that, 'The President is determined that we shall win this war together. Make no mistake about it. He has sent me here to tell you that at all costs and by all means he will carry you through, no matter what happens to him – there is nothing that he will not do so far as he has the human power. My job in coming here, as you know, is to convey as accurate an impression of your war aims as possible back to Washington. I reckon I've had as good an account over the past hour or so as I'm liable to need. Unless you've anything further to add ...'

Churchill sat slouched in his chair at the head of the table and listened, and for a moment Mike thought that perhaps he had not quite heard what Harry had just said. Then the sparse white brows above the red-rimmed eyes glowered, as he stabbed his cigar in Harry's direction and shook his head. 'We seek no treasure, Mr Hopkins, we seek no territorial gains, we seek only the right of man to be free; we seek his right to worship his God, to lead his life in his own way, secure from persecution. As a humble labourer returns from his work when the day is done, and sees the smoke curling upwards from his cottage home in the serene evening sky, we wish him to know that no rat-a-tat-tat,' he rapped on the table for effect, 'of the secret police upon his door will disturb his leisure or interrupt his rest. We seek government with the consent of the people, man's freedom to say what he will, and when he thinks himself injured, to find himself equal in the eyes of the law. But war aims other than these we have none.'

At this point, Churchill paused, puffed in quiet satisfaction and looked directly at Harry Hopkins. 'Well, sir, what in your opinion will the President say to all this?'

Mike glanced across at Harry, who thought for a moment, then in his inimitable, sardonic manner replied: 'Well, Mr Prime Minister, I don't think the President will give a damn for all that.'

He paused again, and threw a glance at Mike, before looking

straight back at Churchill, 'You see, we're only interested in seeing that that goddamn sonofabitch, Hitler, gets licked.'

Mike suppressed a quiet smile. He couldn't have put it more succinctly himself.

Chapter Twenty-five

Moira and Sandy Cameron, Ken's parents, were only too delighted to receive Beth's telegram telling them she was arriving for a few days on Tuesday 14 January. They had warmed to Lara's mother immediately at their first meeting, the day before the wedding, and had been perfectly genuine in their open invitation to drop in and make their home her own any time she felt like escaping the terrors of war-torn London. The fact that Beth had herself been a victim of the bombing made them even more determined to make sure she felt at home.

Sandy came to the station to meet her train and carry her case the few hundred yards to their Victorian, grey-stone semi-detached house at the beginning of Long Lane in Broughty Ferry, Dundee's picturesque fishing village and most northerly suburb.

'My, but you're looking well, considering what you've been through!' he beamed at her, his pale blue eyes crinkling at the corners as he shook her warmly by the hand. He was a 'nice' looking, as opposed to 'good-looking' man in his early fifties. He smelt, not unpleasantly, of pipe-tobacco, as he hugged her warmly before carrying her case up the station steps.

The smell of the sea assailed her nostrils as they emerged from the stone staircase on to the pavement. A glance towards the bottom of the street told her they were only yards from the water, and a fresh breeze sent tendrils of brown hair flying across her eyes as she endeavoured to keep up with her host as they hurried through the cobbled streets.

Now she was here, it was everything she had hoped it would be from the photographs and postcards Ken had shown her, and more. Low, whitewashed fishermen's cottages clustered round the small harbour and, despite the cold weather, a group of old men, too advanced in years for war service or seafaring, clad in the traditional dark-blue jerseys and fustian trousers, stood in a small knot at the end of the street, solving the problems of the world, while their wives and daughters-in-law sat just inside the open doors, baiting the lines for the next day's catch. Without exception, all nodded and passed the time of day as the pair hurried by, their heads bent into the gusting wind.

Piles of empty creels lay along the quayside and, seeing her eye them curiously, Sandy commented, 'We'll maybe see if we can get hold of a lobster or two for you to take back to London, Beth. You'd like that fine, I've no doubt.'

She smiled broadly in return as they paused at the foot of King Street and she gazed back at the castle perched on its rock above the harbour. A ray of watery sunshine was striking the ruined battle-ments and sending golden spangles across the quieter waters of the harbour, where a dozen or so boats lay at anchor. The day's catch had already been unloaded and was on its way to the fish-markets down South. 'It's another world up here,' she murmured, half to herself, and Sandy smiled quietly as he heaved her case up from the pavement and they continued on their way. It may not have the glamour of London, but he wouldn't swap old Broughty for all the capital cities of this world – no, not even for Edinburgh itself.

'I'm no quite sure what's on the menu for tea tonight, but Moira's been baking all morning, rationing or no rationing,' he informed her proudly as, a few minutes later, they walked up the flag-stoned path to the Camerons' front door. 'Having you here has been the excuse for almost as much fussing as when Ken comes home; though, heaven knows, that's pretty seldom these days.'

The door opened immediately they appeared at the garden gate. Moira Cameron, dressed in her Sunday-best Fair-Isle twin-set and pearls, had been watching for them at the sitting-room window and had rushed to open the door as soon as the grey head of her husband showed above the tall hedge. She came forward to give Beth a warm hug. 'Beth, it's lovely to see you again – and wonderful that it's us you should think of at a time like this! Come away in, hen. There's a rare fire going in the back kitchen and the kettle's on.' The fact that Beth was a former Countess cut little ice in the Cameron household. The Presbyterian Church believed as strongly as the American Declara-tion of Independence that all men – and women – were created equal, and Moira was every bit as devout as her husband.

The whole house exuded a feeling of warmth and comfort. The coals in the shiny black kitchen range were blazing merrily as Sandy took Beth's case upstairs and she accepted Moira's invitation to shed her hat and coat and take the chair nearest the fire. A pair of large, white pottery 'Wally Dogs' gazed balefully down at her from either end of the mantelpiece and a mahogany dresser stood against the far wall: the melodic sounds of Joe Loss and his orchestra came from the wireless on its highly polished top.

Moira Cameron went over and switched it off as soon as Beth sat down. 'We'll no hear ourselves speak for that thing,' she said. 'Sandy and I have it on most of the time, I'm afraid. We can't afford to miss any of the news broadcasts.'

Beth knew exactly what she meant. It must be nerve-racking having your only son constantly in the front line, and every snippet of information about RAF manoeuvres must be eagerly pounced upon. A comfortable silence fell when the music ceased, and Beth settled back in the chair. She felt at home here in the Camerons' modest home. It was a place where she could gather her chaotic thoughts and come to terms with what was happening to her and those she loved. It seemed a million miles removed from London and the sharp end of the war – a haven of relative peace in the present battlefield of her life … Yes, it would have been a good idea to come here for a few days even if Jan hadn't been in the area.

She watched as Moira set about piling newly-baked shortcake biscuits on to a plate, then proceeded to pour three cups of tea, leaving an empty cup sitting in its saucer by the teapot. Looking at her, it was easy to see where Ken got his looks from, for his mother's tightly-permed hair was a shining corn colour, despite her forty-five years, and her clear skin still bore the traces of last summer's freckles across the bridge of her nose.

'It was a dreadful thing to hear in your telegram of your house being bombed,' Moira said in an awed voice, as she handed across Beth's cup and saucer. 'We can't really imagine how awful it must be for you all, living down there amongst all that bombing. It only takes one to land in or around Dundee and it's the main news story in the *Courier* the next day! God only knows how we'd cope with air-raids every single night. It doesn't bear thinking about, so it doesn't!' She shook her head, aghast at the very thought, as she took the first sip of her own tea. 'By the way, Beth, you never said if you've managed to get somewhere else fixed up for yourself and Lara.'

Beth took a sip of her own tea and nodded thankfully. 'Oh yes, Lara's old boss at the American Embassy has arranged for us to move into one of their flats for the time being. Lara's already moved in, in fact. We've been very lucky really – spare accommodation is like gold in London at the moment, with so many buildings reduced to rubble.'

'We have to thank the Good Lord when it's only the buildings that are damaged,' Sandy said, coming in at the tail end of the sentence. 'It could easily have been yourself or Lara, heaven forbid … By the way, does Kenneth know yet?'

'I – I presume Lara's written to him by now,' Beth said, reaching for a biscuit from the proffered plate. 'Poor boy, that's the last thing he needs to hear. News like that can only add to his worries.'

'Aye, if you ask me, those poor laddies in the fighter squadrons are having the worst of it,' Moira put in. 'If I'd known they were to be so badly off for equipment compared to the Germans, and that the casualty lists were to be so high, I'd never have let him go.'

'You'd have had the devil's own job to stop him,' Sandy eased himself into his favourite rocker at the opposite side of the fire to Beth, and reached for his tea. 'Why, I'd be up there with them myself if I'd been a wee bit younger!'

'A wee bit younger, is it? Just listen to the man! Why you're a quarter of a century late if you're a day, Sandy Cameron! Your flying days are well past, my lad. And a good thing too!' his wife laughed. 'But I feel right sorry for the young ones, all the same. They haven't had much of a start to married life. Your poor lassie can surely count on one hand the number of weeks she's spent with Kenneth since they were married last year. In fact, I was just saying the other day to Irene, his cousin Alan's fiancée, that if she has time for a honeymoon she can consider herself lucky. Not that she's got much hope of a wedding even, poor thing. Not till that General Rommel's lot's on the run from our lads in North Africa and they get some well-deserved leave.' She glanced at the clock on the dresser. The mention of her sister's boy had jogged her memory. 'Cissie's awful late, is she not, Sandy? She said she'd be over half an hour since. It's just as well I didn't pour her tea.'

'Do you want me to take a wee walk along the road and see what's happening? She's probably fallen asleep in front of the fire, peering over that knitting of hers. I keep telling her it's high time she got her eyes looked at – walk right past you in the street these days, she would.' He got up again with a sigh and reached for his tweed jacket hanging on the back of the door. 'I'll need this – it's perishing out there.'

When he had gone, Moira Cameron's brow furrowed. 'I suppose I shouldn't worry about her like I do, but she's not been herself of late, what with her arthritis and angina and the rest of it. We're trying to persuade her to get one of yon Tan Sad chairs, with the wheels, but she'll no hear of it. Says we're trying to make her into an invalid

216

before her time, when she's as hale and hearty as any of us. But she takes far too much upon herself – always organizing this and that for the Kirk funds. I know what's at the back of it, of course. It's to take her mind off Alan – that's her laddie – being away out there fighting in North Africa. Real depressed she gets about it at times. It's especially hard when you're a widow and have no man to share your worries with ... But you'll know all about that, Beth, having been twice widowed yourself, I mean.'

Beth gave a reluctant nod. 'I don't know what I'd do if Lara had been a boy and was now in the front line like your offspring. Life must be a constant worry about them.'

'Oh, aye, you can say that again! It's got to the stage that we never miss a news broadcast and I find myself scanning the papers every day for the latest RAF news – not that they tell you very much. Well, only what they want you to know ... But, listen here, this is depressing talk. Look what I've looked out for you to take back!' She got up, went to the dresser drawer, extracted a piece of paper and handed it to Beth. 'It's a recipe I tried the other day for an eggless, fatless walnut cake. It's maybe not quite as good as the real thing, but when you're hungry you'll have a hard time telling the difference. I know you've got a harder job getting fresh eggs in the city than we have up here, so it might just come in handy if you've folk coming, or the likes of that. Pop it in your handbag and take it back with you.'

Beth smiled her thanks and looked down at the neat, curling handwriting. 'Four cups of flour; one cup of chopped walnuts; one good cup of milk; one cup of sugar; four teaspoons of baking powder and one pinch of salt. Mix the flour, sugar and chopped walnuts together. Add the salt and baking powder, then the milk. Mixture should be slightly wetter than for an ordinary cake. Leave to rise for ten minutes. Bake in greased cake tin, in a slow oven, until risen and brown ... Sounds good. Thank you, Moira dear, I'll certainly try it.'

She had no sooner dropped it into the back pocket of her handbag, when the door burst open and Sandy reappeared. From the expression on his face it was obvious something was wrong.

Moira's hand flew to her mouth. 'What is it, Sandy, for God's sake? It's not Cissie, is it? Nothing's happened to her?' Since learning of her sister's angina last year she had lived in fear of it ending up in a heart attack.

He shook his head as he fought to catch his breath. 'No, it's not Cissie, Moira. But you better come. It's Alan. She's just received the government cable. He was killed last week, near Tobruk.'

'Dear God – no!' The colour drained from Moira Cameron's face.

Her heart went out to her older sister. Cissie had been like a mother to her when their own died just before Moira's tenth birthday. She would rather bear any pain herself than see Cissie suffer. Tears sprang to her eyes as she turned to Beth. 'I'm sorry, but I'll have to go to her.'

'I'll come with you.' Beth got out of her chair and laid her cup on the table and, grabbing her coat from the back of an empty chair, she followed the two of them out the back door and round the narrow shingle path that skirted the side of the house.

Cissie's house was three doors down and almost identical to her sister and brother-in-law's, except it was painted green to their brick-red. The front door was still ajar, as Sandy had left it, and she hurried after him and Moira through the narrow hall into the front room, where Cissie sat slumped in the chair nearest the fire. She held a buff-coloured cablegram in her hands which shook visibly as she stared vacantly ahead of her. She made no reaction to their entrance, but another great tear fell from her left eye and trickled down her cheek, as her younger sister flung herself down on the carpet at her feet and took her hands in hers.

'Cissie … Cissie …' Moira could say no more, only repeat her sister's name over and over as she squeezed her hands in hers.

Cissie's little Cairn terrier, His Lordship, lay resting his head on his mistress's tassled slipper and was making a little whimpering sound deep in his throat.

'He was only twenty-one … Just a laddie, Moira, just a laddie …'

'I know, Cissie. I know.'

Beth hung back, aware she was in danger of intruding on a very personal, private grief. Her eyes travelled round the neatly-furnished sitting-room, with its high-backed three-piece suite and the beautifully embroidered antimacassars; and the walnut display cabinet, containing a collection of Indian ivories that indicated Cissie's late husband Archie's lifetime spent in the service of the P & O merchant shipping line. A framed photograph of Alan, her only son, sat in pride of place on the mantelpiece. He was a good-looking young man, with fair hair and an open, friendly face. He reminded her of his cousin Ken. Just twenty-one he had been. What a waste. What a terrible, terrible waste.

They remained the best part of an hour with Cissie. Sandy made her a hot toddy with whisky and lemonade, insisting it would do her more good than all the cups of tea she could drink. He then left to go round and fetch Dr MacKenzie. He had a feeling his sister-in-law would need even more than a glass of toddy before today was finished.

A subdued Moira took Beth back to their own house and saw her settled into the spare bedroom upstairs, before going back next door to await the arrival of the doctor. She called it the spare room, but it had obviously been Ken's room, for most of his childhood relics still hung on the walls. The floral wallpaper was covered in framed pictures of early aircraft from the days of the Royal Flying Corps – the type of machines his father had flown, plus one or two vintage German ones – a black-and-white photograph of Halberstadt CLII hung alongside a watercolour of a Fokker DR 1 Triplane. A picture of Sandy Cameron himself, in front of the cockpit of a Sopwith Pup, taken at Farnborough during the Great War, had pride of place above the bed. Beth leaned forward for a better look ... Yes, Sandy Cameron had been a handsome young man in his day. And, looking at the flimsiness of the aircraft he flew, no doubt a very brave one too – just like his son.

As she wandered round the room, acquainting herself with her new surroundings, she could almost feel the presence of Ken at her side. She prayed inwardly that someone up there would keep him safe – that he wouldn't suffer the same dreadful fate as his cousin Alan.

She opened the door of the large Victorian wardrobe to hang up the few items of clothing in her case, and saw that the floor of it was packed with Ken's now redundant sports equipment and piles of well-thumbed books. Beth picked up one at random, *White Fang*, by Jack London, and opened it. On the first page was an ornamental sticker stating that the Grove Academy was awarding Kenneth Cameron, of Form IIIA, the first prize in Latin. Nineteen thirty-four the date said. Ken would have been fifteen. It seemed a lifetime ago.

She sat down on the edge of the bed and thought of her own life with Lara and Jack then. It had been so comfortable and secure she had thought it would go on forever. Never in her wildest dreams did she imagine that, within a few years, Jack would be dead, Lara married, and Jan back in her life – or that they would all be involved in this awful war.

She thought of Cissie sitting there alone in that little house a few doors away. What was left for her now? With her husband dead and her only child killed in some faraway desert – she might never even know his last resting place – how would she cope with the coming years? In her own part-time job as a voluntary ambulance driver, Beth had seen the effects of just such a tragedy. So many women felt that suicide was the only answer when all they had to live for was taken from them. 'Please don't let that happen to Cissie,' she whispered. 'Please, not to Cissie ...'

She had intended taking a bus into Dundee that afternoon and calling at Jan's hotel to let him know she had arrived, but the events of this morning had drained her of all the excitement she had felt on the journey up to Scotland. The world had impinged, had brought reality into the dream. And maybe that's all it was in the end – a dream. Could anyone really recapture their youth? For, if they were to be really honest with themselves, that was exactly what they were doing, meeting here like this. They were searching for the people they once were: a young man and woman from what they now called 'the Lost Generation' – the young people who had reached maturity in the tragic, turbulent years of the Great War ... The war to end all wars, the papers had called it. Her lips twisted into an ironic smile at the thought.

She got up and walked to the window and looked out across the roof-tops to the grey waters of the River Tay.

No matter what misgivings she might be having, she was here now and had to make the most of it ... What would she say when they met? How should she act? Should she be quite casual and let him make the running? Or should she simply forget about appearances, remembering only that he was the man she loved and very soon might never see again? Maybe the answer would be obvious when they were actually face to face. But right now she simply hadn't a clue.

Chapter Twenty-six

Jan Jarosinski's brow furrowed. Although his meetings with the Lord Provost and the other councillors in Dundee's city chambers had been amicable in the extreme, and they had expressed a sincere desire to launch a similar campaign of Polish fund-raising as their opposite numbers in Aberdeen, the Count's own mind had already moved on to other things. General Sikorski had given him one more assignment while here in Scotland. He was to make contact with the Duke of Linlathan, at his country home just outside the city, and try to persuade him to use his influence with Churchill to guarantee the safe release of the Polish Gold Reserve.

He lit a cigarette and paced the floor of his room on the third storey of the Queen's Hotel, overlooking the River Tay. It was going to be no easy task. The bulk of the Bank of Poland's gold reserve, about eighty tons in all, had been transported, soon after the outbreak of war, via Romania, Turkey and the Lebanon to France. On the Fall of France in June 1940, it was then removed from its hiding place in Angoulême to the port of Lorient and loaded on to the French ship *Victor Schoelcher*. Its original destination had been the French West Indies, but after Pétain's capitulation, the captain received orders to change course for Dakar in West Africa. As far as they knew, the gold had then been offloaded and moved inland to Fort Kayes. The whole operation had been master-minded by the British Government who, in effect, still held the key to the coffers. But the funds of the Polish Government in Exile in London were now at a low ebb, and release of some of the money would prove invaluable to the Polish cause. For a start, it was an essential prerequisite to the formation of Canadian and American Polish Army contingents – a scheme that Sikorski and his colleagues in London were keen to get off the ground.

'Linlathan's got Churchill's ear, Jan,' Sikorski had told him, just before his departure for Scotland. 'I feel that as one aristocrat to another, the Duke would be sympathetic to what you have to say. You will be the ideal person to press our cause for at least a partial release of the gold reserves.'

What could he do but agree? Inwardly he had cursed the idea, though. He was not at all convinced that anything he had to say would have the least influence on the Scottish Duke. And he was even less convinced that anything the Duke had to say would have the slightest influence on Churchill. But you had to clutch at straws these days, he appreciated that. What he was convinced of, however, was that time spent with the Duke would interfere with the precious hours he could spend with Beth, if she came. Now his business with the Lord Provost and the city fathers was finished, he had made an appointment to spend tomorrow with the Duke at his castle to the north-west of the city, then tomorrow night he was due to set off back to London. That only left tonight …

He glanced out of the window. It was still not four o'clock, but already the long shadows of evening were drawing in, and the sky to the west, over the grey waters of the river, was a flaming orange, as the sun set like a ball of crimson fire behind the distant hills of Fife.

He would lie down for an hour or so, he decided, then bath and dress for dinner. If he had to take it alone, then so be it. It was her decision. If she came, then he would have salvaged something from the horrors of this war – a priceless memory to take back to the motherland with him this weekend. If not … He stubbed his cigarette out roughly in the ashtray. That, he could not even bear to contemplate.

It was six-thirty before he awoke. He had slept longer than he intended, so he spent little time in the white-tiled bathroom adjoining his room. He looked intently at himself in the mirror above the sink as he combed his grey hair into place. The past few months had taken their toll. Fine lines fanned out from the corners of his brown eyes and a deep furrow lined the skin of the high brow. And the scar – that terrible scar remained – a souvenir of the Gestapo that he would carry with him for life. He touched the still livid skin gently with his fingertips. What could she have thought when she first set eyes on him again? He wished he was younger – that they had met again ten years ago, when he was still in his prime. Even if she did arrive now, and he doubted it, for it was already almost too late, it would be an old man who would welcome her. A man drained of almost all passion, but a deep, abiding love for his native land, and the memory of a woman with whom he shared the most beautiful summer of his life all those years ago.

As he settled the last hair into place, then adjusted his bow tie in the mirror, a faint tapping sound came from the door of the outer room. He glanced at his watch. It was just after seven. It was rather late for room service. An excitement mounted within him that he found hard to contain as he slipped the comb back into his hip pocket and left the bathroom, crossing the bedroom floor in response to a repeat of the faint tapping.

He knew immediately his hand touched the door-knob who it was. Even before the door opened and they stood face to face, he knew it was her. She was standing there, in a nipped-waisted, dark-blue woollen coat and matching hat. Her eyes were wide with anxiety as they looked up into his. 'Hello, Jan,' she whispered. 'I came.'

'I knew you would. I knew you would come.' There was no question of shaking or kissing hands as he buried his face in Beth's hair and held her close. She smelt of summer flowers, and trembled in his arms as they stood in the open doorway of his room. He had waited a lifetime for this moment, when he could hold her once again in his arms. He had wondered in his mind for the past few days how it would be if she came. Would they shake hands and talk about her journey like casual acquaintances? Would embarrassment cloud the elation of their first meeting? There had been no question of it. He had opened the door to see her standing there and their eyes had met and said all there was to say.

The feel of her in his arms sent surges of desire through his body that he had feared had long since gone for ever. But he had to control himself. She was nervous, he could sense it. He held her at arm's length and looked down at her. 'You're pale, *kochanie* ... You've come a long way to be here. Have you eaten?'

She nodded. 'I'm staying with Lara's in-laws, in Broughty Ferry. I've told them I'm visiting an old friend for dinner this evening in Dundee ... But they still gave me a lovely tea of fresh fish. I must admit, I could hardly eat a thing, though.'

He understood. His own appetite had vanished without trace. 'I – I've reserved a table in the dining-room, but I could cancel it ...'

'No, no ... I'm sure I can force something down, even if it's just a glass of wine.'

He gripped her tightly by the elbow as they made their way down the stairs to the dining-room, and across the elegantly-columned room to a table in the window alcove. The black-out meant that there was no river view, however, merely thick black cotton blinds where they should have been watching the city lights sparkling on the waters of the River Tay beyond.

They decided to forgo the soup, and Jan ordered steak pie and roast potatoes, with caramel custard for two to follow, plus a bottle of the finest claret in the house. The waiter poured the first drinks, then departed, and Beth hoped her nerves would not be too obvious, as they raised their glasses in unison. 'What shall it be, Beth?' he asked softly. Then, seeing her shake her head, he looked thoughtful. 'We have a saying in Poland: Youth lives on its hopes; old age on its memories ... Let us drink to both, my love, for we have each in plenty ... To hope for the future, and in memory of the past!'

They touched glasses and took their first sips of the red wine in unison. Their eyes met over the top of the glasses and both felt the same tingle run down their spines. Two decades may have passed, but they had done nothing to dissipate the spell that still bound them.

'We have another saying in Poland, *kochanie*,' he said softly: 'Youth is made rich by its dreams of the future; age is made poor by its regrets of the past ... We will make up for those regrets this night ...'

She trembled visibly beneath his gaze. 'I believe so, too, Jan,' she whispered. 'I wouldn't have come otherwise.'

Despite the shortages, the prime Angus steak in the pie was delicious, and she watched him eat with relish. At times, in the lamplight, she could see the young man in him again, for the subdued lighting softened the deep furrows that marked the high brow, and helped disguise the long scar that ran down the left side of his face. Looking at him was like looking at Poland personified: a country once as handsome and proud as any in the world, its fine countenance now scarred and disfigured. Perhaps worse, more painful than the physical scars were the mental ones: it was a country betrayed by its friends. 'I know we declared war because the Germans invaded Poland,' she said wistfully. 'But I wish we were doing more ... I – I wish you didn't have to take the risk of going back there yourself. Can't you trust our government to do what's necessary?' It was a flimsy shot in the battle to make him change his mind about going back, but it was all she could manage.

He paused, his fork half-way to his mouth, and there was an infinitely sad look in his eyes as he shook his head. There was so much she didn't understand, and so much he could never discuss with her. His country had never been in greater peril, and the actions of her own government recently had only added to the danger, not subtracted from it.

Just before his own arrival in London, the others in the Government in Exile there had received information that Churchill was ready to give his support to Soviet proposals for the recognition of the annexation of the Baltic States of Lithuania, Latvia and Estonia. This was in direct contradiction of the Prime Minister's declaration on 5 September last, when he announced that the British Government would not recognize any territorial changes in operation during the war.

One could only surmise that Moscow's pressure on this matter had arisen from the Soviet wish to unfreeze the assets of the Baltic States, which remained locked in British banks; and also to get their hands on part of the Merchant Navies of these states, which at present were in the service of the British. As far as Jan was concerned, in bowing to Soviet wishes, the British were creating a dangerous precedent by which, to gain the Soviet Union as an ally, they were willing to ignore the sanctity of the territorial boundaries of those states that bordered the USSR – and his own country had one of the longest.

He laid his fork down on the side of his plate and leaned across and took her hand. 'My darling Beth, if only governments were as loyal an ally as you. But we can trust no one in this war ... No, not even our own people, for there are those who, although born and bred in Poland, suddenly declare themselves to be *Volksdeutsch*, and work for the Germans, and those who give their services to the Soviets ... To survive as a nation, there must still be those of us willing to dedicate our lives in the service of only one mistress – our own country, Poland.'

Only one mistress ... Beth attempted an understanding smile. Little did he realize the irony of those words. She should not have spoken. She should know better than to question him on a matter so enshrined in his heart. Their time was too precious. She must lighten the mood. But no topic she could think of had a particularly light side to it.

'Tell me, where are you living here?' he asked, as he took a sip of the wine. 'With Lara's in-laws, you say?'

So she told him of her arrival at the Cameron household and of the terrible loss the family had received news of that morning. Then, as the meal progressed to the coffee stage, he told her of his meetings with the Lord Provost and the city fathers, and of his impending meeting with the Duke of Linlathan the following day. 'There is so much to do, so many people to see, before I leave your country,' he said with a sigh. 'I wish I were younger. I wish I had the energy I once had ...' His voice trailed off, as a wistful look came into his eyes.

Beth was silent for a moment, they were getting back on to thin ice, but she could resist the question no longer. 'Do you *have* to go back to Poland?' she asked. 'Does it have to be *you*? Isn't there someone else – a younger man perhaps, who could go instead?'

Jan took a sip of his coffee and shook his head. 'But why should it be anyone else? Why not me? You could say, why should a younger man, with so much more to lose, be the one to put his life at risk? Why not an older one whose life is already almost past?'

'Don't talk like that! Don't ever say that! You have years still ahead of you and you have everything to live for!'

He looked at her, a sad little smile playing at the corners of his mouth. 'Really, *kochanie*? And what might that "everything" be? Another two decades as Leni's husband? Another twenty years of wishing it were you lying there next to me in bed every night?'

'It was not of my choosing, Jan.'

He sighed. 'No, that is true. It was not of your choosing – or mine. We were victims of fate. And maybe that is part of the reason why I am going back to Poland. A man cannot remain a victim all his life, Beth. There comes a time when you cannot just stand by and let life happen. That time has come for me, my love.'

She averted her eyes, gazing past him at the backs of the heads of the party at the next table. It had always been this way, hadn't it? Poland had always been, and would always be, the first and greatest love of his life. 'And what about when this war is over, Jan? What then?'

He knew exactly what she was thinking. What of them? What did the future hold for them? Another twenty years of loneliness? 'I cannot answer that, *kochanie*. Not yet.'

She knew it was the only answer she would get; the only one he could give.

They lingered long over their coffee. The conversation became more personal, more intense. Both knew what the coming hours had in store. His eyes glowed, dark and luminous in the lamplight, as they gazed into hers. Every so often, their hands would touch across the white damask of the table-cloth and a tremor would run through her. Then, finally, when every last drop of coffee was emptied from the pot, and the waiter was hovering quite obviously in the background, he glanced at his watch. 'Eight-thirty,' he said quietly. 'I think they're waiting for the table … ' Then, sensing her extreme nervousness, he smiled reassuringly and squeezed her hand. 'A walk by the river would be lovely this evening, don't you agree?'

She nodded, a little shame-faced, as she replaced her used napkin on the side-plate. She felt like a young girl again, a silly young girl who had never known what it was to be with a man. She stole a look at him as he rose to help her on with her coat. This was no ordinary man; this was a man in whose company she was proud to be; a wonderful human being she happened still to be in love with, heart and soul.

There was a sky full of stars, and the evening air was sharp and pure as they emerged from the front door of the hotel into the Nethergate. It was the type of night they would dread back in London; the type that meant that the sirens would soon be going and the *Luftwaffe* would be over them at any moment, sending shivers of dread down every spine as they huddled in the shelters below ground.

But this wasn't London, this was Dundee; and there was no *Luftwaffe*, only Jan. He put his arm around her as they walked the half-mile down to the steep path past the station that led to the banks of the Tay.

The moon was still quite full and glowed, an almost perfect sphere, in the sky above them. The mouth of the river, less than a mile from the wide expanse of the North Sea, lay stretched before them. There was nothing to be heard but the lapping of the waves. No sound of anti-aircraft batteries; no ominous, deadly drone of the *Luftwaffe* overhead. The river lay like burnished steel beneath their gaze. It would still be here, ebbing and flowing in the moonlight, when this war was a mere page in the history books of the future. When evil men like Adolf Hitler were expunged from the face of the earth. Or would that ever happen? Perhaps there would always be others to take their place. Perhaps peace was an illusion: something to yearn for, but something that they would never know again in their lifetime.

She shivered in the frosty air and he held her closer. His breath was warm on her cold brow as he whispered, 'I wish this night could go on forever, *kochanie*. I wish it would never end – that there could be no more tomorrows, only tonight ... and us ...'

He took her fingers and raised them to his lips, then, hand in hand, they walked the few hundred yards back up the path that led to the hotel, and his room ...

Chapter Twenty-seven

Beth stood in the middle of the hotel room, her heart pounding furiously in her breast, as Jan turned out the main light and switched on one of the small bedside lamps. Its crimson shade gave the room a rosy glow, and she thought of the new nightgown and robe that lay, not yet unpacked, in the case in Ken's old room in Broughty Ferry. It had come as a shock to learn that Jan was returning to London tomorrow – that it was tonight or never for them.

When they had divested themselves of their outdoor clothes, he produced a bottle of Polish vodka from the bedside cabinet and two glasses. 'It should really be whisky here in Scotland,' he smiled. 'But I feel my own country's spirit warms the soul like no other.'

Beth returned his smile. It was a lovely way of putting it. But it would take a lot more than a glass of vodka to warm her soul after tonight. She accepted the glass with a murmur of thanks. They stood facing each other in front of the fireplace, where a two-bar electric fire gave off scant warmth to the chill of the room. He looked down at her, his brown eyes serious in the pale, drawn face. 'Many years ago, my Beth,' he said softly, 'I said three words to you that I had never said to another woman. I told you I loved you – that I would always love you. I was a young man then, and many things have happened in both our lives, but the truth of those words remains. Whatever happens in the future, I want you to remember that. I loved you then, I love you now, and I will always love you. While there is breath left in my body, my heart will be beating for you – for Poland and you.'

She closed her eyes in a vain attempt to stem the hot tears that spiked the surface of her eyes. He was speaking the truth. She had no doubt about that. And it would always be like that: he would love both her and his country until his dying day. But both loves were equally futile. His country was dying – being bled to death by its ancient enemy, Germany; and he was still tied, by the law and his

Mother Church, to his wife. The reality of both was immutable. All the wishing in the world could change nothing. He could never be hers, and he was leaving her tomorrow to go home to die, to die in the service of his dying country.

'Don't cry, my love. Don't cry ... ' Suddenly his arms were around her, the untouched glasses cast aside as he rained kisses over her wet cheeks. 'Don't cry, Beth *kochanie* ... Not tonight ... '

She clung closer to him, her fingers clutching at his hair, his shoulders, her breath coming in gasps as his lips moved hungrily over her face. His skin was rough on hers, and all the time he was murmuring words of Polish that needed no translation. He was pouring out his heart to her and her own heart was responding, beat for beat, as their bodies moulded as one. She was scarcely aware of them casting off their clothes, or of him carrying her to the waiting bed.

He laid her gently on the satin coverlet and looked down at her, his eyes devouring every inch of her body. Her skin gleamed pale and luminous in the lamplight. Despite the intervening years, it was still the body of the young woman he remembered. The dark hair that lay like a halo around her head on the white pillow was still as dark, still as brown. His fingers reached out and stroked the silken strands back from her brow, then moved down tenderly towards the long curve of her neck, until his fingers touched the pale swell of her breast and he felt her tremble slightly beneath his touch. She held her breath as his hand moved down across the flat plain of her stomach to the firm flesh of her thighs. She gasped aloud as he began to stroke the white, sensitive skin of her inner thigh.

Her hands went up and clutched at him, pulling his face down to hers. 'My love, my love ... ' She could wait no longer. After all these barren years even another minute was too long. 'Love me, Jan ... Love me ... ' She was crying the words as the full weight of his body moved above hers.

He was resting on his elbows, his hands clasping the sides of her wet cheeks as his eyes gazed down into hers. He wanted to look at her, to imprint this moment on his memory, this moment he had waited for for so many long years ...

Their bodies moved in perfect unison, as passion mounted on passion. His eyes remained locked in hers in a visual embrace so intense that she thought she would drown in their golden-brown depths, as together they spiralled higher and higher until, finally, their love exploded in a cry of *'Kocham cie ... Kocham cie ...'* It was all the Polish she knew. All she needed to know ... 'I love you ... I love you ... ' The salt of their tears mingled on their lips as they gasped the words they had not uttered for so long, so very long ...

Moira and Sandy Cameron had waited up for her, and were sitting in front of the dying embers in the kitchen range as Beth's taxi dropped her at their front door in Long Lane, at a little after eleven. They looked at one another, then rose together at the sound of the car door slamming, and Moira busied herself brewing a fresh pot of tea while Sandy went to welcome their guest home.

To her relief, Beth found that they had little interest in how her own evening had gone. They were much more concerned with Cissie's state of health next door. 'I begged her to come and sleep here,' Moira sighed, as she handed Beth her cup of tea. 'Begged her, so I did. She knows we've got the bed-settee in the front room, but she'd have none of it. Said she'd rather be in her own bed.'

'Well, you can't force folk into doing what's good for them,' her husband put in. 'Is that not so, Beth?'

Beth nodded, a trifle too energetically. Despite her deep sympathy for Moira's sister, she found it hard to concentrate on anything or anyone but the man whose bed she had just left. 'Oh, yes, yes it certainly is. I should think she just wants to be alone with her own thoughts tonight ... You know, to come to terms with what's happened.'

'Aye, you're probably right.' Sandy leaned back in his chair and lit his pipe, filling the air with the pungent aroma of 'Old Virginia', as he puffed the golden tobacco into life. 'It's been one helluva day, so it has. Wouldn't you agree, Beth?'

Beth looked across at him over the top of her coffee cup and gave a wry smile. Sandy Cameron had never said a truer word.

She slept little that night, her body tossing fitfully in the strange bed as her mind remained locked in that third-floor bedroom in the Queen's Hotel. 'Jan ... Jan ... Jan ...' In the strange twilight world between waking and sleeping, she was vaguely aware of herself crying his name out loud. The taste of him was still on her lips, the scent of him in her nostrils. Why did it have to be like this? Why?

She sat up in the bed, her body, in the newly-bought nightgown he would never see, glistening with sweat, despite the chill of the night. She raised a hand to her cheek: it was wet with tears. A noise from the bedroom door made her look round in the darkness as she heard the handle turn.

'Are you all right, Beth? Is there anything we can get you? A wee drop of something to make you sleep, maybe?'

Beth could scarcely make out the figure of Moira Cameron in the darkness, but recognized the anxiety in the other's voice. 'No, no thank you ... I'm fine, honestly.'

Moira paused in the doorway, unsure whether to take her word for it, or to bring a wee glass of whisky all the same. The sobbing had been something terrible. It had kept both her and Sandy awake for the best part of an hour. Mind you, it was just to be expected, what with being bombed out of house and home and all that. 'Well, if you're sure ... But just give us a cry if there's anything we can do, now. We're just next door, the pair of us.'

'Thank you. Yes, I'll do that ... ' Beth lay back with a sigh as the door closed quietly once more in the darkness. 'The pair of us.' The whole world was in pairs, but her and Jan. And, in the eyes of the world, even he was part of a pair, she thought bitterly. Did Leni Jarosinska know how lucky she was? Did she ever stop to think that there was someone who would give all she possessed to change places with her? Her mind went back to the buxom figure with the peroxided blonde hair. It was hard to feel real hatred towards Jan's wife; it was a feeling more akin to a deep sadness that filled her soul. Leni's marriage to Jan had been a mismatch from the start, just like her own marriage to Hans Heinrich. The world was full of them – good people bound together in bad marriages. Maybe if, one fine day, a new world were to emerge from the chaos and destruction of the old, things might be different. People might be less willing to remain tied to loveless relationships, less bothered by what the world and its neighbour might whisper over the garden fence. Maybe ... Maybe ... But, by then, it would probably be too late for them.

Their love had been born of a passion that had burst into flame during that long hot summer of 1920; that summer in Silesia when the green grass along the banks of the Praszkawarthe had baked golden beneath the sun's rays, and dragon-flies had darted like diamonds above the sparkling blue of the waters. That summer when they had lain together in the long, dry grass and gazed up into the cloudless blue of the sky and believed that what they had found in each other could last forever.

He had been young then – the Master of Jarosbork – a tall, rather intense young man with brown eyes that sparked gold at the centre and titian hair that blazed a fiery red in the summer sunshine, and a laugh that echoed in the hills, and that still haunted her to this day.

Perhaps that had been the main difference between Hans Heinrich and Jan. Hans Heinrich did not laugh. Liesel, his beloved first wife's death, and the Great War had seen to that. But how could she have known that at the time? Who was there to explain to a naïve twenty-year-old that her new husband's coldness could have had a very human reason behind it? No one; there had been no one. So she had carried the hurt inside her as, day by day, the ice she felt in her husband's heart chilled the warmth in her own. And that chill had remained until she had come face to face with her fate, in the tall, spare figure of Count Jan Jarosinski.

She was not sure to this day what it was that had first attracted them. She had seen better looking men, it was true, and, no doubt, he had met more beautiful women. Nor was it the fact that he was one of Upper Silesia's most noble aristocrats, for the von Lessing family could trace their ancestry back just as many years, and Wolfsberg was every bit as fine a castle as Jarosbork. No, it was none of those things. It was that indefinable something − a vital spark one suddenly recognizes in another's eyes that tells you that here, above all others, is your kindred spirit, the one person you would choose to share your life with to the end of your days.

To the end of your days ... The words had a bitter ring to them as she lay back on the pillow and stared into the darkness. She could not, she must not allow herself to think of death. To live was to hope and both of them still had their lives − though, God knows, plenty of others didn't.

She began to pray, but not the mechanical reciting of the Lord's Prayer that she had done each night since childhood. She began to pray in earnest, to implore God, if there was a God, to hear her plea. 'Keep him safe, Dear Lord. Keep him safe on his journey back to Poland. Don't let him die ... ' She could not ask for him to be returned safely to her, for, in the eyes of the Lord, he belonged to another woman. But surely, if something survived after death, if the spirit really did live on in a far better place than this, then someone, somewhere was listening? Some greater power than a mere mortal such as herself could comprehend was out there somewhere, far above the pain and agony of this war, and would hear her plea. He had promised her they would meet again, just as he had done that day long ago and far away in Silesia. But times were different now. A human promise was a frail thing in this tortured world. If there was a God somewhere above this hell, let Him hear her now ...

She rose at six and slipped out of the house, long before either Moira or Sandy had stirred. She needed to breathe the fresh air of another day in her lungs before she faced them across the breakfast table.

They lived only a few paces from the mouth of the river, where the

Tay swept into the turbulent grey waters of the North Sea. Of their own accord, her feet began to walk towards Broughty Castle, the mighty stone edifice perched on its great crag of grey rock, gazing outwards towards the battlefields of Europe. The words of an old ballad rang in her head:

Grey rocks and greyer sea,
And surf along the shore –
And in my heart a name
My lips shall speak no more.

The high and lonely hills
Endure the darkening year –
And in my heart endure
A memory and a tear.

Across the tide a sail
That tosses, and is gone –
And in my heart the kiss
That longing dreams upon.

Grey rocks and greyer sea,
And surf along the shore –
And in my heart the face
That I shall see no more ...

Chapter Twenty-eight

Shortly before seven o'clock on Wednesday 15 January 1941, as Beth packed her case in the bedroom of the Camerons' neat, semi-detached home in Broughty Ferry for the return journey to London, and Count Jan Jarosinski said farewell to his wife and colleagues at the Polish Embassy before departing for his homeland, a special train made its way towards Thurso, on the bleak, windswept north coast of Scotland.

It was pitch-black outside the tightly-shut blinds of the carriage windows, and a blizzard was raging across the snow-covered landscape but, inside the specially chartered Pullmans, the collection of eminent travellers were already at breakfast.

The train was the one specially assigned to the Prime Minister, Winston Churchill himself, and his fellow passengers included the most remarkable collection of men ever to be gathered together in such unusual circumstances.

The British contingent included Anthony Eden, the Foreign Secretary; Ernest Bevin, the Minister of Labour; Lord Beaverbrook, the Minister of Aircraft Production; Major General Sir Hastings 'Pug' Ismay, Chief of Staff to the Minister of Defence; and Lord and Lady Halifax, the new British Ambassador to the United States and his wife.

The five Americans who shared a carriage were Harry Hopkins, President Roosevelt's special envoy; General Raymond Lee, US Military Attaché in London; Rear Admiral Robert Ghormley, US Assistant Chief of Naval Operations, with his aide, Assistant Naval Attaché Edward Cochrane; and Colonel Mike Adams, of Military Intelligence.

By the time the train arrived in Thurso, breakfast was almost over, but Harry Hopkins was still waxing lyrical across the table about his long conversation with the Prime Minister that had lasted into the early hours that morning. Despite his earlier misgivings about the British leader, he now found himself with a growing regard for the old man and had been keen to impress on him that, although he and others were doing their best in Britain's cause, there was still considerable opposition in the United States to aiding one side over the other. 'I wanted to get across to the guy that although FDR and the rest of us hope to have the Lend-Lease bill passed into law by the end of February, there's still one hell of a lobby against it.'

'It's the big names that are gunning for it we have to worry about most,' Mike agreed, and the others around the table concurred. They knew exactly who he was referring to – the likes of Colonel Charles Lindbergh, the Atlantic flyer, who made no secret of his admiration for Germany; Father Charles Couglin, the popular, right-wing radio priest; Herbert Hoover, the powerful head of the FBI, and Joseph Kennedy, the last Ambassador to Britain, who had left behind him a legacy of bad feeling with his anti-war statements. Yes, the America First campaign that was being waged by the isolationists to keep the United States out of the war was a powerful lobby, all right.

'You reckon they're still able to do us real damage?' Harry queried. 'You think folks really take account of what they say?'

Mike shrugged. 'Who can say? You can never really tell what's going on in other people's minds. Which one of us has a clue what a dirt farmer in Iowa thinks about it all – or some guy knocking his guts out in General Motors in Detroit? They've all got their own opinions and they're perfectly entitled to them. I only know what I think of them ...'

'And that is?' Ray Lee asked.

Mike grinned and thought for a moment. 'Let's just say, if I were the infamous Dr Spooner, the best description of Lindbergh and that lot I could think of would be a bunch of "shining wits!"'

Harry laughed aloud while the others grinned. They couldn't have put it better themselves.

As they finished the last of their toast and marmalade and the cigarettes were passed around, Mike brought up the sensitive issue of Roosevelt's request to the FBI to investigate the financing of the America First campaign.

'That's a field of investigation you may want to get involved in yourself, once you're back in the saddle in Washington, Mike,' General Lee remarked, which brought an abrupt change of subject immediately. Mike had no wish to get involved in anything to do with the FBI: too many men, braver than himself, had come unstuck endeavouring to trawl the murky depths of Hoover's organization.

'I'll take a rain-check on that one, if you don't mind,' he said, leaning across the table to accept one of Harry's cigarettes. 'What else emerged from your early morning perusals, Harry?' The quicker the subject got back to more general matters, the better.

Harry was only too happy to expand and, despite his lack of sleep, Mike had rarely seen his friend more animated as he declared that two major points had emerged from the conversation last night: Churchill was convinced that the danger of a German invasion of Britain had now passed and that any day now Hitler would begin his push into the Balkans. It was the only option left open to the Nazis, and it was this eventuality they must prepare for. For his part, Harry had been willing to be convinced, and was now keen to sound out his fellow countrymen on the idea before they all disappeared across the Atlantic that afternoon, whilst he was left to accompany the old man to Glasgow, where the Lord Provost had arranged a dinner in their honour.

He had not been too pleased by the news that Mike was to accompany his chief, General Lee, and the others back to the States. He had got used to having his company in his dealings with the British, and the thought that he would now be left alone with the Limeys was not the situation he had hoped for. To Mike's relief, he did not press the point too hard, however. Had he done so, Mike might have been persuaded to stay on a few more days in deference to his old friend's wishes. As far as he was concerned, though, the sooner he was on his way back across the Atlantic, the better.

The late-night conversations and early breakfast meant that all those present in the carriage were suffering from a distinct lack of sleep but, despite the yawns, the conversation was still going strong on the Balkan issue when, shortly after seven, the train drew into the tiny fishing port of Scrabster.

As they drained the last dregs of the breakfast coffee from their cups, Mike yanked the blind up and peered out into the darkness. A fierce wind was blowing the snow horizontally across the outside of the glass, making it impossible to distinguish anything but his own face staring back at him.

He lit another cigarette and settled back in the plushly-upholstered seat as the conversation carried on around him. This was the last he would see of Britain: darkness and blinding snow against a bleak landscape. How appropriate. It suited his mood exactly. Despite the *bonhomie* of the carriage, there was an emptiness at his core that he knew nothing could fill. He would go through the motions all right, say all the right things at the appropriate times, and no one would ever know what the leaving of this beleaguered land had cost him.

Any minute now they would draw into the tiny station and make their way down to the harbour, where a destroyer was waiting to take them to Scapa Flow. There the British battleship, the *King George V*, was waiting to ferry him and several others among the train's occupants back home across the Atlantic, and to carry Lord and Lady Halifax to their new life in the British Embassy in Washington.

Although he was unhappy at the thought of leaving Britain, once the decision had been made, it was a relief to be on his way at last. He was glad he had run into Lara's mother the other day, in that tea-shop in Oxford. And the fact that she had confided such a personal secret to him gave him a peculiar feeling. In some strange way, learning that Jan Jarosinski was Lara's real father meant a lot to him. It meant he shared a common heritage with her. It was Polish blood that ran in both their veins. The only trouble was that he knew it and she didn't. And she was never likely to find out, not from him anyway ... No, he would not apply to come back to this country again. Not while this war lasted, anyway. And if, one fine day, many years from now, he were to return, then maybe, just maybe, he could smile quite casually if he were to run into her and Ken Cameron on some crowded sidewalk – outside Harrods, say ... If Harrods was still standing, he thought wryly. If anything was still standing ...

It was two o'clock in the afternoon when they left behind the stormy waters of the Pentland Firth and entered the comparative calm of the approaches to the vast, land-locked bay of Scapa Flow. The sea, glimmering like pale steel and crested with white horses, was still distinctly choppy as the destroyer thrust its way up the narrow channel through a succession of three booms, the gates of which were opened by guard-ships and immediately closed behind them. Once past the third set, they turned sharply to port, rounded a headland and entered the great anchorage of Scapa Flow, where the British Fleet had spent most of the last war.

The snow was lighter now and the wind had abated slightly, but the surrounding landscape of barren hills was bleak in the extreme. A bitter north-easter was blowing, stinging the faces of those who braved the wind and chose to remain on deck. Only a handful of ships lay at anchor, and Mike deciphered the name *Repulse* on one particularly fine looking ship, as their own passed within hailing distance. The bulk of the British fleet, he knew, was in the Mediterranean, and his mind went back to the Saturday morning at Ditchley when news had come in of the attacks on them by German dive bombers. It would be no joke to be a sailor in the British Navy right now, especially at this time of year.

As it came into view, it was obvious to all that, like their own vessel, the *King George V* was pitching badly in the steep chop, and Mike saw Harry's face turning grey at the thought of boarding yet another item of British Naval hardware. It had been arranged that the Prime Minister, along with Harry and several others, would board the vessel to say their farewells before it sailed for America. Then they would return to London, via Glasgow, where Harry himself had an appointment with the King the following day. Churchill, however, harboured no squeamish feelings about the boarding plan, as he beamed his approval of the great grey battleship in which he had implicit faith. 'There is our shield!' he declared. 'If that should go, we'd all be for it!'

Mike exchanged a slightly raised eyebrow with Ed Cochrane. If that should go, then they would be for it before anybody! He could not be sure what the U-Boat success rate was in the Atlantic at the moment, but whatever it was, it was too high for him!

Mike and Ed, closely followed by the others, clambered up the gangplank of the *KGV*, as everyone seemed to be referring to it, right behind the Prime Minister and Harry. Churchill was even dressed for the occasion in a dark-blue reefer jacket and nautical cap, and they could hear his distinctive voice regailing his companion with his thoughts on the North African campaign as they fought to keep their footing on the wet wood in the gusting wind. Harry, being no sailor, slipped and fell heavily and ended up being unceremoniously hauled on board the badly pitching vessel by the scruff of his neck, while the Prime Minister continued his dialogue as if nothing untoward was happening.

Once all the Downing Street party were on board, the Prime Minister turned to have a last word with the Halifaxes, to Harry's ill-disguised relief. 'Goddam brass monkey weather this!' Mike muttered across to him, as they huddled inside their greatcoats on the heaving deck of the ship. 'I bet you're some glad you're heading back down south this afternoon.'

Harry, chilled to the bone and miserable, and wearing a borrowed pair of 'Pug' Ismay's flying boots to defrost his frozen toes, could only nod bleakly as he made to sit down on a cumbersome object on deck. He was promptly hauled off by an irate Chief Petty Officer, 'I wouldn't sit there if I were you, sir. That's a depth charge!'

It was four-fifteen in the afternoon before those who were returning to London along with the Prime Minister left. Mike and the others watched from the rails as they boarded a pinnace and disappeared in a shower of white spray back to the mainland. The great anchor was hauled up on the *King George*.

Once outside the anchorage, the battleship took a north-west course, with four destroyers standing station, one straight ahead, two to port and one to starboard. Most chose to remain on deck as they headed out to sea. Bob Ghormley was standing next to Mike and the Rear Admiral could not disguise his delight. He had just been informed that the US Navy Department had relented and was to allow the *KGV* to make for port in Annapolis. This meant that they would be arriving in the United States to a guard of honour welcome. Mike attempted a responsive smile. The last thing he wanted was to dock to any kind of a celebration. They were heading out to sea for ten days in a huge steel crate, trying their darndest to avoid Hitler's marauding U-Boats. One and a half weeks of certain seasickness and freezing weather awaited them. Hardly a cause for rejoicing, even if the whole darned US Navy was to stand to attention as they came down the gangplank.

It was 23 January, and the sun was shining from a clear blue sky as they entered the placid waters of Chesapeake Bay. The ship's radio announced that two American Admirals, plus an aide, together with the British Naval Attaché, were waiting to board at Cape Henry, and that the President himself was waiting to greet their arrival at Annapolis. There Lord Halifax was to be officially received and the required photographs taken for posterity.

After the farewell dinner on board that evening, they were all invited to the wardroom where, after several drinks over the eight, they were presented with a certificate for crossing the Atlantic in the *KGV*. Mike took his and, after carefully folding it, slipped it into the inside pocket of his dinner jacket. He was in no mood for tall tales and the type of mess room reminiscences the occasion demanded. He needed time to breathe: time to come to terms with being in home waters; with being back home.

He slipped out and wandered up on deck. The night sky hung low like a canopy of black velvet above him as he leaned on the rail and cast his eyes to the heavens. The stars were so brilliant he felt he could reach out and touch them. The only sounds were the lapping of the waves and the faint strains of the ship's orchestra still playing in the dining-room. He was home at last. He was back in America. God bless it.

The salt air was clean in his lungs as he took a deep breath and leaned over the rail. The music from down below seemed to swell in his head, as the musicians went through their repertoire of war songs. They were all singing along with it now, their voices carrying on the still night air and, almost unconsciously, Mike began to join in:

> 'We'll meet again,
> Don't know where, don't know when,
> But I know we'll meet again
> Some sunny day ... '

His voice tailed off. He could sing no more. He fumbled in the pocket of his dinner jacket for his cigarettes. It was funny how this cold air brought tears to your eyes.

Chapter Twenty-nine

'There's no reason for you to apply to get back to the Foreign Office proper now, you know, dear.' Beth looked at her daughter across the breakfast table in the small kitchen of the flat in Lower Belgrave Street. 'Now that Mike's gone back to the States, I'm sure you'd be very happy staying on working for the Americans. You must admit, you found it very congenial at Princes Gate.'

Lara shrugged. 'You're probably right, but I've told them at the Foreign Office that I'm reporting for work this morning, and report I will. Anyhow, I'm rather hoping that I'll get taken on again in Downing Street.'

'But there's no guarantee of that!'

'True, but I've heard on the grapevine that one of the secretaries in the Garden Room is leaving to get married.'

'And you really think you might get the job?'

'I'll try my best.' Lara glanced at her watch. 'But sorry, Mum, I don't have time to discuss it now. I'm late already. Just keep your fingers crossed for me, will you? I should know one way or another by the time I get back tonight.' She took her last sip of tea and grabbed her handbag from an empty chair. 'Try to get out for a bit today. I don't like to think of you being cooped up all alone here during the day.'

Beth smiled reassuringly. 'Don't you worry about me. I've got plenty I can be getting along with!'

They exchanged pecks on the cheek before Lara disappeared out of the door and Beth was left alone in the unfamiliar kitchen. She let her gaze wander round the bare walls and the kitchen cabinet with its almost empty shelves. Since she got back from Scotland a few days ago, she had had neither the energy nor the inclination to set about buying the necessary artefacts that make a house into a home. Anyhow, she doubted if the type of things she would want would even be available these days. It was coupons for just about everything. And, to cap it all, their ration books had been lost in the bombing and neither of them had got round to applying for emergency ones. No, this place, grateful though she was for it, would never be home. In fact London itself no longer felt like home with Jan gone.

Since she had got back from Dundee, her thoughts had returned more and more to Silesia. Jan was back out there doing his bit, and what was she doing? A few hours a week in voluntary ambulance driving, and the odd bit of fire-watching – it wasn't very much. Surely someone in her position, with her background, could do more? She was a fluent German speaker for a start – surely that meant something? She frowned and toyed with the handle of her empty cup. It was something she had kept pretty quiet about of late but, when she came to think about it, it must be a skill that could be put to good use. But how?

She got up from the table and began to clear away the breakfast things as she put her mind to the problem. One thing was certain, she didn't particularly want to remain in London. She wanted to do something concrete, something positive to help bring this awful war to an end.

As she ran the hot water into the basin and immersed the dirty dishes, she found herself being drawn more and more to the idea of offering her services to the SOE.

The Special Operations Executive was still a highly hush-hush operation, designed to offer assistance in defeating Hitler in the occupied countries. She only knew of it herself by picking up bits and pieces from various private conversations over the past few months and, while she doubted if she was exactly special agent material, surely she could be of use as a translator at first? Then, with a bit of luck, she might get trusted with a foreign assignment later on. Until then, she could make herself quite useful in a secretarial capacity, she was sure of it. She had even been known to turn her hand to typewriting now and again when Jack was still alive.

As the morning wore on, the idea continued to grow in her mind. She knew, or at least guessed, that the headquarters of the organization were in Norgeby House, in Baker Street, so what was to stop her calling over there this afternoon and offering her services? But would they accept her at face value? Maybe the whole thing was so hush-hush that she would simply be told she had come to the wrong place and be shown the door. Who did she know with enough clout to make even the Secret Service sit up and take notice? Jack, of course, had had many old friends in the corridors of Whitehall, but most were now retired ... Her face lit up. Bar one! The Prime Minister himself! Dare she? Dare she bother the country's busiest and most important man with such an issue? Of course not! But there was always Clementine. Winston Churchill's wife was one of the most highly-regarded people in London, and Beth knew that above all Clemmie was fiercely loyal to her husband. She, more than anyone, appreciated the people who had remained loyal to her husband during his 'wilderness years', and no one had been more loyal than Jack Mallory. Yes, she decided, she would call Clementine and ask if she would put in a good word for her in the right quarters in Baker Street.

By a stroke of good luck, the Prime Minister's wife was home for lunch when the call went through to Number Ten Downing Street. And, no, she didn't mind at all talking to Mrs Jack Mallory. 'Beth, dear, how *are* you? I heard about that terrible bomb on Atholl Square. It didn't hit your house, by any chance?'

'I'm afraid it did,' Beth replied. 'But Lara and I are trying to put that behind us now. Actually, that's the reason I'm calling. I've decided it's no use sitting about moping and dwelling on our misfortune. I want to go out and do something concrete for the war effort.'

'Good for you!'

'And what I was really wondering was if you'd be kind enough to put a good word in for me in a certain quarter.'

There was a laugh at the other end. 'My dear, if you really think that anyone'll listen to me, I'll be delighted! Where is it you want to work?'

'I'd like to work in Special Operations Executive HQ in Baker Street.' She held her breath.

'That sounds awfully exciting. You're not planning on being this war's Mata Hari, by any chance?'

'Good heavens, no! If I can make myself useful by simply making the tea, I'll be quite happy. And I can speak fluent German, remember, which may come in handy.'

There was a pause on the end of the line, as the other woman cast her mind back. 'That's right! You were married to that German Count before Jack, weren't you? My goodness, I'd quite forgotten. Well, with that background, I should think you'll be a jolly sight more useful to them than as a mere tea-maker. I'll get on to it right away. By the way, Beth dear, how is your daughter these days? I saw her once or twice last summer when she was working for Winston, but for some reason she simply disappeared.'

'It was a purely temporary post, unfortunately. It's been mainly that type of work she's been given for the past year. In fact, she's been working for the American Embassy for the past few weeks,' Beth explained. 'But she's given that up now. To tell the truth, she's gone back into the Foreign Office today to see if there's any chance of getting posted back to Number Ten.' Then realizing that it sounded as if she was asking for a double intervention on her behalf, she added quickly, 'But I wouldn't want you to think I'm telling you that to ask for a second favour!'

A light laugh sounded over the line once more. 'Nonsense, my dear! What are old friends for? But, look, I must dash now. Winston was up in Scapa last week to see the Halifaxes off, and came back with the most rotten cold. I simply must see that he takes his medicine before he disappears for the rest of the day – and night!'

Beth gave an understanding smile. It must be no joke being married to such a man. They exchanged the friendliest of goodbyes, and as she replaced the telephone in its cradle, a shiver of suppressed excitement ran through her. She had no doubt that Clemmie would act on her suggestion, and it could mean the opening up of a whole new way of life, which was exactly what she needed right now. Since Jan had left, she felt like she had come up against a blank wall in her life. But, rather than stand and look at it, she was doing something positive. She was enlisting the help of an old friend to help her climb over it.

She decided that it would be better to wait a day or so before presenting herself at Norgeby House. Mrs Churchill might not get round to her request right away. And she was in two minds whether or not to tell Lara of her decision when she got home that evening. The problem solved itself, however, as Lara was bursting with news of her own day. She was to get her wish and return to Number Ten Downing Street in two weeks' time. 'Isn't that just wonderful, Mum?'

Beth hugged her daughter in delight. 'I couldn't be happier for you, Lara dear!'

They sat down to a meal of Woolton Pie. With Mrs B. dead, and having neither the heart nor the space to get a replacement cook, Beth and Lara were having to take it in turns to prepare food. And this evening the meal was a Lord Woolton special. The Minister of Food had become very adept at concocting recipes for the British housewife using little more than thin air, and tonight's meal consisted of vegetable pie and Oxo gravy. Beth thought wryly of the prime Angus steak she had only toyed with that evening in the Queen's Hotel in

Dundee. What wouldn't she have given for a portion of it for her pie this afternoon!

Lara had brought home a bottle of cheap sherry by way of celebration. They had just finished their meal, and Beth was in the process of pouring two drinks, when there was a ring at the doorbell. 'Whoever can that be?' She looked up at Lara. 'You're not expecting anyone, are you?'

'Not that I know of ... I'd better answer it, though.'

She returned a minute or so later with a puzzled look on her face. 'There's a man at the door asking to see you.'

'Did he give his name?'

'It's a Brigadier Colin Gubbins.'

Beth caught her breath. The name rang a bell in her mind. She was sure she had heard Jan speak of him before. Hadn't he been over in Poland during the Nazi blitzkrieg of September 1939? And wasn't he now something to do with this SOE – something high up at that? Her heart beat faster as she poured another sherry and said quietly, 'You'd better ask him to come in.'

Colin Gubbins turned out to be a slight man with a military bearing, a small, neatly-clipped moustache and greying, curly hair. Amongst the ribbons adorning his chest could be seen both the DSO and the MC. A pair of keen dark eyes looked curiously at Beth as the introductions were made. 'I'm told you already have contacts in Occupied Europe, Mrs Mallory,' he said, moments later, accepting a sherry with a nod of thanks.

'Oh really?' Beth looked surprised.

'Count Jarosinski, amongst others, so I'm informed.'

Beth drew in her breath and almost spilled the drink in her hand as she made to sit down. 'Your sources get their information in a very short time, I see.' How on earth had he found out about Jan?

The visitor nodded and gave a quiet smile, but made no comment. 'I am also informed you have personal, intimate knowledge of both Poland and Germany, having once been married to a Silesian member of the German aristocracy, Count Hans Heinrich von Lessing, no less.'

'He was my first husband.'

'And your second was Jack Mallory.'

She nodded. 'You do your homework, I see.'

Colin Gubbins smiled. 'We have to in this business. But there's no reason for you to feel threatened by it: with a pedigree like yours, and a personal recommendation from the PM's wife herself, I think we can talk business. We need all the knowledgeable staff we can get our hands on at the moment in Norgeby House.' He turned to Lara. 'I understand the young lady here has had high security clearance herself and has worked at Number Ten in her time.'

Lara nodded and smiled, wondering what was coming next. The visitor certainly seemed to know his stuff.

'You wouldn't fancy coming along with your mother when she joins our happy band, Mrs Cameron?'

'Good heavens, no! All that cloak and dagger stuff's not for me, I'm afraid. Politicians may be a peculiar breed, but I love my work, and I'm too glad to be back amongst them to consider leaving again.'

'Lara has been working for the Americans over the past few weeks,' Beth explained.

The Brigadier's brows rose in interest. 'Really? I trust our trans-atlantic cousins treated you well? Although you'll have been working overtime of late, no doubt – what with the Hopkins visit and Ray Lee and Mike Adams leaving for the States. There's been quite a bit of toing and froing in their Embassy recently.'

Lara tensed. Even hearing Mike's name spoken made her stomach turn over and, desperate though she was for any up-to-date news, she deliberately avoided mentioning him. 'I'm afraid I never had the pleasure of meeting Mr Hopkins when he was over here,' she replied lightly, 'but I did hear rather a nice story about him today ... I was doing some letters for Tom Johnston, the Scottish Secretary of State, this morning, and he was telling me he was seated next to Harry Hopkins and the Prime Minister during a dinner at the Station Hotel in Glasgow on their way back from Scapa Flow last week. At the end of the dinner, he said, as Harry Hopkins got up to leave, he looked down at the Prime Minister and said, "I suppose you wish to know what I'm going to say to President Roosevelt on my return? Well, I'm going to quote you one verse from the Book of Ruth, in the truth of which both Mr Johnston here's mother and my own Scottish mother were brought up: 'Whither thou goest, I will go; and where thou lodgest, I will lodge: thy people shall be my people, and thy God my God.'" Then he added very quietly, "'Even to the end' ... " Tom Johnston said that the Prime Minister had tears in his eyes as the American left the room.'

The Brigadier nodded, obviously moved by the story. 'It would seem that Hopkins is on our side all right. And it's certainly good to know who your friends are at a time like this, wouldn't you agree, Mrs Mallory?'

Beth nodded. Her heart still too full to speak. That quote from the Book of Ruth she had read to herself in bed last night. Perhaps, unconsciously, that was the reason behind her decision to apply to join SOE. 'Whither thou goest, I will go … thy people shall be my people …' 'I intend to offer myself to the service of Poland, Brigadier,' she heard herself saying. 'In whatever capacity you choose to use me, my loyalty to the cause, and to the Polish people, you must never doubt.'

When Brigadier Gubbins had gone, Lara looked quizzically at her mother. Her overt declaration in support of Poland's freedom had come as something of a shock. It was the first time she had ever heard her mother come near to professing her true feelings to an outsider, and it was not to the Polish people *en masse* she had been referring, but to one man. 'You really love him, don't you? That Pole – you really care for him?'

'Yes.' There was little point in lying.

'Did you love him when my father was still alive?'

Their eyes met and held. Beth felt the burden of over twenty years of guilt weigh heavy on her heart. The injustice of letting her live her life believing Hans Heinrich to be her father was undeniable. 'Your father is not dead, Lara dear.'

'You mean he's alive – in Hitler's Germany?' The words were almost shouted at her.

'I mean he's still alive in the service of Poland.'

She could see confusion flicker in the hazel of her daughter's eyes. Then the colour drained from her face as realization dawned. 'You – you're telling me that that Pole was my father?'

'*Is* your father, my dear,' she corrected. 'Jan Jarosinski *is* your father.' And, as she uttered the words, she prayed inwardly that she was correct in using the present tense.

They stared at one another from across the room. Two women from different generations, bound by a tie of blood that now stretched taut across a blood-stained Continent. A few weeks ago the younger would have raged of infidelity and dishonour, but today she stood silent. She too knew what it was like to love a man who was not your husband. 'I hope you find him,' Lara whispered. 'I hope, by the time this awful war is over, that you find each other again.'

Beth nodded, her heart too full to speak. It was *his* eyes gazing back at her from her daughter's face. And she understood, Lara understood. 'I hope we both find what we're looking for, Lara dear, when this awful war is over.'

Lara turned to face the window and stared out over the roof-tops. She made no reply. There was none to give. It was already too late for her. Mike had gone.

BOOK TWO

'The Crystal Spirit'

Your name and your deeds were forgotten
Before your bones were dry,
And the lie that slew you is buried
Under a deeper lie;

But the thing that I saw in your face
No power can disinherit:
No bomb that ever burst
Shatters the crystal spirit.

George Orwell

Chapter Thirty

In the late evening of Saturday 9 January 1943, President Franklin D. Roosevelt, Harry Hopkins, and a select party of advisers, including Major-General Mike Adams of Military Intelligence, boarded the Presidential train at a secret railroad siding, alongside the Bureau of Engraving and Printing, in Washington. So secret was this departure that the train's usual complement of porters, waiters and cooks was substituted by a crew of Filipino sailors from Shangri-la, the President's weekend retreat in the Maryland hills.

Roosevelt himself had never been in better heart and, despite his doctor's reservations, he was raring to go. He had been looking forward to this trip more than any other throughout his time in the White House. He would be the first President to leave the United States in wartime, and the first since Abraham Lincoln to visit an active theatre of war.

Rumours abounded in Washington that the President was about to go abroad, and various possible destinations around the globe were bandied about. But few knew the truth: he was heading for Morocco, where the ancient white-walled city of Casablanca was to provide the setting for a conference on war strategy between the Americans and the British Prime Minister, Winston Churchill, and his advisers.

The train left Washington with all the blinds securely closed. Most of the passengers turned in almost immediately for an early night. They were to spend a long, sleepy Sunday travelling down through the Carolinas and the old cotton fields of Georgia, before the train pulled into Miami, Florida, in the early hours of Monday morning.

Like most of the others aboard, Mike Adams had slept little that night, and their call to breakfast at four-thirty in the morning came as somewhat of a relief. He never could sleep on trains and, despite the comfort of the Pullman, the incessant, rhythmic clatter of the wheels seemed to pound in his head every time he switched off the light above his bunk and attempted to doze off.

At breakfast he found himself sharing a table in the dining-car with Admiral Ross McIntire, the President's doctor, Captain John McCrea, his Naval Aide, and Admiral William Leahy, who was feeling far from well. Harry Hopkins had chosen to remain in his carriage: plagued with chronic stomach trouble, hearty breakfasts and the prospect of the forthcoming flight did not mix for the President's favourite envoy.

In Miami, in the darkness of the early morning, the party transferred to a Pan American Boeing Clipper. Mike, being one of the tallest and brawniest there, helped carry the President on board the plane. After seeing him safely strapped into his seat, he sat alongside him and Harry Hopkins as, at just after six in the morning, they taxied out of the harbour and headed towards daybreak and the waiting continent of Africa.

The President's good humour was infectious and spirits were high aboard the plane. Mike had never been to North Africa before, and was looking forward to the change after being desk-bound for two years in Washington. He had come a long way as far as his career was concerned since he left Britain two years ago this month. A Lieutenant-Colonel to a Major-General in under two years. Who would have believed it? Certainly not Joanne when he ran into her back in New York over Christmas. 'So we're a two-star General, are we? With so much gold around, I thought for a minute you were the doorman!' she had said, smiling sweetly and eyeing the gold insignia on his shoulders. They were standing on the sidewalk outside 'Le Pavillon' restaurant on East 55th Street. 'I'm impressed.' She had looked up into the eyes of the young Lieutenant on whose arm she rested and murmured, 'Aren't you, honey?' He was not the same guy she had divorced Mike to marry, but that came as no surprise. Men were dispensable commodities in her book – always had been.

The junior officer had looked so embarrassed that Mike had taken pity on him and changed the subject before he had a chance to speak. 'If you're heading inside for lunch, I'd recommend the Monsieur Souté's Dish of the Day. It's excellent.'

'Mike likes to think of himself as something of a gourmet,' Joanne explained to her companion, the sweet smile still in place.

'A glutton with brains is what she means,' he had corrected. 'It's been real nice to meet you, soldier.' The young man had attempted a watery smile. Mike knew exactly how he felt. A two-star General was something akin to God Almighty to most young officers at the foot of the military ladder … And now he was one himself. Wonders would never cease. He settled back in his seat and closed his eyes; the drone of the aircraft engine had a wonderfully soporific effect after yesterday's constant clanking of the train.

After lunch, most of the party dozed in their seats and, to his surprise, for he was seldom one to cat-nap, Mike too fell asleep for a couple of hours. He awoke just in time to prepare for the landing in Trinidad, where they were to overnight at the American naval base.

They were billeted at a hotel run by the Navy and, after cocktails and an early dinner, most of their party retired to bed at just after nine o'clock. They were to leave before daybreak and would need the sleep. Once again the call to breakfast came at just after four o'clock the following morning, and Mike rose feeling surprisingly refreshed. He showered and dressed before going downstairs to enjoy a leisurely breakfast with Admiral Jesse Oldendorf and General Henry Pratt, who were acting as their hosts during the stop-over.

Just as they were about to begin the meal, Doctor McIntire announced that Bill Leahy was running a high temperature and would have to be left behind. There was an immediate murmur of sympathy around the table. Mike regretted the loss, for though Bill Leahy might not be from the same service as himself, he could always be relied upon to talk sense; and his kind of clear-headedness was going to be needed where they were going. The Americans and the British might now be staunch allies in this war, but that certainly didn't mean that they always saw eye to eye on how the fighting should be carried out.

Once airborne again, the flight was smooth and uneventful, with the plane cruising at around 9,000 feet, so that even the worst air-travellers amongst them managed to keep their drinks down. They landed at the Brazilian port of Belem at three-fifteen in the afternoon. The United States had established a Ferry Command post there, with a permanent staff of 250 Americans to service the bombers on their way to Africa.

Their stay was brief, and for that they were thankful. At this stage in the journey, they simply wanted to get it over with. They were driven to the Officers' Mess, where they were served with a generous glass of rum, and Mike met up again with one or two old acquaintances from Washington. To his utter astonishment, he also spied the young Lieutenant he had met that day in New York with Joanne. The young man was obviously at great pains to avoid eye contact, so Mike obligingly ignored him and concentrated his attention on the others.

The flight to Africa took eighteen and a half hours, and it felt like it by the time they eventually landed at the old slaving port of Bathurst at the mouth of the Gambia river in West Africa. The cruiser *Memphis*, on which they were to spend the night, was berthed in the docks alongside an American destroyer.

The warmth of the tropical sun hit them full in the face when they emerged sweaty and crumpled from the plane, and Mike wished he had thought better than to wear his best dress uniform for the trip, but at least everybody else seemed to be in much the same state. A dozen or so curious children, with eyes like black olives in their round brown faces, ran behind them shouting, 'Gum, chum!' as they made to board the waiting vessel but, sadly, only two packets could be produced. 'Do you reckon they'd know what to do with an Alka Seltzer?' Harry asked, only half-joking. It was all he could come up with from the depths of his jacket pocket.

'Dirt, disease, and a very high mortality rate, I would say, if I were asked to categorize this place,' was the President's farewell comment on the town as they drove out the seventeen miles to the airport next morning for the last leg of their journey, and the others agreed with him to a man.

There were about one dozen big bombers standing on the airfield, and their crews had built a big ramp for the President's wheelchair to be pushed aboard the Douglas C-54 transport plane that was waiting on the runway for them. Mike did the honours and was rewarded with one of FDR's special grins. 'It's your brawn, not your brains, you've been brought along for, you realize that, don't you?'

'Glad to be of service, in any capacity, Chief.' He meant it, too, for his admiration for Franklin Roosevelt had grown tremendously since he had returned to Washington two years ago, just in time to see him pilot the Lend-Lease bill through Congress, to finally become law on 11 March 1941. That had been no mean feat, and he doubted if there was another man in the whole country who could have accomplished it. There were those who doubted the wisdom of the country breaking with precedent to allow the President to run for a third term in office last year, but his re-election was surely the best answer possible for all those doubting Thomases. Right now, they couldn't have a better man at the helm, and he had more than a suspicion that the man they were about to do business with, Prime Minister Churchill, felt the same way too.

Once firmly strapped in, Mike settled back in his seat with a book. Ahead lay seven hours of the Sahara desert, before they sighted the snow-capped peaks of the Atlas Mountains, and finally reached the fertile fields of North Africa and their destination.

The journey was every bit as uncomfortable as they expected and, to a man, they were all relieved when they finally touched down at the airfield about fifteen miles from Casablanca. A scorching sun was still high in the sky as they descended the aircraft steps and squinted down, through the shimmering heat, to the small reception committee waiting at the foot of the steps. Mike recognized the unmistakable figure of General George Patton, who was in charge of operations at Casablanca, and Mike Reilly, the President's bodyguard, who had obviously flown on ahead. The young man in the Lieutenant's uniform standing beside him also looked vaguely familiar. It was the President's son, Elliot, who could scarcely disguise his relief at the plane's safe arrival.

The airfield was situated only two miles from the place chosen as the venue for the Conference, so the final leg of the journey took less than ten minutes. The two Roosevelts, plus Harry Hopkins, were allocated a special armoured car, the rear windows of which had been blacked out with mud, to take them to their waiting villa, and Mike and the others followed closely behind in Army jeeps.

Both the British and American delegations were to stay in the Anfa Hotel complex, now known to all as the Anfa Camp, situated some five miles south of the city. The President and the Prime Minister were allocated modern villas within the hotel grounds, less than fifty yards from each other, with the remainder of their respective parties living in the hotel itself.

As they drove through the Anfa gardens, with their green velvet lawns, colourful flower-beds and sweet-smelling orange groves, Mike could not help feeling a tinge of apprehension at meeting the British again face to face. He had tried, and for the best part succeeded in putting that island and its people out of his mind over the past two years – at least, from a personal point of view. From a professional viewpoint, the British had been on his mind almost every waking minute as he sat in his office in the Pentagon or, increasingly often, in the White House itself, and deciphered exactly what to make of the intelligence reports that came in daily from the war zones.

The hotel and its grounds had been turned into something akin to a fortress for the duration of the Conference, but it still retained its look of leisured luxury, with its dazzling white walls, wide balconies, and breathtaking views of the endless blue Atlantic. If one ignored the fact that they were surrounded by what seemed like miles of barbed wire and had every move scrutinized by heavily-armed soldiers under the gimlet eye of General Patton, you could almost feel you might even enjoy yourself here.

Mike's bedroom overlooked the villas of both Heads of State and, after relaxing for fifteen minutes under a cool shower, he wandered out on to the balcony and lit a cigarette. Two figures were strolling round Mirador, the Churchill villa, stopping every now and then to chat. From where he was standing, it was impossible to mistake the Prime Minister's smallish, rotund figure, and his companion he took to be Churchill's doctor, Sir Charles Wilson, who usually accompanied the old man on most trips, at home or abroad. The Prime Minister was to dine with Roosevelt in the Presidential villa this evening, with Mike and the others joining them after they had met with their British opposite numbers for a pre-dinner drink in the hotel bar. The thought of socializing in less than an hour's time did not exactly fill him with joy. All he really wanted to do was to lie down beneath the mosquito net on his bed and go straight to sleep.

Thank God he had packed a spare uniform, he thought to himself some forty minutes later, as he patted the last hair into place in front of the dressing-table mirror. Apart from the darkish circles under his eyes from the disrupted sleep of the past few nights, he looked almost human again. It was odd really, he could not remember having had any grey hairs to speak of when he left London two years ago, but it was impossible to ignore the streaks of silver at the temples now. Not that he minded, really, for at not yet forty, he must be just about the youngest of the advisers here today, on either side.

The hotel bar was a sea of faces when he walked in through the open door five minutes later. Many of them, such as Eisenhower and Patton, he knew of old, but several of them were unfamiliar. Then, from the far end of the room, a hand shot in the air, and he recognized the tall, moustached figure of Harold Macmillan, the British politician whom he had met at several Embassy social occasions during his short stay in London. Macmillan was talking to Edward Forbes-Hamilton, an even older acquaintance, once on the British Embassy staff in Washington.

He threaded his way through the throng to shake hands with the Member of Parliament for Stockton and the diplomat. 'Harold, nice to see you again! And you Ed. What on earth brings you two out here?'

'You may well ask, old boy,' Forbes-Hamilton grinned. 'The PM, in his infinite wisdom, has sent Harold here over to be some sort of political adviser to Ike, and I'm to lend moral support.'

'You're kidding!'

Macmillan gave a wry smile and his companion's grin grew broader as he added, 'The good General seems to think so too! But I can assure you the Prime Minister is deadly serious. So one does one's best, you know. *Nitor in adversum*, and all that ... ' He broke off to glance over Mike's shoulder towards the doorway. 'Good Lord, there's one of the best reasons for putting up with all the sand and flies round here with a good grace! I'll introduce you ... '

Mike was aware of Forbes-Hamilton signalling once more towards the open door, but was too hemmed in to turn around.

'Mike – or perhaps I should say General Adams – allow me to introduce you to one of the most important people in the whole of the British delegation – and perhaps the most unsung: Mrs Lara Cameron.'

Mike felt his jaw drop open as he turned to gaze into a pair of equally astonished hazel eyes.

Chapter Thirty-one

Lara stared up in amazement at the man in front of her. 'Mike ...'
Her voice tailed off into a croak as her eyes took in the face now
smiling back into hers. He looked older since they last met: his hair
was greying at the temples; the dark brows above the brilliant blue
eyes looked shaggier and had the odd silver hair; but that same quirky
smile had not changed. It still made her heart turn over.

'Hello, Lara.'

'I didn't realize you two already knew each other.' Harold Macmillan sounded almost disappointed as he stood between the two of
them and looked from one to the other.

'Lara used to work for me a couple of years back,' Mike said by way
of explanation, his eyes never leaving her face.

'Oh, really? I never knew you'd worked in the States, Lara ...' The
dark brows above the heavy-lidded eyes rose in surprise, then
Macmillan's gaze moved back to the open door. 'But, look, since you
two are obviously old friends and colleagues, we'll leave you to
"*recherche du temps perdu*" and all that, if you don't mind. I see Ike has
just come in with old Blood and Guts and we really must have a
word with him.'

For a split second, Mike's eyes darted to the doorway through
which Eisenhower and Patton were now strolling, deep in conversation. 'Sure, Mac, you go right ahead. And you, Ed.'

They watched the tall figure with its military bearing and his
smaller companion set off across the room, then Mike took hold of
Lara's elbow. The touch of his fingers on her bare skin made her jump
slightly. 'Let's get a drink,' he said huskily, guiding her through the
throng towards the bar. Then, seeing too many people there he knew
personally, he said quietly, 'On second thoughts, you head on out to
the terrace; I'll bring the drinks out.'

He had not even bothered to ask her what she was drinking, she thought wryly, as she watched him head over to the bar. The palms of her hands were damp with nervous perspiration, and she wiped them dry on the white moygashel skirt of her dress as her eyes remained glued to his retreating figure. He looked good in uniform; he wore it with an easy grace. A leader of men, born to the part, she thought, and felt a curious pride inside her.

Her heart raced as she walked as casually as possible out on to the terrace, where a warm breeze was blowing in from the Atlantic Ocean only a stone's throw away. She leaned on the white balustrade and gazed out to sea, sucking the salt air deeply into her lungs in an attempt to calm her chaotic thoughts and racing pulse. Enormous waves were pounding the rocks down below, the wind sending great clouds of white foam into the air. The swirling waters seemed to complement the turmoil in her mind. She should have known; she should have been aware there was a chance he would be here. She should have been sensible enough to realize it and circumvent it ...

But she *did* know. A pang of guilt ran through her. That was the awful part of it. Something deep inside her had told her that there was a chance, just the slightest chance, that he would be here as part of the American delegation. But, when the opportunity came to accompany the Prime Minister out here, she had jumped at it. She had no rational explanation for it. It was as if she was deliberately playing Russian roulette with her feelings, with her very life ...

The British delegation had arrived two days previously, and on more than one occasion she had found herself making discreet enquiries as to who would be accompanying the President when he arrived; but even General Patton himself could not enlighten her on that subject. 'I'd go as far as to lay a bet on Harry Hopkins, ma'am, but as to the others ... Well, I guess it depends on who the President reckons can stand up to your lot best.'

Her heart had leapt at the mention of Hopkins's name. She knew Mike was a long-standing friend of the special envoy, so there was a chance, just the slightest chance ...

'Pink champagne!'

His voice made her head jerk round, the breeze blowing strands of titian hair into her eyes. 'How lovely!' She ran a controlling hand over her wayward locks, and wished she could do the same to her heart as she held out her hand to accept the drink. 'I haven't had this since ... '

'Since the last time?' He grinned down at her. 'It's been a long time, Lara.'

'Two years to the day – almost?' She blushed into her drink.

'If this was the movies we'd have the days, hours and minutes calculated too.' His mouth quirked slightly at the side in a semblance of a smile, but there was a tone akin to wistfulness in his voice.

'Cheers!' She got in the salutation quickly, before he could provide any other. Her eyes moved to the two gold stars glittering on his shoulders. 'Congratulations are in order, I see – a Major-General no less. I'm filled with admiration.'

'Don't be. It's still the same guy underneath.'

Their eyes met and held. There was no mistaking the innuendo and she could feel a delicate sweat break out under her armpits. Why did he have this effect on her? Why him? Why not Ken? Dear God, why not Ken … ? 'I don't have to ask you how you've been since we last met,' she said, as lightly as possible. 'The gold stars speak for themselves. I – I'm glad things have worked out so well for you.'

He looked straight at her, a quizzical sort of look, as if trying to read beyond the pleasantries. 'Your – your husband, he's still fine?' His voice was husky as he spoke and he cleared his throat before taking a gulp of the vodka in his hand. How's your husband? Is he alive or dead? That was what he wanted to know … that was what he really wanted to blurt out, and he felt shame colour his cheeks beneath the remainder of last summer's tan at the knowledge.

'Ken's fine.' She stared down into her drink, running her finger around the rim of the glass. It made a musical note which echoed in her head and only underlined the momentary silence that had fallen between them.

'See much of him?' Why was he torturing himself like this?

She shook her head regretfully. 'It's getting on for two months now since he had any leave. I did hope he'd manage a day or so at Christmas, but it didn't work out … ' She paused, not really wanting to continue in this vein. Guilt flooded through her at the mere mention of Ken: a guilt for what might have been with this man standing beside her. 'And you – your divorce, it went all right?'

He gave a mirthless half-laugh. 'Sure. I'm footloose and fancy-free once again – have been for the past nine months.' He gave a wry grin. 'You don't realize how short a month can be until you're paying alimony! But don't get me wrong, I'm not complaining. You learn from your mistakes in this world.' His grin grew broader. 'I guess I couldn't remain a thing of beauty and a boy forever for the rest of my life, now could I?'

She attempted a smile in return. He was doing what he always did: joking to cover his real feelings. Just what *had* she been like – Joanne – this woman to whom he had just given her freedom? She could not imagine how anyone could ever divorce him by choice.

The sound of movement from the bar caused them both to look round. 'It looks like they're serving dinner,' Mike said, taking hold of her arm once more. 'They'll have place-cards set out, no doubt, and I'll probably end up being seated next to one of your British guys who wants to talk war the whole darned time.' He glanced at his watch. 'It's quarter to eight now; the meal should be over by eight-thirty or nine. If I can get away, can we meet for a drink afterwards?'

She caught her breath. 'Where ... ?'

He grinned. 'The choice is hardly unlimited! Ever tried getting out of this barbed wire? You'd have old Georgie-boy down on you like a ton of bricks!'

He was right. General Patton had been running the camp like a top-security Stalag and was becoming the butt of many jokes amongst those of them on the inside. 'Point taken,' she smiled. 'In that case, I'll be right here. But don't be surprised if you don't make it because you get a call to Dar es Saada tonight.'

'Dar es Saada?'

'The President's villa. Mr Churchill is going to be there, and he's in a rather talkative mood tonight!'

Her prophecy was to prove all too accurate. She was seated at the other end of the dining-room from Mike who, after the dinner, was called to the President's villa, along with Dwight Eisenhower, Harold Macmillan and several others. Harry Hopkins, who was staying there with Roosevelt and his son, had obviously dined with them and the Prime Minister.

She stood at the back of the room as they filed out, laughing and chatting amongst themselves. She thought for a moment Mike was going to turn and catch her eye, but his tall frame was lost in the crowd of other uniformed figures. It was going to be a long night for some, she could see that.

Reluctantly she made her way up to her room and wandered out on to the open balcony. If she craned her neck enough she could just make out the front door of Dar es Saada. Slats of light from behind the shutters of the front window nearest the hotel indicated the room where the talking must be going on. She stared at it through the falling darkness as a curious maelstrom of emotions whirled in her head.

In a way, she had almost wished this situation upon herself; but now it was here she could feel a panic growing within her. She no longer trusted herself. Britain and the bombs – the whole reality of the war and her marriage to Ken – seemed a million miles away. This was the reality now; this strange foreign land, with its sun and sand,

and the man in the two-star General's uniform who was behind the white-painted shutters and mosquito netting of that window down there. A shiver ran through her at the thought.

She stifled a yawn. It had been a long day. But although her body was tired, her mind was still too alive to think of sleep. A glance at her watch told her it was almost nine o'clock. It was too early for bed, but she had no inclination to go back down to the bar alone. She sighed and wandered back into her room. She would write a letter to Ken.

Forsaking the writing paper she had brought with her, she sat down at the dressing-table and wrote instead on the elegant cream vellum supplied by the hotel. The words did not come easily. Was she simply attempting to purge her guilt feelings by writing messages of love across the page? It was as if she was writing to a stranger – a stranger whose name she bore.

She paused, the pen an inch or two above the page, and closed her eyes as she tried to picture her husband's face. The sandy hair appeared before her closed lids, and the freckles that peppered the bridge of the nose and cheeks, but the actual features remained a blur. No matter how she tried, she could not conjure up Ken's face. She rubbed her eyes. She was tired, that was all. Too much had happened over the past twenty-four hours; too much had happened over the past two hours ...

She got up and walked over to the bed, kicking off her shoes before pulling back the mosquito netting and lying down on top of the white cotton bedspread. She stretched out and closed her eyes. A faint breeze from the open balcony door fanned the bare skin of her face and arms. As she drifted into that strange half-world between consciousness and dreaming, it became a human breath. Another face swam before her; a face without freckles; a face with thick, dark brows above bright blue eyes and a funny quirky grin. She whispered his name in the cool twilight of the room, as a solitary tear squeezed beneath her closed lashes and trickled down her cheek. 'Mike ...'

It was five o'clock in the morning before she awoke, and a pale, watery sun was streaming in through the still open doors of the balcony to penetrate the drapes of netting around the bed. Lara sat up and gazed about her as if in disbelief. It had been a troubled sleep and, instead of feeling rested, a strange, nervous anxiety pervaded her being.

She focused her eyes on her dress and groaned out loud: the white moygashel was a mass of creases, and the back felt damp with perspiration. 'Drat it ...'

She sat up fully on the bed and slipped her legs over the edge as she fought her way out of the mosquito nets. The marble tiles felt cool beneath her stockinged feet as she gazed around the room. Something white lying on the floor in front of the door caught her eye. She padded across and picked it up. It was a carefully folded piece of hotel notepaper. Frowning, she opened it out and, at once, the familiar writing leapt up from the page at her and she gave a small gasp as she began to read:

Dearest Lara,
    You were right. (You usually are.) I'm writing this at just before three in the morning, having just got back from the President's place. I've got to go downtown at 2.30 this afternoon to see Patton at his office in the Shell building. I figure on being back here by 4. Can you get away and meet me out front about then?
                                                          Mike

She read it, then reread it. Could she? Her heart raced. For the two days they had been here she had never been called upon to take notes in the afternoon. She refolded the note and thoughtfully chewed at her lip as she walked out on to the cool morning air of the balcony. Yes, there was a chance, just a chance ...

An almost mystical stillness lay across the landscape as she gazed out across the sleeping compound. One solitary figure – a gaffir, an old man bent double with age and a lifetime spent in the service of others, and dressed in traditional arab robes and head-dress – led a small herd of scrawny, cream-coloured goats across her vision.

Below her, in two of those white-walled villas, two of the three most powerful men in the world slept, while half a world away the other – a half-crazed Austrian by the name of Adolf Hitler – dreamt his own dreams that in the cold light of day would turn into a living nightmare for untold millions.

She thought of the man she now knew to be her father, Jan Jarosinski, thousands of miles away in the blood-bath that was Poland. What had become of him? Was he still alive? There had been no word or sign from him since he left England to return to Poland two years ago. Her mother had attempted to assuage her anxiety by working all hours at the SOE office in Baker Street, but the wound caused by his leaving had not, and would not heal.

What would this year bring? Would any of them still be alive at the end of it? So many of those she knew and loved had already gone. Her grandmother, Emily Sanders, had passed away after a bad bout of pneumonia last winter and, two years ago next month, Ken's beloved Auntie Cissie had taken her own life two weeks after learning that her son Alan had been killed in North Africa. The list was endless, and would go on and on, until this bloody war was brought to an end. And the two men with the power to do it were still asleep less than a stone's throw from where she now stood. 'Please God, give them the strength to do what's right. Help them make the right decisions this coming day and in the days ahead ... '

As she spoke the words she knew it was not only the two Heads of State she was praying for. Her fingers closed tighter around the piece of paper in her hand. The words applied equally to herself.

Chapter Thirty-two

Lara shielded her eyes with her hand and squinted through the pale January sunshine into the windscreen of the dark blue Peugeot 302 as it drew to a halt beside her. There was no mistaking the face smiling back at her from behind the wheel. 'Mike!'

He raised a hand in greeting, then leaned across and opened the passenger door for her to get in beside him.

'I didn't think you'd get away.'

'Neither did I, to tell the truth,' he grinned, as he threw the car into gear and they moved off smoothly in the direction of the camp entrance. 'God, that guy Patton sure can talk! He's either a military genius or a nut, I can't make up my mind which.'

'Probably both,' Lara smiled, as she smoothed the skirt of her dress over her knees and made herself comfortable. 'You had an interesting afternoon, I take it?'

Mike gave a bemused shake of the head as he recalled the meeting he had just come from. 'You know, he's made this city into one vast storehouse for all sorts of things. He's not only got almost a hundred million gallons of fuel stored in dumps around the place, and such things as a million burlap covers to make sandbags, but he's been stashing away thousands of cases of Mum deodorants! I reckon he figures that if the Germans invade Casa, then at least the inhabitants will be sweet-smelling as they fight them off!'

She laughed. 'Nothing about this war surprises me any more. You know, I took my mother out for a meal in Belgravia just before I flew down here and there was a notice displayed very prominently on every table stating: "Dining-room customers who wish to go to the shelter should tell the waiter who will present their bill immediately"!'

'Opportunists!' Mike grinned, in a mock shocked voice. Then the smile faded slightly, 'How is it over there these days, anyway? Pretty hairy, I guess.'

'We survive,' Lara answered quietly. 'At least most of us do … It's like a different world coming here. Just leaving the war behind for a week or so is quite an incredible feeling; to go to bed and know you'll be able to sleep right through till morning is bliss!'

They were leaving the compound now and the two military policemen on guard at the gates sprang to attention and saluted smartly at the sight of the Major-General behind the wheel. 'I thought we'd take a trip out along the coast road towards Rabat,' Mike said, touching the peak of his cap in response. 'It's about a sixty mile drive. How long do you reckon you've got before they miss you?'

'Actually, I've got the rest of the afternoon off,' she replied, still somewhat amazed at her good fortune. 'I think his doctor has insisted that the Prime Minister take it easy for a few hours, before his session with the President this evening, for he actually suggested that I should take the opportunity to slip out and do a bit of sightseeing and shopping if I felt like it.'

'Great! Couldn't be better!'

It was raining now, a soft, gentle rain, not uncommon in Morocco at this time of year. The sound of it on the roof of the car had a lovely soporific effect as Lara leaned back in her seat and gave a contented sigh. The nerves she had felt waiting on the steps of the hotel a few minutes ago had all but vanished. She was comfortable in his presence; it felt right, somehow.

As the car sped northwards across miles of red earth, sparsely covered with tufts of yellowed, dry grass, she relaxed even more as he told her something of the history of the land they were travelling through. She gazed out through the windows in fascination as they left the concrete and glass of modern Casablanca far behind and entered the real Morocco of small villages, where Barbary fig cacti stood sentinel over clusters of conical-shaped huts, like giant thatched beehives, and baggy-trousered 'fellahs' bent over wooden ploughs, harnessed to unwilling, moth-eaten mules or camels, as they attempted to scratch a living from the barren earth.

He had obviously read up on the country before coming out here, and she was content to let his voice flow over her as he explained how this ancient land had proved such a temptation to its Mediterranean neighbours over the centuries. Here Carthage had set up trading colonies; Ancient Rome had invaded as far as the Pillars of Hercules, then, with the decline and fall of the Roman Empire, the Vandals had swept eastwards, followed by Byzantine emperors and Turkish sultans who, despite their great wealth and power, had never succeeded in conquering the Moors. 'They have a saying out here,' Mike said: 'The Tunisians are women; the Algerians are men; but the Moroccans are lions. We could do with a few of them against Attila Hitler and his Hun battalions right now!'

Lara gave a wry smile. She knew that as far as this war was concerned, the worst was probably yet to come. 'Will you stay on in uniform when this is all over, Mike?' she asked, in a quiet voice. 'Will you go on being a General when peace finally returns?'

She felt, rather than saw him smile. He was silent for a moment or two then, just when she thought he was ignoring the question, he said softly:

> 'No longer forward nor behind
> I look in hope or fear;
> But, grateful take the good I find,
> The best of now and here ... '

It was her turn to be silent as he turned to her with a strange half-smile on his lips. 'One of our best poets,' he said. 'John Greenleaf Whittier. Pretty apt, I reckon.'

It was still raining, and the windscreen wipers were making a tiny squeaking sound as they swung backwards and forwards in front of her gaze, wiping the rain from the dusty windscreen. She repeated the words in her head as he reached inside his jacket pocket for a cigarette. He lit it with a quick flick of his lighter, then opened the window, as he inhaled the thick white smoke. It trickled out slowly from his nostrils and mouth as he said gently, 'I've stopped looking forwards any more, Lara. The future, if there is a future, is in God's hands – if there is a God ... ' He gave a mirthless laugh. 'The whole darned world is full of "ifs" right now. All we can do is to take each day as it comes ... If we never get the chance to be alone with each other again, we'll remember these few hours this afternoon. Moments out of time, that's what they are. Moments we'll remember when the world has moved on and taken us with it ... '

He glanced around at her and she turned her head abruptly to stare out of the side window so he would not see the tears that had sprung to her eyes and were glistening in the soft grey light of the afternoon.

They reached the outskirts of Rabat just over an hour later. The rain had turned the white city to a shimmering silver and deepened the foliage of the palms and magnolias to a deep, glossy green as they sped quickly through the 'bidonvilles' – the shanty towns – on its outskirts.

Mike slowed up as they entered the bustling, palm-tree lined streets of the city itself, so Lara could soak up the atmosphere of the 'ville nouvelle', whose straight modern boulevards led on in the distance to the narrow, winding streets of the 'medina'. There, the flat, tightly-packed roof-tops were interspersed with those of the mosques, whose slender minarets pointed like accusing fingers towards the grey-blue of the heavens.

Lara gazed entranced at the fine old houses with their green-tiled porticos, arched, columned windows, and painted wooden balconies adorning the upper storeys. 'Nice, huh?' Mike said, hearing her murmurs of admiration. 'You could say that Rabat is to Casablanca what Washington is to New York,' he mused, as they drove slowly along the Boulevard Misr, then turned right into the Boulevard el Alou. 'The seat of Government was transferred here in 1913, and it looks like a good move to me. It doesn't seem to have the brashness or bustle of Casa: it's more sedate somehow; it's got more dignity.'

After several consultations of a map he had propped up on the dashboard, and at least one wrong turning, he eventually pulled the car up outside a massive fortified gateway built of a dark-red sandstone, and switched off the ignition. 'I've always wanted to say this,' he grinned. 'Ever since seeing Rudolf Valentino in *The Sheik*, as a small kid back in the Bronx … Come on, Lara … Come with me to the Casbah!'

'What?'

The grin grew broader. 'The Casbah – we're here. This is the gate to it.' He got out of the car and bounded round to open her door. 'They don't allow cars to enter the Casbah itself, so I've been told,' he said, as he helped her out and locked the door behind her. 'The streets are just too narrow. We'll have to go on foot. Do you mind?'

She looked up at him. He looked even more handsome than usual, with his cap tilted at a rakish angle over the shock of dark brown hair. She would be proud to walk anywhere with him. 'Lead on, MacDuff!' she laughed, misquoting Shakespeare. 'I can't wait!'

They walked arm in arm up a wide cobbled ramp, passing a battery of old bronze cannons, then on through the portal itself into the tangle of steep, narrow alleyways and cobbled lanes that was the Casbah.

Soon they were surrounded by an entourage of brown-skinned, bare-footed children, tugging at their sleeves and shouting, 'Guide, M'sieur? Guide, Mam'selle? Je suis bon guide!'

'Now I know how the Pied Piper felt!' Lara laughed, clinging tighter to Mike's arm as they moved deeper into the old markets with their eye-catching displays of traditional gold and silver Berber jewellery; breathtaking fabrics shot through with metallic threads;

aromatic sweetmeats; intricately woven rugs and beautifully engraved brass-ware.

They stopped outside a goldsmith's, where the sound of a tinny hammering greeted them from inside the open-fronted shop. 'Let's take a look inside.' Mike gripped her hand more tightly as they squeezed their way past the long, narrow counter into the back-room where an old man sat bent over a workbench littered with a dazzling display of half-finished objects.

At first, Lara was as fascinated by the craftsman himself as with his wares. The finely boned face appeared wrought out of tanned brown leather and the black olive eyes were red-rimmed from a lifetime of straining against the dim light of the shop as he glanced up briefly to acknowledge their presence, then continued with his work. His bony fingers twisted slender strands of gold wire into traditional arabesque patterns, then, with the aid of a tiny chisel and hammer, the intricate designs were inlaid into pieces of specially carved wood.

They watched in fascination for several minutes, then Mike's fingers squeezed Lara's even tighter. 'Choose one,' he said softly.

'I – I couldn't!'

'Go on, please, Lara – choose one.'

She shook her head regretfully. 'I – I couldn't – really … '

'Then I will!'

As the old man looked on, Mike picked up several pieces and examined them closely. Eventually his fingers settled on a gold-link necklet, with a pendant of brilliant diamond locked inside a cage of gold filigree. He held it up to Lara's neck and nodded in satisfaction. 'Perfect. Just perfect,' he said, turning to nod at the craftsman. 'We'll take it.'

She watched mutely as, in faltering French, he settled up financially, placing several notes into the bony hand and waving away the old man's attempt to give change. She could feel her heart beating faster as he walked back over to where she was standing. He smiled down at her. 'Turn round and lift your hair.'

She did as she was told, and felt him slip the gold necklet into place. When he fastened the clasp, his fingers lingered on the pale skin, then he bent down and tenderly placed a kiss on the nape of her neck.

As she turned to face him, her cheeks burning, that funny, quirky grin on his lips was belied by the grave look in his eyes. 'They say diamonds are forever,' he said softly. 'And if nothing seems forever in this crazy world right now, maybe in years to come this might remind you of this moment – of us … No longer forward nor behind, Lara, my love. The best is now and here … '

They spent the best part of an hour in Rabat, but the poignancy – the intimacy – of that moment was not repeated. And, as they made the long return journey back to the Hotel Alfa and reality, Lara could not make up her mind whether to be sorry or relieved. It was as if the incident in the goldsmith's shop had never happened. In fact, if it hadn't been for the diamond glittering in its golden cage around her neck, she would have sworn she had imagined it. If anything, Mike was even more jokey than usual, which she found a relief at first, then slightly unnerving. What exactly was going on behind that passive expression as he whistled softly to himself, his fingers drumming rhythmically on the steering-wheel as the miles sped past and the gentle rain gave way to a soft grey light? If it wasn't for the small nerve flickering beneath the faint stubble at the edge of his jaw, there was no indication that he was anything but completely relaxed.

It was just after seven-thirty when they passed through Security at the gates of the compound. There seemed to be very few other people around. 'Let's hope they haven't started dinner early!' Mike commented, as he drew the Peugeot to a stop outside the main entrance to the hotel.

Lara murmured her agreement, although inside she knew she could not eat a thing. She sat quite still as he switched off the ignition, half-expecting him to say something – make some allusion to what had passed between them this afternoon. But instead, he leapt from the driving-seat and strode round the bonnet to open her door.

'Ever the gentleman,' she smiled wryly, as he took hold of her hand to help her out.

He held on to it and looked down at her as he shook his head. 'Never that, Lara honey. I told you before, I'll never be that.'

She stood on the step and watched as he got back into the car and drove off in the direction of the Presidential villa. Her fingers reached up and touched the glittering jewel around her neck. 'The best is now and here,' she repeated softly. Was that really true? Was this all she would ever have of him? She glanced down at the gold band glittering in the pale, winter sunshine on the third finger of her left hand. A great emptiness welled within her as she turned and walked slowly up the stone steps and in through the front door of the hotel.

Chapter Thirty-three

Lara stood on the balcony outside her hotel bedroom and watched the bevy of photographers and reporters, each with high security clearance, make their way to the lawn behind the President's villa. A press conference had been called and around fifty war correspondents and photographers flown in specially from Algiers. They were to inform the world that not only were the American President and the British Prime Minister here in Casablanca in person, but they had been for over a week, and they would now be issuing a joint communiqué of their talks. The battle-hardened correspondents could hardly believe their eyes or their ears. This was front page news. The whole place buzzed with excitement.

Lara watched from her place above the throng with a faintly bemused expression. Ten days had passed since their arrival here; over a week of soft rain showers and pale sunshine, interspersed by hours of note-taking for the Prime Minister. Ten days in which she had seen little or nothing of Mike. The lack of communication had opened up a great hole in her world. Distance she could cope with – the two years they had been separated by the Atlantic Ocean had become bearable with time – but knowing he was here, only a few yards away, and to be acting like virtual strangers ... It was almost more than she could bear. Did he realize? Had he any idea just what she was going through right now, as everyone made their preparations to pack up and leave?

Mike Adams was well aware. Every day that had passed since their trip to Rabat had been as painful for him as for her. Knowing she was here – sleeping at night in a room only a hundred yards from his own – had brought a peculiar agony which had often resulted in his pacing the silent corridors of the hotel in the dead of night. His steps would slow as he passed her door and, if there was a chink of light showing beneath, he would pause and wonder ... Should he knock?

Should he risk it? Often his hand would be only inches from the smooth wood panels, then sanity would prevail ... What the hell was he playing at? She was someone else's wife and intended to remain that way.

He felt in his pocket for his cigarettes and extracted one from the pack and lit it. He stood leaning against the wall of the President's villa and watched the chairs being set out on the lawn under the scrutiny of Patton's security men. The whole place buzzed with activity, reflecting the tenor of the week that had gone. Thank God, these past few days had been busy – so busy, in fact, that he had had little or no time to dwell on his own personal problems. His boss, FDR, and Churchill had had a problem of their own which had taken up an inordinate amount of his time: how to get the two French Generals, Henri Giraud and Charles de Gaulle together to patch up their differences before the end of the Conference. Both men were now installed in villas right next door to each other, and close by those of the President and the Prime Minister, but although Giraud, whom the United States and Great Britain were willing to recognize as High Commissioner in French North Africa, was not opposed to conferring with the acknowledged leader of the Free French forces, based in Britain, de Gaulle would have none of it. In fact, he had pointedly ignored his neighbour and fellow countryman since he had been here. Giraud he simply did not acknowledge, any more than he acknowledged the existence of the government in Vichy.

De Gaulle had been persuaded to fly out to the Conference at the last minute, believing he was to take part in the talks. His hosts had other ideas, however. The American and British hope was to get some kind of *rapprochement* on record between the two French Generals. But, to the increasing frustration of the American and British leaders, on discovering that Giraud had also been invited to the proceedings, de Gaulle was refusing to play ball.

When it became obvious that Robert Murphy, the President's political representative, and Harold Macmillan, his British opposite number, had had no luck with the recalcitrant guest, Mike had gone with Harry Hopkins to the de Gaulle villa the previous afternoon, at Roosevelt's request, to try to persuade him to see reason. They found, however, that the tall Frenchman was intent on delivering his own lecture to them. Didn't they know, he had declared, that his forces were the only French Forces that were fighting for the liberty of France; that only they represented the true spirit of France? The Marshal Pétain who now headed that puppet of the Nazis, the Vichy Government, was not Marshal Pétain, the Great War hero – that

Marshal Pétain had died in 1925. The one who now masqueraded under his name was a weak, vain character with the spirit of a grandfather. General Giraud, he declared, he would have no truck with, for that man owed his own position out here to the despised Vichy Government.

And so the argument had gone on, bouncing back and forth, and Mike could not help feeling a grudging admiration for the man as he had stood there, reminiscent of a human giraffe, sniffing down his considerable nose at Harry and himself. They were two distinctly lesser mortals in the Frenchman's eyes, despite the fact that neither of the Americans were under six foot, or weighed less than a hundred and sixty pounds. But it wasn't size that counted with de Gaulle, it was breeding, and as neither Mike nor Harry could match his own claim to direct lineal descent from Joan of Arc, they reckoned perhaps the only man in the vicinity to match up was the British Prime Minister. And so Churchill had spent most of this morning with de Gaulle, and the Americans could only keep their fingers crossed that the old man would have better luck than they had had.

Mike took another drag of his cigarette and scanned the faces milling around the lawn, as the cluster of war correspondents and photographers grew increasingly impatient for their story. He glanced at his watch. It was just before twelve o'clock, they should only have minutes to wait. But was the British leader having any luck?

He wandered over to the main body of the group, where people were standing around in small knots discussing the possible contents of the coming communiqué. Giraud had arrived half an hour ago and had made it clear he was intent on obtaining a confirmation in writing that the Allies would supply his Army. He would be willing to come to any concordat with de Gaulle if he was promised that. He was now deep in conversation with Eisenhower, on whom Roosevelt had fobbed him off.

They were all gathering on the lawn now: war correspondents, politicians, secretarial staff, as well as military men. Mike ground his cigarette into the grass and straightened his cap. The photographers would be called into action any minute now, and there they would all be, recorded for posterity, whatever that might mean.

He wandered round to the front of the Dar es Saada villa and glanced into the window. The tall, stiff-necked, patrician figure of de Gaulle dominated the room and, at a much lower level, the back of Churchill's bald, pink head was obvious through the mosquito netting. But it was not the Prime Minister who was doing the talking, he noticed, as Roosevelt's clipped East Coast vowels carried through the open window. The President was obviously using the last few minutes in an attempt to try to talk some sense into the obstinate Gallic head.

Two of Patton's military policemen were guarding the front door and several other plain clothes security men lurked in strategic places around the garden. Mike nodded to a couple of them and then noticed the tall, *soigné* figure of Harold Macmillan just inside the front porch, with the slightly shorter, bald-headed figure of Ed Forbes-Hamilton beside him. He raised his hand in greeting and the two Englishmen strolled over to join him.

'They've got "*le grand Charles*" cooped up in there with the two Emperors,' Macmillan commented, with a nod in the direction of the villa. He had taken to referring to the President as the 'Emperor of the West' and Churchill as the 'Emperor of the East' and was obviously relishing the thought of the leader of the Free French being unquestionably outranked and, hopefully, out-talked. 'I just hope your man, FDR, isn't too soft on him. According to Hopkins, Roosevelt is very taken by the "spiritual" look in "the Gaul's" eyes ...' he added drily, raising his own eyes to the heavens at the very idea.

Ed Forbes-Hamilton's face was creased in a smile. 'Before we left them to it, the President was reminding de Gaulle of how in the American Civil War brother had fought against brother, and explaining how he and Winston expected him to think of Henri Giraud as a brother!'

He glanced from Mike to Harold Macmillan whose bespectacled, heavily hooded eyes had narrowed in amusement at the recollection. 'I tell you, Adams,' he continued, 'there was nothing spiritual about the look the President got for his trouble! Nobody, absolutely nobody, can look down a nose like our French chum in there!'

'Nobody has a nose to look down like de Gaulle!' Mike grinned in return. It was funny how over the past couple of days the Frenchman had become the main talking-point of the Conference and, although they all joked about him, nevertheless there were few here who did not retain a grudging admiration for the haughty General.

Macmillan gave one of his laconic smiles and glanced over his shoulder at the gathering throng on the lawn, then Forbes-Hamilton followed suit, commenting to Mike, 'They seem to be congregating thick and fast over there. Fancy a walk over with us to join them? We know some of those press chaps of old, and you can pick up some jolly useful stuff from them.'

Mike gave a reluctant shake of his head. 'You two go on over. I'll stretch my legs for a bit longer and join you later.'

He watched the others depart to join the crowd jostling for position on the lawn behind the house. They looked an incongruous couple: the elegant figure of Macmillan alongside the smaller, slightly stooped figure of the diplomat, but then the whole place seemed full of incongruous figures, from the leaders downwards. Roosevelt, Churchill, de Gaulle, Patton – every last one of them was larger than life and just as unpredictable. Some days it seemed more like a mad-house than a conference to help decide the fate of the world – and this was just one of those days. The whole place was giving him a feeling of claustrophobia. There were too many people in too small a space. The babble of noise was making his head throb.

He strolled down the front path and out of the gate, nodding in passing to George Patton, who was on his way in to see the President. How that guy got away with wearing those pearl-handled revolvers as part of his uniform he would never know. But then, the sonofabitch always was a law unto himself.

The humidity was high after the morning's rain and his collar felt uncomfortably tight. He wished it wasn't obligatory to be in uniform practically the whole time. He paused on the sidewalk outside the garden gate and ran a finger around the inside of the offending collar. His gaze wandered across to the hotel opposite and something pale-blue and fluttering caught his eye. A young woman in a full-skirted sun-dress was leaning on the balcony looking his way.

He raised a hand to his eyes as his pulse quickened. His eyes narrowed as he squinted into the sunshine. 'Lara!' He could swear it was her! Even at several hundred yards there was no mistaking that red hair flaming in the midday sun.

He began to walk towards the figure that made a backwards movement as if to retreat into the bedroom behind, then changed its mind and remained standing. It was her all right. His stomach gave a distinct lurch as he fixed his gaze on her. He raised his hand in greeting and she responded. His pulse quickening even more, he beckoned her down. She paused, clutching the balustrade, looking down at him. He gestured again. She paused a moment longer, then disappeared in through the open door behind her.

She was coming. She was on her way down. He could feel his heart beating in his chest as he waited, impatiently tapping the leather sole of his shoe on the bottom step. It would be the first time they had met face to face since the trip to Rabat. It wasn't that he had deliberately avoided her: there had quite simply never been an occasion when they both found themselves off duty together. At least, he presumed that to be true, for he had never seen her around in the bar, or

275

anywhere in the swimming-pool or grounds. He could have called on her, of course, but that took ... Well, it was more than courage; that took a certain resolve to carry their relationship forward, and he was not at all certain that was a good idea. In fact, if he was honest with himself, it was one helluva bad idea. Yes, he had steeled himself on more than one occasion and carried on walking past that closed bedroom door, to go back to his own room and sit out on the balcony beneath the stars and smoke away the hours until dawn. And so the days and nights had slipped past, until here they were on the very last day of the Conference ...

It took several minutes for her to reach the forecourt of the hotel, and her face was flushed as she ran lightly down the steps to join him, but it wasn't all from exertion. She had caught what little sun had been around during the past ten days and her pale, freckled skin was a delicate shade of pink across the nose and cheeks. She smiled as casually as possible, tossing her hair back from her face with a rather jerky gesture. She was as nervous as he was, he could see it. 'I thought you'd be at the press conference.'

'So I should be,' he admitted, glancing at his watch. It had just gone twelve.

They stood facing each other at the foot of the steps. A silence fell. There was so much to say, yet both were at a loss for words. 'I guess it'll all be over very soon ... The conference, that is.' It was Mike who spoke. His voice was husky, gruff almost.

She nodded and attempted a smile. 'Yes, I suppose it will.' She looked up and met his eyes. They were a deep blue in the bright sunshine and as serious as she had ever seen them. Small lines crinkled up from the corners and the short tufts of hair showing beneath his cap at his temples were speckled a silver-grey. He looked older – older and more vulnerable somehow. He was going back to America and she might never see him again. A panic welled within her. England and her marriage to Ken belonged to another world. In this world there was only her and the man standing beside her. 'The best is now and here', the words he had quoted to her on the journey to Rabat, rang in her head. It couldn't end, not yet, not like this ... 'The PM wants the President to go on to Marrakesh with him after this,' she heard herself saying. 'Perhaps you could help persuade him. He would enjoy it. You all would.'

One dark brow quirked upwards. 'Marrakesh? What on earth for?'

'The view.' It sounded ridiculous, but it was quite true. The Prime Minister had told her only last night that he wanted the President to join him in a trip to see the sunset tinting crimson the snow on the distant Atlas Mountains – an unforgettable sight that he had witnessed himself on a previous visit six years earlier. 'The perfect end to a momentous trip, Lara, m'dear,' he had said, and her heart had quickened at the thought of a few more precious hours in the vicinity of the American delegation.

'The view?' Mike repeated, half in disbelief. 'Well, it makes a change from visiting feuding French Generals, I'll give you that. In fact, it sounds like it could be fun.'

'You believe there's a possibility the President will agree to it, then?'

He smiled. 'If Winnie has managed to get that Gallic giraffe to shake hands with Giraud for the press guys, FDR just might be amenable to taking a pleasure trip this afternoon.'

'You mean de Gaulle.' It was her turn to smile. 'That would be quite something. The General's not exactly known for bowing to anyone's wishes – especially if that someone is English – unless there's something tangible in it for France … But you could perhaps put in a good word for the Marrakesh idea yourself, if you get the chance. It would be worth the effort, I'm sure it would.' She hoped fervently that she wasn't sounding too desperate, too keen to spin out their time together here in North Africa.

'Sure … I'll wax lyrical about the joys of another Arabian night with old Winston. Who could resist that?' He smiled down at her with that familiar old quirky grin that never failed to make her heart turn over.

She gave a small nod of thanks and forced a smile to her lips as she glanced past him in the direction of the villas. 'Speaking of Winston and the rest, I suspect it's time you were rejoining them all on the lawn – if you want to be captured for posterity and find yourself on the front page of all the newspapers tomorrow, that is.'

He sighed. 'I'll take a rain-check on the latter, if you don't mind. But, you're right, I'd better get on over there.' He half-turned, then paused, as if unsure what exactly to say or do. 'Well, till later, then … '

'Till later … ' She watched him turn and head back in the direction of the Presidential villa, a tall, broad-shouldered figure who walked with a casual grace in the dress uniform. 'Till later,' she repeated softly. How much later? An hour? A day? A year? A lifetime … ?

The press conference was well underway by the time Mike reached Dar es Saada. It was taking place on the terrace, with Churchill and Roosevelt seated side by side in two chairs. Between them stood the unmistakable figures of the two French Generals, de Gaulle and Giraud. And to Mike's utter amazement they were shaking hands. An impromptu cheer went up from the reporters and photographers, who vied with each other for the best position to capture the moment for their editors and posterity. Half of them did not succeed first time round and a cry went up for a repeat performance. To everyone's surprise, the Generals obliged.

'Well, wha'd'ya know!' Harry Hopkins's voice said in Mike's ear. 'God knows what we've had to promise the sons of bitches to get this recorded for the world and his wife to see over the breakfast table tomorrow morning.'

'Promises come cheap. It's delivering that causes the problems.'

They were joined by Ed Forbes-Hamilton, who was delighted with the scene he had just witnessed. 'Joan of Arc will probably be turning in her grave at the sight of her illustrious descendant shaking hands with a man associated with Vichy,' he commented, 'but, I must admit, I'm jolly pleased. It suits our book very nicely at the moment.'

'If I recall correctly, she'd have great difficulty doing that,' Mike said with an ironic grin. 'She was burned at the stake, remember ... But I take the point. Political as well as military expediency is the name of the game at the moment, nobody can deny that.'

They watched as de Gaulle and Giraud, their duty done, walked off the terrace in opposite directions, then the President began to speak. He began by stressing the close unity between the Americans and the British at their meetings over the past ten days, then continued to emphasize, 'that it is our determination that peace can come to the world only by the total elimination of German and Japanese war power. Some of you Britishers know the old story – we had a General called U. S. Grant. His name was Ulysses Simpson Grant but, in my and the Prime Minister's early days, he was called "Unconditional Surrender" Grant. The elimination of German, Japanese, and Italian war power means the unconditional surrender by Germany, Italy or Japan. That means a reasonable assurance of future world peace. It does not mean the destruction of the population of Germany, Italy and Japan, but it does mean the destruction of the philosophies in those countries which are based on conquest and the subjugation of other people.'

'Unconditional surrender,' Forbes-Hamilton said, with a shake of his head. 'The PM's not going to be exactly thrilled to hear that phrase trotted out. If you ask me, that's the President talking off the top of his head. You Yanks have a habit of rushing in where angels fear to tread. If you want something you go for it and to hell with the consequences. But I'm not criticizing – I admire you for that, I really do.'

He looked straight at Mike as he spoke, and the American gave an ironic half-smile, as a picture of a young woman in a pale-blue sun-dress filled his mind. The guy might be a brilliant diplomat, but he'd never know how wrong he was.

Chapter Thirty-four

Lara found it almost impossible to relax in the back seat of the limousine as it headed along the dusty road that linked Casablanca with the ancient desert city of Marrakesh. Marrakesh: the very name inspired fantasies of waving palm trees, exotic souks, and white-robed tribesmen aloft the camels of their desert caravans as they headed for the legendary oasis city. But it was not merely the fact that she was heading for that particular fairy-tale city that made Lara's heart beat faster, it was the fact that she would have a few more precious hours in the vicinity of Mike.

Unknown to her when she spoke to Mike of the proposed trip earlier in the day, the Prime Minister had already convinced Roosevelt of the desirability of making the 150-mile journey, and the announcement of their impending departure was made directly after the press conference. Although many of the entourage had moaned at the prospect of such a journey in the heat of the afternoon, now they were under way, in Lara's car at least, there were few complaints at the unexpected jaunt. Three others from the secretarial staff were travelling with her, and she was content to let them chat amongst themselves as the Citroën sped along in the middle of the convoy of cars that was taking Roosevelt, Churchill and most of their staff to spend their last night together in Marrakesh.

It was a good five hour drive between the two cities, they were reliably informed. And, to Lara's amazement, at 100-yard intervals across the desert, an American soldier stood to attention at the roadside as the fleet of cars containing their President and the British leader sped past. 'There must be thousands of them,' she said, incredulously, as she peered out of the side window. The road ahead was dotted with American sentries as it snaked upwards across the sandy desert scrub. 'But at least it makes you feel secure.' This feeling was reinforced when they stopped half-way for a picnic lunch provided by the British, for, as they sat at the roadside enjoying the cold ham, chicken, and fresh fruit, Allied fighter planes circled protectively overhead.

'I wonder what they'd make of this back home – or even what Hitler would say if he could see us now!' the girl sitting next to her remarked as the wine glasses were refilled. 'It does seem rather incongruous, don't you think? Here we are, sitting in the middle of the desert, guzzling wine and all the rest of these goodies, with the leaders of the free world and their advisers, while a world war is taking place somewhere out there at this very moment.'

The others agreed. And, for Lara especially, today was a day to remember in more ways than one. From where she was sitting throughout the picnic, she could see the main body of Americans seated on rugs about fifty yards ahead. Throughout the meal, as the wine and whisky flowed freely, and the cold ham and chicken was passed around, she found herself stealing glances in their direction, hoping for a glimpse of Mike. At the beginning of the meal she thought that he might leave the others and come down to join her, but that hope did not last long. What could he say? What could she say, with so many other eyes and ears around the white damask table-cloth that lay spread out on the dusty brown earth?

Towards the end of the meal, as she sipped her third glass of wine, the tight group of figures that made up the main American picnic began to break up and people began drifting over from the British contingent. Randolph Churchill, the Prime Minister's son, who had been sitting at the next table-cloth to them, got up to go back to his car to search for a book on Machiavelli he felt might be of use to the President. 'With Harry Hopkins as his special adviser, I should think FDR needs all the Machiavellian tips going,' she heard someone remark, and was about to leap to Harry's defence, when the voice from behind her added, 'but he's a jolly decent chap from what I can make out.'

Lara's eyes darted back towards the Americans. The tall figure of Averell Harriman, Roosevelt's special envoy to Russia, was standing next to the Presidential car. When he moved off, she could make out the gangling frame of Harry Hopkins leaning against the bonnet. She had warmed to Roosevelt's special envoy at their first meeting. He reminded her of her favourite film star, Jimmy Stewart, both in looks and manner. As she sipped her wine and continued to gaze as casually as possible in his direction, an equally tall, but more broad-shouldered man in uniform got up to join him. Lara's heart stood still as he positioned himself so he was looking straight down the road towards where she was seated. Was it him? Was it Mike? At this distance, with so many top-ranking American uniforms around, she could not be sure, but as a delicate sweat broke from every pore of her skin, a small voice inside her prayed that it was.

The uniformed figure continued to look their way, forcing her to shift round slightly so that she was no longer facing him. She was sure the others around her were noticing her manoeuvres, and she felt like a foolish young girl again. This was the type of behaviour one associated with a twelve-year-old schoolgirl, she told herself impatiently, as she sipped her wine and attempted to keep her eyes on her companions seated on the ground around the makeshift table.

The conversation was, as usual, about what was happening on the war front, and of the great advances being made by the Red Army at Stalingrad. On the Voronezh Front, the Soviet offensive was continuing, with the capture of Valuyki and Urazavo, and news had just come in that morning of the loss of Gumrak Airport by the Germans in Stalingrad, leaving them completely cut off.

Lara found her thoughts following the conversation back to Europe and across the blood-stained continent to Poland and the man she now knew to be her father, Jan Jarosinski. What had become of him? She wished now she had been more understanding, had taken the trouble to get to know him better, that man whom her mother had loved for a lifetime. The Christmas of 1940, when she had first got to know him, and had first met the man called Mike Adams, seemed a million light years away now. So many things had happened since then, so many people had died, or simply disappeared, and the end was still not in sight.

'Well, if we can't be in the front line like our menfolk, at least we're in the front line of all the decision making, and that counts for something. It stops you going mad out of total helplessness!' It was one of the others who spoke – a small, bespectacled girl in her early twenties, whose fiancé and brother were both fighting out here in North Africa with the Eighth Army. Although not part of the conversation, Lara found herself murmuring her agreement. That was a consolation all right, but she would find it cold comfort on the plane home tomorrow, knowing the man she loved was heading in the opposite direction across the Atlantic Ocean.

A feeling of desolation grew within her as she helped the others tidy up the remains of the lunch and make their way back to the car. Was this how it was going to be once they finally got to Marrakesh – a few snatched glimpses and then goodbye? She felt cheated and distinctly on edge as she settled back in her seat and waited for the convoy to get under way once again.

As the fleet of cars crossed the Oum er Rbia and began to wind its way upward towards the rocky pre-Saharan steppe, Lara's eyes remained fixed on the passing countryside in an effort to stem the train of bleak thoughts that clattered through her head. The landscape around them had taken on a quite different hue. Gone was the white sand of the coast and the square, flat-roofed, white houses. Ahead of them lay what seemed an endless wasteland of brown, dusty rocks and dry, khaki-coloured earth that made up the great Rehamna plain. Occasional clusters of brown, mud-brick houses appeared in their field of vision, as indistinguishable from their background as the odd camel that lumbered past in the distance. Here and there a Barbary fig tree cast its branches towards the pale, watery sun, the whiteness of its leaves startling against the reddish-brown landscape of the steppe. In the distance, other faint white specks appeared from time to time: flocks of emaciated sheep who scoured the bare limestone and shale hills and barren canyons in search of vegetation that did not exist. And still, at 100-yard intervals, young American soldiers stood to attention at the roadside as the cars sped past, and the fighter planes patrolled the heavens overhead.

The minutes turned into hours and the conversation in the car tapered off into a comfortable silence as, one by one, the passengers began to doze in the heat of the pale sun that beamed down on them from a steel-grey sky. But Lara found it impossible to sleep: her head was too full of what might have been; what might yet be ...

Then, suddenly, on the far horizon, below the snow-capped Atlas Mountains, appeared a mirage. She was convinced that was what it was as she wound down the car window and, shielding her eyes with her hand, peered into the distance. An oasis city was shimmering in the afternoon sunshine, a city of dazzling white, ringed by orchards and palm groves of the deepest green. So this was Marrakesh, the city of her dreams – and it was no dream. 'We're almost here,' she informed her sleeping companions excitedly. 'Wake up, girls. We're almost here!'

The Prime Minister and President, they learned, were to be sharing a villa on the edge of the town, lent by an American lady, a Mrs Taylor; while the rest of them were billeted in a nearby hotel. When the convoy rolled up at their destination, to her surprise and pleasure the Prime Minister singled her out to take the dictation for the cable he intended sending to the Cabinet in London before relaxing over dinner. 'But first come and join us on the roof, m'dear,' he said.

'You'll see a sight you'll never forget. Something to tell your grand-children: I shall most certainly be boring mine about it when we get back to London town!'

They had arrived just as the sun was setting and she accompanied the Prime Minister and Sir Charles Wilson, his personal doctor, up on to the flat roof of the villa. They were followed by the President, who was cradled in the brawny arms of two of his aides. His paralysed legs dangled lifelessly beneath him, but his face was alive with expectation.

'It must be the most lovely spot in the whole world,' Churchill murmured, as the small group stood side by side at the edge of the roof and gazed at the heavens changing colour behind the mountains. The snow on the high peaks had turned from white to a luminous gold, and the whole sky seemed to blaze from crimson to burgundy, then to deepest purple, with streamers of gold bright enough to dazzle the eyes and make Lara gasp with delight as the elderly man standing beside her dabbed his eyes. The Prime Minister was never one to be ashamed of human emotion and the tears ran freely down his cheeks as they gazed in awe at the sight before them.

'I haven't painted a picture since this damned war began,' he confided to Lara, as they made their way back down the winding staircase, 'but I'll do one from here before I leave.'

'Will you give it to the President?' she asked, surprised at her own temerity.

He looked at her in surprise, then a smile broke on his lips. 'Do you know, I might just do that!' The idea seemed to appeal to him and he was still smiling broadly as she accompanied him into the well-furnished room that had been designated as his.

It took less than ten minutes for him to dictate the telegram and another ten for her to type it up before she took her leave and made her way over to the hotel she was to share with the rest of the staff.

As the secretaries were regarded as the bottom of the pecking order, Lara found herself in a small room at the bottom of the building, next to the cleaning cupboards. The other girls in the delegation had a room on the floor above, but they had to share. One of them came down for a chat and offered to swap with her, but Lara declined, thankful that she was lucky enough to retain her privacy. She had an idea that the next few hours would not lend themselves to the good-natured banter of sharing with her colleagues.

Although uplifted by the past half-hour, the journey had been tiring; she felt hot and sticky and made straight for the small bath-room next door to her room. An archaic-looking shower with a brass head like a giant watering-can hung over the ancient bath. She looked at them both and opted for the shower. The water felt cool against her skin as she soaped herself down, then twisted and turned beneath the refreshing spray. They had been told to meet in the hotel dining-room for dinner at eight – that gave her exactly one hour to dress and make-up.

She chose a cool, white linen dress, with a pleated skirt and matching jacket and tied a long scarf in white shot-silk round her hair, leaving the tails hanging loosely over her shoulder. Hot climates did not agree with her, she decided, as she examined herself critically in the dressing-table mirror. It looked as if someone had flicked a paintbrush of amber paint across her nose, she thought in despair, attempting to disguise the offending freckles with a liberal helping of Air-spun powder. A bright coral lipstick was then applied carefully, before darkening the long fair lashes and arching, feathered brows with a brushful of brown mascara. She was in the act of reaching for her eye-shadow when a knock at the bedroom door made her look up. She sighed impatiently. It was probably one of the girls wanting to borrow her shampoo or soap.

Pulling on a pair of white, sling-back sandals, she hurried over to the door as the knocking resumed. 'I'm coming! I'm coming! Keep your hair on!'

She threw the door open to look straight into the amused eyes of Mike Adams. He held his cap in one hand and patted his head with the other. 'It's still here – though there's maybe not quite so much of it these days!'

'Mike – I'm so sorry!' She stepped back and looked up at him in a mixture of surprise and sudden panic. 'I – I was just going down to dinner.'

'And I was just going to ask you to change your mind.' He continued to smile down at her. 'Let's give the hotel food a miss, Lara. We're not liable ever to be here again – not together, anyway. Let's go out and see what Marrakesh has to offer.'

'Go *out* to dinner?'

'Why not?'

She could think of no good reason, nor did she want to. 'That would be lovely – absolutely lovely!'

Mike had ordered a taxi to take them to the Djemaa-el-Fna, the huge square where it seemed that all the mysteries of Arabia had gathered together for their amusement. As they were dropped off on the crowded pavement, they were met by the long, wailing song of the muezzins calling the faithful to prayer from the magnificent

Koutoubia minaret which dominated the square, and from the myriad number of other less grand mosques in the vicinity. Men in all types of garb made their way to pay their homage to Allah: turbaned Souassa; white-robed camel drivers; wild, pale-skinned Berber tribesmen from the High Atlas, and tall, eagle-nosed Tekna tribesmen from the lower Dra hurried alongside smart, Western-suited businessmen towards the beckoning minarets.

'You can almost smell the camel dung, can't you?' Mike said, taking her hand in his as several wild-haired, six-foot desert tribesmen wafted past.

She agreed. The whole place reeked of the odours of the desert. They were standing on the edge of a sidewalk café, where the old men sitting at the tables, smoking their kif pipes and drinking from the small glasses of thick green tea, seemed to evaporate into thin air at the sound of the muezzins' call.

'I reckon somewhere a mite more salubrious would suit us better, don't you?' Mike said, casting an eye around them, then taking her arm and guiding her through the hurrying throng.

They ended up in a French restaurant in one of the numerous small alleyways that led off the square. It reminded her of all the pictures of French cafés she had ever seen. The table-cloths were of red gingham, as were the matching frilled curtains that hung at the narrow windows. Framed sepia photographs of French theatre and music-hall stars hung from the whitewashed walls. Lara recognized Sarah Bernhardt and a brooding Charles Boyer, but most of the others were unknown to her. Brass lamps hung from the low-beamed ceiling, their red shades casting a warm rosy glow around the room, which contained only one other couple, seated at a table at the far end by one of the two windows.

They were shown to a table for two in a small alcove by the other window. A candle in a red glass stood in the centre of the table-cloth and, on sitting down, Mike lit it with his cigarette lighter. 'Romantic, huh?' There was no mistaking the irony in his voice.

Whether it was because of the long journey, or simply the fact that she was so nervous, Lara found her appetite had completely vanished when the waiter came to take the order. 'I'll leave it to you,' she said, as Mike handed the menu across to her. 'But nothing too heavy, please. I think I ate too much on the picnic this afternoon!'

He scanned the gold print for a moment. '*Deux Crèmes Senegale, s'il vous plaît, et deux Oeufs Soubise ... enfin, deux Petit Pots de Crême au Café ... Merci.*'

'*Merci, M'sieu.*' The waiter, a small, dapper Frenchman with a

Hitler moustache, bowed deeply and disappeared in the direction of the kitchen.

There was bottled Vichy water on the table and Mike gave a wry smile as he poured two glasses. 'Just as well ol' Charlie-boy de Gaulle isn't dining with us, huh?'

Lara smiled. 'I'm so thirsty, I'd drink it if it came from Hitler's kitchen sink!'

Mike snapped his fingers and another waiter appeared at his elbow. A bottle of pink champagne was ordered. 'A special drink for a special occasion,' he said softly, as he poured the first two glasses and handed her one. '*Nos plaisirs les plus doux ne sont pas sans tristesse*, Lara ... Over the past two years I would have given all I possessed to be here with you now. But now we are here ... ' He shrugged his shoulders. 'It's like prolonging your own death throes – and I'm no masochist.'

She looked down at her drink, her mind searching in vain for something meaningful to say; something that would tell him that she understood, that she felt just as he was feeling right now. But the words would not come. Anything she could say would sound trite: that she was married; that it was right they should have remained only good friends. A good friend ... She smiled ruefully as she took her first sip of the sparkling drink and looked across at him. Never, never could he be simply a good friend.

They spoke of the war in North Africa, and of the news coming through of the Eighth Army's entry into Tripoli in the wake of the German retreat. Then, when they had exhausted the subject of Rommel's prospective defeat, the conversation turned to more personal matters. 'Did your mother tell you I met her in Oxford before I left Britain?'

'Yes, she did. She went straight up to Scotland after that, to stay with Ken's parents for a few days, but I can't say that it did her much good. I've never seen her so depressed as when she got back to London.'

'That's understandable.'

She looked at him curiously for a moment. 'Why do you say that?'

'Didn't the Count leave for Poland about then?'

She replaced her coffee cup thoughtfully into the porcelain saucer. Her old boss was nobody's fool. But then she'd always known that. 'I should have said something,' she said quietly. 'I should have made it easier for her, but I just couldn't bring myself to, somehow. The time never seemed quite right – or when the subject did come up and the opening was there, I would be too preoccupied with my own problems.' She gave a wry smile. The major problem in her life was sitting across the table from her right now. It hardly seemed possible. 'I – I believe she'd like to confide in me, but the words don't seem to come, on either side.' The smile returned, more wistful this time. 'Typical English reserve, I expect.'

He reached across and took her hand. 'Don't be too hard on yourself … ' His eyes found hers as he said softly, 'It could be you weren't exactly up to coping with other people's problems. As you just admitted, you had other things on your mind.'

His eyes were a dark navy-blue in the lamplight and she could feel her heart beating faster as the pressure of his fingers on her own increased. He knew only too well what those other things on her mind were … Other things such as his own departure from British shores. 'It – it was a difficult time for all of us,' she found herself saying in a quiet voice.

'But life had to go on.'

She nodded. 'What else was there to do … ? What else *is* there to do but carry on?' The despair in her voice was unmistakable.

He had no answer. There was a choice and they both knew it. Both had gone over it a million times in their minds and had rejected it a million times. He could not ask her to leave Ken and return to America with him, any more than she could consider doing it. They were caught like two flies in the tangled web of fate. Yet, as he looked at her across the table, he knew he loved her with a passion he could know with no other woman, and from what her eyes were telling him, he knew that she felt the same.

His eyes left hers to gaze upwards at the shining crescent of the moon in the darkening sky. The moonlight lent an ethereal glow to the world. This was a night like no other; a night he would remember for a lifetime. His mind went back to another moonlit night when he had stood on the ship's rail as it took him away from Britain – away from her. 'We'll Meet Again' the band had been playing, and they *had* met again. Strange things could happen in this world. But if life had taught him one thing in this war, it was to live for today.

'No longer forward nor behind, the best is now and here … ' Lara's voice, soft and hesitant as she repeated the words he had once said to her, broke into his reverie. She gave a nervous smile as their eyes met once more.

'How did you know what I was thinking?' His voice was huskily low as his hand pressed hers. She had no need to reply. They were two separate people, but with two separate hearts beating as one this night, and they both knew it. 'Let's go, my love,' he said softly. 'Let's get out of here … '

Chapter Thirty-five

Mike's arm went around Lara's shoulders as they left the restaurant and re-emerged into the cool evening air. She shivered slightly. 'Cold?' he asked, holding her closer.

She shook her head. 'It must be nerves,' she joked, but it was the truth, for her mouth had suddenly gone dry and her lips stuck to her teeth as she attempted a smile. What happened now? How would this evening end? A few moments ago in the restaurant she had read the message in his eyes, as he had read it in hers. He wanted her as she wanted him. There was no question of it.

Sensing her disquiet, he pressed her to him in a comforting squeeze, but said nothing. He was feeling the same and the knowledge disconcerted him. Men of the world were meant to take this type of situation in their stride, but here he was, sweating like a freshman on his first date beneath the cool cotton of his shirt. 'Fancy a walk, or would you rather go back to the hotel for a drink?'

He was looking down at her, studying her face, but she avoided his eyes. At any other time she would have been delighted to explore the mysteries of this fairy-tale place; but not tonight. Tonight she did not want to share him with the jostling crowds attired in their flowing djellabas and cloak-like burnooses. Tonight she would share him with no one. The thought drifted into her head, then solidified into an unshakeable decision. 'The best was now and here', but not for much longer ... for a few precious hours at the most, then they would go their separate ways, never to meet again. 'The hotel, please,' she said softly, and heard him draw in his breath. His body tensed against hers, then he held up his hand to a passing taxi.

An ancient Peugeot drew up alongside and he held the door open for her. He gave the driver directions in French to the hotel, then settled back beside her in the worn hide seat. The interior of the cab smelt strongly of Turkish cigarettes and the windows were caked with dust, making it almost impossible to see out. In the semi-darkness, Mike was little more than a dark shape looming beside her as he made himself comfortable. She felt a tremor run through her as his arm slid back around her shoulders. He felt close, so very close, and smelt of pine-scented soap and tobacco. Her senses seemed curiously awakened. Every scent, every movement was heightened. Occasionally, as the taxi turned a corner more sharply than usual, she would be thrown against him, and found herself apologizing far too profusely; and he would smile quietly to himself and hold her that bit tighter.

After a few minutes, as they left behind the crowded maze of narrow streets around the Djemaa-el-Fna and headed towards the outskirts of the town, she was aware of his humming a haunting tune under his breath; a tune she had heard him hum before on the journey to Rabat.

'What are you humming?' she asked, more to ease the tension inside her than out of real curiosity.

'It's called "As Time Goes By",' he answered. 'It's from a Bogey movie called *Casablanca* I saw back in New York just before I flew out here.'

'Casablanca – how appropriate!'

She felt rather than saw him give a wry smile. 'In more ways than one. I'd catch it when you get back to London, if I were you.'

She sensed he wanted to say more, but thought better of it. 'I'll do that,' she promised, and felt him squeeze her tighter in response.

Dinner was over when they got back to the hotel, but the place was alive with well-known faces. Harold Macmillan waved to them from a crowded table in the centre of the lounge. 'Fancy joining them?' Mike asked half-heartedly, as he returned the greeting.

Lara shook her head, her face colouring as she did so. She was already anticipating the next question.

'Then ... ' He looked uncomfortable for a moment. 'Well, do I have to ask?' When she made no response, he came out with the question that had been uppermost in both their minds ever since they left the restaurant. 'Your room or mine?'

Panic welled within her as she looked up at him. His eyes were smiling down into hers, offering a confidence he did not feel. Both knew this was the moment of truth and the slightest wavering on either part would be fatal. She took a deep breath. 'Mine will be cosier.'

'I see what you mean by "cosier",' he grinned, as she opened the door on the tiny room a few minutes later. 'You sure they haven't put you in one of the closets by mistake?' He was on the point of making a joke about 'cupboard love', but changed his mind. It would have been out of place, somehow.

There was an unopened bottle of the ubiquitous Vichy water on the dressing-table. Lara glanced across at it, then back at Mike. 'I'm afraid that's all there is,' she said with an apologetic shrug of the shoulders. 'No vodka, I'm sorry to say.'

'I don't need that, Lara,' he said softly. 'I don't need anything else tonight ... Not now ...'

They stood looking at one another in the sparsely furnished room. He took a step towards her and, despite her resolve, she took a defensive step backwards. He paused and stood quite still looking down at her. 'Don't you want to, Lara? Don't you want it too?'

Unwanted tears sprang to her eyes as she nodded emphatically. 'Yes, yes Mike, I do ...' There was nothing, absolutely nothing on this earth she wanted more.

He came to her and gently wiped the tears from her cheeks. 'Don't cry, my love. Don't cry ...'

She gazed up at him, her eyes swimming. Why was she crying? Not for Ken – certainly not for Ken. Her husband was now merely a dim memory that belonged to a past life that had no relevance to the here and now. And not for herself, for this was the moment she had dreamt of in every dream, waking and sleeping, for over two years. She was crying for what might have been – for all those moments like this one that they might have shared if things had been different. She was crying for the future that did not exist ...

She was not aware of them shedding their clothes, only of the strength of his arms around her as he carried her naked through the mosquito net and on to the bed.

His body was as she had dreamt it to be – firmer and stronger than Ken's, with a mat of dark curling hair on the broad wall of his chest. He was sweating – they both were – and his skin seemed to glow in the soft grey light that permeated the room from the open shutters of the window. He lay down beside her on the bed, leaning on one elbow and devouring her with his eyes.

She moaned softly, her slim body quivering on the cool cotton of the sheet as he reached out and traced the contours of her face with his fingertips. His hand moved down the pale curve of her neck to rest on the firm swell of her breast. 'You're beautiful, so very beautiful ...'

His head moved down towards her and she opened her mouth to accept his. He kissed her slowly, sensuously, his tongue sending shivers of sensation through her, making her clutch at the short dark hairs at the nape of his neck and writhe impatiently on the bed beneath him.

'I love you, Lara ... God help me, I love you ...' He raised his head, his eyes gleaming as they gazed down into hers. Her own were still wet and he kissed the tears that spiked the curling lashes. He tasted the salt on his tongue as his mouth moved down her neck and across her breasts, leaving trails of fire over her naked skin.

'No, Mike, no ...' Her protests were gasped into the silence of the room as her nails dug into the smooth flesh of his shoulders. He ignored them and she was glad: her spirit soared higher as his hands and lips awoke feelings within her she had never imagined possible. Her body had become an instrument of sheer sensation that he was tuning with the touch of a maestro.

They came together slowly, beautifully, as if it had always been so – as if they had been sculptured from one flesh, their bodies moving in unison in the pale moonlight. Her nails left trails of blood across the bare skin of his back, but he felt no pain as he repeated her name over and over and poured forth his love as he had never done with another woman.

When it was all over, and she lay exhausted in the crook of his arm, she was aware of his cheek wet against hers. Like her, his mind was on the coming day; the coming weeks and months; the coming years. Her fingers found the fine gold chain around her neck – the one he had given her that day in Rabat. 'A diamond is forever', he had told her. But nothing was forever in this world: they both knew that.

She felt him lean over and light a cigarette, inhaling deeply on the smoke. He expelled it slowly and watched it drift slowly to the ceiling. His eyes closed and his grip on the tube of tobacco increased. He should be feeling triumphant at this moment. He had got her into bed, hadn't he? A grim smile quirked the corners of his mouth as he took another drag of the cigarette. He had fed his body this night and starved his soul. He had given it what it desired more than anything in this world, only to take it away again. For the rest of his life he would crave for what he had known this night, for it would never come again. A love like this did not happen twice in one lifetime, not to ordinary mortals like him. She would be leaving him tomorrow, to go back to her own country – to her own husband. And what of him? What did life hold in store for him? He would return to the States with the President and the others and do his darndest to see this Nazi menace defeated, then who knows ... ? Maybe he would come out of it a three or four-star General, maybe not. And, to be honest, he didn't really give a damn.

She was not aware of falling asleep, only of the emptiness of the space beside her as she sat up in confusion on the dishevelled bed. He had gone ... Dear God, he had gone! She scrambled to her knees and tore back the net drapes that enveloped the bed. Only her own clothes were lying where they had fallen on the rush mat by the bed. He had gone all right. He had gone ...

A long, low groan as from an animal in pain came from the very depths of her being as she stared in utter despair at the closed door. There had been no goodbye – nothing. All that remained was the taste of him on her lips; the scent of him in her nostrils, and a wrinkled, damp patch on the sheet beside her.

'Dear God, dear, dear God ...' She buried her face in her hands as great racking sobs shuddered through her. She cried as she had never cried in her life, for the despair within her was complete. He had given her no chance to plead with him to stay, to say that it was him she loved more than life itself, to beg him to take her back to America with him.

She stared bleakly into space. Was it possible? Was it really possible that it could be done – that she could leave everything of her old life behind and follow him? She thought of the elderly man watching the sun set behind the mountains with her on that roof tonight, Winston Churchill, the leader of her country. What would he think of her if she was suddenly to give up her job – she a married woman, with a husband at the sharp end of the war back in Britain? She thought of her mother back home in London: with her stepfather and grand-mother dead, and Jan Jarosinski gone from Beth's life, Lara was all she had left. It would break her mother's heart if she were to go too ... And, last but not least, what of Ken?

Her mind a whirl of conflicting emotions, she got out of bed and walked naked to the window, gazing up into the starlit sky. What of Ken? Her tear-swollen eyes stung once more as the open, boyish face of her husband swam before her. She had deceived him. She was an adultress – a scarlet woman, some would say. But, strangely, she felt no guilt, only a deep, deep sadness that it could not have been different. She loved Ken, yes, it was true; but she loved him in quite a different way from how she felt about the man who had just walked out of her life. Ken was the good friend she had married because it was the thing to do – the handsome young man in the dashing fighter pilot's uniform who was good fun to be with, who had asked her to marry him when the whole world was upside down and young men and women were rushing to the altar as if there was no to-morrow ...

She frowned into the darkness as the tears ran freely down her cheeks. That was it, wasn't it? That was exactly why she had married when she did. With Hitler's bombers poised above Britain, they had all believed that there might be no tomorrow, so what was the point in delay?

'Forgive me, Ken. Forgive me,' she whispered into the emptiness of the lonely room. She had done an unforgivable thing of which she was bitterly ashamed. But it was not what had taken place in this room tonight – she could never be ashamed of that – it was in marrying a man she could never love as he deserved to be loved. It was in marrying Ken Cameron.

Chapter Thirty-six

Lie in the dark and listen.
It's clear tonight, so they're flying high –
Hundreds of them: thousands perhaps,
Riding the icy moonlit sky –
Men, machinery, bombs and maps,
Altimeters and guns and charts,
Coffee, sandwiches, fleece-lined boots,
Bones and muscles and minds and hearts,
English saplings with English roots
Deep in the earth they've left below.
Lie in the dark and let them go.
Lie in the dark and listen.

Lie in the dark and listen.
They're going over in waves and waves,
High above villages, hills and streams,
Country churches and little graves,
And little citizens' worried dreams.
Very soon they'll have reached the bays
And cliffs and sands where they used to be
Taken for summer holidays.
Lie in the dark and let them go.
Theirs is a world we'll never know.
Lie in the dark and listen.

Lie in the dark and listen.
City magnates and steel contractors,
Factory workers and politicians,
Soft, hysterical little actors,
Ballet dancers, reserved musicians,
Safe in your warm civilian beds,
Count your profits and count your sheep,
Life is passing above your heads.
Just turn over and try to sleep.
Lie in the dark and let them go.
There's one debt you'll forever owe.
Lie in the dark and listen.

'What's that you've been listening to, dear?' Beth's voice called from the depths of the armchair by the fire in the sitting-room. 'It can't be as bad as that, that it warrants switching the wireless off, can it?'

'Oh, it was just Noel Coward reading his latest poem.' Lara tried to keep her voice at a casual level as she stared down at the now silent wireless on the kitchen dresser. What she had just heard, as she washed and dried the supper things, had cut her to the soul. She did not normally switch off the radio half-way through her favourite poetry programme, but that particular poem had reached its target. Never a night had passed since she returned to London from Morocco two weeks ago but she had done just that: lain in the dark of her room at night and listened to the distant drone of aircraft overhead, and wondered if one of them might be Ken.

She had had only one letter from him since getting back: things had been pretty quiet, he had written. He had been spending a good part of his time teaching raw recruits to fly at No. 9 Elementary Flying Training School at Southam in Warwickshire. He would rather be on active service, naturally, than be put out to pasture in a 'cushy number' like this, but you had to take your turn. Anyway, he had informed her, he stood a better chance of getting some leave shortly, if they left him where he was.

Lara sighed audibly as she folded the damp tea-cloth and laid it on the draining board before joining her mother in the sitting-room. She sat down in the armchair at the opposite side of the fire and opened that week's copy of *Woman's Own*. After skimming through it, she returned to the problem page. Somehow reading about other people's problems seemed to put your own into perspective.

Among the pleas for advice on how to cope with the bombs, and the best way to bring up children who had never known their father, was a letter from a young woman in Yorkshire whose husband had been overseas for a year or more and who had now discovered she was pregnant. Lara closed the magazine abruptly and stared in front of her. It was as if someone had poured a jug of cold water down her spine.

'Are you all right, dear?' Her mother looked across from the other chair, frowning slightly at the stricken look on her daughter's face.

Lara nodded dumbly. 'Do we have a calendar, Mum?'

Beth continued to look at her curiously, the bodkin in her fingers poised above the sleeve of the Air-force blue jumper she was sewing up. 'There's one in the kitchen drawer. It came from Ken's Mum and Dad in Dundee, but I'm afraid I've never got round to putting it up.'

She watched in concern as Lara hurried from the room, a curiously fixed expression on her face.

The calendar lay in the drawer beneath a pile of neatly folded tea-cloths and had a picture of two Scottie dogs attired with tartan tammies and scarves on it. Lara flicked open the date pad, tore out the leaf for January and stared down at it. When did she last have her period? Her teeth dug into her bottom lip as she attempted to cast her mind back. She really should keep a note of that sort of thing ... Wait a minute, didn't it arrive on the day she met Judy in town for lunch? That would be when ... ? About the end of the first week in January, if her memory served her right. Oh God, oh, dear God ... What was today's date? She stared down at the small black numbers of February: today was Saturday 13 February. The thirteenth – how appropriate, how very appropriate! Her period was due over a week ago. A chill of fear ran through her. Surely not? Surely it couldn't happen just like that, on the first and last time she had ever made love with Mike?

'Are you sure you're all right, dear?' Beth appeared in the doorway, a distinctly concerned look on her face.

'No, I'm fine, Mum. I'm absolutely fine.' Lara replaced the calendar in the drawer and slammed it shut. 'I – I was just checking up when I'm next due to meet Judy for lunch, that's all. For one awful minute I thought I'd missed the day.'

Beth gave an understanding smile. 'I've done the same myself before now. You've too many things on your mind, my girl, that's your trouble. Mr Churchill works you far too hard; I've a good mind to have a word with Clemmie.'

'No, don't do that, please!' Lara took her mother's arm and guided her back to the sitting-room. 'I enjoy my job, you know that, and I don't mind the hard work – it helps take my mind off other things ... By the way, how's your own work going these days? You don't say very much about it.'

Beth's brow furrowed as she sat back down in her chair and picked up her knitting once again. 'I can't, Lara dear, you know that ... ' The frown deepened. Could she tell her? Was this the time – the opportunity she'd been waiting for to broach the idea that she and her boss at SOE had been discussing on and off for the past week or so? She took a deep breath. 'Lara dear, there *is* something I've been meaning to discuss with you since you got back from Casablanca. How would you feel about me going abroad for a bit?'

'Abroad?' Lara's brows rose in surprise. 'Where abroad? And what does "a bit" mean?'

Beth bit her lip, her fingers fiddling nervously with bodkin and wool. 'Poland, actually. And I've no idea how long for. For however long I can be useful, I expect.'

'Poland!' The name exploded from Lara's lips as she stared down at her mother. 'You must be joking – there's a war on there, for heaven's sake!'

'There's a war on here, too, don't forget.'

'It's hardly the same thing. Poland is a blood-bath, you know that.'

'They're suffering far more there, it's true. And that's the reason I feel I have to go.' Beth was trying desperately hard to keep her voice calm to defuse the situation. This was exactly the reaction she had feared.

Lara did not know whether to laugh or cry as she sat down heavily in the chair. She couldn't be hearing properly. This was a quite ludicrous conversation. 'But what could you do, for heaven's sake? What on earth good would an English woman do in war-torn Poland?'

Beth shook her head. 'But that's just the point – I wouldn't be going as an English woman. I'd be going as a Silesian German: a genuine *Volksdeutsche!*'

Lara gaped at her in astonishment. It was getting worse by the minute. 'What on earth for?'

Beth laid the bodkin down in her lap and leaned forward in her seat, her eyes shining. 'It's not as ridiculous as it sounds,' she said quietly. 'We've been sending quite a few agents into Europe over the past two years, to carry out all sorts of tasks. But very few have been sent into Poland, for one very good reason: while plenty can speak French, very few are fluent in German or Polish.'

'But you don't speak Polish either. At least, not that I know of.'

'True, but I'm a fluent German speaker. In fact, Hans Heinrich used to tell me I spoke better German than most genuine *Deutschers!*'

'What has that got to do with going to Poland?'

'Everything,' Beth said emphatically. 'The Nazis, particularly the Gestapo, are doing terrible things in Warsaw, and we know from reports coming into headquarters that far worse things are planned …' She paused, as if searching for the right words to convey the urgency of the situation. 'What we, and the Government in Exile need to know is exactly what those plans are. In short, we need someone to penetrate the highest echelons of the German High Command in Warsaw to obtain the information we need if Poland is to survive.'

Lara groaned out loud, as she looked in a mixture of disbelief and despair at her mother. 'You're not telling me you are that person?'

'That's exactly what I'm telling you.' Beth clasped her hands together on her lap and leaned forward in her chair, as her voice took on an almost conspiratorial tone. 'Who else could be better fitted? Not only do I speak fluent, accentless German but, having been an authentic German Countess, I'm completely *au fait* with everything required to carry out that role for a second time. I shall be the Countess Lisa von Wolfsberg!' She gave a short laugh. 'It's not too far removed from the truth.'

'Good God, you've even got a name picked out!' Lara stared at her in a mixture of horror and disbelief. 'You're really serious about this, then?'

'Completely.'

'And when does this – this "escapade" take place?' She hardly dared ask.

'They've given me until the end of this weekend to think it over. I've to let them know my decision when I report for work on Monday morning. When they'll finally decide to send me, I'm not quite sure. There are such things as a safe house to be arranged, and the time and place of the drop, but it'll most certainly be sooner rather than later.'

Lara stared at her blankly and shook her head. What could she say? Her mother wasn't a child; she was old enough to make her own decisions in this life, and this was something she obviously felt strongly about. Strongly enough to risk her life. 'What can I say?' she asked bleakly. 'What on earth can I say?'

Beth gave a rueful smile. 'Good luck would suffice.' She got up, laying down her knitting on the cushion, and went over to where Lara was sitting, kneeling down to take her hand. 'Trust me, Lara dear. This is something I have to do. You do understand that, don't you?'

Lara nodded. She understood all right. 'It's something you've been thinking about for a long time, isn't it?'

Beth lowered her eyes. 'For two years.'

There was no more Lara could say. Her mother had made up her mind when Jan Jarosinski left that she would follow him out to Poland. She had not the slightest doubt about that. And she understood the feelings behind that decision. When you loved a man more than life itself, then life without him became meaningless.

Her eyes clouded at the memory of waking in the heat of a Moroccan night to an empty space in the bed beside her. No one could know that agony unless they had been through it, unless they too had loved a man as she loved Mike Adams, and as her mother loved Jan Jarosinski. A wave of tiredness overcame her, mentally and physically. She extracted her hand from her mother's and got up wearily from the chair. 'I think I'll go through to my room for a bit and drop Ken a line.'

Beth watched her get up and walk through to the bedroom, and a feeling of relief swept through her. She understood. Lara understood.

She sat down in the chair her daughter had just vacated and gazed into the dying embers of the fire. While relieved for her own sake, a feeling of disquiet filled her for Lara. Something had happened out there in North Africa, she was sure of it. Lara had been distracted since getting back, spending far too much time staring into space, with a look akin to real pain on her face. Whenever Beth tried to broach the subject of the Casablanca trip, her daughter would quickly turn the subject to something nearer home. She was hiding something, there was no doubt about it. Hiding something or someone. And that someone could only be Mike Adams.

Her mind went back to that day in the Oxford tea-shop, and how she had warmed to the tall American with the disarmingly lop-sided grin and quiet way of talking. If things had been different, she would have more than welcomed the idea of having him for a son-in-law. But, despite her affection for him, she could not forget that her first loyalty lay with Ken. Half the trouble lay with this dratted war, she was sure of it. If he had been able to get home more often this probably would never have happened. But life was full of ifs right now. You simply had to close your eyes to them and get on with it. And, hopefully, that was what Lara was doing at this moment. She knew what it meant to those at the sharp end of the war to get letters from home. They were often the only contact the boys in uniform had with their loved ones and, in all probability, Ken was sitting on his own bed right now writing one to her.

Beth was wrong. As Lara sat down at the knee-hole dressing-table in her room, her husband was not in fact in the 'cushy number' of the Training School at Southam. Four days ago he had been assigned to the highly secret 161 Squadron, which had been formed to carry out the 'special duties' required of it by the Special Operations Executive.

In August 1941, the Chiefs of Staff had decided to do something constructive in carrying out Churchill's declared objective to 'set Europe ablaze'. Three Halifaxes and ten obsolete Whitley bombers were assigned for these 'special duties' of dropping agents and supplies into Occupied Europe, and by 14 February 1942, Squadron No. 161 was set up at the secret aerodrome of Tempsford in Bedfordshire.

But now, in February of 1943, an allocation of twin-engined Lockheed Hudson light bombers from Burbank in California had joined the other aircraft in the hangers, as part of the Lend-Lease deal. Their arrival had caused much talk amongst the crews, who were looking forward to trying them out. Only this month the aircraft's adaptability had been more than proved when one was landed in a small field in France to drop off five secret agents, and had succeeded in taking off again within minutes with vital reports from the French Resistance.

Ken's own reaction to joining the squadron and what was unofficially known as 'The Cloak and Dagger Mob' was ambivalent. On the one hand he was relieved to have left Southam and the monotony of day after day spent teaching his skills to eager young men who seemed to be getting younger by the week, and he was stimulated by the thought of sharing in the excitement of the operational sorties behind enemy lines; but on the other hand he was tired – dog-tired – of this war and its daily death toll. The past few years had seen most of his pals bite the dust. Someone had told him recently that of the crews who had been flying since the beginning of the war, only ten in a hundred were expected to have survived until this year. Ten in a hundred – and the odds were shortening all the time.

As well as the dropping of agents and supplies, one of 161 Squadron's main tasks was the rescuing of agents on the run from the Gestapo. By the end of 1942 a special department of the SOE, known as D F-section, had been set to this task and had organized an intricate system of escape routes across enemy territory. Most of these routes involved long and highly dangerous journeys through occupied France, across the Pyrenees, and on into officially neutral, but unofficially unsympathetic Spain. These escape routes were linked by 'safe houses', provided by extraordinarily brave individuals who risked certain death should they be discovered, and it was to one of these houses that tonight's sortie was headed. One of the Free French's most important agents was holed up in a small farmhouse just outside Issoudun, some seventy miles due south of Orléans. It was their job to get him out.

Ken glanced at his watch. It was five minutes to 2000 hours. Five short minutes to go to the bog for the umpteenth time in the past half-hour; time to glance through well-thumbed photographs and letters; time perhaps to write a short note to be left in a convenient place in one's locker – a note that could always be torn up later, once you had returned safely to base. But, for some reason, he didn't much feel like writing a note tonight. Maybe it was tiredness, or maybe he had just got sick of the sameness of the routine. Whether he was flying with Number One Squadron, or Number 161, the routine and the emotions were the same. And tonight, despite the normal, stomach-churning nerves, he was strangely bereft of emotions.

He pushed the wallet back into the pocket of his flying jacket and yanked up the zip. The only thing he could put this feeling of depression down to was the fact that today would have been Alan's birthday. News of his cousin's death in North Africa just over two years ago had had a peculiar effect on him. When he had got the letter from his mother informing him of it he had been strangely untouched by the news – numbed, most probably, by the deaths of dozens of his friends that had gone before. But as the months wore on he had found himself brooding more and more about the young man who had been more of a brother than a cousin to him. Why Alan? What had he ever done to anyone to deserve an end like that? He hadn't even wanted to go to war. All he had ever wanted to do was to get married to Irene, buy a little house in Broughty Ferry and teach from nine to four in the history department of the Grove Academy, where their mutual uncle, Willie Coull, had taught for well nigh thirty years before him.

His father's letters had been depressing of late. His mother had stopped writing many months since. She had gone into a decline since his Aunt Cissie's suicide two years ago, unable to come to terms with finding her beloved sister dead on the bathroom floor when calling in on their way to the Kirk one Sunday morning, just a couple of weeks after Alan's death. His father was doing his best to cope, of course, but the strain was becoming obvious as the letters got shorter and the news of his mother more perfunctory. 'Mum's fine and sends her love' spoke volumes, when once his mother's activities would fill pages. So now it was just his dad and His Lordship who would set off each morning for the day's shopping, leaving his mother alone in her self-made prison behind the net curtains of the sitting-room window. His jaw clenched as he thought of how it had been only a few short years before, and how it was now … That bastard Hitler had a lot to answer for!

'We're scrambling now, Scottie!' It was the voice of Taf Ellis, the wireless operator, that roused him from his gloomy reverie.

Ken got up mechanically, adjusting the straps of his parachute as he followed Taffy out on to the concrete. The two big hangars, a drab olive green and brown during the day, loomed black and threatening in the gloom. In the distance, about 500 yards away, almost invisible in the semi-darkness, was an odd, barn-like structure, with what looked like a pigeon loft beside it. It was in there that the British agent they would be dropping would be receiving his last minute instructions. Poor sod – no matter how fed up he was with his own job, he knew he wouldn't fancy changing places.

'Did you get a chance to see the notice-board tonight?' his companion asked, as they broke into a jog.

'No, why?' No news was good news as far as he was concerned right now, and he avoided the board as much as possible.

'You're down for leave next weekend, you lucky bugger!'

'You're joking!'

'Want to bet on it?'

'Christ Al-bloody-mighty!' For the first time that day a wide grin spread across Ken's face. Next weekend – just one short week and he'd be seeing Lara again! He broke into a run, tossing his leather helmet into the air and catching it as he let out a whoop of pleasure. 'Taffy, man, somebody up there is smiling on me tonight!'

His friend gave a wry laugh as he panted up alongside him. 'Just keep your fingers crossed it's not a bloody German, boyo!'

Chapter Thirty-Seven

'You are my sunshine,
My double Woodbine,
My box of matches,
My Craven A ...'

'Sing it for real, boyo. Sing it for real!' Taffy Ellis yelled back over
the roar of the engines to the ruddy-faced Yorkshireman they would
be dropping within the next half-hour. It was his favourite song of
last year, and he and Gwen had shared the last dance to it in the
church hall round the corner from his Auntie Annie's in Pontypridd
last Christmas Eve.

'The other night, dear, as I lay dreaming,
I dreamt that you were by my side,
Came disillusion when I awoke dear,
You were gone, and then I cried –
You are my sunshine,
My only sunshine ...'

No one saw the Dornier approaching. All Ken was aware of was a
blinding flash, someone screamed, then everything went black. The
world had exploded in a man-made fireball that was plummeting to
earth. Then he was fighting for his life. He had to get out of the
burning cockpit. He was aware of fighting his way out of his seat
belts and wrenching open the cockpit hatch, only to find that he was
still attached to the interior by his radio and oxygen leads, as the plane
continued its flaming, downward spiral. As it gathered speed, his
head was jerked backwards so violently that he felt his neck had
broken as his helmet was wrenched from his head.

Then suddenly he was free-falling through the freezing blackness.
There was complete silence, except for the whistling sound of the
wind in his ears as he tumbled out of the night sky.

His hand automatically groped for the metal D-ring of his ripcord. He was aware of snowflakes drifting past his eyes. It was bitterly cold, but there was an intense burning sensation in his hands and face. And all the time he was falling, falling ...

There was a sharp crack in the darkness above him and his parachute snapped open. He continued to drift downwards in the blackness. In the corner of his eye, to his far right down below, he could see a patch of orange flame. Was it the Hudson? And where were the others? For God's sake, where was Taffy? He squirmed in the smouldering harness – his eyes, the only living things in the scorched mass that had once been his face, searching the darkness.

He was still searching when the ground came up and hit him.

He was still lying there, at ten o'clock the following morning – a motionless heap in the grassy hollow of a French hillside, only a few yards from the banks of the River Loire, and almost half a mile from the burnt-out wreckage of his plane.

At the same time in far-off London, Beth knocked nervously on her boss's door.

Barney Huntly-Crawford was a tall, bald-headed Scotsman who had been standing in for her usual boss for the past few weeks. He had come to the SOE via the Foreign Office and, although not as personally well acquainted with the situation in Warsaw as her past boss, Colin Gubbins, he was a listener. And the more Beth talked, the more convinced he became that the idea was a sound one. The Polish Government in Exile were desperate for all the up-to-date information they could get hold of on Germany's plans for their country, and Whitehall, as well as the Americans, were becoming increasingly edgy about news filtering through regarding the treatment and extermination of Jews in occupied Europe, particularly in Poland, which had one of the biggest Jewish populations.

From the verifiable information they did possess on 'Operation Reinhard' – Hitler's 'final solution' to what he regarded as the Jewish problem in Europe – things in Warsaw were becoming critical for the remaining Jews in the city. What they knew for certain was that by the late autumn of 1941, the SS in Warsaw had rounded up around 400,000 Jews and sealed them into an area approximately two and a half miles long and a mile wide around the old medieval ghetto. Since then their sources informed them that the majority who had not died of disease and starvation within the ghetto had been transported to concentration camps, most of them to Treblinka, where they had been systematically exterminated, usually in specially constructed gas chambers.

'The latest information we have is on Himmler's personal visit to Warsaw last month,' he said quietly. 'From what we've been told he was not too amused at finding some 60,000 Jews still alive in the ghetto and has issued orders for what they euphemistically call "resettlement" of those remaining to be completed by the fifteenth of February.' He glanced at the calendar on the wall beside him: it read Monday 15 February 1943. A bitter smile twisted his lips as he drew on his pipe. He lapsed into silence for a moment, giving Beth a chance to butt in.

'All right, it's probably already too late, but surely it's still better to do something now, even if it *is* too late for the majority, than do nothing at all,' she protested. 'Presumably you read the translations of the Mikolajczyk reports over Christmas as well?'

Huntly-Crawford's bony fingers fiddled with the pen on the blotter in front of him, then he removed his pipe from the corner of his mouth and relit it. He had read the Polish Minister of the Interior's reports all right. The Foreign Office had received them on 3 December and he had been given a copy shortly afterwards. No one who read them could be left in any doubt that the information coming out from the Polish Underground was correct. Dreadful things were happening over there. The Mikolajczyk documents had contained detailed descriptions of the liquidation of the Warsaw ghetto; the report of a Polish policeman inside the ghetto; a report on the extermination camp at Belzec, and many other horrifying details that underlined all too clearly the desperation of the situation out there at the moment.

Knowing he would be taking over a section of SOE for a few weeks at the beginning of the new year, he had had a long talk with Colin Gubbins, and had been informed by him that one of his staff was keen to go out there. He had spent most of Christmas mulling over the situation, wondering if he really could justify to himself the dangers involved in sending over a woman into that deadly cauldron that was now the Polish capital. But if not a woman, who else? A man would be spotted almost immediately and could prove a costly mistake. In Beth Mallory he had a woman who not only spoke fluent German, but had actually been what she would purport to be – a German Countess.

He looked at her long and hard for a moment, then said quietly, 'How soon can you go?'

She drew in her breath sharply. 'As soon as you can send me.'

He looked thoughtful, tapping a gold-inlaid front tooth with the stem of his pipe, as his eyes searched her face for any trace of doubt.

Then, seeing none, the hint of a smile crossed the lipless mouth, and he scribbled something in a pad on the desk in front of him. 'You're a very brave woman, my dear. We'll see what we can do for Wednesday night. If we can fit in the basic parachute training before then, you're on.'

Wednesday night! She had to stop herself from gasping aloud. That only left tomorrow to put her things in order. She got up from the chair in front of the desk, wiping her damp palms on the fine plaid of her skirt before holding out her hand. 'Thank you, sir. I won't let you down.'

He smiled, holding on to her hand for a trifle longer than necessary. 'I know that, Beth. I hope we can say the same.'

He sat staring at the door as it closed behind her. Was he doing the right thing? There was no way of knowing. But there was no denying the situation in Poland was desperate and, more importantly, she was as keen as mustard to go. He had had no doubt in his mind what her answer would be this morning. In fact, so convinced had he been that he had spent the weekend sounding out safe houses in the Warsaw district. Out of several possibilities he had come up with one that suited admirably: the home of a teacher on the outskirts of Warsaw. They would arrange for him to be present at the drop to guide her to the house, then she would take it from there. The best plan would be for her to book into the Hotel Torun, the Germans' favourite haunt in the Polish capital, and play the role of Countess for all it was worth. The higher up the Gestapo ladder she could climb regarding her acquaintances, the better the information she could hope to glean. He had no doubt about her ability to carry out the role. Beth was an intelligent woman and far better agent material than many of the young idiots straight from university that they often got lumbered with.

If her boss was confident in her abilities, Beth was far from certain as she made her way home that evening. What on earth was Lara going to say now that she had been given the green light to go? And what about her German – was she still up to it? She was bound to be rusty after all these years. There was no doubt what her bedside reading was going to be tonight and tomorrow night. She was relieved that Lara was on days this week, so she would at least have tonight and tomorrow evening with her. The late hours the Prime Minister kept were taking their toll of his secretarial staff, and recently he had arranged for them to have one week purely on days per month. The gods must be smiling on her that it was Lara's turn.

She was home first that evening and, as she prepared the meal of scrambled eggs with what was left of the dried egg powder in the packet, she turned on the wireless, feeling it important to keep up with what was happening at the moment, particularly in Eastern Europe. The news from the Soviet Union was still good. The Russians had captured Volchansk and Chuguyev and were now within a day's march of Kharkov and, in the South-west, Lozovaya had fallen to Vatutin's troops. There was no mention of Poland, however, and she couldn't decide if that was a good thing or a bad thing. Her mind was still on the Eastern Front when she heard Lara's key in the lock at just before seven o'clock.

'You beat me to it again!' Lara threw her bag down on the kitchen dresser and sat down heavily on a chair, pulling off her shoes with a sigh of relief. 'These have been killing me all day!' She looked up at her mother as Beth turned off the cooker and began dishing up the food. 'What's the smug smile for? Don't tell me you've actually got real eggs in there!'

Beth gave a rueful smile. 'Afraid not – but it *is* all milk, with no water added!' She placed four heaped spoonfuls on to the slices of toast and passed one over to Lara before sitting down herself. 'For heaven's sake, take your coat off before you eat!' She watched as Lara slipped off her coat and hung it on the back of the door, then rejoined her at the table. 'I've had some quite exciting news today, Lara dear.'

Lara paused, a forkful of the egg half-way to her mouth. 'It has nothing to do with what you were talking about on Saturday, by any chance?'

Beth nodded excitedly. 'Yes, it does. I'm going, Lara, I'm going!'

Lara felt the colour drain from her face. 'Oh God ...' Then, seeing the excitement begin to fade from her mother's face, she attempted a reassuring smile. 'No, honestly, I'm really happy for you ...' She took a deep breath and hoped the good Lord would forgive her for such a bare-faced lie. 'Have you any idea when?'

'Probably Wednesday.'

The smile froze on Lara's lips and her stomach lurched. '*This* Wednesday?'

'If they can arrange it in time.'

'Whew!'

Beth leaned across and squeezed her hand. 'You *will* be all right won't you, dear? You *will* be able to manage on your own?'

Lara assumed a bravado she did not feel. 'Of course I will! I'm a grown girl now, remember.'

'Anyway, Ken should be due back any time now, shouldn't he? You'll be looking forward to that. It's months since he's been on leave.'

Lara's grip tightened on the cutlery. 'I'm hoping he'll get at least a forty-eight-hour pass this month.'

'You will give him my love when you see him? There are so many people I'd like to see before I go. I – I'd like to have gone over to Portland Place and said goodbye to them all at the Polish Embassy, but Barney thinks it's too risky. I mean, it's all right that the Ambassador knows, and of course General Sikorski, but he doesn't trust the likes of Leni to hold her tongue.'

'Leni? You mean Jan's wife?' She could not bring herself to refer to him as her father. 'I didn't know she was still here.'

Beth finished a mouthful of toast and nodded as she poured two cups of tea. 'There was never any question of her returning to Poland. It would be far too dangerous.' She could have added that Zbigniew Kador had played no small part in Leni's decision to remain in England. As the only Pole to survive the bombing of their home in Atholl Square, he had benefited from her ample shoulder to cry on. Then, once Jan had returned to Warsaw, they had seen more and more of each other. In fact, shortly after her husband left, Leni had moved into a small flat in Highgate and Zbigniew Kador had moved into another in the same block within weeks. She had run into Leni once or twice over the past couple of years, usually in Harrods, or one of the big Oxford Street stores, but Jan had never been mentioned. For her own part, she would love to have asked after him, but the words would not find their way to her tongue. She found it no easier when it came to enquiring about his welfare at the Embassy, and so she would be arriving in Poland, in two days' time, not knowing if he was alive or dead.

'How is ... ' Lara searched for the right word and decided on his title, 'the Count, anyway? Will you be meeting up with *him* in Poland?'

Beth shrugged as she took a sip of tea. 'Warsaw is a big place, and I don't even know if he's still there.' She could have added 'if he's still alive' but could not bring herself to utter the words. To voice her deepest fear was to give it authenticity, somehow.

'Will you be able to get any messages home? I hate the idea of not hearing from you.'

Beth frowned. It was something she hadn't even thought of. 'I honestly don't know. That's something I'll just have to play by ear, I'm afraid.'

'It seems to me there's an awful lot you'll be playing by ear over there.'

The two women looked at each other across the table, then Beth said quietly, 'All of life's like that at the moment, isn't it? There's not one of us can say for sure where we'll be, or what we'll be doing in the future – not as long as this war lasts.'

Lara nodded and stared down into the brown, steaming liquid in her cup. It was true. The whole world had begun to disintegrate that autumn three and a half years ago – countries and families were ripped apart, never to be put back together again. Not in the same way, anyway. For, whatever happened when this war was over, none of them who had lived through it would ever be quite the same. 'In a way, I envy you,' she said and, to her surprise, she meant it. 'At least you're going to be doing something positive with your life from now on.'

'But you're doing something positive, too. What could be more positive than working for the Prime Minister, for heaven's sake?'

'Oh, I know, many people would give their right arm for my job, but it's not quite the same. In Downing Street I merely react to decisions taken by other people; out there you'll be making your own decisions. You'll be waging your own personal war against the Germans.'

'Not against the Germans, Lara – at least not against all of them. Against the Gestapo.'

'They'll give you a gun, of course. Will you be able to use it?'

Beth swallowed the mouthful of tea and replaced the cup in the saucer with a clatter. 'If need be.'

Lara stared at her. 'I don't know if I could – take a human life, I mean. How would you live with yourself afterwards?'

Beth tensed in the chair. Her daughter was asking the very questions she had avoided asking herself since the idea of going over there had begun to germinate in her mind. 'I don't think I can answer that question,' she said slowly. 'It's something I will have to come to terms with when the time comes.'

'Are you afraid of death?'

'No, I'm not afraid of death. I'm afraid of dying, yes, but I'm not afraid of death itself. Your grandmother and I talked about it quite a lot just before she died. She told me she regarded it as simply the opening of a door into another room – a door through which so many of her loved ones had already gone before.' She gave a bitter-sweet smile at the memory. 'She was so absolutely certain my father was waiting for her there that she almost convinced me too.'

'Almost … ?'

Beth gave a strained smile. 'Well, if nothing in this life is for certain, I don't see why anything in death should be either, do you?'

'Do you know this is quite the most depressing conversation I've ever had in my entire life!'

'You're quite right. What we need is cheering up!'

'Any suggestions?'

'Well, one of the girls at work did say something about a very good film being on at the Gaumont this week. She went with her sister when it was on at the Odeon last week and swears they wept buckets! We could always catch the second house.'

'That's the best idea I've heard all day. Did she say what it was called?'

'Well, oddly enough it was quite topical, although she swears it has nothing to do with the Conference. It's called *Casablanca*.'

Chapter Thirty-eight

Dawn came, and with it a pale winter sun that did little to melt the ice that had formed on the singed fur of what was left of his flying jacket and around the burnt rags that clung to his half-naked body. His fur-lined flying boots had become flimsy leather slippers.

Ken lapsed in and out of consciousness, aware that he was still alive; but the knowledge brought him no joy: his hands had swollen horrifically and he was conscious of his face being the same, for he could barely open his mouth to attempt to shout for help. But far worse than the swelling and the pain was the sight of the skin that hung in layers from the grotesquely swollen flesh. He had been sick on landing, and the stomach-turning stench of burning flesh and hair still clung to his nostrils, or what was left of them …

That was the worst part, he decided, in the infrequent moments of lucidness – the not-knowing what was left of him. He had seen burn cases before: young men with nothing left of a face or body but livid masses of congealed flesh. And even when the burns were minor, the consequences were often fatal. One of his own squadron at Tangmere – a quiet-spoken bloke from Carlisle by the name of Bill Bragg – had landed with his kite on fire two years ago and Ken had been one of the first on the scene. The glycol was still pouring out of his engine as they pulled him from the cockpit. His helmet was off and his hair was on fire as the ambulance boys struggled to get him out of his harness. He didn't look too bad, considering. Lucky bugger, they had said when they got back from visiting him in hospital that night. He had been sitting up in bed and joking with them. Next day he was dead. Died of shock. Quite common, the doctors said. Bill Bragg's face swam before him …

He was only semi-conscious when the dog found him. It was its master shouting in guttural French that brought him back across the invisible line to reality. The farmer cursed the animal for straying too far from the narrow track that linked his farmhouse with the pasture on the far side of the river. It was the parachute he saw first, sprawled across the clump of whins that had sheltered Ken from the worst of last night's snow.

'*Mon Dieu!*' The elderly man gazed in horror at the sight before him. Then the horror turned to panic as a sound was emitted from what had once been a mouth.

'*Anglais,*' the prostrate figure did his best to gasp. '*Anglais. Aidez-moi … Pour l'amour de Dieu, aidez-moi …*'

Wednesday 17 February 1943 was a cold, clear night in London, and Beth held her daughter close to her as she said her goodbyes on the front doorstep of their block of flats in Lower Belgrave Street. 'Don't cry, my dear … Please don't cry …' Her own voice broke with emotion as she stroked the mass of shining red hair resting on her shoulder.

'I'm not crying,' Lara protested, as the tears ran freely down her cheeks and on to the fur collar of her mother's coat. 'Why can't I come with you to the airfield? Why do we have to say goodbye here?'

'You know why, dear.'

It was true. She did. No one was allowed to accompany agents to the top secret airfield where they would take off into the dangers of Occupied Europe. 'I shall miss you.' She clung closer to the smooth black worsted of her mother's coat.

'Time now, ma'am, I'm sorry to say.' The young airman who had been assigned to drive Beth to the waiting plane moved uncomfortably on the edge of the pavement. 'It's time we were going.'

Lara clung on even more tightly for a moment, then dragged herself away to kiss her mother on both cheeks. 'God go with you, Mum. Tonight and always.'

'And you, my dear. And you …'

Then she was gone – vanished into the dark interior of the black Rover that would take her out of Britain, out of Lara's life and on into the unknown.

Lara watched until the car had disappeared into the darkness of the street then, slowly, very slowly, she turned and walked back in through the main front door of the block of flats.

The flat seemed frighteningly empty as she walked from room to room, pausing longest in her mother's bedroom, with its chintz curtains and bedspread and the matching frill around the dressing-table. Everything spoke of her presence, everything; from the silver-backed brush and comb set to the well-chosen water-colours on the walls.

It hadn't been easy starting again. Picking up the pieces after the bombing had been a long and often heartbreaking experience. And it was funny how many little things one needed to replace – things that it had proved impossible to obtain because of the wartime shortages. But it wasn't the mundane, everyday things that one missed. It was the other things – the personal, very private items that no money, no amount of searching, could ever replace – the photographs and small items of jewellery, each one redolent with memories.

In many ways they had been luckier than most who had been bombed out for, when her grandmother had died, they had inherited all her precious, family things, including the family album. It still lay where it had lain for the past fifty years – on the small side-table by the fireside in the house in Oxford, for Beth had been quite unable even to contemplate selling what had been her childhood home.

A thoughtful look crossed Lara's face. Perhaps she would spend her next leave up there. She needed time to herself, to come to terms with what was happening to her life. Yes, she would check up tomorrow when she was next due a few days off. They had been promised the extra leave because of all the additional hours of overtime put in over the period of the Conference. With a bit of luck, it might be sooner rather than later.

The following three weeks passed in a numbed daze. The worst part of it was that she could confide her fears about her mother to no one. Beth's mission, like everything associated with the SOE, was top secret. But her concern for her mother was not the only worry on her mind as February passed into March, and the snow showers and sleet gave way to blustery winds and longer evenings in which to sit alone in the small flat and pray to a God she scarcely believed in that her period would come, and that she would hear before too long from Ken. She had never gone so long without a letter from her husband and, although not unduly worried, she resolved to do what she had been so loath to do up till now – get in touch with the aerodrome at Southam and put her mind at rest. She would telephone tomorrow from work. At least the telephone lines from Downing Street could be relied upon to work, which was more than could be said for most public phone-boxes these days, with so much bomb damage around. And there was one other thing she had to do the next day. She was due a return visit to her doctor to receive the results of the pregnancy test she had requested the previous week.

She got up earlier than usual the following day, looking her best coat and hat out of the wardrobe to don before the visit to Dr Munro's surgery. Somehow it seemed important to look her best.

She was in the act of securing the jaunty blue felt hat with its curling ostrich feather to the back of her head, when a loud knock at the door made her stab the pearl-topped hat pin into the skin instead of her hair. 'Blast it!' She rubbed the painful area of scalp and glanced in the vague direction of the noise. Who on earth was that at this time of day?

'I'm coming! I'm coming!' she called in irritation, as she carefully poked the long pin through the felt and into a lock of hair at the back of her head. 'That'll have to do!' She paused for a second longer to adjust a tuft of red hair that stuck out too far in front of one ear, then walked quickly into the hall.

'I told you I'm coming!' It was hard to disguise her irritation as the knocking became more persistent. 'Good God – what do you want?' She stared in a mixture of disbelief and impending panic at the telegram boy on the step.

'Telegram for a Mrs Kenneth Cameron,' the boy said, handing over a buff coloured envelope.

Lara's hand trembled as she took it. No one who had lived this long through the war could be in any doubt what it signified. She felt physically sick.

'You have to sign for it, missus, then I have to wait to see if there's any reply.' The boy thrust a piece of paper and a pencil at her and mechanically she signed her name. 'You'd better open it, missus.'

Lara continued to stare down at the envelope in her hands. He was right. Her fingers shook as she tore open the back flap and pulled out the official-looking sheet of paper.

Missing. Presumed dead …

They were the only words that registered as she stared down at the small black print. She leaned back on the door jamb for support as the words continued to swim before her eyes.

'You all right, missus?'

She nodded. Her throat had closed and the words would not come.

'Is there any reply?' The boy shifted from one foot to the other and looked at her curiously.

She shook her head.

'You sure?'

She nodded, wishing he would just go and leave her alone. She backed into the hallway and closed the door in his face, then leaned against it and reread the words. There was no mistake. Ken was missing, presumed dead ... But how could that be? How could you go missing teaching raw recruits to fly over the English countryside? It didn't make sense.

She folded the telegram and placed it deep in her coat pocket. She could not cry. She wanted to scream – to beat her fists into the wall and scream at the top of her lungs. Why Ken? Why him? For God's sake, why him?

She walked into the bedroom and picked up her handbag. Suddenly it was very important to get out of the flat. She had to be with people. If she stayed in here all alone she would go to pieces, she was sure of it. Oh God – the doctor ... She remembered her appointment. She stared at her white face in the mirror. Could she bear two pieces of traumatic news in one day?

Her gaze fell on the silver marcasite brooch in the lapel of her coat – a present from her mother last Christmas. If anyone had courage she did. And she wouldn't let her down. Whatever courage was needed to get through this day was nothing compared to what her mother needed for her work in Poland.

It took half an hour to walk from her flat to the doctor's surgery. Dr Munro was an elderly Scotsman who reminded Lara of an older version of Ken's father – a fact that lent a bitter irony to the situation as she sat in the chill of the ante-room and waited for her name to be called.

'The doctor's ready for you now, Mrs Cameron.' Within minutes, the white-coated receptionist held the door open for her to enter, and Lara walked hesitantly into the plush, wood-panelled office.

Dr Munro sat behind a large, leather-topped desk, and half-rose in his seat to lean across and shake her by the hand. There was a wide smile on his face – something the good doctor was not known for. 'Well, Mrs Cameron, it's good news we've got for you today, to be sure!'

Lara sat down on the edge of the high-backed chair, her hands clasped in her lap in front of her. 'Good news?'

'You're pregnant, lassie! Have the good grace to raise a smile, will ye!'

Pregnant ... She leaned back in the chair and drew in her breath sharply, letting it out slowly as she shook her head. 'No ... Please, no ...'

Dr Munro looked puzzled. 'Now what sort of attitude is that? If I had a shilling for every young woman of your age who came here in tears because they couldn't conceive a bairn, then I'd be a rich man by now!' He shook his head at the memory. 'I don't know what to make of some of you young folk these days, I swear I don't. I'm sure your husband will be pleased as punch even if you're not. Is that not right now?'

Lara shook her head as a maelstrom of emotions whirled in her mind. She could not tell him of Ken's presumed death, for there was no way her husband could have been the baby's father. But nothing on earth would bring her to utter Mike's name. 'It – it's come as a bit of a shock, that's all, Doctor.'

The elderly man nodded, his face softening. 'Aye, that I can believe. Conception is often the last thing on a young couple's mind at the time …' His eyes twinkled and he gave a polite cough before they turned serious once more. 'I can appreciate your apprehension though, my dear. Wartime is hardly the best time to be thinking about bringing new life into the world.' He looked thoughtful for a moment, then continued, 'But maybe we're all hostages to fate in one way or another, no matter when or how we enter this life. Are you keeping fine in yourself at the moment?'

Lara nodded. 'Yes, yes, I'm fine.'

He gave a satisfied nod. 'I'm glad to hear it … But I'll have you back again in a couple of weeks all the same. You may not be feeling any effects as yet, but by the end of this month you'll know there's two of you, I can assure you of that. But I'll not have to teach the likes of an intelligent young woman like you the facts of life, I'm sure.'

Lara managed a strained smile. If only he knew. If only he knew. For all the closeness with her mother, they had never once broached the subject of pregnancy or childbirth. In fact, she was as ignorant as most schoolgirls in that regard.

Dr Munro stood up and proffered his hand once more. 'Well now, away with you and break the good news to that mother of yours and your husband – the lucky lad. It'll be beers all round in the officers' mess tonight, I've not the shadow of a doubt!'

He had not the slightest idea why the young woman in front of him burst into tears.

Chapter Thirty-nine

Beth listened to the drone of the aircraft fade into the distance as it turned and headed back for England and left her alone in the centre of the Polish field. The drop had gone according to plan and, apart from a few bruises, she had landed unscathed. But never in her life had she felt more alone.

She could feel the blur of tears in her eyes as they scanned the darkness around her. Was it fear, or fatigue? Perhaps a mixture of both. She clasped the rolled up bulk of the parachute closer to her and a shiver ran through her once more.

Someone should be here – her contact. They had told her he would be waiting somewhere out there in the night. She could feel her heart palpitating beneath the thick woollen underwear she had worn specially to fend off the Polish cold. What if no one came? What if he or she, whoever it was, got the time wrong? What would she do then? It never happened, they said. These operations were planned and executed with military precision, by military personnel. But she was not military personnel. She was simply a woman who, in a moment of sheer madness, had volunteered for this assignment. Immediately she felt shame at her panic. It had been no moment of madness that made her volunteer for this mission and, whatever happened, she would see it through to the end.

She stared around her into the darkness, her apprehension growing, despite her resolve to remain calm.

Then, suddenly, a pin-point of light appeared in the distance. It grew bigger as she stared at it. It was moving this way. She stifled a gasp and felt the hairs at the nape of her neck stand on end. Every muscle in her body was frozen, riveted to the spot. Her mouth was dry. 'Please God, please don't let it be the Germans ... Please God ...'

The shape behind the shaded light was tall and bulky – threateningly bulky – as it drew nearer. Then, when about fifty feet away, it spoke. '*Schmetterling?*' a man's voice hissed in a hushed tone.

For a split second the German word meant nothing, then reality dawned. It was the code. '*Ja … Ja … Motte.*' A wave of relief swept through her as she stammered out the correct rejoinder.

The man drew nearer. He was tall and thin-faced, the bulk of his figure being made up by the heavy, dark tweed overcoat he wore against the cold of the night, but she could distinguish very little of his features in the semi-darkness. 'Frau Gräfin von Wolfsberg?'

'*Ja … Ja … Sie sind mein Kontakt?*'

'We will speak English, if you don't mind. Speaking German, I feel I must wash my mouth out afterwards. You understand?'

Beth gave a nervous laugh. 'Yes – yes, I understand.'

He took the bundled parachute from her and, stuffing it in a sack he produced from beneath his overcoat, he took her by the arm and led her back across the field in the direction of the tall hedge.

'Before the war I taught both English and German for my living,' he said quietly. 'In those days I was not too much ashamed of the German part of my work; now it will haunt me to the grave.' He gave a shallow laugh. 'To make my shame complete, it is now the only language I am allowed by the Nazis to teach.' The bitterness in his voice was all too evident and, as he spoke, his eyes darted around him, peering into the pale moonlit landscape as if expecting to see that which he most feared any second. Beth could feel the tenseness in his fingers as they gripped her forearm through the thick sleeve of her warmest winter fur. He kept the shaded beam of his torch pointed to the ground as they picked their way across the rutted, frosty earth.

After several minutes they came to a break in the hedgerow and he helped her through. She almost tripped over something dark and bulky sitting at the side of the dirt track.

'It belongs to you, no?'

She stared down at it. 'My case! You found it!'

His finger went to his lips at her exultant outburst, then he managed a strained smile and said softly. 'That was why I was a few minutes late in getting to you: it was important to see exactly where it landed … Unfortunately cases, like supplies, cannot call out and inform us where they land. It is very easy for them to fall into enemy hands if they are not found immediately.' He lifted the case with his right hand and said, 'Hold on to the back of my coat, if you please, Countess. I have a vehicle. It awaits not far from here.'

His English had a quaint sound to it, as if it had been learned from text books a generation or two out of date. She did as she was told, relieved to be in capable hands.

It was not easy to maintain her balance, for the frost had made the ground slippery underfoot and her leather-soled shoes slipped occasionally on the rutted track. It had obviously rained in the past twenty-four hours, for thinly iced puddles lay in wait at intervals for the carelessly placed foot.

She was beginning to think that 'not far from here' did not mean quite the same to a Pole when, at last, they came to a small copse. She heard a horse whinny softly in the darkness as they approached. Her companion disappeared into the trees and reappeared almost immediately leading an old mare hitched to a hay wagon. Within seconds the case and parachute had disappeared into the animal feed and the man had mounted the wooden plank that served as a seat at the front of the cart.

'Give me your hand!' She obeyed, and was hoisted up beside him. 'I will take you to my home,' he said, 'then I will return the cart to its owner. You will be safe with us tonight.'

Sitting beside him on top of the cart, she felt almost unbearably vulnerable and prayed inwardly that it would not take too long to reach their destination. Back home in London she had imagined this moment so often and had actually looked forward to the excitement of it, but out here in the freezing reality of Occupied Poland it was quite a different story altogether. She could feel her heart beating erratically in her breast, and her fingers gripped the wooden plank beneath her as if her life depended on it.

In the distance she could see the lights of Warsaw. Nearer at hand they passed individual houses, some with a huddle of out-buildings, that she took to be small farmsteads. 'Is – is it a small farm like that you live on?' she heard herself whisper above the steady creak of the wheels as they trundled over the hard ground.

He nodded, then gave an almost apologetic shrug. 'Perhaps a farm would be – what can I say – too "grand" a word. It was my parents' home. They are both dead now.'

'I'm sorry.'

'I too am sorry,' he said in a tight voice. 'They died on Polish soil – but desecrated Polish soil. In Auschwitz … They were Socialists,' he added, by way of explanation.

A shiver ran through her. She was silent for a moment, then reached across and touched his arm. Words would be futile. There could be few who had not heard of the notorious death camp to which the Nazis had sent countless thousands of Poles, mainly of left-wing persuasion, to be followed by untold numbers of the country's Jewish population.

Their conversation, hushed and awkward as it was, came to an end, and before long the cart turned off the lane along which they had been travelling and juddered uncomfortably for about 100 metres along a deeply rutted dirt track, even narrower than the one they had just left. Eventually it creaked to a halt outside the door of a long, low, thatched building. No lights were evident, and at first Beth could not tell if it was a barn or a house.

The young man jumped down and disappeared in through the front door, leaving Beth perched on top of the cart alone. Her teeth chattered in the darkness and she could not be sure if it was through fear or the bitter cold. Probably both, she decided, as she clasped her gloved hands around her in a personal bear-hug and gazed fearfully towards the closed door. To her ill-disguised relief, the young man re-emerged a minute or so later with a young woman at his side. She was holding a small baby wrapped in a blanket. 'This is my wife,' he said proudly. 'To you she will be Katya – and I will be Vanya.'

Beth smiled down at the two young faces in the doorway. She would probably never learn their real names, nor they hers, but they were prepared to risk their lives, and the future of their child, for her. It was a humbling thought.

After helping her down, and removing the parachute and her case from their hiding place in the hay, he carried them both inside, then returned to remount the cart and disappear into the darkness. They watched him go, then Katya touched her gently on the arm and indicated for Beth to follow her inside.

Once the door had been securely shut behind them, the young woman led her into a small but cosily furnished living-room. A heavy, dark-wood dresser stood against one wall, its top strewn with sepia-coloured family photographs in carved wooden frames, and beams of the same dark wood ran at intervals across the low ceiling. A series of empty hooks hung from them, just above head-height – a reminder of the days when meat was not an almost unknown commodity in people's lives.

The floor was bare but for a rag rug that lay in front of the hearth; the floorboards had a dull, well-scrubbed look to them. A meagre fire burned in the grate and the room was little warmer than the chill night they had just left outside. The young woman saw her look at the almost empty grate and shook her head. 'Fuel – it is not possible now. Maybe one day some wood, one day some coal. Some days nothing. Many people – in Warsaw and Praga – they have nothing.

To live they burn their furniture ...' Her eyes glanced to an empty space against the wall opposite the dresser, where the floorboards still retained some of their original polish, and Beth wondered what family treasure that had once stood there had now gone up in flames against the bitter cold of the past winter. The young woman saw her look and sighed deeply, 'Life it is very difficult for us now – for all Poles.'

She spoke English haltingly and had a soft, lisping voice. Beth looked at her. Her round, almost childlike face would have been pretty, but it was now prematurely pinched and careworn around the mouth and eyes. Back home in Britain she would be a typical young mother, but life over there was so very, very different. She thought of the relative comfort in which she lived in the flat in Lower Belgravia Street with Lara. For the first time she felt almost ashamed. They had suffered – yes, it was true, but in England there was at least sufficient food on the table, scant though the rations might be, and no one died of the cold any more. And most importantly of all, there was no Auschwitz or other camp looming as a constant threat in the background; no Gestapo lurking round every corner.

There was one place set at the table in front of them, with an empty bowl and spoon, and a plate next to it on which a much too generous chunk of brown bread lay.

Katya motioned for her to take a seat in the chair in front of the bowl, as she lifted a heavy black iron pot from what was left of the fire. 'Soup,' she said, with a hesitant smile. 'I hope you like.'

Beth watched as she dished up a plateful of what looked like a thin potato soup into the plate, and indicated for her to take up the bread and spoon and begin. There was no sign of any place set for either Katya or her husband, and Beth had the awful feeling that she was being invited to eat what would have been their own main meal of the day.

'Please – eat.' The young woman insisted, standing over her.

And so she began. She was not in the least bit hungry. Nerves and a queasiness born of the long plane journey had put paid to any appetite she might have had. The soup was barely lukewarm and not particularly pleasant tasting, and the bread gritty, but it was offered with love and that was how she must accept it. She finished every drop. 'Thank you, Katya, that was lovely. Most welcome.'

The young woman beamed. 'After so long a journey, you must have hunger, no? And tired, yes? Come.'

She indicated for Beth to pick up her case and, after lighting a candle, led the way out into the narrow hallway and up a creaking, winding stair towards a tiny attic room in the eaves of the house. Beth had to heave the case up the staircase step by step, and was quite out of breath by the time they reached the small door at the top.

She followed Katya inside, ducking her head as she did so, and looked around in a mixture of relief and apprehension. A rough wooden bed, containing a straw mattress and a feather quilt and pillow, lay between the rafters along one wall. On a wooden chest by the bed a ewer containing water for the morning wash stood in an enamel basin. The only other furniture was a wooden, rush-seated chair. A mouse scuttled between the chest and bed, disappearing into the darkness of the eaves. Beth quailed inwardly and pretended not to notice.

'I hope you will have comfort,' Katya said, with a shy smile, as she moved the baby to her other hip in order to fold back the feather quilt.

It was a touching gesture, intended to make her feel at home. 'Thank you, my dear. I'm sure I will.' They stood by the bed smiling awkwardly at one another, and Beth knew the poor girl would not relax until her guest had disappeared beneath that eiderdown for the night. She put down her case with a sigh of relief. 'Well, goodnight, Katya. And thank you ...'

She undressed quickly, afraid to put it off too long in case the candle went out: there was barely an inch of tallow left in the holder. She prayed the mouse would not reappear and lay listening for it as she pulled the quilt up around her chin and snuggled down in her underwear in the unfamiliar bed. After a minute or so of silence she began to relax and her thoughts returned to the young woman and her husband downstairs.

Thank you, she had said. Thank you ... Two little words that could never express what she now owed to these two young people this night. And there were so many of them – all over Occupied Europe there were Vanyas and Katyas risking their lives in the fight against this Nazi menace that was polluting their world.

There was a tiny skylight between the rafters in the eave just above her head, and she stared up into the starlit sky beyond the dusty glass. It was as if she had come full circle. A whole generation ago, in the wake of the war they said would end all wars, she had come here to this part of Europe – had travelled across blood-soaked lands to take her place as a member of the German aristocracy in Silesia. 'Countess Elizabeth von Lessing.' She whispered the name into the silence of the tiny room. It hardly seemed possible.

She thought of Hans Heinrich. If he were still alive she would still be here, but she would not be lying in the attic of this peasant farmstead, listening to the mice scurrying in the ancient wooden rafters around her head, she would be lying in the sumptuous splendour of the master bedchamber in Schloss Wolfsberg – she would be a part of this cancer that was destroying all that she had ever held dear. Yes, she would still be a genuine, real-life German Countess, instead of the mock one she was now purporting to be.

She took a deep breath and clutched the quilt tighter around her as a shudder ran through her. It was true what they said – life often was stranger than fiction. But she was no character in a book or a play. This was a real life drama she was acting out and it would call for the best acting performance of her life. Not only her own life, but those of so many others depended on it – not least the two young people and their baby downstairs.

She would leave here in the morning, she decided. She would take her case and head for the heart of Warsaw itself. They had advised her in London to head for the Hotel Torun. The owner was known to be sympathetic to the Government in Exile, and the place was a known haunt of the highest-ranking Gestapo personnel.

Yes, tomorrow she would be on her own and her work would begin in earnest. She would not put this young couple's lives at risk one moment longer than was necessary. They told her at SOE headquarters that she must stay in the safe house no longer than she could help. Overnight was the maximum they preferred … Yes, tomorrow she would move on into the city itself. Tomorrow she would leave Beth Mallory behind and, for better or worse, become a German Countess once more – Countess Lisa von Wolfsberg. Her heart quailed at the prospect.

Chapter Forty

'Countess von Wolfsberg? *Ach, ja,* I have been advised you would be requiring a room.' The ruddy-faced man behind the reception desk of the Hotel Torun looked at Beth curiously from over the top of his pince-nez spectacles – a look that froze the blood in her veins.

What did he mean he had been 'advised' she would be requiring a room? Who had advised him? While they had instructed her at SOE headquarters that this was the hotel she must book into, they had said nothing about informing the owner of her arrival. Fear washed over her in waves and, despite the bitter cold of the hotel foyer, she could feel her skin break out in a hot flush beneath her warm woollen underwear.

Pan Jozef Gluck seemed to sense her anxiety and gave a reassuring smile before he reached behind him and took a key from the wooden rack on the wall. 'You are in luck, Countess. We have one of our best available – a rare occurrence these days – Room 17. I hope you like it. If you have any cause for complaint, I am here most of the day – and most of the night when our German friends are in festive mood.'

He spoke fluent German with a pronounced Polish accent, and Beth thought she could detect the faintest trace of irony in his last remark. 'I – I'm sure everything will be perfect, thank you.' It was odd to be speaking German again and she hoped her nervousness did not show on her face as she attempted a casual smile and took the key from his outstretched hand to slip it into the pocket of her fur-coat.

The landlord snapped his fingers at a young boy hovering in the background, and the youngster walked smartly across to pick up her case. 'Room 17, Roman,' his master directed him in Polish.

Beth followed the youngster across the foyer towards the lift. It was on its way down from one of the upper floors and she waited apprehensively for its arrival. At last it appeared: an ancient, wrought-iron contraption that creaked its way downwards to arrive with an almighty jolt at its destination. The iron bars of the door concertinaed sideways to disgorge its occupants: two high-ranking Nazi officers whose pale brows rose in unison at the sight of the attractive, dark-haired woman before them. '*Morgen, gnädige Frau.*' Two perfect bows were executed as she slid past them with a studiously gracious smile.

She glanced across at the young boy beside her as the lift creaked back into life and moved slowly upwards. He was looking past her, out through the bars of the cage. To him she was just another top-drawer German – probably the wife of one of the top Gestapo chiefs who had arrived in the city on a brief matrimonial visit. How little he knew! How could he imagine the rate at which her heart was beating beneath all this finery, or the film of nervous perspiration that bathed her body as she played her new role to the hilt?

The boy carried her case to the appropriate door and accepted the proffered tip with a sharp, Prussian click of the heels of his well-worn shoes and a deep bow. He had obviously picked up quite a few tips other than the purely monetary from the hotel's German clients, she mused to herself, as she turned the key in the lock and pushed open the door.

The room was large, with a rather ugly four-poster bed at one end and a *chaise-longue* covered in faded red velvet in front of the empty fireplace. A large, double wardrobe and dressing-table on the same heavy Gothic lines as the bed sat along one wall; a marble-topped wash-stand and two easy-chairs on either side of the mantelpiece completed the furniture. The walls were covered in a heavy flocked wallpaper depicting overblown tea-roses in a faded pink against a cream-coloured background, and two etchings in narrow black frames hung on either side of the mantelpiece, with a much larger one above the fireplace itself. Beth walked over to look more closely at them. They were all of Silesian castles, very similar to Wolfsberg and Jarosbork. The sight of them sent a shiver down her spine.

It took her a little over half an hour to unpack and freshen up, then, suddenly, for the first time since her arrival the previous night, she was hungry. That the hotel had a good dining-room she had little doubt, for the German High Command would not frequent a place that provided anything less than the best. It had been unnerving enough just running into those two Nazis in the lift without heading straight back into the fray, but she had not come here to hide away in her room, she told herself sharply, she had come here to elicit all the information she could to send back to London. And, anyway, she was absolutely famished.

Replacing her favourite black felt hat, trimmed with the swirl of ostrich feathers, she forced a smile to her lips in the dressing-table mirror. At all costs she must look completely relaxed in the company she was about to enter. 'Heil Hitler!' Her right arm shot out in the ubiquitous salute, to be reflected in all its absurdity in the mirror in front of her, and her laughter rang out in the silence of the room. At last the smile on her face was perfectly genuine! She picked up her handbag from the bed and hooked it over her arm. Her entry into German society, for the first time in a generation, was about to take place.

The longcase clock in the foyer was striking twelve as she passed it on her way to the dining-room. The ground floor of the hotel was alive with the black uniforms of SS officers, interspersed with occasional flashes of the field-grey of their *Wehrmacht* counterparts – almost each and every one of them a perfect specimen of Aryan manhood. And almost to a man they reminded her of Hans Heinrich.

The dining-room, like her bedroom, was pure Gothic, with touches here and there of French Rococo. Large, ornamental gilt mirrors adorned the walls on top of the burgundy and gold embossed wallpaper, and an enormous gilt and crystal chandelier hung from the centre of the elaborate plaster rose in the middle of the ceiling. The tables, set from two persons upwards to twelve, were covered in white damask cloths, the cutlery and napkins laid out with immaculate precision on top, and a crystal vase containing fresh flowers adorned each one, making Beth wonder where on earth they were obtained at this time of year.

The head waiter appeared at her side immediately and, to her surprise, was already acquainted with her name. 'Countess von Wolfsberg – *Wenn ich Sie bitten darf...*'

She followed him across the plush Persian carpets and smiled graciously as he held out a chair for her at a table for two in the far corner of the room, where she gratefully buried herself behind the tall, leather-bound menu as nerves fluttered disconcertingly in her empty stomach. All eyes in the room were on her, she was certain of it ... But no, she was being silly. The German officers who happened to be looking her way were merely looking with the same degree of curiosity reserved for any good-looking woman who happened to be dining alone.

She decided to forgo the soup, and ordered a portion of *Sauerbraten*, followed by *Apfelstrudel* and fresh cream. 'And a half carafe of white wine, please,' she added, closing the menu and placing it back beside the cut-glass water jug. 'A light Moselle will do nicely, thank you.'

The food, when it came, was surprisingly good. She finished the *Sauerbraten* with relish, was half-way through the *Strudel*, and had just been served with her coffee when a tall, jackbooted figure appeared at her elbow; two black leather heels clicked audibly as the Obersturmbannführer executed a perfect bow and murmured, '*Gestatten Sie, gnädige Frau?*'

Her spoon hit the gilt-edged dish with a clatter as she glanced up at the tall, immaculately uniformed figure.

'Obersturmbannführer Walter Schellendorf, my good Countess von Wolfsberg. It is a pleasure to make your acquaintance.'

Beth half rose from her seat and proffered her hand to be kissed. 'You – you know my name?' The words came out in a hoarse whisper as she gazed up into the palest of blue eyes.

He smiled across at her as he took the seat opposite and signalled to the waiter. 'I regard it my duty to acquaint myself with all newcomers to the hotel, my dear Countess – especially one as charming as yourself, if I may be so bold.'

Beth attempted a smile and took a large sip of her wine as her new companion ordered himself a cognac.

'And one for the lady, too, *mein Lieber*.'

'Oh, no, really …'

He held up his hand and waved the waiter away. 'I insist. It's a special consignment that has been brought over from Paris. You must try it.' It was an order given with the most charming of smiles.

Beth replaced her wine glass on the table and toyed with the stem. Now the questions would begin. Her mouth had gone quite dry and she moistened her lips with her tongue as she forced a smile to her lips. 'The food is quite delicious here, isn't it?' It was quite the most inane of remarks, but she could think of nothing better.

Her companion smiled, and a gold inlay glinted in a front tooth. 'Old Gluck knows what's good for him. We pay him well and he comes up with the goods. Business is business, even in wartime, my dear Countess.'

The cognac arrived and he raised his goblet across the table to meet hers. '*Prozit!*' They drank in unison. 'And what brings you to the Hotel Torun, may I be so bold as to ask? I trust you are not in Warsaw for the scenery!'

Beth gave a wry, but mirthless smile. The smoking remains of what was left of Poland's once beautiful capital city was a terrible testimony to what he and his kind had done. 'No, it is not the scenery. I was staying on one of our family estates in the east and ... '

'Don't tell me – you had to flee the advance of those murdering Soviet swine!' His contempt for the Red Army was all too obvious as he took another swig of the cognac. 'You left it late, my dear Countess. It could have been your undoing. Had you no man to advise you it would be suicide to remain so long in the firing line?'

Beth could detect a personal interest behind the perfectly innocent question. She gave a slight shrug and pushed the now empty *Strudel* dish from her. 'My husband did not survive the last war, Herr Obersturmbannführer.'

'You are quite alone in the world, then?'

She nodded. 'I have not been blessed with children. My staff, the workers on my estate, were my family ... I – I fear for their safety now I have gone.' She was warming to her story now. There was no way he was in a position to check up on it. The lands to the east were in ferment, with the Soviet troops advancing towards the lands claimed by the Reich with every day that passed. The *'Ostflucht'*, the long, continuing flight to the West from the large *Junker* estates of East Prussia, was the ideal vehicle for her cover. To check up on every single *'Volksdeutsch'* refugee aristocrat was a task beyond even the Third Reich's considerable, but rapidly dwindling resources. 'I thought I might stay here for a short period ... You know, wait and see how the fighting progresses. I have faith our troops will regain my land for the Fatherland before too long, and I would prefer to be here when it happens rather than in Berlin.'

He nodded. He could not argue with that. To do so would be to deny that the *Wehrmacht* was in anything other than complete control on the Eastern Front. 'Then while you are here we must make it our duty to see that you are treated as befits your status, my dear Countess. You have plans for tonight?'

Beth drew in her breath, not quite sure what was coming next. 'Well ... No, nothing specific ... '

Walter Schellendorf finished his cognac in one last gulp and signalled for another. 'Good! In that case you must join us. We are having a small soirée in the ballroom here tonight. You must be our guest.'

Once more the invitation was given as an order rather than a suggestion and she found herself nodding in agreement. 'That is very kind of you. I should be delighted.'

He went on to tell her of his home in Wedel, just outside Hamburg, and of his despair in going home on leave last summer to discover that his parents' home in Altona had received a direct hit during an RAF bombing raid. 'They are swine, the British,' he said

329

bitterly. 'They pretend to be oh-so-civilized, but practise concentrated terror bombing raids on our cities. It is terrible how many women, children and old people have perished. My grandparents died in Lübeck during just such a raid in March of last year.'

He shuddered at the thought, and Beth's own mind went back to March 1942 when Lara, who rarely commented on what went on behind closed Cabinet doors, had been unaccountably upset at reports on the wireless and in the newspapers about the fire-bombing raids on Lübeck. 'They said it would go up like a tinder-box,' she had said bitterly. 'All those medieval wooden-framed houses ... All those poor people ... ' There were no perfect goodies and no complete baddies in war: Beth had learned that much long ago. The rights and wrongs of war were never black and white, but rather dirty shades of grey, just like the shattered skyline of this tortured city.

It was almost half an hour later when her uninvited companion took his leave, with a promise to look out for her in the hotel ballroom that evening. The dining-room was now filling up and, grateful though she was at finding her first encounter with a Nazi officer a relatively painless one, rather than find herself going through the same experience again, she decided to make her way outside to take a look at the city in daylight.

What she found horrified her. More streets appeared to be smoking ruins than were actually left standing, and not even the grey mist that hung in wraiths along the banks of the Vistula could disguise the grim sight on its left bank of the nine feet high, two-brick-thick wall, its top studded with broken glass, that snaked its way for eleven miles around what was now the Jewish ghetto. From what she had heard and read before coming out here, she knew only too well what was going on behind its forbidding walls. It had been built by Jewish money, the Germans levying taxes on the Jews to pay for its construction by forced Jewish labour. Its twenty-two exits were constantly guarded, and very few who entered its grim portals were ever allowed to leave, except by cattle trucks headed for the dreaded camps of Auschwitz, Treblinka, Chelmno, Belzec and their like.

It was a relief when it disappeared from sight as she walked quickly along Rymarska Street towards the relative sanctuary of the Saski Gardens. Despite the wall and its hidden horrors and the wholesale destruction around her, Beth could sense a heart still beating within the city. Yes, despite its wounds, Poland's historic capital was still very much alive. Her eyes scanned the roof-tops. HE could be out there somewhere. 'Jan ... ' her lips whispered his name. Would they –

could they – ever find each other in this war-torn city? For all she knew he was no longer here. He might even be dead. A shudder ran through her at the thought. But it was a possibility that had to be faced: after all, countless thousands had already died, and many more had simply disappeared, were still disappearing, without trace from these rubble-strewn streets, and from every other town and village the length and breadth of the country.

Her boss at SOE had told her that she would be contacted by a member of the Underground soon after her arrival in Warsaw, but even that was no real comfort. No one used their own names, or those of friends or colleagues. The less one knew, the less one could disclose under torture. It was as simple as that, so there could be no question of saying, 'Oh, by the way, you don't happen to know of a Count Jan Jarosinski here in Warsaw, do you?'

She sighed inwardly and pulled the collar of her coat up around her cheeks to ward off the chill of the late-winter breeze that eddied down from the river a few streets away. She had walked enough for this afternoon. A good rest was what she needed before she faced the massed ranks of Hitler's favourite sons in the hotel ballroom this evening. Lunch with the Obersturmbannführer had been but a dress rehearsal: tonight she would be on stage for the real thing.

Chapter Forty-one

Beth wore the one evening gown she had managed to squeeze into her suitcase to the soirée in the ballroom that evening: a pale-blue taffeta affair with a straight skirt and one shoulder bare. On its single strap she fastened a rose fashioned out of white silk and was in the act of pinning a similar one in her hair when a knock at the door made her look round in surprise. Who on earth could it be?

Aware of her heart beating much too fast, she hurried across to open it and found herself face to face with Roman, the young boy who had carried her bag up to her room. He gave a perfunctory bow and held out a small cardboard box on a silver tray. 'For me?' She lifted the box and stared down at her name written in blue ink across the top. It was for her all right. 'Thank you, Roman.'

She waited until she was back inside the room before opening it, and gasped in astonishment at the exquisite jewelled bird that lay within. It appeared to be some exotic creature such as a flamingo in flight and was composed entirely of minute gems, which from the look of them could only be genuine rubies and diamonds.

She lifted the shimmering creature out of the box and laid it in the palm of her hand then, totally bemused, searched the inside of the container for some clue as to where it had come from. She found the answer inside the lid in the form of a neatly handwritten note:

My dear Countess von Wolfsberg,
   Please accept this small token of my esteem, in anticipation of a mutually agreeable association.
                    Heil Hitler!
         Your servant,
         Walter Schellendorf

Good God, it was from him, that German! What was he trying to do – buy her friendship? Or, even worse, buy her body? She shuddered inwardly at the thought, but it was a situation she was aware she would have to come to terms with at some time when she took this assignment.

She sat down heavily on the edge of the bed and stared at the brooch in her hand. He would be waiting downstairs for her now, resplendent in his SS uniform. Her heart sank as she gazed down once more at the sparkling bird in her hand. What was she expected to do – wear it? And where had it come from? Even on an Ober-sturmbannführer's salary, Herr Schellendorf could not possibly afford to go dishing out jewels like this to recent acquaintances. Her frown deepened. It was looted, very probably, from one of those wretched people who had ended up just another statistic in Hitler's 'final solution'. She felt dirty – contaminated – as if by just holding it she was somehow condoning the method by which her benefactor had come by it.

She got up from the bed and walked to the window. A light snow was swirling in flurries past the dusty pane. The whole of the cityscape looked as bleak and cold as she felt inside. She sighed deeply, turned to the mirror on the dressing-table, and set about removing the silk rose from the shoulder of her gown and replacing it with the shimmering bird.

Her face looked pale as she examined it in the mirror; there were dark shadows beneath her eyes – a testimony to the lack of sleep over the past few nights. If anything, they made her eyes appear even larger and more luminous against the pale skin of her face. It was a face that would not see forty again but, in truth, it did not look it. The only concession to age was in the faint lines that fanned up from the corners of her eyes when she laughed. She always referred to them as her laughter lines, preferring that to the uncomplimentary crow's-feet.

A touch of rouge to her cheeks and two applications of a new Coty lipstick brought immediate life to her features, and she could feel her confidence oozing back as she patted the last stray hair into place. She would be leaving Beth Mallory behind in this room a few seconds from now and the Elisabeth von Wolfsberg who would take her place should possess all the confidence endemic in the Master Race.

The ballroom was full when she entered at a little after eight o'clock. At one end a dinner-suited three-piece band was playing a sentimental Lehar waltz and a few couples were dancing at that side of the floor. Along the far wall, laid out on white-clothed tables, was the most sumptuous buffet that Beth had seen in many a day. No matter how starving most of the population of this city might be, their Germanic masters lacked for nothing ... Nothing, perhaps, but female companionship, for there were very few women in the room, and most of them were decidedly on the matronly side. Wives of the higher command, most likely, Beth decided, as she made to sit down on one of the gilt chairs that were ranged along the wall nearest the door.

'Countess!'

She looked up to see the tall, elegant figure of Walter Schellendorf striding towards her, the silver oak leaves on his collar glinting in the light of the chandeliers. She responded uncomfortably to his 'Heil Hitler', then allowed her hand to be kissed. 'Herr Obersturmbann-führer ... '

His eyes moved from hers to the jewelled bird on her shoulder. 'You like it?'

'I – it's very beautiful,' she flustered. 'But I really don't think it would be correct, or appropriate, for me to accept such a gift.'

'Nonsense!' he laughed. 'What could be more appropriate than presenting one exotic creature in flight – my "*Ostflüchtling*" – with another?' He moved closer to her as his voice lowered intimately. 'I have met many refugees from the east since coming to this city, my dear, but none so beautiful. You make my little trinket pale into nothing in comparison.'

Colour suffused Beth's cheeks, but she was spared having to think of a suitable rejoinder as his hand found the small of her back and he guided her on to the dance-floor. If there was one thing she was learning about Obersturmbannführer Schellendorf, it was that he did not waste time on waiting for replies to invitations. What the Obersturmbannführer wanted the Obersturmbannführer got, it was as simple as that.

He danced well and, to her surprise, Beth found herself actually enjoying the evening as it progressed. He proved a stimulating companion, conversing knowledgeably on most of her favourite composers, and waxing particularly lyrical over the works of Wagner, to whose festivals in Bayreuth he had been taken by his parents from an early age. Learning that she herself had seen *Die Niebelungen* performed there before the war clearly delighted him and sent her already considerable stock soaring in his estimation.

'What other nation can claim such genius, *Liebchen*? Wagner, Beethoven, Schubert ... ' he made an expansive gesture with his hands. 'Who can dare deny that we Germans have contributed more to this world's civilization than any other people?'

'None,' she had murmured, 'none at all,' and wondered at the incredible paradox of a nation that could indeed produce the world's greatest composers and philosophers, yet also let loose an evil like National Socialism on the world.

She was introduced to most of the higher ranks present, and to three of their wives, plus one very beautiful, fair-haired young woman who spoke German with a distinctly Polish accent. Marysia, it transpired, was a *Volksdeutsche*, and had the appropriate papers to prove it, but had been born and brought up in Praga, the poorer suburb of Warsaw on the east bank of the Vistula. She had been invited to the soirée by a certain Sturmbannführer Fiedler, but seemed to spend as much time dancing with his colleagues as with him. Towards midnight, Beth found herself standing alone with her as they waited for the men to replenish their plates from what was left of the buffet.

'You are an old friend of Herr Schellendorf – betrothed, perhaps?'

The question took Beth unawares and she glanced across at the young woman in surprise. 'Good heavens, no! I – I don't really know him. I only arrived in the city today.'

The young woman's immaculately groomed brows rose, and a quiet smile flickered at the corners of her lips. 'Walter likes beautiful women. He collects them as some men collect beautiful objects – butterflies, perhaps. But not to stick on a board on their wall and to admire. No, Walter does not waste time admiring beautiful objects … he uses them.'

The studied smile on Beth's lips froze and a thousand questions poured on to her tongue, but she had to bite them back, for the men were returning with plates heaped with the last of the cold ham and chicken.

'Perhaps we could meet for coffee sometime – get to know one another better?' the young woman said softly. 'I work in "Sofia's", the gown shop on Straka Street.'

No more was said, and Beth did not even acknowledge having heard the comment, but mentally filed it away in her mind as they were swept once more into the boisterous company of the men.

It turned out that Walter was leaving the next day for Lodz, but hoped to be gone only a day or so. That he was taken by her there could be little doubt: he hardly left her side all evening. Had she not been so nervous, she might even have been flattered, for the room was not short of top brass to congregate around. In fact, for a short period around ten o'clock, Hans Frank, the black-browed, thickset German Governor General of Poland himself was there, accompanied by SS Brigadeführer Jürgen Stroop, the Major General of Police.

Beth had read of such men in the reports from the Polish Underground that reached them at the SOE offices, but to be actually standing there right next to them, even to catch their eye on occasions and have the odd remark addressed to her in person ... Well, at times she could scarcely believe what was happening.

If only those left behind back in the office at SOE could see her now. To say things were going to plan would be to put it mildly. They were going better than in her wildest dreams, she told herself, as she joined in the polite laughter at each and every one of Herren Frank and Stroop's mildly funny jokes. Neither, by any stretch of the imagination, could be termed good-looking men, but there was something about that uniform, with its silver oak leaves and looped silver lanyard shimmering against the black jacket that commanded attention and seemed to turn the most insignificant of men into titans.

There was no doubt that the entire company was on its best behaviour when the highest ranks were present but, once most of them had gone, the drink flowed even more freely, and the dancing dwindled to only the keenest of couples, who showed their expertise in executing intricate quicksteps and foxtrots around the whole circumference of the dance-floor.

Beth's companion, however, was well beyond such activities and was content to indulge his taste for fine cognac on one of the plushly upholstered, gilt-legged sofas, as he forsook his passion for classical music to regale her with tales from his childhood in the great Hanseatic port of Hamburg.

As the hours ticked past, his memories of long, lazy summer days sailing on the Binnen Alster gave way to disclosures of a more intimate nature, as he told her of past loves and of the wife he had discarded three years ago on discovering the fact that she was a 'Mischling'.

'I would not have believed a woman could be so deceitful,' he said, almost petulantly, as he swirled the golden liquid of the drink around in his glass. 'To let me marry her and only then, weeks after the wedding, discover she had a Jewish father!' He shook his head at the enormity of the crime. 'All she told me before our marriage was that he was born and brought up in Wedel and had won an Iron Cross in the Great War ... '

'And had he?'

'Of course. But not a word about the fact that her grandfather was a Rabbi ... ' He took a mouthful of the cognac, swirling it around on his tongue to savour the full flavour of the drink before swallowing.

'It was not that she told outright lies, you understand, *Liebchen*. She simply did not tell the whole truth. How can there be trust in marriage with such a wife?' His eyes searched hers, seeking confirmation of the injustice that had been perpetrated against him.

Beth was silent for a moment then, averting her gaze, asked quietly, 'What became of her after the divorce?'

Her companion's mouth hardened, and he answered through gritted teeth. 'She went to England. I received a letter. She said she felt no bitterness ... No bitterness – can you believe it?'

'But you still do.'

'*Aber natürlich* ... And why not? The woman nearly ruined my career.'

'You don't miss her, then.'

He laughed out loud – a cold, mirthless laugh that was at odds with the hint of hurt that lurked behind the pale blue of his eyes. 'Miss her? How could I miss such a woman with so many other beautiful creatures in this world?' His hand reached out and touched Beth's cheek. 'So many other beautiful creatures ... '

They were joined moments later by Hans Fiedler, the pale, rather sickly looking young man who had accompanied Marysia, the *Volksdeutsche*, earlier in the evening. The neglect he had suffered at the hands of his pretty blonde partner had resulted in a few glasses of wine too many, and the only way they could escape his company was to take to the dance-floor.

For over half an hour they circled the room. The cognacs had put paid to any real attempts at dancing, but her partner seemed more than content to hold her in his arms as he hummed the familiar waltz tunes into her ear.

Finally, however, he had had enough and, as they filed out of the ballroom at a little after two in the morning, his arm tightened around her waist. 'It has been a memorable night for me, *Liebchen*. A memorable night ... ' His lips nuzzled her ear. 'I should not be gone for long in Lodz. There is little left to be done there now the town has been completely rid of its Jewish menace. Thanks be to God that Warsaw will be completely free of Jews too before long.' He used the word '*judenrein*' – to be completely cleansed of Jewish people – and Beth froze inwardly. They all talked as if it was some deadly pest they were ridding the land of, instead of human beings – men, women and children like themselves. But she remained silent. Her job was to listen.

He accompanied her in the lift to the third floor, then walked with her along the corridor to the door of her room. As they walked he held her closer to him, his lips murmuring incomprehensible endearments into her hair.

They stopped outside her room and he looked down at her. 'The Great War, you said ... Your man was killed in the Great War ... ' He had both arms around her now, and she could smell the sweet stench of cognac on his breath as she braced herself for what was coming next. 'Tell me, *Liebling*, what have you done with yourself for all those years: not lived as a nun, surely?'

She tensed in his arms, unsure of the right way to play it.

'Come on, you know what I feel about women with secrets. You can tell me ... There must have been someone – on the estate, perhaps – someone man enough to keep you happy?' He thought he was smiling affectionately down at her, but it turned into what Beth could only think of as a leer as he sensed he was getting near the truth. 'You are here now, *mein Schatz*. You are safe with your own people. You are safe with Walter ... ' His lips moved down to kiss the damp skin of her brow. 'I will protect you ... I will be everything you need in a man – a real man ... '

He was kissing her passionately now, his tongue almost choking her as his hands reached roughly for the fastenings at the back of her gown.

'No, Walter ... Please!' She succeeded in pushing him back sufficiently to gasp for air and plead, 'Not now – not tonight! ... ' She searched wildly for an excuse, then resorted to that used by women since time immemorial. 'It – it's not the right time ... You understand? A few days, perhaps, but not tonight ... '

He lunged backwards under the pressure from her hands, supporting himself against the wall at the side of the door as he looked down at her. He was doing his best to remain upright and steady, to retain his dignity. His pale blue eyes narrowed as if weighing up the truth of what she was saying. 'Not tonight, you say? The lady is "indisposed" tonight.' He was silent for a moment, his eyes searching hers for any sign that she was telling less than the truth, then he took hold of her right hand and lifted it to his lips. 'But you will no longer be "indisposed" in a few days, when I return from Lodz – correct, *Liebchen*?'

She nodded bleakly and attempted a disarming smile. 'Correct.' Oh God, what was she letting herself in for?

He pulled her to him once more and kissed her roughly. His mouth tasted and smelt of a revolting mixture of cognac, *sauerkraut* and nicotine. In any other circumstances than these – in another time, another place – she might have found him an attractive man, with his muscular, six-foot frame, thinning, but still fair hair, and clean-cut features. But not now – not on her first night in Warsaw ... Not ever. Dear God, not ever ...

'Curse the female of the species,' he murmured between kisses. 'Curse their beautiful bodies for being "unavailable" when a man needs them most ... But in a few days you say, *Liebling* ... A few days, you promise ... ?'

'I promise!' She wrenched herself free of his embrace, one part of her aghast at hearing what she had just said, and another willing to promise him anything that would make him go back to his own room and leave her alone for the night.

One more prolonged kiss saw him on his way, staggering back towards the lift, a tall giant of a man well used to having his way with any woman of his choice. She felt her legs begin to give way beneath her as she fumbled in her handbag for her key.

Once inside the door, and with it safely locked behind her, she slid as if in slow motion to the floor and sat there, leaning back on the closed door for support for what seemed an eternity. Every ounce of energy had drained from her. She was a shell, a beautifully dressed shell, with the taste of an SS officer's kiss still on her lips. She began to laugh – a little giggle at first that turned within seconds into hysterical laughter, and ended up a few moments later in tears; scalding tears that ran down her cheeks and into the corners of her mouth, their salt taste mingling with the taste of the man who had just left.

The whole world had gone crazy. What was she doing here risking her life for God only knew what end? What were all those poor people doing behind that wall out there – starving to death, being beaten and tortured, gassed to death, in the name of racial purity? What was so pure about a race that would do that to its fellow man, would somebody tell her that?

One man could explain. One man could explain everything in this world so that she could understand. And he was out there somewhere – if not in this city, then in this land. For this was *his* land – this was Poland. And that was why she was here – why she was here sitting on the floor in this ghastly room crying her eyes out.

Chapter Forty-two

Beth's first few weeks in Warsaw passed uneventfully, a definite anticlimax, she decided: after the excitement of her first twenty-four hours in Poland, she had been tempted to think that that was how things would go on. After dinner on the night following the soirée, she had ventured into the cocktail bar area of the hotel alone, but the sight of one or two ladies of dubious reputation already seated there had made her courage fail and she returned to her room after finishing her first drink. The fact that 'ladies of pleasure' were allowed to frequent the cocktail lounge waiting for German officers was decidedly off-putting, for in no way would a lady of her breeding choose to be seen in the company of such females, and this cut down her opportunity for striking up acquaintances considerably.

Those Germans she did come into contact with over the next week were polite and exchanged the time of day but that was all: the camaraderie she had enjoyed with them at Walter's side on her first night in the hotel had disappeared in the cold light of the following day. She had mixed feelings about the Obersturmbannführer's absence, for on the one hand he was the perfect entry permit into the highest echelons of Warsaw's Nazi society, but on the other his return would pose a harrowing problem for her. He would expect her to keep her promise ...

Almost every night since she had left him on the doorstep of her room she had lain awake wrestling with the problem in her mind. Her boss at SOE had tried, as tactfully as possible, to raise the question of her possible personal relations with individuals within the Nazi circle she hoped to penetrate, and while he was too much of a gentleman to actually suggest that she sleep with any one of them in order to get information, she knew the thought was uppermost in his mind. At their last meeting he had told her: 'Many of us in this war have to do things we would not dream of doing in peacetime, Beth –

things we would be shocked even to contemplate, indeed be bitterly ashamed of under any normal circumstances. But war is not a normal circumstance, and those of us who participate actively in it must be prepared for such eventualities – and accept them. You do realize that, don't you?'

She had nodded emphatically. 'Of course I do. I wouldn't be volunteering to go otherwise.' Brave words indeed.

Those of Walter's friends she came into contact with after his departure, she had asked as tactfully as possible when he was due back in the city, and was continually told, 'Any day now', but she could tell by the shrug of their shoulders that they really had little idea. As the 'few days' turned into weeks, she came to the conclusion that things were probably not going quite as smoothly in Lodz as was hoped.

It became increasingly obvious that something would have to be done if her mission here was to be a success. Her hesitant attempts at striking up relationships with other Germans had not got beyond the superficial stage, so she resolved to seek another means of entry to the charmed circle of German social activities within the hotel. Her thoughts returned to the pretty blonde *Volksdeutsche* with whom she had chatted that first night. Marysia – that was her name, wasn't it? And where was it she said she worked? 'Sofia's' on Straka Street … Yes, that was it. She would take a walk there this afternoon. The catalyst for this decision was the remark by Pan Gluck, the landlord, on her way down to breakfast one morning that there was to be another soirée that night. With Walter still absent in Lodz, Marysia might just be her entry into it.

As soon as breakfast was over she set off. She was quite familiar with most of the main streets that made up the city centre now and, on her excursions out of the hotel, she seemed to spend more time looking at the people than the street-signs. Their hunger-ravaged faces haunted her. Never in Britain had she seen anything like them, but never had Britain suffered as Poland was suffering. Small children stood on street corners begging, or hawking the few items of worth that were left in the family home to bargain with. She knew that many people had sold all they possessed merely to stay alive, and often even that was not enough: corpses littered the pavements in the mornings – human skeletons who had run out of the meagre means required to keep body and soul together. In her expensive fur and with her healthy complexion she was the exception rather than the rule as she hurried past the war-torn buildings, averting her eyes from the beggars and the endless food queues at the soup kitchens.

At least now they were well into March the weather should be turning warmer soon – a fact that might bring some meagre comfort to the inadequately clad beggars who spent their days huddled at the corners of Pilsudski Square and around the Poniatowski Bridge, or any other place likely to yield a few zlotys; or to the growing numbers of homeless in the city who sought shelter in the ruins of burned-out houses. Poland's capital was teeming with refugees, mainly from the fighting in the east: bent-backed with their pathetic bundles they shuffled on rag-bound feet in unending columns along the pavements of the once elegant Nowy Swiat and Krakowskie Przedmiescie, heading God only knew where. It was the children that upset her most as they stared ahead of them with unseeing eyes, their pinched faces a hundred years old, their childhood long gone, stolen from them by men in grey and black uniforms who stood at every street corner, Mausers at the ready, shouting orders in a language they did not understand.

She had little difficulty finding Straka Street, which turned out to be a once affluent small avenue of shops in the centre of the Stare Miasto – the Old Town – where the few picturesque, pastel-painted houses on the small squares that remained intact were a poignant reminder of what had once been, and the great brick edifice of St Jan's Cathedral, where Hitler now stabled his horses, was a painful reminder of how things were now. A chalk drawing of a tortoise on the cathedral wall, similar to other drawings on walls all over the city, was a trenchant reminder to Poles not to work too hard. Industry aided the enemy. Beth suppressed a quiet smile at the sight of it. It was funny how a crude cartoon could lift one's spirits.

Straka Street itself seemed to have suffered less damage than most of the adjoining streets, and she found the shop easily. But, to her consternation, like most of the others in the row, it was closed, and seemed to have been that way for many months.

She stared disconsolately at the drawn blinds on the window, feeling her journey had been for nothing, then her eyes moved to the brown varnished door. Although there seemed to be no sign of life, there was no harm in knocking, she decided.

Her fingers clutched the brass lion's head between the heavy oak panels and she rapped it hard four times on the plate beneath; then, when there was no response, she did it once more. There was still no sound from within and she was just on the point of turning away when, to her surprise, the flap of the brass letter-box opened and two bright blue eyes stared up into hers.

'Countess!'

'Marysia, is that you?' She stared down at the letter-box in astonishment, then the eyes disappeared and she could hear the rattle of chains being removed from behind the door.

'Countess – you came!' Marysia was scarcely recognizable as the sophisticated young woman she had met on the arm of an SS officer the previous week. Instead of the fashionable evening gown, she was attired in a pair of men's trousers and had on a thick, hand-knitted blue jumper over a checked shirt. Her once elegantly coiffeured hair hung long and loose over her shoulders and a pencil was stuck behind one ear. 'Come in – do.' She seemed genuinely pleased to see her.

Beth followed her into the main body of what had obviously been a very exclusive dress shop, although the models were now bereft of clothes and the neatly stacked, glass-fronted drawers of the tall cabinets were depressingly empty.

Marysia saw her looking around and gave a helpless shrug. 'Everything has gone,' she said in a matter-of-fact tone. 'One has to eat ... I am only glad my grandfather did not live to see me exchange the last of his personal creations for fifty kilos of potatoes.' She gave a wry smile, 'He may well have witnessed it from above and inflicted some kind of heavenly retribution, for almost the whole two sacks were rotten!'

Beth followed her on through a door hung with a heavy, red velour curtain into what had obviously been the hub of the business – the workshop. Three long trestle tables dominated the room, but only one sewing-machine remained: an ancient Singer, with the most beautiful enamelling on its shiny black body. 'It was his favourite machine,' Marysia commented, reaching out to touch it as one would stroke the head of a favourite child. 'I will have to be down to my last crust before that goes.'

She paused in front of a large cabinet, still half-full of dress patterns and other dressmaking artefacts. Here she turned and, to Beth's surprise, looked her straight in the eyes, and in a low voice uttered the word, '*Schmetterling.*'

Beth gasped in surprise and took a defensive step backwards, only to have her companion put a comforting hand on her arm and repeat the word. Marysia was nodding expectantly, as if to tell her it was her turn now; she was waiting for the correct reply.

A myriad of conflicting thoughts ran through her head. Was it a trap? Marysia was an admitted *Volksdeutsche* after all – and a known Nazi sympathizer. Perhaps they had caught Vanya, or someone else in the Underground network, who had given her password away? Sweat broke out beneath her armpits and across her brow as she looked into the other's eyes. They were smiling back into hers as the word was repeated once more – more insistently this time, '*Schmetter-ling*, Countess, *Schmetterling*!'

Barney Huntly-Crawford's voice rang in Beth's head. 'Remember, you will be contacted by one of the network within a few days of your arrival in Warsaw. Be prepared. Your contact may be the person you least expect it to be ...'

'*Schmetterling*, Countess, *Schmetterling*.'

'*Motte!*'

An even bigger smile engulfed the other's face, then Marysia threw her arms around her. 'Thanks be to God, I was beginning to think I had been misinformed! My orders were to make contact with you immediately, which I did, thinking you would call here during that first week. I should have gone back to see what had happened to you, but things have not been working exactly to plan these past few weeks. But, then, do they ever?'

She gave a helpless shrug, then turned to the cabinet in front of them and proceeded to open one of the doors, pushing her hand inside and feeling around. Beth presumed she was looking for something on one of the shelves until, to her astonishment, the whole thing swung out towards them revealing an open door in the wall behind. 'Come,' her new friend said, taking her hand and leading her through the wall. 'Follow me.'

Beth obeyed, too bemused to do anything else, and found herself at the foot of a wooden staircase. There was barely room for the two of them to stand side by side. She held her breath and pressed herself against the distempered wall as Marysia gave a hefty tug and pulled the cabinet back into place behind them.

Seemingly unconscious of Beth's shocked state, 'You were lucky to get me in,' her companion remarked as she led the way up the narrow flight of stairs. 'I was just on the point of leaving when you knocked, otherwise I would never have heard you.'

Beth followed her in silence, still too dumb-struck to participate in small talk. The staircase seemed to go up forever, and she could feel her thighs begin to ache. But eventually they arrived at a narrow door at the end of the top flight of steps. Marysia opened it and she followed her inside into a long narrow room that appeared to have been partitioned off from a much bigger attic. A wooden table stood in the centre of the room with six bentwood chairs around it. On the floor in the far corner was a makeshift bed of straw, with two old coats serving as blankets. A few books and personal effects lay around, but the only other furniture was a large wooden chest that reminded Beth of a coffin.

'Welcome to the den – Daniel's den!' Marysia said with a smile. 'My grandfather's name was Daniel – Daniel Fischer ... You remember the Bible story?' The smile grew somewhat sheepish. 'The lion's head on the door was my grandfather's idea. It was the trademark of the firm. He had it on all the invoices, everything. But, to be honest, the Jewish connotations became something of an embarrassment, to say the least, when the Nazis invaded.'

Beth's astonishment grew. 'You mean you're Jewish?'

Marysia gave a rueful smile and shook her head. 'That's the ridiculous part of it – our family were genuine *volksdeutsch* but, before all this anti-Semitism got out of hand, Grandfather actually thought it was no bad thing to be thought of as Jewish. In the dressmaking profession it was almost a mark of respectability. People expected the best if you were a Jewish tailor or dressmaker and, certainly in this city at least, before this damned war messed everything up, they would prefer to give their custom to a Jew than a German.'

Beth shook her head in bemusement. Was nothing in this city what it seemed to be? 'But how did you get involved with ... with ... ?'

'With the Underground?' Marysia took a packet of German cigarettes from the pocket of her trousers. 'Smoke?'

Beth shook her head.

Marysia extracted one for herself and lit it, drawing the smoke deeply into her lungs, and gave a wry smile. 'Grandfather did not approve of women smoking.'

'You were very fond of him, weren't you?'

Marysia nodded. 'He brought me up, he and Grandmama Sofia. My Papa was killed in the war, the last war, and my mother died giving birth to me and my brother.'

'You're a twin?'

She nodded. 'My brother is all I have left in the world.'

'Is he – is he ... ?'

'Is he in the Underground too?" Marysia finished the question for her. 'Of course.'

'He got you into it?'

She laughed and shook her head. 'He tried his best to keep me out, but I am as stubborn as he is ... Anyway, my best friend and many of our other friends from University were already part of it.' She hoisted herself up on to the edge of the table and flicked some specks of ash from the navy worsted of her trousers, then looked across at Beth.

'You must be very brave – all of you – to be so young and yet to risk everything, to lay your life on the line before you have even lived it.'

Marysia shook her head and looked down at the burning end of the cigarette between her fingers. 'When my brother joined in September '39, just after the Germans invaded, Grandfather was dying and he thought long and hard about telling him he was fighting the Germans.' She paused, her eyes misting over as memory took her back to the quietness of the small bedroom in the flat downstairs and the look in the eyes of the old man whose frail head had lifted from the pillow as he took his grandson by the hand. 'Fight for Poland, Marek,' he had said. 'Fight for your country, my boy. Better to die on your feet than live the rest of your life on your knees.' 'Grandpapa approved,' she said. 'That mattered more to him than anything.'

'You all have your allotted tasks, presumably – in the organization?'

Marysia's eyebrows rose. 'You do not imagine I frequent the Hotel Torun by choice?' She gave a strained smile, then her eyes turned serious. 'Did Walter ask you to sleep with him?'

Beth was taken aback, but nodded. 'Yes. Yes, he did.'

'And did you?' The blue eyes looked straight into hers.

'I – I …'

'Please forgive me for being so rude, but it *is* important. You must get close to them – very close – to gain any information of worth. I have learned much to help my friends in the ghetto, but the only information that has been worth a damn has been gained in bed.' She stared down at the burning tip of her cigarette. 'I make love to the enemy so my lover can live a little longer. It is a small sacrifice. Each day is a bonus.' She looked across at Beth, her eyes defiant, yet searching the other's face for understanding. 'There are so few left in the ghetto … So few …'

'Your boyfriend is Jewish?'

Marysia nodded. 'When one joins the Underground one makes a choice which branch to join. Most choose to join the *Armia Krajowa* – the Home Army – who concentrate on getting information back to Sikorski and the others in London, but I chose to help the Jewish Fighting Organization – the *Zydowska Organizacja Bojowa*. It arose from the sea of blood that engulfed the ghetto between July and September last year and it will go on fighting – to the bitter end. And it will be bitter, there can be no doubt about it. The SS and their Ukrainian lackeys will see to that. That is why our work has never been more important. Things are going to happen soon in this city – terrible things – and it is our duty to find out exactly what and when … You are going to the soirée tonight, aren't you?'

'That's why I'm here. I hoped you could gain me entry.'

Marysia flicked a column of grey ash into a glass ashtray on the table beside her. 'No problem, if you're sure that's what you want.'

'Do I have a choice?'

'That depends.'

'On what?'

'On why you came out here in the first place.' She drew on the cigarette and looked searchingly at Beth. 'Either you have an overwhelming love for your fellow man in general over here – or for one man. Tell me, Countess, which is it?'

Beth could feel her face colour. Her *Volksdeutsche* friend might be young in years, but she was no fool when it came to human nature. She sat down on the edge of the wooden chest and gave a wan smile.

'He is a Pole, then?'

She nodded.

'He is in this city?'

Beth shrugged helplessly. 'I only wish I knew.'

Marysia stubbed the remains of her cigarette out in the ashtray beside her and said consolingly. 'Perhaps that is a matter for another day ... You ask if there is a choice of how you can be most useful to the Underground out here. It is quite simple really: if you wish to gain information worth sending back to London then you must be prepared to sleep with the enemy in the hope of learning new facts that may or may not be useful ... '

'Or?'

'Or you do something practical for those left in that hell-hole they call the ghetto. They need all the help they can get in there – now more than ever.'

'But how on earth can you get in there to help? How can anyone get over that wall?'

Marysia gave a knowing smile. 'That you will no doubt find out soon enough ... As for tonight – you really want to go?'

Beth swallowed hard. 'I must,' she said quietly.

Marysia nodded. 'I feel it could be worthwhile. I understand a new contingent of SS has just arrived from Berlin. No doubt they will be missing their womenfolk ... '

Beth shuddered, and was to shudder many more times throughout the day after leaving 'Sofia's'. One half of her was relieved and excited at discovering that Marysia was her contact in Warsaw, but the other half felt almost physically sick at the prospect of what lay ahead. It had been spelt out in no uncertain terms today what was expected of her. She might have got out of sleeping with Walter that first night in Warsaw, but tonight there would be other Walters there. Tonight there could be no excuses ...

347

Chapter Forty-three

Lara drew the car up in front of the Queen Victoria Hospital and stared up at the serried ranks of windows; they stared back at her – row after row of unblinking eyes in the pale spring sunshine. It had taken her just over an hour to drive down to East Grinstead from London, an hour in which she had tried and failed miserably to make sense of her chaotic thoughts.

It was a little over a week now since she got the telegram informing her that Ken was missing, presumed killed, a week in which she had battled gamely to come to terms with the two most traumatic pieces of news she had ever received: the information that she was expecting a child, Mike's child, and that in all likelihood she was now a widow.

She switched off the ignition and sighed as she slipped the key into her handbag. If only her mother was here. If only she had someone to talk to. Even her friend Judy was no longer in London. She had taken herself off to Wales to live with Dai's parents.

The lack of someone close to confide in she had felt most acutely this morning when yet another telegram arrived from the Air Ministry. She had just been setting off for work when it came, and the sight of the now familiar buff envelope in the telegram boy's hand caused her heart to lurch uneasily in her breast. Her fingers had shaken as she opened it, so much that she had torn the flimsy paper of the telegram itself as well as the envelope. She was certain it was to inform her officially that she was indeed a widow, that Ken's body had been found. How wrong could you be? Ken was not dead ... Yes, that was what it said all right. Ken was not dead – he was a patient in the Special Burns Unit set up by the New Zealand plastic surgeon Archibald McIndoe in the Queen Victoria Hospital at East Grinstead. That was it – nothing more. No information as to his condition or how and where he was found.

She got out of the car and took a deep breath. She had not even taken time to inform them in Downing Street that she would not be in this morning. Instead she had unearthed her mother's car from the garage just off what was left of Atholl Square, where it had remained since Beth's departure for Poland, filled its tank with petrol with the few precious coupons she had amassed over the past few months, and set off at breakneck speed to get down here.

And now here she was. She gazed up at the windows once more. He was in there somewhere: just how badly injured he was she had no idea ... But standing here like this was no way to find out.

Clasping her coat around her against the chill March breeze, she set off at a brisk pace towards the main door. Inside she was confronted with a notice-board giving directions to the various departments, but there was no mention of the Special Burns Unit. She stopped a young nurse, who was only too happy to oblige her with the relevant details. 'Have you got a relative in there?' The question was innocent enough.

Lara nodded. 'My husband. I've just been informed.'

A curious expression came over the young woman's face, an expression that Lara could not quite comprehend. There was both pain and pity in the candid grey eyes that looked back into hers. 'Good luck to you both,' she said softly, before continuing on her way down the corridor.

Lara watched her disappear through the swing doors at the end, then continued on her own way. It did not take her long to find the unit and present herself to the sister in charge.

'Mrs Cameron ... Oh yes, your husband arrived from France two days ago.'

So it was France he was shot down over. 'How bad is he?'

The sister, a grey-haired, briskly efficient looking woman in perhaps her middle fifties, gave a strained smile. 'The patients who are brought here for special treatment by Dr McIndoe are not at their best, Mrs Cameron. You must be prepared for that. But there is no better place in the country for treating burns victims, I can assure you.'

Burns victims – so that was what Ken was now, was it? He was no longer a number in the RAF, but a 'burns victim'. 'May I see him?'

The sister glanced at her watch. It had just gone eleven, the doctors' round would be over by now. She rose from behind her desk. 'I think that can be arranged, if you care to follow me. Your husband is quite lucid.' Then, seeing the look of concern on Lara's face, she continued, 'So many of them aren't when they first arrive ... shock, you know – or simply the sedation we require to give them in the early stages. But I wouldn't worry yourself in that regard. I spoke to your husband only a few minutes ago myself. He is remarkably cheerful, considering ... '

The last sentence was left hanging in the air and reverberated in Lara's brain as she followed the sister down what seemed endless miles of corridor and through a pair of metal swing doors.

Within a few minutes, she found herself in a small ward where most of the beds were filled with what seemed to be long rows of Egyptian mummies – figures swathed in white bandages, lying or propped up at awkward angles against the pillows. The sight made her gasp aloud and, as her eyes began to focus on individual beds, she found herself grasping the sister's arm for support. Those who had had the bandages removed were no longer recognizable as human beings. Where faces and hands had once been were now livid masses of raw, swollen flesh. Features and fingers no longer existed. She thought she was going to faint.

The sister's voice sounded in her ear. 'Courage, my dear. It is vitally important that you register no shock. The poor boys have enough to contend with without their relatives going to pieces.' She patted Lara's hand, which was still gripping her arm. 'Your husband's in the end bed on the left-hand side. Come with me ...'

How she got to the other end of the ward she did not know. Her senses had numbed and she was conscious only of being propelled along by the superior strength, mental and physical, of the older woman on to whose arm she still gripped as if for dear life.

'Here we are ...' They halted by the very last bed on the left-hand side of the ward. 'My goodness, he seems to have dropped off for forty winks. That's not like him. I'll leave you to waken him, if you don't mind, my dear. There's a new admission due in any minute and I've a few things to attend to before then.'

'Th-thank you, Sister.' Lara's eyes were fixed on the face on the pillow. This was Ken? This was her husband – the man she had married just over three years ago? A feeling akin to panic gripped her. She wanted to run – turn tail and flee from this awful place with its rows of mutilated mummies. This was not Ken. How could this possibly be Ken? Ken was a handsome young man with hair the colour of ripe corn and open, friendly features. And freckles – Ken had freckles ... Bitter tears sprang to her eyes. Where were those freckles now in this mass of bright red melted flesh that had once been the face she loved?

He stirred on the pillow and made a soft moaning sound like a small animal in pain. She wanted to reach out and touch him – but where? What could she touch? The whole of his body visible above the regulation grey hospital blanket was swathed in bandages – all except his face and hands, or what was left of them. A bandage was fastened around his scalp and small tufts of dark brown frizzled hair stuck grotesquely from the raw skin of his scalp.

But it was his face that made her insides tie themselves into a knot so tight that she thought she would double up from the physical pain. His face was simply a hugely swollen mass of raw flesh. He had no eyelids left, no eyebrows or eyelashes, and where his nose and lips had once been were two twisted apertures in the flesh with a larger one beneath. Where his face ended and his neck began was impossible to say, for the whole mass was so swollen as to be unrecognizable as a human head, let alone her husband's.

'Courage, my dear ... the poor boys have enough to contend with without their relatives going to pieces ... ' The sister's words echoed in her brain. It was true. My God, how true that was!

She sat down so heavily on the chair by the bed that the resulting squeak made the swathed figure on the bed stir and the head half-turn towards her. For a moment there was silence, then a sound was emitted from where lips had once been. 'Lara ... '

She sensed rather than recognized it was her name he was uttering. 'My love ... ' Her lips whispered the words, as she sat rooted to the spot, desperate to reach out to him, yet unable to move from the spot.

'You came ... '

The words were only just intelligible and she nodded. 'I – I only heard this morning ... I came straight away.'

His eyes were still there. The only part of him untouched by the inferno that had been his aircraft. They fused with hers. The pain in them was almost too much to bear. 'Not a pretty sight, eh, girl?' They had not allowed him near a mirror, but he only had to look at the others to know.

She looked down at her hands clasped tightly in her lap. There was a moment's silence. An uncomfortable silence. 'They – they can do wonders now – the sister told me so. This is the best place in the country she said. Probably in the world ... ' Her voice trailed off. What more could she say? It all sounded so hollow. They only had to look around to see what the future held.

She sat for another half an hour by the bed. She talked to him of the past – their life together – recounting small incidents that might make him smile inwardly, although what was left of his lips could not show his mirth. It was important, vitally important, that she keep talking – to do any other would risk breaking down, and that she could not bear to do. It was obviously painful for him to try to communicate himself, but she was conscious of his eyes never leaving her face. She did her best to meet his gaze, but it was not easy. She feared her own features might register the continuing shock she felt at the sight of his. She deliberately avoided any mention of her trip to Casablanca. She had simply blotted it out of her memory since receiving the telegram this morning and would not allow her mind to wander in that direction. She also avoided telling him of her mother's departure for Poland. It would only worry him and he could do without that. She had just reached the subject of Judy's decision to move in with Dai's parents when the sister returned to inform her quietly that the doctors had orders that the patients must not be tired out by overlong visits, especially in the initial period of their treatment.

Lara stood up and looked down at her husband. 'I'll be back tomorrow, my love. I'll come every day, even if I have to walk here ... '

The pained, haunted look in the eyes softened and she could swear she could see the glisten of tears. 'Good on you, girl ... '

She held his gaze for a second or two longer then, feeling the hot rush of tears to her own eyes, she turned and walked quickly from the bed, stopping only to give a backward glance at the door of the ward, and a tentative wave of her hand in the direction of his bed.

'You held up very well, my dear,' the sister said, as they walked together back down the corridor. 'So many, especially the very young wives, break down. It makes it all the worse for their husbands, you know. Heaven knows, most of them are not much more than boys themselves.'

They had stopped outside her office and she turned to Lara. 'You'll have a cup of tea before you go home. I'm sure there are plenty of questions on the tip of your tongue that you're dying to ask and I'll do my best to answer them. Although this is still a relatively new branch of surgery, you realize that.'

Lara nodded mutely as she followed the uniformed figure into the small office. Questions – what questions? What was she supposed to ask? How long would it be until he was the same good-looking young man she had married three years ago? Her lips formed a bitter smile as she seated herself on the metal chair in front of the desk and watched as the sister set about pouring the already prepared tea.

She handed Lara a cup and sat down behind her desk, leaning forward with her hands clasped in front of her. 'It must have come as quite a shock, I realize that, my dear. It always does. But things have improved quite dramatically in this field since Dr McIndoe took over.

When I began in plastic surgery, not so long ago, they were still using tannic acid and tannic jelly on the burns with some quite horrific results. The tannic acid solidified over the burns, which they believed was a good thing, but as well as sealing out the air, it sealed in the bacteria, so that all the pus and germs were locked inside to do real damage.' She grimaced at the memory. 'The infection rate in those days was horrific, I don't mind telling you. But we didn't know any better – the only other method in common use then was to paint the burns with gentian violet, which made everything go rigid, but not much else. Not before time, when he came on the scene, Dr McIndoe stopped all that sort of treatment and introduced such things as saline baths.'

'Saline baths?'

The sister nodded. 'We discovered after treating the burns victims from Dunkirk that all those who had been immersed in the sea before being brought to us did much better than those who hadn't been exposed to salt-water. So Dr McIndoe stopped all the tannic acid and gentian violet treatments and concentrated on saline baths in the first instance.'

'And afterwards ... What then?'

'Well, once the burns are on the mend, we begin to think of reconstructive surgery. Quite honestly, there isn't a better plastic surgeon practising today.'

Lara shook her head. 'But Ken's face ... his eyes ... he has no eyelids left ...'

The sister shook her head. 'Your husband will have eyelids again. Never fear.'

Lara stared at her dully. 'How?'

'Quite simply, a single layer of epidermis will be taken from elsewhere on the body – the arm or the leg, perhaps – to form new eyelids. That's basically how it's done: fine layers of skin are taken from healthy parts of the body to rebuild the destroyed features. I must warn you, though, we are not in the beauty business. This is a hospital, not a beauty salon. Our main aim is restoring normal functions, such as the opening and closing of eyes and mouths, and restoring the functions of the hands. We are not here to make Clark Gables of them.'

Lara nodded and gave a mirthless smile. 'I understand that. How – how long do these operations go on for?'

The sister shook her head. 'We can't put a time-scale on any patient's treatment. From the time the burns heal to the time we can begin the reconstruction can be anything from five days to five years, depending on how bad the case is. Some of our worst cases can expect to come back for many years for corrective operations. Scar tissue has a tendency to tighten and pucker over the years and that must be put right.'

'And Ken's case ... He's one of the worst?' She knew the answer before the sister opened her mouth.

'We have had worse, it's true ... But, yes, your husband is very badly burned indeed. In fact, he's lucky to be alive.'

'Lucky?' Lara gave a bitter laugh. 'You call that lucky?' She shook her head in a despairing gesture.

'Would you rather he'd died?' the other asked sharply.

Lara coloured. 'No – no, of course not,' she said quickly. 'But what about *them*, Sister? Does anyone ever ask them how they feel? Does anyone ever ask them how they feel about it?'

The sister's lips tightened. 'Many take a long time to come to terms with their injuries, it's true. Most are very young men, Mrs Cameron. Very young men indeed, with their whole lives ahead of them. It's our job here in the hospital to come to the aid of their physical injuries; it's the job of their families to help them come to terms with the mental scars.'

She looked straight at Lara as she had looked at so many young wives over the past few years. Little bits of girls, most of them. How in heaven's name were they supposed to come to terms with this ghastly carnage to their menfolk themselves, let alone provide the bulwark for their husbands to cling to? A bell rang in the office and she got up immediately. 'That's for me, I'm afraid,' she sighed. 'It's been so nice to meet you, my dear. I only wish it had been under more auspicious circumstances ... If there's anything I can do for you in the future, don't hesitate to ask.'

Lara got up from her seat and watched her go. 'If there's anything I can do for you in the future ...' What could anyone do for her now? What could anyone do for Ken? She wanted to scream – bash her fists against the clean grey paint of the office walls and scream until there was nothing left inside her to hurt any more.

Her face, already pale, drained of all colour. But there would be something left inside her. She was carrying Mike's child, and no matter how horrific Ken's external injuries, she was sure there was nothing wrong with his mind. There was no way on earth this baby could be his, and very soon he would know it ... She pressed a hand to her already rounding stomach and sank back against the desk for support. 'Oh Christ, oh my God ... What have I done ... ?'

Chapter Forty-four

Ken stared up at the ceiling. He had lain like this for hours since his arrival at East Grinstead two days ago and stared at that same spot between the ceiling and the top of the wall, with its tiny imperfection of flaking grey paint. There was little choice, for he could not move the position of his head on the pillow without help. Tears swam in his lidless eyes and it was impossible to blink them back.

Two nurses – pretty girls in their early twenties – walked briskly down the ward and out through the swing doors by the side of his bed. They aimed two cheerful smiles in his direction, but he could not respond. What remained of his features were locked in this immobile mask of hideous burnt flesh. What did they really feel when they looked at him – at any of them cooped up here in this horror side-show to the main hospital block? It was impossible to say – impossible to know what really went on behind the smiling masks and jolly banter they reserved for the particularly gruesome cases. And that's what they were, there was no mistake about it.

He heard a car start up outside the window behind him and he wondered if it was Lara on her way back to London. That meeting with his wife was what he had been dreading every conscious moment since the accident. He had watched her eyes, listened to every nuance in her voice to detect the horror she must be feeling at the sight of him. She must be one helluva actress, that was for sure, for there had been little to indicate what was really going on behind those wide hazel eyes. Nothing except the fact that almost everything she had said to him had avoided the thing that was uppermost in both their minds – the future. Recollections about the past and a recounting of the trivia of everyday life was one thing, but they did not touch on the real issue uppermost in both their minds. How the hell were they going to cope with this?

'Go well for you, mate, did it?'

The voice was from the next bed. His eyes glanced sideways. He could just make out the cage beneath the bedclothes that covered the bottom half of his neighbour's body. Lucky blighter – the flames had only reached as far as his chest. He was almost unmarked from the neck up. 'Yes ... Yes, thanks ... ' His voice tailed off. He had no inclination to share his thoughts on what had just passed between him and his wife.

'Nice looking girl, your wife ... Held up really well by the look of it.' He had a South London accent. Croydon most probably. 'Some don't, you know. We've seen some pretty awful scenes in here, I can tell you. Bloody good job I never took the plunge myself into matrimony. Dunno how any girl would have coped with the prospect of an old man on roller skates ... '

He gave a mirthless half-laugh. 'That's what it would've amounted to, you know, if they'd had their way at that last place I was at. Wanted to take my legs off at the hips, they did. Bloody roller skates I'd have needed to get around after that. A trunk on roller skates – that would've been me. Until Archie McIndoe stepped in that is. He came round to have a look at the worst of us burn cases over there and asked how I felt about losing my legs ... Well, I ask you, what was I expected to say to that? I told him straight, I did. Said I'd come into this war at six-foot-one and I was bloody well coming out of it at six-foot-one. "We'll see you do, son," he said – and he's doing his damndest to keep his word. But what I want to know is, what the hell's going to happen to us all when this shooting match is over? What then, Jock? What then?'

It was a rhetorical question and he lapsed into silence for a moment or two. 'You reckon they'll find a use for us when it's all over?' The continued silence from the next bed prompted him to muse over the answer himself. 'If you ask me, they'll put us in one of them homes ... You know, the type of place they put all those poor buggers from the last war in. They'll hide us away in a room making bloody poppies. Well, I won't stand for that ... ' Then, realizing the irony of his last remark, he gave a bitter laugh. 'I'll sit on my arse, or what's left of it, and tell them what they can do with their bloody poppies! What do you say, Scottie? Am I right – or am I bloody right?'

The distorted aperture that was once a mouth twitched slightly. 'You're too bloody right, mate. Too bloody right.' Ken's answer, though slurred, was said with a vehemence that surprised even himself. No one was going to shut him up in any bloody home either when this was all over. He would see to that ... But what was the alternative? A wave of despair engulfed him. No one who had been here for more than a few minutes could fail to see what the future held – and it wasn't a pretty sight.

Just look at them: the cream of this country's crop of young fliers. All the beautiful young men, Hugh Dowding's beloved 'Brylcreem boys', who had been more than a match for Goering's *Luftwaffe* in the skies over the Channel throughout the long hot summer of 1940. Just look at them now ...

He felt the sting of tears in his eyes once more as his thoughts went back to those heady, early days at Tangmere and the small pub in Chichester, The Dolphin, if he remembered rightly, where they would congregate for that well-earned pint after a particularly hairy skirmish with Jerry. Closing time was officially 10.30, but the local bobbies were good about turning a blind eye. Most of them had been in the trenches in the first war and knew what it was all about.

He thought of his father and how proud he had been to know that his son was following him into the air-force blue. What would he say if he could see him now? Broughty Ferry and his family and friends in Scotland seemed a long, long way away. He stared hard at that peeling spot in the paint on the ceiling. Could he ever go back there? Could he ever go anywhere again? How would people react at the sight of him?

Lara's face swam before him. The bloke in the next bed was right. She had taken it well – bloody well, considering ...

But that was for now: how would she feel in a week's time, a year's time? How would she cope with a husband that not only no longer bore any outward resemblance to the man she married, but who would bear no inner resemblance either. And he *would* be different, there was no doubt. The war had seen to that. And it wasn't only him. The war had changed the lives of everyone. He thought of his cousin Alan lying dead somewhere out there in North Africa. What had he ever done to deserve to die at twenty-one with his whole life ahead of him?

A long, moaning sound came from the corridor beyond. Some other poor blighter was being brought in, to be patched up for what? The future was a prospect he could not even contemplate. He wished he could close his eyes. Just for a few seconds. Dear God, he would give anything to close his eyes. Maybe Alan was one of the lucky ones ...

Lara returned to her empty flat and headed straight for the bedroom, where she threw herself on top of the patchwork quilt and stared up with unseeing eyes at the glass light-fitting above her. She felt numb, completely numb, body and soul. What she had seen today had shocked her to the core. If she had any feelings left she should feel anger – real anger at what this war had done. Only three and a half short years ago she had actually felt excitement at the prospect of a war with Germany. How young and stupid could you be?

It was all disintegrating – everything. Until this morning she was just coming to terms with the fact that she was probably a widow, and now, not only was her husband alive, but ... but ... She could not even bear to think about Ken, to recollect the pain in those grey-blue eyes that gazed back into hers from out of that livid, swollen mass that was now what was left of his face. But worse, much worse than having to come to terms with his deformities was the fact that all the time she sat there at his bedside she was nursing a secret, a secret that would soon become all too obvious. Yes, she had committed the most heinous of all sins against him – a sin the guilt of which she would carry with her throughout her life. She was carrying another man's child.

Her eyes closed as a deep sigh ran through her body and, despite her determination to blank him out of her life, her thoughts returned to Mike. Where was he now? Back in Washington, probably. Back at his desk in the Pentagon making decisions on which other men's lives hung. Other men like Ken. The poor bloody infantry of this war who simply carried out the orders. If they said jump in Downing Street or the White House then you damn well jumped, even if that jump meant you losing your life, or every scrap of skin on your body ...

Would she ever see him again – that tall American with the quirky, lop-sided grin? No, she must not even ask herself such a question. Not now. Especially not now. Her future was bound up with another man – her husband – who now lay in that iron bedstead in the Special Burns Unit at East Grinstead. There could be no question of harbouring any secret longing for the past and Mike. Ken needed her as much as one human being could ever need another. To dedicate her life to his welfare was the very least she could do. Perhaps the only way she could ever begin to make up for the great wrong she had done him.

Her hand automatically went to her stomach. It was in there – her child – Mike's child. How big was it now? As big as her thumbnail, perhaps? But it would not always be so small. With every passing day it would grow bigger until the day next autumn that she held it in her arms and looked down into its eyes ... 'Please don't let it be a son,' she whispered. 'Please don't let it look like him. Don't make it any harder for me, Dear Lord ... Please ...'

She began to be sick the following morning. Just when she

thought she was going to escape with relatively little morning sickness, a great wave of nausea swept over her as soon as her feet touched the bedside rug at a little after seven o'clock. It took all of half an hour for it to subside enough for her to continue her preparations for work. She would have to tell them soon. It would be stupid to wait until it became too obvious to hide. She was not too sure what the regulations were regarding pregnant women on the Prime Minister's staff in Downing Street, but she was certain she wanted to hang on to her job as long as possible. She would go mad mooning about this flat on her own otherwise.

Over the next few days her life took on a different routine. She asked to be excused from late-night duties taking notes in Cabinet because the most important thing in her life now was keeping her promise to Ken in visiting him every day. Most days she had to travel down to East Grinstead and back by train but, just occasionally, she would find a few precious petrol coupons in her desk drawer. She could not be sure who was putting them there: it could be any one of at least a dozen people, for all in the office were full of sympathy about the terrible tragedy that had befallen her husband, but she had a sneaking suspicion it was the Prime Minister himself. Never one to hide his feelings, Winston Churchill had been visibly upset to hear of Ken's accident. It was as if he took on some personal guilt for the dead and wounded. She remembered her stepfather, Jack Mallory, remarking once that Winston still carried the deaths of thousands of British soldiers at Gallipoli during the Great War like a great cross on his back, and certainly the sufferings of the boys at the Front, in all three services, seemed to affect him just as deeply a generation on.

As the weeks of March dragged by and the mornings became less chill, and the breeze turned more playful as she walked the few hundred yards from the bus stop to Number Ten Downing Street each day, she wished more than ever that her mother was still at home. She had gone down to SOE headquarters on two or three occasions over the past few weeks to find out if there had been any word from her but, apart from the news early on that the drop had been successful, she had heard nothing.

Sometimes she thought she could not cope with the worry any longer. She longed to tell someone – anyone – of her concern, but she had been sworn to secrecy by Beth. Her mother had made her promise that the story she was to put out was either that she had gone to Scotland to stay with relatives, or she was living up in Oxfordshire, in her old family home. But just what *was* happening over there in

Poland? And did her mother have any idea just how worried she was about her?

Barney Huntly-Crawford, who had by now returned to the Foreign Office but was still in touch with things over at SOE, had proved to be a never-ending source of comfort. 'Of course, you have nothing to worry about, my dear. No news from our agents in the field is positively good news. It means they are out there ferreting away on our behalf and haven't fallen into the hands of our Nazi friends, otherwise we'd have heard about it in no uncertain terms. There's nothing that old Himmler likes better than broadcasting that his Gestapo chums have nabbed yet another of our men – or women, as the case may be. You can rest assured your mother will be doing her best to keep out of German hands – and succeeding admirably.'

Had Beth heard him she would have given a wry smile, for not only was she doing her best to fall into German hands, tonight she would probably end up doing her best to fall into their arms into the bargain, if that was what was required to gain the information they so badly needed back in London.

She was relieved that Marysia would be by her side when she walked into the hotel ballroom in a little over an hour's time for, although she had made quite a wide circle of acquaintances amongst the Germans who frequented the Hotel Torun, it gave her an immense sense of comfort to know that in this strange city she had not only found a friend, but one who was working towards the same end as she was herself – the defeat of this terrible scourge of National Socialism that had brought such misery to them all.

She dressed with special care, doing her hair up on top of her head and fastening it there with one of the white silk roses that she had brought with her from England. She had slipped Pola, the chamber-maid, a few zlotys to run an iron over her evening gown, which had been so badly creased during its first airing on the night of her arrival in Warsaw.

Her mind returned to Walter Schellendorf, the Obersturmbann-führer who had swept into her life that first day, only to sweep out again with equal suddenness almost immediately. She had to admit to a certain relief that he had not returned from Lodz and, if what Marysia said was correct, he might not now return at all, for a new contingent of Gestapo officers had just arrived, who no doubt she would have the dubious pleasure of meeting tonight.

Marysia was waiting for her at the door of the cocktail lounge as she made her way downstairs at a little after eight. Her *volksdeutsch* friend was looking stunningly attractive in an ankle-length, figure-hugging dress of plum-red velvet; her blonde hair was long and loose, falling in a silken curtain over one eye, reminiscent of the popular Hollywood star, Veronica Lake; and the ever-present cigarette was being puffed elegantly through a long ebony holder. 'Countess!'

'Marysia!' The two women embraced and kissed on both cheeks. 'You look quite beautiful!' Beth stood back and regarded her new friend with approval.

'Thanks be to Grandfather. This is one of his creations.' Marysia looked down fondly at the gown that clothed her model's figure. 'I am very lucky. He used me to model all his latest creations on and I usually got to keep the odd one or two … But enough about me. The important thing is that you should shine tonight …' She glanced around her and lowered her voice, 'Have you seen them yet?'

'Them?'

'The new lot that have arrived this week … Have you seen them?'

Beth shook her head. 'Not that I know of. Although, I must confess, they all look alike at a distance.'

Marysia gave a quiet smile. That was certainly true. With their blond, blue-eyed, Teutonic good looks and athletic frames within the black SS uniforms, they could have all been cloned from the same ideal of Aryan manhood. 'I'm not sure exactly how many new ones have arrived,' she said quietly, 'but the three I've already met must have made Herr Himmler rub his podgy little hands in glee when they joined up.' She glanced towards the door, then looked at her watch. 'If I'm not mistaken they're already in there. Care to meet your new lover?'

It was a joke, but the fixed smile that Beth had worn since entering the cocktail lounge froze on her lips. There was many a true word spoken in jest.

She followed Marysia out into the main foyer. They paused by one of the tall pot plants that stood in elaborately-gilded jardinières around the marble-tiled floor and watched for a second or two as the other guests filed in through the ballroom door.

'Ready?' Marysia gave a reassuring smile in her direction.

'As ready as I'll ever be.'

The two women walked side by side into the ballroom, already alive with the sound of the band at the far end and the lively chatter and laughter of the assembled guests. White-coated waiters were serving drinks from silver trays and they both accepted a glass of Sekt with a smile of thanks.

Although she had spoken nothing but German since she arrived in

Warsaw and had even trained herself to think in German over the past few weeks, Beth suddenly found herself resorting to English in her thoughts. It was anxiety, she knew, for her mouth was dry and nerves clutched at her throat as Marysia said excitedly, 'There they are – look – over there!'

Beth clutched the stem of the wine glass ever tighter and watched with growing apprehension as her friend raised her arm and waved to a small knot of tall, black-uniformed men on the other side of the ballroom. They appeared to talk amongst themselves for a moment, then three of them broke away and strode leisurely across the room towards them.

'It's the tallest one I've got my eye on,' Marysia murmured. 'He's quite a specimen, don't you agree?'

Beth's eyes moved to the object of her friend's approval. He was well over six feet tall, with unusually blond hair, even for a German, and strikingly brilliant blue eyes. He looked to be in his middle to late twenties and in any other circumstances would have made a perfect match for the young woman by her side.

All three officers bowed in unison, then the older of them, a thin-faced man in his late forties, held out his hand and kissed both of their right hands in turn. 'My dear Frau Fischer,' he said in a voice that betrayed his Swabian origins, 'how nice to make your acquaintance again. I don't believe we have had the pleasure of meeting your friend here.' The pale grey eyes glanced approvingly in Beth's direction.

'This is the Countess Elisabeth von Wolfsberg,' Marysia said proudly. 'She is one of our poor *Flüchtlinge* from the East. The Russian swine have swarmed over her estates and forced her to flee to Warsaw for sanctuary. Is that not correct, Countess?'

Beth's eyes were fixed on the tall young man in the middle of the group, whose blue eyes were looking with equal curiosity into her own. Marysia had to repeat her question. 'Oh, yes, yes, that's quite correct.'

Marysia gave a strained smile and prayed that her companion was going to live up to the expectations she had for her this evening. 'I'm sure the Countess will be able to recount her harrowing story to you in full later on but, in the meantime … Countess, allow me to present SS Gruppenführer Wilhelm Gerhardt. Herr Gruppenführer, perhaps you would be so kind as to present your two colleagues.'

'*Aber gewiss*, my dear young lady. Countess von Wolfsberg, allow me to introduce SS Obersturmführer Martin Dickmann …' The smallest of the three men stepped forward and kissed Beth's hand, 'I am honoured, Countess ... '

Then the Gruppenführer's eyes turned to the taller of his two companions. 'And last, but by no means least, I'd like you to meet someone who knows this part of the world only too well. I believe his family has been resident out here for several generations ... Countess von Wolfsberg, allow me to introduce SS Obersturmbannführer Count Otto von Lessing ... '

Chapter Forty-five

'Countess Elisabeth von Wolfsberg ... What a remarkable co-incidence. Wolfsberg is my family home in Silesia. You know of it, perhaps? There may be some connection?' A pair of ice-blue eyes looked down quizzically into Beth's, the fair brows above rising in curiosity as Otto von Lessing raised Beth's hand to his lips.

Beth could feel the colour drain from her face as she met his gaze and allowed her hand to be kissed. She could have been looking into the eyes of Hans Heinrich, his father, himself: the resemblance now he was a grown man was uncanny. 'I – I do believe I may have heard it spoken of ... ' Her mouth had gone quite dry and she answered with the greatest difficulty. 'In Silesia, you say?'

'Yes, but, alas, I do not get too much time to attend to estate business these days. I have to leave it in the capable hands of my uncle. The Reich is a demanding mistress – you would agree, would you not, Herr Gruppenführer?' He turned to the superior officer at his side.

'Most certainly – and it is our privilege to serve such a mistress.' SS Gruppenführer Wilhelm Gerhardt's answer was emphatic, but his eyes were on the younger woman, Marysia, by Beth's side. Marysia, in turn, was paying scant attention to the two shorter men. She had eyes only for the tall, imposing figure of Count von Lessing, whom she was observing with scarcely disguised interest.

But Otto von Lessing had scarcely noticed, his eyes were fixed firmly on the older of the two attractive women before him. There was some-thing strangely familiar about her; something he could not quite put his finger on. It was as if he knew her from somewhere, but that was absurd. She was from the East – a refugee, so they said. What could she know of Wolfsberg? She was probably only being polite in saying that she may have heard of it. And yet – and yet ... Curiosity got the better of him. 'May I have the honour of this dance, Countess?'

Marysia gasped faintly at Beth's shoulder and she herself could barely disguise her surprise, and dismay, as the young Count von Lessing held out his arm to escort her to the dance-floor.

He danced well, very well, as he swept her round the floor in the centre of the dozen or so other couples already making the most of the music. He held her at arms' length so he could look into her eyes as he asked, 'You know Warsaw well, Countess? You have been here before, perhaps?'

Beth shook her head. 'I travelled little in the past, I'm afraid. The estate was my whole life ... '

'And now it is over – that part of your life?'

She shrugged helplessly in his arms. 'One has hope.'

He continued to look down into her face. She was older than him, quite a few years older, but he felt strangely drawn to this pale-skinned, beautiful woman with the sea-green eyes that seemed unable to hold his gaze for more than a second or two. He had had his fill of younger women. They had no consciences – no souls. And the younger and more beautiful they were, the less they could be trusted, the more they made one suffer.

He closed his eyes for a moment as he drew his partner closer to him and they glided slowly round the floor in time to the music. A face appeared before his closed lids. The face of a strikingly pretty young woman appeared before him; a young woman who had held his heart from the time he was old enough to traverse the winding path that divided his estate of Wolfsberg from her father's of Jarosbork. Yes, Anna Jarosinska had been the love of his young life – until the day three Christmases ago, when he had managed a few precious days leave at Wolfsberg and she came back from Warsaw and told him that she was in love with another man – a Jew.

He tensed, gripping Beth tighter to him, as the pain and disgust he had felt at that moment surged through him once more. A Jew – she had rejected him for a Jew! The humiliation of that moment he would carry with him to the grave. What could a Jew – an *Untermensch* – give her that he couldn't? How could a Jew love her as he had loved her? How could she? How could she even contemplate such a union? Didn't she know she should have been flattered that he, from one of Silesia's oldest families – much older than most of the *Junkers* of Prussia – should choose her from all the young women available to him? Granted she was from one of Silesia's oldest *Szlachta* families, but the Polish land-owning upper class of Silesia could never rank in importance to those of genuine German stock. Most young women in her position would have gone down on bended knees and thanked God for the chance of such a match – but not she. Not the daughter of Jan Jarosinski.

He could have got his own back, of course. The opportunity was there, when her father was arrested and brought into Pawiak prison. Yes, he could have got his own back then, all right. But what did he do? Instead of shipping him off to Treblinka or Auschwitz, or even shooting him out of hand, which he would have been perfectly at liberty to do, he let him go. Let him go – just like that. It was a weakness, there was no denying it. Sentimentality for the past should never be allowed to cloud one's judgement about the present. But he had been younger then. It wouldn't happen now. No, now he had found himself posted out here for the second time in this war, he would not be so soft-centred. They had been sent here by Reichs-führer Himmler to do a job – a man's job – to rid this city of the last remnants of its Jews and any other recalcitrant Poles who were hindrances to the final victory of the Reich. He would do that job with pride.

Yes, he had had enough of young women. When he needed a woman in future he would go for one like this emerald-eyed creature in his arms: an older, cultured woman who would attend to his bodily needs and leave his heart intact.

He stole another glance down at his partner's face. How old was she? Fortyish, maybe? Her skin was curiously untouched by the years, except for a few fine lines that fanned up from the area of those sea-green eyes. Her hair, piled so elaborately on top of her head, still shone with the nut-brown glow of youth. He imagined himself running his fingers through it – stroking the pale, creamy-white flesh of her neck. Her body felt soft and supple in his arms and, as he drew her closer to him, her perfume filled his nostrils, and he felt the throb of desire in his loins.

It was almost a month since he had had a woman. 'You'll be all right in Warsaw,' they had told him in Berlin. 'The whores are of a much higher class now than when you left. The city has been filling up with refugees from the East who would sell their souls, never mind their bodies, for a few cigarettes and a decent meal.' And it was true, there were many more good-looking women hanging around this hotel and the few others favoured by the German High Command in the city. He could see that old roué Gerhardt had his eyes on that blonde piece, Marysia, and it was never politic to win out in the female stakes over your superior officer. No, this one in his arms would do him all right tonight. Women, like good wine, often improved with age – they had learned more tricks, were more experienced in the ways to please a man. Yes, his Countess from the East was not a bad bet for a good time tonight. By the looks and feel of her, she would do very nicely indeed. And the more he thought about it, the more aroused he became. But even here it was not done to simply haul the lady of one's choice off to bed. Rituals had to be observed ... A drink perhaps, some intimate conversation. Then another drink, and another ...

The dance had come to an end and, before the band started up again, Otto took Beth's hand and raised it to his lips. 'Shall we sit this one out? If I remember, Countess, they do a very nice champagne cocktail at the bar ... You must be thirsty – dancing is thirsty work.'

Beth's heart sank. He had taken a fancy to her, it was obvious. She felt sick at the thought, but managed a passable smile as she took his proffered arm and followed him across the dance-floor in the direction of the cocktail lounge beyond.

He led her to a low, plushly upholstered, two-seater sofa in one of the window alcoves and, after seeing her comfortably seated, he summoned a waiter to bring two of Pan Gluck's special cocktails – his own version of Turk's Blood – a potent mixture of champagne and best burgundy; an aphrodisiac par excellence. 'And make sure there are replacements on the table before we finish these,' he commanded the young man who brought them. 'We don't frequent this establishment to spend half our time going thirsty, while you and your like loll around.'

The young man bowed politely as he took his leave and, as Beth watched him return to his bar duties, she could imagine the curses he was invoking beneath his breath at this typical example of Teutonic boorishness. She glanced across at Otto, who was leaning back in his chair as if he owned the place. He was so like his father in looks, yet never in her wildest dreams could she have imagined Hans Heinrich behaving in such a manner. They must have done it to him – Himmler and his like – those terrible people at the SS training establishment, who taught them that to wear that black uniform was to rule the world.

She was aware of her features hardening into a frown the more she thought of the harm that had been done to a whole generation of Germany's finest young men. She forced a smile to her lips as she accepted the proffered glass of the blood-red wine. 'To what shall we drink?'

He raised his glass to touch hers and their eyes met. 'First, as always, we must drink to the great and glorious victory of the Third Reich!'

'To the great and glorious victory of the Third Reich!' Beth thought she would choke on the words.

Otto smiled. 'And now –

> *Trinke, dass die Nase glänzt*
> *Hell wie ein Karfunkel,*
> *Auf dass du eine Leuchte hat*
> *In das Daseins Dunkel!'*

This time her smile was genuine as she lifted her glass to drink to the nonsense verse about drinking till your nose shone like a jewel to light you through life's darkness. For a few fleeting seconds it was not the black-uniformed SS Obersturmbannführer that was seated next to her, but Otto, her beloved stepson, the blond-haired, blue-eyed, angelic child she had had to leave behind on her return to England. The gentle child that his uncle, Carl Christian, had insisted on sending to military academy in Potsdam, to turn into this perfect specimen of German manhood. She was sick at heart at the thought.

But would it have been any different if she had remained at Wolfsberg? Could she have stopped him from serving the Fatherland? Could she have salvaged the soul inside this black-shirted body? She must stop torturing herself like this … She must concentrate on the present. 'You plan on being long in Warsaw?'

'As long as it takes.'

Her blood froze. 'As long as it takes … ?'

The blue eyes across from her hardened. 'To do the job … to rid this city of its pestilence.'

'Its pestilence … ?' She repeated his words once more, her heart beating faster.

'The Jews and the other *Untermenschen* who have polluted it for far too long.'

She shifted uneasily on the soft seat. 'And – and just how do you intend carrying out this "cleansing process"?'

His eyes narrowed as he looked at her closely, then he smiled. 'That, my dear Countess, you will find out soon enough … It is not for pretty women to worry their heads about men's work.' He downed half his glass in one gulp and replaced it on the table. 'But enough of this formality – if we are to get to know each other better, perhaps we should begin now.' He reached across and took her hand in his. 'Your name is Elisabeth, they say. May I call you Lisa?'

'If I may call you Otto.' She whispered the words, as her pulse-rate increased. There was no mistaking the look in his eyes. There was no mistaking along what lines his mind was already running. His hand was still on hers. She looked down at the long, smooth-skinned fingers – pianist's fingers, she used to call them. Just like Hans Heinrich's.

To increase her discomfort, he began to tell her about his home in Silesia – about Wolfsberg. 'My mother died when I was born and my father died when I was very young,' he said quietly; then his face hardened. 'My stepmother, an Englishwoman, deserted me and went back to England, so you could say I was an orphan three times over.'

Her fingers tensed beneath his as the words found their target. She wanted to cry out 'No – no, that's not true!', but could not. She was a total stranger to him, a stranger from the East, she must remember that. But a combination of guilt and curiosity would not allow her to let the subject rest. 'Is – is she still alive, your stepmother?'

The broad shoulders shrugged. 'Perhaps. She must still be quite young. She married again back in London – a much older man, by the name of Mallory, I believe … ' Memory misted his eyes for a moment, then they found hers once more. 'Her name was Elisabeth – the same as yours, but she called herself Beth … ' He was looking at her intently now, his eyes taking in the gleaming crown of glossy brown hair, the wide green eyes set against the pale skin, as realization dawned. 'Yes, that's it! That's who you remind me of! I couldn't understand it when we first met – I was sure I knew you, sure we had met before. But that's why – you reminded me of her – of my stepmother!'

Beth went hot, then ice-cold. The smile came with difficulty to her lips. 'Should I be flattered hearing that I remind you of your mother – albeit your stepmother?'

He had the good grace to colour slightly. 'My dear Lisa, forgive me. Of course I could never think of you as a mother figure … Never.' He moved closer on the sofa, replacing his drink on the small table beside them as he took both her hands in his and lifted them to his lips. 'You could be many things to me – many; but a mother – never!'

It was less than an hour and several glasses of Turk's Blood later when he suggested they adjourn upstairs to her room, taking a fresh bottle of champagne, and one of burgundy, with them. 'It's becoming far too crowded in here,' he said, indicating the bevy of 'ladies of pleasure' and their hangers-on around the bar with a dismissive nod of his head. 'We can get to know each other so much better in more intimate surroundings, wouldn't you agree?'

She looked at him through the haze of wine. His eyes seemed so blue – so very blue, and the expression in them was so like Hansi's. So very like Hansi's. He reached out and touched her cheek, his fingers moving down to gently stroke her lower lip and, of their own volition, her lips kissed them. He had moved even closer to her now and seemed to tower over her on the soft cushions. He might be in a uniform she despised, but he was one of the most attractive men she had ever met ... Every inch a man. And so like Hansi. So very like Hansi ...

His eyes were gazing down into hers and she was swimming in their deep blue depths. She had drunk far too many cocktails much too quickly, and with each one her inhibitions about their former relationship were receding. He was stroking her neck now and breathing more heavily. His breath was warm on her face. Her eyes moved to his mouth, with its well-drawn lips and white, even teeth. It began to speak softly, intimately, in her ear, as he leaned forwards and drew her to him, '*Bist du bereit, Liebling*? Are you ready for it, too ... ?'

She was not aware of answering, only of his arm encircling her and helping her to her feet. It remained around her as they made their way up the stairs to her room. It seemed the most natural thing in the world.

It was still daylight outside and she walked unsteadily across the floor to close the curtains, but he held up a restraining hand. 'No – don't do that. Let the light remain. I want to see you as you take that beautiful gown off ...' His voice was husky, almost unrecognizable, as desire took command of his vocal cords and pulsated through his body. 'I want to watch – watch every movement ... Come here, *Mutti* ... Let me help you ...'

He was joking as he called her by the childish name for Mother. It obviously amused him that she reminded him of his stepmother. It added a certain forbidden spice to what was about to occur. But, despite all the drink, it stabbed her to the core. She stood quite still in the middle of the floor and gazed across at him. The face of the small boy she had once known and loved and the grown man mingled into one in her sight. If only he knew ... If only he knew ...

He poured two more glasses of the cocktail from the new bottles and brought one across to her. They drank them quickly, greedily, standing up in the middle of the room. Then he took her glass from her and placed it with his on top of the mantelpiece. 'Come here, *Liebchen* ... Come closer ...'

She walked slowly into his arms, gasping slightly at the touch of his lips on the bare skin of her shoulder. His hands were clumsy from the drink as they fumbled with the fastenings behind her gown. A momentary panic engulfed her. But this was what she was here for.

Or was it? How could she have imagined in her wildest dreams that she would come here to this foreign land to be made love to by her stepson? It was an obscenity: an obscenity against Hans Heinrich, his father; an obscenity against all she had held dear.

Her head swam as his hands worked feverishly to undo the tiny hooks and eyes. If it was acceptable with a stranger – why not with him? He was no blood relation, after all. He was simply an extremely handsome man from whom she could learn things that could save the lives of countless people … Perhaps save the life of the man she loved.

She closed her eyes and let out a low moan of despair as Jan's face swam before her – a moan of despair that the man in whose arms she was held took to be of pleasure, and his teeth bit harder into the soft flesh of her neck as he tore at the remaining catches of the gown. 'Ahhh … ' He let out a small cry of triumph as it slipped down over her breasts and landed in a shining heap around her ankles.

He lifted her out of it and carried her to the bed, lying her down on top of the quilt and gazing down at her silently for several seconds, revelling in the sight of the pale, creamy flesh that was soon to be his. Then, slowly, very slowly, his eyes never leaving her prostrate figure, he began to remove his own clothes. First the black jacket of the uniform was cast aside, then his shirt and tie. Then, as she watched, his hands began to unbuckle the leather belt of his trousers.

When he was down to his underpants he walked over to the edge of the bed and continued to gaze down at her, as if by prolonging the anticipation he was increasing the pleasure. She was lying back on the pillows, her brown hair spread out around her head. She had on a pale-pink brassiere and French knickers, one stockinged leg was bent at the knee and her arms were above her head as if in total sub-jugation. At last he spoke. 'Turn over,' he commanded, his eyes on the swell of soft white flesh imprisoned in the shiny pink of the brassiere. 'Turn over … Let me remove that for you … '

He slid on top of the bed beside her as she obeyed his command. Impatient now, his breathing laboured as desire became his master, his fingers wrenched roughly at the small metal fastening. Then it was off and her back was bare. His eyes devoured the smooth expanse of fair skin and his right hand reached out to touch her shoulder, lifting the thick curtain of brown hair back from the curve of her neck.

Suddenly he froze, his eyes riveted on the two small rose-red birthmarks at the side of her neck. He was no longer in this stuffy hotel bedroom in Warsaw but transported in his mind to another time, another place. He was back a quarter of a century ago in the small, four-poster bed in his nursery at Wolfsberg. He was being read to by a beautiful young woman, with nut-brown hair and eyes the colour of emeralds, a young woman whose hair would always be done up in a bun, so that in the summer, when she wore her prettiest, low-necked lace blouses, the small boy's eyes would fix on two such rose-red marks. He would lie there beneath the covers staring at them as her voice read through each of his favourite fairy tales in turn: Rumpelstiltskin, Hansel and Gretel, Big Klaus and Little Klaus ... He could remember them all as if it were yesterday, just as he could remember those marks. They were part of her and he had loved her. Oh, how he had loved her. But she had failed him, just as Anna had failed him.

And now she was back. By what means and for what reason he could not imagine. But it was her. He had no doubt about that. His fingers reached out and touched the birthmarks, trembling as they did so. Then they tightened around her shoulder as he turned her roughly on her back to face him as his other hand reached for her knickers and pulled them down, casting them roughly aside, as he shed the last remnant of his own clothing.

He would make love to her – the only mother he had ever known, the mother who had deserted him when he needed her most. He would make love to her now ...

There was no gentleness in his lovemaking. He made love to her roughly, cruelly, on the soft bed, causing her to cry out in pain as he entered into her. And as his passion reached its climax all the hurt, all the hate that had been hidden deep in his heart for all these years came spilling out of him, as his voice, throaty with emotion called out, 'Damn you, *Mutti* ... God damn you, *Mutti* ... Damn you, Beth Mallory ... God damn you to hell ... !'

Chapter Forty-six

Beth froze beneath him on the dishevelled bed. He knew ... Otto – he knew ... ! A wave of panic engulfed her.

He was lying on top of her, panting, his skin bathed in a film of perspiration, his face buried in the pillow at the side of her head. His body was still locked in hers. Terror filled her soul. She could not move a muscle, even if she had wanted to. Then he groaned and pulled himself up on his elbows, so that he was looking straight down into her eyes. 'Deny it, *Liebchen*, if you wish ... But the evidence is there. It *is* you, isn't it? It *was* you who married my father then ran out on me as a child.'

She was pinned against the mattress, his eyes only inches from hers. In the half-light of the evening they glinted a steel-grey. His voice was little more than a hiss. What could he mean – the evidence is there? She had taken such care to remove all labels from her clothes – remove any item from her possession that could be construed as originating in England. She had to play for time. 'I – I don't know what you mean, I swear I don't.'

'You can swear all you like, but you can't fool me.' A look akin to distaste disfigured the handsome features of his face as he swung himself off her immobile body to kneel beside her on the crumpled quilt. 'What are you doing here? Spying, is that it? You are a British agent?' He spat the words out, jerking her head back to face him as she attempted to avert her eyes from his. 'Answer me, damn you. Answer me!'

'I – I am not this woman you think me to be,' she stammered, pulling herself up on the pillow. 'My name is Elisabeth von Wolfs-berg ... I – I am from ...'

The slap rang out. 'Don't lie to me, *Mutti*!' He used the name now as a term of abuse as his eyes glared down into hers. 'You are Beth Mallory – formerly von Lessing und Wolfsberg.' He shook his head in derision. 'It wasn't very clever of you, was it, using the name of our home as part of your cover? You could have chosen something more original! But then you British always were amateurs at most things, weren't you?'

He reached down to the pocket of his discarded trousers and extracted a packet of cigarettes. He took one out and lit it, drawing the smoke deep into his lungs as he looked down at her petrified face against the feather pillows. 'I could shoot you now, you know – this very minute – and nothing would be said, except "Well done, Herr Obersturmbannführer." I would have killed one of my country's enemies – a spy – and would be commended for it, perhaps by the Reichsführer himself. Who knows, I might even be rewarded by a transfer back to Berlin.' He blew a perfect smoke-ring into the air and watched as it drifted lazily to the ceiling. 'Give me one good reason why I shouldn't.'

Beth caught her breath, the blow from his open palm still stinging the skin of her left cheek. Was he serious? He certainly looked it. What was she to do – confess that she really was his stepmother and rely on their past relationship to save her, or simply attempt to bluff it out? She was ice-cold, but a sheen of nervous perspiration covered her body. God, what a dilemma!

'I'm waiting, *Mutti*. Give me one good reason why I shouldn't kill you right now.'

'You would be making the most terrible mistake.' She struggled up further on the pillows. The room was freezing cold and gooseflesh covered her bare skin. She had nothing on but her suspender belt and stockings. Her teeth began to chatter and she fought to keep them still, to retain at least a particle of dignity.

He reached across and lifted her fur coat from where it was lying over the back of a chair and threw it towards the bed. 'Put that on. If you die of pneumonia you will be no good to us. Corpses cannot supply information.'

His words struck terror into her heart. She knew only too well how the Gestapo interrogated information out of their victims – what went on in those dank, dark cells in their headquarters in Szucha Avenue.

She scrambled down from the bed and slipped the coat over her naked body. The satin lining felt cold against her bare skin and she began to shiver once more. Her shoes were lying by the side of the bed where they had been discarded earlier. As he reached for his own clothes, she slid her feet into them. Although all but naked beneath, the outer garments gave her some vestige of dignity back.

She sat back down on the edge of the bed and watched in silence and growing fear as he dressed slowly in front of the dressing-table mirror. He was watching her in the glass, his eyes darting towards her huddled figure every so often. She now knew what it meant to be panic-stricken: she felt totally immobile, mentally and physically, drained of all energy, all emotion. The sight of him fully dressed a few minutes later, in that awesome black uniform, sent a physical shiver through her that he was quick to notice.

He walked slowly back to where she was sitting and stood over her. She looked so small, so vulnerable sitting there, fear oozing from every pore. Her once elaborately piled up hair was hanging long and loose over the fur collar of the coat, making her look far younger than her years. Could this really be the woman whose return he had yearned for all those years? Could this really be her, the only mother he had ever known?

He continued to stare down at her, struggling to identify the dream figure of his memory with this flesh and blood creature who now sat shivering before him. Surprisingly, making love to her tonight had brought no satisfaction, merely a strange sense of disgust when it was all over. Instead of exorcizing the ghost of the past, he had defiled something – not her, for he felt almost nothing for this virtual stranger who sat staring up at him with those fear-filled eyes – he had defiled a memory. He had defiled his own childhood, for childhood, once it is over, exists only in the memory. And Wolfsberg, in those golden days before the spartan hell of the military academy at Potsdam, was all he had known of happiness in this life. He could never get close to his uncle – Carl Christian was himself a product of that loveless upbringing – but for a few golden years he had had Mutti Beth. Then, when she disappeared from his life, he had found Jan Jarosinski at nearby Jarosbork – Onkel Jan, whose small daughter Anna later came to mean … His features froze along with his thoughts. How did one define 'everything'? 'More than life itself' would be as near the truth as he could get. Mutti Beth, Onkel Jan, and Anna … Each and every one he had loved. And each and every one had deserted him. And each and every one was now fighting against the only other thing he held dear in this life – the Fatherland itself.

He could kill her now, just as he could have killed Jan Jarosinski the last time they met, just after he had been transferred to this god-forsaken city. Kill her or hand her over to the others to deal with.

'What are you going to do with me?'

The whispered question broke into his musings. He continued to stare down at her, willing the hate to grow within him to make it easier. This was the moment that would test his mettle as an officer of the Reich – an SS officer. This was the moment when he must prove his love for the Fatherland – prove it meant more to him than mere ties of sentiment. Sentiment had no place in war. Part of their task in the SS was to identify enemies of the Reich and deal with them. Others he knew had even denounced their friends and divorced their wives because they had Jewish blood, or were Socialists or, even worse, Communists. The Reich demanded it and it was to the Reich that he was committed body and soul. '*Meine Ehre ist Treue*' – 'My Honour is Loyalty' – the motto of the SS itself, the élite corps whose uniform he was so proud to wear, was branded on his heart. Could he speak it with his head held high after tonight, if he let her go? Could he? Could he?

He had let both himself and his country down when he allowed Jan Jarosinski to go free. If he was to do the same now, what kind of a moral coward would that make him?

A nerve twitched spasmodically at the side of his clenched jaw and his right hand rested uneasily on the cold steel of his revolver. Despite what he had said, killing her out of hand was out of the question, even if he could bring himself to do it. Dead men – or women – did not tell tales, and there was obviously quite a story behind her turning up in Warsaw like this. But if he was to hand her over to the others ... A bitter bile rose in his throat. He had seen the results of their interrogations at first hand.

A bead of sweat broke on his upper lip. She was gazing up at him, waiting for him to speak, her hands clasping and unclasping in her lap. His vision blurred. He could see his old bed in the nursery in Wolfsberg. A voice, a soft voice reading him nursery rhymes in English echoed in his head, 'Humpty Dumpty sat on a wall, Humpty Dumpty had a great fall'. Gentle hands stroked his head on the pillow ... 'As I lay me down to sleep, I pray the Lord my soul to keep, If I should die before I wake, I pray the Lord my soul to take ... ' Soft lips kissed his brow. '*Gute Nacht, mein kleiner Schatz, Schlaf gut ...*'

He blinked his eyes and shook his head, as if to rid himself of the memory. Their eyes met and locked. She was an enemy of the Reich, of the beloved Fatherland. The grey metal of the gun was cold beneath his fingers. Sweat broke beneath his armpits and trickled down his skin beneath the black shirt. '*Meine Ehre is Treue*', he repeated softly to himself. '*Meine Ehre ist Treue*' ...

Then he swung round and strode to the window, to stand, with his back towards her, staring out over the roof-tops. 'Get out,' he hissed through gritted teeth. 'Get out – this second – now! Get back to England – or go to hell – but just GO!'

She did not need a second telling. For a split second she stared at the back of the tall, black-uniformed figure, as if not quite believing her ears, then, clutching her coat shut around her, she made for the door before he could change his mind.

Not daring to wait for the lift, she clattered down the marble stairs to arrive breathless in the hotel foyer. Music and laughter were coming from the open door of the ballroom to her left. She had to get out of here, get as far away as possible. Her life depended on it. But where could she go? In this state there was no question of going back into the ballroom to enlist Marysia's aid. Anyway, to do that would be to write her friend's death warrant as well as her own.

She looked around her in panic. Pan Gluck was standing behind the reception counter a few yards away. She remembered his knowing look and comment on her arrival at the hotel. Could she trust him? She gazed in panic at the balding Pole. It was a chance she had to take.

Half running, half walking, she hurried across the tiled floor towards him. Jozef Gluck's bushy brows rose at the sight of her distraught face. 'I have to leave, Pan Gluck. I have to leave now – immediately … Help me … Please …'

He stared at her hard for a moment, then glanced around him. There was no one within a dozen yards. He looked down at the reservation book on the counter in front of him and began to casually flick through the pages, as if she had never spoken. Then, 'Ten Toporski Street,' he said quietly, without looking up. 'Go now – and don't come back here. Ever.'

Not stopping to thank him, she made for the door, to find herself heading straight into a group of young SS Untersturmführers who had already had a few Schnapps too many that night. She had no choice but to squeeze her way past them and head out into the darkening night.

One grabbed at her arm, and automatically she let go the revers of her coat in an attempt to wrench herself free, only to clutch in panic at the edges of the fur once more. Dear God, she was almost stark naked beneath it!

Oblivious of the reason for her flaming cheeks, with the ribald shouts and laughter reserved for all attractive members of the opposite sex, the young men threw her from one to the other, as Beth clung desperately at the fur that was clothing her near-naked body. 'Please, please … Let me past, please …'

She was beginning to think that the end had really come, that she was about to be found out by this grotesque encounter with these awful, overgrown boys, when a barked command from the street brought the game to an abrupt end. Juergen Stroop, SS Brigade-führer and Major General of Police himself, was standing at the foot of the hotel steps, having just got out of his official car. 'All of you report to me in person – my office – nine o'clock tomorrow morning … ! *Gnädige Frau*, may I offer my sincere apologies on behalf of these young animals!'

He bowed deeply and then signalled to his driver, before turning back to Beth. 'The least I can do is see you arrive safely at your destination and do not risk running into any more louts like these who have disgraced their uniform tonight.'

Beth took a defensive half-step backwards. The last thing she wanted was to end up in the hands of the infamous Juergen Stroop himself tonight. 'That … that's very kind of you, sir, but it really won't be necessary. I – I'm only going a short distance.'

The Brigadeführer waved away her protest. 'Any distance is too far on a cold night in this city … Alas, I cannot accompany you myself, my presence is required here, but my driver will see that you get to wherever you wish to go in the utmost safety.' He opened the back door of the limousine himself and gestured for her to enter.

Her heart thumping, she obeyed, sliding into the sumptuous sanctuary of the soft hide as the door was closed behind her. The SS Chief bowed deeply and watched from the pavement as the car slid back out into the late-evening traffic.

'Where to, *gnädige Frau*?' the driver called over his shoulder as she gazed back in a mixture of fear and relief at the receding figure of the second highest ranking SS officer in Warsaw, and at the hotel itself, where another member of that dreaded band, her own stepson, still remained.

'Topo … ' She corrected herself in time and named another street a good half mile from the one named by Pan Gluck a few minutes earlier.

It was impossible to relax as the car sped through the darkening streets. This past hour had been the most terrifying of her life – worse even than the most harrowing nights of the Blitz. Just where in God's name was she headed? Where and what was waiting for her at 10 Toporski Street?

The car drew up and she got out, aware of the looks of contempt from an elderly couple passing by as the black Mercedes-Benz, its swastika standard fluttering from the bonnet, drew away from the kerb and disappeared down the street. It was cold, very cold, and she was more conscious than ever of her lack of clothes beneath the fur coat.

She began to walk in the vague direction of Toporski Street. Very few people were around at this time in the evening. An armoured car full of German soldiers passed, and one of the young men shouted an obscenity at her. With her high-heeled evening shoes, her fur coat, and her long hair hanging loose around her shoulders, she could only be one thing walking the streets alone at this time of night. A grim smile flitted across her face. If only he could see beneath the protective wrapping of fur! She would have a hard time indeed maintaining she was anything but a 'lady of the night' if she was picked up before she got as far as her destination.

Toporski Street was one of the streets that ran adjacent to the Jewish Ghetto. It was a depressing area of the city that she had rarely entered until now. Her anxiety increased as she turned the corner that led her on to it. What if Pan Gluck was not on their side? What if she was simply jumping from the frying pan into the fire?

Nerves cavorted so strongly in her stomach that she felt physically sick by the time her eyes fell on the number 10 painted in black on the wall by the varnished door. To her surprise it turned out to be a small tobacconists-cum-newsagents. The door was still open and an old man sat behind the counter reading one of the papers.

'*Guten Abend, Mein Herr.*'

'We are closed,' he replied, in badly accented German. His eyes, behind the pebble-spectacles, never left the paper.

She stood her ground. 'I – I have come ... I have been sent by Pan Jozef Gluck of the Hotel Torun.' She held her breath as, for the first time, he raised his eyes to meet hers.

'Joe sent you, you say?'

She nodded, her eyes taking in the almost empty shelves and the black cat that lay curled up on one end of the counter. It had a pink ribbon around its neck; an adornment that looked curiously out of place in this most desperate of cities. The place smelt of the tobacco that it was supposed to sell and a badly-stained *meerschaum* pipe lay on a tin ashtray at the old man's elbow.

He got out of his chair and, to her surprise, he barely reached her shoulder. 'What's your name?'

She paused for a moment, then answered, 'Countess Elisabeth von Wolfsberg.'

His sparse brows shot up behind the wire frames of the spectacles. 'Can you identify yourself?'

She shrugged helplessly. 'My *Kennkarte* – in fact all my papers, all my possessions, I've had to leave behind tonight ...'

The confession cut little ice. 'There are other ways of self-identification,' he cut in.

She looked at him blankly as he took a pencil from behind his ear and began to draw a small sketch in the margin. It was a passable attempt at a butterfly. Realization dawned. She was with friends, all right. '*Motte*,' she said, with a heartfelt sigh of relief. '*Motte* ...'

He lifted the wooden flap of the counter and motioned for her to follow him into the back shop. It was even more cramped than the outer one, with several wooden chairs arranged around a small table and piles of papers on every available surface. 'You need somewhere safe to go,' he said. It was more of a statement than a question.

'Yes, yes, I do. I'm really desperate. The Gestapo know who I am. I daren't go back there – not ever.'

The old man frowned and scratched several days growth of beard. 'That makes it difficult. Very difficult. Have you any objections to going over to the other side?'

'What?'

'The other side,' he repeated impatiently. 'Have you any objections to going over into the ghetto tonight on a mission, until we can get something sorted out for you?'

She stared at him in incredulity. 'Into the Jewish ghetto? You want me to go into the Jewish ghetto?'

'For tonight, that's all. One of our number is going over there tonight and we're short of someone to accompany him. The boy who would have gone with him has been lifted, so I've heard.'

'Lifted?'

'Into Pawiak.'

A shiver ran through her. 'You're all in the *Armia Krajowa*, I presume?'

The old man's watery blue eyes narrowed behind the pebble-spectacles. 'Ask no questions you'll get told no lies ... Anything you need to know about tonight's exercise Wladek will tell you himself.'

'Wladek?'

The old man nodded. 'He's the one you'll be assisting. I told you – the boy's been arrested. You've no objection to taking his place, have you?'

Beth gave a bemused shake of the head. 'No, no, of course not. That's what I came to Poland for – to help.'

A clock in the front shop struck ten, and the old man looked at his watch. 'You'd better be going. Wladek likes to make a start by midnight … You know Freta Street?'

Beth's brows furrowed for a moment. 'Isn't that one of the streets that back on to the Jewish ghetto?'

'It is. Number thirteen, that's the house you want. Tell Wladek you've come to help. If he thinks you're up to it he'll take you. If not, he won't. It's as simple as that.'

Beth looked at him, waiting for him to continue, but he had already opened what looked like an ancient ledger and had begun writing in it. So this was it. She was expected to find this Wladek and accompany him on some awful assignment into the forbidden part of the city. Her heart sank. This was not what she had imagined at all. So much for the safe house where she could have a good night's rest and get over the traumatic events of the past few hours!

The black cat had woken up and come through to investigate the stranger on the premises. With a determinedly brave smile, she shook hands with the old man and bent to stroke it before heading back out into the rapidly darkening night in search of 13 Freta Street.

It took her all of half an hour to get there. Instinctively she found herself ducking into alleyways and doorways to avoid the omni-presence of the German soldiers who seemed to appear out of the semi-darkness as she rounded every corner. By the time she reached Freta Street her legs felt so leaden with fatigue that she knew if she had to walk another step she would simply collapse.

Number Thirteen was a tall terraced house in the middle of a block of seedy looking houses. The whole block looked deserted, with either planks or wire mesh up at the windows. She looked at the flaking brown paint of the front door in trepidation. God only knew what she would find inside. Summoning up all her courage she knocked hard three times, then thrice more, before stepping back to wait. After a minute or so she thought she saw a blind at one of the upper windows move, then a short while later footsteps sounded behind the door.

It was opened by a lean-faced, shabbily dressed man around the same age as herself. He looked at her suspiciously from beneath beetling black brows. 'Yes?'

'Wladek?'

He neither confirmed nor denied it. 'What do you want?'

'I – I've been sent here from Number Ten Toporski Street.'

'Identify yourself.'

'Motte.'

The brows rose a fraction of an inch. So this was the British agent they had said was in town. He had expected a man. 'Schmetterling.'

He stood aside to allow her to enter.

The door was locked and barred behind them and she followed him down a narrow staircase into the cellars of the house. He had a pronounced limp; a war wound she imagined, as he dragged his left leg down the dank concrete steps, one by one. It was almost pitch-black, and she had to hold on to the wall to stop herself from falling headlong after him. The walls felt damp and cold to the touch and, although she could not see, she could tell by the smell they had mould growing on them. Her already low spirits sank even further with every step.

Eventually they reached the bottom and entered the cellars themselves. They consisted of several large rooms packed with large, old-fashioned items of furniture that loomed at her threateningly through the darkness; what looked like old cabin trunks were stacked around the floor. He led the way into the back room and, to her immense relief, lit a kerosene lamp. Immediately the place assumed a ghostly glow which sent an involuntary shudder through her.

He gestured for her to take a seat on an ancient, overstuffed sofa that sat along one wall. 'Why do they send you here?'

The question had an accusatory tone to it which only increased her misery. 'They said I was to help you tonight … Please, Wladek, let me help …'

He frowned and shook his head. 'I am not Wladek. Wladek is not operating from this address tonight. My brother has been picked up. Didn't Mietek tell you? There has been a raid on the ghetto – many killed.' The furrow on his forehead grew deeper. 'You cannot stay here tonight. It is not safe. The Gestapo they are everywhere.'

Tears of frustration and sheer fatigue sprang to her eyes. 'Then where am I to go? Tell me, please? I'll do anything – go anywhere.'

'Old Mietek – he said you were to help in the ghetto assignment?'

She nodded, 'Yes, if that was his name – the old man in Toporski Street said I could help out there tonight.'

The man tapped his front teeth with his thumbnail. 'Sixty-seven Freta Street. The operation is now planned from there. If Wladek thinks you may be of some good, he will make use of you. If not …' He shrugged and did not continue the sentence. 'It is better you go there now. I will walk with you. It is not far.'

As if in a daze, she followed him back upstairs and out into the chill of the night. Her lack of clothing beneath the fur coat brought her entire skin out in gooseflesh as she accompanied him along the darkened street, his lame leg making a soft, scuffing sound as it dragged along the concrete pavement. After several minutes he stopped in front of a door and turned to her. 'It's the top flat,' he said quietly. 'It has his name on the door – Wladek, Wladek Bronski. Knock twice, wait, then knock three times quickly, then twice more, then he will know it is a friend ... Good luck.'

He put out a bony hand and Beth grasped it. 'Thank you. Thank you so much.'

She entered the unmarked door, closing it quietly behind her and wearily climbed the stairs. 'Please let this Wladek be in,' she prayed beneath her breath. 'Please let him be in.' She could not bear to be passed on again to yet another house. Not again, Dear Lord, please ...

When, at last, she reached the top landing, a beam of moonlight penetrated the dirty glass of a narrow window to fall on the small scrap of paper bearing the name, 'W. Bronski.' This was the correct door all right. She gave a deep sigh of relief and knocked hard the regulation number of times, then listened.

She did not have long to wait. After a few seconds came the sound of footsteps behind the door. She could feel her heart thumping in her breast as the bolts were pulled back and the door opened a fraction of an inch.

'Yes?' a man's voice said hoarsely. 'Who is it?'

'I've come to see Wladek,' she heard herself say in a voice choking with anxiety. 'I've come from Pan Jozef Gluck at the Hotel Torun, and 13 Freta Street, and 10 Toporski Street ... ' Her voice was weak with fatigue, 'Please let me in, please ... '

The door opened another few inches and a man's head peered through the darkness at her. There was a few seconds silence, then a gasp as it was thrown open more fully. An arm pulled her into the narrow hallway and the door closed behind them with a resounding click. She peered up at the face that was staring down incredulously into hers.

'Dear Mother of God, I can't believe it ... ' The brown eyes stared down into hers in disbelief. 'Tell me I'm not dreaming. Tell me I'm not dreaming ... '

She stared back into his eyes as tears rushed to her own. 'Wladek? Wladek Bronski?' she whispered, as they cascaded down her cheeks and Jan Jarosinski enfolded her in his arms.

Chapter Forty-seven

'I must be dreaming ... It must be a dream ...' Jan Jarosinski repeated the words over and over as he buried his face in Beth's hair.

She clung to him as if her life depended on it. She had waited over two years for this moment – had crossed a war-torn continent and spent weeks surviving by her wits in this god-forsaken city in the hope, the very slight hope, that one day she might find him again. 'Jan ... Jan ... My love, my love ...' It was as if all the pent-up emotions of a lifetime had erupted to cascade in a flood of tears that tasted salt on their lips as they kissed and kissed again, before he lifted her in his arms and carried her through to the small sitting-room.

He sat down beside her on the settee and held her hands in his as his eyes devoured her. 'How, *kochanie* ... how?' He shook his head. 'I never dreamt – never, not once, that you could come to Poland, to Warsaw ...'

She answered his question with another. 'How could I stay away?' Her eyes swam with tears as they gazed into his. 'I couldn't sit at home in London and not know ...' her voice sank to a whisper, 'not even know if you were alive or dead.'

He reached up and touched her cheek and as he did so her fur coat slipped open, partially revealing one naked shoulder.

A mixture of fear and shame was reflected in Beth's eyes as they met his own troubled gaze. 'Don't ask me, my love ... Not yet ... Not now ...'

He carefully pulled the shawl collar of the coat back over the expanse of pale skin. 'I understand,' he said quietly. And he did. Whatever she had done, she had done for him – and Poland. The time for explanations would come later. The present was what mattered, not the past and all its sorrows. Part of him, the most important part, had died that day he said goodbye to her in that hotel room in Dundee. Life, since returning to his beloved Poland, had been hell, a hell that went on and on and on ... 'But to come here, *kochanie*, to Warsaw ... You know what is happening here in this city?'

She nodded. 'I know, my love, I know. And that is why I came. Warsaw cannot be allowed to die. The Polish people cannot be allowed to perish beneath Hitler's jackboots.'

'Why not the Poles?' he asked bitterly. 'Hitler has already disposed of most of the Jews in Europe. Have you not heard? Have you not seen? Who in this city can be unaware of the transports that leave daily for the camps – Auschwitz, Treblinka, Chelmno, Sobibor? Can you imagine the hell that lies behind that wall over there?' He gestured with his head towards the window and the ghetto wall that loomed tall and threatening out of the darkness beyond. 'They are dying daily by the hundreds over there – starvation, cold, disease ... ' He shook his head. 'I can do little about the first two killers, but about the last one, the disease, I can do my best. But it can never be enough, Beth, never enough ... '

'So that's what you take over,' she said softly. 'Medical supplies ... Why, Jan, why did you get involved?' Was he not in enough danger without risking his life for the Jews, who everyone knew were doomed anyway?

He looked down at her hands still clasped in his. 'Anna,' he said simply. 'Anna is still over there, with her Jew. She will not leave him – ever. It is the least I can do for them.'

So that was it. His daughter, his beautiful Aryan daughter was behind those ghetto walls, with the man she loved who just happened to be a Jew.

'They would almost have finished with medical school – would almost have been qualified by now,' he said, with a despairing shake of the head. 'If it wasn't for the Germans. If it wasn't for this damned war. But now they must work as they would never have worked in a lifetime of doctoring. They must forget they are students and do the work of a whole hospital of physicians in one filthy little room in Kozla Street. They must work every hour God gives to patch up the living dead, only to have the Germans kill them officially, shortly afterwards, in their death factories ... Yes, I risk my life taking them medical supplies. It is the least I can do.'

He got up from the settee and took down a bottle of vodka from the mantelpiece and poured two generous glassfuls. 'Drink this,' he said, handing her one of the glasses.

She took it and looked down into the clear spirit. 'To what shall we drink?' she asked quietly. She lifted her glass and answered her own question. 'What else can it be but – to Poland?'

Polska tak, ale jaka? ... Poland, yes, but what sort of Poland, he thought bitterly? Then, seeing her troubled eyes on his face, he attempted a smile. 'To Poland, my Beth,' he said softly, lifting his glass and touching hers. 'To Poland and the future.'

They drank the pungent spirit in unison, then he sat down beside her once more to talk quietly, intensely, about his hopes and fears for that future, of his love for his daughter whose young life he knew was as doomed as all those others who were at this moment living and dying in the hell behind the ghetto wall. Then for a moment the bitterness and hurt faded from his eyes as he asked softly, 'But, Lara, my love ... How is Lara?'

Beth's fingers nervously smoothed the fur over her knees. How *was* Lara? She remembered the look in her daughter's eyes as they said goodbye on the pavement outside their small flat in Lower Belgrave Street. What was she going through at this moment, not knowing if her mother was alive or dead? 'I wish I knew.' Her voice was little more than a whisper. 'I've had no contact with her since I arrived here in the middle of February.'

'She will be fine,' he said reassuringly. 'She still has her husband, yes? Her Scotsman – he is fine, too?'

Beth smiled. 'Yes, thank God. Ken's just fine. She's very lucky having him. He's a truly nice young man.'

Jan nodded and smiled across at her, but his eyes clouded once more. A Scotsman and a Jew. Two equally fine young men his two daughters just happened to have fallen in love with. Two equally fine young men who just happened to belong to different races, to have been born in different lands, whose futures would be so different, so very different. Ken would return home when this was all over to raise a fine family with Lara, to give himself and Beth fine Scottish grandchildren who would probably never know their grandfather's land, would never know Jarosbork ...

And the Jew, what of Anna's Jew? What of Leon? A knife twisted deep in his heart. Leon would never see that Promised Land he dreamt about; the only land he would ever see was those few square miles within the ghetto walls. Himmler was all set to send in his *Einsatzgruppen* to liquidate the few Jews still alive in this city. Leon would not even see the pink and white blossom fall from the trees in the Krasinski Gardens and the other green and pleasant places in this tortured city. Leon would be dead come summer, and Anna, his beloved Anna, with him.

Nothing was forever any more. Nothing ... But here, out of all this human misery, a miracle had occurred in this city tonight. He reached out and touched Beth's face with his fingertips, as if to reassure himself she was quite real. She had come. She had crossed a whole continent to be with him. Risked everything – for him. He had dreamt of this moment for so long, but never, not once had he believed it could ever come true. '*Kochanie* ... My love ... My only love ... '

They made love, tenderly, slowly, on the soft cushions of the settee. The world and its unending toil of human misery was forgotten for an enchanted hour when nothing and no one existed except each other.

It was as if they had never been apart, had never spent all those long, empty nights alone. They were not two separate, single souls, but one, as breath for breath, heart on heart, they were swept higher and higher on the crest of a love that consumed them body and soul. There was no need for words; they let their bodies speak – express all the yearning, all the love that had been pent-up within them for so long, so very long ...

Finally, when all passion was spent, she lay in his arms and told him of the weeks that had passed since her arrival in the city; of her shock at meeting Otto that evening.

He listened in silence, stroking the soft skin of her shoulder beneath the fur coat they had snuggled under to ward off the chill of the night. He felt a cold sick feeling in the pit of his stomach. She had gone through all that for him, had gambled with her life, been willing to submit to the unthinkable with those bastards just to gain some information that might be of use to his people. And now Otto knew – her once beloved stepson who was now one of Hitler's most despicable henchmen – knew. 'You must never appear on the streets of this city again, *kochanie*, never. It will be too dangerous.'

'You think he will betray me?'

His hand stroked the brown hair back from her brow. He was silent for several seconds. It was a question he could not answer. 'This is something we may never know.'

'But what shall I do? I can't just remain indoors. That's not what I came here for.'

'We must get you back to England as soon as possible.' The words almost stuck in his throat, but they had to be said. He could never concentrate on his own work behind the wall in the Jewish ghetto knowing she was in danger of falling into the hands of the Gestapo. Their net was tightening in the city. Raids, usually in the small hours of the morning, were now commonplace. Screams in the night, glass breaking, the crack of wood as doors were burst open, and always the

hoarse shouts of *"Raus, raus, ihr Saupolaken! Ein bisschen eilig!"* Then
came the distant revving of engines as the trucks with their terrified
human cargoes set off, rumbling over the cobbles, in the direction of
Szucha Avenue. She half sat up beneath the fur and stared down at
him in the darkness. 'No, I won't go. You can't make me. I won't
leave you, Jan. Not ever. Not now that I've found you again.
Whatever life has in store for us, we'll see it through together.' Her
voice, thick and intense with emotion, was quite emphatic.

'You make it hard for me, *kochanie*.'

She gave a half-smile in the darkness. 'I mean to. You won't get rid
of me, you know. I'm here to stay. Where you go, I go … If you go
over the wall tonight, or tomorrow night, then I go too.'

He pulled her back down beside him and kissed her brow as she
snuggled back into the warmth of his arms. 'You are a hard woman to
argue with, Beth Mallory. A hard woman … '

She fell asleep in his arms and awoke to find the pale morning sun
already illuminating the meagre furnishings of the room, and Jan
brewing a small pot of ersatz coffee on the one-ringed kerosene stove
in the walk-in cupboard that doubled as a kitchen.

'Did you sleep well, *kochanie?*' he called through at the sound of her
stirring.

She propped herself up on one elbow, a thrill running through her
at the mere sight of him. So she hadn't dreamt it … It was true. She
had found him! Her heart sang with joy at the knowledge. Dragging
her eyes from him, she glanced at her watch. It was just gone eight. 'I
must have been dead to the world,' she said, with a bemused shake of
the head. 'I haven't slept so soundly in weeks.'

'It'll do you good,' he smiled, handing her one of the cups of
steaming brown liquid he had just poured. 'Drink this. It may not be
the real thing, but at least it's hot and wet.'

She took it gratefully and sipped the contents as she looked up at
him. 'What's on the agenda for today, boss?'

He smiled and sat down on the bed beside her. 'If you are really
determined to be my comrade as well as my love, then perhaps it is
best you learn something of life over the wall for the Jews.'

She made herself more comfortable beside him, and took another
sip of the coffee as a shiver of anticipation ran through her. 'Fire
away. I'm listening.'

He lit a cigarette and drew on it deeply as he began, 'To survive
behind the wall you must be acquainted with how things are over
there. In the past two years over four hundred thousand people have

perished behind that wall – have died of starvation, disease, mass execution, or ritual extermination in Treblinka, or one of the other death camps. Four hundred thousand people, Beth – just think of it.' He paused, the figure hanging in the air between them.

Beth shook her head, trying to comprehend the enormity of the horror. 'But was there no resistance? Surely that number of people can't just allow themselves to be slaughtered?'

Jan gave a grim smile. 'Oh, there were one or two acts of resistance all right, but they came to very little. Last August, the Jewish Underground made an attempt to assassinate Jozef Szerynski, the commander of the Jewish Police in the ghetto, but the attempt failed. The bullet entered his left cheek and came straight out through the right one, without even grazing his tongue, teeth or palate. Incredible, no?' He gave a mirthless smile. 'They said he had the luck of the devil on his side, and who would argue?'

He sipped his coffee and fell silent for a moment, his thoughts returning to one of the many incidents that had prompted the assassination – an incident that he himself had been a witness to. It had taken place on the fifteenth of August last year. The round-ups for the transports to the camps were at their height and he had just delivered a consignment of supplies to Anna and Leon in Kozla Street. He was on his way across the roof-tops to the home of Henryk Zylberberg, one of the founding members of the newly-formed Jewish Fighting Organization, when he was stopped in his tracks. A crowd was gathered in the middle of the street beneath him. He recognized Henryk, his wife, and their small daughter Michaela amongst those forced from their homes at gun point, to become the victims of yet another round-up.

As he watched from his vantage point high on the sloping roof-tiles of a neighbouring building, the men were separated from the women and children, then the children from the women. Most of the little ones, too terrified to protest, allowed themselves to be taken without protest, but little Michaela clung to her mother's hand screaming, 'Mama, Mama!' A German corporal had then grabbed her by the arm and attempted to drag her away. But still the screaming child would not let go of her mother. Finally, the soldier got the little girl by the waist and succeeded in wrenching her fingers from her distraught mother, only to smash the child's head to pulp against the wall of the house.

It was exactly five days afterwards he heard that the Jewish Fighting Organization had carried out their first action, the attempted assassination of Szerynski. And Szerynski had escaped. But did it really make much difference? This city was full of Szerynskis. The child's screams filled his ears. Jan's eyes closed and his jaw clenched at the memory of the lifeless doll that had once been Michaela Zylberberg that was thrown on to the pavement, and of the bloodied patch on the wall that remained, a mute testament to man's inhumanity to man. One memory amongst so many that now scarred his mind from the hell of these past few years.

'Go on, my love. Go on.'

He collected himself and took another sip of the coffee. He met Beth's eyes. They were so full of love, so full of trust. Just how much of this continuing horror could he protect her from? It was a question he could not answer.

'Down to practicalities, my love ...' He reached inside his jacket and took out a pencil and a scrap of paper, which he balanced on his knee. 'I can't claim to be half the artist you are, but this will give you some idea ...'

He did a rough sketch on the page and beckoned her to come nearer and watch as he pointed out the important areas of the ghetto he had marked out. 'The Germans have divided it into three sections, and it is important that you memorize the street names of each one, for to be caught in the no-man's land between them means certain death ...'

She nodded, her eyes serious as they met his, and he continued. 'The first area, what we can call the "shop" area, forms a square bordered on one side by Lezno Street, and on the others by parts of Nowolipie, Nowolipiki, Karmelicka and Smocza streets. This area contains work places controlled by Germans, mainly armaments factories and the like, all manned by Jewish slave labour. The second area is that formed by the big brush factory blocks, with their workshops on Swientojerska and Walowa streets, and part of Francis-zanska Street. Here again the *Wehrmacht*, or their German placemen, are in charge. It is in this area, in Kozla Street, that Anna and Leon work in their makeshift clinic.'

'And the third?'

'The third area is known as the Central Ghetto, and it includes such streets as Stawki, Nalewki, Gesia, Zamenhofa, Mila, and Mura-nowska.' He gave a reassuring smile. 'I don't expect you to remember all these names tonight, but it's important that you at least hear them. This area contains several factories and the offices of the *Judenrat*. The spaces between the separate areas are out of bounds to Jews. In fact, the only people who dare cross them are members of the Underground – the resistance organizations.'

'It's not just you, is it? You're not the only Aryan helping them in there. I mean the AK has been active within the ghetto, hasn't it? I remember "Grot" getting in touch with the SOE in January to say that weapons were desperately needed there.'

Jan nodded. General Stefan Rowecki, code-name 'Grot', their commander-in-chief in the AK, had been on a desperate search for weapons for months, not just for the Jews, but for the Polish Underground itself. 'There are many Aryans risking their lives for others, although I must admit relations between the AK and the Jews could be better at times. But the Jews themselves are not always united; the Jewish Fighting Organization, which is the largest of the resistance groups within the ghetto has to work alongside the Yiddisher Militerisher Farband, and even Betar, the Zionist revisionist youth organization, and I can tell you the sparks often fly at their joint meetings.'

He sighed and sipped the bitter dregs of his coffee. 'All consist of very different men, with very different characters, but one sworn aim – to fight to the death.'

His voice lowered as he looked across at her. 'And that death is only days away, *kochanie*. Stroop, and the SS leader von Stammern, have been given orders by Himmler that Hitler must have a very special birthday present this year. This city must be completely *"judenrein"* – totally free of Jews – by 19 April, the day before the Führer's birthday. Dear Heinrich, our little fat SS slug wants to be able to go to his mad Austrian friend on the 20th and say, "Here you are, Adolf, the present you wanted – Poland's capital is rid of its Jewish menace, just as all Europe will be soon."'

Beth stared down into her cup. It was no more than she already knew. Yet he was prepared to go on risking his life day after day in a cause he knew in his heart was already lost. Surely there could be no greater sacrifice? She reached out and clasped his hand.

They sat in silence for a moment, then Beth said quietly, 'Before the twentieth of April, you say. It doesn't leave us very long.' Suddenly every second counted. She felt almost guilty to be sitting there enjoying her morning coffee with the situation beyond the wall so desperate. 'How soon are you planning on going back over there?'

He glanced at his watch. 'In about one hour's time.'

Her heart beat faster. 'You have a spare set of clothing I can borrow?'

He grinned, imagining her slight figure in his shirt and trousers. 'My wardrobe is hardly extensive, but you can have your pick.'

***

He smiled again when, half an hour later, he saw her dressed for the first time, in his spare dark-blue woollen jumper, grey flannel trousers and tweed jacket. Her long dark hair was piled inside a felt, peaked cap, and she looked for all the world like an eager young boy, as she looked expectantly at him. 'Well, boss, will I pass?'

He forced a sombre look to his face as he nodded slowly and eyed her from head to foot. 'You'll do, comrade. You'll do.'

The medical supplies they were to take with them were carried in two rucksacks strapped to their backs, and he helped her on with hers, making sure the canvas straps were not digging too hard into the soft flesh of her shoulders.

As they made for the door of the flat to make their way down to the cellars, he took something from an inside pocket and handed it to her. It felt cold and hard in her hand and she froze inwardly as she gazed down at it.

'Ever used a gun before?'

She gazed at the .38 Special revolver in her hand. 'They gave me a bit of rudimentary target practice at SOE, but I can't claim to be an expert.'

'I hope you won't have to be. But, for God's sake, don't hesitate to use it if the time ever comes. It's loaded. All you have to do is pull the trigger.'

She made no reply as she took the weapon and placed it in the right hand pocket of her jacket and followed him out of the door.

Chapter Forty-eight

Lara's eyes followed the rotund figure of her boss with more than usual concern as Winston Churchill paced the polished floor of his 10 Downing Street office. He had been overdoing it as usual, and she noted with some anxiety the puffiness around the eyes and the trace of wheeziness in the voice this morning. He had come back from Casablanca at the beginning of the year with a cold and sore throat which, by the end of February, had turned into a bad case of pneumonia. She had made as many tentative suggestions as she dared that he take it a bit easier, only to be brushed aside with an emphatic assurance that he had never felt better. To make matters worse at the moment, he was worried about his wife, Clemmie, who had been ordered down to the south coast resort of Weymouth by her doctor, for a ten day rest at the Royal Hotel. 'She's been doing far too much, you know, Lara. Far too much. But won't be told – and now look what's happened ... ' He was like a man with his right arm cut off. Lara knew he would not function properly until Clemmie was safely back in Downing Street, and she prayed that would come about before the Prime Minister's departure for Washington which was scheduled for two weeks' time, on 4 May.

This morning he was particularly agitated: he was awaiting the arrival of General Wladyslaw Sikorski, the chief of the Polish Free Forces, and Count Edward Raczynski, the Polish Ambassador to Great Britain. The meeting would not be an easy one. German Radio had just put the cat amongst the pigeons by broadcasting an allegation that seemed set to create real problems in an already strained relationship between the Polish Government in Exile in London and Britain's Soviet allies in the Kremlin. Lara knew her boss would need to summon up all his considerable powers of persuasion to pacify the Poles this morning, and she just hoped he was up to it.

She glanced down at the translation of the current bone of contention on the desk in front of her. It was dated three days previously, 13 April 1943, and headed: 'Communiqué issued by Berlin Broadcasting station on the discovery of graves of Polish officers in the Smolensk area.' The text ran:

'It is reported from Smolensk that the local population has indicated to the German authorities a place in which the Bolsheviks had perpetrated secretly mass executions and where the GPU had murdered 10,000 Polish officers. The German authorities inspected the place called Kosogory, which is a Soviet summer resting place, situated 12 kilometres west of Smolensk, and made the most horrific discovery. A great pit was found, 28 metres long and 16 metres wide, filled with 12 layers of bodies of Polish officers, numbering about 3,000. They were clad in full military uniform and, while many of them had their hands tied, all of them had wounds in the back of their necks caused by pistol shots. The identification of the bodies will not cause great difficulties because of the mummifying property of the soil and because the Bolsheviks had left on the bodies the identity documents of the victims ... The total figure of the murdered officers is estimated at 10,000, which would more or less correspond with the number of Polish officers taken as prisoners of war by the Bolsheviks ... '

'Grisly reading, eh?' Churchill remarked, seeing the look on her face as she reread the document. 'Damned inconvenient too. Of course the Russians are denying it vehemently, and why shouldn't they? Who in this world would take the Nazis' word for anything these days?'

'Sikorski and Raczynski would for two,' Sir Alexander Cadogan, the Permanent Under-Secretary of State at the Foreign Office, and the only other person present, put in. 'If it's possible for those two gentlemen to hate any race more than the Germans, then that race must be the Russians. And why shouldn't they? The Russians and Germans have caused more misery in Poland over the centuries than the rest of Europe put together. As they see it there's not much to choose between the two, and who can blame them?'

Churchill grunted. 'Well, as *I* see it, there's a great deal to choose between the two right now. The Russians are our allies and the Red Army and Stalin's cooperation in winning this war is as essential to us as that of Roosevelt and his lot.'

He paused by the desk to snip the end off another cigar and stabbed it in the direction of Cadogan. 'Whatever the truth of this horrific little episode, we have to regard it as no more than that, and do our best to pacify the Poles when they arrive. Sikorski and his band cannot be allowed to rock the Allies' boat – not now, not ever.'

His words still hung in the air when, a few minutes later, Poland's two leaders in exile were shown in. The gravity of their demeanours said it all. They were in no mood to take this revelation lying down.

Churchill, despite his air of affability, was tense as he resumed his seat behind the desk. His stubby fingers drummed on the blotter as the Polish Ambassador launched into a catalogue of grievances directed at the Soviets. 'It is not just this latest report, Prime Minister. Our patience is at an end. Moscow is waiting to devour our land piece by piece and we cannot and will not let it happen.' He waved a copy of the report of the massacre in the air. 'They have already begun with our people – our finest Army officers. How does one replace 10,000 such men? And how does one forgive the murderers, tell us that?'

Churchill grunted. His pale eyes were red-rimmed through lack of sleep and he was in no mood to enter into a heated discussion on the alleged Russian atrocity. He listened with scarcely disguised impatience as Edward Raczynski demanded urgent British action against the Soviets. 'Of course, Ambassador, of course. Leave it to us. I can assure you the matter will be taken up at the highest level.'

'With Stalin himself?' Sikorski cut in.

'Naturally.'

'And immediately?'

'You have my word on it. It is in all our interests that Britain should be allowed to mediate between yourselves and the Soviets on this matter. But we must tread carefully. It will do the Allied cause no good at all to provoke the Kremlin. Their help and goodwill is essential if we are to defeat Hitler.'

Sikorski looked decidedly unconvinced. 'For some of us, Prime Minister, there is little to choose between the Reichstag or the Kremlin.'

The atmosphere remained highly charged as the two Poles joined the Prime Minister and Alexander Cadogan for lunch in a room on the ground floor. Before the war it had been part of the servants' quarters, but was now transformed into a dining-room, its ceiling strengthened since the bombing raids of 1941 by several white-painted wooden beams.

Lara did not join them at the table, but sat quietly in the background taking notes. She required all her wits about her, for Churchill spoke occasionally in French. When English was used, Count Raczynski translated for the benefit of General Sikorski, who spoke little English.

During the soup course, the vexed question of Poland's borders was raised by General Sikorski. The Prime Minister was at pains to point out that while he agreed that Poland's strength and independence must be guaranteed after the war, her Eastern border would have to be revised in Russia's favour. 'You have my assurance that Poland will be amply compensated with former German-held territory in the West.'

Sikorski snorted and said in French: 'What you are saying is you will fob us off with German territory that will very quickly become a bone of contention once the war is over. Need we remind you of Alsace-Lorraine?'

The Prime Minister looked pained and refilled his wine glass from the carafe at his elbow and, as Lara's pencil sped over the page of her notebook, he declared, 'Bismarck is long dead, General. And as long as I live, I shall not depart from the principles which I have always respected, of individual freedom and the rights of large and small states to independence. My government will guarantee that.'

His guests remained silent, and from the looks on their faces Lara could only deduce they were far from convinced. Rhetoric was one thing, action quite another.

When, inevitably, the conversation turned once more to the revelation of the mass graves at Katyn, Raczynski and Sikorski were adamant that they had concrete proof of the responsibility of the Soviet Commissariat of Internal Affairs for the massacre. The Prime Minister listened sympathetically and promised once more to speak to Stalin on their behalf, but emphasized he would prefer to wait until after the major victory he expected in Tunis within the next few weeks.

Lara watched him carefully, looking for the tell-tale signs that he was simply saying what they wanted to hear. She had now spent so much time in his company that she could usually tell quite easily when he was being less than genuine. Within herself she felt distinctly uneasy about Britain's commitment to aiding the Poles. She had been in Downing Street long enough to know that the British were no different from any other country when it came to pursuing their own interests to the detriment of others.

The Prime Minister's assurances appeared to be accepted at face value, however, for, despite their private misgivings, neither of the Poles demurred too loudly and the lunch broke up quite amicably around two o'clock.

On the way out, to her surprise, the Ambassador, Count Raczynski, took Lara aside for a moment and asked quietly, 'You have had word of your mother recently, my dear?'

She shook her head. 'I'm afraid not. To be honest, I haven't heard anything positive other than that the original drop was successful and she left her first safe house the following day for Warsaw.'

The Count's brows rose. 'But that is most unfortunate. I am sure we have had news more recently than that – in the past few days, in fact. Why don't you call at Portland Place when you come off duty? I'm sure something came in from the AK in Warsaw recently that would be of interest to you.'

Lara's spirits rose immediately. 'Why, thank you, Count. I will. I certainly will.'

She watched the two men leave, a wistful expression on her face. They were Poles, just like her own father – Jan Jarosinski – the man she knew her mother had gone to Poland to seek out. Yes, that had been Beth's real reason for going, she was sure of that, despite her initial protestations about serving the war effort and the Polish nation at large.

With the prospect of news of her mother in the offing, the rest of the day seemed to drag past, taken up mainly with the drafting of a letter to Stalin, which Lara noted with concern made no mention of Katyn. Instead the Prime Minister explained that a short pause was now necessary in Tunisia so that General Alexander could regroup his armies in the north, and to make time for Montgomery to bring up the mass of artillery which he habitually used in his battles. Very soon, he pointed out, the biggest battle of the war would begin, and it would not stop until Africa was cleared of Axis forces.

He also commented on 'three good blows' the RAF had inflicted in Europe: on Spezia, Stuttgart, and the Skoda works at Pilsen and Mannheim. Lara noted he seemed to take particular pleasure in giving details of the raid on Stuttgart, which he categorized as 'a flaming success'. The RAF had lost 81 bombers and 'about 500 highly-trained personnel' in those three raids alone, but the losses were brushed aside as Churchill concentrated on impressing his opposite number in the Kremlin that 'the attacks will continue throughout the summer on an ever increasing scale.'

Her fingers froze on the page and she had great difficulty keeping her concentration as she translated the Prime Minister's words into impeccable Pitman's – 81 bombers and about 500 highly-trained personnel ... As she scribbled the details, she was no longer in the elegant office at 10 Downing Street, but back in the Special Burns Unit at East Grinstead. How many Kens would emerge from those raids? How many other young men would lose their lives or, almost worse, would be so badly injured that they became not only totally unrecognizable to their loved ones, but to themselves as well?

It was a question she could never ask – not here in Downing Street anyway. To do so would be to question the very morality of war itself. Aiding and abetting the enemy by lowering morale was what she would be accused of doing, so she must keep silent and ponder on such questions alone in the silence of her room as she lay awake night after night and thought about the future ... The future – a shudder would run through her at the very word.

Her visits to Ken had become even more painful of late. It wasn't that she didn't try. God knows, in those long hours she spent lying awake every night, she would rehearse the right things to say – things that might, just might, jog him out of the terrible depression into which he seemed to be sinking. It was all she could do, but it was not, and never could be enough. Only he could come to terms with what had happened to him – to them and their future after this hell of a war was over. Would it ever be over? Sometimes she doubted even that.

A sigh ran through her as she closed her notebook for the day and said her goodbyes to her boss and the others that made up the cosy little circle of power that was 10 Downing Street. She glanced at her watch. She was almost an hour late in finishing. If she took up the Count's invitation to drop in to the Embassy at Portland Place now she would be late for Ken, yet she was dying to get word of her mother.

Her brow was still furrowed as she hailed a taxi a few minutes later. Would he understand if she came by a later train? He never said anything when she was late, but the hurt in his eyes was plain to see. When you had to spend all day totally immobile in a hospital bed, an extra hour spent waiting for the highlight of your day could seem like forever. Dare she spare the time?

She slid into the back seat of the Hackney and stared in confusion at the back of the balding head in front of her as the driver asked, 'Where to, Miss?'

She took a deep breath. 'Portland Place, please – the Polish Embassy.' She sank back on the worn hide upholstery. She had made the decision. She would just have to be even more profuse than usual in her apologies when she eventually arrived at East Grinstead.

Count Raczynski was preparing to go out to dinner with his wife Cesia and a party of 'Friends of Poland', as he termed it, when Lara arrived. 'My dear, forgive me if I do not stay to brief you personally, but I have left details with my secretary. I told him you might call in and he will have what little news we have written down waiting for you. I fear it is not much, but I expect even a word will be welcome in the circumstances, no?'

Lara nodded gratefully. 'Oh, yes, absolutely.'

She made her way up the sweeping staircase with a lighter heart. Just to know that her mother was still alive was all she asked. Just that. Nothing more.

The Count's secretary occupied a smaller room to the right of his chief's. The door was half-open, but she knocked all the same, and tapped her foot impatiently on the landing carpet as she awaited the invitation to enter. The sooner she got the information, the sooner she could catch the train down to East Grinstead.

'Ah ... *tak* ... Mrs Cameron, the Ambassador said you might call ... ' The secretary looked up from behind the overloaded desk as Lara entered, but her eyes were not on the small, bespectacled man with the thinning grey hair. They were on a much taller, broader figure standing by the window. A tall figure, resplendent in full evening dress. It was the first time in a long time she had seen him in anything but military uniform.

'Hello, Lara.'

'Mike ... ' She mouthed his name rather than spoke it as she stared in astonishment at the familiar, twinkling eyes.

'The information, Mrs Cameron – it is in here.' The secretary was handing her an envelope. She took it mechanically, murmuring her thanks, as her gaze remained rooted on the face still smiling down into hers.

She stood tongue-tied and totally unable to move a muscle, unsure whether to run into his arms or run out of the door.

'You – you have met General Adams before?' the secretary asked tentatively, not quite sure how to read her shell-shocked expression.

She nodded, still speechless, as Mike intervened. 'I have had the pleasure of making the acquaintance of both Mrs Cameron and her mother on previous visits to London,' he said, coming round the side of the desk and extending his hand in Lara's direction. 'How are you, Lara? You look well.'

She had quite forgotten how blue his eyes were. Only three short months and she had quite forgotten. 'I – I'm fine, thank you.' What a relief she was wearing a loose fitting jacket so he could not see the thickening of her waistline. Her hand was in his and his skin was warm to the touch.

'Your hand is cold,' he said, that quirky smile still there.

She gave a shrug of the shoulders. 'It – it's quite cold out, for April.' She gave a slight pull and released her hand from his. They stood looking at one another in front of the bemused gaze of the secretary, as embarrassment sent the colour surging into her cheeks.

'And how is your mother – and your husband?' He was going through the motions and they both knew it.

She took a deep breath. How did she answer that one? 'They – they're fine, just fine, thank you.' She glanced down at the envelope in her hands. This was not the time or place to open it; not with *him* standing there gazing at her like that. She began to back towards the door. She felt confused, angry even, that this should have happened. He said he would never come back here, would never enter into her life again, yet excitement at seeing him again tingled in every pore.

He followed her out into the passage and grabbed hold of her arm as she attempted to flee down the stairs. 'Don't go, Lara. Not yet …'

She turned to face him, her eyes searching his for some vestige of understanding as she pleaded, 'Please, Mike, let me go … Please … I must go …'

'What's the hurry? You can spare a couple of minutes, can't you? Don't tell me you have a train to catch.'

She wrenched her arm from his grasp. 'I have, as a matter of fact. That's exactly what I have.'

He looked at her long and hard, then obviously decided she was telling the truth. 'Where are you headed?'

'East Grinstead.' It seemed useless lying.

'And you were going by train?'

She nodded. 'You know that petrol is almost impossible to come by.'

'I'll drive you.'

'No!' She almost shouted the word. 'There's no need, honestly.'

She was backing away from him towards the stairs, but he followed. 'I know there's no need,' he said through gritted teeth. 'It's something I *want* to do, for Chrissake. Now will you let me drive you down there, or do I have to make a scene?'

She glanced around her in apprehension. He would too, she had no doubt about it. Already people were turning to look curiously at the tall, evening-suited American and the obviously embarrassed young woman blocking the top of the staircase. 'Aren't you going out? You look like you're dressed for this "do" the Count is going to tonight.'

'The "do" can wait.'

She sighed. There was no way she was going to win this argument. But did she really want to? She was sure of nothing any more, but the nervous churning of her stomach as she looked at him. 'All right then, if you insist.'

'Your enthusiasm bowls me over,' he said with a rueful grin as he took her arm and walked with her back down the staircase.

Once outside, it felt curiously comforting to slip into the front passenger seat of the Packard beside him. It was something she had done so often in the past. The past ... She stole a look at him as he drew the car away from the kerb. Without his military cap, the silver hairs at the temple were more obvious now, and his face had a leaner, more careworn look. She wondered if he was taking care of himself enough back in Washington, but daren't ask. That was the sort of personal question that must be avoided at all costs.

For a few minutes neither spoke as he negotiated the worst of the traffic. Then, once they were out of most of the bomb damage and headed for the southern outskirts of the city, he lit a cigarette and glanced across at her. 'So, how have you been these past few months? That's the polite thing to ask, isn't it – now that we're mere acquaintances again?' There was no disguising the bitter edge to his voice.

She took a deep breath and shrugged her shoulders. 'I've been very well, thank you.' She knew her answer sounded unbearably prim, and it was so far from the truth she was almost inclined to laugh. If only he could have witnessed the mornings over these past few months when she felt so nauseated with sickness that she thought she would never make it through the day. Nauseated with morning sickness because of the child she was carrying – his child.

'And your Mom?'

She was silent for a moment, unsure of whether to tell the truth or not. But if she couldn't trust him, who could she trust? 'Mum's in Poland,' she said quietly. 'On a mission for the SOE.'

'Jeee-zuz!' He let out a long low whistle. 'You've got to be kidding!'

She shook her head miserably. 'I only wish I were. That's why I was there tonight, at the Embassy. The Ambassador was in Downing Street today to see the Prime Minister – he told me they had some news of her.' She fingered the precious envelope in the pocket of her jacket. 'I certainly didn't expect to find you when I got to Portland Place.'

He gave a strained smile. 'And you would probably never have known I was in London if you hadn't called in there tonight. I've been here for the past week. I'm heading home tomorrow.'

A wave of disappointment mixed with an irrational hurt flooded through her. Irrational because she knew they had resolved never to see one another again, and he had done no more than keep to that decision. 'I see.'

'Yes, I've been doing some arm twisting back home for the Polish cause and was merely following up over here in person. FDR's been getting edgy. You know that relations between the Soviets and the Poles have been deteriorating these past few months ...'

'So you've been sent over to smooth things out. To tell the Poles over here that Big Brother across the Atlantic insists they kiss and make up with the Russians, or else.'

He gave a wry laugh. 'You're a cynic, Mrs Cameron, you know that? But it's not too far from the truth ... And, hell, I may be half Polish myself, but that doesn't stop me from doing some straight talking to Sikorski and his lot. Even I can see why Old Joe in the Kremlin is feeling pretty aggrieved of late. Look at it from his point of view: we have broken off the convoys; got bogged down in North Africa and let the Red Army do the brunt of the winter fighting in Europe; we've even got him to forswear the cause of world revolution, even though he had sworn over Lenin's dead body never to abandon the concept ... All that and yet still no Second Front. And now, as they see it, the London Poles – reactionaries every last man of them – are belly-aching about not losing an inch of territory in the east, and Sikorski is collaborating with Hitler's gangsters in trying to pin the guilt for the Katyn massacre on them.'

'You've got your work cut out trying to pour oil on all these troubled waters, I can see that,' she said. 'But I get the distinct impression you're quite enjoying it. You're doing what you're best at – playing the diplomat.'

His laugh had a bitter edge to it. 'What is diplomacy but "lying in State"? It just so happens some of us lie better than others, I guess ... Wheeling and dealing, that's all there is to so-called power politics, Lara. Wheeling and dealing.'

'With all this experience, you should make a fortune on Wall Street once this is over.'

He made no reply. He had never allowed himself to think beyond the end of the war any more. The future no longer held any personal excitement for him. Casablanca had seen to that. He changed the drift of the conversation away from himself. 'You didn't say why you're headed for East Grinstead.'

She tensed in her seat. 'I – I'm going to visit Ken.'

'I see.' Her reply was like a physical stab of pain in his guts. He was silent for a moment, then good manners got the better of him. 'He – he's doing OK these days, huh? He's still enjoying the flying?'

She looked down at her hands clasped tightly in her lap. 'He was shot down,' she said in a quiet voice. 'He's in the Special Burns Unit

402

at the Queen Victoria Hospital down there.'

His hands gripped more tightly on the steering-wheel, the knuckles showing white beneath the lightly tanned skin. 'The Special Burns Unit. He's pretty bad, then.'

'He's pretty bad.' Her voice was a whisper.

The conversation came to an embarrassed stop. When it resumed several minutes later it was along totally impersonal lines. They exchanged views on how the war was going in general and what films they had seen recently. The closest they got to an emotive question was when he asked if she'd ever got round to seeing *Casablanca*. She answered in the affirmative and there the subject ended, both longing for it to continue, yet determined not to be the one to break their promise not to make it difficult for the other.

He waited for her in the parking area outside the front door of the hospital. She had protested, but he was adamant. ' ... Anyway, the trains are always full of troops these days. But maybe you kinda like the idea of having your ass pinched at least twenty times in the half-hour journey?' She grinned and shook her head. He usually did have the last word.

He watched her disappear into the main door, a neat figure in her swagger jacket, holding on to her jaunty hat against the fresh evening breeze that twisted her skirt around her slim calves.

Long after she was out of sight, he continued to stare after her, imprinting those few seconds on his memory – one more memory to unlock from his treasure house of memories in the wee small hours of the morning when he lay in his Washington apartment and wondered ... wondered what she was doing, if she was still alone like him, or if she was together again with her husband.

He stared even harder at the closed door and gripped the cigarette between his thumb and forefinger that bit tighter. He would not wish to relive these past couple of months. The pain of that parting in Casablanca was still a livid sore within him; a livid sore that had made him determined not even to try to get in touch during this week in London. It had not been his wish to make the long journey across the Atlantic. On the contrary, when he left North Africa he had been determined never to set foot in England again if he could help it. But events had a habit of overruling personal wishes when you were in this game. The deteriorating relations between the London Poles and the Russians, and Churchill's impending visit to Washington had seen to that. 'There's no one better suited to assess the true situation over there and gen us up before Winnie gets here, Mike,' FDR had said, and who was he to argue with his President?

So here he was. He sighed and drew slowly on the cigarette. Here he was in the worst of all possible situations. Not only had he run into her again, he was sitting here waiting for her to visit her husband in hospital.

How he had hated Ken Cameron – really hated him for being her husband. And now ... His jaw clenched as he exhaled a long stream of smoke through gritted teeth and stubbed the cigarette out roughly in the ashtray on the dashboard ... The Special Burns Unit, she had said ...

And now he felt like the biggest jerk in Christendom.

Chapter Forty-nine

'Who is it? Who brought you?'

Lara had to lean right over the bed to make out the words. Weeks of healing had tightened and puckered the skin around the aperture that had once been her husband's mouth, making speech even more of an effort. She frowned at the question, but her heart was beating faster despite the innocent expression on her face. 'Wh – what do you mean, darling?'

'Who's out there?' His voice, still barely recognizable, had an irritable edge.

She glanced in apprehension towards the window, then back to Ken. A young nurse had been by his bed when she arrived. She must have seen her get out of Mike's car and told him. Embarrassment flooded her cheeks. 'Oh, it – it's only Mike Adams ... You remember – the American I used to work for ...' She was aware of him looking at her intently, staring up at her from the pillow as she continued much too quickly, 'I ran into him tonight, quite unexpectedly, at the Polish Embassy when I went to enquire about my mother.'

There was an ominous silence for a moment. Perhaps she should explain more. But what could she say? How *could* she explain why her ex-boss had dropped everything to run her down here tonight? Then, with relief, she remembered that Ken didn't know Mike had a previous engagement, didn't know about the 'do' being given by the Ambassador.

'Ask him in.'

'What?'

'The American – ask him in.'

The words were quite unmistakable. She stared at him in dismay. This was the last thing she wanted to happen. She forced a smile to her lips as she pulled up a chair by the side of the bed and sat down.

'But, darling ... Well, you know how men are about hospitals. I'm sure he'd much rather wait in the car.'

'Ask him in.'

This time the words had a vehemence behind them that quite shocked her. He didn't suspect, did he? How could he? Mike had been back in the States for over two years. Give or take Casablanca ... She looked across at him, making no move, but the expression in his eyes brooked no further argument. She rose from the seat. 'Of course, my love. If that's what you really want.'

She was sure she heard a satisfied sigh as she hurriedly left the bedside and walked quickly back down the ward and out through the swing doors. She felt numb. Completely numb. God only knew how Mike would react. It was bad enough being asked to face your lover's husband under normal circumstances, but now ...

She was breathless when she reached the car. Mike was leaning with one elbow out of the open window, smoking a cigarette. He looked up quizzically as she approached. 'That was a short visit.'

'He wants to see you.'

'What?'

'He wants to see you.'

'What do you mean, he wants to see me?' The shock reflected itself in both his voice and face. 'How the hell does he know I'm here?'

She shrugged helplessly. 'One of the nurses must have told him. Someone must have seen me get out of the car.'

'Jesus, Holy Mary and Joseph!' He stubbed what was left of the cigarette out, then turned to her once more. 'What do you want me to do?'

'I don't see that we have any choice, do you? He knows you're here and says he wants to see you.'

'Do you think he suspects we're having an affair?'

She grimaced. The expression jarred on her sensibilities. '*Were* having an affair,' she corrected bitterly. 'It's over, remember.'

They looked at one another, their eyes locked in a glance that mirrored the confusion and torment they both felt at this moment, then Mike made a half-hearted attempt at a smile. 'Well, I guess we'd better do as he asks. Can't say I'm exactly looking forward to it, though.'

She waited as he got out of the car and locked it. Now was the time to say something – to warn him about Ken's injuries. This was no ordinary hospital ward he was heading for. This was like nothing he had ever experienced before. She put out a hand and touched his arm

406

as they made for the hospital entrance. 'Mike, I think I should warn you, he looks pretty bad. Very bad, actually.'

Mike said nothing, but his expression was grim as they entered the main door and headed in the direction of the ward.

As they reached the grey metal swing doors of the ward itself, she took hold of his arm once more. 'Wait,' she said softly. 'Wait a moment and just take a look in.' It was important that he prepare himself.

He did as she asked and she was aware of the sharp intake of breath as he peered through one of the round windows. He would not recognize Ken, of course, but just one look at any of those young men in there would make the most war-hardened heart miss a beat. When he turned to look at her he had gone quite pale beneath his tan, and there was real pain in the blue eyes that met hers.

'I'll go in first, you follow,' she said quietly.

They were only part of the way down the ward when they were met by the Sister coming the other way. She glanced at her watch. 'I'm afraid it's rather late for visitors,' she said to Lara, with an apologetic look directed at Mike. 'A couple of minutes at the most is all I can allow tonight, I'm sorry. Normally we're not too strict if visitors miss the proper visiting hours – what with air-raids and cancelled train and bus services, one can't be too strict, but your husband is due an assessment examination tomorrow morning, Mrs Cameron. Dr McIndoe is keen to begin with his surgery as soon as possible. It's important the patients get a good night's rest before such a tiring morning – not too much excitement, you understand.'

Lara nodded. 'Of course, I quite understand. Two minutes it will have to be. I presume you'll fill me in with all the details of any prospective operation when I come tomorrow evening?'

The Sister nodded. 'Just call into my office before you see your husband and I should have some definite news for you.'

'Will that please him – that he's to begin surgery?' Mike asked as they watched the Sister disappear back down the ward.

Lara shrugged. 'I don't know. I really don't.' It was the truth. She no longer knew her husband; she could only make guesses at what went on behind the features of that mutilated face. What was on his mind now, at this moment, as she approached his bed with another man?

They were only a few feet from the bed before Ken's eyes swivelled to look at them. Sensing Mike's discomfort, Lara took the lead in breaking the ice, as she leaned over the bed and placed the lightest of kisses on top of her husband's head. 'You two remember each other, don't you?' she said lightly, forcing a smile to her lips. 'Christmas 1940, wasn't it?'

'How are you doing, buddy?' Mike hovered at the foot of the bed, his eyes riveted on Ken's, the only part of him that was recognizable as the husband of the woman he loved.

'Never better.' It was the nearest Ken had come to a joke since the accident.

'Sister says you're to see Dr McIndoe tomorrow,' Lara put in, relieved that the ice had been broken between the two men. 'She says he may operate soon.'

Ken ignored the interjection. 'You here on business?' His eyes were still on Mike, and the words came out with difficulty; the tightening of the skin around his mouth causing his words to slur and saliva to dribble from one corner.

The American shifted from one foot to the other. 'Yes, I've been here for a week – seeing the Poles mainly.'

'Speaking softly and wielding a big stick.' History had been one of Ken's strong points back home at the Grove Academy in Broughty Ferry.

Mike grinned, recognizing the credo of Theodore, the first President Roosevelt. 'Yeah, something like that. But I'm headed back to Washington tomorrow.'

'And tonight?'

Embarrassment flickered across the American's face as he launched into his excuse for being there. 'Well, I expect Lara's told you, I ran into her at the Polish Embassy and it was the least I could do to offer her a lift ...'

'And take her to dinner,' Ken cut in.

'Pardon me?' Mike leaned forward to catch the slurred words.

'Take her to dinner. It's the least you can do. You're dressed for it, aren't you?'

Mike glanced down at his dinner suit. 'Well, yes, but ...'

'I can't do it myself. I'm tied to this bloody bed,' Ken's voice was saying as Mike caught Lara's eye. She looked away immediately, putting a reassuring hand on her husband's arm as he continued, 'God knows when I'll ever be able to do it again.' Tears sprang to the grey-blue of his eyes as they did so often these days. He could not wipe them away and they ran in two rivulets down the swollen flesh.

'Sure I'll take her out,' Mike put in quickly. 'It'll be my pleasure. She'll have the best dinner in town.'

A satisfied sigh came from the pillow. He had done something for her, even if only by proxy. She came here every evening, never missing one, to sit by his bed and do her best to put some cheer into the sameness of life here at Queen Victoria's. The tiredness in her face and voice was usually all too evident. Heaven only knew when she had last had a meal out in a proper hotel, and she seemed to get on well enough with the American. Yes, he had done something this evening that she would thank him for when she went to bed tonight. She needed something to take her out of herself, some lively company and, from what he could remember, her old boss could provide just that.

At that moment, to Lara's barely disguised relief, a discreet gesture from the Sister at the end of the ward indicated that the two minutes were up. She leaned over and placed her hand on Ken's shoulder. 'We have to go. Sister will be throwing us out if we stay any longer.'

Ken's eyes darted to the direction of the door where, sure enough, the Sister was standing. He looked across at Mike. 'Remember now, the best in town.'

Mike came round the side of the bed. He wanted to reach out, to shake his hand, or simply put a hand on his shoulder, to tell him he understood. But did he? Could anyone ever understand what it must be like to lie there imprisoned in that disfigured carcass? His hands remained helpless at his sides. 'Don't worry, buddy, I'll see that she gets the best dinner in town.'

Ken nodded imperceptibly. 'And champagne.'

'And champagne by the jeroboam, if she wants it.'

'Thanks, mate.'

As they made their way back out to the car, Lara's head whirled. There was no way she could let that happen, no way she could let Mike take her out to dinner. And he would realize that too. He must, surely?

She slid into the passenger seat beside him and waited until the car was on its way back towards London before she put the question. 'You do feel the same, don't you?' she asked, in what sounded like an overly defensive voice. 'We can't possibly do what he asked. It – it wouldn't be right somehow.'

'Too true it wouldn't be right. But it was hardly right when we did the dirty on him out there in North Africa, was it? It was hardly right then ...' He was verbally flagellating himself – and her – for what had happened, and she could understand it. She kept silent and he continued bitterly. 'Christ, what a mess! My life's a mess, your life is a mess and, God help him, Ken's is a mess – the whole goddam world is a mess!'

He reached inside the pocket of his jacket and pulled out a cigarette packet. He lit one one-handed, dragging on it despairingly as he pondered on the situation. He shouldn't have allowed himself to drive her down to the hospital, he knew that now. But hindsight was a luxury neither could afford. What he had seen in that ward had shocked him to the core. That poor guy – that poor, poor guy! 'How the hell will you cope with it?'

She knew exactly what he meant. 'I don't know. I just don't and that's the truth,' she answered helplessly. 'We'll just have to learn to live with it, I suppose. And we won't be the only ones. There will be thousands like us, millions probably, before this war is over.' She paused, then continued defiantly, 'I'll continue to work, of course. I'll earn enough to keep us both.'

'It's just as well you haven't any kids, then, isn't it?'

It was meant as a consoling remark, but it brought her back to reality with a thud. Dear God, the baby ... She glanced across at Mike, but his attention was taken up with an approaching convoy of Army trucks. What on earth would she do about the baby? Automatically her hand went to the growing bulge of her stomach beneath the loose swagger jacket. Already it was becoming too obvious to hide and she had to choose her clothes with care. She stared out of the side window of the Packard as a deep gloom overwhelmed her. The very knowledge of it would kill Ken. She was sure of it. Life was tough enough for him coping with his injuries without having to live with the knowledge that his wife had been unfaithful, was carrying another man's child ... And the father of that child, what of him? Was it fair to allow him to go through life never knowing his son or daughter?

'What do you suggest we do then, disappoint him?'

His voice interrupted the bleakness of her thoughts and she looked round in confusion. 'Oh – the meal ... I – I really don't know. What do you think?'

'If you must know, I think I've already been a big enough jerk to the guy. If I took you out for a meal, I'd only want to make love to you afterwards.'

He was speaking the truth and she knew it. She nodded miserably and stared out of the window as the last of the trucks trundled by.

They barely spoke another word on the rest of the journey back to London. When it was obvious the car was heading straight for Lower Belgrave Street, her brows rose slightly. 'You knew I was still there.'

'There's very little I don't know about you, Mrs Cameron.'

She did not respond. He might very well know her official personal file at the Foreign Office off by heart – American Intelligence had a way of finding out these things – but there was one thing he did not know, and would never know. Her hand moved back protectively to her stomach and the baby within.

The familiar streets sped past, grey and monotonous, some with great gaping holes – reminders of the ever-present threat of the *Luftwaffe* in the darkening skies above them. She would be home any minute now. Home? Her lips twisted wryly at the thought. It was not even her own flat; it belonged to the American Embassy. It was a collection of empty rooms full of furniture that did not belong to her; empty rooms that merely echoed the emptiness in her heart. Her mother was a thousand miles away in an occupied country, searching for her father – a man she had never really known; her husband was lying back in East Grinstead, a prisoner within a mutilated body; and the man she loved was on his way back to America, totally unaware that she was carrying his child beneath her heart.

A light spring rain was beginning to fall. It spattered on the windscreen of the car and ran down the glass in small rivulets of endless tears that mirrored those in her heart. 'Just drop me at the corner,' she said quietly.

He obeyed her request a few minutes later, and they looked at one another as the car drew up at the kerb. He kept the engine running and leaned on the wheel with one arm as he turned to face her. His eyes were a misty blue in the semi-darkness. He attempted that funny, quirky grin that she had once known so well. 'It's been a helluva evening one way or another, hasn't it, Mrs C.?' he said quietly.

She nodded, barely trusting herself to speak. 'A helluva evening, General,' she answered softly, then opened the car door and disappeared out into the night.

Chapter Fifty

The changeable, blustery days of spring gave way to summer and, as the golden laburnum blossoms browned on the trees in St James's Park, and the first roses burst into bloom in the immaculate flower-beds, Lara faced the warmer weather with little enthusiasm. She had got out of the Prime Minister's May visit to Washington by using her pregnancy as the excuse. It was not the whole truth: physically she had never felt better now that the morning sickness was a thing of the past. The real reason behind her decision to remain in London was that she could not take the risk of running into Mike. And run into him she certainly would have done, for the Prime Minister himself was the conveyor of the American's good wishes after his return to London on the morning of Saturday 5 June.

'A fine man that General Adams,' Churchill had commented, as she settled down for her first day's dictation just after lunch the following Monday. 'Speaks some sound common sense. I took to that Hopkins fellow, of course. A straight talker if ever there was one, but it seems to me that Adams has got a firmer grasp of realities – more of a European outlook on things. Make a damned good President if anything should happen to Roosevelt.'

Lara had looked up askance. 'You don't really think it's a possi-bility, do you?' The thought had never even entered her head.

The Prime Minister had looked at her over the top of his spectacles and given a shrug of his ample shoulders. 'Depends, dear girl. Depends on many things. Funny business American politics -- not like over here. Money's the thing across the Atlantic. It costs more almighty dollars than most men could earn in a lifetime to run a Presidential campaign and hope to win enough votes even to get selected. One thing's for sure, though, they'll go for a military man next time round, and if it's not Adams, then it'll be Eisenhower, or MacArthur, or one of the others.'

She had sunk into silence. That Mike might run for the Presidency had never even occurred to her. But what the Prime Minister said had made sense, and a strangely wistful feeling pervaded her mind as she listened to him relate his impressions of this latest trip across the Atlantic. As usual, though, in Churchill's presence, one never had long to dwell on personal issues. He immediately digressed into what he saw as the worryingly mechanical development of American civilization. 'Two Americans came over on the plane with us,' he said, watching a cloud of cigar smoke drift lazily to the ceiling, then eyeing her over the top of his spectacles. 'They were talking about which towns to visit. One said, "I reckon we ought to go see Coventry. They say a naked woman rides through the streets there on a horse." His companion agreed wholeheartedly. "Sure thing. A great idea. I haven't seen a horse in years."'

She was forced to smile and punned, 'You're sure that's not an old chestnut?'

His denial was quite emphatic, then he grinned. 'Old chestnuts, like old wine and old friends, can often be the best, Lara, my dear. Remember that.'

But it was to one American in particular that her mind returned as she hurried towards the station after work on her way to catch the train to East Grinstead. The Prime Minister's remarks about Mike's possible candidacy for the Presidency had shaken her more than she cared to admit. He was moving out of her orbit – way out of her orbit – now. He was a highly respected man both in Washington and London. Many of the Communiqués that arrived on her desk from across the Atlantic had his initials at the foot, and every time she heard his name referred to during a Cabinet meeting she longed to shout out, 'That's the man I love you're talking about, the man who loved me, the man whose child I'm carrying.' But she never did. Instead she remained a silent witness in the background, scribbling into her shorthand notebook, then neatly typing up her notes every evening before catching the train to visit her husband in East Grinstead.

They all thought the baby was Ken's, of course. The whole world thought it was Ken's – except Ken himself. She knew he had suspected something for the past couple of weeks, for her expanding waistline was becoming increasingly difficult to disguise; but try as she might, she could not bring herself to raise the subject. To begin with she had promised herself that she would wait until after his first series of operations, thinking he would feel better once they were under way, would cheer up at any visible improvement in his appearance. But that hadn't happened. Instead he had come out of the theatre to yet more weeks of agony and uncertainty as they waited to see whether the grafts had taken.

She seemed to spend her life saving up every little amusing anecdote she came across to recount to him in the evenings as she sat at his bedside and watched the unbidden tears glisten from time to time in the grey-blue eyes. All too often he was lost in his own thoughts, in a private world she could never hope to enter. All she could do was to sit there and do her very best to bring a smile, if not to his face, then to his heart. One of the main perks of working for the Prime Minister was that there was no better teller of tales in London, and she mentally filed away the one about the two Americans for retelling to Ken later that evening. Then, if her courage did not fail her yet again, she would bring the subject round to her pregnancy.

It began to rain as she walked the last few yards up to the main entrance of Queen Victoria's, and the weather seemed to reflect her mood perfectly as she pondered on the best way to approach the subject. Just how did you tell your husband you were expecting another man's child? Never in her wildest dreams had she ever imagined she would find herself in this situation. But, in a peculiar way, it wasn't the physical act of infidelity that caused her most guilt, but the emotional betrayal. To have fallen in love with another man, more deeply, more passionately in love than she had ever been with her husband – well, that was the really hard part to live with. Not that Ken would see it that way, for he would never know. No one would ever know the feelings for Mike Adams that she kept hidden in her heart. No, all Ken would see was the physical evidence, both now and later, when the infant she carried within her became a living reminder of that betrayal.

By the time she had reached the door of the ward, her courage was disappearing fast. Perhaps she should not volunteer her confession. Perhaps she should let him bring it up. After all, the child was not due till some time in late September. But that was merely putting off the evil moment. Her mind reeled. She was not sure of anything any more.

'Mrs Cameron!'

Lara turned, her hand on the ward door, to see the Sister hurrying down the corridor towards her.

'Mrs Cameron ...' she was quite out of breath. 'I've been waiting to catch you. Would you mind accompanying me to my office, my dear.'

Lara frowned. In all the weeks of coming here she had never been called 'my dear' by Sister Melville before. 'Is anything wrong?'

Her question was ignored as the Sister led the way into the small ante-room that was used for the administration of the Special Burns Unit. 'Sit down, my dear.'

Lara obeyed as a cold chill of fear ran through her. 'Is anything wrong? It's not Ken, is it? He wasn't due an operation today?' Surely she wouldn't have forgotten something as important as that?

Sister Melville did not sit down behind her desk, but perched herself on the edge of the other visitors' chair opposite Lara's. Her hands were clasped in her lap and there was no mistaking she was nervous about something. She looked down at her clasped hands for a moment, then looked up to meet Lara's concerned gaze. 'Mrs Cameron, you've been coming here long enough to know that this is no ordinary part of the hospital. The patients here have special problems. It is not only the bodily wounds they have to come to terms with, but the mental scars of finding themselves locked within a body that no longer bears any resemblance to their own, a body that can very often no longer even function as a body ...' She paused, and took a deep breath before continuing. 'Of course there are varying degrees to which individual patients are affected, but I think you realize your husband was one of the worst to have been admitted here.'

'*Was* one of the worst?' Lara scarcely recognized her own voice. 'What do you mean *was* one of the worst?'

Sister Melville's hands twisted nervously in her lap. 'Ken died this afternoon, Mrs Cameron ... At his own hand.'

Lara stared at her. This had to be some kind of a sick joke. Ken was getting better. Maybe not obviously, but he was getting better. These operations he had been going through – they must have been doing some good. She got up from the chair and began to back towards the door. 'No, I can't believe it. These things don't happen – not in hospital. A hospital's a place where they come to get better – not to commit suicide!'

The Sister stood up too and put out a consoling hand. 'And many of them do, my dear. Many of them do. But there are always those for whom the best treatment in the world will never be enough ... those whose mental wounds nothing and no one can heal.'

Lara shook her head. Not Ken, she couldn't be speaking about Ken. He was always such a happy person before the accident. She could never even remember him complaining of a headache. He wasn't the type just to let himself go under. She searched the other's eyes for some sort of explanation. 'But how? How, for God's sake? He was trapped in that bed. How did he do it?'

The Sister looked at her. There was real pain in her eyes as she said quietly, 'Sleeping pills.'

'Sleeping pills! But don't you watch them taking them?' Lara almost shouted the question.

'We do. Most certainly we do. All our nurses have instructions to watch the patients swallow them.' She made a helpless gesture with her hands. 'We can only deduce he used to secrete them in his cheek and retrieve them when the nurse had passed on with the drugs trolley. If it's any consolation to you, he must have taken at least thirty. That means it was no spur of the moment decision. He must have been saving them, been planning it for at least the past few weeks.'

Consolation? That was meant to be a consolation? All the time she had spent sitting at his bedside over the past few weeks he had been secretly planning to take his own life – that was some sort of consolation? 'Can I see him?'

The Sister shook her head. 'I wouldn't advise it, my dear ... Wouldn't it be better to remember him as he was – remember him as he was before this tragic accident, even? Would he really want you to look at him now?'

Lara stared at her bleakly and shook her head. 'No, I don't suppose he would.'

Sister Melville gave an understanding smile and moved towards the desk. 'You'll appreciate he didn't have many possessions when he was brought in, but what there was we have here.' She opened a desk drawer and produced a paper bag. 'Just a few things,' she said, handing it to Lara, 'but you might like to have them.'

Mechanically Lara opened the bag and looked inside. What was left of Ken's watch – her wedding present to him – lay inside the remnants of his flying boots. She pulled one out. It hung from her fingers – a singed leather slipper that had once come up to his knee. So this was it – this was what was left of him. Bitter tears sprang to her eyes. 'He was only twenty-three,' she heard herself saying. 'Only twenty-three.'

The funeral was held four days later in the RAF chapel at his old base of Tangmere, at the foot of the Sussex Downs. She felt he would have liked that. It was where he had done most of his flying in the early years, where most of his happiest memories had been.

Sandy Cameron, his father, came down alone from Scotland. His mother, Moira, could not make the journey. She had been under sedation since hearing the news. The old man stood, proud and erect at Lara's side throughout the service in the small chapel. At Lara's request, they had not been told it was suicide. In fact, the full details of Ken's death did not go beyond the hospital. He had died in the service of his country, just as surely as if his young life had been snuffed out on that distant French hillside.

The elderly Presbyterian Minister who took the service had a Scottish accent, a shock of white hair, and watery blue eyes that peered at the mourners from over a pair of rimless, half-moon spectacles, which he took off and put on again at regular intervals. He reminded Lara of the family doctor she had known as a child. His very presence exuded a reassurance that she badly needed as she sat, her gloved hands clasped tightly in the lap of her well-worn, grey wool coat. Her meagre supply of clothing coupons would not run to a new black one. He was exactly as she imagined Ken's Arbroath grandfather might have looked, and she wondered if he had known her husband personally.

She found herself listening intently as he spoke movingly of the many thousands of young men who had given their lives, and were still giving their lives, in the skies above Europe. 'Those of us who had the privilege of knowing Kenneth Cameron know he would not have felt this service to be complete without a word for those of his comrades still out there fighting for the freedom we prize so highly. Let us pay tribute to his memory now with a special prayer for those he left behind to carry on the fight he himself so gallantly fought to the end of his young life:

> Lord, hold them in Thy mighty hand,
> Above the ocean and the land,
> Like wings of eagles mounting high
> Along the pathways of the sky.
>
> Immortal is the name they bear
> And high the honour that they share.
> Until a thousand years have rolled,
> Their deeds of valour shall be told.
>
> In dark of night and light of day,
> God speed and bless them on their way.
> And homeward safely guide each one
> With glory gained and duty done.

The Minister's voice shook as he finished the poem and his eyes closed for a few seconds in a silent, private prayer after he closed the leather-bound bible. As they filed past him at the door of the church, instead of shaking her by the hand, he put a comforting arm around Lara's shoulders. It was a touching gesture and one she appreciated.

They moved out to the grave-side, a small group, for only one or two were left of his closest friends, those who had gone through basic training with him. So many had already preceded him – Dai Jenkins, Judy's husband; Judy's brother Bob, too, who was missing presumed killed somewhere over Burma; 'Snowy' White; 'Bing' Crosby, his old boss; Martin Aylmer; Eddie 'Cuppa' Coffey … all gone, the list was endless.

His mother had wanted him buried in the Eastern Cemetery in Dundee, but his father's wishes had prevailed. He had told Lara he felt it would create a pilgrimage spot for Moira that would result in an ever-open wound. Better by far, he had said, that Ken be laid to rest in a place where he had been at his happiest, and, if it couldn't be in his own native Scotland, better it be under an English heaven than in some unknown foreign field that would be the last resting place of so many of his flying comrades. She had readily agreed. He was, after all, their only son. He had been their son long before he was ever her husband. It was right and proper that they should have a say in it.

She clung tightly to Sandy's arm as they congregated around the open grave and the coffin, draped in the Union Jack, was lowered into the soft earth. The elderly man bore himself with a quiet dignity, but she could imagine his thoughts as he took his leave of his only son. His hair was much greyer than when they had last met, and there was an infinite sadness in his eyes that had never been there before. 'Goodbye, laddie,' he whispered, as the coffin, released from its cords by four young men in air-force blue, came to rest in the pale chalk soil, and he bent to scatter the first drops of earth upon it.

Tears stung her eyes, hovering on her lower lashes, before trickling down the pale skin of her cheeks. He was too young to die, much too young. And what agony had driven him to this … ? What mental and physical anguish he had gone through over the past few months she could only guess at. She had failed him; they had all failed him. A great sob welled within her and she bit her lip in an effort to fight it back. He had borne his fate with dignity, it was the least she could do to do the same.

She felt his father's hand give hers a reassuring squeeze, and his voice whisper, 'Courage, lass,' as the Minister's voice echoed in her head: 'For as much as it hath pleased Almighty God of his great mercy to take unto himself the soul of our dear brother here departed, we therefore commit his body to the ground; earth to earth, ashes to ashes, dust to dust; in the sure and certain hope of the Resurrection to eternal life, through our Lord Jesus Christ ... '

Then, just before the small group of mourners at the grave-side broke up, one of Ken's oldest friends stepped forward. Pilot Officer Jock Campbell, from Ken's own grandfather's home town of Arbroath, stood tall and proud in his blue uniform, the silver wings on his breast glinting in the summer sunshine. 'Before we go,' he began quietly, 'I would like to dedicate a few words to Ken and the others we have known and loved, who have worn this uniform and died in the service of their king and country. These words were written by one of us – a young man by the name of John Gillespie Magee, who enlisted as a pilot in the Royal Canadian Air Force when war broke out, and was stationed at Digby in Lincolnshire with one of the RCAF's Spitfire squadrons when he was killed on 11 December 1941. Let his words speak for Ken today, and tomorrow, as the fight goes on without him:

> Oh, I have slipped the surly bonds of earth
> And danced the skies on laughter-silvered wings;
> Sunward I've climbed and joined the tumbling mirth
> Of sun-split clouds – and done a hundred things
> You have not dreamed of – wheeled and soared and swung
> High in the sunlit silence. Hov'ring there,
> I've chased the shouting wind along, and flung
> My eager craft through footless halls of air ...
>
> Up, up the long delirious, burning blue,
> I've topped the windswept heights with easy grace
> Where never lark, or even eagle flew –
> And, while with silent, lifting mind I've trod
> The high untrespassed sanctity of space,
> Put out my hand and touched the face of God.

Chapter Fifty-one

Jan handed Beth the bouquet of lilac blossoms with a smile. 'For you, my love. Lilacs have a special place in Polish hearts. They symbolize the arrival of spring, of renewed hope for the future.'

Beth took them, burying her face in their fragrance. He could think of bringing her flowers at such a time!

'Look for the bloom with five petals,' he said softly. 'Legend says good luck will come to anyone who finds it.'

Good luck – they could certainly do with it. Today, Sunday 18 April, could be the last day for a long time, perhaps for ever, that they could allow themselves such a luxury as taking pleasure in a bunch of flowers. Tomorrow, if their sources were correct, the Gestapo would make an all-out assault on the Jewish ghetto. And they would be there doing whatever they could. She had already made three forays beneath the wall with him, but on each one they had failed to make contact with Anna, or her lover Leon. Now Jan could not rest until he found out what had happened to his daughter. Beth knew he feared she had been a victim of a '*lapanka*' – one of the notorious Gestapo round-ups of innocent civilians – that she had been herded into a truck and driven to the Umschlagplatz, where she would be bundled into the waiting cattle-trucks to be taken off to Treblinka with the other unfortunates.

Yes, these last few hours were probably the last hours of relative peace and tranquillity that they would know for many a day if their AK sources were to be believed. The AK members who came and went from the small flat at intervals brought a sense of comfort. It reinforced the fact that they were not alone, that there were others, many others, actively involved in fighting the Nazi menace within the city.

On the wall of the Catholic church across from their apartment someone had scrawled '*Valeat Deus*' – Farewell to God – in white paint, and sometimes she had begun to believe that the Almighty really had forsaken them. How could any merciful God allow what was happening in this city right now? And it wasn't just in Warsaw. All over Poland, all over Europe, innocent people, men, women and children, were dying – and for what? Because one race had decreed it was superior to all others and these other '*Untermenschen*' must either be subjugated or liquidated at all costs. In the whole history of mankind there surely could have been no greater evil than this.

The last AK member to visit – Jurek, a tall, redheaded boy with a quiet smile – had lifted her spirits initially with the news that a message had been relayed to London reporting that she was safe and well. That would mean so much to Lara. But Jurek's other news had sent a shiver through her and caused a deep frown to etch itself across Jan's brow. A conference was taking place that very day between the police and the Gestapo to draw up the final details of tomorrow's planned assault of the ghetto. 'All SS and German police within the city are on the alert,' he told them. 'And from 6 pm tonight the Granatowa – the Polish police – have been ordered to surround the ghetto with heavy patrols. The Gestapo plans are for the Central Ghetto area to be obliterated first, with the brush factory and shop areas to be let off for the time being. Their idea seems to be that the Jews will take fright at the sight of the central area in flames and go voluntarily to the Umschlagplatz for deportation.'

'Do they know of this behind the wall?' Jan had asked grimly.

Jurek nodded. 'The Jewish Fighting Organization and the Farband have both been informed. Mordekhai Anielewicz is calling a meeting for the Central Ghetto group leaders this evening.'

'They'll need even more weapons.'

Again Jurek nodded. 'More weapons and more medical supplies. Dare you risk it?'

'Need you ask?'

It was just after that that Jan went out and brought her back the flowers. He had been to the church to make his peace with God, she was sure of it, although he said only that he had gone out for half an hour to clear his head. As she buried her face in the flowers, revelling in their heady fragrance, he said quietly, 'It is better I go by myself this time, *kochanie.*'

She looked up at him, aghast. 'No – never!'

He was adamant. 'This time it is the real thing. The Germans and their Ukrainian henchmen will not rest until all trace of human life has been expunged behind that wall. For the Jews it will be a fight to the death.'

'And for you, Jan, what will it be for you? You are no Jew. You have no need to get involved.'

'I am no Jew, so I have no need to get involved.' He repeated her words slowly. 'Did you never read your bible, *kochanie*? Did you never read the parable of the Good Samaritan? He was no Jew either. He was from Samaria. But he did not pass by.' He shook his head and rose to look out of the window, where the grey edifice of the wall rose incongruously behind the blossom-laden trees. 'I too am a man, *kochanie*. I cannot just pass by when my fellow human beings are suffering.'

Tears welled in her eyes as she looked at him. She loved him now as she had never loved him. She felt so small, while he was a giant amongst men. 'I wish I had your courage, my love,' she whispered.

He came over and held her to him, pressing his lips to her hair. If only she knew. He was as afraid of the consequences of this act as any man would be. But an even more powerful emotion than his fear was his hatred of the Germans and what they were doing, not only to the Jews, but to his beloved Poland. He had resigned himself to never seeing Jarosbork again: quite apart from the disputed lands of Silesia, at the end of February 1940, a decree of Marshal Goering's had confiscated all landed estates, large or small, belonging to Poles in the German occupied territories. All property of the Polish state throughout both the incorporated lands and in the territory still controlled by the General Government was transferred to the German state. Homes, factories, public buildings – everything had been taken over by the Germans, so that all Polish property simply ceased to exist. His whole country was simply ceasing to exist – was bleeding to death. Could he pass by on the other side while this was happening? It was not only the Jews he would be helping today, it was Poland herself.

It took Beth most of the afternoon to persuade him that she must be allowed to accompany him on what might be his last trip beneath the wall. But persuade him she did, and at just after five o'clock they set off on the hazardous journey through the tunnel that had been dug from the cellar of their block into the corresponding house on the other side of the wall. They had to travel most of the way on their knees, which were wrapped in thick pieces of sacking but, despite this rudimentary padding, the skin beneath the thick trousers she wore was raw and bleeding by the time they surfaced in the forbidden cellar.

There was an uncanny calm in the air and almost no one visible on the streets. After unloading the small consignment of ammunition, and four old army pistols they had strapped to their backs in the cellar, and handing them over to a grateful JFO official, they headed first for Anna and Leon's small attic room at the far end of Kozla Street.

The door was locked and Beth was aware of Jan's face falling once again as he tried the handle. 'I can't believe it,' he muttered, shaking the door in frustration. 'She has to be in sometime.'

Beth could only look on in despair. Then, to their astonishment, the sound of bolts being drawn back behind the door made them look at one another in expectation.

'Papa!' A pretty blonde girl with a thin, grime-smeared face and filthy clothes, threw herself into Jan's arms.

'Anna ... Anna ...' Jan clasped his daughter to him as if unwilling ever to let her go. 'Anna – where have you been?'

Prising herself from his arms, the young woman led the way into the tiny room and relocked the door. She motioned to them to sit down on a wooden chest that ran along one wall and perched herself on a small window seat. She glanced nervously out through the dusty panes as she began, 'Leon – I've lost Leon ...'

'You mean you don't know where he is?' her father asked.

Anna attempted a laugh, but tears glistened in her eyes as she said bitterly, 'Oh, I know where he is all right. He's lying beneath a hundred other dead bodies on a cart parked over by the Nalewki Gate. Leon's dead, Papa – dead!'

'But how?' Jan looked at her askance. Leon, who was always so careful. Leon dead.

'He was picked up in a *lapanka* on his way back here three days ago.' Her eyes, still red and swollen from recent tears, glanced fearfully out of the window, as if expecting another SS wagon to arrive and hear the dreaded shout of, *'Juden 'raus!'* 'He had been called out to a wounded child on Leszno Street ...'

'But that's in the Central Ghetto.'

'Of course. But what was he to do – ignore the cry for aid? The child, a boy called Chaim, was caught stealing bread and shot by one of the guards. He was bleeding internally. His father knew Leon from University and begged him to help.' She spoke in breathless jerks, her voice falling as she continued, 'Leon was on his way home when he was picked up ...'

'And you know for certain he's dead?'

Anna nodded. 'They tried to stop me, but I had to see for myself.' Then anger flared in her eyes. 'They didn't even give him the chance of being taken to the Umschlagplatz ... He might have stood a chance in Treblinka.'

Jan and Beth were silent. Then Anna gave a bitter laugh. 'Can you imagine? Can you imagine what we have come down to when we regret our loved one didn't have the chance of being sent to Treblinka?'

They sat in silence, each one trying to come to terms with this one death – one death in a city of a million deaths. How infinite was man's capacity to suffer? Did one feel a million deaths a million times more, Beth wondered? Wasn't it Stalin who once said that one death was a tragedy, a million deaths a statistic? She knew the truth of that statement as she sat there in that cramped, little room, with its stench of disinfectant and soiled bandages. Its truth was etched on every feature of the face of the young woman opposite her.

Jan had brought a half-bottle of vodka strapped inside his jacket and, unearthing three old cups from beneath a pile of papers, he poured them all a drink.

'To Jan-Warsaw!' Anna said, and raised her cup before them. Then seeing their puzzled faces, she explained, 'It's the code word for the resistance to this sweep the Gestapo are planning for tomorrow.'

Jan looked surprised. 'You know about that?'

'Of course.'

'You must come back with us, Anna. This will be no place for you when the fighting begins in earnest.'

A horrified look crossed his daughter's face. 'Come back with you? I will never come back until Leon's death has been avenged. I will be at that meeting being chaired by Mordekhai Anielewicz tonight and out there on the streets tomorrow with the others.'

Beth saw the colour drain from Jan's face. That was the last thing he wanted to hear. And she looked so ill, so very ill, and half-starved, like everyone else on this side of that devilish wall. Gone were the pretty rounded cheeks and curvaceous figure that marked her out as her mother's daughter. Instead he was looking at a pale, ravaged shadow of the Anna he knew and loved. He was silent for a moment, then said quietly, 'If that is your wish.' He was too proud a man himself to attempt to impose his will on another, particularly his own daughter.

They had been talking in Polish, but Beth now knew enough to follow all but the quickest of conversations. Up till then Anna had addressed all her conversation to her father, but now she turned to Beth. 'Are you Jewish?'

Beth looked at Jan, who gave an embarrassed cough. 'I'm sorry, Anna, I really should have introduced you. This is an old friend of mine from England – Beth, the former Countess von Lessing und

Wolfsberg although, for German eyes, her *Kennkarte* states she is Countess Elisabeth von Wolfsberg.'

Anna's pale brows rose. 'Von Lessing und Wolfsberg – not *the* von Lessing und Wolfsberg?'

Jan answered for her. 'Beth is Otto's former stepmother.'

Anna drew back visibly, as if a viper had suddenly been introduced into the nest, only to be reassured by her father.

'Beth is over here working for the SOE.'

'The British Resistance?'

Beth nodded, adding wryly, 'But at the moment I feel like our King Canute trying to turn the tide.'

Anna smiled. 'I know that story, and you must not think so. Every small act perpetrated against the Nazis is an act for humanity. No one person can make any impression acting alone – but together we can be strong. Will you come with me tonight? Will you give your support too?'

Beth looked at her, this young woman with Leni's pretty blonde looks and her father's pride and fighting spirit, then thought of herself at that age – the age she had fallen in love with her father, Jan. How naïve she had been, how unworldly, how much of a coward she had been compared to the young women of this generation. Where was her backbone when she suddenly packed up to return home to her parents in England after Hans Heinrich's death? How could she have simply turned her back on the man she loved, the man whose child she was carrying? Then she knew why when Anna asked, 'Did you see anything of my mother in England?'

Leni – Leni Jarosinska had not entered her head for weeks. 'I'm afraid not,' she lied. 'Not personally, that is. But I understand she was quite well and happy when I left London.'

Anna smiled. 'My mother loves London. I wouldn't be surprised if she tries to persuade Papa to settle there when this war is over.'

Jealousy stabbed at Beth's heart. She looked across at Jan, whose face had a set look. A nerve was flickering beneath the pale silver skin of the scar that ran down the left-hand side of his cheek. What was going on behind those golden brown eyes? For her part, it was unthinkable that they should be parted when, or if, they ever came through this hell.

'The future is not ours to plan, Anna – only today. And today we will be with you when you join Anielewicz and his fighters.'

And so they were. That evening they joined the others who congregated in the staff bunker of the Jewish Fighting Organization to hear Mordekhai Anielewicz and the others outline their plans.

As seasoned helpers in the ghetto, Jan and Anna sat with the leaders at the front of the room to be able to contribute where necessary to the conversation, but Beth could only sit at the back and listen in growing fear as plans were made for repulsing the German attack that was planned for the following day.

The Jewish resistance would concentrate its defences at three points: number one, the corner of Nalewki and Gesia Streets, near the entrance to the main ghetto artery; the second point was the intersection between Zamenhofa and Mila Streets; and the third at the crossing of Muranowska and Nalewki Streets, opposite Muranowska Square. The defence of the first two points would lie in the hands of the members of the Jewish Fighting Organization, and the third with the Farband members.

She looked on in admiration at the concentration on the faces of the mainly young men and women as they listened to their leader. Months of near starvation had given their faces a ghostly pallor and stretched the skin taut across the cheekbones. Most could scarcely be out of their teens, but looked much older than their years, and the lack of proper nutrition had drained them of much of the energy required for the mammoth task ahead; but what they lacked in physical strength, they more than made up for in their mental resources.

Outside in the distance, a dog barked. A *Kettenhunde* patrol was passing. The sound of the specially-trained German shepherd dogs with their equally lethal masters never failed to send a shiver down the most resilient of spines.

A thin, wiry young man with a shaggy black beard was talking, informing them of the actions that had already taken place. Weapons had been distributed, and at this point he gave an acknowledging nod in Jan's direction and made reference to the help given by others outside the ghetto. As well as weapons, he said, each action group had received their quota of grenades, ammunition and incendiary fluid. Supplies of food and cyanide were also distributed and, as they spoke, houses were being sandbagged and street passages blocked with furniture. Cushions would be placed at windows in order to deflect the bullets. Beth shuddered inwardly. Cushions against the might of the *Wehrmacht*'s tanks. She could only remain silent and admire their courage.

Just before the meeting broke up, someone reminded the others that this was the night of the first *Seder*, Passover 5703. A night of special prayer and vigil in the Jewish calendar. Miriam, a quiet, grave-eyed girl, who had said little throughout the discussion, produced a plate with a single boiled potato and a glass of wine. No one asked where she had come by them, they were simply grateful they had something to symbolize the lamb-bone, parsley, and other foods used over the last three thousand years on this most special of nights. But there was a murmur of appreciation when she produced a tiny morsel of *matzoh*, the unleavened bread that the Jews had carried into the desert on their flight from Egypt.

They stood together and sang the words of the Hebrew prayer, the *Sh'ma*: *'Sh'ma Yisroel adonoy elohenu, adonoy echod'* ... 'Hear, oh Israel, the Lord our God, the Lord is One ... Blessed art Thou, Lord our God, Ruler of the Universe, that Thou hast given us life and sustenance, and brought us to this season ...'

As the words of the ancient prayer echoed in the silence, Beth glanced round the assembled faces and wondered how many of them would live to see another such season. How many would live to see another day ...

There was silence for several seconds, as each said his own silent prayer, then they each embraced their neighbour, all aware it could be for the last time.

'O czym myslales, kochanie?' Jan asked, seeing her worried expression.

She attempted a brave smile. 'Oh, nothing much. I was just thinking we've come a long way from the peace and tranquillity of the banks of the Praszkawarthe. Will we ever see it again, Jan? Will we ever go back?'

He looked down at her, sorrow and love mingling with a deep determination in his brown eyes as he said softly, 'We will go back one day, my love. One way or another, when this war is over, we will go back. I promise you that.'

As he put his arm around her and they walked slowly to the door, only one other person heard that promise – his daughter Anna. She watched in silence as they disappeared out into the falling dusk, a slight, lonely figure whose blonde hair marked her out as with, but not of the others in the room. He had never looked at her mother like that – never. A frown creased her brow as she got up from the hard wooden seat to follow them.

Chapter Fifty-two

SS marschiert, die Strasse frei!
Die Sturmkolonnen stehen!
Sie werden aus der Tyrannei
Den Weg zur Freiheit gehen.
Drum auf bereit zum letzten Stoss!
Wie's unsere Väter waren!
Der Tod sei unser Kampfgenoss!
Wir sind die Schwarzen Scharen.

The time had come to rid Poland's capital of its remaining Jews. In the darkness of the night the song was sung beneath the breaths of the black-uniformed troops whose badge was the Death's Head, as they goose-stepped their way towards Warsaw's Jewish ghetto.

At 2 A.M. on the morning of 19 April 1943, under orders from SS General Juergen Stroop, the cordon of armed guards that circled the ghetto walls was strengthened by reinforcements of German police and Ukrainian and Lithuanian militia. They stood at twenty-five-metre intervals, machine-guns at the ready.

The SS were set for action: over 2,000 officers and men of the Waffen SS; three *Wehrmacht* divisions, the artillery of which would barrage the houses while the sappers would detonate explosive charges throughout the ghetto; two battalions of German police, and a battalion consisting of Ukrainian and Lithuanian militia. In addition, over 7,000 SS troops were on full-alert throughout the city at large, and twice that number in the surrounding countryside.

As the black-uniformed soldiers of the Death's Head and their Fascist militias were marched in columns through the deserted streets of the ghetto, they were followed by a slow procession of black limousines containing the Gestapo chiefs themselves. In the third car, his features totally expressionless, sat SS Obersturmbannführer Otto von Lessing. He was humming quietly to himself. This was the day

428

he had been waiting for: the day when Warsaw, like most of Poland, would be *judenrein*.

The pale blue eyes scanned the moonlit streets. *He* was out there somewhere – the Jewish pig who had defiled her, the woman he loved. That Jew had corrupted Anna just as surely as his race had corrupted European civilization. What was to happen to them now was no more than they deserved. They had had their chance to volunteer for deportation and refused it, and now their time had run out. By this time tomorrow the ghetto and its inhabitants would be no more, German tanks and guns would see to that. Warsaw would be cleansed of its human cancer at last. And maybe, just maybe, when this was all over, the Poles would thank them for what was taking place here tonight. And maybe then *she* would see sense, would come to realize that instead of with Jewish scum, her future lay with him at Wolfsberg. Yes, he would make her mistress of Wolfsberg. He would even buy back Jarosbork, if that was what she wanted. Her father's castle was now being used as an SS headquarters in the region but, after the fighting was over, he could pull strings. He could give her back Jarosbork – make it part of his own estate of Wolfsberg. He would do that – all of it – for her. But first the ghetto …

Watching the procession of troops and limousines were three people who were figuring large in Otto von Lessing's thoughts at that moment. Jan, Beth and Anna were looking on in silence from their attic room in Kozla Street. They had returned, armed with revolvers tucked into their belts, a small quantity of ammunition, and a few precious Molotov cocktails, to wait for the action to begin.

They had left the commander-in-chief of the resistance, Mordekhai Anielewicz at the headquarters, along with a few close associates, such as Israel Kanal, who had carried out the rebels' first successful assassination. The Fighting Organization's chief battle station was to be on Muranowska Street, under the command of David Apelboim and Pawel Frenkl, while the Farband had groups of between fifteen and forty persons operating in the Central Ghetto.

The plan was to attack the enemy from the windows of buildings located at all crossroads of the ghetto, for a face to face confrontation was out of the question. 'Where do you think we would be best placed when it begins?' Anna asked, drawing back from the window. 'If possible, I'd like to get over to Gesia Street as soon as I can. They have got a small hospital operating at Number Six. They'll need all the help there they can get.'

'In that case, it seems to me we would be best placed at the corner of Nalewki and Gesia,' Jan said. 'That's not too far from here and means we'll be nearby if you need help.' He turned to Beth. 'Do you agree, *kochanie*?'

'Yes. Yes, of course.' Anywhere he went she would go.

'In that case I vote we make our way across there now.'

Movement around the ghetto was confined to tunnels beneath the buildings and streets, through the sewers or, if possible, along the roof-tops, and it took them almost an hour to travel the quarter-mile underground.

As they emerged, filthy and red-eyed with fatigue, in the cellar beneath 33 Nalewki Street, the noise of battle assailed their ears. 'My God, they're shooting already!' Anna brushed the dirt from her trousers and ran to the grating of the cellar to stare up into the darkness beyond.

'You carry on to Gesia Six,' her father said, joining her at the window. 'You'll be needed there sooner than you realize.'

They watched her go, crawling back down into the hole that was now one of the few safe thoroughfares within the ghetto, then Jan held out his hand. 'Come, *kochanie*,' he said softly. 'I think we may be needed too.'

While they had been edging their painful way through the tunnel, a few of those above ground had found it impossible to wait until daybreak before launching their attack on the enemy. As the black-uniformed columns marched their way past the intersection of Nalewki, Gesia and Franciszkanska streets, they had been met by a barrage of bullets and Molotov cocktails. The first attack came from the house above them, to be followed almost immediately by shots from neighbouring houses.

By the time Jan and Beth had run up the stairs to ground level, to their amazement, the Germans were on the run. The SS were actually retreating! They turned to one another and hugged, Jan sweeping her up into his arms and whirling her around, as the rebels around them whooped in delight.

Dead German soldiers lay in the middle of the street beyond their fortified windows. 'Come on, let's go!' a young man named Aaron shouted, and a dozen others followed him out into the road to strip the uniforms off the still warm bodies and relieve them of their weapons and ammunition.

This initial success lent an air of euphoria to the inhabitants of Number Thirty-Three. Was it really going to be this easy? Beth glanced across at Jan. His mouth was smiling, but his eyes expressed his true feelings. She moved across to his side and slipped her hand in his. 'They are young. They celebrate now, but this is only the beginning, *kochanie*,' he said quietly. 'Only the beginning.'

The excitement, however, continued until daylight, and at six o'clock, the fighting resumed again in earnest, culminating in the JFO issuing an order to set fire to all factories and warehouses in the vicinity. 'Anything that is of use to the Germans must go,' was the cry on all lips. The first incendiaries were thrown into a huge, German-run warehouse next door to where Jan and Beth were positioned.

They watched the smoke and orange flames billowing into the streets only yards away, as they lay on their stomachs at a second floor window, their rifles positioned at the ready to pick off any German troops who might round the corner. They had lain here for the past few hours, and Beth could feel every muscle in her body screaming for relief. She longed to get up and walk around – do anything that might relieve the terrible aches in her body and stop herself from falling asleep. But no one else was complaining, least of all Jan.

She could feel her eyes begin to close just as a yell went out from the young man next to her. A German armoured car was down below and the soldiers within were firing in their direction. The sound of the shots jerked her awake, then, suddenly, a terrific pain in her temple was followed by a spurt of blood that covered her rifle and hands. She had been hit, but incredibly she was still conscious.

'Beth!' Jan scrambled from his place at the neighbouring window to reach her. 'Beth, *kochanie*!' He cradled her head in his arm and his free hand searched frantically in his pocket for a handkerchief to stem the blood.

'I'm all right,' she heard herself saying. 'Honestly, I'm all right … '

He made a pad with the handkerchief and pressed it to her temple, then raised it to examine the wound. The fear in his face lessened. It was only a flesh wound, but deep enough, nevertheless. And she was losing a lot of blood.

As the bullets continued to ricochet off the outside wall, he helped her to her feet. 'We've got to get you out of here,' he said, ducking to avoid the splintering glass from another direct hit on the window.

She was too shocked and exhausted to protest as he helped her down the several flights of stairs to the cellar. He knew he would have to get her back through the tunnel to the flat at Freta Street. But how?

They paused at the entrance to the tunnel and he looked down at her, raising her face to his. 'Can you do it, my love?'

She thought of that endless tunnel, hundreds of yards of scrabbling in the dirt and darkness. Then she saw the concern in his eyes. She would do it. She must do it – for him.

It took them twice as long to get back as it had to get there. Every yard was a struggle against pain and fatigue, and often she had to pause and lie down on the muddy rubble to summon up enough energy to carry on. And all the time he was talking to her, murmuring words of encouragement every painful foot of the way.

When eventually they emerged into the familiar cellar below their Freta Street apartment, he hugged her to him as tears of relief flooded down her dirt-streaked cheeks, then he lifted her into his arms and carried her up the stairs to the tiny cramped rooms that were now their home.

But as Jan closed their door behind them and gave a heartfelt sigh of relief, there was no such relief on the face of his daughter Anna. Since arriving at Gesia 6, she had been working all-out to help alleviate the pain and suffering she found within. With most of its fully-trained medical staff already victims of the transports, they were chronically short of helpers. Those who were already there were doing their best, but were almost out on their feet. They could not disguise their delight at her arrival. Her work with Leon over on Kozla Street was well-known throughout the ghetto and she was immediately taken down to the delivery room where several young women were in the throes of childbirth.

She had been in there for several hours when the first incendiary bombs landed on the ground floor. At first she could not believe it. This was a hospital. Surely they couldn't be bombing a hospital? She dashed upstairs to find shells and bullets bombarding the building from German tanks in the street outside. Half the downstairs wards were already in flames. Screams from beyond the door on her left made her run towards it as two German soldiers came rushing out, firing wildly in all directions.

As Anna stood frozen to the spot in terror, they pushed past her and headed for the upstairs rooms. The screaming from behind the door continued, bringing her back to her senses, and she pushed it open, only to recoil in horror. At least half the patients had been shot where they lay, their blood causing deep red pools to form on the white sheets.

Fighting back her own impulse to scream, she rushed back downstairs to the delivery room, only to find the SS had been there before her. The beautiful raven-haired girl whose labour she had been attending was lying naked across her bed, her unborn child ripped from her body by the blade of a bayonet. A newborn baby was lying at the foot of the far wall, its head smashed in. Its mother lay dead beside it, a bullet through her temple.

She staggered backwards, leaning against the wall for support. She had seen many terrible sights since taking up residence in the ghetto, but nothing like this before – nothing. She began to shake from head to foot, then retched violently. But her stomach was starved of food and only a hollow animal sound was emitted from her gut.

As she stood there, with tears streaming down her hollow cheeks, the man who loved her was only a few hundred yards away. Obersturmbannführer Otto von Lessing had been ordered back into the rebel-held streets by his chief, Juergen Stroop, to bring order to the mounting chaos. He had stopped his car in the street outside and had watched for several minutes, waiting until his men emerged into the daylight once more, before entering the bomb-blasted building himself.

What he met there caused him to flinch inwardly for the first time since returning to this god-forsaken city. A red cross had been scrawled on the front door, so he knew he was entering what must be some kind of hospital. But it was now a hospital without patients, for behind the first door he opened men, women and children lay slaughtered in their beds, their red blood soaking the sheets and makeshift coverings on their emaciated bodies and dripping down to form scarlet pools on the stone floor.

His blue eyes darkened at the sight. They were here to cleanse the city of its Jews, but what had happened here a few minutes ago he could not countenance. His men could be too zealous. There was no need for this. No need at all.

His fingers gripped the cold metal of his revolver even tighter. All around him it was as silent as the grave, except for one voice screaming somewhere down below him.

He tensed inwardly, and automatically his black-booted feet began to descend the stone stairs in the direction of the noise. It was a woman by the sound of it. A Jewish bitch going mad. He had better investigate.

He threw open the door of the downstairs delivery room and balked at the sight. *Gott in Himmel*, this was an awful thing – an ungodly thing. His eyes stared in a mixture of horror and disgust at the sight of the slaughtered mothers and infants. Someone would pay for this. He would see to it personally. Then do his best to get out of this hell-hole and get back to the sanity of Berlin.

Miraculously the screaming had stopped. He looked about him for the human being still alive in this carnage. Two blue eyes were staring at him from across the blood-soaked room. Two blue eyes he knew better than any on earth. 'Dear God in heaven – Anna!'

She continued to stare at him, her face twisted in hate, then softly, so softly he had to strain to hear, she began to speak. 'Beast ... Murderer ... Filth of the earth. I spit on you and your kind. I spit on you, Otto von Lessing. I damn you to hell for what has happened here tonight. I damn you to hell for what has happened for countless nights in this ghetto, in this city – in my land. I damn you for what you have done to everything and everyone I have ever loved ... '

'No, Anna, *Liebchen*, no ... ' She had it so wrong. He had not done this deed here tonight. His men – they had done it. Headstrong young soldiers who would now be disciplined. He would see to it. He personally ... 'You don't understand ... '

'Oh, I understand only too well, Herr Obersturmbannführer. I have understood all about this creed for years. I have understood better than you what it would do – and has now done – to my country. What it would do to you. And it has done it, Otto. It has corrupted you just as surely as it has corrupted your race. Corrupted you so much that there can be no redemption in this life. Only God can grant you forgiveness for what has happened here, Otto. Only God ... '

'Anna ... *Liebche* ... ' The word was never completed. The pistol shot hit him in the right temple and he fell towards her as if in slow motion, to sprawl in a grotesque position of supplication at her feet.

She stared down at him, the pistol still clenched tightly in her shaking fingers. She had never killed a human being before. But she had killed him. She had killed Otto. Otto, once more dear to her than any brother, more close than any lover. But she had no regrets. It was he who had given the order for this – this sin against God. And it was he who had come to gloat. She was certain of it. You had to be certain to kill.

She gazed down at the prostrate corpse of the man she had once loved. The black cap had fallen to one side and his blond hair lay in a crimson pool of his own blood. She began to laugh – a crazed hysterical laugh. Then, as the tears streamed unbidden and uncontrollable down her pale cheeks, she walked across his stricken figure and out of the door.

Chapter Fifty-three

The night had been cold for the first week of May, but by mid-morning, the clouds had parted to reveal a warm spring sun: a gentle steam now rose from the grey Warsaw streets. Beth stood by the window of the Freta Street apartment, her fingers nervously fiddling with the frayed edge of the net curtain. He was out there somewhere. Back in the ghetto, probably. She had begged him not to go, pleaded with him to stay with her, rest awhile, and get some colour back into the grey pallor of his cheeks.

But he hadn't listened. He had to go back. 'There's just a chance, *kochanie*. Just a chance she's still there.' Nothing could bring him to believe that Anna had gone, that Zamek Feld had really seen her being picked up by a Gestapo patrol in Gesia Street, a few minutes after the burning of the hospital.

Beth had held him close to her and eased his anxiety with soothing words that told him of course there was still a chance. What if Martin Rosenblum had claimed to have seen her being herded on to that wagon with the others at the Umschlagplatz? People could be mistaken. Anna's was not the only blonde head in the ghetto that day.

But in her heart she knew she was only telling him what he craved to hear. Anna had gone to Treblinka. Dear, brave Anna had been taken with the others to that camp from which there was no return. She was certain of it. A feeling deep in her being told her she would not see Jan's daughter again.

Her eyes clouded and she blinked hard to stop the tears that threatened to surface in the green of her eyes. She had done a lot of crying this past week, knowing he had gone back behind the wall to continue his search, and to offer what little assistance he could to those still holding out against the might of the Gestapo and their Fascist lackeys.

Most of the tunnels had collapsed, and now almost the only means of entering or leaving the ghetto was by the complex network of sewers that ran beneath the houses and streets. He would return home – for that was how they now thought of these two, cramped rooms – soaking wet, and stinking of the effluent of the thousands who still lived and died outside these four walls where she was condemned to spend her days.

She looked around her at the room, with its faded, flowered wallpaper, the heavy Gothic furniture that had seen better days, and the motley assortment of knick-knacks that served as decoration. None of it was theirs; not a single thing could they call their own. All of it had been bought by someone else, all of it, except the lilac blossom that now stood brown and faded in a vase on the table.

A brightly-coloured wooden bowl containing a collection of hand-painted Easter eggs stood on the sideboard, but it was not this past Easter, nor the one before that, that had seen the contents blessed by the priest. Whoever had spent long hours lovingly decorating those small symbols of the boulder which guarded Christ's tomb, and had carried them to the church for the blessing, had gone a long time ago ...

Gone ... She turned the word over in her mind. It was funny how used you became to finding less emotional words for what was happening to people these days. The family who had lived here before the war had 'gone', it was true, but through no wish of their own. That bright-eyed young couple, with their arms around each other and their chubby-faced baby, photographed outside the gates of the Krasinski Gardens, and now gazing down at her from a silver frame on the mantelpiece, had simply disappeared one night almost three years ago. Taken to Szuch Avenue, and interrogated by the Gestapo for the crime of being known Communists, she had been told. And that was the last anyone had heard of them. Like so many thousands of others, they had simply 'gone', never to return.

A deep sadness mixed with a feeling of helplessness flowed through her as she turned back to the window. Who cared? Who in the world cared what was happening over here? Where were the planes from the West – from Britain and America – to aid the Resistance? Where was the outcry back home about the death factories that had been set up by the Nazis on Polish soil? Didn't they know? Didn't they care?

Suddenly England and home seemed a million miles away. It was as if her life in the tranquillity of Atholl Square had never happened, as if she had always been here, bound up heart and soul in Poland's troubles. It seemed incredible to think she had once been married to a

German, to a member of the race that was causing all this heartache to half the world.

The thought of Hans Heinrich brought the face of his son before her once more, and an involuntary shudder ran through her. What had become of Otto? Did he get his wish and return to his beloved Berlin, or was he still here in Warsaw striking terror into the hearts of all who beheld his tall, immaculately-uniformed figure striding through these ancient streets? She should hate him, she knew that. Hate him for what he had become, for how he had used and abused the power vested in him by that uniform. But that was something she could not bring herself to do. Somehow, somewhere, deep within her, there remained a memory of a small, flaxen-haired child, with trusting blue eyes and gentle ways, who would plead for just one more bedtime story, one more nursery rhyme, before she turned down the gas-mantle and left him alone in that huge, sombre bedroom in Wolfsberg.

Little had she known then how life would turn out for them all. That she would be a widow within two years of marriage had never entered her head. She had accepted the fact that Hans Heinrich's health had never been good since his return from the trenches of the Great War and his own doctor had, at first, put down his recurring throat trouble to tonsillitis, aggravated by a weakened constitution. And the despair she had felt at his death from cancer of the oesophagus had been doubled by the knowledge of her growing love for Jan.

'Jan ...' she whispered his name into the silence of the room. 'Where are you, my love? Where are you?'

She should be out there with him. After all, that was why she had come here, wasn't it – to be by his side? She sighed inwardly and fingered the still painful scar on her temple as memories of that day behind the wall when she had been shot flooded back.

She had become delirious after crawling back wounded from the ghetto, and had spent days lying beneath the rough grey blankets on the bed in the next room. It had been touch and go, Jan had told her later. A doctor – one they could trust from the AK – had come and told him she was suffering from some unpronounceable ailment that meant nervous exhaustion. On no account must she be allowed to leave the flat until she was completely well and, even then, she must not be allowed to return to active service.

And so here she was, waiting by the window every day while he continued to risk his life for a people that wasn't his, in a cause that was all but lost.

The past few days had been almost unbearable. Last Tuesday 28

April, he had been involved in the heavy fighting which had taken place around Muranowski Square. Other Aryan Poles had been there, members of the Resistance like him, who fought side by side with the Jews.

A group of Jewish Farband fighters had joined forces with Polish comrades, led by a Major Iwanski, with the declared intention of fighting their way through to the Aryan side of Muranowska Street or, failing that, at least to reopen the tunnel and its exit at Muranowska 6, which had been discovered and closed by the Gestapo.

Jan had joined Iwanski's men at Muranowska 7. But, unknown to them, an informer in their ranks had told the Nazis of the plan. The Germans brought in tanks and men and, after a harrowing battle, many of the rebels lost their lives, including Iwanski's brother, Waclaw: one of Jan's closest friends.

Beth had been horrified at the sight of him, when eventually he staggered into the flat at just after midnight. He had been shot in the shoulder and had obviously lost a lot of blood, but insisted it was only a scratch.

She had protested even more than usual when, after only a few hours' rest, and his wounded shoulder bound, he returned to the fray. Even now, as she stood watching the flames rise from the burning ghetto, she still shuddered to think of that day. For hours she had stood vigil on this very spot, praying to a God she only half believed in as the flames seemed to sear her very soul.

That day, the 29th, the Germans had begun to burn and bulldoze the ghetto in a final attempt to root out the remaining pockets of resistance. Those few fighters that were left knew their only hope was to escape, so a rescue campaign was organized between the Jews and representatives of the Polish resistance on the Aryan side of the wall. Several of their contacts from the AK, accompanied by members of other Resistance groups, came to the flat throughout the day to meet and discuss tactics, so she was kept informed on what was happening. But this only increased her anxiety for Jan.

At 11 P.M. that night, well over an hour after the last contacts had left and as she prepared for bed, an almighty rumble shook the building. She had rushed to the window to see yet another huge fire raging in the ghetto. Giant tongues of orange and white flames leapt skywards, filling the heavens with a luminous pink glow. Who had done it? Was it the Germans, the Jews, or their own people? She was soon to find out.

The rebels had blown up a German warehouse at Leszno 72 and escaped through the sewer. They came up, filthy and exhausted, on the Aryan side of the wall, at the corner of Ogrodowa and Zelazna Street, and Jan had brought several of them to the flat, to share what little they had in the way of food until proper arrangements could be made for them.

All she could offer them was a couple of bottles of Bimber – a rough peasant vodka – and bread coated with a pale yellow substance that was passing for butter in the few shops that remained open.

Never had she seen such ravaged faces as they fell upon the food and quaffed the potent white spirit. The full horror of what they had lived through was etched on every feature. Their eyes glowed like burning coals from out of deeply-shadowed sockets, as they told tales of brutality and heroism that brought tears to her eyes and a cold anger to her soul.

Their stories were made all the more harrowing knowing it was their own families that were involved: their own parents, wives and children that had been deported to the camps, tortured, or killed. Her thoughts had returned to her own family back in London, and to the last Christmas Ken had spent with them. He had recited a poem by Scotland's favourite bard, and Burns's words resounded in her head: 'Man's inhumanity to man makes countless thousands mourn ...' In this city, those words had never been more true.

The lucky ones who had escaped were now on their way out of the city, heading for Lomianka, about seven kilometres away. There they would join the roving bands of partisans who honeycombed the forests around Warsaw, wreaking havoc on the German lines of communication. Before they left, they had all stood together in this small room and, very softly, for they could not risk their voices being heard outside the four walls, they had sung the 'Internationale'. There had been tears in the eyes of almost all present as the last note died on their lips and they turned to hug one another. Brotherhood, and hope for the future, was not dead in this city. She had seen it here, in this very room. She had seen it in the eyes of those men and boys she had bidden farewell to only a few days ago. At all costs she must keep that spirit and hope alive in her own breast.

She reached out and lifted a tattered piece of paper from the table beside her. It had been left behind by one of the young men who had escaped the hell of the ghetto the other night. It was an appeal to the Polish population from those behind the wall. Her eyes scanned the words:

Poles, citizens, soldiers of freedom!
Through the cannons' roar, the German Army bombards our houses,

the homes of our mothers, wives, and children; through the noise of machine-guns we seized from the police and SS men; through the smoke and fire, and blood of the murdered Warsaw Ghetto, we, the Ghetto captives, fraternally greet you.

We know you look at the war we have waged during the past few days, against the occupation force, through pain and tears, with amazement and fear for the outcome of this struggle. Soon you will see every doorway in the Ghetto transformed into a fortress. We may all perish in battle, but we will not give up. We, like you, passionately seek to avenge the crimes committed by our common enemy. This is a struggle for our freedom and yours; for our human, social, and national honour, and yours!

We will take revenge for Auschwitz, Treblinka, Belzec, and Majdanek.

Long live the brotherhood of arms and blood of embattled Poland!

Long live freedom!

Death to the murderous and criminal occupation!

Let the life and death struggle against the German occupation prosper!

Jewish Fighting Organization

Beth looked up from the brave words contained in the statement to the billowing smoke and flames rising from behind the ghetto wall. 'Better to have an end with terror, *kochanie*, than terror without end,' Jan had told her before he left last time.

For the inhabitants of that infernal place behind the wall there was no choice.

She was in bed when he eventually returned to her several days later. The noise of his key in the lock brought her running through to the narrow hallway.

'Jan!' She fell into his arms, burying her face in the filthy fabric of his jacket. 'Oh – your shoulder! Your poor shoulder!' In her relief at seeing him again she had quite forgotten the gunshot wound that still throbbed beneath the matted bandage inside his shirt.

She took his arm and gently led him into the sanctuary of the small living-room, carefully locking the door behind her.

He sat down heavily on the sofa and leant back against the plush cushions. It was the first soft seat he had had in days. His head throbbed and the pain in his shoulder gnawed at him, reminding him he was not the young man he once was: wounds took longer to heal. Wounds to the body and the heart.

'You have been away for so long, my love. So very long.' It was not meant as a reproach, for relief was the only feeling Beth felt as she looked at him. His face, his whole body, seemed drained of all energy, of all life.

He put out his hand and took hers. '*Kochanie* ... You must have been so worried.'

'For you ... yes.' She took his hand and raised it to her lips. Then sat with it clasped in her lap, as if afraid ever to let it go.

She waited for him to speak and at last he did, shaking his head slowly, as he said softly, 'It's all over, Beth. It's all over.' He looked across at her and, reading the unspoken questions in her eyes, he said bitterly, 'She's gone, all right. Anna's gone.'

She clasped his hand tighter in hers. Words would not come.

His eyes burned into hers. 'Treblinka.' He spoke the word quietly, as if invoking some fearful curse. 'That's where she'll be ... Treblinka. Dear God, death itself would have been more merciful ...'

She sat and listened as the hurt poured from him, not only for his lost daughter, but for all the daughters and sons he had seen go to their deaths over this past week. 'They died on their feet, *kochanie*,' he told her. 'They did not go as lambs to the slaughter. In generations to come, their children's children will speak of them with honour.'

She remained silent. Their children's children would never speak of them. The butchers had slaughtered the infants too.

She rose to go into the tiny scullery to prepare him some food, and pour a glass of bimber, the only vodka that was now available. His voice reached her through the parted curtain of the door. 'We must leave here, *kochanie*. Leave here tonight.'

She turned in the open doorway and stared at him. She had no reason to ask why. The Germans were making house to house searches. Nowhere in the city was safe any more. Every minute of the day and night was lived in fear of the tread of jackboots on the stairs outside the door, and of the dreaded knock and shout of '*Polen, 'raus!*' She looked at him fearfully as all sorts of questions tumbled through her mind. 'But where to, Jan? Where can we go?'

'I have an uncle in the East, near Lvov. We can go there – stay on his farm for a time, until we see what happens here.'

'For a time?'

He shrugged as he accepted a glass of the potent spirit and downed it in one. 'Who can say how long it will take until we can come back here, or even return to Jarosbork.' His eyes softened momentarily as he spoke the name. Then he sighed, 'A few weeks, maybe a few months ... Time is meaningless these days.'

He fell silent for a moment, as if pondering on something much bigger than the future of the two of them. 'They sing a song in the ghetto, Beth,' he said quietly. '"*Es Brennt*", it's called ... "It's burning". But it's not only the ghetto that's burning. The whole of

Europe is in flames and we are all fuel for the fire … We will head for Lvov and put our trust in the Soviets pushing the Nazis back into their beloved Fatherland.'

Head for the East – for Lvov … Her head swam. When would it ever end? When would they ever be allowed to live in peace?

Seeing the look on her face, he got up from the sofa and came to her, burying her head against his chest as he whispered words of comfort in Polish that she could only half understand.

But it was enough that she was in his arms. Enough to have him home safe with her at last. She would go with him to that farm outside Lvov – if it still existed. She would go with him to the ends of the earth itself …

Chapter Fifty-four

Major General Mike Adams got up from his seat and yawned, stretching his aching muscles, as he walked to the window of his office. Being desk-bound didn't suit him. He felt suffocated, despite the air-conditioning that whirred softly in the background. A pale, autumn sun pierced the slats of the blinds that shielded him from the outside world and he reached out and gave the cord a tug, jerking the blind upwards and allowing the sunshine to stream into the room. Summer had been and gone and he had hardly even noticed it.

His brows furrowed as he took another drag on the cigarette and stared out over the green slope of Jenkins Hill. He was above it all up here in the Capitol. The war in Europe, even though they were now part of it, seemed a world away from Washington. The defeat of Germany was becoming more of a certainty as the summer progressed into the fall. Her forces in Russia were retreating back towards the Fatherland. Only yesterday, reports from the Eastern Front claimed they had been driven out of Smolensk, and this afternoon there had been word of street fighting in Kiev.

In Western Europe, too, the situation was looking up. Montgomery's British Eighth Army and the Anglo-American Fifth Army had landed in Italy, the Italian Government having surrendered unconditionally on 3 September.

Only in Poland was the situation still fraught with tragedy. The country was a battlefield, its people bleeding to death, and its Jewish population all but annihilated in those camps they were continually getting reports on. And, to add to their misery, the Red Army was rapidly approaching the Polish frontier; but their relations with the Polish Government in Exile in London were still deadlocked. Some in the States and Britain had hoped that General Sikorski's death in the plane crash on the fourth of July would help ease relations

443

between the Poles and their Russian neighbours, but this had not happened. God only knew what was going to happen over there next. It was in His hands.

Mike's eyes narrowed as he continued to gaze out over the nation's capital city. Poland ... the place seemed to gnaw at his insides, no matter how he tried to concentrate his mind on other war issues. He was an American, born and bred, but it was Polish blood that coursed through his veins. The President had joked the other day about making him Ambassador to Warsaw after the war and the idea had an almost irresistible appeal for him, despite the covert approaches already made by both Democratic and Republican elder statesmen suggesting he put himself forward as a candidate for the next Presidential election.

He drew deeply on the cigarette and let the smoke trickle out slowly through his nostrils as he turned the idea over in his mind. It seemed almost sacrilege to imagine anyone other than FDR as President, let alone himself. But everyone knew that, the President's health notwithstanding, the Constitution would not countenance him running for a fourth term. Only the knowledge that it would have been far too disruptive to the country during wartime to change horses midstream had allowed FDR to remain in the White House for a third term.

But he himself for President ... A Polak from the Bronx in the White House? He gave a wry grin at the thought, and turned back to the desk as the telephone gave a shrill ring.

He leant over and picked it up, balancing himself on the edge of the desk as he flicked a column of grey ash in the vague direction of the ashtray. 'Yes? Adams here.'

'Mike – it's Harry.'

The Mid-West voice on the other end of the line brought a smile to his face. 'Harry, well I'll be ... ! How the hell are you?'

'Never better – the old guts apart. Hey, listen here, what do you know about the reshuffles that are going on?'

'You mean Welles's resignation?' Only that morning the President had announced the resignation of Sumner Welles as Under Secretary of State and announced the appointment of Edward Stettinius in his place.

'Hell, no. That was a foregone conclusion.' There was a momentary pause on the line as the President's favourite aide lit another cigarette. 'The Harriman – Moscow thing I'm talking about ...'

The removal of Averell Harriman, Roosevelt's diplomat *par excellence*, from London to fly out as their next Ambassador to the

444

Soviet Union had taken everyone by surprise. 'Yeah ... What of it? Seems to me he's just the guy to talk some sense into Old Joe.'

'You're right and I'm not suggesting otherwise. I just wondered how you'd take to the idea of returning to London in his place.'

There was a long silence on the other end of the line as Mike took a deep breath and let it out slowly.

'You still there?'

'Yeah, I'm still here.'

'Well?'

London ... Lara ... Lara ... London ... A light film of sweat broke on his upper lip and his grip tightened on the stub of the cigarette as he placed it between his lips and drew deeply on the white smoke.

'You've as much experience over there as anyone,' Harry's voice was continuing, 'and the President reckons you'd do a first class job. So what do you say? Will you think about it, at least?'

Mike nodded slowly, his eyes on the green slope of the hill that seemed to stretch into infinity outside his window. 'Yeah, Harry, I'll think about it.'

'And get back to me as soon as possible ... You can't keep the President waiting too long, you know.'

'And get back to you as soon as possible ...' There was a muted click as he replaced the receiver in its cradle. He stared down at it, then out of the window once more. London. Dear God, London...

As his mind flew the thousands of miles across the grey Atlantic, in England's capital itself, a young woman lay in a single room in St Catherine's Maternity Home, W1.

Perspiration stood out in a dull sheen on Lara's brow as she gripped the iron bars of the hospital bed behind her head. She wanted to scream, to yell out her agony to the world, but she had not been brought up to do such a thing. Dignity must be maintained ...

'Aaaaah!'

'Easy, Mrs Cameron ... Easy now. Don't push! You'll do yourself and the baby no end of damage. You're not ready yet.'

The midwife's voice came from somewhere at the foot of the bed. Not ready yet? What did she know? How could she tell what it was like to be having your very insides ripped apart? She wasn't even married! 'AAAAH!'

Her scream was louder this time, causing the midwife to jump back and race for her senior colleague. 'It'll have to be an episiotomy, Sister. And a forceps.'

The scalpel was brought, and the large instrument in surgical steel with the curved, pincer-like ends to encircle the baby's head. And, as

Lara writhed involuntarily on the rubber sheet, one deft incision was made in the red, rending flesh between her legs.

'Aaaaaaahhhh …'

The midwife's hands worked quickly to insert the forceps. The child was already well on its way down the birth canal.

'It's got dark hair, Mrs Cameron,' she called out. 'A beautiful head of dark hair!'

It slid out into her waiting hands and she gazed down at the bawling, lusty scrap of life she had just brought into being. 'You've got a daughter, Mrs Cameron. A beautiful baby daughter!'

She wrapped the child in a waiting towel and handed her to her mother.

Lara gazed down at the infant in her arms.

The midwife stood beaming by the bed and, seeing Lara's own head of bright titian hair, beamed, 'She must take after her Daddy, this one, and no mistake. Spitting image of your husband, I'll bet, isn't she, my dear? He'll be a proud man this day, I've no doubt.'

Lara raised her eyes from the small, screwed up face to meet those of the woman by her side. 'My husband's dead, nurse,' she answered softly. 'My husband's dead.'

And, yes, with her head of thick dark hair, she was the spitting image of her father, but her father would not be a proud man this day. Her father would never be a proud man. For her father would never know.

They brought her a cup of tea which she sipped while they washed and weighed the baby. Seven pounds twelve ounces. Not bad for a girl.

Lara listened as the Sister and the midwife chatted about the latest films they had seen. *The Moon is Down*, with Cedric Hardwick playing a German officer seemed to have gone down well.

'Just let any silly devil try to come out with pacifist nonsense to me after seeing that!' Eileen Brodie, the midwife, declared. 'Our RAF lads saved our bacon by a hair's breadth an' no mistake!' She turned to Lara. 'Don't you agree, Mrs Cameron? As sure as God we don't know what we owe to those lads!'

Lara nodded mutely from the pillow. And that's exactly what most of them were – Ken, and the rest of them – lads. Young lads with their whole lives before them. She felt the hot prick of tears behind her eyelids and blinked defiantly as she took another sip of the tea.

'It's funny what touches you,' the Sister chimed in. 'I heard a really good play on the wireless recently. By Eric Linklater it was. A discussion between Abraham Lincoln, Lenin and Confucius, and a soldier from Tobruk.'

'Confucius, eh?' the midwife looked up from powdering the baby. 'I prefer Humphrey Bogart myself.' She wrapped the infant in a clean towel and brought her across to Lara. 'Did you see his latest with that Swedish actress, Ingrid something or other her name was. Set in North Africa it was ... that place the Prime Minister went to meet the American President last January.'

'Casablanca,' Lara said softly, taking the baby from her and gazing down into its rose-pink face.

'Casablanca – that's right. That's where it was. But it had a really sad ending. He sent her away – made her go back to her husband. He couldn't really have loved her to do a thing like that, don't you agree, Mrs Cameron?'

Lara continued to stare down at her small daughter's face. It was *his* face that looked back at her. *He sent her away – made her go back to her husband ... He couldn't really have loved her to do a thing like that.* She shook her head and looked up to meet the other woman's eyes. 'No, I don't agree,' she answered softly. 'Maybe he loved her too much. And that's what made him do a thing like that ...'

The midwife's brow furrowed beneath its fair fringe and she shrugged lightly. 'Oh well, have it your own way. I never could understand men, anyway.'

'If you ask me,' the Sister put in, lifting the scales back on to their metal trolley, 'not a lot of good came out of Casablanca – either the conference or the film!'

Lara gave a quiet smile and said nothing. If only they knew. An awful lot of good came out of Casablanca – and it was lying in her arms right now.

She remained for a week in hospital: a week of air-raids, during which they had to gather everything up and rush with their babies to the cellars, and periods of calm, during which she had time to reflect on the course of her life that had brought her to this.

Not only was she a widow, but she was now a mother, and the knowledge filled her with a mixture of elation and dread. Dread mixed with an infinite sadness that Mike would never know his child. That this small, delicately formed infant in her arms would never know her father.

The wheel had come full circle. Her own mother had brought her into the world fathered by a man who was not her husband, and had been widowed shortly afterwards. But she would not make the same mistake as her mother. She would tell her daughter of her father – her real father. And if, in years to come, their child wanted to find him, to know him, then so be it. It was her birthright. Something she could not deny her.

How she could ever explain to her child's father, though, was quite another matter. How could she ever explain the guilt she had felt after Ken's death – a guilt that had multiplied ten times over knowing that she was carrying Mike's child? To have written to Mike in Washington, to have confessed all, would have been too easy, and she could not have lived with the happiness that might have resulted. Such happiness at this stage in her life would be unbearable. She would not have deserved it. It would be akin to dancing on Ken's grave.

The same young Irish nurse as had been present at the birth was back on duty the day she was due to be discharged and, as Lara sat with her small daughter wrapped in a shawl, waiting for a taxi to take them back to Lower Belgrave Street, she smiled fondly on them. 'And what will you be calling the wee one, Mrs Cameron?'

Lara paused, glanced down at the sleeping child, and gently stroked the soft downy skin of her cheek. 'I'll call her Beth,' she said softly. 'After my mother.'

The taxi never arrived. A bomb from last night's raid, someone said. It had detonated late and blown a great gaping hole in the road less than quarter of a mile from where they were. Lara could not quite grasp why that should prevent her taxi from arriving. Surely there were other roads leading to the hospital?

She did not wait to find out. Instead she took a bus. Struggling alone with the baby and her overnight bag, she squeezed herself into the only remaining seat on the lower deck. It was right at the front, next to an elderly man on his way home from Billingsgate fish market. The smell was unbearable.

She stared ahead of her, trying not to breathe too deeply through her nose. Everyone seemed to smell these days. Maybe it was something to do with having to spend nights fully clothed in the underground air-raid shelters and in the Tubes. On the back of the driver's cabin straight in front of her was one of the Government's latest war posters, entreating the public to rally to the cause:

> In war a strong defence is the springboard
> from which an offensive action can be launched.
> Lag your hot water tank now!

Suddenly, it all became too much, and she found herself laughing out loud.

The fish porter joined in and ended up pressing a silver threepenny bit into the baby's tightly clenched fist. 'Your old man'll be overseas, eh, ducks?' he said, as he made to get up and signal to the conductress to ring the bell.

Lara found herself nodding. 'Yes, he's overseas.'

'Then you write to him and tell him he's a lucky bloke, you hear. A bloody lucky bloke!'

She waved to him from out of the bus window as he disappeared into the waiting queue at the bus-stop. She couldn't even write to him if she wanted to. She didn't have an address. And nothing would persuade her to ask for one at the American Embassy. Just where was he now, the man who had fathered her child, the man she had once loved? The man she still loved.

As Lara and the baby got off at the nearest stop to their small flat in Lower Belgrave Street, Mike Adams was seated at his desk on Capitol Hill, the black telephone receiver in his hand. 'Get me Harry Hopkins, will you?' he said into the mouthpiece, and waited.

'Hopkins here.'

'Harry – it's Mike ... I've been trying to reach you all day.'

'I've been tied up with George Marshall. You know he's down to be top dog in Europe?'

The proposed appointment of General Marshall to the supreme command of Operation Overlord was now common knowledge in the corridors of power on Capitol Hill, and Mike nodded impatiently. 'It's about Europe I want to talk to you,' he said quickly. 'About London, to be precise. I've thought over what you said the other day about that London posting ... '

'And?'

'And I'm turning it down.'

'But that's crazy! It's a great opportunity.'

'Then I'm crazy. Sorry, Harry, that's just the way it goes.'

'Do I get a reason?'

Mike paused for a moment, then gave a wry half-smile into the phone. '*Cherchez la femme*, old buddy. *Cherchez la femme*.'

There was a gasp at the other end of the line. French was never one of Harry's strong points, but there was no mistaking what his old friend was telling him. 'Not a goddam dame? You're not telling me you're turning down a chance like this for a *woman*, for Chrissake?'

'OK, so I'm not telling you that. Have it your own way. But I'm still turning down the appointment.'

'You're crazy, man. You know that? You're plum loco!'

Mike gave a humourless smile into the mouthpiece of the phone, and pressed the burning stub of the cigarette into the ashtray by his elbow with even more vigour than usual. He stared down at the thin wraith of smoke that still spiralled upwards from it into the rarified atmosphere of the air-conditioning. Suddenly, beneath the freshly laundered army shirt, he was beginning to sweat. 'You could be right, old buddy. You could be right.'

Chapter Fifty-five

The autumn of 1943 gave way to winter and with the snow came more advances for the Allies in Europe. The Red Army continued its huge, relentless pressure on the retreating *Wehrmacht* and the Germans' third Russian winter was as marked by hardship and defeat as had been the first two.

In November, 'the Big Three', Churchill, Roosevelt and Stalin, met at Tehran and, although Mike accompanied the President to the conference, Lara remained in London. Having engaged a competent young woman from East Anglia as a nanny for her daughter, she returned to work at 10 Downing Street six weeks after the birth – too late to have made arrangements for the Tehran trip, even if she had wanted to go.

She had little doubt that Mike would be at the conference in Tehran. The regular communiqués they had been receiving from Washington on the subject all too often had his initials at the bottom left-hand corner. Being back at her desk and reading them brought a curious comfort, the same type of feeling she got after returning home at night and tip-toeing into the nursery to check if the baby was awake or not. Both were tangible links with him. The only links she now had, or would ever have.

But, despite her resolve to put him to the back of her mind and concentrate on building a life for herself and the baby, she found herself eagerly scanning every photograph that came out of the conference, in the hope of catching a glimpse of him in the background. It never happened, and she recalled wryly his reluctance to attend the official photo-calls at Casablanca last January.

She socialized little: a visit to the Alexandra with a girlfriend from work to see Noel Coward's *Blithe Spirit* was the nearest she came to a real night out. But the West End at night held little attraction any more. She found she had company enough in the nights she had to spend in the cellars beneath her block of flats. She came to hate those nights spent underground, huddled in a chair with the baby, praying that the all-clear would go before daybreak and she could at least snatch a few hours in a comfortable bed before getting up and preparing for work.

It was at such times that her thoughts returned to Atholl Square and the nights spent underground with her mother and Mrs Bates, with their Polish guests playing cards in the adjoining cellar. And Humphrey – how could she forget Humphrey ... ? Strangely, it was their old ginger tom that caused her eyes to glisten so often these days. On one of her periodic visits to the Polish Embassy at Portland Place, in the hope of hearing some news of her mother, she had learned one Saturday morning in early October that he had simply gone out on the Thursday night and never come back. That had been the night that thirty tons of bombs had dropped on the area around Grays, Battersea, Hampstead, and Vauxhall Bridge. Could he have wandered into the bombing zone? There was no way of telling. For days she had imagined him lying injured in the ruins somewhere and had even taken a couple of hours off work one day to look. It had been a crazy idea, for trying to find a small animal in the mountains of smoking rubble was an impossible task. But she had to look, never-theless. Humphrey may only have been an old, and not very beautiful household pet, but to her he was something special. Like her he was a survivor – the last link with her old life before the bomb on Atholl Square had shattered it beyond repair. Yes, he may only have been a fourteen-year-old moggy, but to do nothing but wait for news was asking the impossible.

It was at times like that that she understood the compulsion that had made her mother risk her own life and fly out to Poland. To sit at home in London and just wait for news – news that might never come – about the man she loved ... No, there was no way she could have done that. And, despite her own anxiety for her mother's safety, Lara knew she would not wish her back to a life of waiting and worry.

When Christmas came, she gave the nanny a week off and decided to escape from London and its never-ending air-raids by taking the baby to her grandmother's old home in Oxford. It was the worst decision she could have made for, despite her small daughter, she had never felt more alone.

And it was then she missed her mother most of all for, despite her frequent visits to the Embassy and the SOE headquarters in Baker Street, it was months since she had had word from Poland. The last news she had had was from one of Beth's old colleagues at the SOE who had called at the beginning of June to tell her that they had been informed that Beth had left Warsaw in the wake of the uprising in the Jewish ghetto, and was heading east, possibly for Lvov.

The knowledge had chilled her. What on earth would she be heading east to Lvov for? To go east was to head straight into the battle-zone. Everyone knew that the countryside to the east of the Polish capital was awash with blood. She tried to put her worst fears behind her after receiving the news, but every so often they would surface and she would find herself weeping at odd times, in the most unexpected places. The smallest thing could trigger so many memories.

She returned early to London. The thought of ending the old year alone, except for the baby, in that Oxford house that held so many memories was just too much. This year had been the worst of her life. She had lost her husband; her mother; the man who she had discovered was her father; and the man she loved. How much more could this war dish out? How much longer could she simply grin and bear it? She had no answer to that question.

And so December gave way to January and the news from the Eastern Front grew more dramatic by the day. She listened to it avidly, fearing that her mother must be somewhere there in the midst of the battle. But at least the Germans were still on the run. The siege of Leningrad, which had begun in September 1941, ended, with over 200,000 killed by the German bombardment, and over 630,000 dead of starvation and cold. When she heard of suffering on such a scale she felt ashamed of her own small worries. At least she still had a roof over her head and someone waiting at home to give her all the love she told herself she would ever need. Her baby was now her whole world and, with her head of dark curling hair and bright blue eyes, was looking more like her father by the day.

As spring came to London's parks and battered streets, attention in Downing Street was focused more and more on Operation Overlord – the plan for an Allied landing on French soil.

When she was at work, Lara found it easy to put her worries about her mother, and her longing for Mike, behind her. There was so much to be done, and she could be in no better place to know what was going on in other parts of the world. In a very humble way, she felt she was doing her bit for the war effort, but once she had left the activity of Downing Street behind her, there was not a night that she did not pray that this would be the last year of the continuing misery, that this time next year it would be all over and they could breathe freely once more. And, most of all, that her mother would have returned safely home.

But, as the days grew longer and the weather warmer, and she cast off her thick winter coat in favour of a light tweed suit, it seemed that things were getting worse before they got better. There were still air-raids on London, of course, and long nights spent in the cellar beneath the flats, but the damage the *Luftwaffe* was doing was nothing compared to the havoc being wrought by the RAF and the American Air Force across the Channel. British and American raids on Germany were leaving hundreds of thousands dead and millions homeless. She took no comfort in the fact. No one did who valued human life. This war was making killers of them all.

Every time she heard of yet another raid on Berlin, or Hamburg, or any of the great German cities, she thought of mothers like herself over there, huddled in shelters with their children. They did not ask for this war. Nor did most of the young men who found themselves at the forefront of the conflict. She thought of her shock at finding her young husband in tears that day, before he was due to return to the fray. They were not machines, the young men they sent out there to kill, or be killed. Ken had been the gentlest, most unaggressive of human beings.

So often, as time went by and the casualties increased, she felt a bitterness well within her for all those she had known and loved who were no longer there. And, as the fourth summer of conflict approached, and the streets and parks began to fill with servicemen home on leave walking out with their sweethearts and wives, she knew if it wasn't for the baby ... Sometimes, when she felt particularly low, it was easy to understand why so many she knew had put an end to it all.

But that did not lessen the deep sense of shock she felt on the evening of Saturday 10 June 1944. On that day she received a letter from Bridgend, Glamorgan, telling her that it had all finally become too much for Judy. Tuesday 6 June 1944, it had happened. That day would be etched on her memory forever. It was the day when the long awaited Overlord was put into operation; the day the Allies began their assault on the Normandy beaches, and newspaper copy writers were proclaiming to the world that D-Day had finally arrived. It was also the day her friend had taken a bus into Cardiff and headed for the station, to throw herself beneath the wheels of the 3.45 to London. It was depression after learning that, as well as her beloved Dai, her brother Bob, so long listed as missing, had now been officially certified as dead, the letter from Judy's mother had told her.

And so it went on. She felt numbed by it all. The laughter had gone out of life. Even the Allies' successes, such as the fall of Rome, failed to raise any real enthusiasm in her. Who was there left to celebrate with?

The only thing for it, she decided, was to concentrate even more wholeheartedly on her work. So every time a chance of standing in for Marian Holmes, the Prime Minister's other favourite secretary, came up, she jumped at it, secure in the knowledge that the baby was extremely well looked after at home with Nanny.

She had volunteered to stay later than usual on the evening of 15 July when, to her surprise, Stanislaw Mikolajczyk, the Polish Prime Minister in Exile, arrived unexpectedly.

As Lara sat quietly in the background, pad and pen at the ready, he handed the Prime Minister the translations of coded messages just received from Poland. They told of the bitter struggle taking place over there between the advancing Red Army and the Polish Resistance still loyal to the London Government in Exile.

Stanislaw Mikolajczyk's face was as grave as his voice as he said quietly, 'Prime Minister, you must telegraph Stalin immediately and point out to him that our Polish Underground forces have co-operated with the Red Army in the final assault and liberation of Vilna. They must acknowledge such and treat our forces accordingly.'

Churchill puffed thoughtfully on his cigar for a moment, his eyes scanning the papers on the desk in front of him, then he shook his head. 'It would do no good. We'd only be asking for a rebuff. The Russians will never admit that any of your men have ever helped in the liberation of Vilna.'

Mikolajczyk's disappointment was obvious, but he pressed on. 'It is important to us that our troops should be allowed to carry on fighting – that they should be allowed to advance with the Russians towards the West.' Then, seeing the set expression on Churchill's face, he added diplomatically, 'Of course, we fully understand the delicacy of the position in Vilna – in view of the Soviet's declaration that Lithuania is now a Soviet Socialist Republic.'

Churchill grunted. 'I don't know why you go on pressing so hard in this matter of Vilna. You must realize you've got no hope of getting your way on this. After all, you Poles seized Vilna after the last war quite against the wishes of the Allies at that time.' There was silence from the other side of the table, so he continued, 'If you ask me, Poland has already thrown away too many good opportunities of coming to terms with the Russians, and this persistent harping on about Vilna will do you no good at all.'

'Then what would you suggest?' The question was put almost too politely.

'That you take yourself off to see Joe Stalin himself if you're so worried about the outcome.'

The Polish Premier shook his head adamantly. 'That would do no good at all. What the Soviets want is to make Poland the Seventeenth Soviet Socialist Republic. If I went to Moscow it would not change that fact. It requires greater pressure than I can impose for them to change their minds.'

Churchill glared across the table and shook his head. He could not accept that assessment at all. He was not going to risk alienating the Russians at a time like this. If the Poles over here had a grievance, let them deal with it.

And so the argument continued with the London Poles all the following week, with Lara drafting telegrams to Washington on the Russo-Polish situation that she knew would be dealt with by the President's most trusted Polish-American aide; and it was indeed Mike's initials that came back on every communiqué.

But the Prime Minister was rapidly running out of patience with Portland Place and, for Lara, the situation reached a head on 27 July, when word reached London that the Red Army had entered Lvov, which the London Poles were insisting should remain an integral part of post-war Poland.

As Lara's pencil flew over the page of her notebook, taking down the resulting long telegram to Stalin, the Prime Minister looked up and, interrupting his flow, said 'Oh, by the way, my dear, I gather this latest piece of information was transmitted from Lvov by an old friend of your family's from Silesia. Count Jan Jarosinski. Did you know him at all?'

Lara froze. Her father! Her father was in Lvov. But that was where her mother had been headed. She stared across the room as her heart pounded in her breast. 'The – the Count is in Lvov, you say?'

'Well, he certainly was when he transmitted this information ...' The telephone rang. It was Eden calling to arrange a meeting.

Lara waited impatiently until the receiver was replaced a minute or so later, but the Prime Minister's mind was already on other things. 'Now, where were we ... ?'

Her heart sank. She longed to question him on the news from Lvov, but the moment had passed. As her pencil resumed its journey across the page, her mind reeled. Could it be? Could it really be that that was why her mother had been making for Lvov? She had met up with her father – or had gone to join him there ...

Please God, please let it be, she prayed inwardly. Please let my mother and father be together.

Had Lara but known it, there was no need for her prayer. Beth and Jan had been together almost every day since their escape from Warsaw in May the previous year. But, as their daughter sat taking dictation over a thousand miles away, they were already on their way back to Poland's capital city.

For almost fourteen months they had lived and worked on the small estate owned by Jan's uncle, Bogdan, about fifteen miles west of Lvov. Incredibly it had remained almost intact and had survived the worst of the fighting. When they had finally arrived, footsore and weary, at the beginning of June 1943, only the old man and one retainer remained. The estate workers had fled at the first signs of the approaching German army.

The Germans had killed most of the livestock and looted whatever was of use to them on their long trek eastwards, but the two old men they had spared. Jan's uncle told the tale with tears glistening in the faded blue of his eyes. It was only because he was a fluent German speaker, he explained, shaking his head. He had had to lie to them: declare himself to be loyal to that madman Hitler; tell them his family were of old East Prussian *Junker* stock. 'May God forgive me,' he kept repeating. 'Like St Peter denied Our Lord, they made me deny my country. May Our Lady have mercy on my soul.'

Jan had hugged him. 'Of course you will be forgiven, old man!' he had said. 'You have lived to tell the tale, just as you will live to see the day they are driven from Polish soil forever.'

The old man had looked at his nephew with hope rekindling in his eyes. 'You really believe that, Janek? You really believe it?'

Jan had nodded and clasped him around the shoulders once more. 'I really believe it. And you had better believe it too.'

And so they had come to live at Tornow, in the big house on the hill, which was almost completely hidden by the tall fir forest that had been its saviour on more than one occasion as the fighting passed within a mile of its gates.

Beth and Jan had lived as man and wife, and the old man had asked no questions. At a time like this, the old rules no longer applied. You took what happiness you could from life while it was there for the living. It was as simple as that.

They had been there just over a year when Jan took Beth aside on the bright summer morning of 24 July and told her he must return to Warsaw. He had just heard on the radio that, at that very moment,

Soviet troops were taking Lublin in Eastern Poland, marching side by side with General Zygmunt Berling's Polish Division, which was loyal to Moscow. 'Soviet power is liberating my country, *kochanie*. I must get to Warsaw. The rising we in the AK have long planned against the Germans must take place any day now. The Soviets must not be allowed to liberate Warsaw. There must be free Polish guns used first.'

The thought horrified her. 'But why, my love, why? Are we not safer here – much safer? They won't need you there. What difference will one man make among thousands? Why go back to a city that will be a blood-bath any day now?'

He had looked at her with pity in his eyes. 'Because it is *my* city that will be bleeding to death, *kochanie* – the blood of my people that will be running in the streets.'

He had that same look in his eyes that he had had when he told her he was returning to Poland all those years ago. She had known then it was useless to argue. Polska was not only engraved on his heart, but on his soul. If it bled, he bled. She knew that by now. His fear that the Russians would get the credit for liberating his country and claim the soul of Poland as its reward was very real. Nothing on earth would stop him now. 'If you go, then I come with you,' she had said softly.

He had protested, begged her to stay. But she could be every bit as determined. 'If you don't take me with you, then I will simply follow behind,' she had said. And he had believed her.

And so, the following day, they had taken their leave of his Uncle Bogdan and Waclaw, the old man who had served this eastern branch of the Jarosinski family for over fifty years. They had kissed Beth's hand after shaking Jan's, and she had impulsively hugged them both. She knew she might never see them again, but this past year they had become as close as any family. The gesture had touched them and there were more than her own eyes glistening when she turned and followed Jan down the hard-baked path that led to the forest.

They had stood at the gates and waved them on their way – two old men, who had both seen over eighty summers come and go in this beautiful land.

There was a curious feeling in the air that morning. Crickets chirped in the long grass at the edge of the path and bees droned in the wild honeysuckle, whose fragrance almost overpowered that of the pine-forest itself.

The forest was cool and alive with the singing of birds and the sun high above them in an azure sky. It was far too beautiful a day for the killing that was taking place beyond the tall trees of Tornow. Only the muffled sound of gunfire in the distance belied the peace and beauty that surrounded them.

'It's a long way, *kochanie*. A dangerous journey we have ahead of us,' he said to her, as they walked hand in hand into the jade depths of the forest. 'Are you sure you won't regret it?'

Regret it? She shook her head, her fingers squeezing his even more tightly. The words from the Book of Ruth came into her head, and she said softly, in English, '"Whither thou goest, I will go. Thy people will be my people ..."'

'"And thy God my God."'

He finished the sentence for her and, as they walked on in silence, she found herself praying to that same God that He would protect them in whatever trials may lie ahead. And there would be many, she had no doubt about that.

Chapter Fifty-six

Beth and Jan reached Warsaw on the evening of 29 July. The setting sun had seamed the darkening blue of the sky with threads of gold and crimson and a pale moon was rising above Praga, on the right bank of the Vistula, as they entered the city from the east. To Beth's dismay, it appeared the final show-down with the Germans had already begun, for the city echoed to the boom of artillery fire and fires were springing up all around them, where German bombs had found their targets.

It did not come as a complete surprise. Warsaw was surely to be the *Wehrmacht*'s last stand, the place where they would dig their heels in against the Russians' relentless advance from their victories in the East. Everywhere they had stopped during their trek back into the capital, people had talked of nothing else but the liberation of Lublin, and the whole country was cheered by the sight of the defeated German Ninth Army retreating in complete disarray across the countryside.

The Germans had already abandoned many of their main military bases and installations in Poland, and the German civilian population were evacuating the country in droves. On their way from Tornow, Jan and Beth had passed hundreds of carts, crammed with German and *Volksdeutsch* families and their belongings, frantically making their way West, back to the Fatherland, in the face of the advancing Soviets. No longer was it advantageous to have a *Kennkarte* certifying you as a *Volksdeutscher*. Divine retribution was being meted out at last.

The atmosphere throughout the land was electric, and Jan maintained you could almost smell the defeat of Hitler's much vaunted Thousand Year Reich in the clear summer air. 'Poland will be ours once more before the summer is over, my love,' he had told her, and she believed him. They had to believe it, otherwise why had they come?

As they neared the capital, the talk was of the liberation of Warsaw itself and, by the sound of it, the attempt had already begun. No longer was it Soviet aircraft dominating the skies above them, but German Stukas now flew low over the capital, discharging their deadly cargoes of heavy bombs and incendiaries on the population. The might of the *Wehrmacht* was concentrating on the city, with heavy Tiger tanks trundling through the cobbled streets.

They had arrived on the Praga side of the river but, to their relief, they learned that one railway and three road bridges across the Vistula were still intact. 'We must try to get across to the Stare Miasto, *kochanie*,' Jan told her, as they came in sight of the blue-grey water. 'We must make contact with the AK tonight.'

She looked at him anxiously. How much longer could she keep up? She was dog-tired and her feet were so badly blistered she felt another few yards would be her absolute limit. She had tried so hard over the past few days not to be a burden to him, and on the whole they had been lucky, getting lifts in farm carts, or occasionally in trucks, for most of the way. This morning, however, their luck had run out and they had had to cover the last ten miles on foot.

They had stopped at a wayside inn for bread and cheese some time in the mid-afternoon, but now it was over four hours since they had had so much as a glass of water by way of refreshment.

The aroma of brewing coffee, so tantalizing that Beth was certain it could not be ersatz, wafted out to them from an open window of one of the houses they passed. It brought memories of happier times rushing back, and for a moment she found herself having to bite her lip and blink back the tears that welled unbidden in her eyes.

She glanced across at Jan as they hurried through the back streets of Praga towards the nearest bridge. Suddenly, back in his nation's capital, he seemed to have taken on a new lease of life. For the first time since Anna's disappearance, the distant, brooding look had gone and there was an excited gleam in his eyes that she had not seen for a long time as he gave her an encouraging smile and squeezed her hand. 'Courage, my love. We are almost there.'

'But where?' she asked, listlessly, unable any longer to disguise her fatigue as they headed for the bridgehead that would take them to the Old Town. 'Where exactly are we headed, Jan? Where do we go once we have made contact with the AK? Do we attempt to go back to Freta Street?' Suddenly it was important to know. It was important to have an end in sight.

He smiled and shook his head. 'It was never our place to begin with. Now it will be someone else's home – if it's still standing, which

I doubt, seeing all this destruction.' A deep furrow creased his brow as he looked around him. There was hardly a single intact building to be seen. 'No, we will go where we are needed most ... Where we can be most effective against the Germans.'

She gave a rueful smile as she increased her pace to keep up with him. Effective? She was having enough difficulty just remaining on her feet, never mind fighting Germans. She knew he did not mean to be thoughtless. He was excited, that was all. Elated with a new found vigour now that he was back at the heart of things. She knew he had been fretting to get back as the summer had progressed back there in Tornow. Things were about to happen in Warsaw – momentous things that he longed to be a part of.

The uprising against the Germans had been planned long ago by the Home Army, the AK, who were loyal to the Government in Exile in London. It had simply been a case of waiting for the right moment to make the move. And now that the Red Army was on the outskirts of the capital, accompanied by the Polish People's Army, who were sympathetic to Moscow, that moment had come. The AK had to be a part of the liberation of the capital: to allow the Soviets and their Polish sympathizers to take all the credit was to throw their country to the Russian Bear.

It was after ten o'clock and the moon was high in the sky by the time they reached the home of Lech Kinski, in the heart of the Stare Miasto. He had been one of Jan's closest associates before their departure for Tornow and, as his home was nearest, they had decided to make for there. As they climbed the winding staircase to the top flat in the dilapidated block where he lived with his wife, Beth was certain there would be no one at home. Incredibly, not only was he in, but crowded into the tiny living-room were six other members of the AK.

Lech's wife, Stefi, in her fifties like her husband, and with a round, unlined face and a pleasant smile, was dispensing ersatz coffee and potato cakes. Once they were seated, she lost little time in serving the new arrivals. The taste of the hot brown liquid on her tongue was every bit as good to Beth as any of the best, freshly-ground variety she had been used to at home in England before the war. Even the potato cakes tasted as good as they smelt, and Lech proudly disclosed that Stefi had, in fact, bartered her best pair of winter boots for a half-sack of the vegetable that was now like gold in the city.

Their united amazement and delight at seeing Jan again was genuine, and the welcome extended to Beth herself could not have been more friendly. Most of them she recognized from visits to their

Freta Street flat, but Wladek Nowlecki was new to her: he appeared to be the oldest and most senior AK member present. He puffed thoughtfully on a briar pipe, sipping his coffee and listening, for the most part, but when he decided to speak, all listened attentively.

It did not take them long to acquaint Jan with all the facts of the situation as what was left of the evening progressed into night and the coffee gave way to vodka. For their part, the group were most interested in learning what, if anything, they had seen of the advancing Red Army on their way back from Lvov. Rumour had it that it was less than a couple of days' march from Warsaw. On being told by Jan that they had passed Soviet tanks at Radosk, within ten miles of the capital, a murmur went round the room. The Russians were even nearer than they thought.

One man who was not present, but who figured largely in the conversation, was the Commander in Chief of the AK, General Tadeusz Komorowski, code-named 'Bor', a man for whom Jan had a particular regard. A family of minor Polish nobility, the Komorowskis were not quite as high on the social scale as the Jarosinskis but, nevertheless, Jan and Tadeusz had many friends in common, and the two had met occasionally before the war at show-jumping events in Silesia. Since Komorowski assumed command of the Home Army, however, they had met only infrequently. It was his word they would wait for to set the uprising in motion.

Crucial to that decision, however, was the support of the Allies and the Government in Exile in London. 'You have more experience of what goes on over there than any man here, Jan,' Wladek Nowlecki said. 'Maybe you can give an opinion on things in London – on the reaction we can expect. "Bor" has contacted Raczynski and the others, putting the case for the Home Army, but we have had no answer yet. It is essential, if we are not to submit to total Soviet domination, that the AK is officially recognized as an integral part of the Allied Forces, and the civil administration as part of the Allied Military Government. We have made a few essential requests of the Allies that must be met if the AK is to be successful in this uprising.'

'And these are?'

'That British help is forthcoming for the bombing of German-held airfields in the vicinity of Warsaw; for our own Polish squadrons within the RAF to return to Poland, and for the Polish Parachute Brigade to be dropped just outside the city … We expect their reply any day now. What do you feel? Will it be positive?'

Jan took a deep breath and let it out slowly. It was years since he had been in London. How could he possibly know what they were feeling over there? But he could only tell the truth as he saw it. 'I feel we should not set too much store by a positive reply to our demands,' he said, choosing his words carefully. 'The Allies cannot afford to offend the Russians. The Red Army is essential to the defeat of Germany and that is paramount. Their needs and desires must be accommodated.'

'To the detriment of Poland?'

'If need be.'

His words were to prove disappointingly accurate, for the following day, a courier, Lieutenant Jan Nowak, was parachuted back into Poland with the reply from the Government in Exile, stating that the large-scale help requested by the Home Army would not be forthcoming.

Jan and Beth, who had spent the night on the Kinskis' pull-out sofa, heard the news at the AK meeting in the Viktoria Hotel on Jasna Street. Sir Orme Sargent, of the British Foreign Office, had informed Count Edward Raczynski, the Polish Ambassador, on 28 July, that it would be impossible to meet the three requests for assistance in the planned Warsaw uprising. It would be impossible for the Polish Parachute Brigade to return to Poland as it would not be able to fly over German territory without incurring excessive losses. As to the despatch of Polish fighter squadrons back to Poland, this would be a complicated procedure which could not be carried out without the approval of the Soviet Government. And, finally, it would not be possible to bomb the German-held airfields as these were out of the normal operational range of RAF bombers.

They had all looked at one another as the news was read out in a flat, unemotional voice, by Colonel Menter, the officer in charge.

A bitterness welled within Beth. Her own people, the British, were deserting Poland when she needed them most. It didn't make sense. Why had they entered this war in the first place, for heaven's sake? You couldn't simply declare war against Germany because it invaded Poland and then leave the Poles to perish at the enemies' hands. She stared straight ahead of her at the tense, drawn face of the Colonel as he sat down heavily on his chair. For the first time in her life she felt ashamed of her country. May God forgive them back in London, for she never would.

'It looks like we're on our own,' someone said from the back of the room, echoing all their thoughts, and Beth felt Jan squeeze her hand that little bit tighter. He knew what she did not – that the Home Army had to establish a quick and effective victory, for they only had enough arms and supplies for a week, no more.

He looked around the room at the faces of the men who had waited almost five years for this moment, and he knew the meaning of the glow that shone in all their eyes. For years they had watched the destruction of their land and their people by their ancient enemy from the West, but now vengeance would be sweet, whether help was forthcoming from London or not. The story of their mammoth endeavour this summer would be written in blood across the pages of the history books. At long last, the Polish eagle was rising from the ashes to drive out the transgressor.

Then his eyes rested on the face of the woman he loved, as she sat listening to the talk around them. She had risked everything to come here to this country to find him. Yet she asked for nothing in return. Nothing but the knowledge that he still felt as she did. A single silver strand shone amongst the fall of thick brown hair that swept back from her brow. They had come a long way, the two of them – a very long way – from that first summer in Silesia, just after the 'war to end all wars' had ended, and the world looked forward in hope to a future free from strife for them and their children, and their children's children.

Their children ... He tensed inwardly as his thoughts returned to the two girls he had fathered by two very different women. The memory of Anna lay like a scar across his soul. It should have been him. He should have been the one who was manhandled on to that cattle-truck in the Jewish ghetto and taken off to that death camp, Treblinka. He could not bear to think of her these days. The knowledge that she could still be alive there and suffering was almost too much to bear ...

And Lara – what of Lara? Would he ever see her again? Would he ever get to know the young woman who was so much a part of himself and of the woman he loved? It seemed too much like tempting fate to look beyond these coming few days. It was enough to ask that one lived to fight another day. And that was how they would do it – bit by bit, street by street, until the Germans were driven back to the Reich and Poland could once more breathe free.

The meeting broke up with the singing of the old patriotic hymn of Dabrowski's Polish legions. Jan and Beth stood side by side, their voices ringing out in glorious unison with those of their comrades. Her Polish was now as fluent as her German, and she had never felt so much at one with the man by her side as she sang along with him:

Jeszcze Polska nie zginela
Poki My zyjemy.
Co nam obca przemoc wziela
Szabla odbijemy ...

Poland has not perished yet
So long as we shall live
That which alien force has seized
We at swordpoint shall retrieve ...

When the meeting ended, they climbed the stairs to the room they had booked into on the top floor of the hotel. After turning the key in the lock of the door behind them, he took her in his arms and lifted her face to his. 'Do you remember the last time we were together in an hotel room like this, my love?' he asked softly.

How could she forget? That night in the Queen's Hotel in Dundee would be engraved on her heart forever. 'Will we ever see it again, Jan?' she asked softly. 'Will we ever go back?'

His hand stroked her hair. 'Do you want to go back, my love? Do you want to return to Britain? Would that make you happy?'

She shook her head. Nothing in the world could make her as happy as just being with him. And, despite everything, she now had her wish. She would not ask for it to be any other way.

Chapter Fifty-seven

Early on the morning of 1 August, for the first time, Beth accompanied Jan to Mass. The air outside the 200-year-old building was close and sultry, as if a storm was in the offing, and inside the atmosphere was quite claustrophobic. The church was packed with worshippers. The whole city was on edge.

They took their places at the back of the church, next to the aisle, as the aged priest, assisted by two acolytes, knelt in front of the altar and began the Mass with a short prayer: '*In Nomine Patris et Filii et Spiritus Sancti ...*'

The congregation joined in: prayers were said and the patriotic hymns sung that morning with even more fervour than usual. The priest spoke movingly of the massacre at Katyn, causing many in the congregation to weep aloud, and Beth knew that she was in the company of many mothers, wives, and loved ones of the officers that were slaughtered that awful day. He called for their deaths not to have been in vain; for a new, free Poland to rise from the ashes of the old. It was as near a battle cry as it was possible for a man of God in this city to give.

Beth was aware of Jan praying silently beside her for much of the service. His head was bowed and her gaze rested on the scar down the side of his face. So livid a few years ago, it had now faded to a thin, silver line. It was a proud, dignified profile and he would bear the wound with pride in years to come. The Nazis could disfigure him physically, but not spiritually. They could never touch his soul.

He looked like his grandfather, he had once told her – a typical Jarosinski – and she could just imagine all those ancestors gazing down from their gilt frames on the walls of Jarosbork. Would he ever see it again? For a fleeting moment doubt crept into her mind, but she dismissed it immediately. This war had caused so much havoc in all their lives, but it could not last forever. A line from Yeats echoed in her head: 'Things fall apart, the centre cannot hold'. Things had fallen apart all right over the past few years, but it was up to them to make sure that the centre *could* hold. And for Jan and her, Jarosbork was the centre. It had been the centre for almost a thousand years – as long as Hitler had promised his Reich would last. But he was wrong. And Jarosbork would stand for another thousand years. And for a small number of those years, God willing, they would be part of it. They would return to Jarosbork when this nightmare was over, and walk once more along the banks of the Praszkawarthe, where they had walked so many years ago, where they had first fallen in love. Yes, they would return there – he had promised her that. And she believed it, just as, deep in her heart, she had believed him when he had vowed to her that they would meet again, when she had taken her leave of him to return to England.

Yes, she had faith in that but, strangely, she could not bring herself to share his faith in this ceremony they were taking part in. She wished she had his faith in the Church – that she could bring herself to believe more in his God. Was she the only doubter here today?

She glanced around her at the faces in the rows of the faithful, then dropped her gaze to the careworn hands of the old woman next to her, as they ceaselessly fingered the black jet rosary beads, worn smooth with a lifetime of use. She looked down at her own hands lying empty in her lap. It was at a time like this that faith could mean so much.

She closed her eyes and tried to pray, but the right words would not come. What kind of a God was it who had allowed such things to happen as she had witnessed over the past few years?

She thought of Lara back home in London and wished she could have made some kind of personal contact over this past year and a half. Had Lower Belgrave Street escaped the worst of the bombing? Was she well? Had she seen much of Ken of late? She hoped with all her heart that she had. Maybe she was even pregnant. Now wouldn't that be something! For all she knew, she and Jan could be grand-parents!

After the service she waited in the background, by the door, while Jan lit two candles. She could see his lips saying a silent prayer as he took the lighted taper and held it to the wicks of first one then the other. Two white candles in a forest of spluttering flames. Each one carrying the hopes and prayers dear to someone's heart. Two small candles to light the darkest corners of *his* heart. One for Anna and one for Poland. She was sure of it, although she did not ask when eventually he joined her at the door, and he did not say.

Out on the crowded pavement once more, he took her arm and suggested they call in at Malinowski's café for a cup of barley coffee. She agreed at once. Both knew it might be the last normal thing they would do for a long time. The announcement of the rising was due at any moment.

They hurried, arm in arm, along the pavements, past houses where, amazingly, flowers still bloomed in window boxes. Their scent met her nostrils. From the sight of the broken, dust-covered windows behind the blooms, it was obvious that the people who had planted them with such love and care were long gone. To Treblinka, to Auschwitz ... Who could say? The scent of the blooms hanging heavy in the humid air of the city street was as incongruous as perfume on a corpse.

The pavement seats were all taken when they arrived at the small restaurant, but they preferred to sit inside anyway. Why expose yourself more than necessary? They found a table for two at the far side of the counter, next to the fireplace, and both glanced around them anxiously before giving their order to the pretty girl in the peasant blouse and dirndl skirt. A wave of relief swept through Beth; she recognized none of the faces at the neighbouring tables.

Jan reached across and took her hand. 'Happy?'

It was an odd question, but she knew what he meant. 'Very happy.' It was wartime, they were in constant danger, but they were together. It was more than she could have hoped for, and she knew he felt the same.

They had not been seated at the white clothed table for more than a few minutes, and the dirndl-skirted girl had just served their coffee, when the door opened and Beth glanced round in curiosity. It was something she did as a matter of course these days. A startlingly pretty blonde girl entered on the arm of a German officer.

'Marysia!' The name burst involuntarily from Beth's lips, but was heard by no one but Jan because of the babble of voices inside the café.

He tensed immediately at the sight of the German uniform and looked at her curiously, his own stomach knotting at the look on her face. 'You know her?'

Beth nodded mutely as a film of nervous perspiration broke on her skin. The past eighteen months disappeared in a flash. 'I met her at the Hotel Torun,' she said quietly. 'She's with the Resistance. She's one of us.' The last two sentences were meant to reassure herself as much as him.

Jan's brow furrowed. 'You're sure about that?' He darted another glance at the couple who had now seated themselves at a table at the far side of the room, next to the door.

She was not sure of anything any more. An almost uncontrollable urge to flee came over her. What if she had been wrong? What if Marysia was not one of them? What if she was a double agent? What if … What if … 'Can we go?' She had already half risen from the table.

He followed her out of the café, his own pulse racing faster as they squeezed their way through the tightly packed tables towards the door. There was no way they could avoid passing their table, but Jan deliberately positioned himself between the couple and Beth as they hurried past, faces averted.

They had barely reached the outside pavement and had a chance to draw a breath of relief, when the door opened behind them and Marysia appeared.

The colour drained from Beth's face and she took an anxious half-step backwards, but the eyes gazing in delight into her own were smiling.

Marysia clasped Beth by the hand. 'Countess – it *is* you! I can hardly believe it!'

Beth stared at her, her mouth dry. But, unaware of the internal panic she was causing, Marysia looked anxiously from her to Jan. 'Is your friend … ?' She deliberately did not finish the sentence.

Beth nodded. 'You can speak freely here.'

'The Home Army or the People's Army?' Marysia asked in a low voice. It was the most common question amongst Poles these days.

'The former,' Jan replied, glancing back towards the door. Thankfully her German companion had not followed.

'Don't worry about Uwe,' Marysia assured him. 'I told him Beth was my sister-in-law and I have to arrange a night's baby-sitting … He is perfectly harmless, but quite knowledgeable, needless to say. He also speaks quite freely when he has a drink or two too many. Can you get a message back to AK headquarters today?'

'Of course.'

Marysia glanced back at the closed door of the café. 'Uwe is in the Administration,' she said softly. 'There are supposed to be over 40,000 German troops in the city, ready for any emergency. It's no longer true. A number of units have already left the city this month. Less than 13,000 remain. But, most importantly, both companies of the 654th Engineer Battalion remain – they've spent this morning laying explosives on the remaining bridges over the river. For God's sake don't let our men use them!'

She made a move back towards the door, then reached out and

clasped Beth by the hand once more. 'One more thing, Countess – you can breathe more easily these days: you do know your old friend is dead, don't you?'

'My old friend?' Beth's brow furrowed.

'Don't tell me you don't remember the Count – von Lessing, wasn't it?'

Beth drew in her breath sharply. 'Ott ...' she checked herself in time. 'Count von Lessing is dead?'

Marysia frowned for a moment, disconcerted by the shocked look on the other's face. 'Yes, didn't you hear? He was killed in the ghetto during the Jewish uprising there last year.'

Beth shook her head. 'No ... No I didn't hear.'

Marysia's frown deepened at the peculiar expression of shock combined with an almost grotesque fixed smile on Beth's face, but she had no time to dwell on the reaction. 'I'm sorry, I must go now. Uwe will be getting impatient.' She turned to Jan. 'You will pass on the message, won't you?'

'Of course.'

And with that she was gone – back inside the café to keep company with the enemy.

Jan and Beth looked at one another. He knew exactly what she was feeling – the conflicting thoughts that were tumbling through her mind. 'Come, *kochanie*,' he said softly, taking her arm. 'We have a message to deliver.'

She let herself be led through the streets in the direction of the AK headquarters. Memories of that beloved golden-haired child flooded her brain, numbing it to all but the knowledge that she would never see him again; she could never find him when this terrible war was over, could never make her peace, could never find out what went wrong. And something had gone wrong – badly wrong – in Otto's past to set him on the path he chose to follow. But now she would never know. It was over. His short, pitiful life was over before it had hardly begun. His beloved Hitler had seen to that. Hitler and some unknown Jew whose bullet had found its target last spring, before the cattle-trucks rolled up to cart him off to Treblinka with the others. To her consternation, she found herself fighting an almost uncontrollable urge to break down and cry. Otto was dead. She did not want him dead. Dear God, she did not want him dead ...

They relayed Marysia's information back to General Komorowski at the AK headquarters in the Kamler tobacco factory in Wola, the working-class district to the north-west of the city. It was greeted with interest, for it confirmed what they all already suspected.

Very few of those present wore a uniform of any sort, and even Tadeusz Komorowski himself was dressed only in shabby civilian clothes. The men and women who manned the headquarters looked as if they had been at their posts for days. And when Jan suggested they stay and help out, Beth readily agreed.

They were still there at two o'clock in the afternoon when, to the consternation of all present, premature sporadic fighting broke out between the AK forces in the city and their German overlords.

The shooting started first in the Zoliborz district, where it was quickly followed by outbursts in Wola itself, which they could hear from the windows of the headquarters. Reports began coming in of other outbreaks – in Napoleon Square; Kercely Square; Mirowski Square; in Mokotow – the locations becoming more numerous as the afternoon progressed. By five o'clock, the prearranged time of the uprising itself, the city was already alive with gunfire.

Beth was asked to man one of the radio transmitters specially set up, along with receivers, to ensure communication with the outside world was maintained, while Jan conferred in a room upstairs with the leaders. Along with 'Bor' Komorowski and the Home Army General Staff, the Polish Deputy Premier, Jan Jankowski, and other notable politicians were present. The whole building buzzed with excitement.

The leaders' discussion was animated and prolonged. The first plan of attack was for their men to concentrate on all the main German strong points throughout the city, particularly on the Gestapo, Police, and *Wehrmacht* headquarters. The rebel forces were to be deployed according to the strength of the enemy.

On the left bank of the Vistula was the Old Town, the Town Centre and, amongst other districts, Wola, the area near the city centre where they were themselves situated. On the right bank lay Praga. Most of the important German headquarters were situated in the Old Town, or in the Town Centre, so it was on these two parts of the city that most of their troops were to be concentrated.

In the middle of it all, stretching between Leszno, Bonifraterska, Okopowa, Stawki and Miranowska streets, lay the burnt out ruins of the Jewish ghetto, its high wall still a poignant and terrible reminder of what their enemy was capable of, as now the Poles themselves rose in rebellion against their German masters.

Jan came downstairs at a little after four and took Beth aside. He looked drawn and tired, but his eyes were alive with the excitement of the moment. 'It is going to be a long night, *kochanie*,' he said quietly. 'I want you to get some rest.'

She looked at him suspiciously. 'Meaning?'

'Meaning I would like you to return to the hotel and catch up on some sleep.'

'And you? Where will you be?'

'Here.'

'Then I will be here too.'

And so she was. She remained seated at the controls of the radio for most of the night, while the room hummed with activity and the city outside shook with explosions and the sound of gunfire.

Time was of the essence. They all knew it. The Third Reich in Poland was crumbling and as Beth stood at the window and looked out over the darkened city a shiver of anticipation mingled with fear ran through her.

The factory building in which they were situated faced on to Pawia Street, which was now no more than a narrow cul-de-sac closed off by the huge, brooding wall of the ghetto. It evoked too many unhappy memories and she deliberately looked the other way.

The night sky to the west was lit by a flame-red glow, but she knew it was to the east that the citizens of Warsaw were looking with mounting anxiety this night. Would the Soviet tanks now gathering outside the capital cross the Vistula before the Home Army had retaken it in the name of the free Polish Republic? They could only wait and wonder.

Chapter Fifty-eight

It had been a long day and one of the warmest of the summer. The main office at Number Ten Downing Street was stifling, despite the open window, as Lara stared at the Prime Minister in incredulity. 'You mean it? You really mean it? You heard my mother's voice?'

Churchill smiled. 'Would I lie about a thing like that?'

Lara shook her head and sat down unsteadily on the hard chair next to the desk. 'I can't believe it, after all this time I'd almost given up hope.'

The PM nodded understandingly. 'I know it's been hard for you for the past year and a half. I've often tried to elicit some news of your mother myself whenever I've come across any of that lot from SOE, but the trail appeared to have gone cold after she left Warsaw last year.'

'I know. I heard she'd headed towards Lvov, but I couldn't imagine why. She knew no one in that area that I'm aware of. In a way it's a relief to know she's back in Warsaw, even though things are pretty awful there at the moment. She was manning the Resistance radio, you say?'

Churchill nodded and swatted irritably at a bluebottle that buzzed between him and the open window. 'No doubt about it. Almost solidly for the last five days, from what I can gather. She gave her code-name and it was recognized by someone from the SOE at the receiving end who knew she was out there. I was in the room myself this afternoon when the last SOS for aid came over the air from AK headquarters and I heard them comment on it.'

Lara took a deep breath and leaned back in her chair. A light film of perspiration shone on her brow and she fanned herself with her notebook. It was too much to take in all at once. 'She must have gone back to Warsaw,' she said quietly. 'She must have known there was to be an uprising, but it didn't deter her ... At any rate, she's in the thick of it now.' She gave a wry smile. Her mother had courage, there was no doubt about that. More courage than she herself would have had. She looked across anxiously at her boss. 'The calls – the SOS calls you mentioned – what exactly were they about?'

The offending fly was swatted with a copy of *The Times* and it fell lifeless on to the window-sill. The irritating buzzing had ceased, and the Prime Minister gave a smile of satisfaction before turning back to Lara. 'Oh, they weren't personal. Don't worry about that. Your mother wasn't requesting to be lifted out of there. They were general pleas for assistance for more supplies for the Resistance. They're at it all the time just now – calling for help. The Home Army's transmitters have been manned around the clock since the rising broke out. They serve a dual purpose. They inform us here in London what's happening out there and let us know exactly how much they need in the way of ammunition and guns. By the sound of it they're getting pretty desperate.'

He was telling her nothing she didn't already know. Everyone she had met from the Polish Embassy of late had talked about almost nothing else, but she could recall no real decisions having been taken in Downing Street for a special air-lift. She looked at him apprehensively. 'We *are* going to supply them, aren't we?'

Churchill paused in his pacing of the carpet in front of the window and puffed thoughtfully on his cigar. 'It's not as easy as that, as you well know. We've been trying, Lara. By God, we've been trying. For the past three years, we've been sending Halifaxes and Liberators over there, dropping ammunition at prearranged spots, but it's dashed difficult. The pure logistics of the situation are a nightmare for those involved. The BBC Polish service has to signal the drop on a given night by playing a certain tune, then another one if it's cancelled for any reason, and each separate dropping-place is signified by a different tune. You wouldn't have to be tone-deaf, I can tell you! Only the Good Lord knows how they keep track of them all.'

She gave a rueful smile and murmured her agreement. 'How do they know exactly where to drop the stuff so it won't fall into German hands?'

A large puff of cigar smoke floated slowly to the ceiling, then disappeared in the draught from the top of the open window. 'By signalling from down below, that's how. And, believe me, it's not easy for either the pilots or the people manning the flashlights on the ground. Especially when you're trying to drop within a city like Warsaw under conditions as they are at the moment, with most of the place covered in clouds of thick smoke from the burning buildings.

Our RAF bases in Southern Italy have been assigned the job – 148 Squadron and 334 Wing, if I remember rightly – but they won't be thanking us for it. It's a thousand miles to Warsaw and they have to fly over mainly occupied territory to get there. It's a dashed dangerous operation. They have to come in at roof-top height through a barrage of anti-aircraft fire to drop their containers at the prearranged spots.'

There was a moment's silence as both pondered on the bravery involved in such operations. Then, still worried about her mother, Lara enquired anxiously, 'But you're still authorizing flights, aren't you? We can't let them down – not now.'

The Prime Minister leaned over and tapped a thick column of white ash into an ashtray on his desk. 'We've been dropping as much as we can in the parts of the city held by the Home Army, but with the situation so fluid from day to day, there's no guarantee it's falling into the right hands.'

Lara's eyes followed him as he continued to pace the well-worn Indian carpet by the window. She wished she'd paid more attention to the daily reports coming in from the Polish capital. 'But they're getting through, aren't they? Some at least must be getting through?'

Churchill reached across to a file on his desk and extracted a piece of paper. He reached into his pocket for his glasses and glanced down at the neatly-typed page. He understood her anxiety and was keen to relieve it as best he could. He knew how his own daughters would feel if it was their mother caught up in something like this.

Peering through the glasses perched on the end of his nose, his pale eyes scanned the page in his hand as he nodded thoughtfully. 'Seems like bad weather cancelled the operation on the third, but last night two Halifaxes succeeded in getting through and dropped twenty-four containers of weapons into the south-west quarter of Warsaw – about sixty tons in all, it says here.'

Lara visibly relaxed. Sixty tons – it wasn't much against the might of the Germans, but at least they were getting something. Her mother would be relieved. She longed to question him further on the subject, but he had replaced the page in the file and was glancing at his watch. She bit back the questions on her tongue and sat and waited, her pencil still poised above the ever-ready notebook, but it was almost seven o'clock, and Winston had had enough for the time being.

'We'll leave it there for just now, Lara. It's high time you were off home, anyway.' He tapped the end of his Havana in the ashtray. There was just time for a brandy before dinner if he went upstairs now, and he could certainly do with it. 'Who takes over from you tonight? Miss Sherlock, I presume?'

Lara smiled as she closed her notebook. 'Yes, Marian Holmes is on this evening.' He loved his little joke.

He grinned in return. 'Good … a first class secretary, Miss Sherlock. Almost up to your own standard!' He winked. There was nothing to choose between them, but he believed it did their morale good to believe each was his particular favourite. He made a shooing gesture with the hand holding the cigar. 'Now be off with you! Otherwise that young daughter of yours will be growing up thinking she's an orphan. How is she, by the way? Is she walking yet?'

Lara stood up and allowed herself a smile of justifiable pride as she straightened the chair. 'She can get around the room holding on to the furniture now. It can only be a matter of days until she takes her first unaided step.'

'Her father would have been proud of her.'

She flushed as the words, so innocently spoken, struck home. He meant Ken, of course, but it was to Mike Adams that her thoughts flew. It was weeks since she had last seen his initials at the foot of any correspondence from Washington, and the lack of this most basic contact with him had brought a feeling almost akin to bereavement. In fact, if it wasn't for her baby, she really couldn't imagine how she would have got through these past few months. Little Beth had come to mean everything to her and, much as she loved her job, every moment spent away from her daughter she was coming to resent more and more. The child was a living part – the only part she had left – of the man she had once loved, and still loved. No one, except the father of the child himself, could ever mean as much. Her heart lifted at the thought of going home to her. She backed towards the door. 'Well, if that'll be everything, sir …'

He waved her away. 'Yes, you'd better be off with you, otherwise I'll be accused of depriving a child of its mother – and I think I'm accused of enough these days without that, don't you?'

She smiled. He had assumed his gruff voice again, but it was totally belied by the twinkle in the pale blue eyes. It had been a long day for both of them and it was time she was going. 'Well, goodnight then, sir.' She left the room, closing the door quietly behind her.

She almost skipped down the corridor to the cloakroom. Apart from her delight at seeing her daughter again shortly, an enormous load had been lifted from her shoulders. She would rest easier tonight – her mother was alive! She was safe in Warsaw. And, despite the incalculable odds against a Polish victory over the Germans, and the undoubted difficulties involved in getting supplies out there to the Resistance, she could not believe that the Allies would allow them to be defeated. After all, they were dropping supplies, weren't they? The Prime Minister himself had confirmed it. And the Red Army was waiting at the city gates to help out. With the Allies and a bit of luck on their side, they could have the Germans on the run within a week and her mother could be on her way home by the end of the month! Her heart sang with joy at the thought. Yes, it was turning out one of the happiest days for a very long time.

She decided to walk most of the way back to Lower Belgrave Street. The sun was still shining in an almost cloudless sky and for the first time in a long time she actually took pleasure in enjoying what was left of the summer.

That morning one of the typists from the Garden Rooms at Number Ten had told her there was a stall at the Portobello Market that was selling apples *and* plums, and she had gone all the way over there in her lunch hour and queued for ten minutes to buy one pound of each. They now lay in the bottom of the basket over her arm – a delicious weight that would be a special treat for supper tonight. And it would be the first time the baby had ever tasted a plum. A fond smile crossed her face at the thought of little Beth attempting to bite into the soft red flesh.

Yes, those moments were special all right – very special. It was odd really how things you would have taken for granted a short while ago could be suddenly taken away from you. If things had worked out differently she would have been able to spend all day at home with her child like almost every other mother. Having to snatch a few precious minutes in the evening before her daughter's bedtime – a few precious minutes in which to cram so much – was not really her ideal of how motherhood should be.

She thought of her own early childhood – the first few years in Oxford before her mother married Jack Mallory. She remembered gathering the rosy-cheeked apples in the small orchard in her grandparents' back garden, and the swing her grandfather had rigged up in the branches of the tallest apple tree, and she regretted bitterly that her own daughter would not know the pleasure such grandparents could bring. Were all the summers really so golden then? Or did distance lend enchantment like they said? She was sure of nothing any more. It was something she would ask her mother as soon as this awful war was over and Beth was safely home again.

There was so much she not only wanted, but needed to discuss with her. And the relief in knowing that this, God willing, might be possible sooner than she imagined was a wonderful feeling. Perhaps she could even pay a call to SOE headquarters in Baker Street and listen in to the next AK broadcast from Warsaw. With a bit of luck it might be her mother on duty. Just to hear her voice again after so long ... She found herself smiling at passers-by at the thought.

The smile was still on her face when she reached home and was greeted at the door of her flat by a smiling nanny and a gurgling baby.

'She's done it, Mrs Cameron! She took her very first step today! Straight into my arms. Now wasn't that a clever girl!'

Lara gaped in amazement at Sheila Prentice, the fresh-faced, East Anglian nanny. 'No!' Surely not. Little Beth couldn't have taken her first step while she was out at work – that would be too much to bear. Despite her proud boast to the Prime Minister tonight, she had never expected this and, despite herself, a deep resentment welled within her that she should have been robbed of this important moment in her child's young life.

'Aren't you pleased?' Sheila's amber eyes looked at her accusingly. 'She's a very clever young lady, aren't you, my little lamb?' The girl smoothed the baby's dark curls with a protective hand.

Little Beth giggled and gurgled once more, then squirmed in the nanny's embrace and held out a pair of chubby arms towards her mother.

Lara reached out and clutched her child to her. Despite her previous high spirits, she had an almost uncontrollable urge to cry. Poor little mite – both her mother *and* her father had missed one of the most important occasions in her young life. Why couldn't it have happened tomorrow, on her day off?

Small sticky fingers were pulling at her hat, tilting it rakishly over one eye, then the pale-blue felt and feather confection was wrenched from her head and sent sailing across the hall. 'Oh, you little devil!'

Adjusting the baby on her hip, she retrieved the hat and placed it safely on the hallstand before turning to the other young woman with a strained smile. 'I'll take over from now on, Sheila, thanks. Why don't you treat yourself to a night at the pictures?'

Hoisting the baby on to her right hip, she dug into the pocket of her suit jacket, extracted a half-crown and held it out. 'Here – you can tell me all about it when you get back.'

The nanny looked down at the silver coin in the palm of her employer's hand. 'Oh, really – there's no need ... '

'I know there's no need,' Lara insisted, 'but I'd like you to take it. It's been four days since you've had an evening off ... Now is there anything you've got to tell me before you go?' It wouldn't be the first evening the baby had been fed twice because Sheila forgot to mention she'd already done it before she went off duty.

The light brows above the amber eyes furrowed. There *was* something now she came to think about it … 'Oh, yes, just as well you mentioned it. You had a visitor this afternoon.'

Lara sighed. 'You didn't say when I'd be home, did you?' The last thing she needed was for someone to stop by tonight. She was out on her feet. All she wanted was to play with the baby, have a bite to eat, then sink into a warm bath – air-raids permitting – and enjoy one of those juicy red plums lying in her basket.

Sheila made an embarrassed face. 'Well, I did actually.'

'Oh Lord – well, who was it? Did she say?'

'It wasn't a lady, ma'am. It was a gentleman. An American gentleman.'

Lara froze and almost dropped the baby. 'An *American* gentleman?'

The nanny nodded, even more embarrassed now by the peculiar look on her employer's face. The last thing she wanted to do was annoy her just after she had given her an evening off and money to go to the pictures. 'Yes,' she admitted miserably. 'A General Adams, he said his name was. A tall bloke – good-looking too. He said he was an old friend of yours … I hope you don't mind, Mrs Cameron, but he's calling back around eight o'clock this evening.'

Lara's breath caught in her throat. MIND? She hoped she didn't MIND? Colour flared up her neck to suffuse her cheeks. She moved the baby back to her other hip and glanced down at her watch. 'He's calling back around eight o'clock, you say?' Her voice was little more than a squeak. It was already seven-fifty!

The young woman opposite nodded in bewilderment, not quite sure whether the other was pleased or annoyed by the news. 'Yes, that's right, ma'am. You – you know him, then, this American General? He's some kind of friend of yours?'

Lara clutched her child to her. 'Yes – yes, you could say that, Sheila. You could say he's some kind of friend of mine.'

Chapter Fifty-nine

Beth and Jan stood at the window of a top floor flat in Barakowa Street in the Stare Miasto, the old part of Warsaw, situated on an escarpment on the left bank of the Vistula and the only part as yet untouched by the fighting. They looked out over the winding streets of tall, narrow buildings, with their steeply tiled roofs, all endearingly uneven. Each house was painted a different pastel shade, and all had elaborately decorated facades and ornamental doorways. If ever there was a place you could forget there was a war on, this was it. This was the picture book part of the city, the part built within its ancient walls by the prosperous merchants of the Middle Ages and almost unchanged from those days to this.

'My mother's family came from here,' Jan said quietly, his arm resting protectively around Beth's shoulders as they gazed out over the roof-tops into the darkening sky. 'The Romerskis made their money from the Baltic, trading in furs mainly.' He gave a wry smile. 'Many of the Jarosinskis liked to refer to my mother's side of the family as part of Poland's "*nouveau riche*", even though the Romerskis had been one of its most affluent families for 400 years. To them, if your family did not date back at least to Kazimierz the Great, you were little more than a parvenu.'

'You're joking.'

He smiled. 'Only partly.'

She knew what he was thinking as they stood there and watched the sun set on the seventh day of fighting in the city. How long would it be before the carnage reached here? How long would it be before the Germans tore the physical heart out of Poland, just as they had attempted over the last five years to tear the spiritual heart from its people?

Yesterday the *Wehrmacht* had launched a large-scale attack from the western side of the city and, all day, in the skies above them,

Stukas had swooped low, dropping their heavy bombs on carefully chosen targets, and sowing their deadly incendiaries by the thousand. The heavy battalions with their Tiger tanks were moving in, closing in on them by the hour. Rumour had it they were already in Grzybowski Square.

The Old Town itself was filling with thousands of refugees fleeing the carnage in the west of the city. All last night they had been coming: whole families fleeing in panic, dragging pitifully few possessions, all they could salvage, behind them. In their wake they left homes reduced to rubble and a sea of flames where once well-loved streets had stood. In this street alone, 5,000 refugees were already crammed into cellars and empty workplaces. 'It can't go on forever,' she heard herself saying. 'Surely the Allies will come to our aid.'

He gave a bitter smile. 'You have not heard the latest news from London.'

She looked up at him, puzzled. She had only been asleep in this borrowed room for less than twelve hours. 'What do you mean, Jan? Has anything happened since I've been here?'

He was silent for a moment. Was there any point in alarming her? He stared out at the red glow in the evening sky. What was the point in lying? He would protect her with his life if need be, but he could not tell her less than the truth. 'We've heard from London that they're calling a halt to their special flights dropping us our supplies. They say it's too costly in RAF personnel. Five of their aircraft were lost the other night.'

'But you are protesting, surely?'

He nodded. 'Komorowski's sent off a very strongly worded signal. It remains to be seen if it'll do any good.'

Beth shivered, but not out of cold. 'It's very near the end now, isn't it?'

He did not have to answer. Beth knew what was going on, that German Panzers were already spearheading an attack on Wola, the district where until today the AK had had its headquarters.

The night before, the Kamler factory they had been using as a GHQ had been under continuous machine-gun fire. Komorowski had ordered its evacuation to Barakowa Street in the Stare Miasto. They were to take over a tall building, once used as a school, only a few blocks down from where they now were.

The route from their old HQ to Barakowa Street lay across the ruins of the Jewish ghetto, and German machine-gunners had a panoramic view of the area from the roof of the old Pawiak prison, so the crossing was far from easy. To add to their difficulties, yet another air-raid was in progress, and the shrill scream of falling bombs mingled with the heavy, earth-shuddering crash of explosives as they dashed in single file from the doomed building.

They were led by Komorowski himself, and a well-armed Polish infantry platoon, as they picked their way across that deadly wasteland that had itself seen more than its share of human carnage. A journey that should have taken less than half an hour had lasted four times that long.

For both Beth and Jan it had been a journey as emotionally fraught as it had been dangerous. Neither had been back in the ghetto since that awful day in May of last year when they had said goodbye to Anna for the last time. The memories of that nightmarish time had crowded in on them. It had been akin to stepping back into hell itself. No word was said, but each knew by the look in the other's eyes. Such memories as those few streets invoked were engraved on the soul.

Instead of accompanying Beth to the new HQ, Jan had insisted she take up an offer of a few hours sleep in a proper bed. The room, in a tall, pink-painted house further down the street, was owned by Lech Poklewski, one of their AK comrades and, like Jan himself, he was becoming concerned at the number of hours she had now gone without sleep.

Jan had promised to return to her that evening, to guide her back to the new headquarters, but now, as they prepared to leave the sanctuary of the room, he was no longer convinced he was returning her to a place of safety. A deep unease had been growing in him over the past few days. When they had arrived in Warsaw he had been convinced that it would just be a matter of a few days; that the Germans would flee the city, just as they had flown other Polish cities over the past week or so. The native population would take up arms – arms supplied in the required quantities by their Allies in London. And they could, if need be, call on the Russians still waiting on the outskirts of the city to help out. But none of it was working to plan. What supplies had been dropped by the RAF had fallen as often into German hands as Polish ones, and now it seemed they had stopped coming altogether. But more worrying than that, the Russians were making no move to come to their aid.

All sorts of reasons were being bandied about for the non-intervention by the Soviets, but in Jan's own mind he was convinced they were now simply content to sit it out and watch the Home Army, still loyal to the Government in Exile in London, fight to the death with the Germans. A city and people on its knees would be easier to deal with than a victorious city and its triumphant inhabitants.

His heart was heavy, and he held her closer to him as he gazed over the roof-tops into the blood-red sky, where the last rays of the setting sun lit the heavens with a fiery glow. The words of the poet echoed in his head: 'He who has chosen the nest on the heights of the eagle, rather than the hearthstone, will know how to sleep when the horizon is red with the storm ...' There would be little sleep in this city tonight.

He had been wrong to let her come. He should have left her there at Tornow. Since arriving in Warsaw he had seen her grow more pale and wan by the day. As long as he remained at his station, she insisted on remaining at hers. He was crucifying her – crucifying the woman he loved for the city he loved. His lips pressed into the soft brown hair over her temple. Cities could be rebuilt, the land could recover. There would be a Poland here in another thousand years, no matter who won this war. But there was only one Beth. Only one woman he would ever love. By some miracle, in all the chaos of this hell they called war, he had found her again and he could not lose her. Not now. Not with the end in sight.

A great load lifted off his shoulders as he made the decision. He would return with her to Tornow and she would wait there for him, safe with his Uncle Bogdan, until the fighting was over. Then he would go back for her and the two of them would return together to Jarosbork.

Yes, at last he had the courage. He would face up to the world after the war was over; he would stand up and say, 'This is the woman I love; the woman I have loved for a lifetime.' He would return to Jarosbork with Beth. He would do what he should have done years ago: hold his head up high and tell the world that this was the woman with whom he wanted to live. With whom he would share his beloved Jarosbork.

He could feel his eyes glisten with unshed tears as he made the decision. It was one he should have made a generation ago. Twenty-five years they had wasted. Now every second was precious.

'We had better go, *kochanie*,' he said softly. He would tell her of his decision in the morning. Tonight was no time to be setting off anywhere. Yes, tonight he would go back with her to their new headquarters, and leave it till the first light of the new day to tell her of his plan. His heart sang at the thought.

As they emerged from the building, they had to duck straight back into the doorway as two Stukas suddenly emerged, as if from nowhere, to rain their deadly cargo down on the houses across the street.

'They must have found out where the HQ has moved to,' Jan gasped, as he shielded her behind him in the doorway and the house directly across from them burst into flames.

The screams of the inhabitants could be heard in the street, and Beth clutched tighter to his sleeve. There were people in there – God help them! 'We've got to do something!' she cried, already making for the pavement outside.

There was no argument. Neither could stand by and watch innocent people being burned to death.

More Stukas screamed down as they ran, doubled up, across the road.

He kept one arm still protectively around her shoulders as they made for the door of the house that had taken most of the blast.

A young girl, in her early teens, ran out of the doorway as they approached. She was in her night-clothes and blood was pouring from a gash down the side of her head. Shock was written all over her blood-streaked face. 'Help! Help – please! My grandparents are still in there!'

'Stay with her. Calm her down. I'm going in!' Jan yelled to Beth as he made for the door. It was swaying, half off its hinges, and black smoke was pouring out in suffocating clouds.

Beth glanced at the distraught girl beside her, then back to the smoke-filled doorway into which Jan had disappeared. She couldn't let him face that inferno alone. She had to help. 'Wait there,' she commanded the terrified girl. 'Don't worry, we'll get them out.'

With that, she ran into the blazing building after Jan. Smoke was billowing downstairs from the narrow staircase straight ahead. The bomb must have exploded in the upper storey. She could hear screaming from a room on the left.

The door was ajar and she pushed it open to see Jan struggling with an old couple in a box bed at the back of the room. The ceiling was half down and they were trapped by the legs by a fallen beam that hung at a rakish angle from the joists above; huge chunks of plaster covered the bedclothes. Despite the choking dust and smoke, the old woman was screaming and her husband was moaning pitifully by her side.

Her own eyes streaming, and choking from the smoke and dust, she worked with him to free them. The heat was intense and it felt as if her eyes and throat were on fire. Every breath seared her lungs and made her choke even more. It was impossible to talk, but there was no need for words. They worked like demons, in complete unison, as he heaved with all his strength to push the beam off the old couple's legs, and she pulled, first at the old woman, then, when she was at last out of the bed, at her husband.

Triumph! At last both were on the floor at their feet. For a fraction of a second she caught Jan's eyes. He was proud of her. She could see it, despite the suffocating smoke. Her own heart burst with pride as she thrust her hands beneath the old lady's armpits and hauled her towards the open doorway. He followed suit with the old man.

The journey to the outside was no more than twelve yards, but it seemed to Beth to be the longest of her life as, choking and spluttering, they fought their way through the searing heat and flames of the hallway to the fresh air, and laid the old couple down on the grey slabs of the pavement.

'*Bogu dzieki! Bogu dzieki!*' Their granddaughter, relief written all over her face, stumbled across to embrace them.

Beth and Jan glanced at one another as they fought for breath. Their eyes were streaming, flakes of soot clung to their hair and clothing, their faces and hands were black with smoke, and they were coughing as if their lungs would burst. But, despite it all, they were smiling. It had been worth it – they had saved two lives.

Beth looked down to attend once more to the two old people at their feet, when the roar of an engine made her look up in panic. But this time it wasn't the bombers returning. A German armoured car was racing along the street towards them, machine-gun bullets spraying from the sides.

Jan saw it at exactly the same time and, for a split second, their eyes met. She was aware of all the emotions she had ever felt for him surge through her and, as if of their own accord, her lips blurted out, 'I love you!'

There was no time to reply, but his action spoke louder than any words as he reached out and grabbed her arm. His only concern was for her. She was his life and meant more to him than his own.

As the armoured car tore towards them, he pulled her to the pavement, and flung himself on top of her, his arm shielding her head from the deadly ammunition that was spraying from the sides of the vehicle.

'Down, my love, keep down! God help us! Keep down!'

But his entreaties went unheard. It was already too late. Before her body reached the cold asphalt a bullet had passed through Beth's right temple. There was barely a mark where it entered, but in the opposite side of her brow there was a gaping, bloody hole.

'Mother of God ... help me ... !' Jan's distraught face turned to the heavens as he cradled her in his arms and let out a long wail of anguish that came from the very depths of his being. Her blood seeped through his fingers and, as he held her head in his hands, his whole body shook with the racking sobs that welled from within him. Her eyes were open and looking straight at him. 'I love you, Beth ... I love you ...'

But she had gone. The light had gone out of his life. What was there left for him now? His tears mingled with the flecks of soot on his face and ran in dirty grey rivulets down the drawn skin of his cheeks as he began to pray out loud to his God.

The world had shrunk to just the two of them on the cold grey pavement. The war and all its misery was no more. He never saw the second vehicle that swept up alongside and dispersed another round of ammunition into the small group on the pavement.

The bullet got him in the back of the neck and he slumped forwards over her prostrate body. He let out a long exhalation of breath, as if giving one last sigh, and his eyelids fluttered for a moment, then closed, his head resting on her bloodied shoulder.

The only one to survive was the young girl. White-faced and bloodstained, she pulled herself to her feet and stared down at the bullet-spattered bodies of her grandparents. They had been shot where they lay. Two old people, well past their three score years and ten. Two old people who had cared for her since childhood – kind, gentle people who did not deserve an end like this.

Her grandfather's spectacles had been knocked half off his face, and automatically she bent and straightened them on his nose, her fingers gently smoothing the flakes of soot from the white whiskers on his upper lip. He was staring up into the darkening sky, a startled expression on his face, as if he could not believe what had occurred in the few minutes since he had gone to bed with Mariana, his wife of the last sixty years.

Numbed with shock, their granddaughter stood up and half-turned, her eyes moving to the other couple lying dead less than ten feet away. They had given their lives tonight for this ...

The man's arms were still around the woman in a gesture of protectiveness, the grey hair of his head resting against her cheek. She wore a wedding ring on her third finger. They were man and wife, most probably. It was a strangely peaceful scene. If it wasn't for the blood oozing from their wounds, they could have been asleep.

She stood for a long time looking down at them, then it began to rain. Large warm spots of rain which fell from the heavens and ran down her soot-blackened face like human teardrops. She looked up to the sky, her eyes glistening, as her lips began to move in a silent prayer.

The angels themselves were weeping for what had happened here tonight.

Chapter Sixty

The knock on the door brought Lara jumping to her feet. The gilt-faced carriage clock on the living-room mantelpiece said two minutes to eight. She caught sight of herself in the mirror above the sideboard. Her face was flushed, her eyes shining, but there was no denying the anxiety in them.

Her hand moved to her hair, pushing back a stray strand from her brow. If only she'd had some notice – a day even – she could have washed it. She had not even had time to change out of the well-worn, light serge suit that she had worn to work day in and day out for the past four summers. A few minutes – that was all the warning she had had. A few minutes to prepare herself for the moment she had dreamt of for so long.

Four more raps of the brass knocker sounded through the small flat, more persistent this time.

It was him … Oh God, it was him! Her heart lurched in her breast. He was waiting out there on the landing. He would be walking into this room – walking back into her life in a few seconds from now.

Taking a deep breath, in a vain attempt to calm her racing heart, she walked slowly out into the hall. There was a sticky stain where the baby had spilt fruit juice on the carpet-runner that covered the linoleum, and the linoleum itself could do with a polish. And how long was it since she had cleaned the bathroom? Her nerves got worse by the second as she paused behind the closed front door. His tall bulk showed as a dark shadow through the opaque glass panel at the top.

Her fingers shook as she turned the latch and pulled the door open.

Their eyes met. She opened her mouth, but no words would come. He was smiling down at her – a tall, broad figure in his Army uniform. He took off his cap and, very correctly, held out his right hand.

'Hello, Lara.' His skin was warm to the touch. Hers was cold and she waited for a comment to that effect but none came. His eyes, still a brilliant blue, even in the dim light from the landing window, were smiling down into hers. There was a slightly embarrassed expression on his face. 'I hope you don't mind me arriving out of the blue like this.'

Mind? He must be joking! She shook her head, determined to remain as calm and collected as possible. He must not know how her insides were churning as she broke his gaze and backed slightly into the hall behind her. 'No – no, not at all.'

There was a moment's silence.

'Aren't you going to ask me in?'

'Yes – yes, of course.' She stepped back almost too quickly and caught her heel on a frayed edge of the hall carpet.

She stumbled backwards and he caught her. It was the closest they had been since that night in Casablanca. He smelt faintly of sandal-wood hair-oil: the familiar scent sharpened the acutely painful memories that crowded into her mind. She could feel her face flame as she disentangled herself. 'I must get that worn bit seen to,' she muttered, backing towards the open door of the living-room.

He followed her, a quiet smile on his face. She was acting as nervy as he felt.

His eyes wandered around the neatly-furnished room that had figured so much in his thoughts since he left England. The furniture was still the same American Embassy stuff that he remembered, but there were homely touches everywhere. Imprints of her personality. He thought fleetingly of his own austere apartment back in Washington. What it lacked was a woman's touch – the woman's touch that was very much in evidence here. His gaze fell on a set of beautifully embroidered cushions on the settee. 'Your own work?'

She blushed and nodded. 'You see what a high life I lead in the evenings when I'm not working.'

The answer seemed to please him. 'May I sit down?'

'Of course.' He was acting so formally that it disconcerted her. She could cope with it better when he was his usual jokey self. She gestured to the settee. 'Please – make yourself at home.' She was aware her cheeks were still flushed, belying the casual demeanour she was so desperately trying to assume. This was not at all the cool, collected welcome she had planned. Nerves clutched at her throat, giving her voice a half-strangled sound as she straightened an anti-macassar on the back of an armchair and said lightly, 'Well, this *is* a surprise. What brings you to London?'

He sat down on the end cushion of the settee and placed his cap on the arm beside him. Its removal had messed up his hair slightly at the front and it fell in a curling, dark quiff over his right eye. He pushed a hand through it to smooth it back into place as he looked across at her. 'You mean, what brings me to break my promise and look you up?'

She blinked at him in surprise, then looked away quickly, avoiding his eyes. If he was deliberately trying to embarrass her he was succeeding. 'I mean what brings you to London,' she said quickly, and much too stiffly. 'Presumably it's to do with your work. Is it the situation in Poland?'

'Partly that, and partly to clarify some points at this end over Operation Anvil, before the next big conference. Harry hasn't been keeping too well of late – his usual gut problem, I reckon – so I'm the Joe Soap assigned to take his place.'

'I see.' That made sense, although a stab of disappointment ran through her at his answer. He didn't sound exactly overjoyed to be here.

'You're clued up on the conference yourself, I take it?'

'Of course.' She herself had typed much of the correspondence that had gone back and forth between the Prime Minister and the President about the forthcoming joint operation in Southern France. And she wasn't surprised someone of his importance had arrived to tie up the loose ends, if Harry Hopkins couldn't make it himself. Everyone knew it was vital to get as many details as possible ironed out before Churchill and Roosevelt met again in person. 'You're going to the next one then, I presume?'

As she spoke, she was backing towards the door, making for the kitchen. A cup of tea could be just what she needed to calm her down – and the sooner the better. Not waiting for an answer to her question, she aimed another at him. 'Tea or coffee? The latter is only ersatz, I'm afraid.'

He got up and followed her. The amused half-smile had gone from his lips and he caught hold of her arm in the doorway. The game-playing had gone on long enough. She had a right to know why he had broken his promise – why he was here. 'Lara, there's something I have to come clean about. I was at the Foreign Office today and spoke to a couple of your old colleagues there.'

'Oh?' Her eyes met his as the flush crept back up her neck to her cheeks. 'Meaning?'

'Meaning they told me about Ken. They told me you have been a widow for over a year ... Why the hell didn't you tell me?'

She twisted herself free of his grasp and rubbed the spot where his fingers had dug into the soft flesh of her forearm. He was asking the one question she herself did not know the answer to. 'You had gone by the time it happened,' she began lamely. 'It didn't seem right to bother you.'

'It didn't seem right to bother me?' he almost shouted the words back at her. 'It didn't seem right to bother me? ... Jesus Christ, Lara ...' He made a helpless gesture with his hands and shook his head in incredulity. 'Look, I was sorry to hear about Ken – genuinely sorry. He was a good guy – one of the best – but didn't you think it might just be of some interest to me that you were now a widow – that you were free?'

They stared at each other across the few inches of carpet. 'Emotional self-flagellation, was that it? You had to punish yourself for what had happened between us while Ken was still alive.' His voice was low as his eyes burned into hers.

'No – no, of course not!' Her protest was much too vehement and fooled neither of them. Then a cry from the bedroom next door increased her consternation.

The unexpected sound brought a puzzled frown to Mike's face. 'You've got a visitor here?'

The question surprised her. He didn't know. He still didn't know! She looked up at him, her mouth dry as she said softly, 'You mean you don't know ... They didn't tell you?' Surely her old friends at the FO must have mentioned the baby.

'They didn't tell me what?'

The initial cry became a full blown wail as little Beth let it be known that she was still awake and in need of company.

'About the baby.' Her answer was a whisper.

He stared down at her for a moment, his knitted brows causing a deep furrow to crease his forehead. Then a most peculiar expression crossed his face and, almost pushing past her in his haste to get out of the living-room door, he set off in the direction of the wailing infant.

The baby was standing up in her cot, facing the door. Lara had dressed her in her best lawn nightie before putting her to bed, and she had never looked more appealing. The sight of her mother caused the noise to cease as if by magic, and her pink, round-cheeked face creased into a broad smile.

Mike gazed down at her, his eyes taking in the dark curling hair and bright blue eyes that looked up curiously at him. Then he looked back at Lara. There was no way on earth that baby could ever be Ken Cameron's child. It was like looking at a much prettier, feminine version of every photograph he had ever seen of himself as an infant. There didn't even seem to be very much of Lara in her. She was an Adamski through and through. He shook his head as if unable to believe the evidence of his own eyes. He had to have it verified. There was no way Lara could lie to him now. 'She's ours, isn't she?' he said softly. 'She is our child.'

Lara nodded. There was no point in deceiving him. The moment she had longed for, yet dreaded, for almost a year had happened. Her daughter was face to face with her natural father. 'She's our child,' she said simply. 'Little Beth is your daughter.'

For a moment there was complete silence, as if he could not quite believe his ears. Then he let out a wild whoop, snatching the startled baby from the cot, clasping her to the ornamental buttons of his uniform jacket, as he pulled Lara to him as well. His arms were around them both and suddenly they were laughing and crying at the same time.

'A daughter! I have a daughter!' He was kissing them both in turn, as he repeated the incredible news, and Lara could no longer make out the elated features of his face, as her eyes glistened and her vision blurred.

The baby, unused to male company and not too taken with the slight roughness of the cheek that pressed against hers, started to yell once more, and Mike reluctantly handed her back to her mother. 'I guess she's a Mommy's girl,' he grinned. 'That'll change – just you wait and see. I'll spoil her rotten – you see if I don't!'

Lara threw him a 'that'll be the day' look as she settled the baby on her shoulder, and they walked back through to the living-room together.

She placed little Beth in the playpen on the floor by the window as Mike reached inside his uniform jacket for a cigarette. His eyes were still on his daughter on the carpet at his feet as he lit the Camel and drew deeply on the calming white smoke. He knew this was going to be some meeting, but he had never expected to find himself a father before the day was over. No sir, he had certainly never expected this!

Lara stood by the window, watching him feast his eyes on his small daughter. The episode had exhausted her as much as it had him. 'Still fancy that cup of tea?' she asked, already knowing the answer.

He followed her through to the kitchen, and sat down at the oil-clothed table as she filled the kettle at the sink and placed it on the stove.

A comfortable silence followed. A silence pregnant with all the questions that tumbled through his head. Questions he knew she would now give the answers to with the simple truth. The time for charades was over and they both knew it. No more games – no more deceptions ... He looked up at her, watching her every movement as she set about preparing the tea. It was the first time he could do so without feeling guilty, without feeling he was trading in stolen goods.

She was every bit as beautiful as he remembered – as he never failed to remember every night when he went to bed alone in the third floor apartment, not a stone's throw from Capitol Hill, that had been his home for the past few years.

Her hair was longer than when he had last seen her and hung over her shoulders in the deep page-boy beloved of so many Hollywood stars at the moment. Her figure was fuller – more rounded and womanly than before. Desire stirred within him as he watched her carry the cups and saucers from the kitchen dresser to the table. It welled within him with the same deep, pulsating throb that he had experienced on almost every occasion since the first meeting in the Embassy Annex in Princes Gate all those years ago. No other woman had ever had this effect on him. Not Joanne, not any one.

She was aware of his eyes following her every move and a quiet smile played at the corners of her lips as she busied herself waiting for the kettle to boil. In brewing the tea she was acting out an age-old ritual, but behind it there was an even older ritual being played out between them. The atmosphere in the small kitchen was electric. They were going through the motions of politeness – she might even begin talking about the weather, she thought, as she lifted the singing kettle from the stove and poured the hot water into the brown earthenware teapot. But he would know what was really on her mind. Just as she knew exactly what was on his, as his eyes devoured her from a few feet across the table.

She handed him his cup of steaming tea and allowed herself the indulgence of meeting his eyes.

Mike was aware of his heart beating faster beneath the thick cotton of his shirt as his mind turned to the one question that had haunted his mind more than any other – the one question that until this afternoon he had thought he would never be able to ask.

But how to do it – what to say ... Here he was a two-star General feeling like a kid plucking up the courage to ask for his very first date. All he had to do was say the words, that was all. Ask one simple question. For God's sake, man, get on with it! He attempted a smile, but it half-froze on his lips as, taking his courage in both hands, he asked quietly, 'Do I go down on my knees or is that considered a mite old-fashioned these days?'

Her grip tightened on the handle of her cup, tipping and half-spilling the contents. The hot liquid ran down her fingers, but she felt no pain as she stared at him. Could it be ... ? Surely not ... 'That's really not necessary, you know – grovelling for a cup of this stuff. It's not even Lipton's best quality tea!'

It was the lamest of jokes but it defused the tension. He stood up and held open his arms. Then suddenly she was in them and he was kissing the tears that had sprung to her eyes.

'Marry me, Lara,' he whispered. 'Marry me now – tomorrow ... Just as soon as they can fix it up. Make me the happiest guy in the world. Be my wife ...'

They were married in St Martin-in-the-Fields four days later, by special licence rushed through the day before he was due to fly back to Washington.

The sun was shining as they walked out into the late summer sunshine of Trafalgar Square and faced the world as man and wife.

They did not bother with a taxi to take them to Rainbow Corner, where Mike had booked a table for two for lunch, but savoured the walk through the crowded streets. All too soon they would be leaving this city, with its bitter sweet memories, for a new life, in a new land across the Atlantic Ocean.

As usual the Rainbow Club was alive with American service uniforms, and Mike got more than his fair share of salutes, as they walked up the broad stone steps and in through the front door.

The sound of music assailed their ears. A live band was playing in the room beyond and a girl vocalist in a white tulle dress was singing Vera Lynn's soldiers' anthem, 'We'll Meet Again'. They could hear the other diners and dancers through the wall join in the chorus. Mike's mind went back to another time and place when he had heard that same song – on the ship taking him away from this land, away from her – the girl who was now his wife.

But there was no time for either of them to get sentimental. The familiar sound of Wailing Winnie, the air-raid siren, blotted out band and singer alike.

He retrieved his cap from the hat-check girl behind the counter and placed it back on his head with a sigh, as Lara smiled wryly. 'This is Britain, General, remember – and there's still a war on.'

He smiled that quirky smile that never ceased to make her heart beat faster as his arm went around her and they made their way down to the cellar to await the all-clear. 'Mrs Adams, honey, I can't think of anywhere on earth I'd rather be.'

And he was telling the truth.

Epilogue

Warsaw, 25 December 1945

Lara and Mike sat, with little Beth between them, on the sofa of their third floor suite in Warsaw's Polonia Hotel. It was one of the few buildings still standing virtually unscathed in Poland's capital city. The furniture was modern, with overstuffed sofas and Art Deco lamps. A metal-legged, black marble coffee table sat in front of them, on which stood two large vodkas ready to drink the toast at the end of King George's Christmas broadcast.

It had taken them fully ten minutes to tune in successfully to the BBC World Service, and the reception on the walnut-cased radio was poor, but miraculously cleared as the sonorous chimes of Big Ben rang out, followed by the halting tones of the British King.

Lara sat up straighter on the soft cushions and gripped Mike's hand. Listening to this broadcast had been important to her. So much of life had disintegrated over the past few years; it was more necessary than ever to cling to the familiar, to the things that had once mattered in that other time, that other world that existed before the war.

As they listened, King George was talking to a world at peace for the first time in six long years. So many families who had once listened together before the war were now no more. Like her own they had lost loved ones whose places in the hearts of those they left behind could never be filled. But like hers also, perhaps a few had found happiness again, and hope for the future.

She clasped her husband's hand tighter and gazed fondly on him and their little daughter ... Beth. It was right that she had named her after her mother. Somehow it lent a meaning to the scheme of things. It was as if, in her child, her mother's life had come full circle. She reached out with her free hand and touched the dark shining curls. Perhaps, one day, if they were blessed with a son, they would call him Jan. Perhaps ...

The King's voice interrupted her thoughts. They were over a thousand miles from London, but it was as if he were talking to her alone as his voice filled the silence of the hotel room ...

'For six years past I have spoken at Christmas to our Empire at war. During all those years of sorrow and danger, of weariness and strife, you and I have been upheld by a vision of a world at peace. And now that vision has become a reality. By gigantic efforts and sacrifice a great work has been done, a great evil has been cast from the earth. No peoples have done more to cast it out than you to whom I speak. With my whole heart I pray to God, by whose grace victory has been won, that this Christmas may bring to my peoples all the world over every joy they have dreamed of in the dark days that are gone.

'This Christmas is a real homecoming to us all, a return to a world in which the homely and friendly things of life can again be ours. To win victory, much that was of great price has been given up, much has been ravaged or destroyed by the hand of war. But the things that have been saved are beyond price ...

'There will be the vacant places of those who will never return, brave souls who gave their all to win peace for us. We remember them with pride and with unfading love, praying that a greater peace than ours may now be theirs ...'

There were tears in Lara's eyes as the broadcast ended and she raised her glass to Mike's. He did not need to ask why. This war had seen the deaths of so many of those they had known and loved. And now, this first Christmas of peace for six long years, they had come to Poland for one reason – to find out for certain, now the war was over, what had happened to her mother and father.

Information from those of the AK left alive after the fighting had indicated that both Beth and Jan had been killed at the end of the first week of the uprising, and had been buried in Warsaw; but rumour was not enough. Lara had to know for certain. She had to hear with her own ears, see with her own eyes, that all hope had gone.

Mike had promised her that once the war was over he would take her to Poland. They would see and hear for themselves what had happened that fateful day in August 1944. And so here they were spending their first day of his precious four days leave in the ruins of the capital city before travelling on to Silesia and Jarosbork, the Jarosinskis' ancient family seat. What had become of it? Was it still standing? Or had it been reduced to a heap of stones like so much of this historic land?

Lara could hardly bear to look next morning as Mike drove the six-year-old Chevrolet belonging to the American Embassy through the rubble-filled streets. Hardly a building was left standing. All but a handful had been bombed or gutted by fire.

She listened mutely as Mike explained that part of the destruction had taken place through Nazi bombing and artillery fire when the Germans launched their first attack on the city in 1939, then the gutting of the Jewish ghetto in the spring of 1943 had added to the destruction. But by far the greatest damage had been done in the two horrifying months of August and September last year when the Germans had driven all the inhabitants out of the city and herded them into the concentration camp of Pruszkow, while they systematically razed the capital to the ground, block by block, house by house, until the only buildings left standing were those, such as the Polonia Hotel, that had housed the German High Command.

Lara did not interrupt once. As she listened her thoughts were totally with her mother and father. It had come as something of a comfort to learn they had been together in Warsaw at the end. But the agony of having no real evidence of their deaths no one could imagine who had not personally lived through such a tragedy.

Mike had been to Warsaw several times before the war and, as Lara stared silently out of the window beside him, his own eyes searched in vain for familiar landmarks as he steered the limousine past the potholes and round the heaps of rubble that lay across every road. Even the once luxurious railway station on Jerusalem Street was reduced to two blackened towers of twisted metal, and the great Prudential skyscraper, once the pride of the city's architects, was now a gigantic pile of stones. Almost nothing had survived. The Poniatowski Bridge, along with all the railway bridges over the Vistula, was completely destroyed, and only a temporary wooden bridge now joined Warsaw to Praga.

At most of the main crossroads, young women in Polish uniforms directed the traffic, assisted by Red Army soldiers. Stalin had got his wish, Mike thought grimly.

It took them over twenty-four hours to reach the small Silesian village that lay half a mile from the gates of Jarosbork. Throughout the whole of the journey they had passed endless processions of pathetic, exhausted refugees, pushing all their worldly possessions in anything on wheels that would move over the hard-packed snow. Small hand-carts vied with rickety bicycles and babies' prams for road space. Where they were headed was anybody's guess, and Mike was aware of Lara having to avert her eyes from the sight of the half-frozen children, their feet wrapped in rags, trudging exhausted through the snow and ice, behind equally foot-weary mothers and grandparents. Fathers were few in Poland these days, as in the rest of Europe. The war had seen to that.

They left the car parked outside the hotel in the village where they had booked a room for the night, and left little Beth asleep in the care of the landlady's young daughter while they went in search of the castle. Mike had suggested waiting till the next morning before visiting Jarosbork itself, but Lara could not rest until she had seen for herself the place that had meant so much to her father.

It was late afternoon when they entered the high stone gates, with their carved stone eagles, and walked up the long tree-lined drive to the castle itself. It loomed out of the already darkening sky, its battlements silhouetted against the heavens as they had been for hundreds of years.

A river, frozen solid, wound its way around the castle, with a small stone bridge across it a few hundred yards from the main entrance.

Alongside the bridge, on the banks of the river stood a white marble column about ten feet high. Hand in hand, they walked up to it and Mike felt Lara's hand freeze in his as they read the inscription:

> Sacred to the memory of Jan Jarosinski
> and Beth Mallory, the woman he loved.
> Killed in the battle for Warsaw
> 7 August 1944.
> *I tam gdzie już łez niema, on łzę Polski złożył.*

'And there, where tears are banished, he still shed Poland's tear,' Mike translated softly.

His arm went around his wife's shoulders. It was journey's end.

'Do you want to go up to the castle itself?' he asked.

Lara turned, her tear-filled eyes scanning the great edifice looming against the darkening sky. There would be nothing there, only the ghosts of people long dead. People who had borne her real name – generations of Jarosinskis, whom she had never known. People like her father and mother, now cold in the cold cold earth beneath this land over which so much blood had been shed.

She shook her head. She had seen what they had come for. She could rest now. They were at peace.

They turned and retraced their footsteps over the small bridge, her hand clasped tightly in his, as they headed back to the hotel – back to America and a new life in a new world, with little Beth.

She would tell her daughter about her grandmother, Lara resolved.

Just as soon as she could understand, she would tell her of her grandmother's love for this land and for the man who loved it too, and was her own grandfather.

Despite her sadness, a great load had lifted from her heart. They were here. They were together and at rest. She could ask for no more. One day she would return and find whoever had erected that monument – old comrades from the Resistance perhaps – and thank them. But not this time. Not this visit. The heart could take only so much, and her heart was already bleeding for this beautiful land and its suffering people.

Lara paused and turned to look back once more on the scene Jan and Beth had loved so much. A soft snow was falling, covering the ravaged countryside in a protective white blanket that hid the scars of war from the eyes, but not from the heart. Another year had come to an end. A year even more terrible than those that had gone before. What the future would bring only God could know. Peace had come to the world, but it had come too late for her father and mother.

Her husband's arm around her shoulders, Lara raised her eyes to the heavens beyond the snow-clad hills. If there really was a life after death, then they were here with her now – her father and mother. She could feel their presence just as sure as if they were standing next to her. Jan and Beth had returned to Jarosbork in body and soul.

They were here and were at peace. She could wish no more for them in this troubled world.